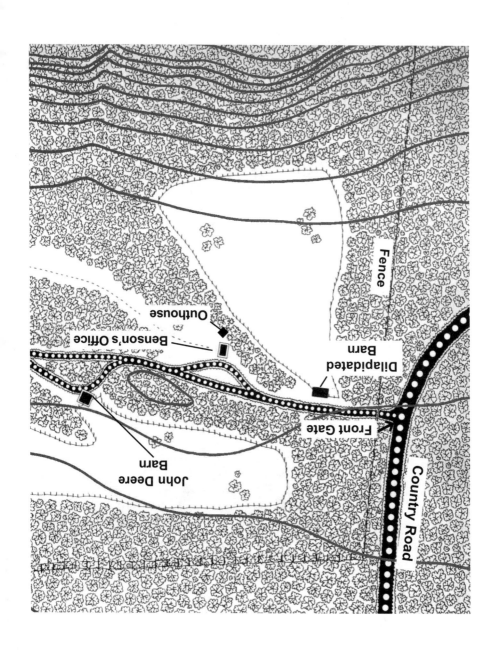

Outhouse

Benson's Office

Dilapidated Barn

Fence

John Deere Barn

Front Gate

Country Road

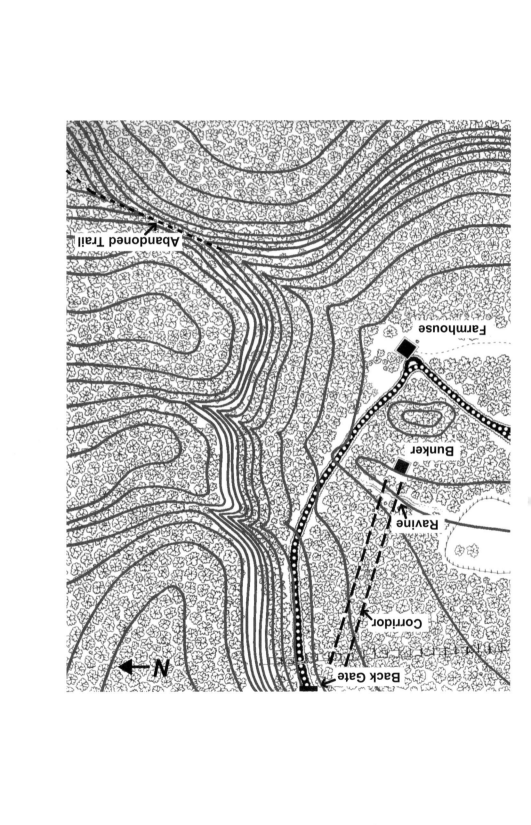

The Undoing

T.R. VILLELLI

BOOK PUBLISHERS NETWORK

Book Publishers Network
P.O. Box 2256
Bothell • WA • 98041
Telephone • 425-483-3040

10 9 8 7 6 5 4 3 2

Printed in the United States of America

LCCN 2005927463
ISBN 1-887542-27-2

Art Work: John Grow
Editing: Carolyn Acheson
Cover Design: Richard Van Lê
Interior Layout: Stephanie Martindale

"It is here we must begin to seek
the wisdom of the children…"

"Talk to God and listen to the
casual reply…"

Dedication

This book is dedicated to my father, Tony Villelli, who, in addition to making sure I always knew that I was loved, provided a constant example of what a true hero is. From helping save the world from the horrors of Nazi Germany to keeping our family together and laughing through the most trying of times, you never let us down. I love you, Dad.

This book is also dedicated to my mother, Arlene Villelli, who raised six children the old fashioned way, when floors were scrubbed by hand and food was brought to the kitchen from the garden for cooking and canning. My entire way of being was influenced by Mom's great sense of humor. And Mom, I still haven't forgiven you for the many times you sewed the sleeves of my tee shirts closed and shortsheeted my bed. I love you, Mom.

This book is also dedicated to my beautiful and graceful Leslie. Without your love and support, neither this book nor I would have turned out quite the same. I love you, Les.

Acknowledgments

A gigantic one-man round of applause goes to Leslie McHenry who had the patience to listen to my chapters, often over the telephone, as each was completed. Her encouragement and insightful suggestions were a tremendous help in keeping my vivid imagination somewhat within the realm of the believable. My gratitude for her love and emotional support cannot adequately be put into words.

A very special thank you goes to Jerry and Esther Hicks and their wonderful Abraham, not only for the fact that much of what they have taught me has had a dramatic effect on the content of this book, but for the way their patient wisdom has changed my life. For those of you who, like me, could stand an occasional infusion of joy, I suggest you look into the teachings of these marvelous people at – www.Abraham-Hicks.com or 830-755-2299.

Once in a rare while, you begin a business relationship and it just "clicks" from the very beginning. That's the way it's been with Sheryn Hara of Book Publisher's Network, Inc. She is my publisher and, I'm happy to say, my friend. I thank you, Sheryn, for your way of pushing me in the right direction without ever being pushy and for your gentle and caring way of being.

My heartfelt thanks go to Carolyn Acheson for her diligent and enthusiastic efforts in editing this book for content and continuity. She made many a valiant effort to keep me between the lines, in spite of my enthusiastic determination to wander off in yet another exciting direction.

Julie Scandora has been a great help with her precision and attention to detail as she edited the spelling, punctuation and grammar, the rules of which I occasionally violated during the excitement of trying to get to the end of a chapter to find out if my characters were going to make it in one piece. It was Julie's observations that inspired me to totally change the ending of the book. If you want to know how it was going to end, you'll have to ask Julie.

I thank Richard Van Lê for the excellent job he did of designing the dust jacket that encases this tome. I insisted on a few items that appear on the cover, in spite of Richard's admonitions to the contrary. Therefore, if there's anything about the dust jacket that seems a bit unusual, please feel free to attribute that to me.

The artwork that appears on the dust jacket is that of one of the most talented artists I know, John Grow of Durango, Colorado. The scene of the Victorian farmhouse and surrounding forest, where a substantial part of the action in my book takes place, was painted by John. He read the entire book in order to be certain that the farmhouse he painted looked as I had intended. He succeeded masterfully.

My sincere appreciation to Stephanie Martindale for her ceaseless efforts in formatting these many pages with patience, understanding and constant good cheer.

And, finally, I thank my wonderful children, Rick, Gina, Maria, and Deanna, my stepdaughter Erin Rose, my brother Dick, and my sisters Sandi, Judy, Linda, and Donna for tons of encouragement and love.

Prologue
1975—Late September

Mom and Dad had tucked the children in for the night.

As little Annie lay in her bed, listening to the sounds of the old farmhouse, she could make out the voice of the weatherman on the radio in the kitchen below her bedroom. She knew that Dad would be anxiously awaiting the latest information on the early snow storm that had been heading their way since yesterday morning.

Annie was warm and cozy under the down comforter Mom had made her last spring for her fifth birthday.

The quarter moon that hung in silvery silence in the autumn sky outside Annie's window bathed the room with a soft glow.

Smiling down from atop the dresser stood Celeste, an elegant porcelain doll, with the most gorgeous emerald eyes. Celeste had been a gift from Mom and Dad last Christmas.

As Annie stared, mesmerized by those hauntingly beautiful eyes, it occurred to her that she was one of the luckiest girls in the world. Never, had she doubted that she was loved. She wouldn't change anything about her parents, except maybe just one thing—she wished they still believed in the magic.

All of Annie's younger friends still knew about the magic. How sad, she thought, that some of her older friends were already beginning to lose the memory of it.

To her surprise, Annie noticed Celeste's eyes were shimmering. Tiny slivers of light appeared to be radiating, pulsating slowly from those beautiful emerald eyes..

She sat up, focusing more intently, searching for some explanation for the unusual display. The shimmering faded, replaced by a bright orange radiance that filled the room, overpowering the pale light of the moon.

Seconds later, Annie was jolted by what sounded to her like the loudest crack of thunder she had ever heard. The room shook violently and glass from her window sprayed across the room in tiny crystalline shards. She heard the sound of shattering glass in the hallway as the light bulb in the ceiling exploded.

Annie felt a terrible pressure in her head, accompanied by a shrill whistle. She clamped her hands over her ears but couldn't keep out the sound. Even with her ears covered, she could hear Mom and Dad shouting in the kitchen but couldn't make out what they were saying above the roar in her head.

Moments later Mom appeared in the doorway, white-faced and trembling, holding Cindy with one hand and Stuart with the other. "Put on your slippers honey. Be careful not to step on any glass. Come to Mommy and Daddy's room."

As Annie headed down the hallway, she glanced out the window. A brilliant reddish-orange glow filled the sky, rising above the meadow just beyond the pine-covered hill to the west and reflecting off of the bark of several of the ponderosas near the front yard.

She walked quickly to her parents' room.

Everyone but her father sat huddled together on the bed.

"Where's Daddy?" she asked.

"He's gone to investigate the cause of the explosion," Mom said. "We're all going stay right here and wait for him."

Annie noticed that the orange glow outside was already fading.

They heard the screen door slam.

"Wait here," instructed Mom, as she stood up. "I'll go see what Daddy found out."

The children sat without speaking, holding each other. Tears rolled down Stuart's cheeks. Cindy did her best to smile. Annie tried to hear what Mom and Dad were saying.

"What in the world's going on?" Mom asked.

"I wish I knew," replied Dad.

Moments later, Mom slipped softly into the bedroom, closing the door behind her. She pulled the children close. "Daddy's calling for help."

After what seemed like a long time to Annie, Dad opened the bedroom door and stepped inside. He had his deer rifle in one hand, his shotgun in the other. He leaned his weapons against the wall, locked the door, and propped the chair from Mom's dresser under the doorknob.

"We're gonna be all right," he said, his voice uncertain.

They sat in silence.

Annie knew what was happening. Not all of the details. But she knew. Annie always knew.

Whatever it was that had caused the explosion meant them no harm. But harm was on its way, nonetheless. Big harm.

Annie watched the clock on the dresser tick off fifteen minutes. All else was quiet.

Suddenly the silence was shattered as a large truck came roaring up the dirt road that connected the farmhouse to the state highway. It stopped in the glow of the floodlight at the far side of the front yard.

Annie ran to the window before Mom could think to stop her. Instead of the county fire truck she had expected to see, she saw a truck like the kind she had seen in war movies. Army men were getting out of the truck. There were a lot of them. They had guns.

Annie knew they meant no harm. The magic told her that.

But harm was surely on its way, big harm.

Annie knew.

Annie always knew.

Chapter One
Thirty Years Later (Saturday)

Late Autumn. Chilling cold. Nobody seemed to mind. For some, it was because the fans were packed so tightly in the bleachers that they generated enough heat to ward off the chill. For others, it was the fact that they had taken care to fortify themselves with a bit of their favorite libation. For most, it was the almost unbearable excitement that filled the air—the kind of tension that causes tiny traces of adrenaline to seep out of the chambers where they normally reside—an anticipation that is somehow both exhilarating and frightening.

The night held the possibility of splendor and the threat of heartbreak. All because in recent weeks the Franklin High football team had raised the hopes of the people of the little town of Sprague to what could be called a fever pitch.

Even Elsie Waller, who for years had left no stone unturned in imparting to her sophomore literature classes her opinions on the barbaric nature of football, had been unable to resist the allure of the stadium. In preparation for the brutality to come, she had supplied her handbag and her cerebral cortex with a half-pint of peppermint schnapps each.

The school board, witnessing the largest crowds in Franklin's football history, had changed the location of the games from the Franklin football field to the nearby community college stadium. For many weeks, in spite of the size of the stadium, the crowds had exceeded the occupancy limits by an unconscionable margin. As Franklin High's chances of advancing to the finals steadily increased, the occupancy limits of the college stadium surely would be violated even more blatantly than in the past.

The superintendent of schools had used two fifty-yard line tickets and a bottle of his best single-malt Scotch to convince the fire marshal to look the other way. Late yesterday afternoon, the fire marshal had upped the ante considerably by requesting that the county spray the gravel road in front of his house with oil. Only an hour before game time, the superintendent of schools had succumbed to that demand.

Holding a Franklin football game on a Saturday night was unusual, but nobody had ever thought Franklin would get this far into the finals—never mind the need to use the junior college stadium. So, many months in advance, the school board had leased the stadium to the VFW for a parade rehearsal on Friday night, causing this week's game to be moved to Saturday.

A victory tonight against Riverton would make Sprague the league champions, an outcome almost nobody believed possible. Franklin was rated the underdog by a serious margin. But that had been the case for the past several games when, somehow, those scrappy young men, outweighed and outclassed by every opponent they faced, had pulled off victory after victory.

As coach Linden had said in a front-page interview with the *Daily Sentinel*, "This is the finest demonstration of team effort I've ever seen."

Everyone knew that each member of the team had given his all. Still, the Lasher twins, Tim and Jaime, and their football magic were the ones who had led the team to victory time after time.

For the first few games of the season, the attitude of most of the fans was, "This just can't continue." Yet, as the home team racked up one win after another, the fans' mood began to slither tentatively down the cold, musky corridors of unfounded hope in search of a modicum of blind faith. Tonight the attitude of the crowd could be best summed up by a statement attributed to Willie Hansen, the school janitor, who allegedly told a reporter, "Hang them statistics! There ain't nothin' that can stop a team with the guts our boys've got."

Besides being brothers, Tim and Jaime Lasher had been best friends as long as they could remember. If the truth were known, they were roughhousing in their mother's womb by the end of her second trimester. In actuality, they had been together long before that.

The two had much in common: natural good looks, uncompromising integrity, a fierce family loyalty, and a burning passion for football.

They had differences, too. Tim was the socialite, the smooth talker, the organizer, the leader. Jaime was quiet and reserved, a deep thinker, dependable, always there when Tim needed him. Together, they had led the team to the finest season in the history of Franklin football.

Tim was the fiery quarterback. He thought fast on his feet. And, my, could that boy throw a football! Jaime could hardly remember when Tim didn't have a football in his hands. He carried it every-where—to school, to picnics, and even to the drive-in theater. He spent hours every week throwing it through an old tractor tire that their dad had hung from the sycamore tree in the backyard of the Lasher farmhouse.

Jaime was—and had always been—the runner. "That kid has one speed—full throttle," his dad often said. Jaime loved the feel of the wind in his hair, the rushing of blood through his veins, the powerful pumping of his heart, and even the aching in his lungs that intensified with every breath. He enjoyed long-distance runs, especially through the forest, where he sometimes imagined the trees to be opposing football players he would dodge and fake. Most of all, though, Jaime liked to sprint. At any moment he might just take off running at top speed to the nearest mail-box or from the school bus to the front gate of the old farm. Over the years he had gotten so fast that, by the time he got to high school, nobody could outrun him, not even Harvey MacGregor, who held the school records in the hundred-yard dash and the four-forty.

The track coach tried every trick he knew to entice Jaime to join his team, but Jaime only wanted to play football. One of the reasons he found football so irresistible was that it allowed him to enjoy a special kind of partnership with Tim. Often, when Tim called a par-ticularly ingenious play, an indescribable rush of energy would course through Jaime's mind and body. He sometimes wondered if he were feeling the same kind of high that kids on drugs bragged about. But no, it couldn't be, for this rush was not only harmless, it was com-pletely fulfilling.

Sometimes the outcome of the play seemed to be of almost secondary importance. It was the creativity behind the play and the extraordinary execution that were so satisfying. Yet, if the plan suc-ceeded, what a thrill he got watching the shocked expressions on the faces of the opposing players.

What Jaime liked best was being on the receiving end of one of Tim's passes. That was the ultimate rush, the thrill Jaime lived for. All those years that Tim had been throwing the football, Jaime had usually been his receiver—the perfect partnership.

On Wednesday afternoon, Tim and Jaime had gone for a walk up to Cougar Ridge, where they spent hours looking down at the town below and strategizing about Saturday night's game, the game of games, the ultimate challenge. They knew the game might go right down to the wire. They knew it might be up to them to make the difference between failure and victory. This challenge was what they had been training and throwing and running and catching for all of their young lives.

Strangely, not until recently had Jaime begun to suspect that all of those years of effort had somehow been preordained, perhaps by some unknown intelligence, to prepare them for this game. As Jaime lay there in the cool grass on Cougar Ridge, a gentle breeze playing in his hair, he thought he felt something beyond his consciousness, something just beyond his grasp, something powerful, some force more noble than anything Jaime had ever experienced at work behind the scenes. That's what Tim and Jaime had come to call it—The Force. Jaime had encountered The Force before, and he could feel it now. Yes, something special was in the air.

Jaime thought about the day he and Tim had first discovered they shared similar experiences with some unknown power. They didn't know what to call it. But the more they talked about it, the clearer it became that they were each describing the same thing, something that allowed them to use their thoughts and feelings somehow to affect the physical world around them.

They discussed for some time what they should call it, wanting to come as close as they could to giving it a name that reflected what it felt like. They considered calling it "God" but dismissed that idea quickly, deciding that "God" carried with it too many false notions. They decided that "The Force" Luke Skywalker had introduced them to, came a lot closer to describing their experiences than did the judgmental, punitive, fickle character they often heard people refer to as "God." From that day forward, the magnificent power source that holds the universe together became known to Tim and Jaime as The Force. It felt right.

So many things had happened to bring Tim and Jaime to this exact time and place—so many apparent coincidences. Long before the twins were born, their father, Michael, had barely escaped death in a Vietnamese POW camp, the only man in his entire platoon to return from the war. The newspapers had called his escape "miraculous."

Then, when Michael returned to the United States, the U.S. Marine Corps experienced a foul-up in one of its secretarial pools and sent Michael to the wrong discharge center—another quirk of fate. Waiting for a flight to the correct location, Michael took a wrong turn while trying to find the snack bar, and stumbled into Sarah, who also found herself somehow in the wrong terminal. Michael and Sarah were married six months later.

More than one doctor had told Sarah, the mother Jaime came to love more than life itself, that she would never have children. Yet, here he was, and with a twin brother as his best friend, a gift from the fertility division of some pharmaceutical empire.

Jaime thought about one night when he and Tim were seven years old. They were supposed to stay at home with a babysitter while their parents went to dinner at a neighbor's home. At the last minute the babysitter called to say she had erroneously scheduled two babysitting engagements for the same night. Their folks had no choice but to take them along. The boys kept themselves occupied watching TV while the adults socialized in the living room. The show they had intended to watch had come on an hour earlier than they had expected, so they missed it. As Jaime flipped through the channels, he happened upon a biography of Rafer Johnson, the Olympic athlete who would become Jaime's hero and inspiration. Rafer Johnson's life of courage and determination, in the face of overwhelming obstacles, was what had inspired Jaime to become a runner. When Jaime ran, he imagined himself as the great Rafer Johnson, pouring every ounce of himself into every stride.

Yes, a lot of coincidences, known and unknown, had converged to bring Tim and Jaime to tonight's game. As Jaime continued to ponder coincidences—a concept his mother referred to as "synchronicity"—he recalled that Franklin High shouldn't even have been in the same league with Riverton.

At one time, Sprague, Franklin High's home town, and Riverton had been in two different counties. Riverton High competed in the

Tri-County League, and Franklin High in the Beaver Creek League. This was the way it had been for as long as anyone could remember.

Then, one fateful night twelve years ago, one of the heaviest rain storms since the turn of the century hit the entire western half of the state. The storm caused tremendous damage, not the least of which was that it washed out the Chippewa Dam, about ten miles north of Sprague. When the dam collapsed, it sent a flood through the town of Sprague, the likes of which no one then alive in the town had witnessed.

After the storm ended and the citizens of Sprague came out of hiding to survey the damage, they were astounded to find that the Elk Horn River, which had flowed along the west side of town forever, had blazed a new trail through Jerry Larson's cantaloupe farm, passed between two high-tension towers, and dropped from a high plateau, forming a magnificent waterfall. It then headed east, making a long sweeping arc around the badlands just beyond that end of town, then curved to the west until it found its way back to its original riverbed about five miles south of town.

The Elk Horn River had always served as the western boundary of Beaver Creek County. When Mother Nature decided to flex her aquatic muscle and reroute the river, however, a heated political debate arose regarding the exact location where Beaver Creek County ended and Silverwood County began.

Some said the relocation of the river made no difference and that the boundary should remain where it always had been, notwithstanding the now-dry riverbed. Others espoused a variable county boundary, capable of relocating from time to time in accordance with the whims of nature. Those in favor of the variable county boundary theory cited as the basis for their position the well-established state law requiring that if a private citizen owned land bordering on a river and the river subsequently changed its course, the boundary of the land owned by such private citizen would be relocated accordingly.

Those in favor of retaining the original boundary, not taking the time to research the legal distinction between a river relocation occurring as the result of a single violent act as opposed to a gradual, long-term process, simply retorted, "Hogwash."

Ultimately, it came down to a vote of the citizens of Sprague as to whether they wanted to remain in Beaver Creek County or to come under the auspices of Silverwood County. The owner and editor of the Sprague *Daily Sentinel*, realizing a new county boundary would put his 640-acre farm in Silverwood County, where property taxes were about half of what they were in Beaver Creek County, promptly published a series of editorials setting forth the many advantages that would accrue to the citizens of Sprague from finding themselves within the friendly arms of the Silverwood County Commissioners. Easily persuaded, the voters stampeded to the polling booths, whereupon the town of Sprague was legally relocated within the benevolent county of Silverwood. The County Commissioners of Beaver Creek sputtered and muttered but, upon advice of legal counsel, decided to confirm the decision of the citizens of Sprague.

So many coincidences, Jaime thought.

Once Saturday night's game had begun, however, there would be no time for reminiscing or philosophizing. It would be time for action—action guided by instinct. Jaime knew it could work to his benefit to let his conscious mind slip into the background and allow The Force to take control. The Force that was not a part of his conscious mind, yet still a part of him.

He had experienced the effects of The Force before. The first time he felt it, he was a fifth-grader riding on a school bus. He was sitting in the front seat next to the window on the right side when he saw an old woman just a few feet away stepping off of the curb and into the path of the oncoming bus. She was staring down at the pavement, concentrating intently on her deliberate footsteps.

When Jaime looked over to assure himself that the driver saw the woman, he discovered the driver was looking in the rearview mirror. Terror gripped him, for Jaime knew the driver could never react in time. In a split second, Jaime did something he had never done before and would never be able to explain to anyone, even if he had wanted to. He saw the old woman safe. He saw the bus missing her somehow. He saw with every fiber of his being that this sweet, little old lady needed help and she needed it right now and there was only Jaime. Small, helpless, eleven-year-old Jaime was all she had.

Jaime was all she needed.

He couldn't decide later whether it was a prayer or a wish or a dream or an act of outrageous will. All he knew was that two seconds later he looked out the rear window and saw the old woman walking across the street in a spot where the bus could not possibly have missed her. Yet, there she was, walking along at her slow, shuffling pace.

Nobody else had noticed the incident, not even the old lady. Maybe, Jaime thought later, that was why it had worked. There had been no other witnesses to add doubt to the equation. There had been only Jaime and the wonderful Force.

As he lay in bed that night after the incident, Jaime kept thinking about the words he had once heard a preacher say, something to the effect that "these things ye see me do, ye shall do likewise." The power of those words sent a chill up Jaime's spine that rushed into his head and seemed to explode inside his mind. This was the most glorious feeling Jaime had ever experienced—a feeling that resonated through every cell of his body. He fell asleep that night suspecting that life was a whole lot more than he had ever imagined.

Jaime knew that, Saturday night on the football field, he would have an opportunity to "do likewise." He would give this game everything he had because that was part of the deal. He couldn't rely on The Force to do it all. He thought of it as a partnership. He did his part, and The Force filled in the parts that were beyond his immediate physical ability. Still, The Force seemed to be a part of him. At seventeen, Jaime found it all very difficult to explain, even to himself. It was just something he knew.

He felt this mysterious power when he ran. He would reach a point where common sense told him he couldn't go any faster, yet something would happen he couldn't describe. He would feel himself driven to increase his speed a bit, as though a gentle hand were pushing against the small of his back. Maybe it had to do with the effects of adrenaline. Maybe it had to do with desire. Maybe it had to do with faith. This unidentified power made him think of Michael Jordan and how he seemed to hang in the air longer than the laws of physics would permit, especially for the basket that would win the game. That same power allowed for the bone and flesh and pretty flowered dress of a little old lady to pass through the steel and plastic and rubber and glass of a fifteen-ton school bus and still be alive and sweet and flowery and slowly shuffling home to the little old man who loved her.

Yes, the Riverton game might be Jaime's finest hour, not for the satisfaction of victory, not for the admiration of the fans, not even for the opportunity to show off in front of Cathy Stevens, the gorgeous little cheerleader whose attention Jaime had been trying to get for months, although any one of these factors would certainly be worth the effort. No, this just might be the night that Tim and Jaime Lasher would get to prove to themselves that this Force they had talked about so often was for real. For years they had discussed it, speculated about it, had doubts about it. The time had come to know.

Jaime had come up with a plan. He hadn't spoken with Tim about what he had in mind, as he was afraid that might ruin the test. For the test even to be possible, a lot of things had to coincide, things out of Jaime's control. But Jaime's entire life had been filled with coincidences. It didn't seem too far-fetched that all of the appropriate circumstances for Jaime's test could materialize, especially if Jaime were to focus his energy and attention as he'd done in the past.

The Franklin/Riverton football game just might be a test of Jaime's ability to affect all sorts of things with the power of his mind.

 # Chapter Two

To date, nobody has been able to build a computer model that will predict the weather perfectly. Because so many variables influence the weather, even the most powerful computers haven't enough room to accept the amount of data necessary to achieve a completely reliable prediction. When it comes to the weather, therefore, we are relegated to the realm of probability rather than certainty.

There is, however, one factor that even those far-thinking scientists, who dream of and work at creating a reliable weather model some day, have probably not yet considered: the effect that the "collective unconscious" has on all of those other variables.

Carl Jung, noted psychologist, coined the term "collective unconscious" to describe the combined mental energy of the inhabitants of this planet. Likewise, as many nuclear physicists or sub-atomic particle theorists will tell you, it has been reliably established that it is impossible for anyone to study a particle of matter without noticeably affecting it with the power of his or her mind. Following this logic, speculation that the weather on this beleaguered planet is affected considerably by the thoughts of humanity seems reasonable.

Our ancestors came to understand this simple fact early on, and forthwith created the effective but sometimes disparaged rain dance. Unfortunately, in recent times most people have forgotten their innate ability to focus their energy and power to affect their physical environment.

Just imagine what would happen if those interested in changing the weather banded together. As soon as the unsuspecting CNN weather lady released her prediction relative to tomorrow's weather patterns, these "cultists" would join hands in small neighborhood groups, focus their collective energies, and completely destroy the weather lady's credibility by replacing her predicted "balmy summer's day" with an unseasonable blizzard.

Be that as it may, on the night of the Franklin/Riverton football game, those variables that inevitably combine to produce our weather, however currently unpredictable, did come together in a most fortuitous manner. A high pressure area over the north Pacific Ocean, combining with a low pressure area over the flat and humid state of Florida, conspired to cause a brisk wind to blow out of the northwest and into the small town of Sprague and the stadium where the scoreboard clock ticked off the few minutes remaining until the game.

This increase in wind velocity initially caused little concern to the residents of Sprague or Riverton. The subsequent long-range effects of this northwesterly wind, however, were numerous, two of which would prove to be significant, to wit: 1. The temperature in the area began to drop precipitously, and 2. The whirling and swirling of the clouds, combining with the arid conditions of the area, caused an abundance of static electricity to accumulate in the heavens. Streaks of lightning began to fill the sky, to the dismay of those fans who had not equipped themselves with umbrellas. These electrical discharges not only leaped from various cumulous clouds to the ground but occasionally shot from cloud to cloud. The resultant display was nigh on to a Disney World fireworks pageant.

As fate would have it, one errant lightning bolt found its way to the precise area occupied by Hans Ruger's newly acquired and expensive irrigation pump, causing it to spin its turbines frantically in a reverse direction before melting down to a relatively valueless glob of metal. This reverse thrusting caused the water, which had been patiently awaiting its release on Sunday morning as part of the annual pre-winter soaking of the pinto bean fields, to surge rearward at breakneck speed.

One might suspect that the result of such an incident would be for the water merely to return to the well from which it had been drawn. However, in its infinite wisdom, the local governmental agency having jurisdiction over such matters had required Hans to install an anti-siphon valve at the top of his well to prevent water from reentering it.

Such a requirement is not unusual and is imposed to keep water that has seen the light of day, and perhaps acquired a dose of giardia or E-coli, from returning to the well and ultimately finding its way into a heretofore pristine underground aquifer. Were this to happen, such contaminated water might end up in the plumbing systems and digestive tracts of unsuspecting inhabitants of the surrounding area, resulting in a dramatic increase in the number of toilet flushes per capita.

In this case, the anti-siphon valve stopped the backward surging water dead in its tracks, resulting in a tremendous increase in the pressure within the six-inch aluminum pipe that connected the well to the former water pump.

Perhaps the high pressure area in the North Pacific and the low pressure area over southeastern Florida would not have had much of a bearing on the lives of Tim and Jaime Lasher, had not Edgar Sphenster been raised by a frugal mother.

Edgar's mother consistently harped on Edgar and his three siblings about such matters as the wastefulness of leaving a light on when nobody is in a room, the wisdom of setting aside a portion of one's earnings for a rainy day, and the need to eat every morsel on their plates to help the starving children in Ethiopia. As a result, Edgar, who detested his mother's harping, nonetheless entered into adulthood with an attitude toward economics reminiscent of Ebenezer Scrooge. In short, Edgar was a cheapskate.

Edgar worked as the controller for Avondale Plumbing and Irrigation Supply. Several months ago, Edgar sought to impress the general manager of Avondale by re-bidding a proposal from a long-time supplier of materials. This re-bidding resulted in a four percent savings on the cost of welding supplies. It also forced the bidder to surreptitiously substitute an inferior welding material for the one that Avondale had used for the preceding thirteen years.

Whether or not the coupler connecting the pipe between the former water pump and the anti-siphon valve would have stood up to the water pressure surge, had Avondale used its traditional welding materials, is a matter of pure speculation. However, the inferior welding material actually used was no match for the immense force caused by the reverse thrusting of Hans's now melted-down turbines. As a result, a gigantic crack formed in the coupler, allowing copious quantities of water to begin gushing from the well. This was possible, even without the aid of a functional pump, because the well was artesian and delivered generous amounts of water to the surface, utilizing only the forces of nature.

No one knew of the leak, nor was anyone likely to discover it until morning, because Hans had given all of his employees the night off to attend the football game.

The water, seeking its own level, as water will invariably do, began its relentless march toward the state highway, where it ultimately began to pool against the highway's shoulder.

Now most people think that "highways" are so named because they are built some distance above the surrounding terrain. They also assume that one of the reasons for this configuration is to keep any substantial quantity of water off of those highways during all but the most tenacious of rainstorms. And they would be correct.

Even Beulah Rigsby, secretary to the chief engineer of the state highway department, would agree with that assessment. Unfortunately,

Beulah was born not only with one toe missing from her left foot, but also with one joint missing from her right pinky finger—a malady that caused Beulah to occasionally have difficulty reaching some of the keys on her word processor keyboard.

If you will wander over to your computer's keyboard and put your right hand in the typing position, you will see that a person with a short pinky finger might not quite reach the plus key on the far right of the upper row and could accidentally hit the minus key. If this should happen, in conjunction with a failure to hold down the shift key, a minus sign would replace the intended plus sign. Sure enough, that's just what happened to the state highway when the civil engineer was designing that fateful strip of asphalt, now rapidly approaching parity with the surface of Hans Ruger's newly acquired pond. The elevation of the surface of that highway was reduced by approximately thirteen inches by Beulah's errant finger.

Had the highway been built to the correct specifications, the water from Hans's leaking coupler would not have reached pavement level until about 11:30 the next morning. By that time, Hans would have undoubtedly noticed a new pond along the highway and would have made haste to close the valve on top of the well. However, being that things are as they are, the water began to come dangerously close to the top of the asphalt by 7:30 Saturday evening.

You will recall that the unusual weather patterns in the area of the Franklin/Riverton football game produced two relevant conditions. The first, static electricity, resulted in the lightning strike on old Hans's well pump. The second, a drastic drop in the air temperature, meant that at just about the time the level of the newly formed pond was approaching the level of the highway, the air temperature in the area, a chilly 24° F, would be driving the temperature of the asphalt rapidly towards a critical 32° F.

Another seeming coincidence is the fact that the intersection of the state highway and Partridge Road, the road that runs to Hans Ruger's ranch house and intersects the state highway a mere twenty feet from the southern shore of Han's recently created pond, had for the last twenty-seven months been well-lighted by two high-pressure sodium highway lights.

It had not always been so, however.

Because of the distance of that intersection from the town of Sprague, and the cost of bringing electrical service that distance, the town fathers had obstinately, and perhaps wisely, refused to provide electricity to such an undistinguished rural crossroads.

However, on one particularly dark evening, a couple of years prior to the historic Franklin/Riverton football game, a busload of Franklin High youngsters had been headed home after a volleyball tournament in the town of Eastridge. As the bus approached the Partridge Road intersection, Melvin Doolittle, returning home from a late night in the fields on his Massey Ferguson tractor, was making a slow sweeping turn off of Partridge Road onto the state highway. Due to the late hour, Melvin's state of exhaustion, and the pint of sloe gin Melvin kept in the tractor's toolbox (a substantial portion of which had found its way from the bottle through the villi in Melvin's small intestine, into his blood stream, and subsequently to his hypothalamus), Melvin's slow sweeping turn was slower and more sweeping than prudence would dictate. The heavy and unlighted Massey-Ferguson swept slowly across the double yellow line and into the intended route of travel of the school bus.

Even if the driver of the ill-fated bus had been paying attention to the road, instead of ogling the kneecap and thigh of the shapely cheerleader seated in the front right-hand seat, he probably wouldn't have been able to spot the oblivious Mr. Doolittle and his slowly sweeping Massey-Ferguson.

Fortunately, every time the bus driver's eyes roamed in the direction of the shapely knee and thigh, a genetic defect in his nervous system caused his right calf to relax slightly, thereby decreasing the amount of pressure with which he depressed the accelerator pedal. Because of the inordinate length of time his most recent knee-and-thigh glance had lasted, his customary pressure on the accelerator pedal had been reduced for approximately twenty-five seconds, causing the bus to decelerate to a modest thirty-three miles per hour.

When, as you have correctly surmised, the Bluebird bus inevitably made contact with the Massey-Ferguson tractor, the reduction in bus speed contributed greatly to the fact that Melvin Doolittle would live to plow another field.

Melvin did not experience the adventure without impunity, however. To the contrary, Melvin found the entire event quite ghastly, notwithstanding the fact that he had adequately buffered, with the aid of the sloe gin, vast portions of his cerebellum from the messages being sent at a frenzied pace from his sensory receptors.

As the Massey-Ferguson did what can only be described as an agricultural double gainer, Melvin came into immediate and unpleasant contact with the plexiglas windshield, intended by those who toil at the Massey-Ferguson design center to protect tractor drivers from being accosted by small airborne creatures traveling in a direction opposite to that of the tractor.

The combined damage perpetrated upon various parts of the school bus and the tractor, when added to that done to Melvin's proboscis, caused a considerable outlay on the part of the various insurance companies involved.

The legal hullabaloo proceeding therefrom, however, paled in comparison to the outcry generated by the parents of the students of Franklin High, who now regarded their precious little ones as an endangered species.

Most of the parents, in total disregard of the contributions the bus driver's wandering eye or Melvin's state of inebriation had made to the scenario, regarded it as a foregone conclusion that none of this would have happened had there been adequate lighting at the intersection.

It was, therefore, quickly decided that those long-awaited high-pressure sodium fixtures would be installed straightaway.

Because of the city's continued refusal to deliver the necessary electrical power, it was determined that those fixtures would be connected to the electrical substation owned and operated by the Farmer's Home Improvement District, affectionately known as FHID. The fact that the association had been formed solely for the purpose of providing power to farm houses and irrigation pumps was disregarded in deference to the overwhelming need to protect school buses from making untimely contact with unlighted farm equipment.

Thus, the two high-pressure sodium fixtures at the intersection of the state highway and Partridge Road were the only fixtures along the entire state highway system in direct contact with the same substation that supplied power to Hans Ruger's recently demised water pump.

After the lightning had succeeded in assaulting Hans's unfortunate pump, it took the route of least resistance, as electricity will invariably do. However, because Hans's pump had been mounted upon four substantial rubber bushings, designed to prevent the vibration of the pump from fracturing the concrete foundation upon which it rested, the pump was grounded by means of a heavy aluminum cable connected to the superstructure of the nearby electrical substation.

For that reason, the path of least resistance proved not to be into the bowels of Mother Earth, as one might have suspected. Instead, the mighty charge found its way along the electrical line and grounding cable from Hans's former pump to the main high voltage lines of the substation. From there it raced to numerous light fixtures and appliances at homes along the route of the power system, taking care not to overlook the towering light fixtures at the highway intersection.

Upon arriving at the site of the light fixtures, the power surge made haste to blow those expensive devises to kingdom come, rendering that intersection, once again, in a state of utter darkness.

Buford Stravinsky was not a patient man. Buford Stravinsky was an angry man. Buford Stravinsky was a man on a mission.

A few days earlier, Buford had, as usual, been watching Monday night football with several of his buddies in a friend's family room. The ever-present six-pack of beer sat nestled safely on the floor between his feet, from which he drew a bottle at approximately fifteen-minute intervals. All had been well in Buford's world on that Monday night.

As the evening progressed and a fresh supply of six-packs was secured, the sounds emanating from that family room increased by a serious number of decibels. As the alcohol and testosterone continued to flow in ever-increasing quantities, the boisterousness of those in attendance reached record heights. Before long, the betting began.

Buford had learned from his father, who had learned from his father before him, that when a matter of disagreement between men cannot be resolved by logic, reasoning, common sense, or popular vote, the laws of masculine conduct require that the disputing parties challenge each other to "Put yer money where yer mouth is."

It is a well-known fact that when the participants in a Monday night football gathering have proceeded beyond the mid-point of their second six-pack—each—then any appeal to logic, reasoning, or common sense is useless and any attempt to resolve the matter by popular vote can only result in a fistfight.

The debate Buford had been engaged in with Andy Teesdale, over the likely outcome of the upcoming Franklin/Riverton football game, ultimately and inevitably reached the point where personal honor was at stake. Buford, while snapping the pop-top on his ninth can of Blatz, uttered the obligatory "Put yer money where yer mouth is."

Some believe that it is genetically encoded in the DNA of members of the male gender that when those fateful words are uttered, the male recipient of the sound waves of that utterance will reflexively suggest an amount to secure the bet, which is beyond his ability to pay without dipping deeply into his wife's household operating reserve.

It seems likely that a complimentary encoding in the DNA of the spouses of all Monday Night football devotees causes them to instinctively know when such a bet has been made, from the mere look in their husbands' eyes. This encoding requires that such spouses, upon learning of the amount of the bet, spontaneously shout out the words "Are you out of your mind? That's more than our next three months' rent!"

Well, as you may have guessed, Buford did, indeed, get himself ensconced into just such a wager on that crucial Monday night.

Later, as Buford tiptoed stealthily through his kitchen door, the overhead lights suddenly came to life, the result of a swift and skillful flip of the switch by his tiny but powerful wife, Lizzy. Before Buford could don his intended look of childlike innocence, Lizzy got a clear and revealing glance into his roadmap-like eyes. She knew. And he knew that she knew. And she knew that he knew that she knew.

His shock at seeing Lizzy suddenly appear before his eyes in the brilliant kitchen light affected his nervous system like a truth serum. Buford blurted out the amount of their household budget he had riding on the outcome of the Franklin/Riverton game without even thinking.

Lizzy instantly and automatically shouted out, "Are you out of your mind? That's more than our next three months' rent!"

Lizzy resisted the temptation to go for the rolling pin and simply but firmly informed Buford that he would be welcomed back in the house when he: 1) redeemed the amount he had risked on the game, 2) presented her with his winnings, if any, and 3) swore on the Good Book that he would never gamble again. She, thereupon, propelled him out the door through which he had gained entrance to the kitchen, locked it quickly, and jingled in front of the windowpane, through which Buford gazed, his key ring which she had had the foresight to remove from his hand before shoving him out the door.

Now, five nights later, Buford finds himself rushing to the football game at the wheel of the Silverwood County oil truck—the truck used for oiling down those county roads which as yet do not sport an asphalt mantle.

Buford's supervisor had sent him out on a last-minute emergency spray job. The superintendent of schools had requested that the gravel road in front of the fire marshal's house be sprayed by the county right away. It had something to do with the occupancy limits at the stadium, but Buford didn't understand county politics and couldn't have cared less. All he knew was that this last-minute assignment was making him dreadfully late for the kickoff of the football game and a substantial portion of his future with Lizzy rode on that game's outcome.

With only eight minutes until kickoff and a good ten miles to the stadium, Buford became a man possessed, possessed of just about everything but good judgment. He threw the transmission into overdrive and put the two-speed rear end into high range. The truck was designed to haul up to two thousand gallons of oil, which would weigh about nine tons, so it had plenty of horse power. With fewer than one hundred gallons left in the tank, the power-to-weight ratio would be about that of a semi-tractor without a trailer or a tow truck with nothing in tow.

He slammed the accelerator to the floor and those four hundred and thirty-five cubic inches of big block torque screamed alive.

Buford noticed that the rear view mirror hung a bit askew, allowing him to look into his own eyes. What he saw frightened him just a little. Staring back at him from that mirror was a sight reminiscent of a line from a poem his sophomore poetry teacher had once read to him that he had all but forgotten: "His eyes were hollows of madness."

A sneer formed on Buford's lips. His teeth clenched reflexively. His right hand squeezed the gearshift knob with crushing pressure. The speedometer indicated eighty-seven miles per hour. In the side-view mirror, he could see smoke swirling out behind the truck, barely visible in the growing darkness. He felt strangely alive.

As he roared down the asphalt at ninety-four miles per hour, determined to see that kickoff, he thought he saw a water pond flash by along the left side of the highway. But no water pond sat along the state highway. Must be his imagination. As he turned to look over his shoulder at the phantom pond, the beastly truck, without Buford's being aware of it, wandered over into the far left lane. Fortunately, there was no oncoming traffic. He was moving so fast that he couldn't verify whether he had seen water or not, especially now that Hans Ruger's pinto bean field was no longer in the range of his headlights.

He rocketed through the intersection of Partridge Road, still in the wrong lane. Something didn't seem right to him. What was it? The lights were off. That's it, those new high-pressure sodium light fixtures that the county purchasing agent had made such a big deal about weren't even on.

As Buford turned to look in the rear view mirror once again, to make sure he had been correct about those lights, the speedometer needle hit one hundred three, and Buford's right knee accidentally pressed against the flow valve of the oil sprayer. Unbeknownst to Buford, the seventy-four gallons of oil remaining in the tank were released onto the asphalt behind the truck, greasing the surface of the state highway for about a hundred yards before the tank went dry.

Thus was the situation along the state highway, ten miles from the Franklin/Riverton football game, at just a few minutes before kickoff time.

# Chapter Three

Quiet. Not a sound…but breathing. Labored breathing. Thirty-three anxious young men and three equally anxious coaches. All but two of the young men in that tense locker room engaged in similar thoughts.

All the training. All the exercising. All the positive thinking. All the pep talks, the praying, the planning, the strategizing. It all came down to this. Tonight. The next two hours would determine whether it was all worth it. The next two hours would give these young men a chance to show whether they had what it takes, to show what they're really made of.

Whether they could walk tall and proud tomorrow hinged on what they would do on this crucial night. There was so much at stake, so much to lose, the tension almost unbearable. Many felt a temptation to run away, to walk out and never come back, anything to get away from the terrible feeling of suffocation, the fear of failure, the terror of having to face their friends tomorrow, knowing they hadn't measured up.

These thoughts alternated with visions of glory, thoughts of victory, thoughts of the surge of joy to be felt when the final gun would go off and the game would be won. The frequent changes in thought were wreaking havoc on the nervous system, causing the digestive tract to feel like quivering, carbonated jalapeño jelly.

The thoughts shared by Tim and Jaime were surprisingly different than those of their friends, calm, controlled, confident. Each knew, instinctively, what the other was feeling.

Strangely, the reason for the difference between their attitudes and those of their teammates had very little to do with their athletic skills but was due to the fact that they didn't place the same emphasis on the outcome of the game. Their identities and feelings of self-worth didn't center on any event or circumstance. Their joy came from the training, the exercising, the strategizing. They savored each moment as it presented itself. Of course, they wanted to win. But victory was only the frosting on the cake. The real joy of living, as they had been taught by their parents, is experienced in giving one's self totally to the present moment, not the past or the future.

Dad had taught Tim and Jaime long ago that the true nature of man is not to be competitive but to be creative. He taught them that real satisfaction comes from personal achievement, not from defeating another person. He taught them that one person does not have to lose for another person to win.

Then why did Tim and Jaime so relish the game of football? Was it not an ultimate form of competition? Jaime had asked himself this question many times. When the answer finally came to him, it didn't come as a single, simple answer. It came as a complex revelation. It was an insight that would affect a vast part of his thought processes for the rest of his life, one that convinced him that his dad's teaching, about man's nature being one of creation rather than competition, was right on.

Jaime realized that his love for football came not from its competitive qualities but, strangely enough, because of the opportunities it provided for him to create. It wasn't defeating the other team that drove him. It was gaining as many yards, catching as many passes, running faster than he had ever run before that turned him on. Even though the other players provided him with the obstacles to overcome in honing his skills, he wasn't necessarily in competition with anyone else. He was being all that he could be. He experienced the elation of just being on this magnificent planet, working with the laws of gravity and momentum, using the power of his mind and the strength of his body to feel. That was it: to feel, to experience.

Football simply provided the vehicle. Unfortunately, because of the structure of society, the vehicles of expression for a seventeen-year-old high-school student are somewhat limited. Jaime expected that, as he grew older and had more of a say in the circumstances of his life, he would find other avenues of expression, perhaps in music or writing or painting or whatever would allow him to be more of what he could be, without the specter of competition looming in the background.

For now, however, the most convenient and available activity that enabled him to work on his growth and skills was football. He didn't need to focus on the defeat of the other team. He had only to be the best that he could be, for himself. In doing so, he would still be a valuable part of the team. And he certainly wouldn't let his team-mates down. In fact, Jaime suspected that his motivation, to be his best just for Jaime, presented the most powerful kind of motive. If his abilities and efforts were instrumental in causing the other team to lose, that came as a result of the nature of the system, not of Jaime's intention. After all, even though Jaime might sincerely care for the members of the other team, he did not trouble himself as to how they reacted to the situations presented to them. That was their concern, their attachment to outcome. The best Jaime could do was always to act from the purest of intentions. The rest was up to the universe to sort out.

Jaime loved to practice what Dad had taught him—that the best way to live is to stay in the present moment. It was okay to plan for an upcoming event. But the real ecstasy comes from the steps along the way. The arrival of the final result in any situation merely indicates that it's time to set a new goal to create a whole new series of exciting present moments.

Tonight, Jaime's mind revolved around the exciting idea that he just might get an opportunity to give The Force an ultimate test.

He glanced over at Tim and there sat his brother, older by four minutes, with that ever-present grin. That smile expressed so much confidence, knowing, conspiracy, and best of all, love that caused Jaime to ache with a longing. He yearned for them to be together always, to never stop being the best of friends, to be with each other for lifetimes to come.

The minutes passed. Jaime sat there, silently, allowing his mind to drift. He thought about nothing in particular, just felt the moment. He glanced over at Tim again. Now Tim's eyes held a distant look, an expression of total concentration and power. Jaime and his parents had come to call this intense state of focus "That Look."

Jaime thought back to the first time he had seen That Look. In those days, Tim was called "Timmy." They were twelve years old up at the rock quarry on the back side of Cougar Ridge on a beautiful, warm summer day. It was the first time they had been allowed to go there without Mom or Dad. The quarry could be a dangerous place.

The pit had been hollowed out on the edge of a gigantic crater that went down into the earth, deeper than anyone had ever been able to measure. The quarry had been there for over a hundred years, originally having been operated by laborers using horses and mules. After the turn of the century, the animals and wagons were gradually replaced by trucks and heavy earth-moving equipment. Over the years, as larger and more powerful machines were developed, the operators of the quarry were able to dig faster and deeper.

An event involving the death of a most unpleasant man named Brute Swenson had caused the massive hole to fill with water long ago, providing a place for young people to gather in the summertime.

Rumor had it that Brute Swenson's ghost inhabited the gloomy depths of the pond.

Many a child had stood on the edge of one of the quarry's ledges, in fear and trembling, as others taunted him or her to leap into the deep, dark, murky, and possibly haunted waters of the quarry pond.

An unfortunate number of children had died at the quarry over the decades since Brute Swenson had plunged to the bottom of what had previously been considered a bottomless crater.

On the day of Timmy and Jaime's first un-chaperoned visit to the pond, their mother had admonished them to be extremely careful. She knew they were excellent swimmers. She knew they were sensible. She knew they were intolerant of any nonsense from less disciplined children. She knew they were obedient. Still, part of a mom's job is to worry needlessly.

The last thing she had said before they left was "Okay, you two scoundrels, I expect you back here by four o'clock. If four-o-one should arrive and I haven't seen those two curly mops of yours, you know I'll be headed for the pond with the chief of police, the sheriff, the head of the state patrol, two fire trucks, an ambulance, and an entire herd of paramedics. So…if you don't want to be embarrassed in front of the entire town, I'd suggest that you glance at your watches frequently."

Timmy and Jaime looked back at Mom as they headed out the door. She stood at the kitchen sink and gave a flip of that long, beautiful hair for which she was so famous.

They sure loved her.

They arrived at the quarry at 1:45. They leaned their bikes against a pine tree and headed for one of the ledges high above the pond. Though far too high for jumping, this ledge offered a great place to be undisturbed. As they lay there in the warm summer sun, a gentle breeze blowing, Jaime felt completely relaxed. That nobody else was at the quarry that day surprised him. Usually, at this time of year at least a few high-school kids would be working on their summer tans.

It was so warm and so quiet that before long, Jaime fell asleep. His rest was not the deep kind of sleep he had when he snuggled into the down comforter Mom had made him for his big four-poster bed. It was an easy, drifting sleep, like one where you wake up a little bit every few minutes and realize where you are and know that all is well, then enjoy the warmth of the sun for a few seconds until you doze off again.

Finally, he drifted into a much deeper sleep. He dreamed about many things. He dreamed about swimming in the quarry pond, all by himself. He dreamed that he saw something deep in the murky depths of the pond. He didn't know what it was, but it seemed strangely familiar. The dark water made it hard see. Its shape made him think of a large prehistoric fish, like one he had seen on the Learning Channel. As it came closer to the surface, Jaime was horrified to see that it had the face of a man, a man experiencing the most terrible agony imaginable. As it drew closer, Jaime thought that he knew the man, but he couldn't remember who he was. Then, the skin around the eyes and mouth began to tear, and the man's skull began to push its way out of the flesh. Jaime tried to scream but only a faint whisper left his mouth. As the fish-man sank back into the dismal depths of the pond, Jaime awoke with a start.

He didn't know how long he had been sleeping, but he knew that something had changed. He felt it in the depths of his soul. For one thing, the bright blue sunny sky had become completely covered with a thick dark layer of thunderclouds. The temperature had dropped dramatically, and goose bumps covered Jaime's body. A strong wind had begun to blow.

Most of all, Timmy was gone.

Jaime glanced at his watch: 3:15! Better head for home pretty soon! Where was Timmy?

As Jaime sat there trying to decide which way to go to begin looking for Timmy, the velocity of the wind increased, and the temperature seemed to drop another couple of degrees.

Then he heard it.

Above the howl of the wind, Jaime heard a faint sound that didn't belong there.

He quickly slipped on his jeans over his swimming trunks and put on his sneakers. He looked around. He couldn't decide which direction the sound had come from. He heard it again. He still had no clue as to its source. He tried to reason it out. Finally, he decided that most likely it had come from upwind. With the wind howling, almost any sound downwind would have been blown away. He headed upwind.

Where the heck was Timmy?

He noticed that both bicycles stood where they had left them. Timmy hadn't gone home. Besides, Jaime knew his brother wouldn't leave without telling him.

That sound again.

It was closer now.

More confident that he was heading in the right direction, Jaime moved a little faster. He found himself on a game trail, leading around to the back of the cliff that formed the south side of the quarry. The intensity of the wind increased.

He heard the sound again, clearer this time. The little hairs on the back of his neck tingled. It sounded like the voice of a woman or a young boy. But, whoever it was wasn't speaking. Jaime tried to give the sound a name. It wasn't a scream. It wasn't a moan. It was a muffled shriek of despair and terror. Jaime started running. He wondered why he was wasting energy thinking about a name for the ghastly sound when someone needed help.

This was the time to take advantage of that blazing speed for which he was already becoming well known. Now, certain that he was heading in the right direction, he began to sprint for all he was worth. Rafer Johnson was with him now. Rafer and Jaime to the rescue.

The branches of the scrub oak bushes tore at his arms and face. He didn't care. *A man on a mission pays no heed to pain! Where did that phrase come from? Never mind, it seems appropriate.*

Then, as Jaime came around a sharp right turn, he stopped dead in his tracks, his legs feeling like warm licorice ropes. A deep ravine blocked his path, too wide to jump. On the other side, not more than twenty feet from Jaime, was the source of those hideous sounds, the scene so chilling it sent shivers up his spine. The wind still roared so loudly that no one had heard him approaching, in spite of the fact that he was chugging like a locomotive.

As he stood there, gasping for breath, he tried to assimilate what his twelve-year-old eyes were seeing. A young woman was tied to a tree. Her arms were behind her, wrapped around the tree's trunk and tied together with a piece of rope. Her head was pulled back, with her chin pointing upward, a strand of barbed wire wrapped around her neck and looped over a branch of the tree, just above her head. In that position, she couldn't lower her head without the barbed wire cutting into her windpipe or rupturing a jugular vein. Her mouth was stuffed with something that looked like a wad of paper. Blood dripped from her nose and the sides of her mouth.

Jaime took this all in in a matter of seconds.

A man stood in front of the woman, a baseball bat in his left hand. The head of the bat was resting on the ground. He appeared to be screaming something at the lady. Spit flew out of his mouth and all over her face and blood-stained blouse.

Jaime could hear nothing but the wind.

The man picked up the bat with his left hand and laid it over his right shoulder. He brought his right hand up to the bat and raised his elbows. He pivoted his torso to the right, just like a baseball player about to hit a grand slammer.

And then Jaime's heart felt like it missed about three beats. For the first time he saw the man's face. It was the face of the fish-man that Jaime had seen in his dream, contorted into the same grotesque expression.

Because of the ravine, Jaime was too far away to help. This poor, terrified woman was about to die, and Jaime couldn't get there in time.

The man pivoted a couple more times at the waist, as if trying to torment the woman further. She looked at the bat, barely able to see it because of the angle of her head. Then she let out that sound. The sound Jaime had first heard muffled by the wind, a sound of frantic terror, a bizarre mixture of insane pleading and defiance. Jaime felt that he might explode with rage and frustration.

Then he spotted a narrow place in the ravine about twenty yards away that he thought he might be able to jump. Just as he started to run, he saw something move. The scene reminded him of one of those drawings where you try to locate an object hidden by the artist among the many busy lines. Jaime hadn't noticed it before. But, something moved. He focused intently on the area of the movement. Then his heart, which had not yet recovered from the recent beat-skipping incident, almost leaped out of his rib cage.

That little movement came from Timmy, the most wonderful brother in the world.

Timmy was about ten feet behind the man, crouched, ready to spring. He paused for a few seconds. At first Jaime thought that Timmy was hesitating for fear of being discovered. Then he saw That Look on Timmy's face, the same look Jaime was seeing on Timmy's face tonight in the locker room. It was a look of fierce concentration, as if Timmy were in contact with another world. Then Jaime realized what Timmy was doing. He was calling forth the power of the universe, The Force. They had talked about this many times before. It was the same force Jaime felt pushing the small of his back when he didn't think he could possibly run any faster, and yet a part of him knew he could.

Timmy was preparing to do something awesome.

Jaime paused for a moment, clenched his fists, gritted his teeth, tightened his neck and stomach muscles, took a deep breath, and shot every ounce of power, energy, hope, faith, and love he had in his being straight toward his Timmy.

Timmy sprang like a madman, screaming a vile epithet. In three bounds, he leapt onto the man, punching, biting, and kicking with a ferocity he'd never known. The man got Timmy in a headlock. Timmy turned his head toward the side of the man's waist and bit down with everything he had, causing the man to let go of Timmy's neck and grab his side, shrieking with pain.

Within seconds, Jaime arrived on the scene with a large tree branch in his hand. With one smack at the base of the man's skull, Jaime knocked him cold.

They quickly untied the woman and used the rope and barbed wire to fasten the unconscious man to the tree. Jaime went for help, while Timmy did his best to comfort the woman.

Anyone who thought Jaime was fast on his feet, should have seen him on a bicycle when he was properly motivated. In a little over twenty minutes, Jaime had returned with a couple of paramedics, a sheriff's officer, and a state trooper.

It turned out that the man with the baseball bat was an escaped prisoner from a state penitentiary in Nebraska, and the lady his former wife. The man had come to Sprague to find the lady and her boyfriend and kill them. He had followed the two of them to the quarry pond to perform his dastardly deeds. The boyfriend's body was found a few hours later.

The boys received a lot of attention over the next several weeks with the Woman's League and the Rotary Club each presenting them with awards for bravery.

The twins relived that day many times over the years. But what Jaime always remembered most about that day was the look on Timmy's face just before he attacked the man.

That was the same look Tim had on his face as the Franklin football team waited in that silent locker room.

Tim was preparing to do something awesome.

Coach Linden glanced at his watch, "It's time, gentlemen."

This was it. Those wonderfully brave, hopeful, and determined young men rose slowly to their feet. An uncommon silence still hung in the room. They quietly came together in the center of the room, football cleats scraping the concrete floor, and joined hands. Coach Linden led them in a brief prayer.

The Franklin team headed slowly down the tunnel to the playing field. Their walk turned into a trot, then into a run, then into a sprint as the team exploded onto the field, the crowd screaming and stomping frantically, the band playing enthusiastically, friends and relatives looking on with pride in their hearts and, for some, a tightness in their throats.

This was it.

Tonight was the night of nights.

 # Chapter Four

At fifteen minutes before game time, Jaime took the field with the rest of the team to do their warm-up calisthenics. Tim stood up front, leading the team, a confident smile on his face. He didn't look like someone about to engage in one of the greatest challenges of his life. To look at him, you would have thought that as soon as the exercises were over, he planned to go for a stroll in the park. In fact, he had said as much to Jaime as they were coming out of the tunnel: "This is gonna be a walk in the park."

Jaime was thinking about how great his life was. Not only was he in the starting lineup for the biggest game in Franklin history, but he was going to play with the greatest quarterback Franklin ever had, who just happened to be his best friend and brother.

And, if everything went the way he hoped, Jaime would get the chance to prove to himself that The Force really existed. That would be no small accomplishment. If The Force is for real, then, very likely, everything else that Jaime had come to believe about how the universe works is for real too. At times, he had been able to rise above the nonsense he had heard from well-meaning but misinformed individuals and see the truth. But, at other times, his view of the truth didn't seem quite so clear. Sometimes, he wondered how he could be right if that meant so many others had to be wrong.

He had considered that maybe there wasn't any real right or wrong, just different points of view or maybe different realities.

But then, he would consider the condition of the planet, the condition of the judicial system, the violence in society, the divorce rate, and all the other insanity. That all seemed to Jaime to indicate that a substantial number of the people on this planet were unhappy. And doesn't that indicate that their thinking is incorrect?

Back to counting blessings. He looked up in the stands. He saw Mom and Dad wearing their goofy bright orange shirts and caps, just so Tim and Jaime would be able to spot them. Now, those are world-class parents. How many kids would give everything they have to be loved the way he and Tim are loved?

Michael Paul Lasher, also known as "Dad," was kind, loving, hard-working, brave, intelligent, and happy, almost always happy, even when there didn't appear to be any reason to be happy.

Jaime thought about a day long ago in mid-July, the summer sun so hot that the corn crop was in serious danger of being lost. That meant a lot to a family that counted on the proceeds from that crop to make the mortgage payments and keep them fed and clothed for another year. On that day, Dad had been up since before sunup, keeping the water flowing as best he could, without any hired help.

He had run out of cash a few weeks earlier so was unable to keep Jim, the hired hand. When the weather turned against Michael, Jim had called and offered to help. He said Michael could pay him later, when he had the money. Dad thanked him but refused the kind offer. Dad said that if he couldn't pay a man in cash at the end of the day, he couldn't rightly accept his help.

But now, with the temperature above 115°, Michael must have wondered if he hadn't been a little hasty in refusing Jim's offer.

He was running from row to row, doing what he could to see that each plant got as much water as possible. Tim and Jaime were too young to help. Mom had her hands full trying to keep the chickens from having heatstroke. She was spraying them down with a fine mist from the hose and adjusting the tarps on the side of the hen houses to take as much advantage as she could of what little breeze there was.

By late afternoon, Dad walked up to the hen house and told Mom that she should go rest for a while. He said the worst of the heat was over and that the chickens would be all right. She offered to go down to the field and help him, but he assured her he had the situation under control and he was more concerned about how tired she looked. He insisted that she go inside and have a little lemonade.

Dad found Tim and Jaime in the house and hoisted them up on his back. He wished he could take them to the pond for a cool dip, but he had drained all of the water from it to use for the corn hours ago. So, he took them to the shade of the big oak tree on the hill. The air started to cool a bit. They played for a long time, Dad with that big old grin of his. From all outside appearances, someone would have thought that he had just won the lottery. They laughed and roughhoused until the sun sat low on the horizon and the lights could be seen shining in the kitchen.

When Mom finally came up to tell them supper was ready, she asked Dad how the corn had done. He looked at her with the best smile he could manage. "The corn died a few hours ago," he said, looking away.

"Oh, Michael," Mom had said. "I know how this must hurt. This means that you're gonna have to hold down two jobs just to get us through the winter, even if I sell all of the preserves and canned fruit I can make."

They were both silent for a minute. When Dad finally looked back at her he said, "Sarah, we've been through a lot worse than this. As long as I've got you and these two scalawags, I'll be fine. My only worry is that these hard times will be too tough on you. I'll be fine."

Mom stood there, with such a look of admiration in her eyes that Jaime just knew theirs was a forever love. Yes, Michael Paul Lasher, known to Tim and Jaime as "Dad," was quite a man.

Jaime looked back up in the stands and saw Mom sitting there with the stadium lights reflecting off of her beautiful reddish-brown hair. She was probably the prettiest mom in the county. Mom was always there to listen when Jaime needed to talk. She was always caring about others, never seeming to mind the hard times, always helping the neighbors, even when she and Dad could have used the help themselves.

And what a cook she was. Jaime had heard it said many times that the most important ingredient in any meal is love. Jaime couldn't remember having a meal in his home that wasn't made with love.

He thought about the days when Mom's hair had been so very long. Sarah hadn't cut her hair since she had been a little girl, except, as she said, "to remove an occasional split end." She would brush it every night before she went to bed. My, how that hair would shine. When she was out in the sun, it was hard to tell just what color it was. Sometimes it looked brown with red highlights. Sometimes it looked dark red. Sometimes it had traces of blonde in it. Jaime remembered how the sunlight seemed to dance on Mom's hair when she moved, especially when she gave it that little flick of her head, as if she was trying to toss it over her shoulder. Mom was a beauty all right. But of all the qualities that made Mom so attractive, it was her hair that always drew the comments.

The longest Jaime ever remembered Mom's hair being was when it came down well past her waist. As a little boy, he liked to touch it. It was so soft. Often she would wind it up into kind of a knot to keep it from getting in the way, especially when she had chores to do.

But when she and Dad went to town on a Saturday night for dinner or a movie, she turned that hair loose and let it do its thing. Dad would stand back with his arms folded across his chest and look at Mom with such admiration in his eyes. He loved the way that hair danced when she walked. He would sometimes tell Mom that he would love her just as much if she were bald. But we all knew that he took a special pride in being with a woman who turned so many heads.

The summer that Jaime was eleven, he came home late one afternoon from helping a neighbor move sprinkler lines to find that Mom had cut her hair.

She hadn't cut it just a little bit. She had cut it a lot. In fact, her hair was almost as short as Dad's hair.

Jaime was speechless. He couldn't think of anything to say that wouldn't hurt Mom's feelings. He just stood there, trying not to stare, but unable to help himself. He thought it looked like Mom had been crying. He didn't say anything. He put his arms around her and held her tight. He felt like crying too. They held each other for a while. He wondered what Mom was thinking. He decided it didn't matter. Whatever was going on in her heart, a hug was the very best thing he could do.

When Dad came home that evening, he couldn't hide his disappointment. It was one of the few times Jaime ever heard his dad speak harshly to Mom. He didn't say anything abusive. He just tried to express a feeling of dreadful loss. Dad left the house, closing the kitchen door quietly. When he came back later, Jaime could tell that he had been crying. Dad walked up to Mom and put his arms around her and said, "I don't know why you did it. But I know you have your reasons. Mostly I feel bad for you. I'm sorry if I got angry. I love you." They stood there, holding each other for a long time. That's the last time Jaime ever heard them talk about it.

Tim had been visiting their cousin Joseph the week that Mom had cut her hair and didn't find out about it until he returned. In typical Tim fashion, he quickly recovered from the initial shock and said, "Hey, Mom, nice neck. I never knew you had one."

Tim and Jaime talked about Mom cutting her hair a few times over the years, but mostly, the topic faded into the background. Mom's hair grew pretty fast and by the time Tim and Jaime were fifteen, it reached down to her shoulders. Jaime knew that Mom had received an occasional dig from a couple of the women in town who were envious of Mom for having the audacity to be happily married and naturally beautiful. But, Mom took it with her usual dignity.

Dad had gotten over the whole thing in a couple of days and was just as proud as ever to be seen with Mom anytime. And he told her that.

Tim asked Mom once whether she intended to let it grow back to full length. She said she didn't think so and that, now that she was thirty-nine, she thought hair down to her waist might seem like she was trying to look younger than she was. Tim said, "Mom, it really doesn't matter. It's just the difference between looking gorgeous and extra-gorgeous." Mom promptly squirted Tim with a can of whipped cream she had been using to cover an angel food cake. This provoked another of the frequent Lasher family free-for-alls. When it was over, they were all laughing so hard that everyone had tears in his eyes.

One night, shortly after Tim and Jaime turned sixteen, they stopped at Kelly's Diner on the way home from football practice for a bite to eat.

They were waited on by a lady they had never seen in Kelly's before. The plastic tag on her neatly pressed uniform said "Helen." Tim engaged her in an animated discussion and soon discovered that this was her first week on the job. When Helen found out that Tim and Jaime were the sons of Michael and Sarah Lasher, she became noticeably silent. Tim decided to pursue the matter and asked her if she knew his parents. She hesitated for a moment and then asked if she might speak to them in confidence. Jaime couldn't imagine what this stranger might have to say that would require confidentiality. Curious, he invited her to sit at their table. She put in their order and returned to join them.

Helen started her story in a hushed and conspiratorial tone. "I don't suspect that you boys knew my Jessica. She was about five years older than you. She was a wonderfully sweet child, quiet and shy. After Jessica was born, I was told that I would not be able to have another child. Gerald and I poured all of our love into that sweet little lady. As with most children who receive lots of love, Jessica grew up with a strong sense of self and an uncommon ability to feel for others. All of our friends and relatives adored her."

She paused briefly, as if trying to compose herself. "I'm sure you can appreciate our grief," she said, "when our sweet Jessica was diagnosed with leukemia." Helen looked away for a moment.

She brushed a tear from her cheek.

"In spite of all of the pain and nausea Jessica endured from the chemotherapy, she was still a teenager and concerned about the opinions of her schoolmates. During her final days, she asked us not to allow any of her friends to visit her. She was terribly embarrassed by the fact that most of her hair had fallen out from the drugs she had to take and that she had lost so much weight.

"One night we arrived at the hospital and found her sobbing quietly. We assumed that it was the pain and offered to call the nurse. She indicated that she didn't need the nurse. When she settled down and was able to speak, she told us that she was terrified of the thought of having all of her friends and relatives see her at her funeral with only a few strands of hair. She said, 'Mom, I want them to remember me the way I was before this all happened. It's bad enough that I've lost so much weight. But, the thought of lying there the way I look now is more than I can bear.'

"We left the hospital that evening in a state of despair.

"I spent days shopping for a wig that might spare Jessica the humiliation that so terrified her. Those that we could afford were disgusting and would have made her look terrible. With all of the money we had spent on medical costs, we couldn't afford one of the fine wigs that are made from real human hair. I began to lose hope.

"Then one evening my husband and I attended a seminar for bereaved parents. We shared with those present our grief at the thought of having to watch our Jessica laid to rest in a condition that was so humiliating for her.

"The very next morning I found a box on my front porch, beautifully wrapped in silver foil and a yellow ribbon. I opened it and found what appeared to be a spool from an antique spinning wheel. Wrapped around that spool was a profusion of the longest, most beautiful reddish-brown hair I had ever seen.

"When we presented Jessica with the hairpiece made from that glorious hair, a look of joy spread over her face, the likes of which we hadn't seen for some time. From that moment on, she accepted the fact that she was close to death with a sense of peaceful resignation.

"That night, after Jessica finished admiring her hairpiece, she fell silent for a long time. Finally she said, 'Mom and Dad, I'm not afraid of dying. I have read a book that one of the nurses gave me, written about people who have died and then been brought back to life. They all report that life beyond this physical world is quite wonderful. I know where I'm going. I know I'll be fine. I just want my friends and loved ones to see me as a happy soul heading for a new adventure. I don't want to be pitied. I have written a letter, explaining how I feel about dying and how I look forward to the next life. I would like Dad to read this letter at my funeral. Now I can die in peace, knowing that all of those people I love so much will be able to understand how I feel. When they walk past my casket and see me for the last time on this plane, they'll see the real me, the way I looked when I was full of fun and laughter. The real me.'

"For a long time, I had no idea where that marvelous gift had come from or how it appeared on my front porch. For months I wanted nothing more than to thank whoever had done such a wonderful thing. Then, a few weeks later, I saw a lady in a clothing store and realized she was one of the volunteers at the bereaved parents meeting. I didn't recognize her at first because her beautiful long hair, which had been so eye-catching at the parents' meeting, had been cut short. Suddenly, I knew I had found my Jessica's savior. When I told her I knew that she was the one, she just smiled and gave me a gentle hug. She asked me to not mention it around town.

"I don't think that telling you what a generous and loving thing your mother did would be considered 'mentioning it around town.' I hope this will be kept between the three of us. I wouldn't want it ever to embarrass your mother. I just had to tell someone. And who better to tell than the two of you?'"

Tim and Jaime talked about Mom and what she had done all the way home that night. They decided that it would be best never to mention what they knew to anyone. For some reason, Mom wanted it to be her secret, and they would honor that.

That night, after the rest of the family was sound asleep, Jaime tiptoed down the hallway to Mom and Dad's room. He stood there a long, long time, watching them sleep. He was thinking how at one time he had believed it impossible to love them any more than he already did. But every time he thought that, something happened that made him love them even more. This night had been one of those nights.

As he stood there, looking down at them both, it seemed to him that Mom looked like an angel, with the glow of the nightlight shining on her hair as it spread across her pillow.

He felt a need to compose a most perfect prayer for her.

When it finally came to him, he felt embarrassed that it sounded strangely like something from a *Star Wars* movie. But, the words seemed so very right. He whispered, "May the God Force be always with you, Mom."

"Yes," Jaime thought, as he scanned the stands once again, his eyes finally coming to rest on those two bright orange shirts topped by the bright orange caps, "that lady up there, the one with the shoulder-length reddish brown hair, that dances in the sunlight when she gives that little flick of her head, that is quite a woman."

Chapter Five

Mortimer Ziffel was a man of many talents, a pleasant and agreeable man. He didn't like to be called "Mort." He said "Mortimer" was the name his mother had bestowed upon him and that made it very special.

Some people jokingly called him "Arnie" after Arnold Ziffel, the pig on the television series, *Green Acres*. He took that kind of teasing with a genuine and robust smile.

Mortimer had been an auto mechanic and handyman most of his life. He could fix almost anything. When someone would ask him if he could fix a particular thing, Mortimer would often reply, "If you're smart enough to break it, I'm sure as hell smart enough to fix it."

Mortimer was a crack shot with a rifle, was known to tie a mean fly for his fly-fishing buddies, and could grow just about any kind of vegetable known to man and grow it well.

Among Mortimer's many hobbies, if hobby is the appropriate word, was refereeing high-school football games. Mortimer was a favorite among the fans, not only because he usually called the plays accurately, but because he had a lot of heart. Everyone knew he cared as much for the players as he did for the sport.

Mortimer lost his wife, Jenny, shortly after their twenty-sixth anniversary to a disease the doctors had never been able to identify. His deep love for her had been obvious to all. They had been unsuccessful in their dream of having children. Mortimer never remarried. He said the kids of the town of Sprague were his family now and that was all he needed.

Mortimer spent a lot of his time looking after those children who seemed in need of a friend. He had helped a lot of kids who were headed for trouble. He had a knack for turning them around and heading them in a better direction. He could always find a few dollars in his pocket for someone in need.

The good folks of Sprague loved Mortimer. They had good reason.

Among Mortimer's many fine qualities was his ability to remain objective about his duties as a referee, in spite of his special fondness for the members of the Franklin High football team. He was so renowned for his fairness that it had never occurred to the coach of the Riverton team to question the appropriateness of Mortimer refereeing the big game. Mortimer was trusted by all.

As the Franklin and Riverton teams went through their warm-up exercises on the field on this chilly Saturday night, Mortimer paced nervously in one of the dressing rooms below ground. He always found someplace to do a bit of pacing before a game, not because he had any concern regarding his ability to do his job properly, but because he was keenly aware of and worried about the emotional turmoil his boys up there on the field were undoubtedly experiencing. Mortimer really cared.

As Mortimer emerged from the tunnel, a cheer arose from the crowds on both sides. With his limp unmistakable, the fans always knew when it was Mortimer taking the field. Mortimer had been injured in the "Big War," as he called it, when a German land mine had exploded about twenty feet to his right, sending several pieces of shrapnel through his right leg. Even if Mortimer hadn't walked with that limp, the crowd would have been able to tell him from the other referees because of the ample tummy that hung over the waist of his white trousers and caused the buckle of his belt to assume a position about four inches lower than that of a man of less portly proportions.

Interestingly enough, Mortimer's rotund configuration did not render him unable to keep up with the action of the game. Apparently, his enthusiasm more than compensated for any negative effects of his stoutly status.

Mortimer never acknowledged the cheers of the crowd, not that he didn't appreciate them. He was simply focused so completely on the task at hand that nothing could distract him.

After a brief discussion with the other referees, Mortimer hobbled to the center of the field, motioning for each of the team captains to join him. As was his custom, he asked the team captains and the other referees to join him in a brief prayer for the safety of the players, Mortimer's kids, in tonight's game.

When the prayer ended, Mortimer cleared his throat and said, "Okay, boys, you know the routine." He removed the silver dollar—the same one he had used for more years than he could remember—from his pocket. He gave it an affectionate buffing on his right pant leg and balanced it carefully on the edge of his right index finger and his right thumb nail. With a high pitched ringing sound, barely audible above the roar of the crowd, Mortimer launched the fateful relic skyward, almost losing sight of it in the glare of the stadium lights. As it reached its apex, the coin appeared to hang in the air a couple of moments longer than Mortimer deemed appropriate, given the inviolability of the laws of physics. In fact, he considered that the coin had somehow slipped into a time warp, its spinning motion slowing down to a fraction of its normal rate, the reflection of the stadium lights from its shiny surface taking on the pulse of a slow-motion strobe light. Mortimer imagined that he heard the coin emitting a sound somewhat like that made by the blades of a military chopper operating in "stealth" mode. All else to Mortimer was complete and utter silence.

After Mortimer had been standing there, for what seemed to him to be several seconds, hypnotized by the slow spinning of the coin, everything suddenly returned to real time, accompanied by the return of the roar of the crowd. The silver dollar hit the ground with a slight bounce, determining forevermore that the kickoff, on this fateful night, would be made by the Franklin High team.

Jaime would have preferred that Riverton make the first kick-off. He was on the receiving squad for Franklin and would have liked nothing better than to catch that ball and unleash his blinding speed on those Riverton boys early in the game. As it was, both he and Tim would have to sit on the bench until Franklin took possession of the ball.

As the teams took their positions on the field, Jaime couldn't help but notice that the Riverton team had an abundance of pretty hefty linemen. Even at a distance, he could see that the Riverton players outweighed the Franklin team by a good forty-five pounds per player. These were big boys. No matter, he thought. As Tim often said, "Skill, cunning, and determination can overcome size and strength any day."

Mortimer raised his right hand above his head, placing his whistle between his lips with his left, ready to signal the beginning of the game. The crowd took a collective deep breath as relative silence settled over the stadium.

Suddenly a loud, deep, screeching sound tore a hole in the silence, as an enormous, orange tanker truck skidded across the asphalt of the parking lot and jumped the curb onto the grass, just fifty feet from the Riverton end zone. The truck spun to the right 180° before coming to rest inches from the end of the Franklin bleachers, the tail end of the truck facing the playing field. The crowd went wild.

The filler cap on top of the tank had been flipped open by the force of the truck jumping the curb. Oil dripped from the sprayers below the rear bumper. The driver of the truck leaped out of the

passenger side door and sprinted into the tunnel beneath the bleachers before anyone could recognize him. Smoke spiraled up from the
tire treads and beads of rubber dangled from the edges of the tires,
the result, apparently, of some seriously aggressive driving. Had anyone been standing in the Riverton end zone, he could have seen from
the lettering on the driver's side door that the truck belonged to
Silverwood County. Buford Stravinsky had arrived at the stadium in
time for the kick-off.

Mortimer shook his head in disbelief and waited for the roar of
the crowd to subside. Noting that the truck was several yards from
the sideline of the playing field, he decided that it posed no danger to
the players. He blew his whistle, signaling the beginning of play.

Buford had scurried quickly to the custodian's closet next to the
home team locker room, removed his coveralls, and hid them in a
laundry basket. He quickly wiped a few oil smudges from his face
with a towel and sprinted up the stairs into the bleachers, where he
took a seat, doing his best to blend in with the crowd.

Seconds later, the toe of Mike Blandon, Franklin's ace kicker,
made dynamic contact with the football resting on Franklin's forty-
yard line, whereupon the pigskin adopted a trajectory and velocity
adequate to deliver it into the eager arms of one of Riverton's
renowned running backs.

That running back took the football to his bosom with an
enthusiasm and intensity sufficient to assure all who were watching
that the appropriate mixture of adrenaline and testosterone had taken
place within his circulatory system. He ran like a man possessed,
bobbing, weaving, faking, and turning, leaving several Franklin
defenders in his wake, sprawled out on the grass and in various
states of somber disappointment.

When he was finally wrestled to the ground by Franklin's last
line of defense, this joyous and enthusiastic running back had traveled all the way to the Franklin twenty-five-yard line.

Three plays later, Riverton scored its first touchdown, followed
by an easy extra point. A mood of solemnity settled over the fans in
the Franklin bleachers. Elsie Waller took a covert swig of schnapps.
Willie Hansen kicked the rail in front of his seat, causing the threads

of the rusty bolt holding the rail in place to strip, allowing the rail to surge forward, striking the left elbow of the Franklin High physics teacher, causing his nearly full twenty-four-ounce cup of Diet Pepsi to slosh across the backs of three female alumni who had driven some distance to see the game.

Coach Linden broke the pencil attached with a piece of twine to his coachly clipboard and threw it in the Gatorade dispenser.

Of all those sitting on the Franklin side of the field, only Jaime regarded the situation with a strange sense of amusement. One step closer to the test.

Riverton's kickoff didn't go to Jaime, but the player who fielded it managed to return it to Franklin's forty-five-yard line.

First and ten. Tim announced a play sent in by Coach Linden that would require Jaime, playing the right end position, to take about ten strides down field, fake to the right, and make a sharp left, heading straight across the field, parallel to the chalk yard-line markers. The left end was to head straight down field for a few yards and then make a sweeping right turn, while the right halfback was to sprint down the center of the field, straight for the end zone. The patterns assigned to the left end and halfback were intended to draw the defending backs away from the center of the field, where Tim hoped to hit Jaime with a short pass. If this didn't work, one or both of the other receivers would, hopefully, be open for a long pass.

As the ball was snapped to Tim, Jaime took off, made a good fake to the right, then turned left, leaving the Riverton player, who was supposed to be guarding him, heading the wrong way. The two deep defending backs, as expected, stayed with the other two receivers, leaving Jaime wide open for Tim's pass. Jaime looked to his left, expecting to see the ball heading for the area just a few feet ahead of him and was amazed to find nothing but empty space. A second glance told him that there would be no pass on this play. Tim had been sacked by two of Riverton's meaty linemen and one enthusiastic linebacker.

On the second play, Jaime again found himself wide open with no football heading his way. Tim had been sacked a second time.

Jaime began to suspect that the reason he had had so much open space, two plays in a row, was that the Riverton team had decided to put its primary efforts into preventing Tim from getting the ball into the air. Jaime figured that Riverton's scouts knew all about Tim's deadly passing arm and had prepared the team well in advance to blitz to keep Tim contained.

Apparently, the Riverton coaches had decided that their defensive backs would be no match for Jaime's legendary speed and Tim's unequaled passing accuracy. Instead, the considerable mass of their linemen and linebackers could be used to their advantage.

Before joining their teammates in the huddle, Tim and Jaime had a brief discussion. Once inside the huddle, Tim surprised everyone by telling them that this time he wanted the linemen to let the Riverton players sack him. As the huddle broke up, Jaime said a few private words to Jim Brewer, the Franklin right halfback.

As soon as the ball was hiked to Tim, he took three quick steps backward, turned to his right, and pitched the ball to Brewer, who lobbed it over the heads of the rushing Riverton linemen into the waiting arms of Jaime Lasher. As soon as the ball was secured under Jaime's right arm, he took off like a shot. The crowd jumped to its collective feet, emitting a deafening roar. Putting a football in the hands of Jaime Lasher, with yards and yards of open field between him and the goal line, caused a sensation reminiscent of that experienced by the crowds in Mudville when Mighty Casey came to the bat.

Touchdown!!!

Extra point!

Piece of cake. A walk in the park.

Riverton and Franklin continued to engage each other in what would come to be known by all in attendance as "the greatest football game of all time." Back and forth they went, with an abundance of spectacular plays, the heavyweights from Riverton shocked again and again by the determination and resilience of the Franklin boys. Emotions ran the gamut from elation to despair as the two teams traded the lead. Just as one team seemed to be taking charge of the game, the other would come back with an amazing and unexpected score. The dynamic duo of Tim and Jaime Lasher had scored twenty-seven of Franklin's thirty-eight points by the end of the third quarter. It was the performance of a lifetime. Assuming the fourth quarter went as he hoped, Gerald Fairbanks, sports editor of the Franklin *Daily Sentinel*, had already come up with the headline for tomorrow's edition. "Franklin High lashes out at Riverton."

By the last three minutes of the fourth quarter Riverton found itself in the lead by six impressive points. Tim had been "sacked" more times than he cared to remember and sported a couple of bruised ribs and a throbbing right wrist. Jaime was not only terribly exhausted, but had done some serious damage to his left ankle in an encounter with one of Riverton's defensive halfbacks.

Franklin had the ball, first and ten, on its own twenty-three yard line. With seventy-seven yards to go for a touchdown and only three minutes left in the game, the excitement among the fans, not to mention the players, hit a record high.

Mortimer had done his usual outstanding job as head referee, but the extra thirty pounds he carried around his mid-section had taken its toll. He was bushed. His limp had become more pronounced. His shirt was soaked with perspiration, in spite of the biting cold in the air. But he didn't really mind. He'd do anything for Mortimer's boys.

Tim knew that he probably couldn't move the ball all the way to the goal line in three minutes running it up the middle. As he had feared, or hoped, it looked as if he would have to rely on Jaime to get the ball a long way down the field in a very few plays. The other team knew that too. The Riverton boys would focus all of their energy on containing Jaime and trying to intimidate Tim.

With both teams exhausted, the size differences of the players became an increasingly important factor.

First and ten. Seventy-seven yards to a touchdown. On the first play, three of Riverton's linemen broke through the Franklin line and crushed Tim for a four yard loss.

Second and fourteen. Eighty-one yards to pay dirt. Tim's right forearm throbbed. His fingers were numb, maybe from the cold, probably from the beatings he had taken. He needed to throw the bomb. But, did he still have enough strength and control? He pondered a moment while his weary teammates dragged themselves into another huddle. He looked at Jaime, who limped noticeably.

Tim announced a pass play he had received from Coach Linden, a long pass to Jaime. Jaime focused his attention on Tim, silently asking if Tim had enough strength left in that arm. Tim shot back a look that said, "I can do it. Can your ankle hold up?" In like manner, Jaime replied, "You bet it can." They smiled at each other with the knowing expressions of exhausted comrades in arms, expressions that only best friends understand. They could do it. Now was the time.

As Jaime walked from the huddle, his mind wandered to The Force, to the Test. Was this the time? He wasn't sure.

As the ball was hiked into Tim's hands, the sturdy Riverton linemen, followed closely by their hefty linebackers, made a devastating crash through the Franklin line, causing Tim to retreat several yards. He planted his feet, bracing himself for the inevitable impact of about twelve hundred pounds of knees, elbows, helmets, shoulder pads, and God knows what else. For a moment, all stood still in Tim's mind. For an instant, there was nothing in Tim's universe but his throwing arm, the football, and that wonderful Jaime kid, that marvelous Jaime, down on the Riverton forty-five-yard line, sprinting for all he was worth. Tim envisioned a slipstream trailing out behind Jaime's body. Then, a fraction of a second before the dreaded impact of those onrushing bodies, Tim ripped loose with the missile of a lifetime. Tim knew in an instant that the throw was perfect, the right trajectory, total follow-through, just enough power, adequate spin on the ball, all followed by a quick shot of flawless intention to the God Force. Then, the rushing bruisers hit Tim with almost crippling force.

Now it was up to Jaime. Jaime had to slow down a bit, keep his velocity constant and moderate, reach up at just the right moment with enough flexibility, followed by a downward motion of his arms so that the ball would not be deflected out of his grasp, then a make quick capture of the ball between his forearms and his chest. All this he had to do while staying ahead of the on-rushing defensive halfbacks in hot pursuit. Jaime was unable to make full use of his celebrated speed, lest he arrive at the intended contact point before the ball, causing it to land behind him. He slowed his pace even more.

Jaime had been so focused on the task at hand from the time he left the huddle that it hadn't occurred to him to send a request for assistance to the universe. He was flying solo.

Jaime glanced over his left shoulder to assure himself that he and the ball were still heading for the same contact point. He was astonished to see that one of the defensive halfbacks was only a few yards behind him and gaining rapidly. Apparently, Riverton had a speed demon Jaime hadn't heard about. By the time Jaime looked over his shoulder again, the Riverton halfback was dangerously close to running him over. Jaime saw the ball, just slightly above and to the left of the halfback's helmet. A fraction of a second before the ball was expected to rush past the defender's helmet toward Jaime's eagerly awaiting arms, the defender raised his left arm, not only blocking Jaime's view of the ball, but coming to rest smack dab in the center of the ball's intended path of travel.

The impact of the ball against the defender's left forearm caused a purple and gray bruise that would not become apparent for several minutes. Its effects in other arenas, however, were more instantaneous, not the least of which were, in their order of occurrence: 1) the deflection of the ball well away from Jaime's grasp, 2) the irresistible impulse of Jaime to shout "Oh, shit!" 3) the release of several joyous words from the mouth of the defender and less than a second later, 4) a collective moan from the stands on the Franklin side of the field, accompanied by sounds of considerable elation from the stands on the opposite side.

The mood was somber as the Franklin team gathered in what promised to be their last huddle of the game. Over eighty yards to the goal line with fewer than thirty seconds remaining. If they were fortunate enough to make a first down, they might have time for an additional play. Their chances of making a first down in one play, under these circumstances, were not good. Their chances of making a touchdown were even worse. Tim called Franklin's last remaining time out.

Tim knelt down on one knee. He had removed his helmet and laid it on the ground. Jaime removed his helmet and stood bent over beside Tim, their faces inches apart.

Jaime whispered, "Let's go for it."

Tim looked at his brother with that knowing grin on his face. "Can we do it?"

Jaime hesitated for a second with a strange look in his eyes. "You bet we can!"

Their eyes locked and each knew instantly exactly what the other was thinking. "The Force; let's do it."

Tim called the team into a huddle. "Okay, guys. This is it. I need enough time for Jaime to get behind their halfbacks. That means you're gonna have to hold their linemen and linebackers out for at least seven seconds. Can you do it?" Those brave and exhausted young men nodded their commitment.

As the team lined up for their final all-out effort, Tim let his mind settle into a bit of a trance. He reminded himself that all those years of tossing that football had provided his subconscious with everything it needed to execute the perfect pass if he didn't screw things up with any conscious doubts. He knew that his best chance of throwing the winning touchdown pass would be if he could focus his conscious thoughts on anything but his performance. So, why not give his chances of success a double whammy by distracting his conscious mind from the physical task at hand and concentrate on sending thoughts to The Force.

He took several deep breaths. He could hear himself shouting the signals to his teammates. But it sounded strangely like someone else's voice. He put everything on auto pilot and focused every ounce of his consciousness on a clear and precise message to The Force. He envisioned a perfect pass leaving the physical control of his fingertips, guided down the field by the power of his mind and into Jaime's waiting arms. He held that thought and nothing else.

He glanced for a split second over at Coach Linden. Linden looked back.

Meanwhile, Jaime had been deeply engrossed in his own thought processes. Over the years, Jaime had had a lot more experience with The Force than Tim. For the past several days, Jaime had used his imagination, his will power, and his determination to pour energy out to the universe, energy designed to assure that tonight's game would reach a point where the outcome would depend on some sort of super-human effort, a point where the passions of the players would reach an unbearable high, a point where Jaime's focus, passion, and intention would be strong enough to induce The Force to alter physical reality.

Jaime thought he had done it before. But, he had never been absolutely certain. He remembered briefly the little old lady with the flowery dress.

Jaime was sure something was about to happen that would provide the incontrovertible proof he wanted so desperately, proof that he had developed the ability to use The Force at will. He didn't know what it was but he knew something was about to happen. He could feel it.

Jaime had done his part. He had thought the thoughts. He had developed the passion. He had refused to allow doubts into his mind. Jaime had more than faith. Jaime knew.

He considered the paradox, the fine line between knowing that The Force exists and that he has the power to command it and yet needing demonstrable proof of those facts, proof that can be obtained only by knowing with absolute certainty. He considered that this is the very same paradox Jesus tried so unsuccessfully to teach the world.

Jaime could hear Tim shouting out the signals, that would set in motion the commencement of the final play of the long-awaited and ultimately critical Franklin/Riverton football game.

Those same signals were being heard by Mortimer Ziffel, who stood at the ready, sweat pouring down the sides of his rib cage. Mortimer reminded himself, one last time, that he mustn't allow his love for those fine Franklin football players to prejudice his conduct in any way.

In the stands, a man and a woman, each wearing a bright orange T-shirt and a bright orange baseball cap, sat quietly praying a silent prayer. The woman gave an unconscious flip of her gorgeous reddish-brown hair with such intensity that it actually came to rest atop the opposite shoulder of the one from which it had been launched. As her face turned toward her husband, he looked at her and each could not help but notice the tears welling up in the other's eyes, reflecting the intense love for those two wonderful boys down on that football field and for each other. She touched his hand most gently, a smile of adoration on her face that caused one of those tears to spill down her beautiful cheek from the place where it had been trying to hide. They each turned back to the action on the field. She squeezed his weather-worn hand warmly. They could hear their Timmy shouting out the signals. They saw Jaime cocked and ready to fire. They each sent out one last silent prayer.

Jaime slowed down his conscious mind and allowed it to focus on the outcome he wanted.

He concentrated intently, not on the process, only on the outcome. Strangely enough, he wasn't thinking of winning. His focus was only on an outcome that would allow him to witness The Force in action—in absolute, irrefutable, undeniable, and glorious action.

Jaime braced himself as Tim finished calling out the signals. The crowd sat quietly, allowing Jaime to actually hear the sound of the ball slapping against the hands of that marvelous quarterback.

Tim wasn't consciously aware of the ball making contact with his hands. He wasn't aware of his rapid retreat from where he had been standing. He wasn't aware of the intense struggle that was being conducted between his teammates and the onrushing Riverton players. His conscious mind was completely submerged in the most glorious vision he could imagine of the perfect pass being magically transformed into the perfect reception, followed by a flawless sprint across the goal line by the most wonderful brother in the world. For those few seconds, nothing else mattered. Nothing else existed.

Jaime shot off like a racehorse, his subconscious in complete control of his body, his conscious mind focused exclusively on sending out the most perfect instructions possible to The Force for a sign, an irrefutable, unquestionable, absolutely certain sign that his beloved Force was everything he believed it to be.

As the ball left Tim's finger tips, he felt his mind take control of the ball, almost as if there were some kind of magnetic link between the frontal lobe of his brain and that mystical football. Tim knew for a certainty where the football needed to land, and he knew without the slightest doubt that it would land there. He knew that Jaime, that always dependable Jaime would be there.

And then it happened, against all odds and in apparent total contradiction to the wishes and powerful intentions of the Lasher twins.

Jaime, attempting to fake the last halfback between himself and the goal line, yielded to the pain in his left ankle, slipped on the wet grass and went down on his side. He went down hard, followed by a complete roll. When he looked up, he realized that the ball had already left Tim's hand and was speeding toward the intended target zone. There was no way for Jaime to be there in time. No way in hell!

And then a wondrous calm settled over Jaime. What was he thinking? Of course, there was time. Jaime realized that he had slipped, for an instant, into the old way of thinking. He, for just a split second, had allowed himself to think in terms of physical cause and effect. He had failed to cling tenaciously to his knowing that The Force was not governed by the beliefs of the Earth plane, those beliefs that we have erroneously come to call "laws."

Wasn't that what Jesus had been trying to demonstrate to his disciples with his numerous miracles? Didn't he say repeatedly, "These things ye see me do, ye shall do likewise and even greater"?

Suddenly, Jaime realized with an absolute certainty that the truth of The Force, the truth of what Jesus had referred to as "The Father," was that its power could not be limited by the laws of the Earth plane.

In an instant, Jaime's mind reverted to the thoughts it had been holding to, so tenaciously, before the fall. He saw himself arriving at the target zone at the same instant that the ball arrived. In total disregard for the laws of physics, the law of time, the law of distance, and the law of gravity, Jaime knew with every aspect of his body, mind, and soul that he was in direct contact with The Force. He knew that The Force was absolutely, positively, and irrevocably all powerful. He was in direct contact with The Father. He felt it. He knew it. There was no possibility of doubt. What Jesus had called "faith" Jaime called "knowing."

Jaime stood there, totally focused on his intended outcome, in a state of absolute faith. This was not faith in any authority figure or in a set of rules or regulations or commandments. It was a pure belief in The Force, in The Father, and in Jaime Lasher as an essential part of The Force, a part of the All That Is.

As Jaime stood there, sensing that something very special was happening, he suddenly realized that everything around him had stopped.

The crowd was silent. The players were no longer moving. The defensive back, who Jaime had just tried to fake, was in mid-fall about to hit the ground. Tim's right arm was extended skyward in front of him, fingers pointed at the football that was suspended in the air, about halfway between Jaime and the goal line.

Jaime looked up into the stands. The crowd sat completely still. Not a movement. A woman in a bright orange T-shirt, with long beautiful hair, was looking intently at the ball high above Jaime's head, her hair in mid-flip. And then, Jaime noticed that almost everyone in the entire stadium seemed to be focused on the ball. Apparently, hardly anyone had seen him fall. Maybe that had something to do with the experience he was having. Sort of like when the little old lady in the flowery dress had passed through the school bus, unharmed, while nobody but Jaime had witnessed it.

Even Tim was so focused on the ball that he probably hadn't yet noticed that Jaime had fallen.

A thought suddenly came to Jaime. It occurred to him that, contrary to what he seemed to be observing, time had not stopped. He realized that his contact with The Force, his command of The Force had affected him only. It had placed him in some kind of a time warp. He speculated that for all of the others in the stadium, time and events were still proceeding as usual. Tomorrow, nobody in the entire stadium would have any sense of anything unusual having happened.

Then, why wasn't Tim moving? Why wasn't Tim aware of the suspended animation that Jaime was observing? After all, Tim was certainly as focused upon and in command of The Force as Jaime was.

Then it came to Jaime. Although both he and Tim had been in approximately the same state of mind, both commanding the same outcome, there was no need for anything Tim had done to change. Tim had performed perfectly. The ball was heading for the perfect destination. Only Jaime had encountered a physical deviation from the intended result. Only Jaime's location, direction, and momentum had to be altered to produce the desired outcome.

Then the ultimate realization came thundering to Jaime's mind. He became aware that The Force could have easily produced a completed pass and a touchdown with little or no modification of physical reality, as understood and observed by those on the Earth plane.

But…Jaime and Tim hadn't commanded a touchdown. They had each put forth the energy of their most passionate thoughts to manifest proof of the existence and power of The Force. Their desire for proof of the existence of The Force and their ability to command it were more powerful than any desire they had to score a touchdown or win the game.

That's why Jaime had slipped. Tim and Jaime had produced an intention that a set of circumstances would occur to each of them that would convince them of their ability to command The Force. Jaime speculated that right now Tim was probably experiencing his own sense of a "suspended animation" with a different set of circumstances that would fulfill Tim's intent to have proof of the existence and power of The Force.

But, what should he do now? Jaime certainly didn't want to spend eternity walking around a stadium full of people looking like the statues in a wax museum. For that matter, perhaps his entire world was in a suspended state. He fantasized that it would be interesting to run up the stadium steps and help himself to a couple of hot dogs and a beer. But that might cause complications beyond his ability to remedy, not that The Force wasn't sufficiently powerful to remedy any situation. It was a matter of Jaime not knowing what to do or think to correct any negative changes he might cause to his world. Perhaps it was only a matter of him instructing The Force to put everything back to where it had been before the fall. But he wasn't sure. He thought it best to deviate as little as possible from his present location this time.

Jaime thought for what seemed like a few minutes in Earth time. He reasoned that if his present world were to start moving again, the football would probably begin heading for the place where Tim had intended it to arrive in Jaime's arms. But the question of how to get it started remained.

Please, God, show me the way.

Then the answer slammed into Jaime's mind with such force that little doubt remained. Jaime knew.

He started running, for all he was worth (which now seemed to be a great deal more than Jaime had ever thought) for the goal line. He imagined that everything was just as it had been before the fall. As he reached what he liked to call "Mach 1," his top speed and approached a point well ahead of the hovering ball, everything suddenly came to life. The roar of the crowd was more glorious to his ears than ever before. The gorgeous reddish-brown hair finished its flip. Dad stood up and cheered at the top of his lungs. Tim's arm came to rest near his right hip. Jaime went back on auto pilot.

A perfect catch. A Tony Dorsett-style, violate-the-laws-of-physics touchdown.

The crowd went wild. The three visiting alumni turned around, in unison, and tossed the dregs of their cola cups on the joyful physics professor behind them, who gave each of them a big bear hug and then proceeded to try to light up his Meerschaum pipe which he had filled with his favorite vanilla flavored tobacco.

Franklin easily made the extra point.

Elsie Waller blatantly finished off her bottle of schnapps, then cheerfully launched the empty container into a distant trash receptacle. She vowed, then and there, to lighten up on the football lecture to her literature classes next semester.

The physics professor was so joyfully moved that he experienced some difficulty maintaining his match steadily above the bowl of his pipe, causing him to use several matches before achieving ignition. As each match reached the end of its useful life, the exuberant professor tossed it overhead, as an extension of his celebratory ritual, in negligent disregard of the possible consequences.

The roar of the crowd exceeded all previous records.

Jaime and Tim were on a dead run toward each other, expecting to come into semi-violent contact somewhere around the fifty-yard line. Mom and Dad were scurrying down the bleacher steps, intending to arrive, as soon as possible, at the same contact point.

Jaime and Tim reached each other just seconds before Mom and Dad got there. In the midst of a most brotherly hug, Jaime shouted, "Did you do it?"

Tim said, "You bet I did! How about you?"

"Yeah!" shouted Jaime.

Before they could begin sharing their respective "suspended" experiences, Mom and Dad arrived. There ensued a Lasher family group embrace, laced with many shouts of joy and a couple more of Mom's tears. In seconds, they were joined by several of the other team members, all shouting and embracing.

They had done it, all of them, an ultimate football victory, a life-changing experience for the Lasher twins. Nothing could possibly go wrong on such a wondrous night.

Almost nothing.

Chapter Six

In addition to being a physics teacher at Franklin High, Isaac Morganstern was a bachelor. He never had had much use for committed relationships. It wasn't that he didn't dabble, on occasion, with a bit of feminine recreation. He was just too set in his ways to allow for the type of compromises required by conventional arrangements such as marriage or going steady.

Isaac liked his little house on his little half-acre out at the end of Hidden Canyon Road. He liked to be able to eat what he wanted to eat when he wanted to eat it, listen to his choice of music, play his stereo as loudly (or quietly) as he wanted, stay up as late as suited his fancy, and sleep in on weekends, all without feeling the anxiety associated with having to perform household chores or modify his schedule or conduct for the satisfaction of someone else.

Over the years, Isaac had grown accustomed to and comfortable with his life of selfish isolation, not that Isaac didn't do for others occasionally. It was just that his life style, basically, centered on Isaac.

On those rare occasions when Isaac did get involved with a member of the opposite sex, the young lovely didn't take long to realize that any relationship with Isaac was going to require uncommon sacrifices necessary to accommodate Isaac's idiosyncrasies. If this knowledge alone was not sufficient to induce any self-respecting lady to decline an invitation to further extend the relationship, Isaac's incessant ramblings, centering on the laws of physics and the theories of those deep thinkers responsible, over the centuries, for bringing such laws to the attention of the less imaginative, would usually send the object of Isaac's affection scurrying for the relative comfort of her bachelorette domicile...alone.

The resultant lack of sexual gratification in Isaac's life caused him to focus the energies normally associated therewith in other areas. In addition to his penchant toward burying himself in the depths of his physics books for hours on end, he almost never was without a lighted pipe either in his hand or dangling from his teeth.

Years of smoking had rendered those teeth a dark yellowish color, accompanied by the usual ashtray-like aroma, frequently known to assault the nasal passages of those who were unfortunate enough to find themselves in the pathway or near vicinity of one of Isaac's exhalations. This was yet another factor rendering Isaac less than erotically appealing to the single ladies of the fine town of Sprague.

Among the many offensive habits fostered by Isaac's state of frequent solitude and abetted by his condition of general unawareness was, as mentioned earlier, that of flipping his spent tobacco-lighting matches into the air. This habit proliferated in total disregard for its ecological implications or the possibility of igniting a nearby flammable substance.

For almost seventeen years Isaac had been enlightening the minds of the students of Franklin High relative to the intricacies of the fascinating, if sometimes incomprehensible, laws of physics. During that lengthy tenure, he never once attended a sporting event of any kind. He, like Elsie Waller, considered most pastimes involving the strenuous use of the human body to be uncivilized. Tonight's game, however, received so much notoriety and fostered so much enthusiasm that hardly anybody, not even Isaac, could resist the urge to be present at this crucial conflict.

When Isaac causally mentioned, to the students of his one o'clock "Introduction to Physics" class, that he was considering being present at tonight's game, one of the more courageous students shouted, "Mr. Morganstern, I hope you don't burn down the stadium with one of your flying matches." Isaac flushed slightly and then informed all present that he took great care never to flip a match skyward until he was certain that it was completely extinguished. This was notwithstanding the fact that he had once allegedly set a stack of papers afire in his classroom. Nobody was present to witness the event other than Isaac himself. But the telltale signs of small traces of ash, plus the faint aroma of burning paper the next morning, gave rise to copious rumors.

The event was punctuated by the appearance of a small fire extinguisher on Isaac's desk the next morning. It was wrapped in a plastic yellow ribbon with the words "Crime Scene" printed thereon.

Another of Isaac's less-than-commendable habits was that he was invariably late for everything. Students typically showed up five to ten minutes late for his classes knowing, for a certainty, that he would not be there until at least fifteen minutes past the hour.

On the night of the Franklin/Riverton game, Isaac's propensity toward tardiness caused him to be seated at the far end of the bleachers, the overcrowding of which caused him, several times, to almost slip off the end of the bench upon which he was precariously perched. This seemingly dangerous, not to mention frightening, situation caused Isaac to experience an uncommon sense of agitation, fearing that his bottom might slip over the edge of the seat to which he was clinging, by judicial use of his right gluteus maximus. This condition of anxiety caused Isaac to increase the tempo at which he ignited his pipe and disposed of his matches to a rate he heretofore had not experienced. Although he was vaguely aware, at some level, that his customary pace of lighting and flipping was being exceeded, he was so entranced by the game that he gave this reality little, if any, serious thought. Actually, the intensity of the game, conspiring with the unnerving proximity of Isaac's bottom to the edge of the bleacher seat, was what drove him to the point where the rhythm of his lighting and flipping would eventually have a dramatic effect of its own on numerous pertinent and far-reaching laws of physics.

As Jaime crossed the goal line to score the wining touchdown for Franklin High, Isaac flipped what was to be not only the final match flip of the game, but possibly the last match flip of Isaac's life. So focused was Isaac on Jaime and his superb catch and dash for the goal line that he paid absolutely no attention to his pipe or the match that was raging out of control in his right hand. He didn't notice that he wasn't holding the match above the pipe bowl. He didn't notice that the flame of the match was a good two inches from the bowl. He didn't notice that he was sucking in air that was not the least bit tainted by the aroma of burning tobacco. Most significantly, he never realized that the match that he absentmindedly lofted overhead was burning furiously, spurred on to even greater intensity by the rush of the oxygen-laden air through which it was passing.

Sometimes we look back at an event, particularly an event having serious repercussions, and wonder just how it was that so many circumstances necessary to bring about the results that unfolded could have just happened all to be in the right places at the right times, or more often, the wrong places at the wrong times.

For those who have come to understand that nothing happens by accident and that, in fact, every event is the result of thought, the apparent mystery is resolved quickly and naturally.

As Isaac Morganstern's errant and fateful match arched overhead, not a single soul in that stadium noticed it, except, that is, for Shirley Merimac, who, because she was wearing her newly acquired azure-blue tinted contact lenses, was momentarily distracted from the game by the glow of the match flame. That match flame, as seen through those contact lenses, caused a slight sparkling aura around the outer periphery of Shirley's field of vision. This simple combination of factors rendered her the only person in the entire stadium capable of verifying the causal role that Isaac's match played in the ensuing events.

Had it not been for the northwesterly wind, caused by the high-pressure area over the Pacific Ocean, in combination with the low-pressure area over the flat and humid state of Florida, Isaac's match, set temporarily free from the normal effects of gravity by Isaac's flip of the wrist, would have landed harmlessly on the damp grass below the bleachers. As it turned out, however, those winds came from the precise direction and moved at the exact velocity necessary to alter the arc of Isaac's match in such a manner as to cause it to fall through the opening atop the Silverwood County oil truck. That oil truck, you may recall, was uncapped by Buford Stravinsky's hasty arrival at the stadium parking lot, followed by a forceful leap over the concrete curb, just prior to its coming to rest alongside the bleachers directly below Isaac Morganstern's smoking pipe, his endangered bottom, and his flying matches.

As Isaac's flaming match arrived at the epicenter of the Silverwood County oil truck's now-empty tank, it encountered a combination of oil fumes and oxygen intertwined in a ratio that made it temporarily incapable of exploding. However, the oil residue remaining on the bottom of the tank, with the assistance of just barely enough oxygen, did begin to burn slowly.

Had the winds in the area been either more or less intense than they actually were, the ratio of gas fumes to oxygen within the tank would have remained such that the oil would have continued to burn at a slow rate until it was totally consumed. However, as the oil continued to burn, causing an almost undetectable wisp of smoke to escape the opening at the top of the tank, the quantity of oil on the bottom of the tank decreased to the point at which air was now able to enter the tank through the pipes leading to the open sprayers suspended below the rear bumper. As the northwesterly winds continued to skim over the opening at the top of the tank, they created a venturi effect, not unlike that in an automobile carburetor, which caused the non-explosive mixture of oil fumes and air to be drawn out of the opening atop the tank.

As the passing winds gradually sucked portions of the oil vapor from the tank, the vapors were replaced by the oxygen-rich air being sucked in through the open sprayers. The oil vapor-to-oxygen ratio

within the tank slowly but surely approached the point at which detonation of the vapor was possible, if not inevitable.

Just after the critical point of explosive potential was reached, a
partially contained explosion took place, causing flames to shoot out
of the opening atop the tank more than a hundred feet into the air.
Those flames did no serious harm, although they caused several fans
sitting at the near end of the bleachers to feel an intense rush of hot
air, which produced a pink glow on the cheeks and foreheads of those
with fair skin for the next several days.

The flames forced out of the sprayers were another matter
entirely. When Buford Stravinsky had spun the truck into the area
next to the bleachers, it had come to rest with its rear end pointing
toward the football field. Fortunately, the truck was angled so the
flames that shot out of the sprayers were aimed toward the
Riverton end zone and not toward the players and fans who were
gathered at mid-field.

It had taken about seven minutes for the smoldering fire on the
bottom of the tank to become transmuted into a full-blown explosion. By that time, hardly anyone remained in the line of fire of the
lethal sprayers. Actually, nobody was in that line of fire—except for
Mortimer Ziffel.

Mortimer had wandered down toward the Riverton end zone to
retrieve one of his referee flags, which had fallen from his pocket just
after the gun was fired signaling the end of the game. As soon as
Mortimer retrieved his flag, he headed back toward the fifty-yard line
to join the exuberant crowd.

As the flames poured out of the sprayers, shooting a good fifty
feet across the field with the intensity of a military flame thrower,
Mortimer was exactly where he shouldn't have been. The flames
engulfed him in an instant. He was dead in a matter of seconds.

Terrified screams poured forth from the crowd. Jaime arrived at
the scene within seconds but it was obvious that Mortimer was
already dead. The sight of the charred body caused such a revulsion
in Jaime that he ran away as fast as he could. He found himself leaning against a goal post and gasping for air. For a moment, he thought

he was going to vomit. But he didn't. He just stood there in total disbelief, his body trembling.

After what seemed like several minutes, Jaime began to regain control of his body. For the first time since the explosion, he was able to entertain a rational thought. The thoughts that assaulted his mind were so hideous, however, that he wished he could return to the relative safety of not being able to think at all.

He stood there in a state of what can only be described as utter despair. He became vaguely aware of a light pressure on his left shoulder. It took Jaime a few seconds to react to that stimulus. When, with uncommon effort, he finally managed to turn his head and lower his eyes to a position where he could examine the source of that pressure, he realized it was Tim's hand.

Jaime turned to face his brother. Tim stood there, tears streaming down his cheeks. Neither one could think of anything sane to say. They did the only thing that made any sense: They held each other and sobbed uncontrollably.

Eventually, the weeping subsided, and they settled into a state of desperate silence.

Tim was the first to speak. They talked quietly, each trying to express his grief, but neither coming close to describing those feelings that so defied description. Neither could remember what the other had said. The words all seemed to run together in an unintelligible jumble.

Then Tim did a most remarkable thing. The faintest semblance of a smile appeared on his face. Not a smile of happiness, but a smile nonetheless. As Jaime stood there, totally puzzled by the look on Tim's face, Tim pulled him farther away from the crowd that had gathered in the area of Mortimer's cremation.

When they were some distance from the crowd, they sat down on the grass. After a brief silence, Tim whispered, "Please bear with me. I know this is a strange time to be philosophizing. But hear me out. I know you saw the same thing I did during that last play. Time stood still. Or it seemed to stand still. Or maybe time for you and me moved at a different rate than it did for the people around us. I don't know what really happened. All I know is that what I saw defied the normal laws of reality, at least of physical reality or what appear to be the laws of physical reality. You and I were able to move while every-thing else stood still. At least that's the way it appeared to me. I think it had to do with The Force. When we were sitting in the locker room, I focused my thoughts on producing a situation that would allow us to determine, once and for all, if we are able to utilize The Force. I suspected that you were having similar thoughts."

Jaime nodded.

Tim continued, "It occurred to me that the power of both of our minds, working together, might be able to create an energy greater than the sum of both energies. I decided, then and there, that I was going to do something awesome before the game was over, some-thing beyond the normal laws of nature, something more wonderful than anything I had ever dreamed of doing. I sensed that with your help I could perform miracles. I think the excitement of the game amplified our focus or determination. I can't explain it. I just felt that the power of The Force was with us.

"I read a book that my friend Leslie gave me for Christmas, called *Einstein's Dreams*. That book contains a lot of little stories designed to help a layman understand many of the laws of time and space that Albert Einstein proved to a mathematical certainty. What happened to us tonight seems to relate, in some way, to those laws, those stories. What we experienced tonight seems to me to be the result of the laws of physics and the laws of nature and the laws of spirituality working together. Or maybe they are all the same law.

"We asked The Force to present itself to us in a way that we would be certain of our ability to direct its power. Well, as you and I have always thought, perhaps The Force isn't only all-powerful but also always knows the best way to achieve a desired result, probably a better way than we imagined."

Tim said, "I think The Force has not only shown us the power of our minds to make time stand still. I think it has presented us with an opportunity to prove that we can move time backwards.

"I believe the two factors most helpful in eliciting the coopera-tion of The Force are desire and faith. In the case of tonight's foot-ball miracle, we already had a decent amount of faith. We also had a lot of desire. I think the combination of these two factors, multiplied by the fact that there were two of us, each having the same desire at the same time, produced an outrageous amount of energy.

"If you think our desire to prove our connection with The Force created a lot of energy, can you imagine the energy we could generate with a motive as powerful as love?"

Now it was Jaime's turn to allow a little smile to creep ever so slowly across his face. Was Tim thinking what Jaime was thinking? Jaime could hardly believe that Jaime was thinking it.

They sat in silence.

What had they done to stop time during the game? Could they do it again? But now they had to reverse time, not just stop it. If they were to bring Mortimer back to life, they had to reverse time! And not only reverse time but actually change the circumstances that led to Mortimer's death before allowing time to resume its forward motion. Were the principles the same? Had the first time been a one-in-a-million accident, a strange, unrepeatable convergence of factors? What were the factors?

Jaime and Tim already had identified desire and faith as essential. But what else was necessary? Jaime remembered his first encounter with The Force and how he suspected that what he came to call his "manipulation of energy and matter" worked because nobody else witnessed the event. And, if others witnessed the event, could his desire and faith be so powerful that it would overcome any resistance? Jaime remembered his readings of the New Testament. Jesus had been able to manipulate matter with the power of his mind, even when others were witnessing. But hadn't he asked those present if they had faith? Didn't he say, "Your faith has made you whole?"

Wow! What a lot to think about!

Then it came to him, one of the grandest realizations Jaime had ever had. By the look on Tim's face, Jaime suspected that Tim was coming to the same conclusion.

All it takes is knowing that The Force is all-powerful and is always willing, without exception, to do our bidding if our thoughts are pure. This is not the kind of "pure" that some relate to morality. It is a clarity of purpose that allows for no doubt, no hesitation, that some would call "commitment." It matched what Jaime had read some-where described as "the empty-handed leap into the void." They would need, simply, absolute trust in the goodness, abundance, and benevo-lence of the universe, in The Force.

Jaime suddenly realized that the factors were not as important as he had originally suspected. It occurred to him that we are always using The Force. We cannot not use The Force. It's simply a matter of whether we use it deliberately or by default, whether we control The Force with our focused intent or allow it to be controlled by our random thoughts or by the power of the universal subconscious.

Boy, this is getting heavy. These are not the thoughts of a typical seventeen-year-old. This stuff must be coming from somewhere other than my mind. But it feels good. It makes sense. It all seems to be fitting together.

Jaime knew that all he had to do was form an intent, enhance that intent with powerful emotion, and then stand back and allow The Force to do its thing without resistance from Jaime, without doubt.

Tim smiled and nodded. They were tracking exactly, thought for thought.

Closing his eyes, Jaime sent forth to "The God of all Creation" a most powerful prayer. It wasn't a request. That would allow for doubt. It was a command from the very depths of his soul, a righ-teous order from his heart, with the abundant love he had for all of creation and, at this moment, for Mortimer Ziffel. With all the love he had for himself, he shot forth an energy that made his body tremble, causing tears to pour forth from his eyes and an almost unbearable tightness to envelop his throat.

Jaime pictured his beloved friend Mortimer as he had been just before the terrible explosion, with that great smile on his face, with his tummy hanging over his belt buckle, with his heart as big as all outdoors. He saw Mortimer perfectly well and whole—and alive. Jaime knew that Tim was doing the same.

Although he wanted to scream out all of the love and pain and joy and glory he was feeling, Jaime held his silence. He just knew. And he knew that he knew. And that was all that mattered.

Jaime had a sense of time passing. But he had no idea how long he sat there. The intensity of his feelings produced a clarity of thought that, for some reason, blurred his concept of time.

When he opened his eyes, there was no sound. He could see the crowd gathered at the center of the field. Everything seemed to be moving normally, but there was no sound. Then he saw Mortimer down at the Riverton end zone. Mortimer bent over and picked up his flag. He placed it in his pocket.

Jaime focused on the oil truck near the bleachers. Jaime saw smoke rising from the opening atop the truck. He looked back at Mortimer, now walking toward the crowd, just thirty feet from the oil sprayers at the back of the truck. Jaime started to rush for Mortimer, hoping against hope to push him out of the way of the explosion that would be happening again in only a few seconds. Then Jaime realized there was no way he could get to Mortimer in time and a feeling of utter uselessness tore at his heart. The silence was unbearable.

Then he heard a sound, barely audible. But in the absolute silence that had inexplicably found its way into this nightmare, that faint sound attacked Jaime's ear drums with a clarity beyond description. He looked in the direction from which the sound had come and saw that its source was the cap closing atop the filler hole of the tanker truck. A burning match hovered just inches above that cap. He looked back toward Mortimer and saw that Mortimer was heading toward the Riverton end zone, his yellow referee's flag still lying in the grass. Somehow, time had moved backward by several more minutes.

The sound of the crowd suddenly burst forth, reaching Jaime's ears in an instant. Time returned to normal.

A lighted match struck the cap that covered the filler hole of the tanker truck, falling harmlessly into the dew-drenched grass beside the bleachers. As the match reached the ground, unnoticed by the fans nearby and completely forgotten by Shirley Merimac of the azure-blue contacts, Jaime looked over at Tim, who was standing on the rear fender of the oil truck with "That Look" on his face.

While Jaime had been realizing and agonizing over the impossibility of reaching Mortimer in time, Tim had been rolling back time in his reality several more minutes. He had climbed onto the fender of the oil truck and simply closed the cap on the filler hole.

Tim jumped down from the truck and headed toward Jaime.

As they met near the thirty-yard line, Mom and Dad came walking toward them, looking a little dazed. Perhaps they were wondering how Jaime and Tim had gotten from the center of the field to where they were now in an instant. Or perhaps Mom and Dad hadn't noticed. Perhaps the Universe had taken care of everything.

As Mom and Dad got to where Jaime and Tim were standing, they all joined in a Lasher family hug. Mom and Dad couldn't stop praising the boys for what they had done.

If they only knew.

Tim asked, "Does anyone mind if I invite Mortimer to join us?"

"Hell, no," said Jaime, without waiting for anyone else's opinion.

Mortimer was heading back from the Riverton end zone, a yellow referee's flag hanging from his pocket and a gigantic look of admiration on his face as he watched "his kids" reveling in their victory. Jaime and Tim ran to Mortimer and, each grabbing one of his arms, dragged him to where Mom and Dad were waiting.

The referee said, "I was hoping I'd be invited to the old Lasher family hug!"

Mom said, "Wouldn't think of having one without you." She flipped her hair and gazed at her two handsome sons with an unmistakable look of pride and love. Dad couldn't say anything. He just stood there looking at his two fine boys. They were all silent for a few seconds. The energy that swirled around their little circle said all that needed to be said.

Jaime glanced at Tim and felt a warm glow near his heart, a glow that got mixed up with a whole lot of other feelings. Tim smiled back, that knowing smile. Yes, they had done something awesome tonight. Or was this just proof that they had been doing lots of awesome things all along?

 # Chapter Seven

Jaime and Tim resisted the temptation to remain in the locker room with their celebrating teammates. They took a quick shower, put on their street clothes, thanked each of the other players for their efforts, and hustled out to the field where Mom and Dad sat on the bottom bench of the bleachers talking with Mortimer.

As the Lasher gang, including Mortimer, headed toward the parking lot, Mortimer stopped for a moment to gaze at the yellow truck parked next to the bleachers. He stood there a few seconds, as if trying to remember something. Then he shook his head and continued on his way. Jaime watched Tim walk to the area between the bleachers and the truck, bend down, pick up a partially burned matchstick, and put it in his pocket.

When Tim looked up, he saw that Jaime was watching him. Tim patted his pocket and smiled.

Mom suggested that this would be a grand opportunity to indulge in a delicious Kelly's pizza, and the gang agreed. Mortimer offered to buy. He and Dad debated the issue for a minute and resolved the matter by agreeing that they would add a calzone or two and split the tab.

Dad thought a restaurant named "Kelly's" seemed like a strange place to find a great pizza. He once said that it made about as much sense as going to a place called "Pitruzello's" for corned beef and cabbage. Nonetheless, Kelly's had the best pizza in all of Sprague, and tonight's meal was no disappointment.

Jaime found himself unable to look at Mortimer without seeing flashes of the charred remains of his dear friend lying on the football field. He was glad to have that sweet old man sitting across from him, alive and well.

He thought about the movie *Back to the Future* and the concern the professor in that movie had had about how altering events in the past could have disastrous effects on the entire time/space continuum. He wondered if what he and Tim had done tonight would affect many other lives besides Mortimer's.

Jaime and Tim would have a lot to talk about. Especially now that they knew for an absolute fact that The Force is for real and, equally important, that The Force responds to thought. What a sense of power! What a sense of responsibility!

As they ate, Jaime and Tim joked a lot with their waitress. Noticing the affection her boys had for Helen, Sarah wondered if the waitress had told them about the gift Sarah had given to Jessica. She had no way of knowing without asking, but she couldn't ask her boys without letting her secret out of the bag. To ask Helen might seem accusatorial. She decided just to let it be.

The little group lingered at Kelly's quite a while, laughing and joking. From time to time, Helen caught herself glancing their way, thinking what a great family the Lashers were. She wondered if her sweet Jessica might be looking down from somewhere in the spirit world, knowing the delight her mom took from watching Sarah and Michael have fun with their two fine boys.

Tim and Jaime walked out of Kelly's with happy taste buds, full tummies and bursting hearts for the football victory of the century, a certainty about The Force, their friend Mortimer alive and well, and the two greatest parents in the world.

As they stepped out into the parking lot, the group noticed how dramatically the temperature had dropped. Mortimer said his right knee told him it was close to 20°. Tim made a crack about wanting to sit next to Mortimer for the warmth Mortimer's ample body would generate. Mortimer grabbed Tim in a headlock and rapped the top of his head with his knuckles.

Tim yelled, "Mom, call the attorney—assault and battery!" Mortimer rapped him one more time for good measure, let go of Tim's head, ran as fast as his portly body could manage, and got into the middle of the back seat before either of the boys caught up with him.

Mortimer shouted through the open car door, "Hey, you two scoundrels—get in here now and close the doors. I need you to insulate this magnificent body from the cold."

Tim and Jaime climbed in and closed the doors. Tim reached down and pinched Mortimer's leg just above the kneecap, knowing that Mortimer was outrageously ticklish. Mortimer screamed, "Sarah, Sarah, make these goofballs stop. They're gonna make me wet my britches."

Jaime attacked the other knee. Mortimer went ballistic, kicking and screaming and laughing and doing his best not to pee in his shorts. Tim and Jaime showed no mercy. Mom got up on her knees, leaned over the seat, and attacked Mortimer's ribs with her fingertips. Mortimer screamed and farted. Tim and Jaime each bailed out of his respective car door.

Mortimer shouted, "Hey, you goons, close those pneumonia holes. It's cold in here!"

Tim yelled back, "Not anymore. You just raised the ambient temperature in the car by 35°."

Mortimer retorted, "You don't even know what 'ambient' means—and close those doors, or I'm gonna lock you out."

Dad was laughing so hard that he had trouble getting the key into the ignition. Mom turned around, buttoned her overcoat, and scrunched down in her seat to avoid the possibility of retaliation by Mortimer. But Mortimer didn't have the energy. Finally the boys got back into the car after eliciting a promise from Mortimer that there would be no retribution.

The drive back to the stadium started out surprisingly peaceful. Then Tim belched, which prompted a series of giggles that grew in intensity and frequency, followed by a burp out of Jaime.

Mom said, "Hey, you bunch of rudenicks."

This was followed by an even louder belch from Dad, which sent everyone into a state of uncontrolled laughter.

Jaime said, "Hey, let's not get Mortimer started again." Where-upon Tim launched another attack on Mortimer's knee, joined shortly thereafter by a similar attack by Jaime. Barely able to speak, Mortimer managed to blurt out, "Okay, you guys, I tried to warn you, I can't hold off much longer. It's gonna get real ugly back here."

Mom was laughing so hard she yelled out, "Mortimer's not the only one who's gonna have an accident. You boys stop it this instant!"

By the time they got back to the stadium, their sides ached from laughing and their cheek muscles needed a rest. Mortimer said, "Are you gonna let me out of this car, or am I gonna have to blast my way out?"

Tim said, "We surrender," and jumped out of the car.

The Lashers said their good-byes to Mortimer, and Michael headed the car toward the state highway. Sarah noticed that her husband was driving unusually fast, but she didn't want to dampen anyone's mood by saying anything. She reached over and took his hand. He gave her a warm smile. Sarah slid over next to him, strapped on the center seatbelt, and rested her head on his shoulder. Michael, in turn, rested his head on hers.

Tim was watching the moon passing behind the few clouds that were in the sky on this cold autumn night. Jaime settled into listening to the hum of the tires on the highway as he thought about the night's events. The family cruised along in silence.

Michael could tell by the weight of Sarah's head on his shoulder and her gentle breathing that she had fallen asleep. He drove on, a contented smile on his face.

He became vaguely aware that he was starting to get a bit drowsy. Had he glanced down at the instrument panel, he would have been surprised to see that they were traveling down the state highway at a rather brisk pace. But Michael didn't look. Michael didn't know. He was in such a happy state that any thought of danger or fear wasn't likely to come into his mind. A wave of drowsiness rippled up from the base of his skull to the center of his forehead. His eyelids lowered slightly.

Tim and Jaime, having succumbed to a variety of factors, were now both sound asleep in the backseat.

Michael fought for a while to remain awake and then somehow forgot what it was he had been fighting for. A tiny droplet of melatonin had been released into that part of his brain that bears the responsibility for ushering the mind out of the conscious world and into the realm of slumber. Michael's chin rested gently against his chest, and his eyelids surrendered.

 Chapter Eight

For as long as Ethel Whorley could remember, her husband had been known as Big Red. Actually, it seemed to her that she and all of her friends and family had always referred to him as Big Red. Sometimes she had to remind herself that his given name was Horace.

One might think that anyone called Big Red would have a head full of red hair. The truth is that Big Red had only a tiny wisp of some fuzzy stuff that he insisted on combing from just above his left ear to the center of his shiny dome and over the years it had faded from red to gray.

The other irony about Big Red was that he was not big at all. He was what some might refer to as a pip-squeak of a man. Big Red was so frail that the only bulge that anyone had ever observed emanating from the sleeve of his ever-present J.C. Penney's T-shirt resulted from the pack of Lucky Strikes he kept rolled up there, just above the area where a muscle should have been.

Now, his wife was another story. Ethel tipped the scales at three hundred ten pounds, stark naked, which, as you might imagine, was not a pretty sight.

Ethel and Horace had long ago settled into a relationship of tolerant hostility. He drove the big rig, and she sat quietly in the passenger seat, usually knitting or working crossword puzzles, not saying much.

Once in a while Ethel would let out a disgusted grunt, indicating that she was recalling some incident, involving what she considered misconduct on her husband's part, conduct that raised her level of revulsion above its normal range. The release of such a grunt within the confines of the truck cab caused Horace to automatically and involuntarily tighten his grip on the steering wheel and depress the accelerator pedal a bit past the point at which he normally held it to maintain the big rig at a speed just four miles per hour above the speed limit.

During his eighteen years as a professional truck driver, Horace had determined that he was highly unlikely to receive a speeding citation as long as he didn't exceed the speed limit by five miles per hour. To Horace, five miles per hour above the posted limit was a magical number preordained by the powers-that-be. It was the speed at which any truck driver became fair game for the state patrol.

Horace reasoned that no self-respecting law enforcement officer would want to risk standing before a judge, having to explain why he took it upon himself to infringe on the judge's valuable time to drag a hard-working truck driver before the bench to answer to a charge of exceeding the speed limit by a mere four miles per hour.

Five miles per hour, however, seemed to Horace to have a different ring to it. He could picture himself standing before the magistrate, hat in hand, shuffling his feet and sweating profusely, while the state patrolman shouted out, "Your Honor, this reckless maniac was apprehended driving a fully loaded eighteen-wheeler at a speed of five miles per hour above the clearly posted speed limit." The very thought made Horace cringe.

Horace's fear of going above his self-imposed "maximum overage" was exceeded only by his terror of dropping below that ideal speed of four miles per hour over the limit. Ethel was not a patient woman. Wherever Ethel was heading—which was almost always in the direction of a gambling casino—she wanted to get there in the very least amount of time, without an unnecessary risk of having to fork out funds from her gambling stash for a traffic citation.

So Horace was required to keep the speedometer needle at least four miles per hour above the posted limit unless there were some mighty good extenuating circumstances, and Ethel reserved the right to decide just what circumstances did or did not qualify as being mighty good. She didn't care if Horace went above his self-imposed five-miles-per-hour point, but if he got a ticket, there'd be hell to pay.

On one occasion, Horace allowed himself to daydream to the point where the velocity of the big rig dropped below the fateful four-miles-per-hour-above-the-speed-limit mark and, moreover, had remained there long enough to attract Ethel's attention. Without hesitating, Ethel summarily lunged across the great divide normally separating them and impaled Horace' right thigh with a number six-teen knitting needle and thereafter immediately informed Horace that if he didn't get the truck up to speed mighty fast and stop his scream-ing, she was going to impale more than his thigh. Horace never both-ered to decipher the exact meaning of that threat, but proceeded with all due haste to return the velocity of the vehicle to the accept-able rate.

After that, Ethel wiped the tip of her knitting needle clean on the front of Horace's white J.C. Penney T-shirt and resumed knitting with an unusually contented grin on her face. The incident was never mentioned again. But for many months thereafter, Horace found quite remarkable his ability to keep the speed of the rig perfectly steady. Horace drove, and Ethel knitted.

On one rare occasion when Horace thought his wife was in an uncommonly good mood, he got up the courage to suggest that per-haps it would be wise to have a cruise control installed in the rig. Ethel informed him that such a luxury was totally out of the ques-tion. She added, as an afterthought, that if she should ever find a shortage in her carefully monitored gambling fund, his hide would be hung on the back side of the trailer in the exact way her daddy had once hung a bear hide on the side of his barn.

Every once in a while, Ethel grabbed one of her ever-present knitting needles and made a lunging motion in the direction of some part of Horace's lower anatomy. She told herself, "This was just to keep his reflexes sharp and to be sure it was understood who was in charge."

On more than one occasion, Horace considered leaving Ethel at a truck stop while he drove on down the highway alone and at peace. But he knew she'd track him down sooner or later, and the likely consequences of such conduct were more than he even cared to consider.

Still, Horace liked to fantasize about the possibility of being free of her tyranny. He just had to restrict those daydreams to times when he wasn't behind the wheel. He decided that his best chance for escape would be to drive off while Ethel was in a restroom. He had no idea what she did in there, but she sure took a long time. Obviously, she wasn't primping.

Ethel would announce each of those restroom visits, by stepping down from the cab, causing the darn thing to lean ominously to starboard, and inform Horace, "Sit tight—I'm gonna go take the big one." He could then count on sitting in the cab for anywhere from twenty to thirty minutes while his beloved did heaven-knows-what. He even fantasized about informing her that her lengthy pit stops were going to make her late for her next casino visit, but he knew he wouldn't have the courage to say it.

Once, while Ethel was "taking the big one," Horace courageously slipped the transmission into first gear, let out the clutch ever so slowly, and began to creep toward the truck stop exit. He had moved only a few yards when he came to his senses. Fearing that Ethel might see his tire marks on the gravel and thereby know he wasn't exactly where she had left him, he quickly backed up. Then he realized, to his horror, that she might see the tracks in front of the tires caused by his hasty maneuvering.

He stopped the truck and sat there, sweat running down his cheeks, waiting to see what would happen. He picked up the lug wrench from under his seat, thinking he might have to defend himself. Then he decided it wouldn't be possible to inflict damage serious enough to stop Ethel, especially through all of that blubber. Besides that, there was the very real danger that Ethel would disarm him and use the wrench to beat him to death. He got out and did his best to erase the tire marks in the gravel in front of all eighteen wheels, keeping a constant eye on the door through which Ethel would emerge once she had finished "taking the big one." He inspected his work through the filter of fear that influenced the neural connectors between his eyeballs and his brain. Those tracks still looked horribly visible to Horace.

As he stood there trying to sort out the vast array of emotions assaulting his bewildered mind, he suddenly realized that all of his fantasies had been only false hopes and he would never be free of Ethel. Never. Ever.

He hurried back into the cab and awaited his fate.

To Horace's great relief, Ethel took almost an hour to do whatever it was she was doing. By the time she came out of the building, the sun was low enough on the horizon that any marks remaining on the gravel were almost impossible to discern. Horace didn't try, or even consider trying, anything like that again.

Now, many years later, Big Red and Ethel found themselves heading down the interstate on a Saturday night. Ethel was fast asleep, knitting needles resting in her lap, barely visible beneath her meaty hands.

Horace was thinking how amazing it was that Ethel, even when asleep, could detect the slightest slowing of the truck. She seemed to be able to tell the difference between slowing for a turn and slowing from lack of concentration. The first was permissible; the latter unforgivable.

Having driven this route a few times in the past, Horace had calculated that he could save considerable time and fuel consumption by taking a triangular shortcut from the interstate he was on and the one he would be intersecting about a hundred and twenty miles ahead. The shortcut would save him about thirty miles, and at this time of night, he didn't anticipate much traffic on that state highway.

Horace wondered if he dared to make such a decision without consulting his wife. But Ethel was asleep, and awakening her for anything short of a genuine emergency was a strict no-no. As the intersection of the interstate and the surface road rapidly approached, Horace contemplated the situation. When he reached the point of impending decision, he had flipped his imaginary navigational coin and courageously decided to take the off-ramp leading to the surface road. He hoped Ethel's always-listening subconscious would interpret his downshifting as a turn and not as a minimum speed violation.

Horace eyed the knitting needles anxiously. Ethel didn't flinch.

To Horace's great relief, the off-ramp from the interstate transitioned smoothly onto the surface road without the necessity of bringing the truck to a stop. As the big rig accelerated gently onto the state highway, the One Eyed Jack tavern and the Sleep E Z motel glided by on the left. Horace shifted smoothly through the gears, bringing the velocity of the rig up to the safety of sixty-nine miles per hour, just four miles per hour above the posted speed limit. Ethel snoozed peacefully.

By now it was completely dark, a moonless night. The eighteen-wheeler was performing well, the tires humming on the cold pavement. Horace was beginning to relax—if the term "relax" is not interpreted too strictly. Blessedly, Ethel remained sound asleep, the only time Horace was ever able to relax.

No more than two miles down the state highway, Horace sat bolt upright as his headlights revealed what appeared to be a pond or a lake dead ahead. To Horace's terror, the very highway on which he was driving seemed to disappear into the water. One might expect that Horace's immediate reaction, or that of anyone in his situation, would be to begin rapidly down-shifting and pumping the air brakes.

But Horace froze. Not a single part of his body seemed capable of responding to the messages his central nervous system was frantically sending. This was a red alert. He knew he must do something and do it fast. But he couldn't move. He had been so preconditioned by Ethel's terror tactics not to deviate from her minimum speed requirements, except under certain specific conditions, that he couldn't react appropriately to the stimuli that were assaulting his sensory receptors at a frenzied rate.

In a split-second after the front tires touched the edge of what Horace thought was a lake, he finally slammed on the brakes as the semi began to slide sideways and then to spin slowly in a counterclockwise direction, the result of a thick layer of ice on the highway that at first had appeared to Horace to be water. The unusually low outside air temperature had converted this body of water, which had no business lying across the state highway in the first place, into one of a truck driver's worst fears—black ice.

Even if Horace could have reacted appropriately, he could have done very little to improve his situation. The black ice rendered the eighteen-wheeler totally out of control. Miraculously, even though the truck was well into a spin, it remained on the appropriate side of the highway, although there was no way Horace could have known that, because the double yellow line separating the two travel lanes was invisible beneath the ice.

To Horace, his surroundings took on a surreal appearance. Everything seemed to be moving in slow motion. All was silent. The engine died as the result of Horace's failure to depress the clutch pedal when he slammed on the brakes. Strangely, Horace felt relatively little fear of an impending crash. He wasn't terrified by the thought that the truck could roll at any moment. He wasn't worried about the possibility of the tractor and trailer jackknifing with the further possibility of the occupants of the cab being crushed by the load in the trailer.

Horace had only one thought, *What is Ethel going to do to me when she finds out what I've done?* Even stranger than that, Ethel remained asleep, her body flowing easily with the slow, graceful spinning of the truck over the frozen pond.

# Chapter Nine

Only a few hundred yards down that same highway, something caused Sarah to stir. Her eyes opened slightly. At first she wasn't sure where she was. Her brief nap was unusually deep, and she had been dreaming. About what, she couldn't remember. She realized she was in the car. She sensed that the car was moving. She looked up slowly, not moving her head from its resting place. As she glanced out the windshield, a tiny white speck began to appear on the far horizon.

With a start, she became vaguely aware that something was wrong. She raised her head. The speck on the horizon was approaching rapidly. It was now not more than a few hundred feet away. As the automobile drew near, the white speck transformed rapidly into a woman standing on the right shoulder of the highway. She was a beautiful young woman with long, reddish-brown hair, wearing something white and flowing, like a long, fine nightgown, her hair blowing in the wind. The woman was motioning to them with gestures that were both gentle and powerful. She was signaling them to slow down, like the way flagmen on highway crews signal you to slow down even though you think you're already going too slowly.

As the car passed the woman, Sarah could clearly read her mouth saying, "Slow down."

Sarah screamed, "Michael!" Only then did she realize that Michael was asleep at the wheel. He awoke immediately and hit the brakes.

Then Sarah realized what she had sensed earlier that seemed strange to her: They were on the wrong side of the highway. The double yellow lines were to her right.

In spite of Michael's judicious pumping of the brakes, the car was still doing ninety-five miles per hour. They must have been traveling over a hundred when Sarah had screamed at Michael.

Sarah saw something ahead. It looked like lights. They were headlights. But they weren't pointing in the right direction. They weren't aimed down the highway, they were pointing off to Sarah's right. The lights were approaching so rapidly that Sarah didn't think Michael would have time to react. She grabbed the steering wheel and pulled it toward her, bringing the car violently into the proper lane.

Jaime shouted, "Hey, what's going on?"

Tim bolted upright.

Just as the car reached the right side of the center-line, Sarah realized that something else was wrong, even though Michael was back in control of the steering wheel. He was trying to aim the car down the right lane, but it wouldn't respond. He turned the wheel gently to the left and then to the right. Nothing.

At least their speed had dropped considerably. Thanks for small favors. Thanks for that woman along the highway. They were down to about sixty miles per hour, but the brakes were of no use. At first Michael thought the brakes had gone out. But then he tried downshifting the transmission. Nothing happened. Sarah held tightly to her door handle, resisting the urge to scream. Instead she said, "Hang on, boys. It's gonna be okay."

Michael realized that whatever was preventing the car from braking must be outside the vehicle. He looked closely at the pavement and saw that the double yellow lines disappeared occasionally. *There must be something on the pavement, something very slick.*

The headlights Sarah had seen only a few seconds ago were approaching rapidly, only now the lights were aimed away from them.

Whatever was the source of those lights seemed to be spinning. Then they disappeared completely as something very large came between those lights and their car.

Fifty miles per hour.

Michael shouted, "Everyone check your seatbelts!"

Forty-five miles per hour.

Michael tried very gently to coax the car as far to the right as possible. Not much response, but a little.

The source of the lights was now only a few hundred feet away and closing rapidly. The lights appeared to be shining off to the left of whatever had come between the Lasher family and the lights for a few seconds.

The thing was now close enough to be visible in the glow of the Lasher headlamps. It was a semi-truck, an eighteen-wheeler heading toward them—backward. Sarah screamed, "Michael! Oh my God Michael!"

Michael tried once again to urge the car to the right, praying that by some miracle they could avoid being crushed by the gigantic trailer heading their way.

Then things got a little better. Whatever was on the highway that had prevented Michael from braking and steering was gone. He felt like he had some control of the car again. The car shot through what Michael recognized as the intersection of Partridge Road. Before he could do anything, however, things got even worse than before. He had no control at all. At least moments ago the car was heading front end forward. Now it began to spin. Ice. They were on ice.

What the hell was ice doing on the state highway? There was no water out here. It hadn't rained for days. And where the hell were the intersection lights?

Michael knew he couldn't have slept for more than thirty seconds. If so, they would have ended up in a ditch or, perhaps, gone off the road into Hans Ruger's pinto bean field.

Michael and Sarah braced themselves. Tim and Jaime were focused on The Force, not saying anything. The car continued to spin in a counter-clockwise direction, now heading backward.

Sarah thought, "If we're going to hit that trailer, it might be easier on our bodies if we hit it rear end first. At least our seats may act as some kind of cushion between our bodies and all of that steel."

When the two vehicles finally made contact with each other, the right rear corner of the Lasher car crashed into the left rear wheels of the trailer. This caused the car to spin furiously. The Lashers all felt the same centrifugal force tearing at their bodies. It felt like their skin was being pulled away by some mighty, invisible force. Jaime thought for a moment that his eyeballs were going to be pulled out of their sockets. They were all screaming. The car spun at a phenomenal rate. Perhaps the lack of traction caused by the ice was what allowed them to spin instead of rolling or, worse yet, flipping end-over-end.

The impact of the car with the rear tires of the trailer was the final factor in forcing the load within the trailer to shift. The shifting of that heavy load caused the trailer to do a complete flip. The flipping of the trailer yanked the tractor up off the pavement and threw it thirty feet into the air, causing it to impact with the earth about a hundred feet down the highway.

Somewhere during this frantic ride, Ethel awoke and began shrieking at the top of her ample lungs, "Horace, you son-of-a-bitch, I'm gonna kill you. What the hell have you gotten us into?"

Horace was still totally paralyzed, in a daze. Like a kid on a Disneyland ride, feeling a sense of false safety fostered by the snugness of his seatbelt harness. He surrendered to the situation, didn't try to fight it. He took some kind of sadistic satisfaction in hearing the obvious torment Ethel was going through.

When the tractor within which Horace and Ethel were entombed finally made its inevitable and forceful contact with Mother Earth, it wasn't a pleasant experience. However, just before that fateful incident, as the truck was spinning on the icy highway and as Ethel was hurling energetic insults at Horace, he turned to her from the security of his seatbelt harness, raised his eyebrows, reached far into the depths of his normally limited vocabulary, and with an eloquence fueled by years of pent-up rage, surprised himself by shouting, "Ethel, you cheap imitation of a beached whale. I have to say that whatever ignominious fate awaits me at the end of this brief journey will pale when compared to what you have put me through all these years. I pray that your abundant remains will smolder indefinitely in the fiery brimstone of hell."

With that, Horace closed his eyes and surrendered to whatever fate awaited him. He started to giggle. The giggle became a laugh. The laughter became so uproarious that tears began to trickle down his face. For the first time in more than twenty years, Horace was a happy man.

As the car, in which the members of the Lasher family had gone on the wildest ride of their collective lives, came to a stop, Tim looked out the rear window and saw the tractor flying through the air at an elevation of about twenty five-feet above the ground. He probably would not have seen it if its headlights had not remained on.

When the tractor hit the ground, it flipped end over end several times, as evidenced by the flashing of the beams of its headlights, and came to rest in the middle of the asphalt, smoke and flames pouring out of the engine compartment. Tim, Jaime, and Michael took off running in the direction of that vehicle, although they had a devil of a time running on the ice.

When they got there, they found two people in the cab, both alive but unconscious. They pulled Horace and Ethel out of the cab, fearing that the fuel tanks might blow at any moment. It took Tim, Jaime, and Michael, using every ounce of strength they had, to drag Ethel's body away from the truck.

Sarah arrived, slipping and sliding, with a blanket and a first-aid kit she had grabbed from the trunk of their car. Jaime found another blanket in an external compartment of the truck.

Michael said, "We'd better get these folks some help right away."

Jaime looked into the cab and saw a CB. In spite of the fire danger, he climbed inside but found it inoperative. The family car was of no use. It had ended up with its rear wheels in the mud of Hans Ruger's recently formed lake, buried up to the axle. It was decided that Jaime, the sprinter, should run to the motel and tavern at the intersection of the highway and the interstate about three miles away. Sarah and Michael wrapped the blankets around Horace and Ethel in a vain attempt to ward off the terrible cold. Tim and Michael

managed to get Horace back to their car, where the heater was running. They were able to move Ethel to the car by laying her on both
blankets and sliding her across the ice. When they got her there,
Sarah had to help Michael and Tim force Ethel's body into the backseat.

As they sat in the car waiting for the heater to do its job, Sarah
suddenly said, "Oh, my goodness, I forgot about the lady along the
highway.... Michael, there was a lady back there. She saved our lives.
If I hadn't seen her flagging us down, we wouldn't have been able to
hit the brakes until after we were on the ice. We probably would have
hit that trailer at eighty miles an hour instead of thirty-five. Oh, my
God, she didn't have a coat on. It looked like she was wearing some
kind of a nightgown. She must be freezing to death. Michael, we've
got to help her."

Michael and Tim jumped out of the car, grabbed a flashlight from
the glove compartment and headed down the highway on foot. The ice
and oil on the pavement made their efforts exceedingly difficult.

Sarah sat in the car, exhausted from the events of this incredible
evening. She looked back through the rear window several times, trying to see Michael and Tim. She wondered how much longer it would
be before Jaime would return from the tavern.

It seemed like a good half-hour before Michael finally opened
her door. He just stood there, saying nothing. Sarah could tell by the
look on his face that they hadn't found the lady.

Her heart sank. "Oh, Michael, it's so cold out there. We can't
just let her freeze to death."

Tim stood nearby, silent.

Michael handed Sarah a box. Printed on the lid of the box, in
pencil, was simply "Sarah."

"I didn't write that," said Michael. "It was like that when we
found it."

Tim nodded.

Sarah placed the box on her lap and raised the lid. Inside she
found a note in the same penciled printing. It said, "Sarah, my most
beloved friend. Whenever you need me, think of me. I'll be there.
Love, Jessica."

Beneath the note, tied in a red satin ribbon, lay a length of hair, Sarah's hair.

Sarah held the note close against her heart. As she looked up at her men, a single tear fell upon that long, reddish-brown hair.

Chapter Ten

The very first thing most people noticed about Chris was his piercing, dark-blue eyes, a highly unusual characteristic in a Native American. Perhaps this stunning feature resulted from a romance between one of Chris's great-great-grandmothers and a Scandinavian explorer.

Over the years, an indentation was formed in the area between his eyebrows, probably arising from his passionate nature. That indentation, combined with those intense eyes, could make him look menacing, especially when he was angry.

At first glance, a stranger was likely to consider Chris dangerous—until Chris let loose with one of his famous smiles. Chris was a charmer. But in his arsenal of remarkable traits, a raging temper prowled, waiting to be unleashed. If Chris was your friend, you were most fortunate. He had an uncommon sense of loyalty. If you were so foolish as to cross him, though, you'd be well advised to make amends fast.

Willing to forgive an oversight or an act of simple stupidity, Chris, strangely enough, was a peacemaker. But once he confirmed a person's standing as his enemy, that person's days as a healthy, ambulatory human being were numbered. Any transgression against one of Chris's family members was an automatic confirmation of such a status.

Chris spent his childhood with his mother on the reservation. His dad had died in the Vietnam War, where he won numerous medals as a fighter pilot. Chris was born just a few months before his dad's death. Much of what he knew about his dad came from stories his mother had told him, and a few newspaper clippings he ran across. Beyond that, Chris knew that whenever his dad was mentioned among family or friends, an obvious feeling of reverence permeated the air.

Although Chris's mother always cherished him, by far the strongest influence in his life was her grandfather. By the time Chris was five years old, he and Great-Grandfather were close friends. Chris never called him anything but Great-Grandfather. After Chris's father died, Great-Grandfather made it his life's purpose to teach Chris everything he could about the old ways.

On Chris's twelfth birthday, Great-Grandfather took him to a far-away canyon, where they spent many days locating, capturing, and taming a wild mustang. It was the largest horse Chris had ever seen with amazing contours, unbelievable strength, intelligent eyes, and a most magnificent head. They didn't break the great beast as so many did to these noble creatures. They tamed him with love and patience.

Chris named the horse Nahimana Tama, from the words of the Sioux language, combining to mean Mystic Thunderbolt. On most occasions, Chris called him Tama. But whenever they were faced with a grave challenge and the stallion needed powerful encouragement or firm direction, Chris used the full name Nahimana Tama with unfailing results.

That horse grew to be more precious to Chris than anything in his world except his family. A day never went by that Chris didn't spend time with Tama. Chris often slept in the barn in the stall next to him.

They often traveled into the mountains for weeks at a time and camped beside quiet lakes and roaring rivers. They provided courage and confidence to each other. When Tama found himself faced with an unusually wide ravine to jump or a risky river to cross, he sometimes looked back at Chris as if to say, "Can we do it, friend?" Then Chris would tighten his knees against Tama's rib cage, lean close to the horse's ear, and whisper, "You bet we can!" And they always made it—always. It was as if their combined wills were all-powerful.

If Chris wasn't quite sure they could handle a perilous situation, he paused for a moment, took a deep breath, and sent his soul soaring to Great Spirit, just as Great-Grandfather had taught him. He commanded his heart to open wide to the Great Mother/Father of all creation. In seconds, he felt the sense of peace and confidence that always came to him from contact with Great Spirit. Then he knew, beyond any doubt, that they could do it. Tama knew too.

When Chris wasn't in the mountains having a wild adventure with his horse or attending the Christian school, which he disliked but went to out of respect for his mother, he was with Great-Grandfather. They spent hours walking in the desert, where Great-Grandfather taught Chris the identity and healing powers of the various plants along the trail. He taught Chris how to make weapons, tools, and utensils out of the simple, natural materials they gathered as they walked and talked.

They spoke for hours about Great Spirit, Mother Earth, Grand-mother Moon, the four directions, the tree spirits, and other wonders that sent Chris's imagination racing. Chris learned of the power of prayer, which was far different from what he had been taught in the Christian school. He came to understand his ability to influence matters beyond his physical reach, using the power of his mind. He learned that he could influence the circumstances of his life by choosing an outcome and aligning the vibration of his thoughts and feelings with that outcome.

Chris regarded Great-Grandfather with a combination of awe, respect, unfailing obedience, humor, and love.

One day, Chris and Great-Grandfather were sitting on top of a huge boulder, looking down upon a beautiful clear lake that had formed in a volcanic crater high in the mountains, watching the reflections of clouds roll by. It seemed to Chris that Great-Grandfather remained silent an unusually long time. Chris wondered what he was thinking, but he had learned not to disturb Great-Grandfather when he was pensive.

After some time, Great-Grandfather stood up and slowly folded his arms across his chest ceremoniously. He said, "My son, Great Spirit has instructed me that the time has come for you to learn how to direct the energies of the non-physical world with the power of your mind into the realm of the physical." He asked Chris to focus his attention on a small cloud directly overhead and to hold the thought of making that cloud disappear.

Chris had witnessed Great-Grandfather perform so many wonders that it didn't even occur to him to question the feasibility of such
an undertaking. He relaxed into the effort and allowed himself to be
guided by Great-Grandfather's soothing voice.

From his many discussions with Great-Grandfather, Chris knew
his job was simply to have faith. This was not the kind of faith that he
was taught about in the Christian school, not faith in a god who sits
in the clouds and decides to grant the wishes of some but not those
of others. The faith that Great-Grandfather taught Chris was more
of a *knowing*, a knowing that Great Spirit does not decide—it simply
acts in accordance with our desires. Our job is to align our thoughts
and our feelings with the goal we have chosen. Once we have achieved
this alignment, and assuming we don't cancel it out with a contrary
thought or feeling, the outcome is a certainty.

The only variable on this plane of relativity is the time that passes
between our thought or feeling and the physical result. The more
perfect our alignment and the more clear our intention, the more
quickly the result will appear in our material world.

With these thoughts, Chris relaxed his body and cleared his mind.
He then put forth his intent to vaporize that little cloud with as much
clarity and emotion as he could gather. He was distracted for a
moment by the thought that it seemed a waste of Great Spirit's time
to be messing around with a tiny cloud when more serious matters all
over the world needed attention.

He then remembered Great-Grandfather's lecture about the infinite power of Great Spirit and Great Sprit's utter inability to render
judgment about any matter, large or small. Chris refocused his energy
and, after a few minutes, thought that perhaps the cloud had gotten a
little bit smaller. He wasn't sure. He quieted his mind once more. He
told himself, "I know. I know I have the power. I know the power of
the God Force is with me. I know it will grant my every wish if I just
have faith. I choose to see that little cloud growing smaller."

And then he was sure the cloud had gotten smaller.

And then he wasn't so sure.

And then, yes, it clearly was smaller and less dense. It wasn't the bright white it had been. It was almost as if he could see through it. Yes, he could. Yes, it was smaller. And then *it was gone!*

He jumped up and looked at Great-Grandfather, waiting for a reaction. Slowly a grin started to form on Great-Grandfather's weather-worn face. His eyes began to twinkle and a small tear ran down his cheek. He said, "I remember the day I made my first cloud disappear. I was with the medicine woman of our tribe. She was so happy that she pulled me to her bosom and held me there until I almost suffocated."

Chris asked Great-Grandfather to tell him how this happened.

Great-Grandfather explained that clouds are often used for introducing young searchers to their powers because it helps them develop faith in their abilities. The ephemeral nature of a cloud is what makes it easy to imagine that it's changing. Such an imagining allows for a bit of faith sufficient to move a bit of energy. That energy causes the cloud to become a bit smaller. The observation of that phenomenon then causes another increase in faith. The increased faith then causes a little more energy to be released and on and on until eventually the cloud is gone.

Chris was so excited that he spent the rest of the afternoon zapping clouds out of existence. It didn't always work. When it didn't, he found that he was allowing doubt to enter his mind. Then he refocused and tried again. Eventually he got to where he could do it consistently.

Great-Grandfather cautioned Chris to resist the temptation to demonstrate his newfound talent to others. He told Chris that to do so would carry the danger of involving the ego, which would put tremendous pressure on a person to perform, which would give rise to the possibility of doubt entering the mind that likely would block the power, causing failure, which would produce more doubts, and so forth.

Great-Grandfather told Chris that he would do well to practice these matters frequently until he had such confidence that no doubts could enter his mind. With repeated practice, the faith and the power would expand the ability to affect physical objects in items of a greater solidity than clouds. He told Chris that if someday he were called upon to use his powers in the presence of others, he should do so only with a compelling reason and that he would have to take great care to keep his ego out of the way. He reminded Chris of how much trouble Jesus had gotten himself into by allowing others to witness his energy manipulations.

He added that such powers were admired and respected many thousands of years ago but that in more recent times those demonstrating these powers were feared and considered to be in league with Satan. Women had been burned at the stake, he told Chris, for simply using the power to heal others.

Great-Grandfather explained that many great books prophesized turmoil and devastation toward the beginning of the twenty-first century and, for those who would survive, the world would enter into what Jesus called the thousand years of peace. Great-Grandfather told Chris that when that time arrives, those who have mastered their power will be revered and sought after as teachers rather than feared and crucified.

Chris vowed silently to develop his power to its maximum potential but to keep it to himself unless it was desperately needed. At that time, Chris had no idea what its maximum potential was.

 **Chapter Eleven**

When Chris was nineteen, Great-Grandfather died.

Chris refused to allow Great-Grandfather to be buried in a public cemetery. Everyone knew better than to challenge Chris's decision on this matter, even though his mother feared the authorities would object. Chris would do what Great-Grandfather would have wanted. Chris made the arrangements for a gathering where friends and relatives would have an opportunity to pay their respects and to console one another.

That night, after everyone had gone home, Chris wrapped Great-Grandfather in a beautiful blanket and fastened him securely to a travois that Chris had built the night before. He attached it to Tama with heavy leather thongs, and together they headed up into the mountains to fulfill Great-Grandfather's commitment to honor the old ways. As Chris rode, he thought a lot about Great-Grandfather and the many memorable times they had enjoyed together.

Chris recalled how Great-Grandfather had told him, only a few weeks earlier, that he had accomplished everything he had set out to do in this lifetime. He told Chris that his life was totally fulfilled and that he was prepared and eager to experience, once again, the great joy and freedom of the spirit world. He said he felt particularly easy about making his transition from the Earth plane, especially now that Chris was old enough to look after his mother, Maria. Maria was Great-Grandfather's only granddaughter.

He asked Chris to think of him often after his departure. He promised he would always be there, ready to help Chris in any way he needed.

Great-Grandfather had died alone in front of his fireplace, resting in the easy chair he had enjoyed so often. He held his war bonnet close against his chest. A most gentle smile graced his weather-worn face.

Chris and Tama rode on in silence. The great horse clearly understood Chris's feelings. Chris smiled as he remembered his mother telling him that, when he was born, it was up to Great-Grandfather, as the elder of the tribe, to name the baby. Chris's parents had already decided that the name would be "Christopher" if it was a boy and "Elizabeth" if it was a girl. Still, Great-Grandfather had the duty and honor to give the child an Indian name. In the old days, the elder, shortly after the birth of a child, customarily looked out of the entrance of the tepee where the child had been born, and whatever he first saw provided the basis for selecting a name. As a result, history is filled with colorful names such as Sitting Bull, Running Bear, and Eagle Feather.

On the morning of Chris's birth, Great-Grandfather was summoned to the home where his granddaughter was in labor. His presence was requested for the purpose of providing comfort to his granddaughter and also to be available for the momentous task of naming the child. As soon as it was announced that this was a boy, Great-Grandfather walked ceremoniously to the door, glanced outside, and seeing nothing that impressed him, announced, "Great Spirit has suggested that I think on this for a while."

Several days later, Great-Grandfather announced that the name he had selected was Roaring Thunder. Nobody openly questioned the decision of the proud old man. Still, many wondered about the basis for such an unusual name, especially considering that not so much as a drizzle had dampened the air for many days.

As the years passed, the matter of Chris's unusual name slipped into the background. The advent and blossoming of Chris's well-known hot temper seemed to render the name quite appropriate.

One day, while Great-Grandfather was enjoying the benefits of a small dose of peyote, he took it upon himself to invite young Roaring Thunder into his cabin. He directed Chris to have a seat. Great-Grandfather gazed at the ceiling of his little home, as if looking through it to the heavens, and announced that Great Spirit had commanded him to make a revelation to young Chris. He then asked, "Have you ever wondered, my son, about the source of your Indian name?" Chris nodded eagerly.

"Well, my fine great-grandson, you may know that it was I who gave you that name. I didn't give you that name on the day of your birth as is the custom. It came to me several days later while I was standing over your small bed observing you intently. I was looking for a sign from the heavens. You are probably not aware that, at the time of your birth, your beloved mother had quite a habit of consuming a variety of spicy foods, often with an abundance of jalapeño chilies in them. Since you were receiving your nourishment from your mother's breasts, it was only natural that a certain amount of the juice of the mighty jalapeño would find its way into your young and sensitive digestive tract. As a result, as I was standing over your bed, imploring Great Spirit to send me a sign regarding the Indian name to be selected for you, there came a great escaping of a most thunderous and odorous gas from your tender body. The name Roaring Thunder came to mind immediately." Great-Grandfather laughed and slapped his knee so hard that he almost fell off of his stool.

Chris laughed, too, and in his laughter was reminded of the great joy that a long, heartfelt laugh can produce.

Chris smiled at the memory of the story even in his great sadness. Out of deep respect for Great-Grandfather, Chris and Tama
moved slowly along the trail. Their journey took all night and most
of the next day. When they arrived at the canyon Chris had selected
to be Great-Grandfather's final resting place, he took care to perform
the ceremony as he had been instructed. When it was completed,
Chris spread his arms, raised his eyes toward the heavens, and as the
sun began to disappear behind the mountains, he sent forth, from the
very depths of his soul, a cry that thundered down the walls of the
canyon and out into the great desert, where Great-Grandfather had
taught him so many wonderful lessons.

Chris entered into a state of mourning that lasted for days. He
cried and laughed and thought and prayed. The crying was not out of
concern for Great-Grandfather but for himself. Chris knew for a certainty that Great-Grandfather was now in a state of glorious freedom. He was without pain, without worry, no longer confined by the
limitations of this physical plane. Where he was now, there was no
time or space. Everything happened instantly. If you wanted a double
cheeseburger with large fries and a chocolate shake, all you had to do
was think it and it would appear. And you never got indigestion. You
had no worries about cholesterol. And you were free of any concern
about getting fat.

The only negative about the place where Great-Grandfather now
resided was that, with the absence of time and space, it didn't provide
the same kind of opportunities for learning that we provide for ourselves on this Earth plane. The time lag between our thoughts and
their physical manifestation on Earth is what allows us to experience
what we already know when we are in the world of spirit. Great-
Grandfather had explained this to Chris long ago. Chris knew that
death was nothing to be feared.

The tears that Chris shed were for himself, for the void he felt in
his life without Great-Grandfather. He knew his grief would dimin-
ish over the next many months. After that, he would look forward to
being reunited with Great-Grandfather in the spirit world, where they
would have many great belly laughs discussing how they had each

done in fulfilling their roles in this lifetime and what each of them had learned.

When Chris returned home, he was without Tama. Nobody asked what happened or what became of the great beast. His mother knew Chris would have seen to it that Tama would be safe and happy in his new home. In truth, Chris did spend many hours observing Tama's tentative approach to the herd of wild horses. He watched Tama slowly work his way into the herd, using body language to establish dominance over the weaker horses and submission to the leaders. The confidence Tama had developed from the many adventures he and Chris enjoyed would serve him well as he gradually gained the respect of the other horses and ultimately became the alpha horse, leader of the herd.

Chris knew instinctively that this would happen. He also knew that Tama would grieve for him for a while. But he was certain that Tama would be happy back with the herd, where he could live out the remainder of his life in the comfort of the companionship of his own kind. Chris had many great adventures ahead of him that would not allow him to stay at home to tend a horse. It was best for them both.

Anyone who has spent years on the back of a fine horse cannot easily be content with an automobile as his or her only means of transportation. There is something about feeling the awesome power of a fine horse between your legs that is hard to do without once you've experienced it. Shortly after Chris made the difficult decision to leave Tama in the wilds, he began to feel a longing.

At first he thought his loneliness for Great-Grandfather was what was disturbing him. But, after considerable reflection, he was able to make a distinction between his feelings over the loss of Great-Grandfather and his yearning for the return of the outrageous sense of power he had felt when he and Tama were confronting their fears amid the challenges of the great outdoors. In those days, he hadn't liked to admit that he had fears. But it was the truth!

He recalled several lessons that Great-Grandfather had taught him about fear. One was that, in the end, there are only two human emotions, love and fear. All of the other negative emotions are only variations on fear. Second, fear was created to keep us safe; it is nothing to be ashamed of. To have fear is not unmanly. To be without fear is to be stupid. A courageous man is not without fear. He is the man who confronts his fears and does what he knows is right in spite of his fears. Finally, one of the greatest acts of courage is to acknowledge the truth, no matter what the consequences.

Yes, Chris and Tama had both been afraid. That was a fact. That was the truth. And wasn't facing those fears and conquering them what made them feel alive? Wasn't overcoming those obstacles together what made them such great friends?

Chris had to face the reality that owning a horse at this time in his life wouldn't be practical, no matter how strong his craving. Even more important, it wouldn't be fair to the horse to be deprived of the frequent attention and companionship that is so important to herd animals. So, it was decided.

But how was Chris going to satisfy the need for power, the need for the thrill, the need for speed?

A motorcycle! Of course! Motorcycles don't need constant attention. You can leave them in the garage for weeks all by themselves. They are relatively inexpensive, get great gas mileage, and have low insurance rates. Power! Speed! Freedom!

The next day, Chris got a ride into the city. All three of the motorcycle dealers were on the same street within a few blocks of each other. He spent the day test driving many different brands and models. The Harleys tempted him. No doubt, Harleys have the look, the sound, the image. But when it came to performance, they didn't measure up to the foreign bikes. He drove Suzuki's, Kawasaki's, Yamaha's, Husqvarna's, BMW's, a Maico, a Bultaco, a Ducati, and even a Motoguzzi.

Then it happened. He visited a Honda dealership. The minute he walked through the door, the Honda beckoned to him. It stood out from all the other motorcycles, sort of the way a book at the bookstore seems to jump out at you, as if it's asking to be read. And you know for sure there's something in that specific book that is meant for you to read.

Well, that's just the feeling Chris got there in the Honda show-room. It was love at first sight.

A 2005 Honda CBR 1000-RR, just about the fastest street-legal machine you could buy on a showroom floor. A ten-minute test drive was all it took. Talk about power! Smooth. Zero to one hundred thirty-five in about ten seconds. And sure-footed. The faster it went, the steadier it felt. It didn't have the heart of a horse. It couldn't love you back. But until Chris was ready to settle down, this would do just fine.

A few months after Great-Grandfather returned to the spirit world, Chris's mom began dating a man from a nearby town. His name was Clint, and he was a cowboy. He was remarkably fit for his age and rather handsome. Chris liked him. Within a few months, Mom asked Chris if it would be all right with him if she and her cowboy were to tie the knot. Chris assured her that she didn't need his per-mission but that he certainly appreciated being consulted on the mat-ter. He said it was fine with him, then jokingly added, "Just be sure Clint understands that if he ever mistreats you, he's a goner." Mom laughed and said she would convey the message.

A week before the wedding, Chris moved out. He set up tempo-rary living quarters on the piece of land high in the mountains that had been left to him in his father's will. The property was one hun-dred sixty acres, covered with beautiful ponderosa pine, aspen, and scrub oak. A small stream flowed through the forest and tumbled over the cliff that marked one boundary of the property. From this cliff, Chris could look out over the entire valley and see the small town where he and his family had lived all of his life.

Chris's new home consisted of a tent, a fire ring, a wash basin, a mirror, a few tools, and a sizeable pile of firewood. Chris didn't need restroom facilities for now. Mother Nature provided several thou-sand acres of open-air outhouse. Chris did, however, provide him-self the luxury of a few months' supply of toilet tissue. As he told his mom, "I may be a rugged mountain man, but I'm civilized."

Fortunately, an abandoned logging road came through Chris's property. It was still in good enough shape to allow Chris to ride his

Honda from the main highway to his campsite. In the winter, Chris would leave the Honda covered in the forest and get to town and back in his Jeep.

For the past three years, Chris had had a job in town as an automobile mechanic. He worked only twenty-five hours a week, but that was all he needed for food, gasoline, an occasional shirt or pair of Levi's, and dinner once a month at the Edgewater restaurant for him and Mom and Clint. He did his own vehicle maintenance.

During the three years since he had started his job at the auto repair shop, he had managed to save about five hundred dollars a month, primarily because of his very low overhead. Of the eighteen thousand dollars he had put in his savings account, he had spent half of it on his Honda.

Shortly after Chris moved onto his mountain top property, he began making plans to build a more permanent, more comfortable home. Over the next many months, he built a log home using timber that grew on his land and that he milled with a portable lumber mill he borrowed from a long-time family friend. On the weekends, he borrowed Clint's pickup to haul the larger and heavier materials he bought at the True Value store in town. He had to ask a couple of his friends to help, once in a while, with the heavier tasks. Most of it he was able to handle himself.

After his first month of construction, using only some basic hand tools, Chris's mom and Clint showed up one Saturday morning with a Honda generator, a Skil worm-drive power saw, a Makita power drill, and one hundred feet of extension cord. Chris thanked them at least ten times, until finally Clint said, "We just wanted to be sure you got the job done before winter so you wouldn't move back in with us." The three of them had a good laugh.

Chris served them a delicious elk stew that had been simmering over the campfire, and Clint broke out a six-pack of Dos Equis from the ice chest in the back of his truck. It was a fine family event—one of many that Chris would remember when the going got tough. From that time on, the construction job moved along quite nicely.

His new home was a source of great satisfaction for Chris. It had one bedroom, a bathroom, and one large room that served as the kitchen, dining area, and living room. Chris constructed a fireplace using moss rock gathered from the property. Above the bedroom and bathroom was a small loft.

Lighting was provided by gas fixtures attached to two small propane tanks, which also powered the propane refrigerator Chris purchased from a motor-home supply store in the city.

Chris built a small greenhouse, made of glass panes he hauled up from town, three or four at a time, in his backpack. He grew a variety of vegetables and herbs. The herbs were for cooking and for medicinal purposes.

The stream that flowed past his front door provided plenty of year-round drinking water. Chris installed a seventy-five gallon water tank on the hill behind the cabin. The water flowed by gravity down to the cabin with enough pressure to allow for comfortable showers. The tank was supplied with water diverted from the stream several hundred yards uphill, where the stream was quite a bit higher than the tank. Surplus water from the tank overflowed into a pipe that returned it to the stream. Chris constructed a leach field some distance from the cabin to take care of waste water. All in all, it was a nice, low-maintenance, trouble-free, ecologically sound system, taking advantage of the natural topography and the laws of physics and nature.

Heat was provided by a system of radiators connected to three solar panels on the roof and a heat collector in the flue of the fireplace. This enabled Chris to be comfortable most of the time without building a fire. When he did build a fire, the system collected much of the heat that ordinarily would have escaped up the chimney and distributed it throughout the cabin.

As Chris stood in front of his new home, admiring his work and feeling a profound sense of satisfaction, the thought flashed through his mind that it sure would be a fine home to share with a lovely woman.

Chapter Twelve

On the Thursday morning just prior to the Franklin/Riverton football game, Chris awoke to a glorious sunny day. A slight breeze coaxed the fragrance of pine trees from the forest in through his open bedroom window. The thought of a scrambled-egg and hash-brown-potato breakfast played around the edges of his consciousness, causing him to salivate slightly. Before long, the eggs were scrambling and the taters were browning.

After his hunger was satisfied, Chris took a quick shower, pulled on a pair of blue jeans, and sauntered out to the ponderosa log he had placed in his front yard for sitting and thinking purposes. He sat on the log, cogitating and looking out over the cliff at the town below.

The sun shone gently on Chris's body. He was strong, with solid muscles and good definition. The strenuous work he had done on the cabin firmed up the fine physique he had perfected as a high school wrestler, football player, and weightlifter.

Before long, the magnificent sunshine, the majestic view of the valley below, and the contented state of Chris's stomach combined to cause a notion to form in his eager young mind. That notion, together with a longing he hadn't yet identified, resulted in a full-blown idea. This, he decided, would be a great day for a motorcycle ride over Crestline Pass to the city of Winston. A ride through the pass would be breathtaking this time of year. Besides, he hadn't been to the big city in a long time. Who knows what wonders awaited him there?

Chris put on his riding boots and took his motorcycle helmet from the shelf. The helmet matched his motorcycle almost perfectly, with several brightly colored racing stripes running from the center of the helmet just above the Plexiglas face shield and spreading out to the sides and back. Chris picked out his favorite shirt and put it into the tank pack on his bike. He decided the weather was too warm not to expose his upper torso to the wind and sunshine. He would put on his shirt upon arriving in the city. In the meantime, his body could soak up all the rays it wanted.

As Chris headed up into Crestline Pass, an awesome feeling of freedom pervaded his being. The roar of the one hundred fifty-six horses at his command was exhilarating. The aroma of the pine forest was delectable. The sunshine was intense. The air was stimulating. The Honda was responding magnificently. All of his senses were being tantalized. He had the undeniable feeling that he and his motorcycle were one, that he and the highway were one, in fact, that he was one with all of creation.

It took Chris two glorious hours to get to Winston. As he dropped down from the high mountain pass into the valley below, the air temperature rose dramatically. By the time he got into the heavy traffic, it was about 85°.

He stopped for a red light. As Chris sat there waiting for the signal to change, a burgundy-colored convertible pulled up on his right. He glanced at the driver.

There, in this very same city, on this very same day, sitting at the very same traffic signal, was the most beautiful woman Chris had ever seen. She had long, dark brown hair, high cheek bones, almond-shaped eyes, and the cutest little nose in the solar system.

Chris's heart began to do strange things. It stopped for a few seconds. Then it started again, all by itself. It raced at triple speed, stopped again, and did a hiccup. It spun around, doubled in size, and returned to normal. Finally it fell to the bottom of Chris's abdominal cavity.

The light turned green. The burgundy automobile accelerated. Chris stood paralyzed. A man behind him in a Subaru honked politely. Chris forgot which lever was the clutch. He stalled the engine. The Subaru honked more insistently. Chris fumbled with the shift lever. Mercifully, the engine started again. Chris let out the clutch lever too fast. The rear tire spun, creating a smoke screen in front of the Subaru.

The Honda roared up to the next signal. Chris had to skid to a halt to avoid colliding with a man in the crosswalk. He was now beside the burgundy convertible in which sat the woman of his dreams. He looked straight ahead. After what seemed like forever to Chris, he slowly turned his head to the right and sneaked a glance at the woman. She was staring directly at him. He smiled. She remained expressionless. His heart fell from the bottom of his abdominal cavity into his left boot.

The signal changed. The burgundy dream machine moved on. The impatient Subaru man, formerly behind Chris, had shown the good judgment and presence of mind to relocate to a position behind the burgundy convertible. As a result, he was able to proceed along the street at a respectable pace while Chris continued to fumble with the controls of his formerly well-behaved motorcycle. He killed the engine again. By the time he got it started, he had to race to the next signal to arrive there before the goddess in the burgundy machine departed. This time he was able to bring his steed to a stop without depositing an abundance of tire rubber on the pavement. He tried to look cool. Once again he glanced in the direction of the queen of the universe. Once again she was looking his way. He smiled. She remained impassive.

By the time Chris survived two more signals and another abrupt stop for an elderly woman in a crosswalk, he suddenly had two simultaneous realizations. The first was that the princess with the dark brown hair couldn't possibly have seen the wondrous smile he had flashed repeatedly, because his face was hidden behind the tinted Plexiglas shield of his helmet. This, he prayed, accounted for her lack of response. The second realization was that, because of the effects of the abundance of stimuli that had accosted Chris's psyche during the past several minutes, he completely forgot his resolve to don his shirt upon arriving in the big city. This resulted, to his great embarrassment, in his making his first contact with the lady of his dreams in a state of semi-nudity, not at all the image he wished to convey. He vowed to make no more stupid moves with his motorcycle in the presence of his beloved.

As Chris was attempting to recover a modicum of composure, he suddenly realized that there remained but one traffic signal before the thoroughfare, upon which he was conducting his courtship, would become an open highway. As the love of his life sped off, shaking her head almost imperceptibly, Chris yanked his favorite shirt out of the tank bag in which he had sequestered it and pulled it on without removing his helmet, thereby rendering the neckline five sizes larger than the manufacturer intended.

He headed slowly toward the fateful traffic signal with a firm resolve not to make any more of a fool of himself than he already had. The brown-haired beauty had already stopped for the light, and a Dodge pickup had assumed the position directly behind her. To Chris's dismay, the Subaru now occupied the position to the left of the burgundy convertible, making it extremely difficult, if not impossible, for Chris to effectively continue wooing the maiden. To make matters worse, the right turn signal of the burgundy convertible was broadcasting the intention of its captivating driver to head in a direction legally prohibited to Chris from his present lane.

In total disregard of his recent vow to refrain from performing any actions that might further discredit him in the eyes of his prospective sweetheart, Chris pulled up to the left of the Subaru and made a right turn in front of both the Subaru and the convertible, a maneuver that headed him in the direction indicated by his beloved's turn signal and causing him to commit seven traffic violations simultaneously.

He proceeded slowly down the side street, waiting for the burgundy chariot to follow. To Chris's horror, his rear view mirror revealed that, against all odds and in total disregard of the laws of decency, the lady was proceeding on her original course. She didn't turn right. But how could this be? Didn't she realize that it's illegal to proceed in a direction other than that indicated by one's turn signal? Was she not aware that the man of her dreams was now fading into the distance, not even visible in any of the numerous mirrors attached to her vehicle?

By the time Chris had maneuvered his Honda back to the original thoroughfare, the convertible was nowhere in sight. He drove up and down the street, carefully dividing his attention between the search for the lady and due concern for the safe operation of his vehicle. He explored several cross streets, nothing. He drove more slowly, taking care to search each parking lot, still nothing.

Finally Chris ran out of places to look. And besides, the lady was probably home by now, sipping a daiquiri and making a stir-fry.

Or, heaven-forbid, having dinner with her boyfriend, or, worse yet, her husband. Chris's mind dove into a downward spiral of increasingly agonizing possibilities, some of which bordered on an invasion of the lady's privacy.

Then he broke into a laugh. He laughed and he laughed. He laughed until his smile muscles began to ache. He was laughing at the situation. But, most of all, he was laughing at himself. *Chris, you crazy Indian. Here you are, acting like a jilted lover over a lady you've never met.*

He had acted like a crazy man over a lady he didn't even know. For all he knew, she might be a spoiled rotten little brat. She might be ornery, hot-tempered, malicious, or hateful. She might be a serial killer. What right did such a nasty woman have to interrupt his previously peaceful day? He laughed again.

He enjoyed a nice, long, relaxing lunch, followed by a two-hour nap in one of the city's beautiful parks. He did a bit of window-shopping and purchased a few items he couldn't get in his home-town. He kept hoping he might run into the brown-haired damsel who had so captured his heart, but had no such luck.

Chris decided to spend the night in town. Only about an hour of sunlight remained, and he didn't like going back through the pass after dark. There was too much of a chance of hitting a deer or an elk. Hitting a large animal on a motorcycle is serious. He'd get a nice motel room and a good night's sleep.

After he got settled at the Best Western, Chris realized that the night was still young and he was too keyed up to sleep yet. He rode his motorcycle to a cocktail lounge a few blocks from the motel, parked his bike on the street in front of the bar, and secured his helmet to the theft-proof helmet holder on the left side of the Honda's seat.

Chris slid into a booth and ordered a Corona. The lounge was almost empty.

For years, Chris had noticed that when he had a few bottles of beer or a couple of shots of whiskey, his thoughts expanded. At those times, his mind seemed to venture into realms that normally were beyond his reach. He often got some of his best ideas when he was drinking. Chris had been drunk only a couple of times, and he didn't like it. He liked to be in control of himself at all times. He was especially aware that his hot temper had to be chaperoned by his conscience.

So Chris usually drank moderately, if at all. He never drank to escape from reality. He liked to think that he drank to explore new aspects of reality. Usually though, he drank just to unwind.

Before long, Chris was midway into his second Corona. He felt himself relaxing. His thoughts turned, naturally, to the lady in the ill-mannered Burgundy Beast that didn't even have the decency to obey its own turn signal. Chris laughed.

What was going on? Chris had met lots of beautiful ladies in his life. And, although he appreciated a gorgeous face or a dynamite body, he didn't let those qualities override his good judgment. Chris was one of those old-fashioned guys who looked for true beauty, the kind that's on the inside.

No doubt, what first got his attention was often a pair of beautiful eyes. But if a new relationship didn't promise a great deal more than physical attraction, Chris was quick to walk away. If Great-Grandfather had taught him anything, it was that true beauty is found in the soul.

So what was it about the lady in the burgundy automobile? What caused Chris to act like a schoolboy on his first date? He hadn't even heard her voice, hadn't looked into her eyes. Perhaps it was some unusually intense hormonal secretion. Perhaps the lady reminded him of someone else, someone for whom he had once cared. He didn't think so.

He ordered another Corona.

By the time Chris reached the bottom of that third bottle and while he was chewing intently on a lime wedge, he detected the onset of a mild buzz. He wandered over to the jukebox. His eyes settled immediately on his all-time favorite song, "Unchained Melody," by the Righteous Brothers, Bobby Hatfield and Bill Medley. The fact that, out of more than two hundred selections on that jukebox, his eyes settled immediately on his very favorite, the one that fit his mood perfectly, was the kind of coincidence that Chris often experienced when he was drinking. This phenomenon was what Great-Grandfather called "synchronicity." Chris put a quarter in the jukebox and pushed the buttons for his selection.

He had once asked Great-Grandfather why drinking alcohol seemed to cause his awareness to expand. Great-Grandfather offered his opinion that the moderate use of substances like alcohol or peyote tend to set aside the mental blocks we acquire during our formative years and allow us more direct access to our Higher Self.

The music began, hauntingly, "Oh, my love, my darling, I've hungered for your touch, a long, lonely time…." It sent goose bumps up Chris's back. He was getting "twitter-pated"—a term his mom used to describe an intensely romantic state, a term Chris first heard in the great Disney cartoon *Bambi*.

Chris thought about the woman again. What was it about her?

Then the alcohol caused Chris's body to release a tiny droplet of whatever hormone nudges wider the opening of the door that sometimes blocks the corridor between the conscious and the subconscious. The memory of a discussion Chris and Great-Grandfather had once had, when they were canoeing on the Seminole River, came to him. Great-Grandfather had told Chris about what he called "Spirit Lovers," explaining that some people call them "soul mates." He said this term refers to couples who have been together, and very much in love, over many lifetimes. He said Spirit Lovers are best friends in the spirit world. When they choose to have an adventure on the Earth plane, they sometimes take a long time and make many painful mistakes before they find each other.

Chris couldn't help but wonder if this might have something to do with the way he was instantly and powerfully attracted to the lady in the convertible. He often saw attractive ladies with nothing more than a fleeting interest. But to react the way he had, almost out of control, utterly twitter-pated, was not normal, not for level-headed Chris.

From the jukebox behind him the music continued to tug at Chris's heartstrings, coming dangerously close to bringing tears to his eyes. Chris focused all of his attention on the words of the song.

The song ended. The feelings it aroused in Chris were so intense that its ending caused him to feel a strange combination of relief and yearning.

He sat spinning his Corona bottle in lazy circles on the table, almost hypnotized by the reflections on the glass. The room was quiet.

The only light Chris could see in the dark lounge, other than the light above his table, was the glow from the jukebox.

Then, it started again.

The same song.

That same haunting melody.

But Chris had put only one quarter in the machine, made only one selection. Why was his favorite song in the whole world playing again? The goose bumps returned with a vengeance. The tiny hairs on the back of his neck stood on end. Tears threatened again.

Chris turned toward the jukebox. His eyes were not yet adjusted to the darkness. He saw only the jukebox, heard only the music.

Then his heart leaped as he noticed a hand resting on the selection buttons, a beautiful, lightly tanned hand with raspberry fingernails. Attached to that delicate hand was a slender arm with the slightest hint of fine, downy hair. Chris could see nothing more. His heart pounded. The hand remained motionless.

He rose and moved slowly as his eyes began to detect a form beyond the light.

The hint of a silhouette floated just beyond the brightness, the outline of a high cheekbone, the hint of almond-shaped eyes, the almost imperceptible image of the cutest little nose in the solar system.

It was his dream woman. Or was it? It had to be.

Chris placed his hand, palm up, in front of her, a subtle invitation. She reached out with that gorgeous hand and laid her fingertips upon his. Chris thought he sensed a shiver run through her body.

He smelled her perfume. Obsession! His favorite. He stepped closer. She was still in the shadows. He could feel warmth radiating from her body.

He felt her other hand rest lightly on his shoulder. He reached out and gently touched her waist. They began to move with the slow rhythm of the music. She whispered, "Is it you?"

Chris said, "What do you mean, 'Is it me?'"

She said, "Never mind—I can see by the size of your shirt neck that it's you."

Chris looked down at the shirt he had stretched over his motorcycle helmet. He laughed. She laughed.

He held her more closely. She didn't resist. He touched his cheek ever so gently to hers. Her cheek was soft and warm. Her aroma was intoxicating.

They danced slowly. He brushed his lips against the base of her neck, the tip of his tongue touching her skin lightly. He felt her tremble. This was happening too fast. He decided to back off and dance like a gentleman.

Mercifully, the song ended. "Thank you, Great Spirit," Chris breathed. "Another minute and I would have been fumbling with the buttons on her blouse."

Chris led her to his table. They introduced themselves. Her name was Wendy. Chris invited her to have a seat. They sat there for a long minute, staring into each other's eyes, neither knowing quite what to say.

Wendy finally broke the silence. She explained that Chris's conduct on his motorcycle had gotten her attention and piqued her curiosity. She was disappointed when he performed his crazy right-turn-from-the-left-lane maneuver. She thought she'd never get to find out who was lurking behind that Plexiglas face shield, but she was late for an appointment and couldn't stop. All she knew for sure was that a man on an impressive motorcycle with an outrageous helmet and a splendid physique was doing strange things that she hoped were for her benefit.

She was on her way home when she noticed his motorcycle and that fabulous helmet parked in front of the lounge. Although she had never done anything like this before, she felt an uncontrollable urge to stop and see if she could meet the man who had so aroused her curiosity.

She had intended only to take a quick look and leave. But when she walked into that lounge and heard the ending of her favorite song, something happened that she couldn't explain. She just had to play it again. And when she looked up and saw Chris walking toward her, she knew that something very special was about to happen. The instant their fingertips touched, a surge of energy ran through her body like she had never felt before. From that moment until the song ended, it felt as though her entire being was subject to some power beyond her control. If the song had lasted a bit longer, who knows what might have happened!

Chris confessed to having the same experience.

They agreed that this warranted further discussion, but not until each of them had time to cool off. They decided to meet again on Friday night, eight days from tonight, for dinner at a restaurant Wendy knew, which they hoped was bright and respectable, the kind of place where they could talk quietly, with their emotions under control.

As Chris walked Wendy to her car, he realized that he wanted to put his arms around her more than he had ever wanted anything in his life. Wendy felt the same way. With almost superhuman effort, they managed to say goodbye without touching.

They decided not to exchange telephone numbers so their only possible contact would be to meet at the specified restaurant. That way, if either of them decided this entire situation was just too crazy, all he or she had to do was fail to show up, and it would be over.

Chris's soul literally ached for Wendy. He could think of very little else. What mattered to him most in the whole world was that she would be there on that Friday night.

 # Chapter Thirteen

Chris stood in front of the cocktail lounge, watching the tail lights of Wendy's convertible disappearing into the night. He stood hypnotized, unable to take his eyes away from the spot where her car had faded into nothingness.

It was Thursday night, eight days until he was to meet Wendy again.

His reacting this way wasn't like Chris. He was usually well under control. But he wasn't at this moment. He fantasized that Wendy would be coming back down that street, any second now, yielding to the same almost irresistible attraction that Chris was feeling. But she didn't. It was probably just as well.

There was no way he was going to sleep now. In spite of the fact that he had paid for his motel room, and in spite of the risks involved in riding over the mountain pass after dark, Chris decided to head for home. The next best thing to being with Wendy would be a midnight ride on the Honda. Chris couldn't think of anything that would better suit his mood than the roar of those one hundred fifty six horses, powering him through the graceful curves of the high mountain road.

He walked over to the Honda and put on the leather chaps and jacket he had brought with him as protection against the cold air he would encounter on the mountain pass. He threw his leg over the seat and sat there smiling as he put on his helmet. With both hands on the handlebars, he raised the kickstand and pressed the starter button. The engine came to life with a throaty rumble.

The thrill of being on the back of this mighty beast, eager to respond to Chris's every command, was a perfect compliment to his existing state of exhilaration. Things couldn't get a whole lot better.

Pausing for a moment, he wondered what it must feel like to be at the controls of a fighter plane. He smiled. No, it couldn't be much better than this.

Chris sat there for a while, just thinking. Certainly he had feelings deeper than this, like his love for Mom, his respect for Great-Grandfather, the joy he had felt looking into Wendy's eyes. Those were treasures beyond description. Those were feelings a man would die for.

Motorcycles and fighter planes were in a different category. Most men wouldn't die for them, although many had. Still, there was something almost alive about them. Chris thought about the "romance" the American public has been enjoying with the automobile for decades. He thought about the reverence and respect he felt for his hunting rifle, the rifle Great-Grandfather had given him for his 14th birthday. He thought about the joy he felt holding a well-balanced throwing knife in his hand.

One summer Chris and Great-Grandfather had spent many hours reading a book about Albert Einstein. As Chris recalled, Einstein believed everything that exists is made of the same stuff and that this stuff is, ultimately, energy.

Chris revved the engine, slowly released the clutch lever, and the Honda rolled smoothly down the street toward the beckoning mountain pass. Great-Grandfather had told him to never ignore his feelings, that feelings are far more reliable than thoughts. Great-Grandfather said, "Never override your feelings with thoughts. Follow your feelings. They will always lead you to the right place. Just be sure they are really your feelings." The feelings Chris had for his motorcycle were nothing like what he felt for his loved ones, but they were feelings nonetheless, and powerful feelings at that.

As the city street rose to become a mountain highway, the Honda began to climb with ease. Chris had the bike in fourth gear. Even in fourth, a turn of the throttle could cause his head to be pulled back with considerable force.

He began thinking of Tama, that wonderful beast he loved so much, with the heart of a lion.

As Chris banked powerfully into each turn, the bike responded to his wishes. It took such a slight, almost undetectable change in Chris's body position to cause the Honda to turn that he fantasized he was actually doing it with his mind, not his body. He tried banking into several turns without changing his body position at all. It felt like the bike was responding to his thoughts. Sort of like vaporizing clouds. Maybe just his imagination.

Chris used to think sometimes that Tama was responding to his thoughts, just pure thoughts, without any intentional physical signals. He even wondered if Tama could read his mind. But that was an animal. Certainly the same principles didn't apply to non-living objects. Then he remembered that Great-Grandfather had told him everything has consciousness, even objects that seem to our limited sensory receptors to be inanimate.

By the time Chris arrived at his cabin, he was relaxed and ready for some serious sleep. He parked the Honda next to his Jeep, stretched his arms, and looked up at the millions of stars twinkling in the jet black sky. He thought about Wendy and wondered if she might be looking at those same stars. A week from Friday seemed like a terribly long way off. Chris had no idea how long it would prove to be.

Before retiring for the night, Chris stood for a while admiring his Jeep C-5. It was one of the great joys in Chris' life. He had replaced the stock engine with a fuel-injected 427-cubic-inch Corvette V-8 that he modified considerably. With the help of a friend, he installed an Iskanderian 800 rpm high-lift cam, solid lifters, heavy-duty rocker arm springs, and a Hays 3,200-pound racing clutch. He modified the exhaust system to relieve a great deal of back pressure. As almost an afterthought, he installed an air-filter system, designed to allow plenty of air into the mighty engine, and replaced the stock sparkplugs with tri-tips. The C-5 was a screaming machine.

Friday morning, the day before the Franklin/Riverton game, Chris awoke early.

The sun had just begun to break over the mountaintops. Before he could even remember what day it was, thoughts of Wendy flooded his mind. He rolled over, wrapped his arms around his pillow, and just lay there with his eyes closed and a big grin on his face.

He finally turned loose of the pillow, sat up, and gave his scalp a vigorous rub. Then he showered, dressed, and took considerable time making himself a delicious breakfast of chorizo and eggs, accompanied by some of Mom's homemade tortillas. He cleaned the kitchen and went outside to sit on his favorite log and gaze down at the town below.

Now, he just had to figure some way to make it all the way to next Friday night without going crazy.

Chris sat there for a long time soaking up the warm sunshine, thinking about Wendy, picturing those beautiful, almond-shaped eyes, that gorgeous smile, that cute little nose. He knew he wouldn't make it to next Friday this way. As pleasurable as those thoughts were, they only made him yearn for the real thing, to be holding Wendy, smelling the aroma of her perfume, feeling the touch of her fingertips. Better find something to take his mind off Wendy or he'd be a basket case before nightfall.

Then it came to him.

What better way to keep himself busy and his mind occupied than a few days in the wilderness? When Chris was in the forest or the desert, he kept himself so busy that he didn't have much time for his mind to wander. He was constantly doing something, that required his concentration, like marking his trail, calculating his location and direction, watching for possible dangers, deciding on a safe location to spend the night, setting up camp, cutting firewood, building a campfire, cooking his dinner, and much more.

Being in the woods made Chris feel particularly alive. The fresh air and the smell of the trees gave him an unusually powerful hunger. So what if it was almost winter? He had a heavy sleeping bag and lots of warm clothing. Besides, he was a tough guy, wasn't he?

Yeah, a few days in the mountains would be just the thing to keep him distracted until next Friday night. And if he just happened to think about Wendy once in a while, what better place to really get into his feelings?

Chris knew just the place. Not far from Great-Grandfather's burial site. Not far from where he had released Tama.

Chris called his boss and made arrangements for a friend of his to cover for him next week. Then he took several hours gathering his camping and fishing gear, making sure everything was in working order, loading his supplies and equipment into the Jeep, giving the cabin a thorough cleaning and securing it. Finally he headed out for a few days of what he hoped would be a grand experience.

He followed the state highway for quite a while. Then he drove along a county road for a few miles before turning off onto a gravel Forest Service road. As that road wound its way high up into the mountains, Chris recognized the trail where he and Tama had crossed the Forest Service road as they had made their slow, sorrowful trek to Great-Grandfather's final resting place.

The haunting memory of that journey caused Chris's throat to tighten. He felt tears beginning to form. He shook it off and concentrated on the road. He knew there were no accidents. He sensed that he was on this road, at this time, heading for a particular destination for a powerful reason. He could feel it. Yes, he wanted to distract himself from the yearning to be with Wendy. But there was more. He felt something compelling was pulling him along that beautiful mountain road, another kind of yearning. He didn't know exactly what it was. But maybe it was better this way. Chris loved the unknown, the feeling that an adventure lay ahead of him. It almost frightened him. But that was part of the excitement. Maybe he would be able to forget about Wendy for a little while after all.

The Jeep wound along the gravel road. Chris was lost in thought. The trees were beautiful this time of year, the leaves displaying shades of yellow, orange, and dark red.

The sun began to sink behind the mountaintops to the west. The road became more difficult to see. Chris turned on his headlights.

A vision of Great-Grandfather's face flashed through Chris's mind, appearing to be a reflection in the windshield, just his mind playing tricks.

He rounded a turn and was suddenly enveloped in a patch of fog. The temperature must be dropping. He slowed the Jeep. He thought he saw a large animal off to the side of the road, just out of range of his headlights. He stopped. But when he looked closer, nothing was there. Just the shadows and his headlights reflecting off tree trunks. He continued on his way.

Chris felt chilled. He turned on the Jeep's heater. Instant warmth blew out from under the dashboard. Still, for some reason, he couldn't shake the cold. Even as the cab of the Jeep became obviously warm, a chill kept hovering around him, causing goose bumps to ripple up his spine and neck.

Before long the sun was completely gone and the forest took on a new feeling. It seemed to be closing in on both sides of the road. The same forest that had felt so inviting only a while ago now seemed ominous and threatening. As Chris rounded each curve, the blackness that was hiding just around the bend seemed to be waiting for him, preparing to pounce on him and his little Jeep.

Wow, this wasn't the wilderness Chris knew. He was on excellent terms with the forest and all of its creatures and mysteries. Something was different tonight. Something Chris didn't like at all.

He stopped the Jeep and sat there thinking for a few minutes. He was very aware of the darkness all around him, especially behind him. He fantasized that if his headlights were to fail, he would disappear into the darkness forever. He felt a need to get moving, fast, as if something were lurking behind him ready to attack. He fired up the Jeep's powerful engine and let out the clutch quickly, spinning its huge off-road tires, throwing gravel out behind him, digging way down through the gravel to dark brown native soil.

As the Jeep sprang forward, Chris had the haunting feeling that he had left something bad behind him, something very bad. He felt the chill again. Trust your feelings, he told himself.

For the next several minutes Chris drove uncommonly fast, skidding into several curves. He didn't know why he was doing this. He just felt a need.

After a while he began to relax a bit, and whatever had spooked him seemed to ease up. He began to laugh. "Chris, you crazy Indian," he told himself. "What the hell's the matter with you?"

He drove for a few more miles and began to realize that he was on a part of the roadway that didn't seem familiar to him. The more he concentrated on it, the more he became convinced that he had never been here before. He rounded a curve and came face to face with a gigantic oak tree. An oak tree that was grotesque beyond words. Not only had it been badly deformed, as if it had grown up under some terrible stress, but it obviously had been struck by lightening. It had a huge scar on its trunk that was charred and weather-worn. But mostly its terrifying appearance was caused by the unnatural twisting of its limbs. The tree was so hideous that it took Chris' breath away. He slammed on the brakes and skidded to a halt just inches away from it.

Chris reflexively threw the Jeep into reverse and backed away from the tree as fast as he could. When he had backed up about twenty feet, he stopped and sat there staring at the tree. He thought it probably didn't look quite so awful in the daylight, but here in the dark with just the headlights shining on it, it looked disgusting. One thing Chris knew for sure, he had never been here before. He had never seen this tree, ever.

Searching for a word to describe the feeling that tree evoked in him, he came up with "omen." That tree is some kind of an omen. It related to the chills he was feeling and the terror he felt earlier as he tried to catch a glimpse of whatever he thought he saw in the forest.

He definitely had never been here before. He must have missed the turnoff to the place he planned to camp.

Chris turned the Jeep around, intending to head back in the direction from which he had come. A tingle ran up his spine. The gruesome tree was behind him, unlighted by the headlights. It was so large that, even at this distance, its twisted branches were looming above the Jeep in the darkness, its presence very apparent to some sense Chris couldn't describe. He kept moving.

At last he saw a few trees that seemed slightly familiar. With more confidence now, Chris proceeded along the road. He didn't know how long he'd driven before he found the turnoff to the lake where he intended to spend the next few days.

Within minutes Chris arrived at the lakeside campsite he knew so well, from so many wonderful camping trips he had taken with Great-Grandfather. The familiarity helped him relax. He quickly set up his tent, unrolled his sleeping bag and, with the aid of his flashlight, made his way back to the Jeep, where he removed his fishing gear and retrieved his Beretta 9 millimeter pistol from beneath the front seat. He leaned his fly rod against a nearby ponderosa, paused to enjoy the moonlight shining on the lake for a few minutes, then crawled into the tent, zipping the flap shut behind him. Having the Beretta in his sleeping bag gave him a sense of security, helped him to relax more.

Chris lay there, concentrating on the sounds of the night. Nothing unusual. Perhaps those things that had spooked him earlier were the result of an overactive imagination.

If Chris had not been so focused on finding the turnoff to the lake, he might have noticed that just a few feet beyond that turnoff were the scars on the road that the tires of his Jeep had made earlier.

What Chris wouldn't have noticed, even if he hadn't been looking so intently for the turnoff, were the eyes watching him from deep in the shadows.

# Chapter Fourteen

Chris awoke the following morning to the sound of raindrops tapping on the canvas above his head. The overcast was so heavy that at first he thought the sun had not come up yet. A glance at his watch told him it was actually morning. He looked out the flap at a newly formed stream trickling past his tent.

By the time Chris got cleaned up and had organized his equipment, the rain had stopped. But the weather remained cold and cloudy. He decided to spend the morning climbing to the top of the mountain on the other side of the lake. It would give him a bit of aerobic exercise, offer some great views, and help the time to pass while waiting for the sun to break through the overcast.

He put on his waterproof climbing boots, a heavy parka, and a windbreaker. He grabbed his hunting knife and waterproof matches. He headed down the trail that would lead him around the lake to the base of the mountain. After a few minutes, he paused, as if trying to remember something. And then, not knowing what he was after, he turned and headed back to the campsite.

As he arrived at the tent, he realized that the pistol in his sleeping bag was what he was after. It was almost as if the Beretta had been beckoning him. Perhaps it was just a subconscious fear that it might be stolen from the tent in his absence. In any event, it wouldn't hurt to have it with him. Great-Grandfather told him it was a lot better to carry a weapon you didn't need than not to have one when you needed it.

With the pistol tucked in the waistband of his jeans and protected by his windbreaker, Chris headed down the trail a second time.

As he began his ascent, it seemed to be a lot steeper than he remembered. Perhaps it was because he had aged about five years since the last time he had been here.

The cloud cover had dropped since Chris first observed it from the opening in his tent flap. The clouds were now so low that they covered the top of the mountain. It seemed to Chris that they had gotten darker.

As he reached the cloud base, he noticed that it was not as clearly defined as it appeared from down below. Some of the rocks and trees were totally covered while others, at the same elevation, were in the open. He observed canyons of clear space between areas completely covered with mist. This created a surrealistic atmosphere. It made Chris wonder what it must feel like to fly an airplane around big, puffy clouds constantly changing shape with their many dead-end corridors. He wondered if one of those cumulus clouds he and Great-Grandfather had vaporized contained a pilot in his Piper Cub and whether the pilot's family was still wondering what happened to him. Chris laughed out loud, his laughter echoing down a canyon.

He walked for a while, mostly inside the clouds. Eventually he realized he had lost his bearings. Chris, who always prided himself in having a compass in his head, couldn't believe he was actually uncertain of his position. He wasn't really lost. He had nothing to worry about. He knew, from years of hunting and tracking, that all he had to do was head downhill and he would come out of the cloud cover and ultimately end up back at the lake. Only by going uphill did people who were lost often make their situations worse.

He thought for a minute and decided to continue uphill, in spite of the possibility of getting really lost. His confidence in his outdoor skills tilted the scales in favor of pursuing an adventure rather than returning to the relative safety and comfort of his campsite. In search of a trail to the top of the mountain, he wandered through several small canyons. He hoped he would eventually rise above the cloud cover and enjoy a long bask in the autumn sunshine, perhaps with a view of the desert below on the far side of the mountain.

When Chris stopped to catch his breath, an uncomfortable feeling enveloped him, a most unusual sensation, partly physical and partly emotional. Then his muscles tensed as he realized it was the same feeling that had overtaken him last night on the road when something in the darkness had spooked him. He stood still, barely breathing, not even blinking, trying to identify that feeling. It grew more intense. He knew instinctively that the source of his uneasiness was somewhere behind him, in the mist. Something told him he was being watched.

As he headed uphill once again, he experienced an urge to run. But, unlike last night, when he felt certain his Jeep could outrun whatever he imagined to be lurking behind him in the forest, he now had only his two legs to rely on. Even though he was a strong runner, he knew of several inhabitants of the forest that could run down any man. If something was really there, and if it was an animal, Chris reasoned that his best chance for escape would be to move quietly and attempt to outthink it.

Chris worked his way up the mountainside to a point about four hundred feet above the mountain's base. It took all he had to keep from gasping for air, but he didn't want to release any sounds that would make it easier for whatever might be pursuing him to get a lock on his position.

Pausing for a few minutes, listening for any unusual sounds, and providing time for his breathing to settle down, Chris checked his waistband. The Beretta was still there. He decided he had better hold it in his hand where he couldn't lose it and where he could use it quickly if he had to. He shoved the ammunition clip all the way into the handle of the pistol until the lock snapped, pulled back the slide, and let it go as quietly as he could, loading a round into the chamber. He left the safety on, knowing he could snap it off in an instant.

Chris wished he had brought his 44 Magnum. A 9 millimeter could provide adequate protection against a human being, but the forest harbors some predators that would only become more aggressive when they are injured by something as small as a 9 millimeter.

As he continued up the mountain, working his way around a thick stand of scrub oak, he came to what seemed to be a dead end. The more or less level terrain upon which he was walking was blocked by a gigantic granite boulder, surrounded by fog. To one side was a steep uphill cliff. To the other was a steep downhill cliff. No place to go except to retrace his steps. He looked back, not really wanting to return the way he had come. He heard something that sounded like footsteps, large footsteps. He heard branches snapping.

Chris did his best to calm himself. He asked himself what Great-Grandfather would do in a situation like this. This was an excellent time for guidance. He closed his eyes, trying to control his trembling, trying to be quiet.

Great-Grandfather had told him that each of us has a Higher Self, that our Higher Self is part of the God Force. He had said we are all one. We are one with all of creation, including the light beings, who are focused at this time in the physical world as well as those who are focused in the world of spirit. Great-Grandfather had said each of us is what he called a part of the One, just as a wave is a part of the ocean. Just as a wave emerges from the ocean for a time and then returns to the whole of the ocean, we light beings emerge from the God Force, occupy our physical forms for a time, and then return to it. And just as the wave is never separate from the ocean, we are never separate from the God Force.

These recollections returned to Chris in a matter of moments.

He also recalled Great-Grandfather's telling him that our Higher Self will interfere with our physical reality only rarely and only in matters of extreme emergency. However, it often sends us urges and intuitional insights to assist us in achieving our objectives. "The trick," said Great-Grandfather, "is to get very clear about what those objectives are and then have absolute trust that our Higher Self will guide us in what it knows to be our best interests."

Chris didn't know whether his Higher Self would consider his present state of agitation an emergency, but he sure wouldn't mind a little insight regarding his current situation. With as much calm as he could muster plus every ounce of concentration available to him, Chris tried to disregard the crunching sounds that were growing closer by the second. He said the following silent prayer. "Dear Higher Self, which is a part of me and a part of the God Force, please know that among my many objectives is a firm desire to stay alive for a long, long time. So please do what you can to help me get my ass out of here in one piece. Thank you."

Chris stood there, waiting for an inspiration. Nothing came.

The footsteps or hoof-steps or paw-steps or whatever were no more than two hundred feet behind him. He heard breathing. Maybe it was more of a snorting. He focused his energy.

One hundred fifty feet.

He clicked off the Beretta's safety. Sweat was dripping down the sides of his rib cage.

One hundred feet.

Then, for no apparent reason, a sense of total calm came over him. The trembling stopped. His breathing returned to normal. He wondered if this was the calm he had read about that a man experiences just as he is about to die.

He closed his eyes and focused one more time. Seventy-five feet.

The footsteps stopped. Chris opened his eyes. Strangely, instead of looking in the direction from which the terrifying sounds had come, Chris looked at the area between the granite boulder and the uphill cliff. He wondered what had prompted him to look there. He saw for the first time what appeared to be an opening, a surprisingly large gap he hadn't seen before. Perhaps it had been buried in the cloud cover. It was a space between the boulder and the cliff about two feet wide and six feet high. He couldn't make it out with any clarity. It could have been an actual opening or just an illusion caused by the cloud cover that was all around him.

Why had the footsteps stopped? Perhaps a predator was savoring the last moments between the time it realizes that its prey is trapped and it makes the kill.

The footsteps started again. Only now they were running. Whatever the hell it was was racing, crashing through the underbrush. Chris sprinted for the opening like a madman. He didn't dare to slow down, knowing that whatever was behind him would probably catch him in a matter of seconds. If that dark space in the center of the cloud cover was only the illusion of a cavity, Chris was going to have one gigantic headache. But, compared to the alternative, the risk seemed reasonable. Chris was running hard as he entered the hoped-for gap, and the realization that he didn't come to an immediate bone-crunching halt confirmed that it was an opening after all.

Chris stopped quickly, recognizing that his good luck, in finding empty space instead of what could have been solid granite, probably wouldn't hold for long. Besides, he couldn't see a thing. As he continued forward at a walk, arms extended in front of him, he realized he was in some kind of a cave. His vision improved slightly, but not enough. What little light was entering the cave didn't help him to see what was surrounding him. His only clues came from his sense of feel. Whatever it was, was cold and damp and covered with something slimy. Chris stopped. He had reached the end. It was a dead-end cave.

Please, God, let whatever's following me be too big to fit in here!

A second later, what little light had been seeping into the cave disappeared completely. Chris looked back toward the opening and realized it was covered, obscured by something very dark and very large. He could see small traces of faint light around the outer perimeter of whatever was blocking the entry. He observed the thin rays of light on the right side of the object getting larger and smaller in an exact opposite rhythm to the widening and narrowing of the light rays on the left side of the object. To Chris's horror, he realized that the light phenomenon he was observing had to be caused by the creature swaying from side to side. It was walking toward him. Obviously (and unfortunately) in spite of its size, whatever he was about to make an intimate acquaintance with was not too large to come into the cave.

Come on, Higher Self, don't fail me now. Chris used every last bit of self-control he had to calm himself, to think.

One thought: He had all but forgotten the pistol in his hand. It would be hard to miss his target. Even if his aim wasn't perfect, the bullet would probably ricochet off the granite wall and ultimately make contact with the beast. The clip held twelve rounds, maybe enough to cause sufficient pain to discourage whatever was heading his way from continuing on its mission, maybe sufficient firepower even to encourage it to go away.

He fired two shots. The sound was deafening. He covered one ear with his free hand and did his best to cover the other with his opposite shoulder. This left him with his gun hand above his head. He fired two more rounds. His ears were ringing so loudly that he couldn't hear whether his adversary had reacted to the shots or not. What he thought might have been a roar was overwhelmed by the echoing of the blast from the pistol.

Another thought came to him: his waterproof matches. Chris reached into his pocket and found the plastic, screw-top container. He had to put the gun back in his waistband against his back so he could unscrew the lid from the match case. He almost tried to strike the first match on the cave wall, and then remembered the slime. That would be a sure way to guarantee that a match won't light. He remembered how Clint Eastwood often struck a match on his beard stubble or, better yet, on the beard stubble of the bad guy. No such luck. Not with Indian stubble. It occurred to him that he had forgotten to put the Beretta's safety back on, a good way to shoot his butt off. No time to do that now. He would have to take his chances.

Then Chris remembered that inside the cap of the match container was a small, circular patch of sandpaper-type material for striking matches. He hoped the beast had stopped. He couldn't hear anything. For all he knew, it was right next to him. He struck the match. The initial flare caused his night vision (or, in this case, his cave vision) to take a nosedive. He held the match above his head, out of his line of vision. Within seconds his vision returned. What he saw caused his blood to run cold. There, not more than five feet from him, were two gigantic, hostile eyeballs, reflecting the flame from his match.

 **C**hapter Fifteen

Whatever it was that possessed the malevolent eyes staring at Chris, it seemed to withdraw a few inches from the sight of the flame.

What difference does it make, five inches or five feet, I'm dead.

Even before Chris finished his thought, he heard laughter, not a whispered laughter—a big booming laughter. It was Great-Grandfather's voice, saying, "Where did I go wrong? Great Spirit put me in charge of your spiritual education, and at the first sign of a little danger, you resort to negative thinking! What's this 'I'm dead' stuff? Didn't I tell you that nothing happens by accident, that there are no coincidences, that everything that comes into your experience is the result of your thoughts? So what's to be afraid of? After all, it's all an illusion, isn't it? Didn't I teach you anything?" Again came that same booming laughter that Great-Grandfather called his "great belly laugh."

Chris struck another match. The eyeballs were still there. Not moving.

That voice has got to be my imagination. But it wasn't. And Chris knew it was Great-Grandfather speaking. Even though Chris was practically deaf from the sound of the pistol shots, he had heard the words. Maybe they didn't reach his brain through the normal physical channels. But it was Great-Grandfather's voice nonetheless.

"Okay, Great-Grandfather, I'd really like to chat with you, more than you'll ever know, but right now I've got a situation on my hands. Could you give me a little insight? NOW?"

"Listen my son. Listen with your heart. Listen to your soul."

Chris struck another match. The beast didn't move. It just watched, apparently mystified by the fire.

Chris thought he heard something else. It wasn't really a sound, but an impulse, a feeling, an urging. It wasn't quite clear.

He tried his best to give no thought to the beast confronting him. He didn't even light another match.

Then the words came to him: "You that have eyes to see, open them that you may see the glory of God, the glory that you are."

Against all impulses of common sense, Chris turned his back to the beast. There on the back wall of the cave near the floor, he saw a faint light. He bent down and saw an opening he hadn't noticed before, probably because his eyes hadn't fully adjusted to the darkness. It was about two feet high and two feet wide. It appeared to be about fifteen feet long with a source of light at the far end. Chris got down on his hands and knees and began crawling toward the light. Just as he entered the opening, the beast let out a mighty roar, audible to Chris, even above the ringing in his ears. He scrambled as fast as he could.

It was too late. He felt a terrible burning pain in his right calf. It had a hold on him. Chris grabbed onto the sides of the small tunnel and tried with all his might to break free from the beast's grasp. But he was being dragged backward. The pain was excruciating. He rolled over on his back and braced his other foot against the top of the tunnel while pressing his left hand against one wall. This forced his right shoulder against the other side. Using all his considerable strength, he was able to wedge his body so tightly against the tunnel walls that he temporarily stopped the beast from dragging him back into the larger cave. With great effort he worked his right hand under his back and grabbed the butt of the pistol. As he pulled it out of his waistband, the friction of the gun between his back and the tunnel floor pulled the trigger back far enough to release the firing pin.

He couldn't decide later what hurt more, the bullet tearing skin off of his left buttock or the flame from the firing chamber burning a quarter-sized blister in the small of his back. In any event, the pain pissed him off so completely that he sat up, slamming his head against the top of the tunnel. He screamed and pumped the remaining seven rounds of 9 millimeter copper-clad lead into whatever part of the beast was available through the opening at the end of the tunnel. The claws withdrew from his calf. Chris screamed again, not from the pain in his calf, his buttock, or his back, but from the pain in his ears caused by those last seven shots.

The beast let out a horrible roar, almost as deafening as the pistol shots, but all Chris heard was a high-pitched ringing.

He rolled over and snaked his way to the end of the tunnel, where he found a patch of sunlit grass. He pulled himself out and sat there shaking, trying to inspect his wounds. To his amazement, the damage to his calf was no more than three inch-deep claw marks. The damage to his butt was less serious than the damage that same shot had done to his ego. The burn on his back was the most painful of all but would result in no more than a lifelong scar. Blood ran down his forehead. He would need some stitches and a tetanus shot.

But how the hell was he going to get home? He wasn't about to head back to camp, knowing that a wounded monster of some type was probably roaming that side of the mountain and probably pretty upset.

Chris decided that as soon as he got back to civilization, he would call the Department of Wildlife and suggest that they send some professionals to find and destroy whatever had almost killed him.

At least, he was now above the cloud cover. It was warm up here. He would listen to his own good advice and head downhill this time; only he would be sure to do it on this side of the mountain, as far away from the beast as possible.

It was still before noon, he reckoned, and although it was going to be mighty painful, Chris was sure he could make it back to the main road, and probably hitch a ride to the ranger station he had passed on the way up. From there, he would call the Department of Wildlife, ask the ranger to take him to his Jeep, load his stuff, and get to a hospital for those stitches.

Chris headed down a small canyon that he thought would lead to the main road. Shortly after he entered into the shade of the forest, the canyon he was following split into three smaller canyons. The one to his right seemed to be the least steep of the three.

The thought flashed through his mind that he was out of ammunition. And the smell of blood would be easy to follow. Better keep moving.

Chris traveled steadily, though slowly and quietly, on the watch for any motion in the underbrush. He stopped every few seconds and studied his surroundings. All seemed peaceful enough. Still, a killer was out there. And he was seriously handicapped without his sense of hearing and without any ammunition.

He estimated that he had descended about two hundred feet, about halfway to the main road.

Then terror grabbed at his gut as he thought he saw something dark brown in a thicket just ahead and to his left. It might be just a boulder or a gigantic tree stump. He stood still. He couldn't hear anything with the ringing in his ears. Nothing moved.

Then several grouse erupted from the forest floor just to his right, flying in front of him, causing about a teaspoon of adrenaline to surge from the tiny glands atop Chris' kidneys.

As a slight breeze moved up the canyon, Chris detected the unmistakable aroma of *bear*! He had hunted bear and skinned them. The acrid smell of bear is something one can never forget. The same aroma can fill the air when a bear has been running, or when it has been injured. There was a bear nearby, no doubt about it. Whether it was that dark brown object Chris saw ahead on the trail remained to be determined. The possibility that it was the same beast that had almost killed him in the cave was such a terrifying prospect that he tried not to think about it.

He reflexively reached for his pistol and then remembered that he had no cartridges. Bile was rising in his throat. He thought he was going to puke. He forced it down. Not a good time to be making noise. Not a time to be doing anything but getting the hell out of here as quietly as possible. He turned back uphill, hoping to find another route to safety. Maybe he could circle around the mountain and make it back to his campsite. Not likely.

Maybe the bear he had smelled was just a harmless black bear cub. But he didn't think so. The aroma was too strong.

He continued up hill, looking back every few seconds.

Then Chris heard a terrifying roar, audible to him in spite of the thundering in his ears. He spun around, and there stood the beast on its hind legs, a twelve-foot-tall grizzly. Even at this distance, Chris could see that its chest and belly were covered with blood.

Chris took off at a dead run, ignoring the pain that was tearing at his body, knowing there was no way a man on foot could outrun a grizzly. But what else could he do?

What was a grizzly doing in this part of the state? No grizzly had been reported here in more than fifty years. The grizzlies stayed on the other side of the Continental Divide....What a strange thing to think just before dying. Dying? If Great-Grandfather could only hear me now! Come on, Higher Self, do your thing.

Chris ran like a madman, not looking back. He remembered how angry he got when the movie starlets being chased by the bad guys kept looking back to see if they were gaining. Chris would shout to them, "Don't look back—run like hell. Looking back only slows you down." He didn't look back. He ran like hell.

He expected about half a dozen claws to rip his back apart any second. He imagined he could hear the grizzly right behind him, feel his hot breath on his neck. He ran with every ounce of strength he could muster, totally disregarding the pain.

Chris had run only about a hundred feet, but it seemed like a hundred miles. He figured the grizzly had been about two-hundred feet behind him when the race started. That meant that if the grizzly were running about three times as fast as Chris—which seemed like a reasonable assumption, given the grizzly's apparent wounds and loss of blood—the claws should be tearing Chris in half in about ten seconds.

Then he saw it. On the horizon, about thirty feet ahead of him, a silhouette was outlined by the afternoon sun: a horse. A big sturdy stallion was standing broadside to Chris, facing to Chris's left. What in the world was a horse doing up here in this high country? And why was he standing still? Didn't he know he was about to be run over by a raging human being and one crazed grizzly bear?

Well, if that horse is crazy enough to just stand there, there must be some reason. Had someone hobbled it? Was it tied to a stake? It didn't matter. All that mattered to Chris was that something was there. Something is always better than nothing, even if the something is of no apparent use. But what could he do with a horse? Hide behind it? Certainly the horse wouldn't let Chris ride it—especially as soon as he came to his senses and got it through his thick skull that a grizzly was chugging toward it at about thirty-five miles an hour.

In seconds, Chris reached the stallion. He dove behind it, crazily thinking that at least the horse would absorb the shattering blow of the grizzly, maybe cause the grizzly to become dazed by the impact.

Then Chris's heart almost leapt out of his chest. This very stallion, standing in the path of an on-rushing grizzly, was the most awesome animal Chris had ever known. Nahimana Tama.

Tama, the beast Great-Grandfather and he had caught and trained and loved for so many years was just standing there, not hobbled, not tied to a stake but held there only by the love he had for the man who had released him to the wilderness. Chris had released his mighty body, but not his heart. In that instant Chris knew Tama was his forever.

Chris grabbed two fists full of mane and threw his body, injuries and all, onto the back of the mighty animal. Tama didn't wait for Chris to dig his heels into his flanks. The instant he knew Chris was on board, he bolted—just as one gigantic paw tore a deep gash through the top of Tama's left flank.

Tama ran in total disregard for his injury. All he knew was that the human he loved was in danger and that he was the only chance they both had of outrunning that bear.

Chris didn't try to guide Tama. He understood that the horse knew what his job was and how to get it done. They ran like the wind. The two of them became one, Chris leaning into the turns to help Tama keep his balance. The grizzly was never more than fifty feet behind them. Tama had to dodge the small trees in their path. The grizzly simply mowed them down, never flinching.

They ran for mile after mile, foam running from Tama's mouth, all the way down his neck and under his broad chest, as his thundering hooves pounded the earth. Sweat poured off his body. So slick was his coat that Chris had to fight hard to stay on Tama's back. Tama's heart was beating harder than Chris had ever felt it beat before.

The horse didn't know what a heart was, but he knew, instinctively, that something was wrong. He knew he was damaging his body. But he couldn't stop. His human was in danger. His only fear was that whatever was wrong with his body might stop him from delivering Chris to safety. Chris knew, too. He could feel the heart pounding, right through the horse's rib cage. Chris knew they couldn't go on. That loving heart couldn't take much more.

Chris looked back. The grizzly was still there, maybe dropping back a few yards. It was hard to tell. But he knew he had to slow Tama down, knew that if he didn't that noble heart was going to explode any minute. Chris leaned back, his signal for Tama to stop.

As insane as it might sound to anyone who had not known this wondrous creature, Chris would rather that the two of them die fighting that crazed grizzly than to have Tama's heart shattered because of his love for Chris. He leaned back further, more insistent this time. Tama didn't ease up a bit. He turned his magnificent head ever so slightly to the left and glanced back at Chris. That look said it all.

Tama looked straight ahead once again, determined to achieve his goal, to save his human.

Before Chris could decide what to do next, he saw a ravine coming up fast. He couldn't tell how wide it was, or how deep. But he knew it was wider, much wider than anything Tama had ever jumped before. He didn't know if Tama could turn in time.

Tama looked back once again, just like in the old days, and asked, "Can we do it, friend?" Chris leaned forward, his mouth inches from Tama's ear. "You bet we can Nahimana Tama," he said, "you bet we can."

Chris wrapped his arms around Tama's neck, partly to keep from falling off, but mostly to let Tama know that Chris was with him all the way. He shouted, "We're one now, my dear friend. Go for it, mighty beast."

In spite of the distance he had already run and in spite of the almost unbearable pounding in his chest, Tama increased his speed beyond anything Chris had imagined possible. They were flying, literally flying. Tama left the ground at the very edge of the ravine. It felt to Chris as if they were floating. He glanced down and thought they had moved into some kind of time warp. Everything seemed to be happening in slow motion. The flight seemed to last for minutes, although it was only a few seconds.

When they landed on the far side, Tama's weary legs couldn't stand the impact. They folded under that heavy chest as Tama tucked his head down and rolled end over end, throwing Chris off his back.

Chris was so concerned that Tama had broken his neck that he hardly felt the scrapes and bruises he had sustained. By the time Chris got back to where Tama was lying, the horse was breathing so hard that Chris thought he couldn't possibly live. Blood was pouring out of Tama's mouth and nostrils, spraying with each breath.

Chris knew he had to get Tama on his feet and help him to walk it off, just as a long-distance runner has to walk it off after a race. Chris tried and tried to get the horse on his feet, but Tama was too exhausted. Or, perhaps, the horse knew more than Chris. Chris decided to let him be for a few minutes.

He ran to the ravine, not knowing what to expect next.

There at the bottom lay the grizzly, his body contorted from the fall of about fifty feet. Its neck was obviously broken. Apparently it had been so crazed that it hadn't heeded the danger of the gigantic ravine. Even at this distance, Chris could see steam rising from the grizzly's coat in the chilly evening air.

Chris ran back to Tama. From many years of watching kindly old Dr. Fernandez, the town's veterinarian, he knew he had to get Tama cooled down fast. From all those years he and Great-Grandfather had wandered these mountains, he knew that a stream ran nearby, but he couldn't remember exactly where it was. He studied the terrain and guessed at where that stream would most likely be. He got down on his knees and laid his cheek against Tama's neck. He couldn't believe the amount of heat coming out of that faithful horse. He could feel the pounding of that big old heart. Chris choked back the tears. *Don't die on me now, friend. Help is on its way.*

With that, Chris took off running for all he was worth in the direction he hoped the stream would be. There it was! He took off his clothes, except his shorts and shoes, and soaked them in the ice cold water of the stream. Within minutes he was back by the horse's side, carrying his clothing, including his long johns, in his arms. The ice cold water against his arms and chest, plus the cold air, caused a shiver to run through his body.

In seconds he had his shirt and long johns wrapped around Tama's neck, where he knew they would help cool the blood flowing through the jugular veins. Chris knew not to put any cold water on the long muscles, for fear of causing them to cramp.

He sat down, lifted Tama's head off of the ground, and rested it on his lap. Chris squeezed as much water as he could from his blue jeans into the horse's mouth, hoping to stave off dehydration. Tama gulped it down. Chris squeezed some more water into his mouth, taking care not to give him too much at one time for fear it would cause stomach cramps. Then he laid the horse's head back on the ground and used his blue jeans to sponge Tama's rib cage. Great amounts of steam continued to rise into the air from the horse's trembling body.

Chris turned his shirt and long johns around, placing the wettest sides against Tama's neck. He swabbed the rib cage once more before returning to the stream. Before he left, he told Tama to stay where he was.

This time he returned with a rusty one-gallon can he had found in a small ravine and filled with water. *Thank you, Great Spirit, for those jerks who throw their trash in the forest.*

Once again Chris slowly poured water into the horse's mouth. Then he poured some water onto his shirt and long johns that were still wrapped around Tama's neck. He kept this up until it was so dark that he thought he probably couldn't find the stream, or worse yet, not be able to find Tama.

During all of his efforts to cool down the horse and get sufficient water into his system, he hadn't given much thought to the wound in Tama's flank. Luckily, the large chunk of flesh the grizzly had torn from the body was still held on by considerable skin. It appeared that no major veins or arteries had been severed, although it looked like the horse had lost a lot of blood. Perhaps the adrenaline coursing through Tama's body had caused the blood to coagulate more readily than normal. Chris gently pressed the chunk of flesh back into the gaping hole from where it had been removed. The horse shuddered violently.

"Easy, friend," Chris whispered, "I've got to do this." As gently as he could, Chris moved the large piece of flesh back and forth until it fit back into its rightful place. He hoped that sufficient blood vessels and nerves were still intact to keep alive that part of the muscle that had been torn away until it could heal and reattach itself.

From his years with Great-Grandfather, Chris knew that Great Spirit has provided herbs for every conceivable condition and situation. If he could only remember which herbs to use for a flesh wound. He would think about that while he went for help. He told Tama to stay where he was, that he would be back with help soon. Tama seemed to understand—or else he was just too exhausted to move.

Chris took off running downhill toward where he believed the road was. It was now dark, so he didn't dare run too fast for fear of knocking himself out against a tree trunk or a boulder. He kept his arms crossed over his face just in case.

Please help me, Great Spirit. My best friend is in trouble. I've got to move faster than this.

Then, almost as if on cue, Chris looked over his shoulder and saw a light rising above the horizon: the moon. Wonderful Grandmother Moon was here to help. Chris kept moving. Within a few short minutes, there was sufficient moonlight to actually help. In another few minutes, Chris was able to see enough to allow him to run faster. He couldn't see much on the ground, but he could see major obstacles.

Soon after reaching the road, Chris was able to flag down a vehicle, even wearing only his underwear. He told the driver what had happened, and the driver let him use his cell phone. Chris called Dr. Fernandez at his home and told him of the situation. The Doc told Chris he was on his way in his Land Cruiser with everything he needed. Chris said he would mark the trail with rags tied to trees from the road to the meadow where Tama was. He picked up a large rock and set it at the edge of the road so he could locate the canyon that led to the meadow when he would return with his Jeep.

Chris thanked the driver for letting him use the cell phone, and he started running toward his campsite. The driver backed up quickly, caught up with Chris, and offered to drive him there. Chris accepted gladly.

Before long Chris was back at the spot he had marked with the rock. A fresh change of clothing covered his shivering body. He wished he could wait here for Doc Fernandez, but he didn't want to leave Tama alone for too long, especially with the real possibility of coyotes or, even, wolves being attracted to the scent of Tama's blood. He cut the bright orange tarp he used as a windbreak whenever he went camping into long narrow strips and tied the first one to the trunk of an aspen tree beside the road. Then he headed the Jeep up through the canyon, stopping every fifty feet or so to mark another tree.

Ten minutes later Chris was back at the meadow.

Tama was gone.

# Chapter Sixteen

"Oh my God!" screamed Chris, "Oh my God! Tama's gone."

He removed the flashlight from the glove box. He felt in his waistband for the Berretta. It wasn't there. Then he remembered he had used his Levi's to soak up water to help cool down Tama. The Berretta hadn't been there then. It probably fell out of his waistband during the race with the grizzly.

Maybe he didn't need it. Maybe Tama was just over the next rise, grazing on some high mountain grass. Not likely. Tama wouldn't disobey Chris without good reason, especially when every aching muscle in his body told him to stay put.

No, something compelling had to have happened for Tama to leave this place.

In desperation, Chris screamed, "Great Spirit, help me find my horse. He needs me."

Chris shined his flashlight at the spot where Tama had lain. No mistaking it. This was the place. Grass flattened. Blood stains on the ground. Even Chris's shirt and long johns close by.

Then he heard a voice. He couldn't tell where it was coming from or what it was saying.

A strong wind began to blow, causing little dust devils to spin in the glow of Chris's flashlight.

He heard the voice again, stronger this time. It sounded like, "Follow the wind."

"What do you mean, follow the wind?" yelled Chris, "Who are you?"

"Follow the wind."

Chris looked around, totally frustrated. He had to find Tama. He searched the area for hoof prints. He found them in the dusty earth and began to follow them up a slight rise.

The wind increased dramatically, erasing the hoof prints that were within the beam of Chris' flashlight.

"What do you want?" Chris screamed, assuming some link between the voice he had heard and the intense wind that seemed intent on making his job more difficult.

As if in response, the wind increased.

Follow the wind. What the hell does that mean? Could Great-Grandfather be trying to tell me something? Is Great Spirit attempting to answer my prayer?

"Follow the wind," came the whispered reply.

Okay, maybe I'm supposed to walk in the direction the wind is blowing. But that's not the direction the hoof prints were going. "I don't have time for this," he screamed.

He stood there, trying to decide. He turned in the direction of the wind.

Walking slowly, Chris looked for a sign or something to make sense out of what he was experiencing. He continued to walk in the direction the wind was blowing, searching desperately for a sign.

Then he saw something shining in the distance, reflecting the beam of his flashlight. He ran toward it, hoping it had something to do with Tama.

The Beretta! It was his Beretta! In an instant the wind stopped. All was calm. The moon shined brightly overhead.

The total silence was almost eerie—but welcome.

Chris picked up the pistol, still not believing what he was seeing. It was his, all right. It must have stayed in his belt through the entire ride until Tama collapsed and threw Chris off his back. It was a good fifty feet from where Tama had landed.

Chris ran for the Jeep, yanked open the glove box, and removed his box of 9-millimeter cartridges. He slid twelve cartridges into the clip, shoved the clip into the handle until it snapped into place, pulled back the slide, and chambered a round. He put the box with the remaining cartridges into his right front pocket, checked to be sure the Beretta's safety was on, and ran to where he had last seen Tama's hoof prints.

To Chris's relief, he picked up the trail quickly. As it turned out, the blast of wind that had crossed the trail erased only a few dozen hoof prints. He followed the trail over a small rise and into a shallow canyon. His flashlight thoroughly searched the canyon floor. Nothing there. The trail led up another hill and disappeared into a narrow opening between two boulders, each about fifteen feet tall.

Chris shined the light into the gap. He could see nothing but blackness as far as the beam would reach. He stepped cautiously into the opening, holding the flashlight above his head so as not to blind himself with light reflecting off the boulders. Then he felt what he and Great-Grandfather used to call that "creepy" feeling. Something wasn't right. He could feel a tingling all over his body, as if each of his hair follicles was a small antennae, locking onto a warning signal.

He stepped forward, out of the other end of the narrow passageway, and stood quietly for a few seconds, listening in the cool night air, his breathing shallow. A droplet of cold sweat trickled down his right cheek. He heard something, barely audible, breathing. Something was breathing. He tried to determine the direction of its source. It seemed to come from nowhere in particular. Then his stomach muscles tightened as he realized it was coming from several sources.

Chris shined the light in front of him. He was in a meadow. There were no trees, just a tiny field, totally surrounded by boulders, the ground covered with tall grass and small bushes. It was almost like a hideaway. The breathing was everywhere, louder now, and only a few feet away.

Then he noticed a light flickering at the far end of the meadow, a reflection. As he moved his flashlight, the reflection flashed off and on. He stepped a few feet forward, his heart beating frantically, sweat running down his sides, his hands shaking. He clicked off the safety and walked several paces in the direction of the reflected light.

The reflection moved. A few more steps toward it and the reflection seemed to separate, becoming two reflections. Eyeballs, they were eyeballs. Chris was sure of it, about fifty feet away.

The sources of the breathing seemed more distinct now. Some were on either side and above him. Chris summoned his courage and turned his flashlight in the direction of one of the sources of the breathing.

A wolf. A gigantic gray wolf, hunched on top of the boulder to Chris's right, breathing heavily, saliva dripping from its jaws.

He moved the light a few feet to the left. Another wolf.

Within seconds, Chris spotted several more wolves on the ledges above him.

He flipped his light back to the first set of eyeballs he had seen at the far end of the meadow. He kept the beam steadily on those eyeballs as he started to back toward the opening behind him. Those eyeballs began moving toward him. As they drew closer, the breathing around Chris grew more rapid, more intense. The eyeballs stopped, close enough now that Chris could make out the animal's body.

It was Tama, that courageous creature, waiting for a command.

Chris hesitated, afraid that any sudden action on his part would cause the wolves to unleash the feeding frenzy he knew they were anticipating. They wouldn't wait much longer. They had probably been ready to strike Tama just before Chris arrived. Now they were reevaluating their situation. It wouldn't be long.

He took a chance by making a clicking sound with his mouth. A sound he and Tama knew meant "get on your mark." He saw Tama's massive chest muscles tighten and followed that with a second signal, two kissing sounds. That meant "get set." Tama lowered his head a few inches and leaned forward. Chris could picture the muscles in Tama's hind quarters tensing.

There would be only one chance, Chris knew. He clicked on the Beretta's safety, tucked it into his belt, and pulled his belt a notch tighter.

Sweat continued to pour down his sides, a few drops trickling from his chin.

His lips were dry.

Then, with his attention focused on absolutely nothing except the task at hand, he let out a piercing whistle. The great beast surged forward with all its might. Chris shoved his flashlight into his front pocket with the lighted end shining upward. Within seconds, Tama traveled across the meadow. As he roared past on Chris's left side, Chris, with the help of the light beam shining upward from his pocket, leaped up, grabbed two handfuls of mane, and rolled his body over the top of Tama's back.

The instant he was mounted, Chris yanked the flashlight from his pocket and aimed it straight ahead, enabling Tama to see the opening between the boulders.

"Go, Nahimana Tama!" yelled Chris.

The wolves sprang, two of them landing on the horse. One clung to Tama's back with its fangs only inches from Chris's ear. Chris pulled the Beretta from his waist, flipped off the safety, reached over his shoulder, and pumped two rounds into the wolf's chest. The wolf fell from Tama's flanks with a terrible roar. The other wolf was balanced on Tama's head, its front claws buried deeply in the horse's neck, its rear claws flailing in the air, trying to get a hold on Tama's muzzle while it snapped its fangs at Chris's face. Chris shoved the Beretta into the wolf's mouth and blew the back of its skull off.

Tama ran with all his might, the wolves in hot pursuit.

In less than a minute, Chris realized the horse couldn't go on any longer. Tama's pace began to slow. The surge across the meadow and out through the narrow opening had taken most of what little energy remained in Tama's body.

Chris decided he had to stop. He wouldn't kill his best friend. He slipped the Beretta into his belt and the flashlight back into his pocket. He leaned forward and cupped his hands over Tama's eyes. Even with the heart this creature had, he couldn't keep running without his vision.

Tama came to a stop, not for lack of will, but a trusting that, in spite of all evidence to the contrary, his human knew what was best.

The wolves were only about a hundred feet behind and charging hard.

Grabbing the Beretta and the flashlight, Chris got down on the ground on his stomach and planted his elbows wide, his hands coming together at the point where the handle of the pistol and the flashlight met. It was an awkward position from which to shoot, but the best he could do on such short notice. Chris knew that Tama was a big target for those on-rushing fangs, but he didn't have time to do anything else.

The first two wolves arrived at the same instant, both leaping side by side over Chris. He managed to blow a hole through the heart of the one on the left, but the one on the right got past him.

A third wolf came into the beam of his flashlight. Chris shot twice, the second bullet tearing a hole in the animal's lung and ripping out one kidney.

In a split second, two more wolves shot past, one on either side of Chris. He couldn't get a shot off at either of them.

Chris heard the frantic sounds of the desperate battle going on behind him. He spun around, his light and pistol ready for more action.

Then a set of headlights flashed over the crest of the hill, a hundred feet away. Within seconds, gunfire rang out. One wolf collapsed instantly.

Two to go.

One was on Tama's back. The other was snapping at his right rear flank. Tama was bucking and twisting, just like Chris had seen horses do at the rodeo. He spun and kicked at the wolf on the ground. Chris couldn't get a shot off without the risk of hitting Tama. Apparently, whoever owned those headlights was having the same problem.

On the third spin, Tama caught the wolf on the ground in the center of its rib cage, tearing the animal in half.

The wolf on Tama's back was relentless. The claws of all four paws were sunk deeply into Tama's ribs, and the jaws held the back of Tama's neck firmly in a vise grip, dangerously close to severing nerves in the horse's neck.

Chris then did something that surprised him when he later had time to think about it. He screamed with all his might, "Great Spirit, help my friend, or I'm gonna have to kill him."

Then an amazing idea came to Chris. He let out a loud whistle, the kind guys used in the old days when expressing appreciation for a pretty lady, the one they called the "wolf whistle." It was the signal he and Tama had used to mean "stop." Chris had even trained Tama to come to a screeching halt from a dead gallop by putting his rear end down on the ground and sliding to a stop.

Tama instantly came to a complete stop. Not a muscle moved. He looked like a bronze statue. Even the wolf lay paralyzed, unable to comprehend what had brought his wild ride to an end.

Chris leveled the Beretta's sights on the wolf's forehead. The instant the bullet left the muzzle of the Beretta, an 8-millimeter bullet was working its way up the twenty-three-inch barrel of Doc Fernandez's deer rifle. Both bullets struck the wolf at the same instant, spinning it in mid-air above Tama.

The horse collapsed.

Doc Fernandez ran to the horse as fast as his legs could carry him, his medical bag banging and clanging in the air.

Neither man spoke.

Doc gave Tama an injection. Chris rummaged through the bag and found the equipment for making sutures and a tube of antiseptic ointment. Chris covered the large wound on Tama's flank with the antiseptic and began stitching the wound closed.

Doc applied some kind of ointment to the claw and fang marks all over the horse's body and stitched those that needed it. He gave Tama another injection and then administered an IV saline solution.

The two men labored for nearly half an hour, neither saying more than was necessary to facilitate the repair of Tama's damaged body.

As soon as the two men had done all they could for the horse, Doc walked toward his vehicle, sensing Chris's need to be alone with Tama.

Chris lay down beside the injured animal, wrapped his arms around his wounded neck, and whispered something in the horse's ear. Doc could hear Chris sobbing. He knew the horse would be all right. Love is a powerful healer.

Finally Chris sat up and just sat there looking at Tama for a long time.

Doc came over and put his hands on Chris's shoulders. He said, "Why don't you go on home. It looks like you've had quite a day. There's not much more that you can do tonight."

He surveyed Chris's body and instructed, "You'd better stop by the emergency room at Mercy Hospital and get those wounds attended to and then get home for some rest. I would consider it an honor if you'd allow me to spend the night here with Tama. It's been a long time since I've been in the presence of such courage and love, not since my wife died. You know I'll take good care of him. I've got everything I need."

He added, "In the morning, I'll call for help on my cell phone. I'll get my assistant, Randy, to bring the horse trailer up here. We'll take Tama to my home and look after him there until he's ready to be released to the wild again. We'll be there all day tomorrow whenever you're feeling well enough to visit."

Chris paused for a moment. He nodded his head slowly. He hugged Doc, found his Jeep, and headed down the canyon.

He knew of a roadhouse along the state highway that would be open. His body and mind could use a couple of Coronas. Then he'd drop by the hospital for a few stitches and a tetanus shot before heading home.

It had been quite a day.

 # Chapter Seventeen

Some distance from the little town of Sprague lived a man named Chas. He was what many would call a scoundrel, bad to the bone, evil to the core. It was rumored that he was born bad.

Chas had no desire to do anything that was for the benefit of anyone but himself. He was selfish. He was cruel. He was hateful. What made dealing with him even more perilous was that he was charming. He was clever. By the time he was five years old, Chas had learned that he could usually have whatever he wanted by using his charm, his cuteness, and his clever mind. All he needed was someone who was programmed to please, someone who had learned at a young age that survival depends on pleasing others—in other words, the majority of the modern human race.

Chas learned to capitalize on this common condition early. With so many susceptible victims and his complete lack of integrity, it was a natural evolution and a source of great delight to him to become a consummate bad guy. By the age of nine, Chas—who at that time was called "Chuckie"—had begun to take sadistic pleasure in torturing animals. His mother, being in complete denial, told those reporting Chas's atrocities to her, "Oh, he's just all boy." Her failure to accept her maternal responsibilities ended up causing many people a great deal of suffering at the hands of Chas.

At about the age of twelve, Chuckie decided it was time he had a grown-up name. His mother suggested that "Charles" would be nice. Chuckie told her to mind her own business. He thought "Chas" had a nice ring to it. It sounded smooth, slick, sophisticated. Just the image Chuckie needed to attain his already carefully planned objectives. He informed his mother that he would no longer respond to "Chuckie," and that if she knew what was good for her, she would drop that silly name from her vocabulary. Chas announced this in the kitchen, where his mother was visiting with her friends, Thelma and Blanche. Chas's mother responded to his proclamation by saying to the ladies, "Oh, he's just all boy."

Chas spent a lot of time schmoozing the tough guys on his high school campus. He knew their weaknesses and the right buttons to push. He heaped all of his abuse on the geeks and the intellectuals and those suffering from terminal timidity. As a result of this carefully reasoned strategy, Chas was able to vent his hostilities while avoiding getting his ass kicked—which might have done him some good.

During his teen years, Chas had many run-ins with the law. But the legal system being what it is, Chas didn't pay any serious consequences for his conduct. If the system had functioned properly, it might have been instrumental in counteracting some of the damage done to Chas's warped mind by his mother's permissiveness.

The condition of our judicial system did not escape Chas's ever-watchful eyes. He discovered that, although masterfully structured by our forefathers, the system was not intended to function in a society where a substantial part of the population no longer valued personal integrity. With many judges lacking courage and many witnesses having no qualms about lying blatantly on the stand, the judicial system has been rendered virtually impotent. In fact, he concluded, it had become a weapon by which those without integrity could easily abuse others without consequences.

Chas learned to use the system to his advantage with style. He could use his charm to twist the truth to a point where even a judge with the best of intentions wouldn't know who to believe. Chas found the system to be particularly effective against honest people. When he got on the stand and used his way with words to spin his web of deceit and the other party got up and told the truth as he best knew it, the judge, not knowing who to believe, often took the easy way out instead of insisting that the truth be determined and chose a position about mid-way between the two divergent testimonies. This usually resulted in Chas getting less than what he had asked for but way more than what he should have received—which in most cases should have been nothing. He, more often than not, found a way to get his innocent victims to pay for his legal costs.

He developed quite a reputation for devastating good people in court, without needing a reasonable legal basis. Often, when someone received notice that Chas was suing him or her, that person settled out of court to avoid the terrible emotional stress and outrageous legal costs that likely would result from tangling with Chas.

Perhaps a lot of this judicial abuse could have been avoided had Chas's attorney had the integrity to refuse to participate in these charades. He justified his conduct, however, by telling himself, "If I don't take the case, someone else will, and besides, doesn't our form of government guarantee every citizen his day in court?" And, finally, "Who am I to judge what is right and wrong?"

During the rare discussions Chas's attorney had with his own conscience, he didn't dare to approach the issue of the tremendous amount of money his association with Chas had accrued to him at the expense of innocent victims. That would be dangerous territory to venture into and might raise moral issues beyond his ability to rationalize.

Chas regarded all members of the opposite sex with the same abundance of disdain he heaped upon his own sweet mother. He regarded women, especially ladies, as essentially weak and obviously placed upon this planet for his own enjoyment and exploitation. As a result, he left quite a trail of broken hearts in the wake of his amorous excursions.

Somewhere along the way, Chas made contact with the infamous Herpes virus. It didn't occur to him to allow this to slow him down in his unending quest for personal pleasure. As a result, many of the damsels who favored Chas by surrendering their chastity inherited not only a broken heart but also a lifelong battle with the aforementioned virus. This included the obligation to inform future suitors, to their great embarrassment, that they were infected with the malady.

That infants born of these ladies would be subject to this virus was of no concern to Chas. He rationalized that the primary law of the universe was the law of survival of the fittest, which meshed nicely with other rules of conduct to which Chas subscribed, including, "Let the buyer beware," "Every man for himself," and "There's a sucker born every minute." He had absolutely no use for certain other slogans, such as "Do unto others...."

One motto, of which Chas was originally unaware but which ultimately made its appearance in his life, was the oft-quoted, "You can't fool all of the people all of the time." Sooner or later, enough people within a given geographical area would catch onto Chas's true nature and avoid future contact with the fraud. When this situation reached the point where it became difficult for Chas to function profitably or lecherously or both, he would relocate to a new area, doing his best to cover his trail.

Of Chas's many unconscionable exploits, there was one of which he was particularly proud. He was at a financial low point in his career, sitting in a cocktail lounge in one of the more affluent neighborhoods of the community he was then victimizing. A well-dressed but noticeably unattractive woman entered the tavern, accompanied by several equally well-dressed companions. As they made their way to a large booth in a secluded alcove in the back of the tavern, Chas noticed that their passing caused quite a stir among the clientele. He inquired of a nearby cocktail waitress as to the identity of the lady with the sizeable and gasp-invoking entourage.

He was informed that her name was Samantha Higgins and that she was the heiress of the estate of a financial giant of the New York garment district. She was well known for her generosity to countless charities.

Chas thought the term "heiress" had quite a nice ring to it.

As he observed the woman, now seated with her friends, he became aware that her right eyeball made movements independent of those made by her left eyeball, causing her to look cross-eyed a good part of the time. This, added to her abundant proportions, caused Chas to experience a mild wave of revulsion. He had to choose between his disdain for the lady's physical attributes and his propensity toward financial advantage. His inherent greed carried the day.

Chas informed the waitress that he would be leaving the lounge and that he would return shortly, and he demanded that she retain the table for his continued use at that time. He headed for his Volvo. In the trunk he had a device he had acquired from the old lady who supplied him with an occasional false passport or driver's license. The mechanism was a small printing device that allowed him to produce business cards that looked surprisingly like they had been printed professionally. This device had set him back more than two thousand dollars but had returned Chas many times that amount over the years.

The title he bestowed upon himself on the second line of his freshly printed business card had something to do with a religious organization. The third and fourth lines bespoke that organization's avowed purpose (in addition to the saving of souls, of course) to be that of helping those who had been cursed with various afflictions of the eye.

Upon returning to the restaurant, he instructed the waitress to deliver a second round of "whatever those ladies in the alcove are having" with his compliments. As almost an afterthought, he said, "Oh, by the way, I do suppose it would be courteous of me to send a little message." On the back of the freshly printed business card he wrote, "Just a thank you from one of your many admirers for all of the wonderful things you do for our community." He admonished the waitress, "If you expect a tip from me, be sure it is clearly understood that my generosity is directed toward the lady in the ivory blouse."

Chas waited expectantly for the drinks to be delivered. When this was accomplished and the waitress got out of his line of vision, he waited for the fat lady to acknowledge him. When she finished reading the note, she paused for a moment, showed it to the ladies on either side of her, then looked up and began scanning the room. When her eyes finally reached the area where Chas sat, displaying his most humble but eloquent smile, he couldn't tell where she was looking.

He began making casual movements designed to attract attention. But those two discordant eyeballs continued to roam about the lounge in his general vicinity and never found their target. He wanted desperately to give the woman a friendly, conspiratorial wave, but timing was everything. To act too hastily would appear presumptuous. To respond too slowly might convey an array of negative attitudes ranging from sloth to indifference.

Chas wanted to rush over to that table, smack her on the side of the head, and realign those errant eyeballs here and now. He determined, in the secret and squalid depths of his treacherous mind, where his most dismal schemes were spawned, that, henceforth, this woman would be known as the "Cockeyed Porker."

Ultimately, neither of those two mal-aligned orbs rested upon Chas's grinning countenance, leaving him looking and feeling like a consummate boob. The portly woman with the visual inadequacies and the ivory blouse resumed the lively conversation with her numerous associates, leaving Chas sniveling in the shadows. He quickly downed two more Chivas on the rocks, left the waitress a grossly inadequate tip, and began a slow, ponderous shuffle toward his aging Volvo.

As he was fumbling with his car keys, the waitress, temporarily setting aside her angst over the lousy twenty five cent tip, shouted across the parking lot, "Hey, asshole, I got somethin' for ya'."

Assuming that she intended revenge, Chas increased the pace of his attempt to unlock the car door. He hoped to finalize this endeavor before the waitress was able to wreak retribution on his person. He was not the least bit assisted by the fact that he had consumed six shots of Chivas during the preceding ninety minutes.

Just as the tip of his key was within striking distance of the orifice, Chas felt the cold, clammy paw of the vengeful waitress on his shoulder. He spun around, forearms raised in a protective gesture over his face.

The waitress said, "Here, jerk, the lady in the corner booth asked me to give you this card." As the waitress stood there trying to decide how one man could be such a loser, Chas read the card with trembling hands. The name "Samantha Higgins" was embossed on the front. On the back, she had written, "Please call for an appointment. I wish to confer with you regarding your organization."

Chas was so elated that he reached into his pocket, pulled out a dollar bill, and quickly tucked it into the cleavage of the profusely endowed waitress, giving her left breast an amiable pat while he winked his most sincere wink. The waitress, with virtually no hesitation, leaned forward, grabbed Chas's lapels, stretched her right leg far out behind her, and with a look of profound satisfaction, brought the knee of that same leg forward with unparalleled swiftness (not to mention accuracy) to a contact point in the very epicenter of Chas's groin. The momentum of the knee, backed up by the mass of the tibia and fibula of the waitress's lower right leg, caught Chas's left testicle between her kneecap and Chas' pubic bone, causing the formerly egg-shaped testicle to assume a shape previously unknown to modern geometry.

When Chas regained consciousness, the waitress and the dollar bill were nowhere in sight. It was dark. He was in agony beyond the ability of all currently known word forms to describe, including Sanskrit and hieroglyphics. He did, however, find, impaled with a swizzle stick and fastened to the zipper of his urine-soaked britches, the business card of Samantha Higgins. He would have smiled if only it would have been anatomically possible.

The next day Chas found himself seated in the waiting room of the luxurious offices of Samantha Higgins. After a brief wait, she greeted him personally and with enthusiasm. This time her left eye did settle upon the central portion of Chas's face, although he was never quite certain what visual wonders were being conveyed to her brain by the right eye.

Within weeks, Chas had weaseled his way into the heart and confidence of Samantha Higgins. Theirs was an energetic courtship. Chas was the benefactor of Samantha's financial generosity. Samantha was the recipient of Chas's unending flow of words of praise and adoration. Fortunately, because Chas refused to have intimacies with Samantha, on the grounds that he was saving himself for their wedding night, she escaped the fate of those numerous other ladies who had been the recipients of Chas's viral contributions.

If the truth were known, Chas would have been willing to consummate the relationship with the sweet and munificent Samantha for the sake of extending the length of her generous courtship rituals, in spite of his disdain for her physical appearance. But his recently deformed testicle had not yet resumed its original contours, rendering any attempt he might make at copulatory expression far more excruciating than any thought of the loss of his current financial advantage.

By the time Chas had worn out his welcome and Samantha's advisors discovered that the religious organization with which he was allegedly affiliated did not exist, Chas had milked his position for all it was worth, ultimately bilking Samantha out of several hundred thousand dollars. Samantha's legal staff would have made short work out of the unscrupulous Chas—had they known where to find him.

Prompted by years of experience in the field of deviousness, Chas had demonstrated uncommon foresight when he printed the business card that was instrumental in securing his relationship with Samantha. He not only used a fictitious address, but he also gave a false name.

As soon as Chas figured out that Samantha was on to him, he sent her five dozen roses, charged to her MasterCard, along with a note informing her that he regarded her as a "gullible, fat, ugly, cross-eyed porker with the sex appeal of a medium-sized radish."

Samantha reported her MasterCard stolen and spent the next several days crying herself to sleep, not over the loss of Chas but, rather, over the loss of a substantial part of her dignity.

Within a few months, Samantha was able to resume a normal, healthy lifestyle, aided immeasurably by the efforts of a capable therapist. Samantha ended up a much wiser woman.

Chas often told the story of Samantha, which he thought made him look like a big man in the eyes of his listeners. If he weren't so distracted from reality by his own illusions of self-importance, he might have observed that many of those listening to his tale walked off shaking their heads and thinking the world would be a better place without the likes of Chas.

Somewhere along the way and long after his encounter with Samantha Higgins, Chas married a lovely lady named Cynthia. He wanted a woman with social position and great looks to show off to his friends and to keep his ego inflated. Cynthia fulfilled these requirements and, furthermore, came from a strong financial background. She was everything Chas needed.

He had researched Cynthia's background so he would know just what would melt her heart. It was only a matter of keeping up his false front until he had her where he wanted her. After that, he couldn't care less what she wanted. Once a guy had a woman committed, she was easy to control. He had taken care to convince her that he was Mister Wonderful. He went to great lengths to portray to her the image of a spiritually advanced being. He said the right things. He used the right words. And he was, oh, so sincere.

Six weeks after their wedding, Cynthia announced to Chas, with great pride and a look of ardent love in her eyes, that she was with child. She just knew Chas would be delighted, too. Having a baby was something she had looked forward to for years. And now her dreams were all coming true. She had a wonderful, loving husband and a child soon to arrive, to whom she would devote her life. And in a year or two, they would certainly have another. Life was good.

Chas wasted no time in informing her that she must be "the dumbest woman in the world." How could she be so stupid as to let herself get pregnant? Didn't she know that babies were the kiss of death for someone of his importance? Well, she could just march her worthless butt down to the abortion clinic and get the problem solved.

That she refused to do.

How, he asked her, was she going to impress his business associates with Cynthia sporting a bulging gut?

Cynthia cried most of the night.

When Chas woke up the next morning, he headed to the kitchen to raise some hell over the fact that he didn't smell his breakfast cooking. If she thought she was going to withhold her services to get even with him for rejecting her stupid pregnancy, he'd show her a thing or two. He'd not only make sure he got his breakfast, but he'd see that it was cooked to his liking and that she experienced a little pain in the bargain. He wasn't accustomed to anyone telling him "No!" and he didn't intend to start now.

Where the hell was she? He went to the guest room. He figured she must have gone there to cry her little eyes out. He'd show her.

She wasn't there either.

When he finally realized she wasn't at home, he devised a plan to teach her a lesson. By the time he and his attorney were finished with her, she'd regret that she had ever messed with him. After all, who was she to turn on him after he allowed her to share his life? Some women sure had a lot of nerve.

That afternoon, just as Chas finished conferring with his attorney by phone but before he could put down the receiver, the doorbell rang. He walked to the door, the phone still in his hand.

There stood a young man of considerable size with the build of a weightlifter. He wore a pair of wrap-around sun glasses. Chas decided he must be some dumb delivery boy. He opened the door and said, "Can't you see I'm on the phone?" He tried to slam the door, but the young man blocked it with his foot.

Chas began to tremble, partly from rage but mostly from fear. Who was this bag of muscles anyway? He decided to bluff, a tactic he had perfected over the years. "Listen, ass wipe," he said, "this is my attorney on the phone, and if you don't get the hell out of my house right now, I'm gonna have the police here in about one minute."

Unfortunately for Chas, at just about the time he finished that statement, a voice blared out of the earpiece of the receiver, "If you wish to make a call, please hang up and dial again." Chas quickly covered the earpiece.

The young man approached Chas, who was dangerously close to peeing his britches. The man removed his sun glasses. Chas suddenly realized that this man was Cynthia's brother, Scott. Chas had met him at the wedding.

Scott informed Chas that Cynthia had called him early this morning and told him about Chas's reaction to her pregnancy. Upon hearing that unpleasant news, he covered over three hundred miles on his

Harley, in a little over three hours, just to have this meeting. This was one angry man. He told Chas that if he ever messed with Cynthia again, he would hunt him down and settle the matter man to man. Scott demanded that Chas grant Cynthia a no-contest divorce with Cynthia getting a hundred thousand dollars to cover the expenses of having and providing for the baby, plus what he called "my sister's pain and humiliation." He gave Chas two hours to come up with a cashier's check and a signed agreement, making sure Chas knew that failure to comply as instructed would result in the ante being raised by another hundred thousand dollars for what the man called a "being an asshole" fee. This increase in penalty would be accompanied by a complete remodel of Chas's face.

Chas was almost in tears. Who was this barbarian to confront him with physical violence? Hadn't he heard of the judicial system? Didn't he realize that the court was where civilized people settled their differences? Chas had never been defeated before. But what could he do against a brute who used such uncivilized tactics?

Cynthia got her no-contest divorce. Cynthia got her hundred thousand dollars. Cynthia was never bothered by Chas again.

Chas needed desperately to soothe his wounded pride. He wanted a woman. And, by golly, he'd have one even more beautiful than Cynthia. After all, beautiful women were plentiful and easy prey for a man with his talents. This time he'd find a real woman. He'd find someone who would make him look good and also knew how to take orders from a man.

Two months later he met Gail. She was every bit as pretty as Cynthia and was already past her child-bearing years. She had recently received a substantial sum of money from her deceased husband's life insurance carrier. To Chas's delight, she was uncommonly shy, almost timid, the kind of a woman around whom a man could feel comfortable. Gail displayed the vulnerability that is not uncommon for a woman who has recently lost a life partner. This would be a piece of cake.

The only problem with Gail was that she had a kid, a seventeen-year-old daughter named Becky. The more Chas thought about this complication, though, the more he began to see its advantages. Even though having a daughter in the family wasn't ideal, in Chas's way of thinking, it could have some benefit, someone else to order around, someone else to do his bidding. And, as frosting on the cake, Becky was mighty fine looking. Chas began to think of the pretty young friends Becky would probably have overnight for slumber parties and all that. Yes, this could be all right.

Three months later, Chas and Gail were married. Now he could have it all.

Chas had no idea what he was getting into.

# Chapter Eighteen

Daryl Harrington's workplace was antiseptic. Every aspect of his environment was artificial. At fourteen stories below the surface of the earth, some type of mechanical device had to supply every human necessity, from the buzzing lights above his desk, to the elevator music piped into his room, to the very oxygen he breathed for nine hours a day.

When Daryl was first assigned to the CIA's Decoding Division, he was somewhat unnerved to consider that even the air he was allowed to breathe depended on a bank of high-powered fans that were wired in rotation many stories above his office. If one fan were to malfunction, the second in the series would kick on automatically, allowing for such a brief interruption in the air supply down on level Fourteen-Minus that the lapse would be essentially undetectable, except, perhaps, for a slight and temporary drop in barometric pressure. The second fan, likewise, was backed up by a third.

One might conclude that a double backup was overkill. But the division of the General Accounting Offices that had approved the contract for construction of the underground facility didn't concern itself with engineering or policy matters. As long as the cost, overall, was not more than triple what such a facility would cost in the private sector, the bureaucrat in charge would most likely bless the contract with his official little bureaucratic stamp of approval. He would do so expecting that an appropriate gift would be delivered anonymously to the side door of his flat in the city, courtesy of the construction contractor benefiting from the juicy plum of a contract.

Daryl found himself occasionally wondering what precautions had been taken to assure that an adequate supply of oxygen molecules would continue to surround the alveoli of his lungs in the event the power supply to those redundant fans was interrupted for more than a few minutes. He also wondered how the scanning device that allowed him to enter the elevator that brought him to and from Level Fourteen-Minus—which required a combination of his access code plus the scanning of the iris of his right eyeball—would function without power.

Strangely, Daryl was also required to use the same code and scanning procedure to enter and to be released from his cubicle. When Daryl asked his supervisor, Ron Tate, the reason for needing to use a security device to leave his room, the supervisor told him that it was the bookkeeping department's shortcut method of tracking working hours. Daryl didn't buy that story. But the look in Tate's eyes said clearly, "Don't ask about that again."

On occasion, Daryl's friends kidded him about his working fourteen stories beneath the earth's surface. A buddy commented that Daryl's workspace was where he would like to be in the event of a nuclear war. Daryl thought about that. He decided he would probably rather die as the result of instant vaporization with one last, deep, delicious breath of fresh air than to die a slow death from oxygen deprivation, alone and lonely, trapped in his dreary cubicle, trying desperately to use the power of his lungs to suck air through the fourteen-story-high intake duct. Occasionally, the fluorescent tubes above Daryl's desk flickered, causing him to take a deep, reflexive breath, wondering if this might be the big power outage that would result in his dreaded entombment.

Daryl didn't like the CIA. Actually, Daryl didn't like the federal government. He loved his country and most of what it stood for. He believed, however, that the government our forefathers had so brilliantly designed to serve and protect the people of this nation had, long ago, overstepped its bounds.

He often thought of the millions of volumes of statutes and court decisions that imprisoned the ordinary person in a maze of rules and regulations. He frequently found himself frustrated and angry over the fact that the middle-class working person spends several months of each year laboring just to support a massive governmental structure, the primary purpose of which has become to perpetuate and expand its existence and "to serve and protect" only as a token gesture to keep the common person placated.

After frequently asking himself why he worked for an entity that he considered so corrupt and destructive to the American way, Daryl came up with three answers. First, he hoped he could become part of the solution by being one of the good government employees who actually gave an honest day's work for his pay. Second, he loved decoding. He found it truly exciting, sort of like playing a gigantic combined chess-and-crossword-puzzle game. Third, Daryl had a sense that in his position with the CIA, even as a lowly decoding agent on the Fourteen-Minus floor of some obscure federal facility, he might have an opportunity to make a real difference sometime.

As intelligent and observant as Daryl Harrington was, he didn't notice that the pattern in the acoustical tile, fastened with some type of mastic to the concrete ceiling above his head, had one slight irregularity. Even if Daryl had been interested in that pattern beyond a quick occasional glance, he probably wouldn't have been able to detect the tiny microscopic mini-cam inserted into one of the decorative holes in the tile. That mini-cam was connected to a length of fiber-optic cord that ran, along with twenty-seven other fiber-optic cords, through a series of ducts and conduits to a top-secret room in an underground bunker some distance from the building where Daryl labored. Those fiber-optic cords fed into a series of recording devices that kept a permanent record of all activity in Daryl's room, as well as twenty-seven other rooms in the decoding department.

Nobody bothered to observe those recordings on a regular basis. They were available, however, in the event of a suspected security violation. There was also a monitor in that top secret bunker capable of being switched to any one of the twenty-eight cables, allowing immediate observation of the activities in any of those rooms.

When Daryl wasn't in the depths of the federal facility, he usually chose to stay to himself. He preferred an evening of working in his homemade electronics lab or hacking his way into some obscure computer database to a night out with his fellow bachelors.

On the weekend before the Franklin/Riverton football game, Daryl was spending his Sunday morning engaged in a series of reminiscences, not the least of which was related to how he had managed many months ago to hack his way into the central design computer of Astral Electronics Corporation, using an inexpensive, over-the-counter CAD-type system to unravel the intricacies of the inner workings of Astral's numeric-code, and iris-scan activated security device. Daryl discovered that, in spite of the complexity of the electronics within the device and the care that had been taken to render those electronics difficult, if not impossible, to fool, the mechanical aspects of the device were quite simple and straightforward.

The main weakness of the device as it was installed, was that the manufacturers had designed it to prevent access *to* an area, not to escape *from* an area. As a result, the exterior of the device facing the outside of Daryl's cubicle was made of a material that was nearly impenetrable—impervious to drilling, welding, or even blasting. Unbeknownst to Daryl, the walls of his cubicle, as was true of all other walls on the Fourteen-Minus floor, were made of concrete.

Astral Electronics Corporation, being a part of the private sector, was motivated by a strong need to show its board of directors a substantial annual profit. Had Astral been able to sell its security devices directly to the Federal Government, it would have simply tripled the price of the device and cast the entire thing from the impenetrable material. But, because the general contractor who had built the building acted as a buffer between Astral and the government and because that general contractor wanted, of course, to maximize his profits, Astral was forced to compete with two other suppliers. This caused Astral to cut every corner possible, as it assumed its competition would do. Astral determined that the additional cost of casting the device in two steps out of two different metals, would cost far less than the substantial savings that would accrue from using a much less expensive material in five of the six surfaces of the device. Astral actually determined that it could save about nine hundred net dollars per unit by using this process.

As a result, the side of the device intended to face the interior of the room to be secured was constructed of a rather ordinary grade of steel, subjecting itself to the possibility of numerous types of assault. But who would ever need to break out of a room that hadn't already used the proper identification to gain access into the room in the first place?

With these thoughts in mind, the marketing department of Astral felt confident in certifying its product as adequate for the purposes intended. The general contractor, well pleased with the surprisingly low price of the device, made haste to accept Astral's proposal and to sign a contract for the purchase of more than three hundred of these devices.

Daryl was shocked to discover how readily he could hack his way into Astral's main computer. He suspected that the information relative to the numeric code reader and the iris scanner was secured by a much more formidable protection system. All he needed, however, was a picture of the simple mechanics activating the slide bolt once the security code reader and iris scanner had been satisfied. To his further surprise, it was a simple solenoid device, easily activated by a 12-volt direct-current generator, such as a series of dry-cell batteries or a simple AC/DC transformer.

In the event of a power failure, all Daryl would need to gain freedom from his cubbyhole was a small, self-contained, battery-operated power drill with a carbon-tip bit, a can of 3-in-1 oil, eight D-cell flashlight batteries taped together end to end, two lengths of small-gauge electrical wire with tiny alligator clips attached, and a penlight.

Smuggling these devices past the electronic security scanner into his office had been quite an adventure for Daryl. He asked Ron Tate for permission to bring a Ghetto Blaster to work, to replace the elevator music that had driven everyone in the building to distraction for months. Ron saw no harm in granting such a request. Besides, he had grown quite fond of Daryl over the months and didn't mind bending an occasional rule for Daryl's benefit. The blaster was equipped with eight D-cell flashlight batteries, and it was easy to hide several lengths of electrical wire within the blaster's frame, along with the alligator clips.

The penlight was no problem. Daryl just slipped it into the plastic pocket protector on his shirt—the type worn by engineers and electronic geeks for generations—along with his pens and pencils.

Daryl purchased a straight-handled, high-speed, electric drill. He removed the vacuum bottle from his Thermos and replaced it with the drill and several bits. His old Thermos bottle, one he used to take hot lunches to school way back in his grammar school days, was made of metal, unlike today's plastic bottles. This, he hoped, would prevent the scanner from detecting its contents. Just to be sure, he made a trial run, putting harmless metal objects in the Thermos. If caught, he planned to say that apparently his nephew had been playing with the Thermos. Nothing was detected.

He used the same method with the oil.

The most difficult part of the project was the charger for the drill. It was too wide to fit into the Thermos. Without it, though, the drill eventually would lose its charge and possibly not be ready to use in an emergency situation.

After some thought, Daryl realized that the heart of the charger was the transformer that plugged into a 110-volt wall outlet. That would easily fit into the Thermos. The base of the charger—the part that was too large for the Thermos—could be disassembled. The contactors and other metal parts would be removed and smuggled into his room in the Thermos shell. The base itself could be walked right past the detector in one of Daryl's pockets. Being made of plastic, it wouldn't even cause a blip on the detector's screen.

Now that he had resolved the problem of how to escape from his office in the event of a power failure, Daryl was more at ease. He did, however, wonder occasionally what would happen to him if someone in the higher echelon were to discover that he had smuggled forbidden objects into the building. At best, he surmised, he would be reprimanded. At worst, he would lose his position. He could live with either of those possible outcomes. Certainly, nothing would happen to him like what is portrayed in those James Bond movies. This is, after all, the land of the free.

Still, a slight concern occasionally danced around the edges of his mind.

Ever since the end of the Cold War, an event that Daryl suspected was more likely a trick by the Soviet Union to lull the United States into reducing its military might and surveillance efforts than it was an historical fact, Daryl's workload had been reduced and modified. Rather than decoding top-secret messages intercepted from the Soviet Union by the CIA or Great Britain's MI-5, Daryl spent most of his time puzzling over innocuous dispatches from what the CIA called "minor threats to world peace," such as nations along the North African coast and the Middle East.

Because of tricks he had learned from, of all the unlikely places, the Internet, Daryl became extremely efficient at deciphering codes originating from the Far East. Over the past several months he had gotten involved with a group of computer wizards and hackers who liked to fool around with solving puzzles. The identities of all of these individuals were kept secret. This involved a circuitous and extremely complex method of making contact with each other, using code names. The person who originated the ingenious communication system used the code name *El Jefe*, pronounced "el hay fay," the Spanish word for "Chief" or "Leader."

On the day Daryl stumbled upon this intriguing network, he was invited to participate, with the understanding that nothing he would learn from the others could, in any way, be used for any purpose detrimental to the people of this nation. He was led to believe that *El Jefe*, and *El Jefe* alone, knew the identities of every participant. *El Jefe* would be able to locate and deal with any one who violated the rules.

Daryl was informed that the very fact he had found his way into this network demonstrated his uncommon skills in the science of hacking. He was also told that almost every other member had discovered this network as Daryl had, through an opening that was provided for that purpose. It was a one-time opportunity. Once someone discovered this entrance and used it, it would thereafter be forever closed to him. From that moment on, a member could gain access

only by using his access code. If the access code were ever terminated for "mal-performance"—which meant a violation of any of
the rules of honesty and integrity required by *El Jefe*— the member
whose access code was revoked would never again be able to gain
entry to the network.

To prevent any member from allowing someone else to use his
access code, every log-on required instantaneous answers to a series
of questions, which no one would likely know except the member or
someone in his family. Daryl didn't know how *El Jefe* collected all of
this private information, but it could include items such as the name
of a member's sophomore-year English teacher, the names of his
aunts on his father's side of the family, the color of his Uncle Chuck's
tractor, the year he made his First Communion, his undergraduate
grade point average, his sister's telephone number, and so forth.

This security measure was coupled with a camera connected to
the member's computer, provided by *El Jefe* at the member's cost. The
camera relayed a live picture of the member's face, making it unlikely
that someone else could be answering those personal questions.

Imperfect as this security system was, it seemed adequate in view
of the fact that this network was composed of a bunch of private
citizens just playing games, for the most part. They had a common
interest in using the information they discovered to harass various
groups they considered less than honorable. These included a few
departments of The Federal Government. Because *El Jefe* could re-
voke members' access at any time he suspected a violation of his
rules, it seemed likely that everyone would play the game honestly.

From his conduct, Daryl thought *El Jefe* probably considered
himself some sort of Internet freedom fighter. *El Jefe* made it clear
that he considered some departments of the United States Government fair game, as enemies of the common man—in particular, the
IRS and the FDA. This opinion, although somewhat unorthodox,
didn't seem too far removed from Daryl's own beliefs. *What the hell. I
can always back out if I don't like what I learn about this group.*

Since that first day, Daryl was surprised and pleased to find that
the participants in this Internet fraternity were friendly, intelligent,
and, in his view, acted with uncommon integrity. He assumed that *El*

Jefe checked thoroughly into the backgrounds of his associates and "eliminated" those who didn't live up to his standards. By "eliminate," Daryl didn't mean to imply anything evil, only a change in access codes to prevent undesirables from participating.

Chapter Nineteen

Ever since Becky's dad had died, she felt as if she'd grown closer to her mom. She and Gail had always been good friends, but her dad's death had given them something very special in common. They both missed him terribly. For Becky, no one could ever take his place. He had always been Becky's hero.

Becky inherited her mom's great figure. Her beautiful brown eyes and long brown hair had a bit of both Mom and Dad in them.

She worried a lot about Mom. Mom didn't have a very strong self-image. She always tried to please everyone, without a lot of thought about what she wanted for herself. She had been raised by overbearing parents who trained her always to put herself last.

Becky believed that pleasing others can be fine within limits and when dealing with people who care and won't take advantage. But in the outside world, it can sometimes be a fatal flaw. Dad always did a good job of protecting Mom. Now it was up to Becky to help keep her mom from being walked on by the controllers of the world.

A little over two years after Brad's death, Gail met Chas. She hadn't been looking for anyone, having resigned herself to remaining single for a long time or maybe forever. She didn't think she would ever find another man as wonderful as Brad or, just as important, a man Becky would like.

But when Chas came along, Gail's thinking underwent a rapid and drastic revision. This man was so perfect. He was so sweet and gentle. He had such integrity. And he didn't seem to mind at all the idea of helping raise Becky. He would never be able to take Brad's place, but it seemed he might be able help fill a bit of the void in Gail's life.

Gail was particularly pleased to learn that Chas had a background in child psychology. He told her he had recently retired from that profession after a distinguished career. Such a background certainly had to be of benefit to a man intending to become a stepfather.

He had gone out to his Volvo and returned with one of his business cards. He handed it to Gail with much fanfare, bowing deeply and saying, "Child raising expert, at your service."

Gail was eager for Chas to meet Becky. When Gail first suggested the possibility, Chas didn't appear to be quite as enthusiastic as Gail hoped he would be. But as soon as Chas got a look at Becky, his enthusiasm rose to the occasion. In fact, it seemed he couldn't keep his eyes off of Becky. This pleased Gail to no end. Yes, Chas was definitely stepfather material.

But Becky didn't like Chas. She didn't like him at all. She particularly disliked the way he looked at her. But she knew Mom thought he was wonderful. She didn't feel she had the right to stand in the way of her mom having the companionship she obviously craved.

At first, Becky tried to force her feelings into the background, and she pretended to be pleased with Chas for Mom's sake. Perhaps it would be all right. She would do everything she could to help it work. But she still felt it wouldn't.

Over the years, Becky had found that her instincts were a lot more reliable than any logic she might attempt. In the old days, whenever she wanted to make a decision, she would make a list with the pros on the left and the cons on the right. Whichever row was more compelling usually dictated her decision. Her decisions proved to be correct about a third of the time, if she was lucky.

Then she read a great book about the power of the subconscious mind. She learned that the subconscious observes and remembers everything that has ever happened in a person's life, even while an unborn infant is still in its mother's womb, even when a person is asleep. She also learned that, in moments of deep contemplation, an individual's subconscious can link itself with the Universal Subconscious and draw from vast, almost unlimited, sources of knowledge.

Among other things, the individual subconscious mind is a gigantic database. The conscious mind, by contrast, remembers only a small fraction of the data with which it is presented, and not for very long. The puny conscious mind is almost powerless by comparison with the subconscious. With one exception! The subconscious mind doesn't make decisions. As powerful as it is, the subconscious only takes orders from the little conscious mind.

This made Becky think of the gigantic machines she had seen on television, used to move spacecraft to the launching pad. One of these tremendously powerful machines, being several stories tall and capable of moving thousands of tons of equipment, is controlled by a man whose size is miniscule by comparison. All of the muscle is in the machine. But it responds without hesitation to the little man at the controls, whose strength is nothing compared to that of the machine. She thought this was a great metaphor for the way our conscious minds can create the kind of life we choose through its intelligent use of the subconscious. Just as the little man controlling the gigantic rocket mover has to rely on the gauges and meters that keep him informed about the status of the machine he's operating, our conscious minds have to rely on our instincts, which are the messengers of information from the all-knowing subconscious, to provide it with accurate information it can use then to properly instruct the subconscious. Yes, Becky's subconscious knew what it was doing. It didn't make mistakes. Her instincts were reliable. Chas was no good.

It didn't take long for Becky's feelings about Chas to be substantiated. Little by little, it became obvious to her that Chas was a phony. But Mom didn't see it. She acted more and more like a schoolgirl with a crush on a teenage idol.

Then the worst possible thing happened: Gail and Chas were married. Becky was not consulted. The decision was made quickly; then Gail and Chas went on a brief vacation to Las Vegas.

Chas had used his almost irresistible power of persuasion to convince Gail that he and Becky were getting along wonderfully and that Becky had confided in him that she would be very pleased if he and Gail were married. Gail could hardly wait to get home to share the wonderful news with Becky. Chas moved in immediately and took control of Mom.

When Becky heard the news, she did a great job of hiding her feelings. But the damage was done. Anything she might say regarding her true feelings would only hurt Mom.

Becky could tolerate Chas's lies and exaggerations. She could put up with his laziness. She could even try to accept the fact that he made a lot of demands on Mom. But the way he looked at Becky made her skin crawl. She tried to avoid any incidences. She didn't walk around the house in her nightgown any more. She kept the bathroom door locked when she was showering. She kept her bedroom door closed when she was dressing. A couple of times she hinted to Mom that she was uncomfortable around Chas, without getting too specific as to why. Mom said that it would just take a little time. Adjusting to a new family member takes a lot of effort on everyone's part.

But Becky knew this wasn't the kind of situation that time would cure. "Chas has an evil mind," she told herself. "A man is capable of making personality changes if he really wants to, but if he doesn't have integrity, there's no hope. And Chas has no integrity."

As the weeks passed, the situation grew worse. Mom continued to fall for more and more of Chas's nonsense. He grew more and more aggressive toward Becky. It soon became obvious to Becky that part of his plan was to drive a wedge between Becky and her mom. He probably noticed that Becky had quite a strong will and feared that she might hamper his efforts to work his way into a position of total control.

Becky finally decided that it wasn't doing her mom any good to keep trying to maintain peace with Chas. If he did intend to come between Becky and her mom, he wasn't only a dirty old man, but he was also one who didn't really have Mom's best interests at heart.

Becky realized she couldn't change Mom's opinion about Chas. Mom would just have to figure that out for herself, over time. Becky resolved that she would take no more abuse from Chas, period. Out of pure dislike for the man, Becky decided to keep to herself most of the time.

Erroneously mistaking Becky's reticence for deference to his superior intellect, Chas began taking cheap shots at her on a consistent basis. When Gail meekly questioned the wisdom of his treatment of

Becky, Chas reminded her of his professional background, assuring her that Becky needed to be brought down a notch or two. Gail yielded to his superior knowledge in the matter and resolved to stay in her place, although it still didn't feel right. Brad had never had to employ such tactics. Becky always seemed like a perfect child.

About three months after Chas moved in, he made a fatal mistake.

He had been riding Becky harder and harder. His warped sense of relationship had him convinced that, if he tormented her long enough, Becky would eventually come to accept him as being in complete control of the family. Through some bizarre twist of logic, Chas concluded that this would stimulate Becky to welcome his amorous advances. All he needed was a bit of time and the right circumstances. No woman had been able to resist his charm before, least of all a young and inexperienced beauty like Becky. She would be putty in his hands.

One afternoon Chas came home after having consumed several martinis at the men's club he had joined—at Gail's expense, of course. He hadn't yet found a job worthy of a man of his talents. Besides, Gail had plenty of money. Brad had been thoughtful enough to die with a substantial insurance policy. Yes, Chas had done all right this time. He had a beautiful wife, who knew how to take orders, plenty of money to allow him to live as he deserved, and the tantalizing certainty of a little stepfatherly incest in the offing.

He stepped out of his Volvo and briefly noticed that he had parked too close to the edge of the driveway, causing him to step into the muddy flower bed. He cursed a bit as he tried to pry his Gucci loafers from the mucky soil. Finally he left one shoe behind, slowly filling with muddy water, and staggered down the driveway, giggling and reciting a line from a long forgotten childhood nursery rhyme: "one shoe off and one shoe on."

As he rounded the corner near the back door, he noticed that Gail's car wasn't in its usual parking place. He looked in the garage and saw that it wasn't there either. Then he remembered, hazily, that Gail had told him she was going to have her hair done this afternoon. He struggled to fathom the relevance of this recollection, which seemed to bear some import to his present situation.

Then his eyes widened slightly, his eyebrows began to rise, and a smile began to encroach on the area where he had formerly displayed a bit of a frown (the result, undoubtedly, of the recent Gucci-in-the-mud incident). Thereupon, a notion began to form in the Netherlands of his vacuous mind. At first it simply flirted with the outer fringes of his consciousness. Within seconds, however, it began an assault in earnest on his lightly anesthetized frontal lobe. Finally it exploded into a full-blown revelation: Gail was gone! And probably would be for some time! Opportunity!

Chas's libido had been well lubricated by the frenetic undulations of the topless dancers at the men's club. "In fact," he mused, "I'm already partly undressed," although his buddies at the club wouldn't consider the unintentional removal of one Gucci loafer by Gail's damn flower bed as a salient step in the seduction process. Chas laughed out loud. All he needed now was for Becky to be at home, and he would have all of the ingredients for a little carnal interlude.

Becky was at home. She was standing in the family room, where she had paused for a moment to watch something that caught her attention on a television talk show. Chas tiptoed quietly toward Becky until he was standing behind her, just inches away. He put his finger up to his lips, as if reminding himself of the appropriateness of stealth.

Becky felt his presence. She felt the hair stand up on the back of her neck. She spun around to confirm her suspicion. Sure enough, there he was, so close she could smell the booze on his breath. Before she could step back, he put his arms around her. His right hand moved quickly down to her bottom, pulling her body tightly up against his. His left hand moved up to her right breast. He bent down and made a pitiful attempt to kiss her.

For no particular reason, neither Gail nor Becky had bothered to mention to Chas that Dad had taken care to see that his little girl was well prepared for the eventuality of any unpleasant or dangerous encounter. When Becky was nine, she and Dad enrolled in a martial arts course. They found it to be so much fun and such a confidence builder that they signed up for a second class. Five years later Becky had her black belt in tae kwan do. Two years after that, she received her second black belt, in Arnise, a form of karate that doesn't place a lot of emphasis on the high kicks that most people associate with Karate. It is, however, the kind of skill a person would be mighty glad he had mastered were he to find himself surrounded by four knife-wielding hoodlums in a dark alley.

Chas acquired an abundance of wisdom, if not a complete education, in a matter of seconds. Becky made a half-turn to her right, raised her left leg up high and away from Chas, and brought the outside of her left shoe down sharply against the shin of Chas's left leg, just below his knee, removing about eight inches of skin from Chas's shin as her leg moved powerfully downward. As her foot hit bottom, she heard the bones in Chas's left foot shatter. Chas bent forward, screaming in agony. Becky returned her left foot to its original position in front of Chas, facing him head on. She then stretched her right leg as far behind her as she could and spun powerfully to her left, raising her right knee and slamming it solidly into the left side of Chas's rib cage. The sound emitted by the breaking of Chas's ribs was reminiscent of a deck of large playing cards being shuffled with unusual dexterity.

Later, Becky wondered if she would have gone easier on Chas if she had had more time to think about it. She decided not.

As Chas lay gasping on the floor, Becky made a most fateful decision. She would leave the house before Mom returned. She would leave Mom a note, explaining that she was all right, that she was going to stay with her aunt for a while. She would say that she didn't care to discuss what had happened to Chas, but that Mom had best do some thinking about whether she wanted to stay with a man who had obviously offended her daughter enormously.

Becky knew Chas was in no shape to tamper with the note she would leave taped to the bathroom mirror. She knew he would make up some lie about what had happened. Mom knew that Becky could take care of herself and that she would find her way safely to her aunt's house. Becky needed time to sort this all out. And she certainly couldn't do that around Chas. Besides, she was seventeen and had been thinking it would soon be time for her to move out on her own.

She would be graduating from high school this spring at the top of her class and had more common sense than most.

Mom didn't know that Becky had spent most of the money she normally kept in her room on Christmas presents last year, so she would assume that Becky would have adequate money for transportation and food. Becky didn't have a car. Mom would think she had taken a taxi to the bus station and a bus the rest of the way.

Becky needed a few weeks to think. Then she would do whatever was necessary to protect Mom. She didn't think Chas would cause any more trouble. Bullies are always cowards. Chas was both. He wouldn't want to tangle with Becky again. She quickly packed her backpack and took what few dollars she had left in her drawer. She wrote her note to Mom and taped it on the bathroom mirror. The note indicated where Becky was going and admonished Mom to be very careful when it came to Chas.

She walked to the family room where Chas was lying on the floor, whimpering. When he saw her approaching, he tried to turn to protect his injured ribs from further attack. She assured him that she meant him no further harm, at least at this time. She warned him that if he ever harmed her mother, she would give him another martial arts lesson. He assured her, repeatedly, that he would never anger her in any way.

When Becky got to the front door, she paused, walked back to Chas, and said, "If I come back and find that you're still playing with Mom's head, you're going to experience pain the likes of which you've never imagined. As I see it, you've got a big decision to make. You can either get out of our lives and go play your games somewhere else, or you can get yourself a lobotomy and start acting like a man. Frankly, I don't think you've got it in you. But, it's your choice. Just remember—I'll be back."

Becky walked out the front door and headed for the interstate. She decided to take the trail through the forest. She didn't want to run into anyone she knew just now.

Chapter Twenty

At just about the same time Chris was embarrassing himself on his Honda for the benefit of the princess in the burgundy convertible, Daryl had been on the verge of making a discovery that would change his life forever. On this particular Friday afternoon, Daryl found himself with several hours to kill, the result of having broken a code in about three hours that was expected to take him at least a full day.

Although he did most of his personal computer work at home, he decided to spend the afternoon hacking in his office. After all, his work was done. The government had gotten its money's worth. Daryl couldn't leave his office until 5:00 p.m. Best of all, he had at his disposal one of the most powerful computers in the nation.

He decided to have a little fun.

The first few minutes found him searching through some old dead files in the CIA archives. Nothing more was required than the security clearance that came with his position. He stumbled across some of the messages he had decoded in his early days with The Company. Rather basic stuff.

So buried was Daryl in his search for new challenges and off-limits information that he had failed to notice that the small hand of the clock above his desk had passed the 5:00 p.m. mark. Although other floors had shifts that went until the building was locked at 7:00 p.m., all members of the decoding division had, as usual, left the building.

Then he decided to do something a little more interesting. He had been fooling around in an old section of the archives, off and on, for several weeks. From the difficulties he had in gaining access to this area, he had a hunch that something sensitive was buried there. He proceeded with caution. After all, he could be dangerously close to messing with something that could get him into hot water.

Before long, Daryl found himself becoming a little more adventurous. He tried a couple of avenues that led to "Access Denied" messages.

Eventually he found himself in an area that seemed strange and foreboding. The messages did not simply say "Access Denied." They offered warnings Daryl had not seen before in all his days of hacking.

Daryl finally stumbled upon a message that read, "You are not authorized to search this archive. Your presence will be reported to your supervisor and noted on your employment record. Leave this area immediately. Failure to do so will result in your dismissal as well as further sanctions."

Daryl hit the "escape" key several times, backing completely out of the area. He was a little shaken. He sat there thinking. "What," he wondered, "is hidden behind that notice? It must be something very important to national security."

Then an idea hit him. Perhaps he could do a search on that file, using some of the techniques he had learned from his buddies on the Internet. He could at least find out when it had been created, the last time it was modified, and the size of the file. All, he hoped, without anyone knowing he had done so. Just in case, he would use a few tricks he had learned to keep whoever might be monitoring that file from knowing it was his computer that was doing the searching.

It took Daryl a while to create a different path to that same file. To his surprise, the file was created in 1975. The last update had also been in 1975. It was not an active file and not very large.

Once Daryl had the file folder on his screen, the temptation to try to open it was irresistible. It seemed doubtful to him that anyone would be actively monitoring a file that was more than thirty years old. But it could be linked to some kind of alarm system.

He decided that the dangers involved warranted a consultation with the best in the field of super hacking. He backed out of the archives and jumped on the Internet. Within minutes he was in contact with *El Jefe*. The big guy was pleased with an opportunity to tweak the nose of a federal agency. He logged on to Daryl's computer with his Lap Link and, before long he and Daryl were working hand in hand, so to speak.

They sent messages back and forth over the Lap Link while they took turns running their respective keyboards. They took care to ensure that, if their intrusion were detected, it would be impossible for their identity and location to be determined, or, as *El Jefe* corrected in one of his messages to Daryl, "*almost* impossible."

Using several of *El Jefe's* best tricks, it still took nearly an hour to get into the file. For quite a while, Daryl sat observing, allowing his teacher to run the keyboard and mouse.

Then, suddenly, there it was—the screen filled with coded nonsense. Daryl sat there in awe of *El Jefe's* ability to decode the document so quickly. Daryl thought he himself was good, but he could hardly keep up with what was happening on his screen.

Within twenty minutes, the code was cracked and the contents appeared before Daryl's eyes in plain English. From the speed with which the words scrolled across the screen, Daryl knew *El Jefe* was speed-reading the contents. Daryl had to hustle to keep up. By the end of the fifth page, Daryl shouted, "Holy shit!!" He knew his accomplice was certainly unleashing comparable expletives.

What Daryl read caused the muscles in his neck and shoulders to tighten. The story unfolding before him was bizarre, terrifying beyond anything he had experienced. His hands were shaking. He wondered how his friend at the other end of the Lap Link could continue to operate his computer.

When the ghastly story was concluded, Daryl was perspiring. His breathing was shallow. The main text was followed by an appendix, in a different kind of code. Daryl waited for *El Jefe* to begin decoding the appendix.

But instead, a message from *El Jefe* began to scroll across Daryl's screen. The message caused Daryl's already heightened state of agitation to increase dramatically. It read, "I suggest that you download what appears on your screen onto a memory stick, take it with you for your protection, and get the hell out of there, NOW!!"

Daryl suddenly thought about *El Jefe's* earlier correction— "*almost* impossible."

A drop of cold sweat trickled down Daryl's right temple. He began rummaging through his lower desk drawer, looking for a memory stick, when suddenly all went black except his computer monitor. The computer and monitor would be powered for a while by a large UPS power backup and surge protector.

There was almost total silence, no hum from the overhead fluorescent lights, no sound from the tiny refrigerator where Daryl kept his fruit juices. He sat there feeling a combination of disorientation and terror. Then the tightening of his stomach muscles increased as he realized that the all-encompassing silence included the absence of his favorite sound: the fans. The fans had stopped. His source of blessed oxygen was gone.

⬥   ⬥

In a top secret bunker, some distance from the cubicle where Daryl's intense drama was taking place, a pair of fingers rested on one of three tripped circuit breakers. The heading above the vertical row of breakers read, "Floor Fourteen Minus - All Circuits." The labels on the three tripped breakers read, "Lights," "Security Latch," and "Air Supply Fans."

⬥   ⬥

Thoughts raced through Daryl's mind. *Was this the accidental loss of power he feared? Was it related to his hacking into the CIA's secret files? Should he let El Jefe know what was happening? How long did Daryl have until the oxygen would run out? Did he have time to download the file before attempting to extricate himself from the cubicle that was soon likely to be his tomb?*

Daryl decided that the laws of probability and statistics weighed heavily against the possibility that this power outage was just a coincidence. He would have to assume that his situation had a deliberate cause. If so, what other steps were being taken to ensure that what he and *El Jefe* had discovered would never become public knowledge?

He decided to do the downloading.

The UPS unit would keep the computer operating only for about half an hour, at most, after the power went out. He unplugged the UPS unit from the wall outlet, just in case whoever caused the power outage had some method to direct a power surge through the building's electrical lines, with enough voltage to override the UPS unit's surge protector and melt down the computer.

He jumped over to his keyboard and shot off a message to *El Jefe*, "Someone's on to us. My power and air supply have been cut off. Download a copy of the documents, if you can."

He decided not to disclose his plans of escaping his cubicle, in the likely event that his messages were being monitored.

In the far-away bunker, the man who had flipped the circuit breakers, intending to cause Daryl Harrington's untimely demise, glanced at the monitor connected to the mini-cam in the ceiling of Harrington's room. As he suspected, the screen was blank. The lighting in the cubicle was inadequate for the camera to function. The man left the bunker, deciding to head quickly to a nearby pub, where he would have plenty of witnesses as to his whereabouts this Friday evening. When Harrington's body is discovered Monday morning, he thought, there will be lots of questions. He wanted to have a sure alibi when the shit hit the fan.

The man wiped his fingerprints from the circuit breaker handles. He then took the stairs to his office several floors above the bunker and quickly tidied up his desk so it looked like it had been left in a routine manner rather than in haste. As his last official duty of the day, he went into the control panel of his computer and reset the internal clock, making it twenty seven minutes earlier than real time. Then he logged off, intending to show anyone conducting an investigation that he had left the office half an hour earlier than he actually did. The first thing on Monday, he would reset the computer's clock to real time.

He decided to do the same thing, quickly, quietly, and hopefully unnoticed, with the large clock on the wall at the back of O'Leary's Pub, just before asking someone without a watch what time it was. He then would make a big deal about the time so that person would likely remember that he was there half an hour before he actually was. The man had learned a bit about deception during his many years with the federal government.

Nobody was allowed access to Floor Fourteen-Minus over the weekends. Cleaning and maintenance people were permitted only during the week and only in the company of a member of the security team. The man would return very early Monday morning and reset the breakers before anyone else was likely to be in the building. The coroner would set the time of Harrington's death as having occurred late Friday evening, long after the man had taken great care to be well noticed at O'Leary's Pub. He assumed that Harrington would manage to live an hour or more in the oxygen-depleted environment.

He considered the advisability of driving to the building, where Harrington was undoubtedly now gasping for air, and checking the fans to be sure they were, in fact, off. He thought better of it, though, not because Harrington's cubicle was some distance away but, rather, because the farther he was from the scene of the termination, the better. It would be just as well to let someone else discover the "accident."

Before leaving his office building for the weekend, the man ran down the several flights of stairs to the underground bunker for one last look around to be sure he hadn't left anything that would connect him with the incident. He found nothing.

He backed out of the bunker door, taking one last glance to be sure all was in order before turning off the lights and locking the door. If he had turned off the lights before that last glance, he might have noticed a faint flicker of light flash across the monitor attached to the mini-cam in Daryl Harrington's office.

With the aid of his penlight, Daryl had downloaded the documents onto a memory stick and removed the batteries, wires, and alligator clips from his ghetto blaster. He then removed the oil can, high-speed drill, and carbon-tip bits from where he had taped them to the back of his desk.

With the penlight held between his teeth, he drilled eagerly into the steel plate of the door lock. Within ten minutes, he managed to dull three drill bits. The fourth one succeeded in providing a half-inch opening into the inner cavity of the lock without slipping into contact with the solenoid. Daryl used the side of the rotating bit to scrape the insulation off the two wires connected to the solenoid. Then, with the aid of tiny needle-nose pliers from his computer hardware maintenance kit, he attached the miniature alligator clips to those wires. He quickly taped the eight D-cell batteries together in one long row, using seven strips of duct tape. He laid the tube-shaped row of batteries on his lap while he held one wire against either end. The solenoid hummed and clicked once. When he released the wires, the solenoid, being spring-loaded, snapped back into place.

Daryl knew he might not be able to activate the solenoid more than a few times, assuming it would require considerable amperage each time it was engaged. Just a few uses might completely drain the batteries.

He was becoming painfully aware of the oxygen draining from the room. He slowed his breathing, trying to ration what precious air remained.

Making sure he had the memory stick in his front pocket, Daryl grabbed a few of his personal things. He decided to leave the tools of his escape behind to sort of tweak the cheek of the CIA.

Daryl held the row of batteries under his arm while, once again, he touched a wire tip to each end. The solenoid hummed and clicked back, pulling the steel bolt into the door and out of the strike plate in the door frame. Daryl quickly pulled the door open before the bolt could snap back into place.

As soon as the door opened, Daryl was reinvigorated by the fresh supply of air in the hallway. He took several deep breaths. The oxygen he was appreciating so greatly had remained in the corridor after the fan stopped only because no human beings were present to convert it to carbon dioxide.

Daryl could hear the air fans humming on the floor above. Apparently the power had been turned off on his floor only. Of course, whoever had turned off the air supply to level Fourteen-Minus would not have wanted to kill the people in the rest of the building. Too messy. Too hard to explain. Not necessary. Not efficient.

This would account for the fact that the elevator was working.

Whoever was behind the attempt on his life had probably planned for the possibility of such a situation even as the building was being designed. The building design provided for the ability to shut off life-giving air to any one of the floors in the building separately.

Just as he was about to enter the elevator, Daryl decided that whoever had been observing him and trying to kill him would likely have all normal methods of exit watched, just in case, but maybe not. Perhaps, whoever it was, was so certain that the system was foolproof that he didn't feel a need to take additional precautions. Why involve anyone else? It would be too messy, too hard to explain. Not necessary. Not efficient.

Still, Daryl didn't feel like taking any more chances than necessary. He decided not to risk using the elevator. Instead, he moved to level Minus-One, using a series of circuitous maneuvers that included several different stairwells and corridors. He suspected that if anyone were looking for him, that person would most likely be waiting for him on the ground level, as that was the only floor that had doors leading to the outside.

On level Minus-One, Daryl slipped into an air-conditioning duct designed to dump large quantities of air into a storage and maintenance room. Once inside the duct system, it took him quite a while to find a run that would provide him access to the ground floor. As soon as he had located that duct, he had to shinny up it by pressing his back against one side while he planted his tennis-shoed feet against the opposite side. By the time he had risen the twelve feet to the next floor, he was winded and had to rub out a cramp in his left calf.

He began looking for a route to the ground floor women's restroom. He knew there was a door right next to the ladies' restroom that led to the parking lot. If he could manage to get into that restroom and then to the exit door, he would have quick access to the parking lot, although a bar alarm would probably sound. He hoped he could sprint from that door either to his car or, if that appeared to be under surveillance, to the stairway to the subway where he would likely get lost in pedestrian traffic.

Daryl finally found his way, by trial and error, to an air diffuser that opened into the sought-after restroom. It was located in the wall near the ceiling. Luckily, the diffuser cover was large enough to admit a small person. Luckily, too, Daryl was in good shape, with a thirty-two-inch waist, no beer gut, and flexibility that, he hoped, would allow him to bend his shoulders in such a way as to slip through the opening.

He had to wait a few minutes until no ladies were present in the room. Then he kicked off the air diffuser cover, a rather noisy event that echoed around the tiled room as the cover bounced off of a metal partition and landed atop a toilet seat. He waited a few seconds, sweat dripping from his chin. When nobody came to investigate, he slipped down onto that same seat, bending the diffuser cover but not stepping into the toilet bowl.

As he stood there, steadying himself, two ladies came into the restroom. Luckily, only one of them used a toilet, and she didn't investigate the stall where Daryl was perched on the lid. The other woman had apparently been invited along to the restroom for her conversational value.

Daryl stood there praying they would leave quickly. They didn't. In fact, they eventually decided to light up cigarettes, while they discussed the romantic endeavors of one of their friends.

Daryl glanced at his watch. It was now almost 7:00 p.m. In a few minutes, all exit doors, except the main entry, would be locked for the night and, in this case, for the weekend.

If he could get out before seven o'clock, he could slip out the side door next to the restroom. After that, the only way out would be through the main entry. He would have to walk past the security guard. He didn't know if that would be a problem or not. In any event, he'd much prefer to leave through the service door, even at the risk of sounding the alarm. Better to be able to make a run for the subway than to be accosted by a group of security guards or, worse yet, a bunch of the CIA's hoodlums.

Daryl stepped down from the toilet, opened the door, and walked past the two smoking ladies as if it were the most natural thing he'd ever done. He couldn't resist the temptation to say, "Evening, ladies." They both stood there, mouths agape. As Daryl left the room, he heard them laugh and resume their conversation.

He slipped out the side door. As he remembered, the door was locked only from the inside. It was used for food and equipment deliveries, allowing access from the outside only during business hours and only to those having the proper code.

Sure enough, the alarm sounded as soon as he opened the door. Daryl got as far away from the door as he could, as quickly as he could. Once in the parking lot, he slowed his pace and walked nonchalantly toward his Mustang. He resisted the urge to glance around, wanting to look casual.

Now he was going on pure instinct. As he approached his car, it "felt" okay. He decided to risk it and placed his key in the lock. It opened silently - no explosion, as his vivid imagination had feared, no tackling of his young body by a group of muscular brutes looking like the Denver Broncos' defensive line in business suits.

Daryl sat in the driver's seat, hands trembling. This was the last chance for a block of C-4 to end his young life. He inserted the key in the ignition, turned it one click forward. The stereo blasted out one of his Credence Clearwater favorites, causing his heart to take a major leap. He turned off the CD player, breathing heavily. One more click forward and the engine came to life. He was still alive.

Had Daryl looked around a bit as he crossed the parking lot, he might have noticed a very large black man, with piercing brown eyes and a scar running from his left earlobe to the underside of his jawbone, standing beside an elm tree. The man had followed Daryl's every movement, his focus intent. Daryl might have found it interesting to see that the man had a tattoo on each of his massive forearms. One was a tattoo of a battleship and the words "Proud member of the United States Navy." The other was a heart with a dagger piercing it and a single drop of blood dripping from the dagger's tip. Below it were the words, "For my brother Mikey. Get us the hell out of Vietnam."

Chapter Twenty-one

It was a warm, sunny day. And, in spite of the unpleasant encounter she had just had with Chas, Becky found herself enjoying the walk and feeling proud of the lesson she had taught him.

She allowed her mind to drift, taking in the scenery and enjoying the abundance and variety of sensual stimuli in the forest. After a while, a long forgotten memory surfaced, the memory of an unusual event that had happened when Becky was in the eighth grade.

In those days, Becky's most special and closest friend was Rachel. Becky and Rachel had been friends since the second grade, sharing each other's deepest secrets and talking for hours on the phone.

They were both hard workers and well-liked. Of the two, Rachel had the better grades, although Becky was not far behind. While Rachel was a pretty girl, Becky was what Rachel called "gorgeous." They were both lanky, but there was no doubt in the vivid imaginations of the eighth grade boys that something spectacular was likely to develop over summer vacation. Those eager young men would simply have to wait a while. It was still April, and spring vacation was just around the corner.

The girls were both close to their fathers. Becky's father, Brad, and Rachel's father, Doug, were good friends. The girls had been hinting for some time that a father/daughter camping trip would be a lot of fun for all of them. The men teased their daughters, contending that camping was a guy thing and if their fathers were ever to be so foolish as to weaken and take the girls on such a trip, the girls would undoubtedly whine and complain and want to go home after one night of sleeping on the hard ground. The girls begged and pleaded, alleging that they could handle the discomfort just fine, including the lack of bathing facilities—as long as they could bring real toilet paper.

Actually, Becky and Rachel had been hard-core tomboys for years. Their dads knew the girls would probably handle a camping trip better than they would themselves.

A couple of weeks before spring break, Becky awoke to find a large box adorned with a big blue ribbon sitting in the hallway just outside of her bedroom door. An attached note read, "Happy camping, Jungle Girl!" Inside she found a sleeping bag, an air mattress, and a two-man tent, along with a handwritten invitation that read, "You and your pal, Rachel, are cordially invited to attend a knock-down, drag-out, no-holds-barred, for-men-only, canoeing trip along the Santa Rita Flowage with the two best outdoor guides in this or any other forest in the continental United States. P.S. You bring the toilet tissue."

Becky was elated. As soon as she heaped abundant hugs and kisses on Brad and Gail, she called Rachel to tell her the news. Rachel was already in her own state of euphoria, having found a similar package, on the counter of her bathroom. The girls determined that it would be fun to share one tent, agreeing that it would be cozy and warmer that way.

For the next two weeks, the girls planned and packed and packed and planned until Doug informed Rachel that they were going to have to carry whatever they took in backpacks about three miles into the forest from where the truck would be parked. With the men lugging the canoe, the girls would have to carry a substantial part of the rest of the equipment. Thereupon, the girls unpacked and planned and planned and unpacked, until the pile of items they intended to take was down to a manageable size. The food planning was left to the men.

The girls' moms showed no interest whatsoever in participating in any activity as "barbaric" as a canoeing trip. They considered the upcoming absence of their families a rare chance to goof off and have some fun of their own.

The men and their tomboys departed on Friday afternoon immediately after school got out, intending to return the next Thursday evening. Everyone was in a festive mood.

By the time they had driven the seventy miles to the parking area and hauled all of their gear to the banks of the Santa Rita Flowage, it was close to sundown. They had to hustle to set up camp while they still had some visibility. They built a campfire inside a ring of large stones the girls had put in place while Doug and Brad put up the tents.

The effort it took to put the camp in order plus the late hour conspired to create some serious appetites. The smell of the fir and aspen trees along with the crackling of the campfire put them all in a great mood for a full and satisfying meal under the stars.

Brad announced, "Well, ladies, by tomorrow night we should have some fresh fish to eat. But tonight I'm afraid it's gonna have to be dry cornflakes." A joint moan came forth from the lips of the girls.

"Hey, Brad, did you hear a whine? Or was that a grumble? It sounds like our hearty campers aren't pleased with our menu planning."

Becky apologized, "Sorry, Dad, but I'm *so* hungry."

Rachel added, "Yeah, we'll be fine. I was just sort of craving some meat."

"Well, ladies," Brad said, "never let it be said that Brad and Doug don't know how to treat their fellow campers." Whereupon he and Doug went over to the canoe and removed a collapsible fabric cooler they had tied to the underside of one of the seats. From under another seat they removed a cast iron Dutch oven with its lid taped in place. They brought these items to the edge of the campfire and, grinning ear to ear, revealed, with much fanfare, that the Dutch oven contained potatoes, carrots, onions, garlic, celery, bell peppers, mushrooms, a turnip, a rutabaga, a parsnip, a bay leaf, and a zip lock bag full of seasonings. The cooler contained a large, tender piece of beef back strap (sometimes known as filet mignon), two cubes of butter, and a bottle of Moosehead beer. Brad explained that, in celebration of the presence of two of the finest daughters in the county on this their first annual father-daughter canoe trip, he was about to favor everyone with his famous camp meat stew.

The girls took a couple of hunting knives and set about cutting and slicing the vegetables and the meat. The men arranged the hot coals in the middle of three rocks they had placed in such a way that the Dutch oven would be supported securely and high enough above the fire so as not to burn the stew.

When all was ready, Brad placed a cube of butter and the cubed backstrap in the bottom of the hot kettle with a portion of the seasonings and stirred the meat until it was browned exquisitely. He then put in all of the vegetables except the mushrooms, saving them until just a few minutes before everything else was cooked to perfection. As soon as he added the mushrooms, he placed the second cube of butter on top of the stew and, after it melted, he poured in the bottle of Moosehead and the rest of the seasonings. The aroma was irresistible.

Brad stirred and smiled. The others smiled and salivated.

The aroma wafted through the forest

Coyotes howled in the distance, cries of agonizing envy.

From his backpack, Doug produced a loaf of his wife Cheryl's homemade dill rye bread and yet another cube of butter.

A feeding frenzy followed. They all fell asleep that night with joy in their hearts and an occasional expression of gratitude to the goddess of culinary delights in the form of a gentle burp.

<hr />

The Santa Rita Flowage is a series of interlocking lakes, ponds, rivers, and streams, covering several thousand acres within a fairly dense forest. For the most part, a canoe is easily navigated throughout this system of waterways because most of the bodies of water involved are at about the same elevation. For this reason, there are very few waterfalls, and the few that exist are small enough so a canoe can easily manage them.

An outdoor person can look forward to a peaceful day upon the waterways, paddling his or her vessel with confidence, as long as he or she avoids a couple of notable hazards. One of these is the legendary Glory Hole.

<hr />

There was a time, farther back than most people can possibly imagine, even in the deepest recesses of their most exuberant flights of fancy, when the earth had no mantle, that is, no hard surface.

In those days, the earth was one gigantic glob of molten matter. Over periods of time almost beyond comprehension, the outer peripheries of that molten glob, which has since come to be affectionately known as "Mother Earth," began to cool. After billions of additional years, the surface took on a less volatile consistency, ultimately assuming a modicum of hardness.

As time went on, the earth, as hundreds of trillions of tons of swirling, revolving, rotating, and seething lava will sometimes do, went through a series of geological changes. These changes included the shuffling to and fro of various gigantic tectonic plates. These plates inevitably collided with one another, much like the participants in a bumper car carnival ride, which facilitated the resultant rising and falling of land masses. As these land masses participated in an almost unending series of bumps and grinds, a variety of mountain ranges, deep ravines, islands, and bodies of water were formed.

Eons later, the movements of the land masses slowed a great deal. With surface movements becoming less frequent and less violent, along with thousands of other changes, atmospheric and otherwise, conditions were right for a host of creatures to evolve and occupy this galactic island. Eventually that scourge of the planet, man, made his appearance on the scene, introducing, among other things, the concept of time.

Mother Earth, erroneously deciding that man was of a value somewhat greater than the dinosaurs (which she had extinguished with a flick of her geologic wrist), caused the undulations of her crust to subside to the point where man has been able to survive for hundreds of thousands of years, notwithstanding his penchant for self-destruction.

Many thousands of years ago, about the time that man was making such wondrous discoveries as fire and the wheel, our little patch of land, now occupied by the Santa Rita Flowage, was at the bottom of a vast saltwater sea.

Beginning to think she might have made an error in assessing the value of man as being greater than that of her other creatures, Mother Earth did a tiny tectonic pirouette, intended to throw the fear of Zeus into mankind. This resulted in the raising and lowering of numerous mini land masses accompanied by countless earthquakes, volcanic eruptions, and tidal waves. The vast majority of the members of the human race, while scared into untimely eruptions of their own, concluded that, while the gods must be angry, it certainly had nothing to do with them. Whereupon mankind continued on its original trajectory toward self-destruction and planetary debasement and continues to do so to this day in spite of countless admonitions and warnings from innumerable quadrants of the universe, both physical and metaphysical.

As almost an afterthought, the tectonic gyration that Mother Earth unleashed on her troublesome human occupants did a geologic hiccup beneath the sea that, at that time, covered the area now known as the Santa Rita Flowage. That seismic burp caused a fracture in the supporting structure of that ancient sea, allowing all six hundred trillion gallons of saltwater to rush into the bowels of the earth, where it made contact with the molten innards of the planet. Because of the volume of that water, it took several minutes after contact with the molten substance for it to turn into steam and attempt its return to the surface of the earth. Mere seconds prior to the leading edge of the resultant steam ball reaching the underside of the earth's crust, the gaping wound in the bottom of the now relatively dry ocean bottom slammed shut, entrapping that high-pressure steam ball beneath the surface of the earth.

Just as water must seek its own level, steam, under pressure, will migrate to any available outlet. In this case, the nearest outlet was in an area now known as Yellowstone Park. That ancient steam ball has been performing faithfully ever since.

When the gaping wound mentioned above slammed shut, the fact that it was not pivoting on hinges like a well-hung door allowed it to close in a position somewhat different from the one from whence it originated. As a result, the easterly portion of said gaping wound came to rest at an elevation seventy-eight feet higher than its opposing fragment. This created a cliff seventy-eight feet high and seven miles long.

Thousands of years later, water began flowing through the area from the run-off of the snow-capped mountains to the north. The Santa Rita Flowage and its surrounding breathtaking evergreen forest were formed, including a waterfall with an approximate height of seventy-five feet, falling into a gigantic crater, which the years of water flow dug into the soil at the bottom of that waterfall.

This waterfall and the churning cauldron at its bottom were named the "Glory Hole," a source of much pleasure for the many tourists and locals beholding its beauty each year. It has been the inspiration for countless photographs and paintings. The sound erupting from its crater is almost deafening. And it has taken millions of lives of animals and humans over the centuries.

Fortunately, the U.S. Forestry Service, the Army Corps of Engineers, and the Department of the Interior combined forces to publish literature warning those enjoying the splendor of the Flowage to keep a safe distance from the Glory Hole waterfall. In their combined and expensive good judgments, they also constructed a barrier of steel cable and steel netting across that river at a distance of about one hundred yards upriver from the waterfall. This well conceived but poorly constructed structure was intended to allow the river to continue its meanderings in a relatively unobstructed manner while, at the same time, it was hoped, stopping any hapless boater headed toward the grizzly plunge from continuing on his course. This was accomplished by using a screen with a large enough mesh to allow most debris to pass through it while trapping the largest logs and branches behind another huge cable stretched across the water several yards upstream from the net. The large items stopped by that cable are removed on a regular basis, using an old Navy tugboat.

Such a safety device has no way of discerning an errant boater from other forms of debris heading downriver. Items not stopped by the cable upstream from the net but too large to slip through the mesh of the net are often caught in the net. As a result, the net sometimes becomes burdened with a variety of floating objects, an overabundance of which tends to clog the net, putting a tremendous stress on both the steel cables and the steel netting.

One might wonder, "Wouldn't a boater being caught in the steel net, likely be drowned in the water flowing through the net?" This thought occurred to representatives of the previously mentioned governmental agencies. But they decided that being caught in the net with a decent chance of rescue was preferable to an "E" coupon ride into the Glory Hole, with death almost a certainty.

At the time of Becky and Rachel's canoeing and camping trip, the tensile strength of one of the steel cables on the safety net was succumbing, inexorably, to the ravages of several years of tension, rust, temperature change, and an untimely lightning strike to one of its anchor bolts. With an abundance of debris accumulating in the net supported by that cable, it was only about two thousand pounds away from snapping.

On the day following the camp stew feast, Becky, Rachel, Brad, and Doug were enjoying the morning wonders of nature, including the chirping of birds, the ecstasy of a relaxing squat in the woods with genuine toilet tissue, the gentle sighing of the wind through the pine boughs, and a breakfast of bacon, eggs, and buckwheat pancakes with real maple syrup. The scents floating on the gentle breezes that drifted from time to time through the campsite added immeasurably to the campers' contentment. Those breezes carried the scents of wildflowers, pine needles, aspen leaves, an occasional wisp of smoke from a distant campfire, and that tantalizing, musky aroma of an ancient forest that defies description.

The anglers spent the morning exploring the avenues and byways of the Santa Rita Flowage, with their cameras clicking and their ever-present fishing gear trolling in the wake of the swift and silent canoe.

By early afternoon, Brad and Doug, doing what fathers must inevitably do, decided to retire to the comfort and security of the tiny, roll-up, nylon, pocket-sized hammocks that they had squirreled into their backpacks and that now hung beckoningly from a gathering of Douglas firs.

Before long, each man was hiding from the realities of city life under his respective fishing hat, hammock swaying gently in the warm afternoon breeze. Pulse rates, blood pressure levels, and brain wave frequencies hit an all-time low.

Becky and Rachel debated whether to retire to their tent. They considered dragging their fathers' sleeping bags to stack upon their own fluffy bags, thereby creating an ultimately comfortable napping zone. They could further assure their absolute comfort by zipping down the tent flap, practically eliminating the possibility of the inconvenience of an occasional pesky fly. The temptation was almost irresistible.

But doing what young daughters must inevitably do, they decided that napping was a waste of valuable time.

As they silently launched their canoe into the eastern end of the Santa Rita Flowage, a strange feeling of excitement crept up the back of Becky's neck. She sat in the rear of the canoe, paddle poised. Rachel turned to look back at her best friend. The look that passed between them, as their eyes locked for a moment, was more than one of ardent friendship, there was a sense of something neither of them could name. The words that whispered in Becky's mind were "conspiracy," "danger," and "high adventure." Why these words would occur to her on such a warm, peaceful day was not apparent, unless her magical friend was trying to tell her something again.

She and Rachel lost track of time. They paddled a while. Then they leaned back and let the canoe glide with the current. They made numerous turns down tree-lined corridors that opened into large lakes. They went down a couple of small waterfalls.

Becky had left a note fastened to Dad's tent flap, telling him that they had gone for an adventure on the Flowage and that they would be back long before sundown. Now sleep was tugging at Becky's mind. She glanced at Rachel, who hadn't spoken for a while. She couldn't tell if Rachel was asleep. Everything was so warm and so quiet. The sun was playing hide-and-seek between the tree branches. When Becky closed her eyes, she was fascinated by the sunlight and shadows as they played on her eyelids. For some reason, the insects that had been so noticeable back at camp were nowhere around. She dipped her hand in the water. It was comfortably cool. She tapped her fingernails on the side of the canoe to see if Rachel would look back. Nothing.

A couple of small deer were standing at the edge of a pond, watching the canoe drift by. They didn't flinch.

Sleep was beginning to overpower Becky. Why not? She slipped down onto the floor of the canoe and rested her head on the seat cushion. She thought about tying the canoe to a tree branch while they snoozed. But why bother?

Just after Becky dozed off, Rachel looked back. She slid down onto the bottom and propped her seat cushion between her head and the side of the canoe.

There was no current. The canoe was still. The sun was warm. Just a half-hour nap and they'd head home. Becky had taken care to memorize the route they had taken. Besides, she had a good sense of direction. She could just about point to where the two greatest dads in the world were snoozing.

All was well in Becky's world.

Chapter Twenty-two

Becky's rest was fitful. Even though she had nothing on her mind, she awoke periodically and peered through tiny eyelid slits. She thought she might have been dreaming. Actually, she *was* dreaming. She dreamed of cruising down a mighty river in an old side-paddle steamer. She smelled the water, felt the breeze on her face. The sun's rays and shadows continued to play on her eyelids.

The sun was lower on the horizon now. There was a slight chill in the air. She smelled the smoke of a campfire. Sleep wouldn't turn loose of her. It was so compelling. It felt so good.

She dreamed that she saw a sign through squinted eyes, floating past in the water. There were harsh words. As she turned, someone screamed her name. A woman threw a drink in her face.

Becky sat bolt upright in the canoe. Water splashed over the side. Rachel was screaming her name.

It was almost dark. She could barely see the faint glow of a pink and gold sunset. The water was black. They were moving fast.

Rachel climbed over the seat that had separated them and held Becky closely. She screamed, "Where are we?"

"I don't know, but wherever we're going, I don't want any part of it." Becky jumped up on the seat and spun around. She began paddling for all she was worth in the opposite direction from where the canoe was heading.

Rachel took her cue from Becky and climbed back up on the other seat. She was now in the rear of the canoe. She paddled like a mad woman.

Despite their efforts, it soon became apparent that they couldn't overcome the force of the current. The edges of the lake were coming closer. The waterway was becoming narrower, and the water was moving more swiftly. They were no longer on a lake. They seemed to be in a river, a mighty fast river. It was now only a couple hundred feet wide. They couldn't possibly overcome the current. Their only hope was to make it to a shore and grab onto something.

Becky shouted to Rachel to head for the riverbank on their right. Rachel couldn't hear her. The water was roaring. The sound behind them was almost deafening. Becky pointed to the riverbank. Rachel nodded. They both dug in.

Becky mouthed a silent prayer that she knew came out as a scream. She couldn't even hear her own voice. The prayer was, "Please, my magical friend, don't fail me now."

They were sixty feet from the river's edge. She could barely see it. The sun was gone. She was paddling so hard she thought the paddle would break.

She looked back for a brief second at her friend. Rachel was paddling with a look of such determination in her eyes that it could have scared Becky to death if Becky weren't already scared beyond that.

Then, against all odds, they hit something. They hit it so hard that it almost threw them out of the canoe. "Thank God," Becky thought. "It must be a boulder. Maybe it has slowed our momentum enough to allow us to paddle to the river's edge."

Then she saw it, a gigantic cable just above Rachel's head. She made out a net of some sort. It made her think of a chain link fence, only with a much larger mesh. Rachel saw it too. The canoe began to turn sideways and to take on water. The bottom of the canoe rose up onto the net, forcing the girls' upper bodies down into the river. Becky's mouth filled with water. She coughed it out. It filled her mouth again, this time getting water in her lungs. She blasted it out. Still choking out the water, she stood up on the side of the canoe, which was now under water, to try to rise above the waves that were grabbing at her. She looked at Rachel. Rachel was doing the same but she had been able to reach up and grab the cable at the top of the net. Becky did the same.

Becky was nearer the edge of the river than Rachel. She motioned for Rachel to come closer to her. Their only chance was to hang from the cable and work their way, hand over hand, to the river's edge. They could put their feet through the holes in the part of the steel net that was above water, to lighten the load on their arms. There was no way that Becky could communicate this to Rachel. The roar of the river was too great. But Rachel seemed to understand Becky's plan anyway. She put her feet on the net and began moving toward Becky, one hand ahead of the other on the gigantic steel cable. The cable was so large that it was hard to hold onto. It was wet and slippery. One false move and she could fall into the lower portion of the net and be pinned against it under water by the force of the current.

Don't think about it! Just keep moving!

Becky continued inching toward the river's edge. It was only about twenty more feet. She guessed that it might take two minutes to get there. Her arms ached. Her hands were numb. Her shoulders felt like her arms were being pulled out of their sockets. She could stand any amount of pain for two more minutes. *Come on, girl—what are you made of?* She thought of Rachel. Was Rachel strong enough? If Becky looked back and Rachel was gone, Becky would die. Cancel that thought! She looked back. Rachel was there, holding on like a trooper.

This time Becky sent forth a real live, genuine, silent prayer. The very best, most honest, most loving, most earnest prayer Becky could make: *Please, my magical friend, for me and Rachel. Don't fail us now.*

Then she saw something that filled her heart with terror. Whoever the fool was who designed this net ought to be shot. The cable they were hanging onto didn't go to the edge of the river. It was fastened to a concrete pylon in the water, about ten feet from the river's edge. Or maybe the river had widened since it was built. It didn't matter. All that mattered was that, if they got to the pylon, they had nowhere to go. They couldn't get around the pylon. It was in raging water. There was no way to climb up on it. Their only hope was to hang onto the cable until help came. But what help? Nobody knew where the girls were. Nobody could see them in the dark. Nobody could hear them above the roar of the water. And they couldn't hang on more than ten more minutes at the most.

All right, Becky girl. This is it! What are you made of? Remember what Dad always says. We are pure love. We are part of the God Force. When we have no way to turn, always ask, "What would Love do now?" When we have a life-changing decision to make, ask, "What would Love do now?"

She turned around as best she could without losing her grip. Her very best friend in the whole world was holding on with superhuman effort. They were only inches apart. She didn't know if Rachel realized they had nowhere to go. She must think it strange that Becky was turning away from the river's edge.

Then Becky closed her eyes. She called forth her power, the power of the God Force. She gathered all the love she could summon into every aspect of her being, her body, her mind, and her soul. She didn't ask for help this time. She issued a command, not to some outside force that was separate from her; she spoke from the depths of her soul to the power that was herself, as part of the God Force. She commanded the Universe that she and her beloved Rachel would survive this terror not by means of some plan that Becky had in her head but by whatever means the Universe might choose.

Becky was certain of her outcome. She would leave the details to the Universe. All she had to do was come from a position of pure love, faith, and trust. It all seemed so clear now. She just knew they would be saved.

She pulled herself up with one arm, shocking herself with the strength of her little girl's body. With her other arm she grabbed Rachel in the most perfect hug she had ever given. Then the most wondrous thought flashed through her mind. This Rachel, whom she loved with all her heart, was part of her. They were both part of the same God Force. They were one.

She pulled Rachel close to her with a strength she never knew she had. She put her mouth close to Rachel's ear and screamed, "Don't worry, dear friend; we're all right now."

As those words reached Rachel's ear, Becky saw a look in Rachel's eyes that told her Rachel understood. Becky could hold on to the cable no longer. She wrapped her arms around Rachel's waist and locked each of her hands around her opposite wrist. Rachel did the same. They slipped beneath the water and were instantly pinned against the net with a force so great that neither of them could move. They clung fast to each other, best friends forever.

As Becky came close to losing consciousness, the twenty-five-year-old, rusted, weather-worn, lightning-abused, cable assaulted one last time by the power of Becky's prayer, snapped, allowing the top of the steel net to drop below the surface of the water and swing rapidly downstream. Becky and Rachel were released to the current.

The girls rose momentarily to the surface, letting them gasp in several breaths of fresh air. They clung tightly to each other as the churning current pulled them back under the water. Becky thought, "Thank you, my magical friend!"

All Becky knew was that they were spinning out of control beneath the surface of a rushing river so powerful that nothing she could do with her body could make any difference. Strangely, the phrase, "Go with the flow," resounded through her mind. For some equally strange reason, if she could have breathed, she would have laughed.

Everything seemed to be moving in slow motion. She expected that they would strike a rock at any moment. But they didn't. *Thank you, my magical friend!*

Becky thought about a parable she had read and loved at the beginning of a book by Richard Bach. The parable was about a group of water creatures that had spent all of their lives clinging to the debris at the bottom of a stream for fear of what might lie downstream. One day, one lone, brave creature, no longer able to stand the boredom of bottom-clinging, decided to turn loose of the bottom and trust in the wisdom of the stream to take him on whatever adventure lay in store for him.

The story of that lone, brave creature in the parable touched Becky deeply and came to mind many times after she read it. Becky identified with that courageous stream creature now. She was going with the flow, in more ways than one. Everything seemed peaceful. She thought, "Maybe I've died."

Then she was falling. She couldn't see anything. It felt like a free-fall ride she had been on at an amusement park once. Then she hit bottom with more force than she knew existed. She lost consciousness.

When she came to, she was amazed to find herself floating in the air. She was looking down at her very own body. Her body was lying on the edge of a gigantic, swirling pool at the base of a waterfall. At first she thought she was dreaming. Then the reality of her situation came crashing into her mind. She really *was* dead.

So this is what it's like to die. Not bad. Not bad at all. No pain. Total freedom.

The first thing she noticed was that she could move instantly to any place she thought about. She thought about Dad. Suddenly she was hovering above Dad and Doug. They were walking rapidly through the forest with a large group of men. They all had flashlights. There were three bloodhounds on leashes. They were looking for Becky and Rachel. She called to them. They couldn't hear her. She dropped down and tried to touch them. Her hand went through Dad's arm as if it didn't exist.

She thought about Mom. All at once she was in Mom's bedroom, hovering near the ceiling—actually above the ceiling—looking through it. There was Mom, asleep in her bed, unaware of the night's adventure. She thought about Rachel. Immediately she was hovering above the Glory Hole, looking down at her friend.

Rachel's body was lying on the opposite side of the pool from Becky's body, her legs still in the water. *Poor Rachel, was she dead too?*

Then there was someone beside her, a person of sorts. Becky realized that it didn't have a body, at least not the solid kind of body that Becky was used to. This being shimmered. It seemed feminine or maybe just unusually loving. Becky could see through her, sort of. Becky could feel warmth radiating from the being, warmer and more soothing than anything Becky had experienced before.

This being was telling Becky something not with her voice but with her mind: "It is not your time. You must return to your body. You have more to do on the Earth plane. Your love prayer was more powerful than the power of death. Your will to live is stronger than other forces on the Earth plane that would have thought you dead. The fact that your adventure was not observed by anyone other than you and your friend, plus your friend's faith in you, saved you from having to overcome the negative energy of others. Return to your body. Help will be arriving soon. Because of the power of your spirit and the love in your heart, your friend will live, too. Do not ever be afraid. Be at peace, my friend."

Becky felt a strong pull, like a roller-coaster ride when you start down the first fall. The next thing she knew, she was back in her body, and it hurt a lot. The pain caused her to lose consciousness.

When she awoke, she was in her bed, at home. Mom and Dad were there. She tried to speak but was too weak. Dad said, "Becky, my magical child, you have just lived through an impossible ordeal. You have to rest now and conserve your strength. You're all right. Rachel is alive, too. Nobody can figure how you lived through that fall. The fact that you both made it is beyond all belief. God was certainly watching over you. It was truly a miracle."

Becky lay there, *My power is the miracle, Dad, my power. The God Force is my strength. God is there to create with us whatever we choose. God does not decide. We decide. God loves.* It all seemed so clear. She would never be afraid of anything ever again, least of all, death.

Oh my dear Rachel, I love you. She sent her thanks to the God Force for her life and Rachel's life, but most of all for the way things are, the way they so wonderfully are.

She fell asleep and slept for a long, long time with a most radiant smile in her heart.

⚬⚬⚬

Now, many years later, she was off on a new adventure, one she suspected would teach her many lessons. After all, why was she here on this physical plane if not to learn and experience? How great to learn at an early age that it is all about experiences with nothing to fear.

As Becky continued through the forest on her way to the Interstate, she gave herself a reality check. She understood about the power of the subconscious. She knew about the relationship between the subconscious and the Universal Subconscious. She had even read a book about the power of manifestation. Her instincts were working fine. Her conscious mind knew its limitations and its ability to use the all-powerful subconscious. Most important, she was in contact with The Force, even though Becky didn't yet know it by that name.

Chapter Twenty-three

Even though she hadn't managed to hitch a ride, Becky wasn't sorry she had left home, and the lecherous Chas behind. There was already a chill in the air, and the sun was dangerously close to disappearing behind the top of the mountain ridge to the west.

She knew it was illegal to hitchhike on the interstate. She was afraid that if the state patrol were to pick her up, they'd call her mom, who would probably insist on their bringing her home. So she stayed at the bottom of the freeway on-ramp for almost two hours, hoping to thumb down a westbound driver from among the few who used that entrance.

Becky also knew hitchhiking wasn't the smartest thing to do. But with her considerable martial arts skills, she felt fairly confident. Still, the rapidly fading sunlight made her a little anxious. She was beginning to wonder if she had made the right choice in not going up onto the interstate in the first place. It seemed to her that her chances of running into someone with devious intentions would increase dramatically after dark.

As the sun continued to slip behind the mountains, it was becoming more difficult for Becky to make out the details of the objects surrounding her, which only half an hour earlier had been easy to see. With the increasing darkness and dropping temperature, she decided that waiting at the bottom of the on-ramp, where traffic was so infrequent, was no longer a good idea. She walked up onto the freeway, prepared to take her chances with the state patrol.

The enveloping darkness reminded Becky of a time when she was riding down the interstate with a friend on a dark, moonless night. Her friend turned off the headlights for just a few seconds to startle Becky. It worked. Becky was shocked to find herself speeding down the asphalt without even a hint of visual reference. It took all of her will power to keep from screaming. When her friend finally turned the lights on again, Becky's sense of relief was astounding. They both laughed and tried it again. As much as Becky enjoyed the thrill of those few seconds of self-inflicted blindness, she couldn't wait for the lights to come back on.

Becky moved some distance down the freeway to a location where she thought passing drivers would be more likely to see her. She was now well beyond the glow of the mercury vapor lights located near the on-ramp. Once again she was reminded how dark the interstate could be during those periods between passing automobiles, especially on a moonless night like tonight. It was one of those rare nights when it's so dark you can't even see your own hand.

Suddenly Becky realized she wouldn't be visible to the driver of a passing automobile until a few seconds before it passed her, especially with the dark clothing she was wearing. She began to think about the abundance of rattlesnakes in this part of the country. She thought of the possibility of stepping on a rattlesnake that had stretched itself out on the asphalt, enjoying the warmth that lingers on the pavement at the end of a warm, sunny day. She also considered the profusion of coyotes in the area, usually hunting in packs and looking for a solitary victim.

Over the years, whenever Becky thought about the possibility of something terrible happening to her, she had formed the habit of telling herself that the very fact that she had thought about it probably meant it wouldn't happen. For something to happen immediately after she thought about it would seem to be too much of a coincidence. She realized this was totally illogical, but it still had the effect of making her feel better.

Nonetheless, there was the very real possibility of a big old rattler lurking in the darkness, or a band of coyotes waiting in a storm drain up ahead. The prospect began to shake her confidence.

There was nothing to do about it now except to hope that a kind older woman would happen by soon, a lady whose concern for the safety of a seventeen-year-old girl alone on the interstate, would outweigh her natural caution about picking up strangers. The more Becky thought about the possible natural dangers awaiting her while she was on foot, the more she began to think that almost any ride would do, thank you very much.

Becky wondered how Mom was doing. Mom would be home by now and would have heard Chas's version of what had happened to him. He wouldn't have the nerve to tell the truth. It would be interesting to hear what kind of story a man like Chas would make up to explain why he was lying on the floor with a broken foot, some broken ribs, and several inches of skin missing from the front of his left shin.

Becky resolved to call Mom from the first telephone she found. She wouldn't tell Mom her side of the story now. That could wait until she returned home. She would simply assure Mom that she was safe and that she would explain everything later. Mom would certainly know, without being told, that Becky had a powerful motivation for what she had done to Chas. This alone should inspire Mom to proceed with caution.

Most of the damage had already been done. By marrying Chas, Mom put herself in a situation that would probably take a sizeable and expensive legal action to resolve. As inclined as Mom was to please others, Becky still hoped she would have the good judgment to keep Chas from getting his hands on the proceeds from Dad's insurance policy.

Becky wondered if she had made a mistake by not staying at home until Mom returned and having it out with Chas right then and there in Mom's presence. She thought not. Mom was still starry-eyed over Chas. It would be best to let things take their course. The condition in which Becky had left Chas would serve both as a notice to Mom that all was not right and as a compelling deterrent to any further shenanigans by Chas.

Just as Becky was beginning to feel a little more confident, a pack of coyotes began to howl up ahead. A shiver ran up her back. She opened her backpack, took out her Levi jacket, and put it on.

Passing cars were now infrequent. The minutes that passed between cars seemed longer than they probably were because of the absolute, impenetrable darkness. Becky decided to stand still for fear that she might wander into the traffic lane.

Anxiety continued its assault on her mind in earnest. She stood still, her backpack on the pavement beside her, waiting for the next automobile to come over the hill. It was so quiet. The air was perfectly still.

She thought she heard something in the bushes behind her. She stood completely still, barely breathing. It moved again, probably, nothing dangerous. It moved again, closer now.

Becky grabbed her backpack, considering the possibility of using it as a weapon, fat chance. She took off running in the blackness, expecting to run into something any second. She ran about fifty paces and stopped. Standing still, she struggled to hear above the sound of her heavy breathing. Whatever it was she had heard in the bushes, it didn't seem to be following her. All was quiet again.

Amazingly, she was still on the asphalt, but where on the asphalt? Was she near the shoulder or was she in the travel lane? Fear knotted her gut. Her knees felt shaky. If she stayed where she was, she wouldn't know if she was in the path of an oncoming vehicle until it was almost upon her, probably too late for her or the driver to react.

She began walking in the direction where she thought the relative safety of the bushes awaited. She took five steps, still on asphalt. Five more paces. Still asphalt. Was she walking parallel to the travel lane? Was she walking toward the center divider? She had become totally disoriented.

Headlights appeared, rising over the crest of a hill about a quarter mile away. Next came the sound of an engine, powerful and moving fast. Gears shifted. Was the car on her side of the freeway? Or had she gotten so turned around that she was seeing a car coming from the direction she had been walking toward? She could no longer see the lights of the on-ramp. She had no point of reference.

Where was the shoulder? She had only seconds to decide.

The automobile had gotten dangerously close to Becky mighty quickly. Now it was only yards away and appeared to be heading directly toward her. At least, with the speeding automobile so close, Becky knew for certain where she *didn't* want to be. She knew she didn't want to be anywhere near where she was at this instant.

She heard the screech of tires melting into the pavement and dropped her backpack as she lunged for what she hoped was the edge of the road. *"Help! Please, my magical friend, help me!"* Everything faded into slow motion. Something seemed to be propelling her. A powerful but gentle push, almost a caress, thrust her farther than she thought she could have possibly moved with her own strength. Tires still screeching, the automobile raced past her, only inches away. Becky rolled hard on the pavement. The screeching faded into the distance.

The car that had come within inches of ending Becky's visit to this planet stopped. The powerful machine turned slowly and headed toward her, lights on high-beam, blinding. It turned slightly and stopped a few feet from her, the headlights no longer glaring into Becky's eyes, the ground shaking from the vibration of the car's massive engine.

A man's voice asked, "Are you all right?"

For the first time, Becky considered the condition of her body. Surprisingly, she felt pretty good. Her jacket had taken some of the brunt of her untimely contact with the asphalt, thereby preventing the removal of several inches of epidermis from her forearm. Other than a bruised elbow and a scraped knee, she felt surprisingly sound.

The man turned off the engine.

"I think I'm okay," Becky said softly.

"What in the world were you doing in the middle of the highway?"

Becky tried to explain. The man assured her that she was very fortunate to be alive. "When I first saw you," he said, "you were in the middle of the left lane. I was doing about ninety. I couldn't possibly have stopped or swerved in time. By the time I passed the spot where I first saw you, you had moved all the way over near the right shoulder. I don't know how anyone could possibly move that fast. But I'm sure glad you did."

"Thank you!" Becky thought. "My dear magical friend, thank you!"

As he helped her to her feet, the man offered Becky a ride to the next town. She accepted gratefully, not bothering to mention that she had already decided to get to the next town in his automobile, even if she had to take it by force. For Becky, there would be no more walking on the freeway after dark. *Thank you my magical friend.*

She walked over and picked up her backpack. She hugged it, glad to be alive. As she headed back toward the automobile that had almost brought an early end to her adventure, she was pleased to find that the source of that deep, throaty roar she had first heard coming over the hill was a beautiful Ferrari Testa Rosa. Not a bad way to get to the next town.

As she approached the car, several coyotes let out a chorus of mournful cries. They appeared to be only a few yards beyond the shoulder of the road, near the spot where she had picked up her backpack. She hastened her step and slipped quickly into the passenger seat. The driver wasted no time climbing into his seat and closing the door.

Becky noticed that her hand was trembling. "Oh my magical friend," she whispered, "you never ever let me down, do you?"

"What?" asked the stranger.

"Oh nothing," Becky replied.

Chapter Twenty-four

After a few minutes seated in the passenger seat of the Ferrari, Becky began to relax. Perhaps it was the contrast of the relative safety of the inside of the automobile compared to the terror of walking along the interstate in the darkness. That was part if it, for sure. But there was more. The man who had rescued her from her predicament turned out to be a gentleman.

His name was Jim. He was about forty years old, a vice president of a large construction company specializing in sizeable government contracts.

At first Becky was mildly concerned by the way he had looked at her when he got into the car. What she didn't realize and would probably deny because of her modesty was that the look she had seen was simply Jim's reaction to her uncommon beauty.

Jim didn't have a chance to get a good look at her out on the highway because of the glaring lighting and the shadows it created around Becky's eyes. Under those conditions, she looked like someone who, while telling ghost stories to a group of enthralled listeners, held a flashlight beneath her chin, aimed up at the ceiling, causing her to sport the countenance of some type of demon. The warm lighting inside the Testa Rosa revealed the beauty of Becky's face to great advantage. Becky's looks could easily be described, without fear of exaggeration, as breathtaking.

As soon as Jim began to talk, Becky realized he was a decent person. He made no pretense, no come-on. One of the first things he related to her, by way of casual, get to know each other conversation, was that he was the father of four terrific kids and married to a wonderful woman.

Jim was the kind of person with whom it's easy to carry on a conversation. Their exchange allowed no time for uncomfortable silence. Their discussion was so animated that each of them frequently started to speak almost before the other had finished.

At just about the time the Riverton/Franklin game was nearing completion many miles away, the talk between Jim and Becky turned easily to philosophical matters and then to recent findings in the realm of sub-atomic particle theory. Soon they were deep into the writings of Gary Zukav and Stephen Hawking, discussing how modern physics seems to support many of the beliefs of ancient mysticism.

Before Becky realized it, they had covered the hundred miles to the general area where they agreed Jim would drop Becky off. This was about the point where she planned to head west. She hoped there would be a motel where she could enjoy a safe night's sleep and have access to a telephone.

The highway signs indicated that a truck stop lay a few miles ahead. They thought this would be as good a place as any to part company, assuming a motel was near by. The truck stop was situated at an off-ramp that provided access to a state highway running roughly east and west. There was a small motel nearby. Perfect.

They arrived at the truck stop so quickly that Becky didn't have time before they stopped to thank Jim adequately for having been her knight in shining sports car. She did ask him to wait a couple of minutes while she made sure the motel had a vacancy. She came back quickly and reported that a room was available. Jim handed her a $100 bill with a look in his eyes that said, "it won't do you any good to argue with me." So she didn't. She simply asked Jim if he would mind stepping out of the car for just a minute. She set her backpack on the ground and gave him a big bear hug and a daughterly kiss on the cheek.

Then she quickly headed for the motel, turning back for a second to wave goodbye.

Jim stood there a minute with a big smile on his face, thinking life was good indeed. He had been so surprised by her hug that he hadn't even hugged her back. He thought, "Now that's a fine young lady." Silently, he wished her a safe trip. Then his thoughts turned to his own family. He said a silent prayer that if any of his children should ever find themselves in a situation like the one in which he had found Becky tonight, someone would be there to take his child to safety. In his heart, he knew someone would.

As soon as Becky settled in her room, she decided she had better call Mom. The telephone wasn't working. She put on her jacket and headed for the office. The temperature had dropped a great deal, and fog was swirling around the streetlight. She guessed it was close to freezing.

The woman at the front desk was dressed in her nightclothes, even though it was not yet close to what most people would consider bedtime. She explained that the phones in the entire motel were out of order because a backhoe had dug up the line from the highway to the telephone panel on the side of the building. The phone company had promised to have it repaired by today but rescheduled the work for tomorrow for some reason the lady didn't understand.

She suggested that Becky try the pay phone in the bar next door, in the hallway outside the restrooms at the rear of the bar. "You take care, honey," she cautioned. "Kind of a rough crowd there at One Eyed Jacks."

Becky didn't have much concern about rough crowds. She knew how to handle herself. Still, she decided to keep her coat on even if it was warm inside the bar. No sense attracting unnecessary attention.

She stepped into the air-lock entry to the bar and, before passing through the second set of doors, put up her collar, hoping to further enhance her anonymity. One of the things she had worked on, as part of her martial arts training, was to become as invisible as possible when in potentially dangerous situations. This would be fun.

She stepped through the doors. The smell of cigarette smoke and stale beer hit her instantly and heavily. The room was hot, almost stifling, compared to the outside temperature.

The crowd was large and noisy. About twenty men occupied the main room, with about four more in a side alcove, shooting pool. There was another dimly lighted room with a couple of booths in the back corner to the left of the hallway that probably led to the restrooms. Becky couldn't see if anyone was in those booths. To the right of that hallway was another door, which opened into a small kitchen.

It was obvious that the customers had been heavily into the beer. They were loud and boisterous, using an abundance of language that Emily Post certainly would not have endorsed. Nobody paid any attention to Becky yet. She hoped to keep it that way.

Although she made no moral judgments regarding people who used vile language, she found that it usually went hand in hand with a serious lack of intelligence and, often, a lack of integrity. This wasn't her kind of crowd.

She would just make a quick call to Mom and slip out unnoticed.

Becky headed for the hallway at the back of the room, hoping it would be the one with the pay phone. Luckily, it was, and it did. There were three telephones, kind of overkill for a small place like this. But a better chance that at least one of them would be working.

Becky reached into her jacket pocket. She found only a paperclip, a toothpick, and two sticks of Dentyne. She tried her jeans. No coins. Then she remembered she had taken only paper money from her stash back at home. Her coins were in a large Sparklettes bottle on the floor of her closet.

She picked up one of the phone receivers and held it to her ear, hoping this part of the world had the kind of phones where you could always reach an operator, even without change. She would call Mom collect and hope that Chas didn't answer the phone. No dial tone. She read a little silver placard on the face of the telephone: thirty five cents for a local call, probably the price of admission to speak to an operator.

Maybe she should wait until tomorrow to call Mom. She couldn't do that. Mom would worry herself sick, especially since Becky had indicated in the note she had left on the bathroom mirror that she would call tonight. She couldn't do that to Mom. She could walk over to the truck stop and get change and maybe even use a pay phone there. But that was nearly half a mile down the road.

What the heck! She'd just walk on out to the bar, "proud as punch," as her grandma used to say, ask the bartender to change a five-dollar bill, and make the call. After all, this was America. This was a public place. What was she worried about? Certainly, if there was a rowdy dude out there, his friends would calm him down.

She walked out to the bar, reached into her pocket, pulled out a five-dollar bill, and realized the bartender wasn't behind the bar. Maybe he was using the men's room. Or maybe he was in the back room rustling up a batch of buffalo wings. She stood there trying to look invisible. Hard to do for an seventeen-year-old beauty in a bar full of redneck drunks.

Becky sensed a presence behind her. When she looked over her right shoulder, her right cheek came into abrupt contact with a nose and a stubbly beard, reeking of beer and tobacco.

"My, oh my, what have we here?" A loud, deep voice emanated from the same source as the foul smell of beer and tobacco.

Becky turned around and backed toward the bar until she pressed against a bar stool and couldn't back up any farther. She was now about two feet away from a large, ugly man who was staring at her with glazed eyes. He was clearly having difficulty maintaining his balance.

The man reached over to a smaller man to his right, grabbed him by the shoulder of his shirt, and pulled the smaller man toward him. Then he put his arm around the other man's shoulders and pulled him tight against his own chest. He placed his mouth next to the other man's ear and shouted, "I said, what have we got here?"

The smaller man, obviously in pain from the volume with which the larger man had shouted into his ear at close range, bent over, placed his hand over the abused ear, and yelled, "Dammit, Hank, I wish you wouldn't do that."

By now, the shouting had attracted the attention of several of the other patrons, who gathered around the scene like a band of jackals around a wounded fawn.

Becky braced herself and assumed a modest karate stance, her hands up on either side of her face, elbows tucked tightly against her rib cage, ready to deliver some decisive blows if necessary.

"Well, well, well," Hank said. "What's this? Hey, fellas, I think we got ourselves a Kung Fu wildcat on our hands. Maybe old Hank here's gonna have to tame her a bit."

Hank reared back and lunged at Becky with a wild right-handed roundhouse punch. His swing was intended to catch Becky on the left side of her head.

Becky quickly and firmly extended her left arm, blocking his swing with the mid-point of her forearm. She immediately wrapped her left hand over and around the big man's right biceps, made an abrupt half-turn to her left, pivoting from the waist and smashing the tip of her right elbow powerfully into Hank's right biceps. As Hank howled in pain, Becky extended her right arm slightly and, reversing its direction, delivered a shattering blow with the outside of her flattened right hand solidly to the base of Hank's neck. Hank fell like a rock.

In seconds, four of Hank's companions, incensed by the brutal treatment perpetrated upon their comrade, were all over Becky. The little man with the aching ear dived for Becky's knees, wrapping both of his arms around them and squeezing them for all he was worth, diminishing Becky's ability to maintain her balance enough for the other three men to bring her to the floor and pin her there with the sheer force of their combined weights.

It became immediately apparent to Becky that struggling would be futile. What the heck had she gotten herself into? She hoped they were going to throw her out into the parking lot and have a good laugh at her expense.

She waited. The men held tight. Hank attempted to rise. He got partway up with the assistance of a bar stool and fell back on the floor, letting out a scream of agony. "What the hell did you do to my right side? I can't use my arm or my leg."

Becky tried to explain that it was only temporary and that he would be all right in a couple of hours. But nobody was listening. Several other patrons had joined the gathering. Two of them helped Hank up into a chair, which they situated such that Hank was looking down directly at Becky. He was rubbing his right biceps with his left hand.

Hank growled, "Okay, boys, let's handle this little wildcat real careful. She's got claws." He fought to achieve some clarity in his sedated mind and began orchestrating the proceedings. First he enlisted the help of eight able-bodied men, two holding each arm and two holding each leg. They lifted Becky off of the floor. With renewed incentive, she began struggling for all she was worth. The men were surprised at how difficult she made it for them to maneuver. As she twisted and turned, she caused them to stumble, almost dropping her. At one point, she managed to pull her left leg loose and delivered a crushing blow with her foot to the chest of one of her captors, cracking his sternum and putting him permanently out of the action.

A rather stupid-looking man with more tattoos than his body could comfortably support joined the fracas, replacing the man with the cracked sternum, who was now lying on the floor gasping for breath.

Under Hank's direction, they finally carried Becky over to the pool table. Another man came in from the parking lot with several pieces of rope.

Hank instructed the men to bind her arms and legs to the corner pockets of the table "good and tight." He said, "As soon as you boys got her real secure, we're gonna let Gil over there use that hog sticker he keeps in his boot to remove those fancy britches the little bitch is wearing. Then old Hank is gonna teach "fancy britches" here what a real man can do. She's gonna find out, even with what she done to my arm and leg, that old Hank's still able to do a bank shot into her corner pocket."

Everyone roared with laughter. "The rest of you boys can line up to have turns, if there's anything left after old Hank gets done." A cheer went up from the crowd.

Becky lay there, frantically trying to focus her thoughts. What could she do? The words of the motel attendant rang in her ear, "You take care, honey. Kind of a rough crowd there...." " Nothing Becky had learned in karate class seemed of much use when her arms and legs were tied to a pool table and she was surrounded by about twenty lunatics.

Finally she closed her eyes and relaxed her muscles as best she could, almost an act of surrender, not to the crowd but to the power of the universe. "Okay my Magical Friend, now's the time."

Chapter Twenty-five

Just as the drunken rednecks finished tying Becky to the pool table, a howl burst forth from the back of the room, a scream so loud and savage that the entire room came to a state of complete silence.

In the back corner of the room stood a man with fire in his eyes. From his stance, the fierce look in his bright blue eyes, the muscles that rippled in his upper arms and chest, and his heavy, almost furious breathing, not a person in the room doubted that this was a man to be reckoned with. This man had some serious intent.

Hank said, "Who the hell are you?" His words, intended to be defiant, sounded more like a plea.

The man made no reply. He walked slowly in Hank's direction. The crowd parted, leaving a wide aisle for him to pass.

When he reached a position about ten feet from where Hank stood trembling, the stranger turned suddenly toward the pool table and, with three quick strides, threw himself at the two men who were standing near Becky's right hand. He slammed their heads together with such violence that one of them was rendered immediately unconscious and the other could only lie on the floor, holding his head, screaming.

He then reached down and yanked the end of the rope holding Becky's right hand tightly to the corner of the table, causing the knot to come loose. One hand now free, Becky managed to roll on her side, even though both of her legs were still pinned. She slammed the three middle fingers of that free hand, fingertips tightly bent into a semi-fist, into the carotid artery of one of the men who had tied down her other arm. He lost consciousness immediately while his companion took off running for the front door.

Before the door closed behind him, a young man stepped into the bar. He was a stranger, breathing heavily. Sweat was pouring down the sides of his face.

The stranger paused for a moment as if to size up the situation. He saw Becky, legs still tied to the corners of the pool table. For a few seconds he stared down at the floor, as if in a state of deep concentration. When he looked back up, there was little doubt in anyone's mind that this young man wasn't happy with what he had seen.

He sprang forward with an unbelievable burst of speed, straight for the pool table, where he took out the two men who had tied down Becky's right leg, slamming both of them against the wall. In the process, he managed to hit his own head against the cue rack, causing his forehead to split open and blood to gush from the opening. Through sheer will power, he recovered his equilibrium. One look at the two men who had been standing near Becky's other leg and they both backed off, raising their hands as if to indicate that they wanted no part of whatever the young man had in mind.

Becky had untied her other hand and was busy loosening the bindings around her ankles. The young man took a moment to assure himself that Becky was now free from any constraints and set out in the direction of the large man who appeared to be the ringleader. Hank, with the help of a bar stool, had managed to stand up in spite of the paralysis in his right leg.

The young man charged headlong into Hank's massive gut and made contact at the same instant the blue-eyed madman came crashing into Hank's left side. It wasn't a pretty sight. The double impact almost tore Hank in half. Two of the vertebrae in Hank's back were dislocated, causing him to fall once again to the floor, where he lay screaming.

The madman spun around just in time to catch a hard-charging cowboy, wearing a belt buckle the size of Vermont, with an open-handed blast of his right palm, directly on the point of the cowboy's chin. The cowboy's head stopped in mid-charge while the remainder of his body continued on its original trajectory with little loss of momentum. The cowboy landed flat on his back, about ten feet beyond the point of contact, out cold, with a surprisingly peaceful look on his face. If he had been a cartoon character, three or four small bluebirds would have been flying lazy circles around his head.

Becky was now on her feet. In total disregard for the solicitous looks on the faces of the two men who had recently tied down her left leg, she jumped up on the pool table, positioned herself directly in front of them and, before they could react, did a complete three-hundred-sixty-degree spin to her left, raising her left leg, and blasting her foot against the ear of one of the unfortunate scoundrels. As he dropped to the floor, Becky reached down, grabbed the other assailant by the collar of his Levi jacket, and pulled him forward as she brought her left knee into immediate and bone-crunching contact with his jaw. Several teeth flew from the man's mouth before he slid to the floor.

Those members of the once-boisterous crowd who were still standing headed for the door with uncommon haste. All that could be heard were the moans of the injured. Nobody else remained in the bar, except the bartender, who had managed to stay clear of the entire fracas.

The cocktail waitress emerged from the kitchen, where she had been hiding ever since the mêlée had begun. She brought a first-aid kit with her and started patching up the wound on the forehead of the youngest warrior.

Becky introduced herself to the madman from the back room. He told her that his name was Chris, and that he had been in a back booth having a couple of Coronas after a hard day in the mountains. He said he would have come to her assistance sooner except he hadn't heard a thing because of a fierce ringing in his ears. The only reason he had even found out that something was going on was that he got tired of waiting for the waitress to bring him the beer he had ordered and came out to see what was detaining her.

The young stranger held out his hand to Becky and said, "Hi, my name's Jaime. I came here to use the phone. My family was just involved in an auto accident a few miles down the state highway. I need to call for an ambulance and a tow truck."

Becky thanked both of the men profusely for having rescued her.

Chris and Jaime shook hands. Each felt an exchange of energy. A friendship had begun, an easy thing to happen between two men whose first contact was as comrades fighting a mutual enemy.

Chris said to Becky, "Make your calls and I'll drive you home." Becky explained that she had planned to stay at the motel down the street tonight and then to continue hitchhiking to her aunt's house tomorrow.

Jaime called an ambulance, a tow truck, and the state patrol and arranged to meet everyone at the scene of the accident in a few minutes.

At last Becky got change from the bartender and called her mom. As she was dialing, it occurred to her that Chas would probably be in no condition or mood to be answering the phone. Sure enough, Mom answered. Becky immediately assured her that she was safe. She explained quickly that she couldn't talk long because she didn't have any more change than what she had already deposited in the pay phone. Actually, she didn't want to get into the topic of Chas's broken and battered body until she had a few days to think about it. She again asked Mom to be careful and not to make any major decisions until Becky had a chance to talk with her. Mom indicated an eagerness to meet with Becky as soon as possible. Becky told her that she expected to be home soon, but that she didn't intend to live there any longer, at least not as long as Chas lived there.

She said "goodbye" and hung up with the uneasy feeling that she should have said more. She was worried about Mom but couldn't think of anything she could do for now.

Chris suggested that Becky was probably not safe staying anywhere near the bar. And, as eager as Jaime was to get back to his family, he wasn't about to leave Becky behind in a place like this.

It was agreed that Becky would accompany Chris and Jaime back to the scene of the accident and that they'd figure out later how to get Becky safely to her aunt's house. They stopped briefly at the motel, where Becky quickly explained her situation to the clerk and got her money back.

While Becky was recovering her money, Chris and Jaime sat in the front seats of the Jeep in silence. Although each was sensing the beginning of a friendship between them, they were too exhausted to make conversation. They had each experienced more adrenaline rushes in one day than most men experience in a year.

Jaime began to realize that he had been so focused on rescuing Becky, protecting Chris, and keeping himself alive that he had completely failed to notice something. The fact he had missed was so blatant, so obvious, so overpowering that he would later find it impossible to believe it could have ever escaped his notice.

Now, as he sat there in the front seat of Chris's Jeep, slowly regaining his equilibrium and just beginning to focus more clearly on his surroundings, that fact began to gnaw around the outer perimeter of his mind. Something powerful but still out of reach was stirring, nagging and insistent. It was a strange kind of yearning, a longing, like when you hear an old familiar love song that tugs at your heartstrings but you can't remember its name or who sang it. And you're afraid the song will end before you remember and you'll never hear it again or know its name.

Jaime's eyes focused on some dried water tracks on the windshield. Whatever lay beyond that point of focus was blurred. He became vaguely aware of movement in the distance. It drew closer and brightened. Becky, returning from the motel office, stepped into a circle of light cast by a neon sign.

In an instant, Jaime's eyes refocused, and as Becky's image cleared, he became fully and immediately aware of what it was that had been teasing his mind, what it was that he had failed to notice in the heat of battle and its emotional aftermath. There, before him, stood the most gorgeous woman he had ever seen. Not just pretty. Not just attractive. Not just beautiful, but absolutely gorgeous. How could he have not noticed that before?

Even in her blue jeans and flannel work shirt, there was no doubt in Jaime's somewhat confused young mind that he was in the presence of beauty beyond words. She had the kind of beauty that inspires the artist to paint, the composer to write, and the hero to offer his very life.

Jaime sat bolt upright and hit his head on the Jeep's roll bar. He hardly noticed.

He thought of the scene in *The Godfather* where Michael Corlioni first saw the love of his life and was so overwhelmed with emotion that his bodyguards couldn't help but notice what was happening. One of them commented that Michael had been struck by the thunderbolt.

That's how Jaime felt: as if he'd been hit by a thunder bolt. He opened his door, tried to step out to help Becky into the Jeep, forgot to put his feet out first, and fell to the ground.

Becky bent down to help him up. He smelled her perfume, intoxicating. She touched his arm, gentle. She smiled, dazzling.

Jaime lay there for a few seconds with a silly grin on his face.

Those eyes. Oh, those eyes.

Words from an Elton John song floated through Jaime's mind, "Yours are the sweetest eyes I've ever seen."

He started to stand up, brushing himself off, and smacked his head against the rearview mirror. Becky touched his head soothingly. Instant healing. Becky said, "I think my heroes need some rest."

She climbed into the backseat. Jaime couldn't help but notice how her blue jeans caressed her bottom. He couldn't think of words to describe what he was seeing and decided that it was just as well.

Jaime lay back in the front seat, thinking, "Heroes. Her heroes. She said we are her heroes." The word continued to repeat in his mind.

Chris set a new land-speed record getting to where the over-turned truck had already caused several vehicles to back up on both sides of the highway. From the flashing lights, the emergency vehicles obviously had already arrived on the scene.

He drove down the shoulder of the highway to where Sarah, Michael, and Tim were watching their auto being pulled out of the mud. Damage to the car appeared to be only cosmetic. It could still be driven. Ethel and Horace had been taken to the hospital.

Chris introduced himself and Becky to the family. Jaime stood there grinning. Tim walked over to Jaime and whispered, "Are you all right?"

To which Jamie replied, "I'm just fine, except for that damn thunderbolt." Tim looked over at Becky, then looked back at Jaime and that silly grin. Tim knew.

Back at the Lasher farm, Mom made sure that Becky was comfortable in the guest room.

Chris brought in his sleeping bag from the Jeep and situated himself on the family room sofa.

Michael built Sarah a fire in the fireplace. They sat on the leather loveseat, holding hands and thinking of all that had happened. By the time they headed for bed, everyone else was sound asleep.

Sarah went into Tim's room and made sure he was tucked in. She kissed him gently on the top of his forehead. She felt comfortable that all was well in Tim's world.

She went to Jaime's room and stood there watching him sleeping, breathing so peacefully. On the way home, Tim had ridden with Chris. Jaime and Becky had ridden with Michael and Sarah. The kids told them about what had happened at the tavern. Sarah worried about what affect something like that might have on Becky. But Becky seemed strong.

She couldn't help but notice how Jaime looked at Becky. It made her realize that Jaime wasn't her little boy any more. From now on, things would get more intense. A lot more was at stake. Jaime had a lot more to win, but also a lot more to lose. She made a wish that Jaime's life would be as good as the life she had found with Michael.

What a night this had been! Sarah felt a little chill run up her neck, that old motherly chill. She sensed that a lot more lay ahead.

She bent over and pressed her lips ever so gently against Jaime's forehead, careful to avoid his injury.

She said a most motherly prayer.

Chapter Twenty-six

The morning sun came pouring over the top of the snow-capped mountain range behind the Lasher house. It was one of those mornings when the air is so clear, so clean, so still, that you wonder if some magical force had blown through the valley during the night and sucked every last molecule of haze and dust and pollen and moisture out of the atmosphere. The sun is so bright that the mere thought of looking in its direction would cause you to squint.

A light misting of dew clung to the needles of the evergreens that stood guard over the backyard, enhancing their wondrous aroma.

Sarah's silver-white Persian cat, Whiskey, lay curled up on the sill of the herb window above the kitchen sink, luxuriating in the warmth of the intense sun. The only sound in the Lasher house was the ticking of the grandfather clock in the family room. The face of the clock would have told anyone who had been up and about and cared to look at it that it was almost nine o'clock.

But nobody looked at the face of the clock. Nobody envied the cat's contentment. Nobody smelled the aroma of the dew-enhanced evergreens. Nobody even saw the glorious sunrise. Everyone in the Lasher house was sound asleep from utter exhaustion. Even Michael, who was accustomed to rising at five o'clock in the morning, was dead to the world.

Amazing how a few simple events like an automobile accident, an attempted rape, a barroom brawl, a death-defying race with a grizzly bear, and a couple of time warping miracles can wear people out.

In spite of his state of fatigue, Chris got up long before sunrise and drove to Dr. Fernandez's home to spend several hours with Tama. The doctor assured him that the horse was going to recover despite the incredible damage that had been inflicted upon his body.

When Chris opened the gate, Tama was lying on the floor of the barn. The big horse made a mighty attempt to stand up to greet Chris, but Chris quickly forced him to lie back down. Chris lay down beside the horse and wrapped his arms around Tama's neck. In that instant, Tama relaxed his neck muscles and laid his head on the straw-covered floor with a sigh. They stayed like that for a long time, old friends having survived yet another challenge.

Chris stroked Tama's neck and shoulders, taking care to avoid the deep gashes the wolf had inflicted. Tama's eyes told Chris he understood and appreciated the energy Chris was sending him.

When Chris finally had to leave, he told the good doctor that he'd be back as soon as he could and that, in the meantime, Tama was to have whatever he wanted or needed, regardless of the cost. Doctor Fernandez already knew that.

Chris arrived back at the Lasher home just as the family room clock was striking 9:00. A few minutes later, the crowd began to stir. By 9:30 everyone was awake. By 10:00, there was an all-out scramble for the bathrooms. By 10:45 everyone was seated at the big oak kitchen table, ready to devour whatever Sarah had created for their culinary delight.

Waffles, low in fiber, vitamins, and minerals, high in white flour, sugar, and salt, but delicious, satisfying, irresistible. Every plate was piled high, with plenty of butter, maple syrup, whipping cream and Sarah's homemade boysenberry preserves.

The conversation, as one might well imagine, centered on the events of the preceding day.

Jaime stole a couple of quick glances at Becky when she was looking the other way. Sure enough, she was absolutely gorgeous. She hadn't aged a bit during the night. Now, after a nice long shower, a judicious application of a tiny bit of makeup, and a hundred strokes with a brush through her hair, Becky was once again causing Jaime's heart to do funny things.

As Jaime tried to sneak a third glance, Becky turned her head quickly, almost as if on purpose, and caught Jaime's eyes in mid-stare. He couldn't move. He just sat there, feeling like a kid caught with his hand in the cookie jar. He moved his eyes slightly left and then right but couldn't resist the urge to return them to center, where the vision across the table kept mercilessly pouring out large doses of enchantment.

Becky turned away quickly, relinquishing her hold on Jaime's vision. So abrupt was her release and so intense Jaime's recoil that he unconsciously bent forward at the waist, inserting his right elbow into the soft butter that had been waiting patiently to be applied to a steaming hot waffle.

Jaime froze, elbow at mid-insert. To raise his elbow would be to display it to one and all with its newly acquired calorie-rich coating. So he sat there, looking innocently at the ceiling, trying to decide how he was going to relocate his elbow from the center of the butter dish to the nearby bathroom without detection.

Tim resolved the dilemma by shouting, "Hey, dum-dum, ever try a butter knife?"

If looks could kill, someone might have had to dial 911.

Jaime looked up at Becky. She looked at Jaime, then at his buttered elbow, then back at Jaime. She said, "God, you're cute." In less than a second, Jaime's entire being assumed a consistency identical to that of the melted butter. He started to laugh. Then Becky began laughing. Everyone else joined in. Chris laughed so hard he dropped a forkful of waffle on his lap, whipped cream and all. The laughter was exactly what they all needed to release the tension of the previous day's traumas.

Jaime looked at Becky. She was looking at him. They sat there laughing and staring into each other's eyes. Jaime didn't remember life ever being quite this good.

He risked reaching his hand out to Becky. He held it there, a question dangling in the air. Neither blinked. She reached out slowly and placed her hand in his. He squeezed it gently. She squeezed back, a squeeze more wonderful than Jaime could ever imagine a squeeze could be.

His heart was still doing funny things. Becky stopped laughing. The look on her face was like nothing Jaime had ever seen. It seemed to Jaime as if that look was saying exactly what he was feeling. For just a second, nothing else in the world existed. There was just that face, that smile, those eyes, that look. Jaime knew he would never be the same again.

By the time the breakfast dishes were finished, it was well past noon. Chris and Jaime had decided they would see that Becky was delivered safely to her aunt's home.

Becky protested, assuring them that they had already done more than enough and that she was perfectly capable of getting herself there safely. Sarah insisted that the boys escort Becky. To Jaime's great pleasure, Becky's protestations were not convincing. They were tempered, he hoped, by her desire to spend some more time with him.

Chris suggested that they could save almost a full day's travel time by taking a shortcut he knew that led through a couple of mountain passes, a beautiful desert valley, and across a high plateau. Chris reminded himself that he had to be home in time for his date with Wendy on Friday evening, just five days from now.

He had plenty of gear and supplies left over from the camping trip that had been cut short by his encounter with the grizzly. Likewise, Becky was prepared for almost any conditions they might encounter. Her backpack was well supplied.

Jaime borrowed a duffel bag that Michael had brought home from the war and filled it with an assortment of goodies intended to make their trip enjoyable, including lots of snacks and several plastic bottles of water and fruit juices.

Chris checked to be sure that the two gasoline cans attached to the rear bumper of the Jeep were full. He filled the clip of the Beretta and stowed the pistol under the seat.

The mood was festive as the trio climbed into the Jeep. They all got hugs and wishes for a safe trip from Mom, Dad, and Tim.

While the others were still occupied with their good-byes, Tim stepped to the back of the Jeep, raised the canvas cover, and slipped a few items into Jaime's bag. He zipped it closed and walked around to the passenger door to give Jaime a second hug. He whispered in Jaime's ear, "Hey, little brother, you take care. I had a dream last night about this trip. Just keep your senses keen and follow your instincts. I put a few things in your bag just in case."

Jaime slapped Tim on the shoulder and said, "Thanks—we'll be just fine."

Becky had built a little nest of blankets and sleeping bags in the back of the Jeep, which allowed her to recline in comfort. From her vantage point, she observed the exchange between Tim and Jaime. She couldn't hear what they were saying, but the looks on their faces and their body language caused her to suspect that whatever was said was of a serious nature. She snuggled into her cubbyhole, intending to get a bit of shuteye to help compensate for the stress of last night. Before long, the humming of the tires put Becky in a deep sleep.

During the first couple of hours, Chris and Jaime had some animated conversations. Chris gave an exciting rendition of his adventures of the previous afternoon. Jaime gave Chris a play-by-play account of the previous night's football game, deleting any mention of the metaphysical wonders he and Tim had experienced, not knowing yet what Chris's spiritual leanings might be. A discussion of those experiences would have to wait until Jaime was sure Chris could hear about them without taking offense. From what little Jaime knew about the beliefs of the ancient Native Americans, he suspected that Chris might be open to some of Jaime's notions. But it was too early in the game to risk having his new friend think he was loony.

Eventually the two settled into a comfortable silence, each lost in his own thoughts. They drove on for a few more hours. The sun was now low on the horizon. Becky slumbered peacefully.

As the deep purple of twilight faded into the all-consuming ebony of a moonless night, Jaime turned sideways in his seat and treated his eyes to a long look at Becky, her face lighted gently by the glow of the instrument panel. He thought of how she had squeezed his hand across the breakfast table while the elbow of his other arm had tried to ignore its buttery coating.

That magnificent squeeze was probably a more significant form of communication than the telegraph or the telephone, probably more important than the Magna Carta or the Declaration of Independence. It occurred to Jaime that he might be exaggerating slightly, but not much.

Jaime concentrated on Becky's breathing for a while. Chris pretended not to notice. He knew what Jaime was feeling. It was the same feeling a crazy man on a motorcycle could have for a princess in a burgundy convertible with a misbehaving turn signal.

Five nights to go, five nights until Chris's eyes would be blessed with another opportunity to feast on the glory of Wendy's exquisite face. She had to show up. She just had to.

The trio headed silently into the darkness of the night, each exhilarated by a newfound source of joy, each content with the imagined invincibility of youth.

Chapter Twenty-seven

Becky's restful dreaming was shattered by an explosion of such intensity that it caused her to sit upright and cover her ears with both hands. In spite of the unsettling events of the previous day, Becky had managed to sleep deeply and peacefully—that is, until someone set off what sounded like a bomb next to her left ear. She looked around, trying to get her bearings. In a matter of seconds, she realized she was in her nest in the back of Chris's Jeep. Jaime was now behind the wheel. The Jeep was stopped, its engine off. Raindrops were pelting the windshield. Chris and Jaime were studying a couple of maps by the light of two flashlights. It appeared that they were parked on top of a mountain ridge.

"What was *that*?" Becky screamed.

Chris explained that a lightning bolt had struck a rock outcropping about fifty yards behind the Jeep.

Becky suggested, enthusiastically, that they might consider getting out of wherever they were right away before the friendly skies decided to unleash another million or so volts of static electricity in the middle of their vehicle.

Lightning would be unlikely to strike the Jeep, Chris explained, because the rubber tires acted as an insulator between it and the earth. "Besides" he said, "haven't you heard that lightning never strikes the same place twice?"

Becky disclosed to her two adventurous protectors that neither of those considerations gave her the comfort and security she was looking for. She suggested that this might better be accomplished by the trio relocating itself to a position somewhere other than a mountaintop, preferably at the bottom of some cozy little canyon.

Jaime explained that they had decided to take the trail over this ridge some time before the storm started and that it had come upon them so quickly and with such violence that they had no chance to avoid their current predicament. They were studying two maps. One looked like a USGS trail map or, perhaps, a U.S. Forest Service map. The other looked homemade, written by hand, on what appeared to Becky to be an animal hide.

The downpour increased and became almost deafening as it hammered against the canvas cover of the Jeep. Becky had to shout to be heard from the back seat. She checked her surroundings and was relieved to find that there was, apparently, no water leaking into the vehicle.

Jaime started the engine and steered the Jeep cautiously down the mountainside. Had it not been so noisy, Becky would have asked where they were going. She decided, however, that in view of the difficulty of communicating, she would be content to remain silent and assume that the men had discovered a reasonable route to relative safety.

They wound down the side of the mountain, exercising extreme caution because of the slippery surface condition. Several times, the Jeep began to slide sideways. Each time, Jaime corrected the situation by turning the front wheels in the direction of the slide and applying the brakes gently. Once again, lightning struck dangerously close to the Jeep, this time shaking the vehicle violently. Becky encouraged Jaime to keep moving.

Eventually the slope became more gradual and Becky assumed they were nearing the bottom of the mountainside. Then, two more lightning strikes hit, one on either side of the front fenders, only yards away. Each was so bright that it took several seconds before anyone could see well enough to proceed. At last the Jeep was nearly level, and it appeared, from the limited visibility provided by the headlights, that they were, indeed, on flat terrain. Conferring with his map, Chris said that if they were to go straight ahead, they would be moving in the general direction of their intended destination and that they would eventually get back to a paved road without having to cross over any more high ridges.

Chris and Jaime jumped out and traded seats. Becky felt better now that Chris was at the wheel, assuming that he could probably handle his own vehicle better than Jaime, although Jaime had done a remarkable job. Chris proceeded with care across the meadow—or whatever it was. The grass grew taller, now brushing against the underside of the Jeep. Before long, the tops of the grass were hitting the bottoms of the outside mirror brackets. Becky flinched.

Then Chris stopped and turned off the engine. The rain had moderated to a point where he didn't have to yell to be heard. He suggested that because the grasses were getting taller, they probably were getting into an area where there was normally more water, perhaps a swampland. This time of year, it probably would be dry, with most of the precipitation in the nearby mountains being frozen into snow pack instead of running down the canyons.

Still, this had been quite a downpour, releasing a lot of water on those slopes. Chris rechecked his map, not completely certain of his position. Jaime studied the other map. They both came to the same conclusion at the same instant. They looked at each other without speaking. Becky felt her gut tighten. She didn't say anything.

What those young men had come to realize was that they were sitting in the middle of a dry river bottom, not just any dry river bottom but a river bottom fed by an entire network of normally dry streams, all of which emerged from the very mountains they had just traversed and upon which the violent rainstorm had, only minutes ago, unleashed a savage torrent. Within minutes, unless Mother Earth was dry enough to absorb all of that precipitation quickly, those hundreds of millions of gallons of water would likely be rushing past the Jeep at a depth nobody could predict.

Chris started the engine. He double-checked to be sure the transfer case was in four-wheel drive. The map indicated that they would reach higher ground more quickly by going ahead rather than back. He said a brief silent prayer to Great-Grandfather and shot ahead as fast as he could. They didn't have time for caution. They would have to take their chances and hope that no ravines lay ahead of them, especially ravines full of surging water. The grass grew deeper. It was now slapping the windshield and almost eliminating any light rays attempting to escape from the headlights. Chris roared on, relying on pure faith. Faith in what? Certainly not his driving skills. He said another prayer, this time to Great Spirit.

Jaime was focusing on The Force. Becky pleaded for assistance from her Magical Friend.

If one were to observe the Jeep from a distance, using the proper photographic equipment, one might well perceive the vehicle as being aglow with the energy being generated by its occupants. There was some serious praying going on.

Soon the Jeep's massive engine began to labor and the tires started throwing up water. Becky held tight to the roll cage.

The water became deeper and Chris had to down-shift into third gear to keep the engine from bogging down. The occupants could hear and feel water slapping against the bottom of the floorboard. They heard the rubber of the tires whining against the mud and rocks and grass.

The Jeep began to float. Its occupants could feel the tires touching down on the ground occasionally. Mostly, though, they were floating. Nobody knew how long the Jeep would float before tipping over or filling with water and sinking to the bottom. They were now floating in a solid body of water—a river, a rushing river. A few times, they hit something below the surface. Each time, it caused the Jeep to turn sideways.

Mercifully, the engine kept running and the headlamps remained on, but now only partly above the water's surface.

Chris knew it was only a matter of time before the air intake would go below the surface and about a pint of muddy water would be sucked into the engine, not only rendering it dead but ensuring that it couldn't be re-started. He prayed fervently.

Becky reached forward and took Jaime's hand. She put her other hand on Chris's shoulder, a silent vote of confidence. The Jeep rocked to one side. Water began to enter the door on Jaime's side. Becky felt water soaking through her tennis shoes. They all leaned automatically to the left, trying to use their body weight to help the Jeep right itself. Surprisingly, it helped.

They floated on in silence. Please, God, no waterfalls!

Then the water began to move much more swiftly. Becky thought of her canoe ride with Rachel. She let out a little cry. "Sorry," she said. "just having a little déjà vu here." But it was more than déjà vu.

She realized that the hastening of the water's momentum probably meant the river was either heading downward more rapidly or the river was getting narrower.

The newly-risen moon broke through the cloud cover for only a moment. The trio mutually gasped as they discovered, to their horror that a large rock loomed directly ahead of them. It was a rock wall, actually, several hundred feet wide and reaching about fifty feet into the night sky. But where was the water going? It was heading straight for the rock wall. But how could that be? The river had to turn somewhere. It couldn't run headlong into the rock.

Then, just before the moon disappeared behind the thick layer of clouds, the moonlight, combined with the small amount of light from the headlamps that was still escaping above the waterline, revealed where all of that water from the river was going.

At the base of the gigantic rock wall, just a few feet above the water's surface, was a huge opening, about the size of a Greyhound bus. As the water crowded toward that opening, it roiled and foamed, creating huge waves, which smashed against the wall before circling in a further attempt to find the massive opening.

Jaime sat there, paralyzed. He had no idea where that water went once it entered the Greyhound bus-sized opening. Probably some underground series of caverns and waterfalls, designed by the forces of nature to beat a Jeep full of young people into metal flakes and organic fish food.

Then the moon was gone.

Becky's hold on Jaime's hand became a vise grip. Chris grimaced as her fingernails dug into his shoulder.

As the Jeep approached the opening, it slowed considerably, probably the result of a backwash caused by the water crashing against the rock wall. It seemed to Chris that the Jeep actually began to move away from the wall, likely because of some fortunate cross-current or eddy. Then the Jeep turned ninety degrees to the left, its right side facing the deadly hole.

Chris heard the engine slow down. For the first time since the Jeep began floating, he realized it had been in gear all along. The wheels had been spinning in the water, propelled by the idling of the engine. That slowing of the engine probably meant either that a bit of water had gotten into the air intake or that something was slowing the wheels. Chris prayed it was the latter.

Then the engine slowed way down. Chris touched the accelerator pedal ever so gently. The Jeep lurched slightly. The wheels were touching something. Chris pressed a little harder. The Jeep moved forward, just a few inches. He decided not to risk trying to drive forward for fear that he would break the tires loose from whatever little footing they had attained. He took the Jeep out of gear and set the emergency brake. The Jeep remained still. Becky held her breath. Jaime let his breath out.

Chris grabbed his flashlight and aimed it upstream. He saw a large boulder just fifteen feet from them. Apparently the Jeep tires had touched bottom at the same moment the Jeep had entered the slower water below the boulder. The reduced velocity of the water and, probably, a bit of backflow had apparently permitted what little traction the tires found on the slippery bottom to allow the Jeep to remain stationary for the moment.

Then, in the dim light of the headlamps, Jaime saw a tree, a wonderful, large, strong tree, just a few feet ahead of them. That tree meant three things to Jaime: 1) The Jeep was definitely standing still, 2) There was some hope that they would survive this ordeal, and 3) There had to be someone or something watching over them.

Jaime pointed out the tree to Chris and Becky. He asked Chris, "Do you have a winch on this thing?" Chris assured Jaime that he did. Jaime said, "Tell me it isn't one of those electrical, three-horsepower pieces of junk that you attach with duct tape."

Chris said, "Hell no, compadre, this beast's got a Power-Take-Off winch powered by six hundred eighty horses of big block V-8. We've got enough torque to lift this baby right off the ground if we want to. Our only problem is, how the hell do we get the cable wrapped around the trunk of that tree, considering that there's about ten feet of raging river between it and the winch?"

Jaime suggested that he could work his way over the hood of the Jeep, unwind about thirty feet of winch cable, swim across the ten feet of river, and tie the cable around the tree trunk.

"You gotta be kidding us," Becky said.

Chris advised Jaime that there was no way in the world anyone could swim across that expanse of water. He said, "That water has to be traveling at least thirty miles per hour. Before you could possibly get to the other side, you'd be fifty yards downstream entering that black hole. Besides, you'd be carrying at least twenty-five pounds of cable, which means, at the least, you'd have the use of only one arm for swimming. Think again."

Becky gasped as they slid a few inches.

"I've got an idea," Jaime said, "but I don't have time to explain." He began to open the door.

Becky said, "At least, tie a rope around your waist in case the water gets a hold of you."

Chris instructed Becky to remove a climbing rope from one of the toolboxes behind the front seat. He secured it around Jaime's body, taking care to wrap it around his waist a couple of times and also looping it around both of Jaime's thighs, creating a secure harness. Next he tied a knot just in front of Jaime's abdomen to ensure that the harness would not come undone. He laid the remainder of the rope in a series of loops on the Jeep floor, tying the far end of the rope to the Jeep's roll cage. He then cut the rope at a point about eighteen inches from the knot he had tied in front of Jaime's abdomen and reattached the cut ends, using a slip knot. Finally, he tied a simple knot at the very end of one of the two dangling rope ends.

He told Jaime, "The slip knot will hold unless you yank on this piece of rope with the knot at its end. On the outside chance that the rope is somehow holding you under water, you may want to set yourself free and take your chances with the current rather than drowning. But don't pull on this knotted end unless it's your only chance of escape. We'll have the other end securely fastened to the roll cage. Good luck."

Jaime reached into the toolbox behind his seat, fumbled around in it for a few seconds and took out a large lug wrench. He found a piece of coat-hanger wire in the tool box behind Chris's seat. He folded the wire and stuffed it into his right front pocket. Then he stepped out onto the running board, the force of the current almost shoving his foot off of it.

Becky bowed her head, closed her eyes, covered them with the palms of her hands and said silently, "My Magical Friend, I need you once again. A very brave and wonderful young man is about to do a very dangerous thing. Please be with him."

Jaime leaned over the front fender and inched his body onto the hood of the Jeep. With the wrench in his right hand, he had only his left hand to try to find something to grab onto. He felt a ridge formed into the metal of the hood. Not much. But better than nothing. One little slip and he would get a chance to test Chris's knot-tying skills.

Never before had Jaime clung so tightly to anything. He lay flat as a pancake, imagining that every square centimeter of his body that made contact with the cold metal gave him a better chance of not being washed away by the water splashing across the hood. Slowly he inched his way to his left until he lay astride the center of the hood in relative safety. He relaxed a second.

He put the wrench between his front teeth, a maneuver he knew his dentist would not approve of. Jaime could barely open his mouth wide enough to get ahold of the wrench's handle. But he had it. He then used both hands to pull himself to where he could look over the front of the hood and down at the winch. He reminded himself that if the wrench dropped out of his mouth, he would have to react quickly to catch it before it dropped into the fast-moving water.

The lights of the Jeep, reflecting off the water, were sufficient to give Jaime a clear view of the front of the Jeep and the submerged winch. He saw a space between the front bumper and the frame of the Jeep where he thought he could put the handle of the wrench without danger of its falling through into the water below. Actually, the wrench then would be entirely below water, but Jaime reasoned that its weight, which he estimated to be about three pounds, should keep it from being washed up and out of the opening. He tried it, releasing his hand slowly. It stayed in place. This set Jaime free to use both hands on the winch.

He disengaged the ratchet and began slowly pulling cable from the spool. Twice, the torque of his pulling almost caused him to slip sideways toward the waiting water.

As he pulled each length of cable free from its spool, he carefully coiled it in a neat pile on the hood next to him. The cable, having been wound around the spool of the winch, was relatively easy to coil on the hood. Luckily, the cable was well worn, probably from many years of use. It coiled nicely and didn't spring straight.

As Jaime figured it, about twenty feet of cable would be enough to reach the tree, wrap around the trunk, and fasten the big hook at its end back around itself, with some to spare. He judged that was about the length of the cable lying beside him.

He pulled the wrench out of the hole where he had secured it, reached into his pocket, and took out the piece of coat hanger wire he had placed there. He fastened the handle of the wrench to the heavy-duty hook at the end of the cable.

Jaime stood up slowly and began swinging the cable, with the wrench on its end, in ever-larger circles over his head. He kept letting out more and more of the cable, increasing the size of the circle made by the wrench until the wrench was passing within inches of the tree and barely missing the boulder upstream from the Jeep.

With nearly ten feet of cable out, Jaime needed tremendous strength to keep the wrench moving. The cable bowed slightly because of the wind resistance.

Now what did I learn in my physics class? An object in motion will continue in motion, in a straight line, until acted upon by an outside force. So, at any instant, the wrench is trying to head out in a straight line. The only thing that's keeping the wrench from flying off in that straight line is its attachment to the cable, which is attached to my arm.

So, if I want to wrap this cable around the tree, I have to extend its length enough to allow it to wrap around the tree trunk and an additional amount to allow it to return and hook onto itself. I would guess that to be a total of eight feet.

But I can't release the additional eight feet until after the wrench has passed the tree, or the wrench will strike the tree. Then I must release all eight feet before the wrench makes one more circuit or there won't be enough cable out there to allow the wrench to make it all the way around the tree."

So, since I'm running out of time and before my arm runs out of energy, I'll do the only thing I can think of that may save our lives. I'll stop trying to reason it out and trust the power of the universe to guide me."

Jaime closed his eyes, a scary thing to do while twirling a three-pound wrench at the end of a piece of cable while standing upon a wet Jeep hood right next to a raging river intent upon dragging his body into a probably bottomless black hole if he should make the slightest slip.

Jaime focused his energy, called upon The Force with every bit of faith and determination he could muster, and pictured the wrench flying through the air, being pulled short from its straight-line trajectory by his perfectly timed yank on the cable, circling the trunk of the tree with a slight upward arch, enabling it to rise slightly over the cable leading back to Jaime's hand and then, miraculously, looping over the cable, spinning around the cable three or four times and coming to rest in a position whereby the large hook at the end of the cable (which Jaime had wired to the wrench) would latch onto the cable and connect the Jeep to the tree.

He made one last pass of the wrench past the tree, waited a fraction of a second, released what he estimated to be eight more feet of cable, brought it up short, and pulled back with all his might. He saw the wrench, shining in the glow of the headlamps, begin its orbit around the tree, fade out of sight for a split second, reappear around the far side of the trunk, and rise ever so slightly in an upward trajectory, clear the length of cable extending from his hand to the base of the tree, and quickly wrap itself around the cable, with the hook snapping into its intended position over the cable, just as ordered!

Jaime shouted, "Thank you, my wonderful Force!" just before his feet slipped on the wet hood, his hand lost its grip on the cable, and he shot into the raging, ice-cold waters.

Chapter Twenty-eight

The fast-moving current was going to flood the engine if Chris didn't winch the Jeep out of the river immediately. He wanted desperately to help Becky pull Jaime out of the water and back into the Jeep. But if the engine stopped running, the winch wouldn't work and the Jeep soon would be spinning around an axis that ran from front to rear at the end of the cable attached to the ponderosa. Chris and Becky undoubtedly would be thrown out of the cab and Jaime would drown at the end of his safety rope.

The only way Chris could think of to bring this terrifying situation to a happy conclusion was for him to winch the Jeep onto solid ground first, and then help Becky pull Jaime to safety. The winch, although tremendously powerful, was exasperatingly slow, especially when someone's life hung in the balance.

During the two agonizing minutes it took Chris to winch the Jeep from the rushing current to solid ground, Jaime was under water, fighting to retain consciousness. Becky was pulling with all her strength, but the weight of Jaime's body, augmented by the force of the rushing water, was more than her arms could handle. Even with the adrenaline rush that gave Becky tremendous strength, the rope connecting Jaime to the Jeep's roll cage was sopping wet and wouldn't allow her to get enough of a grip to do any good. She was so frustrated that tears were streaming down her cheeks. She shouted, "Please, please, my Magical Friend! You've never let me down before! Why now?"

Becky pulled on that rope until she felt like her back muscles were going to rip apart. Even then, she didn't let up. She heaved with every ounce of strength she had. But the hundreds of pounds of pressure on the other end were more than she could overcome.

Jaime had been under water almost three minutes now. Luckily, he had filled his lungs before going under. From contests he and Tim used to have when they were in grammar school, he knew he could last as long as four minutes when the stakes were high enough. He held onto that thought with every bit of will power he had. He knew The Force wouldn't let him down. The swirling water buffeted him mercilessly, but he didn't hit anything solid. He knew he had only a few more seconds before he either would pass out or would have to pull the knotted end of the rope, releasing him and sending him on his way to the dark hole.

So focused was Becky on trying to save Jaime that she wasn't even aware of what Chris was doing with the winch. Just as she was about to despair, Chris appeared by her side and grabbed the rope. She could see his muscles flexing and straining. His hands made hers look like those of a little child. She stepped aside, knowing that she would only be in his way. He gripped the rope and managed to wrap it around his fist. He pulled the rope toward him at least a full foot, got it looped around his other fist, and gave another mighty pull, another foot, a long way to go. Jaime was still a good twenty feet from the Jeep.

Jaime reached for the knotted end of the rope near his waist. One powerful pull and he would be released to the current, surging toward the black hole. He hesitated another second, knowing he couldn't hold out much longer. He squeezed the end of the rope with what little strength he had left and began to pull.

Just as the rope started to slip through the knot, Jaime heard a voice.

The words were as clear as if the water hadn't been roaring in his ears, the tone so gentle and peaceful it distracted him from his pain.

He let go of the rope. He was still tethered to the Jeep, floating five feet under the water. He felt himself slipping into an altered state of consciousness as reality began to elude him.

Then he saw a light in the distance, moving toward him. As it drew near, he realized it was the lady in the long white gown who had warned them of the ice and the oil on the highway last night.

"Help me," Jaime prayed.

Jessica smiled.

Chris, his legs now braced against the inside wall of the Jeep, gave one more mighty pull, using all of the strength in his arms, back, and legs. Jaime shot to the surface, gasping frantically for air, pulling the breath of life into his lungs. Becky grabbed for the rope. She and Chris pulled together. They weren't going to let that boy go down again.

In seconds they had Jaime within a couple feet of the Jeep, his trembling legs at last touching solid ground, safe. Jaime lay draped over the fender of the Jeep, coughing and sputtering for several minutes, a crazy grin on his face.

When he was able to resume a semblance of normal breathing, he shouted as loudly as he could, "Thanks, Chris! Thanks, Becky! You'll never know how great it is to be alive!" He looked back into the raging waters and whispered, "Thank you, Jessica."

As Chris helped Jaime into the Jeep, Becky crawled into the back corner and began weeping silently, her back to the boys. "Thank you, my Magical Friend, thank you, thank you."

Chris didn't notice the blood dripping from his hands. He hugged Jaime and wouldn't let go, afraid, through some form of illogical thinking that his friend might slip back into that deadly water. Chris hadn't felt this close to another man since Great-Grandfather had left him. His massive arms held onto Jaime for dear life.

Becky turned and took Jaime's face in her hands. She kissed him gently on the cheek, her hands trembling, with a look in her eyes that Jaime hadn't seen before. The three of them stood there hugging, tears flowing down their cheeks.

Chris said a silent prayer to Great-Grandfather. "Hey you wonderful old man, could you make it a little quicker next time? I almost lost my friend."

He heard Great-Grandfather say, just as clearly as if he was standing next to him, "Chris, my great-grandson, if it had ended any sooner, it wouldn't have accomplished its purpose. Just look around you and see what you've got. All is as it should be."

Chris looked at his new friends. *Yes, just as it should be.*

❦

The rain had stopped. The three friends sat in the Jeep checking the maps. Jaime was wrapped in blankets. The doors were closed and the heater was turned on full blast. Becky asked Chris about the old animal-hide map. Chris told her his Great-Grandfather had left it to him.

Great-Grandfather had made that map while traveling for many years in the mountains and deserts of the area. He liked to tell Chris that it was a magical map, far more accurate than any map he could purchase in a store, with far more important details. He said that whoever read the map would likely find different information on it at different times, depending on what was needed. If you were looking for a safe place to hide, it would show you. If you needed a shortcut, it would appear on the map.

Great-Grandfather jokingly told Chris that he considered having the map copyrighted and published, but he was afraid he would become too rich and famous. "Besides," he had said, "the map won't work for everyone. You have to be pure of spirit. Otherwise it will lead you into dangerous places." On more than one occasion, Great-Grandfather cautioned Chris to be sure to purify his heart before embarking on any adventure where the map would be needed.

Becky laughed, but not in disbelief. She was far too wise to doubt the power of the spirit world. She laughed in delight in having such a treasure.

They drove off, Chris driving, Jaime navigating with the government map. Becky checking occasionally with Great-Grandfather's map to be sure they weren't getting off the true trail.

The rain resumed. They decided it was about time to stop for the night. It had been quite a day.

As they rounded a corner lined with thick evergreens, a gate appeared to their right. Behind it they saw a dirt road that apparently hadn't been used for many years. It wouldn't have been evident that a trail was even there were it not for the gate.

The gate was of unusually sturdy steel, well rusted. A sign announced: "PROPERTY OF THE UNITED STATES GOVERNMENT. TRESPASSING IS STRICTLY FORBIDDEN. TRESPASSERS WILL BE PUNISHED TO THE FULL EXTENT OF THE LAW."

Chris quipped, "Sounds to me like an invitation." He stepped out and walked to the back of the Jeep. He reached into the toolbox attached to the rear bumper, fumbled around for a few seconds, and pulled out what looked to Becky like gigantic pliers. In a matter of moments, Chris's bolt cutter shattered the padlock that had secured the gate.

"What in the world are you doing?" Becky asked. "Do you want to get us shot?"

"This tool was given to me by President Reagan. It's a universal key to all federal padlocks. He told me to make myself at home at any and all federal properties."

Becky said, "You know you're goofy?"

"I know. But with me, challenging the government is a matter of principle. Do you know that over eighty percent of the land in this nation is owned or controlled by some sort of governmental agency? Maybe it's my Native American heritage, but I believe the land belongs to us all. I don't believe in borders or boundaries or gates— at least not where public lands are concerned. I realize that, as a practical matter, someone needs to oversee these lands to ensure that unscrupulous individuals don't waste them. But the government's proper role is as caretaker, for the benefit of the citizens of this fair country. I believe this land should be used and harvested and made to benefit man as Great Spirit intended."

"Besides," Jaime said, "this is the only route I can see on the map that doesn't lead to either a high, lightning-susceptible ridge or a low flash-flood-vulnerable valley. Our personal safety requires that we take this route."

They proceeded through the gate, taking care to secure it behind them.

As they headed up the overgrown trail, Chris said, "The only harm we've caused thus far is we've destroyed a ten-dollar padlock, for which the government will pay two hundred dollars to some favored supplier plus five hundred dollars for the time of some slow-moving bureaucrat to get a new one and put it in place."

Jaime and Becky cheered Chris's statement.

After half an hour of struggling through a dense forest on a barely visible trail, which required moving several trees that had fallen across it, they came into an opening that apparently was once a pasture or a meadow. It was fenced at one time, but most of the fence was lying on the ground, the fence posts rotted and the barbed wire rusted and broken.

A bit farther down the trail, they came to an old two-story hay barn that was barely standing. Part of its roof had completely collapsed, and its walls leaned precariously.

They were considering the advisability of seeking refuge in this questionable structure when Jaime suggested that they consult Great-Grandfather's map. That weather-worn document revealed that the land upon which our stalwart travelers now found themselves had once been a rather large farm or ranch and that there was once a farmhouse about two miles farther down the trail. It was an easy decision to give the farmhouse a try instead of risking a night in the partially collapsed barn.

Ten minutes later they arrived at the site indicated on the map as the location of the farmhouse, and sure enough, there stood a magnificent old house, somewhat shabby and in need of paint, but magnificent nonetheless. It obviously had been a grand structure at one time, three stories high and of decidedly Victorian architecture.

As the trio stopped the Jeep near the bottom of the steps leading to the front porch, they noticed a sign on the front doors. Not nearly as elegantly composed as the sign at the front gate, it simply stated, "PROPERTY OF THE UNITED STATES GOVERNMENT. KEEP OUT."

Chris turned off the headlamps and the engine. The air felt close to freezing. All was silent except for the wind blowing softly through the huge cedars that surrounded the front yard. Chris approached the double front doors and, with the aid of a flashlight that Becky held, once again used his bolt cutter to remove a sturdy, rusted padlock. The padlock secured a cage constructed of heavy-gauge solid steel bars covering the front doors and the casing within which those doors were hung. It seemed strange that anyone would install such a heavy security device over the doorway to an apparently long-abandoned and neglected structure.

To their surprise, once they had broken through the steel cage, the double doors themselves were unlocked. As they entered, a musty smell assaulted their noses, as if the building had been closed for decades.

At Becky's suggestion, the boys gathered several armloads of kindling and a few dry logs they found stacked on the side porch.

Before long, they had a roaring fire going in the fireplace. Happily, the chimney drew perfectly, allowing the fire to burn without filling the room with smoke.

The three sat around talking for a couple of hours. They spoke mainly about their experiences with The Force, Becky's Magical Friend, and Great Spirit. Early in the conversation they decided they all had been dealing with the same power, the power that many called "God." They agreed that the concept of God was often misunderstood.

Before retiring, Chris went outside and moved the Jeep well into the forest, out of sight of anyone who might happen by. They all fell asleep quickly that night, their sleeping bags gathered around the fire, with thoughts of how exciting it was going to be to explore the old house and its surroundings in the light of day. Jaime noticed that Becky placed her sleeping bag close to his. He slept particularly well.

Becky dreamed of the old house. In her dreams it was filled with lots of people, many of them young children. There was something wrong with these people. They were sad, suffering, fearful. Becky couldn't put her finger on the cause, just a feeling that something was very, very wrong. The people were trying to tell her something, but she couldn't understand them. It was as if they were speaking a foreign language, but not really, not any language that Becky could recognize. They reached out to her, pleading. But she couldn't help them. She didn't understand.

Then she saw a tattered old book. In it she knew were the answers or it could lead her to the answers. The book was hidden. Even though she could see it, it kept disappearing, fading out of sight. Then a child came to her, a young girl with terribly sad eyes, motioning for Becky to follow. The girl led Becky down a long hallway, a dark, narrow hallway with lots of turns. Every time Becky thought she was close to where the book was hidden, the little girl disappeared. Then she'd reappear in a different place, gesturing for Becky to follow.

Becky discovered a hole in the floor of a closet. It wasn't really a hole, but a place where she could see through the floor. There was the book. And as she looked upon it, blood began to flow across its cover.

The little girl was gone. Everyone was gone. There was blood everywhere, dripping down the walls, spreading across the floors. And then the blood was gone and the sun beamed in through large windows. There were flowers in a vase on the dining room table. The front door stood open, a gentle breeze flowing in through the doorway, rustling the draperies. Becky looked back at the table and there, in place of the flowers, was the book, covered with blood, the pages blowing in the wind. The pages stopped moving. All was silent. There, written by hand in the center of one blank page, were the words, "God help us."

Becky awoke with a start. The sun shone brightly, lending warmth to the morning air. She sat up and stared at the front door, now standing open, a gentle breeze blowing across the room, rustling the ancient draperies.

She looked up and let out a gasp. All the windows were covered with steel bars.

Chapter Twenty-nine

Daryl Harrington was far too intelligent to return to his home, like some fool in an action movie. He knew the type. He remembered sitting in the audience and saying to himself, "Don't go back to your home, dummy; that's the first place they're gonna look for you. Go hide out somewhere."

That's precisely what Daryl did. He went to a place where nobody would be likely to look, not to some relative's cabin in the woods, not to some friend's home. Daryl went to a motel, far away from the federal facility and far away from his home. He registered under a fictitious name, paid cash, and didn't spend any unnecessary time jawing with the check-in clerk.

On that Friday night in his motel room, Daryl spent several hours considering his circumstances and carefully planning each step necessary to ensure that he would survive the incredible situation in which he now found himself. He considered how ironic it was that the time he had spent in the CIA's decoding department brought him into direct contact with so many facts, events and ideas that prepared him so well to do battle with his adversaries.

Even though Daryl had been valedictorian of his high school graduating class and quite an athlete, he knew that the challenges he was about to face would require strategizing and cunning beyond anything he had ever dreamed of doing.

The first thing he did the next morning was race to his bank and withdraw all of his cash. It came to more than thirty-seven thousand dollars. Going to the bank was risky, but necessary. He was thankful the bank was open on Saturday mornings. He figured the government hadn't had time to take all of its standard precautions. It had been only fourteen hours since the power to his cubicle had been cut off. Whoever had tried to murder him had no reason to suspect that the attempt wasn't successful.

His next move was to contact *El Jefe*. He didn't do so using his own computer. He used a computer at an Office Depot store, far from his motel room and within a local call of his Internet provider. He stayed on the line briefly, telling *El Jefe* of his situation. He asked *El Jefe* if he could break the code used in the appendix affixed to the documents they had uncovered and have the results ready to download over the Internet the next time Daryl made contact.

El Jefe indicated that he was already well under way with that task.

Daryl spent the next few hours checking out several pawn shops that were some distance from his motel. That night, he drove to within a few blocks of one of the pawn shops he had visited earlier that day that had an easily bypassed security system. It also had everything Daryl needed: (1) a Desert Eagle 44 Magnum pistol with several clips full of hollow-point cartridges, (2) two canisters of black powder, (3) some blasting caps, and (4) a spool of fuse line.

He was in and out of that pawn shop in four minutes flat, breaking the glass entry door, prying a door off the gun case, grabbing exactly what he needed, and leaving sufficient cash taped to the cash register to cover the reasonable value of what he had purchased, plus the damage to the building and cabinets. All the while, he wore latex gloves he had acquired at Albertson's so as not to leave a single fingerprint. He wore a plastic shower cap over his head to reduce the chance that a hair or two from his head might fall on the floor, providing the Feds with something to use for a possible DNA trace.

He was out of there long before the owner of the pawn shop arrived to meet the waiting police officers. His scary adventure was building in intensity but somehow Daryl found it invigorating. He was beginning to enjoy this game in spite of its dangerous, even deadly, nature.

Later that night, Daryl abandoned his Mustang in a twenty four hour supermarket parking lot, where he hoped it wouldn't be noticed for a while. He walked a mile to a used car lot and selected a Jeep. It would serve him well for off-highway travel and was easy to hot-wire. He placed five thousand dollars in an envelope and hid it under the soil in a flower pot next to the entry to the office. He would send a note to the owner in a few days, telling him where he could find the payment for the Jeep. He drove from the lot slowly, taking care to obey all traffic laws. Considering this was his first ever auto theft, he was surprisingly calm.

Then he drove across town to a large wrecking lot. He parked in the shadows of a row of trees along the rear of the lot and gained access by climbing a chain-link fence. After roaming the area for quite a while, he located a Jeep that had been seriously damaged. From its condition, he assumed that it was probably scheduled to be crushed and melted down. Fortunately, the registration and insurance documents were still in the glove compartment. Apparently it had been brought to the wrecking lot recently and the paperwork hadn't yet been processed. Daryl swapped the license plates and registration with those of the Jeep he had "borrowed" from the used car lot.

Sunday morning Daryl drove the Jeep through an Earl Scheib paint shop. For $69.95 cash, he changed its color from light tan to forest green.

Next he headed to the Big-O tire shop, where he purchased five chrome wheels and five heavy-duty off-road tires to give the Jeep a new look and maximize its off-road capabilities. As he left the tire shop and was merging into traffic, he looked back and caught a glimpse of a large black man staring at him. The man turned away, but not before Daryl had a chance to observe a scar running down the side of the man's face.

He drove to a True Value hardware store and purchased a stone grinding wheel for his cordless high-speed drill (the only tool he hadn't left at his cubicle in the CIA building), a ball-peen hammer, and a set of number and alphabet dies. Then he drove to an abandoned gas-well road, far from any traffic, and used the grinder to remove the VIN numbers from the Jeep's frame. He used the dies and the hammer to replace those numbers with the VIN numbers of the Jeep from which he had "borrowed" the license plates and registration documents in the wrecking lot.

Daryl splashed water over the area where the new numbers had been hammered into the steel frame, hoping that before anyone would have occasion to check those numbers, they would have rusted to match the steel of the surrounding area. He made a mental note to check those numbers later to see how well they had rusted and to smear a light film of axle grease over the area to help hide the fact that the numbers were recently stamped into the metal.

Now he had a registration certificate and license plates from a non-stolen vehicle. The only flaw he could find in his plan was that, if he were pulled over for a traffic violation, the name on his driver's license wouldn't match that on the registration.

He used a pay phone to contact a long-time friend, Jack Gleason. He told Jack that he was in a predicament and needed his help. Although Jack hadn't been in contact with Daryl for several months, they had spent a lot of time together over the years and were close friends. Daryl knew that Jack trusted him completely and that he wouldn't hesitate to help his friend. Jack was well aware that Daryl was in a top-secret and sensitive profession and knew better than to ask questions.

Daryl asked Jack to go to a temporary-help and answering-service company and rent an answering machine with a private phone line. He instructed Jack to be sure that it was rented in Jack's name, not Daryl's. Jack then was to write down the telephone number of that line and give it to Daryl the next time Daryl called. Jack was to put a message on the rented answering machine saying, "Hello, this is Henry Mathews (the name of the man who had owned the Jeep from which Daryl obtained the registration documents). I will be out of town for the next few months. If this call has anything to do with my Jeep, I have loaned it to my friend, Daryl Harrington. If there's any problem, please leave your name and number and I will get back to you when I return from the Caribbean."

Shortly after he had left the federal facility Friday night, Daryl decided to discontinue his morning shaving ritual so as to sport a full beard as quickly as possible. By Sunday afternoon he was already looking grubby. A trip to the pharmaceutical section of an Albertson's supermarket provided him with the necessary products to change his light brown hair to dark brown.

Sunday afternoon, Daryl purchased a laptop computer with a Titanium processing chip, 100 gigabytes of hard drive, 1 gigabyte of RAM, a CD burner, and a full load of the latest software. He also purchased a zip drive and a device that would enable him to connect his computer to his Internet provider by means of his cell phone.

He sat in the Jeep for a while, rereading the documents he had downloaded from the CIA files. Even though the documents made no mention of geographic landmarks, such as roads or trails, Daryl had been able to pinpoint with a fair degree of accuracy the location of the events depicted, using the military style coordinates in those documents, assisted by the navigational software he had loaded into his new laptop.

Daryl then drove to another computer store where he used one of the demo computers to contact *El Jefe*. He was pleased to find that the task of decoding the appendix, which had been attached to the CIA documents, had been completed. He downloaded the decoded appendix onto a memory stick and printed a hard copy, just in case the memory stick malfunctioned. He took care to erase from the computer's hard drive all of the information *El Jefe* had provided.

When Daryl got back to the Jeep, he took a few seconds to glance over the hard copy. Attached to the appendix was a note from *El Jefe* that simply said, "If this doesn't blow your mind, your mind will never be blown."

Daryl reread the document three times, its amazing significance becoming clearer with each reading. What he held in his hand, unless the decoding was totally erroneous or *El Jefe* was playing with him, was a transmission, intercepted by a NASA deep-space listening facility, from a spacecraft transmitting a distress signal.

The message indicated that the spacecraft had been damaged by a collision with a meteorite. It had a malfunctioning guidance system, as well as other operational problems. To save the craft from being hopelessly lost in space, those controlling it were now utilizing an outmoded device that had long ago been installed in the craft as a backup navigational system. The device had been designed to track signals emitted from quartz crystal transmitters located atop several navigational monuments, known as "pyramids," on the African and South American continents of a minor planet, referred to on the intergalactic navigational charts as "Planet Earth."

The transmission indicated that the craft was being forced, by the limitations of this outmoded navigational device, to seek refuge on Planet Earth until its primary navigational system could be repaired. Those controlling the craft requested assistance in landing it, indicating that their navigational capabilities were so seriously hampered that they required a rather large and level area for an attempted landing.

The response to this request for assistance read as follows: "Your craft is not welcome on this planet. If its course is not changed, it will be shot down. Repeat, remove the craft from the area immediately, or it will be destroyed."

The next transmission from the spacecraft read: "Our communication system does not compute the words 'shot down' or 'destroyed.' These words appear to be from a language not familiar to our decoding equipment.

"Please direct us to a landing area. The damage to our craft has also rendered it without high-impulse anti-gravitational capability. We require a large, flat, level area. It must be landed immediately."

The appendix ended with the statements: "No further communication authorized. Continue tracking. Destroy any occupants. Absolute Top Secret. Code Name: Zephyr."

Although much of what Daryl discovered didn't make sense to him, he now understood the reason for the atrocities that the CIA had committed, as set forth in the document he and *El Jefe* first decoded in his office in the federal facility, the one to which this appendix had been attached.

He sat in the Jeep a long time. What had he stumbled onto? He thought of the implications of what he had read. He felt sure that nobody knew where he was. Still, he looked around, trying to satisfy himself that he was not being watched. He started the Jeep and headed away from the parking lot of the computer store. As Daryl left the lot, the black man with the scarred left cheek stepped back into the shadows.

Daryl took a circuitous route back to his motel, where he quickly loaded his few personal items and headed out to look for a new place to spend the night. If he was ever going to be able to live like a person again, he was going to have to get enough evidence against the Feds to either have the key players sent to prison or make them too terrified to ever mess with him again. He didn't know exactly where he was going with this situation, but he resolved that the bad guys were in for one hell of a fight.

⎯⎯⎯ ⎯⎯⎯

Monday morning Daryl woke up in the third motel he had occupied since his escape from the federal building three days earlier. So far, he had encountered no indication that anyone was on to him.

About the same time that Daryl was leaving his motel room, Becky was stirring in her sleeping bag at the old farmhouse. She was still badly shaken from her frightening dream.

The first thing Daryl did after leaving the motel was to call his friend Jack to get the telephone number for the answering machine Jack had rented. He kept that number in his wallet to present to any suspicious officer of the law.

On the far side of town, a CIA official arrived at his office, close to the federal facility where Daryl's former cubicle was located. Just before driving to his office for the second time that day, the official spent half an hour in the men's room, fourteen stories above Daryl's cubicle, wrestling with a serious and unexpected complication.

Long before sunup, that CIA official had first driven to the building where his office was located and taken an elevator down to an underground bunker. He had entered the bunker and turned on the circuit breakers for the electrical lines that provided power to the lights, air fans, and security system for cubicle 22, on Floor Fourteen-Minus.

He had returned to his office, reset the clock in his computer to real time, and waited until 9:00 a.m. Then he drove to the federal facility where Daryl's cubicle was located, to be available to run interference relative to his anticipated reception of the tragic news that a young man working on Level Fourteen-Minus had accidentally died sometime over the weekend.

When the official stopped at the front desk of the main floor to ask if the weekend had been peaceful, he was told that an unusual condition had been discovered on Floor Fourteen-Minus. He feigned surprise and asked for a copy of the report.

Fully expecting to read that the body of a young employee had been discovered, he was shocked to read that all that was found of any significance on Level Fourteen-Minus was a half-inch hole drilled through the inside panel of the security latch in Cubicle 22 and some electrical wires, batteries, and a few hand tools lying on the floor.

The revelation of this seemingly innocuous information caused a mixture of adrenaline and several survival hormones to flow through the official's circulatory system. He darted for the nearest men's room where he spent some time trying to rally his senses and reasoning skills to enable him to formulate some kind of a plan.

He had to be careful about who he told what had happened, or the extent of the problem, until he came up with a story that would cover his ass.

By the time the agitated CIA official returned to his office, Daryl Harrington was in the process of connecting his computer to his cell phone, reminding himself to stay on the line for no more than three minutes.

Daryl contacted *El Jefe* for the second time that day and found that his mysterious friend had hacked his way into a top-secret communications system of the federal facility where Daryl had worked. He intercepted a communiqué containing the code word "Zephyr," the same word appearing at the end of the appendix he had decoded and delivered to Daryl earlier this morning.

That communiqué set forth three facts of great interest to Daryl.

The first was that the person who had broken into the CIA's top secret files was still alive and at large. He had to be apprehended as soon as possible and held for questioning by the CIA.

The second was that any actions taken in this regard must be approved by the official sending the communiqué, and executed with extreme caution. This indicated to Daryl that whoever was after him probably would not be moving very quickly.

Third was that the decision, made in 1975 to (1) secure the scene of "the incident," keeping everyone out of the area for a long, long time, and (2) destroy all "destroyable" evidence only after any possibility of "political fallout" from the event was practically non-existent, was possibly a serious mistake. The evidence now had to be destroyed as soon as practicable.

Daryl knew it was extremely dangerous, if not insane, for him to go anywhere near the scene of "the incident." He also knew his only chance of getting the hard evidence he needed to get the bad guys and to save his own life required that he go there.

The approximate location of the scene of the numerous crimes, so clinically and callously documented in the secret files Daryl and *El Jefe* had discovered, was now displayed clearly on the screen of Daryl's laptop. Daryl assumed that only a few CIA agents were involved in the present situation. He guessed that whoever had screwed up his attempted murder wouldn't be spreading word all over the hallowed halls of the CIA building. He further assumed that whoever was presently involved would be moving very cautiously so as not to end up being the sacrificial lamb if and when this entire mess was disclosed to the public.

Daryl thought chances were good that he could get to the scene of "the incident" before the Feds got there. It wasn't that he had the physical ability to get there any faster. He was counting on the fact that he was going to be on a dead run while the Feds were having to move slowly and cautiously.

Besides that, a great deal of their energy and manpower was going to have to be diverted to looking for Daryl. A good part of the remainder of their efforts would have to be spent trying to figure out how to destroy the evidence at the scene without attracting any attention. Daryl didn't think the CIA had any reason to suspect he knew where the site of "the incident" was, since the intricacy of the code was far beyond Daryl's decoding abilities. Besides that, they would assume he was running for his life.

If they had known he was heading for the scene, they would have realized they could quickly and easily attain both of their objectives— his death and the continued cover-up of the atrocities—with a single effort. But they only knew that the file had been broken into. They probably didn't know that *El Jefe* existed. They knew that Daryl's level of decoding skill was nowhere near that needed to break the code of their top secret files. But they had to assume that it was just a matter of time before Daryl would deliver whatever information he had into the hands of someone with the necessary skills to do the decoding.

They probably didn't know of Daryl's alliance with his Internet hacker buddies.

They were probably thinking it would be best to devote most of their efforts to finding and disposing of Daryl. His death would allow everything to remain about the same as it had been and buy them the time they needed.

Daryl was fairly sure this incident had gotten them to thinking that they'd better get around to destroying the evidence, including all of the files, as soon as possible. On the other hand, he considered that whoever knew he had discovered the files might not want them destroyed. He just might want a copy hidden away somewhere that only he knew about, to be used to save his hide when all the finger-pointing began.

Daryl hoped these factors would slow down his adversaries enough to allow him sufficient time to locate and remove the evidence he needed once he got to the scene. The thought that his death was probably now their top priority caused Daryl's gut to tighten once again.

They will probably be looking for me in several places, none of which will be near the scene. They will be avoiding the scene like the plague until they are sure that I'm dead and that I haven't passed on any of the information I might have.

Still, when I finally reach the area of the incident, I'll be scared half to death and will be imagining that I'm seeing a federal agent behind every tree.

He filled the gas tank of the Jeep, plus the two five-gallon cans attached to the rear bumper. He stopped by a hardware store and purchased a heavy-duty bolt cutter, a pry bar, a shovel, and a crosscut saw.

Then he went to a sporting goods super store and purchased a pair of binoculars, a camouflaged down jacket and cap, a shoulder holster for the 44 Magnum, a waterproof match holder with easy-strike matches, a Buck hunting knife, a large steel-cased flashlight with six D-cell batteries, a small pocket-sized flashlight, several rolls of duct tape, a backpack, and a spool of nylon cord. And, because he had recently seen the movie *Cape Fear*, he bought a can of cigarette lighter fluid.

Daryl slid into the front seat of the Jeep. He reached under the seat and removed the paper bag containing the Desert Eagle 44 Magnum and the cartridge clips. He checked the clips to be sure each was filled with cartridges and shoved one into the handle of the pistol until he heard the comforting click. He pulled back the slide and released it, watching to see that a cartridge had been securely chambered, then set the safety. He eased the Desert Eagle into the shoulder holster he had strapped on beneath the camouflaged jacket.

He fired up the Jeep and headed out for the place where he suspected the CIA had committed, or at least been a party to, a series of hideous crimes. He didn't know what to expect. He wondered what the hell he was doing. But, deep inside, he knew.

Daryl said a long and sincere prayer to the energy force he had come to respectfully call "Infinite Intelligence." To Daryl, a prayer didn't mean a request. It meant a command, a powerful statement of intent from his inner being to the God Force.

He felt a new sense of confidence that all would be well.

Chapter Thirty

At just about the time Daryl Harrington was leaving his motel room on the Monday morning following his final and hasty departure from his cubicle in the federal facility and a short time before the CIA official was about to discover that his attempt to terminate Daryl had failed, Jaime and Chris were beginning to stir in their sleeping bags on the floor of the old farmhouse.

Jaime looked over and noticed that Becky was sitting up, staring at something. She had a puzzled look on her face. He whispered, "Good morning." She didn't respond or look at him.

"What's got your attention riveted to the far wall?" Jaime asked.

"Look," Becky said. "All of the windows have bars on them. Doesn't that seem strange out here, miles from any city and miles off the main road?"

"Yeah," said Jaime. "Doesn't seem like the kind of place where anyone would feel a need for extreme security."

By now Chris was sitting up, ruffling his hair and adjusting his eyes to the morning light. He listened to the conversation and followed his friends' gaze. Sure enough, every window he could see had bars over it, and not just ordinary bars. These were some kind of heavy-duty hardware.

Chris got up, slipped on his hiking shoes, and walked out onto the porch. Had he taken the time to examine the door frame and hardware carefully, he would have noticed a relay switch designed to send a radio impulse to a receiver many miles away. The switch was rusted from many decades of non-use and didn't perform the task for which it had been designed.

A few minutes later he returned. The crease between his eyebrows, which gave him his famous intense look, had deepened noticeably. Something was obviously on his mind.

Becky informed them that if she didn't find a place to relieve herself shortly, something was going to happen that would embarrass all of them and most certainly her. It didn't seem likely that the plumbing in the old house would be working, so the trio agreed that this would be an excellent time for them to head for the forest to do what comes naturally.

In the interest of privacy, Becky suggested that she head east and the gentlemen do whatever they needed to do in a westerly direction. They divvied up a freshly unwrapped roll of toilet tissue that Becky had removed from her backpack, and left the old house.

As they headed into the brisk morning air under a glorious, clear, sunny sky, Jaime let out an enthusiastic jungle cry. Normally the exhilarating weather would have put Becky in a state of mind as exuberant as Jaime's, but she couldn't shake the mood resulting from her frightening dream last night.

Chris took a deep breath of cool, clear air as he and Jaime started into the forest. Chris didn't say anything while Jaime jabbered on about the weather, the scenery, and the excitement of being in the great outdoors in the company of his friends.

Finally Jaime stopped rambling long enough to notice that Chris wasn't responding to his monologue. "Are you okay?" he asked.

Chris said he was thinking about the house. Something wasn't right. He stopped abruptly. "I know," he said. "I know what's been bothering me. It's those bars. I knew something didn't look right, but I couldn't put my finger on it. Those bars are on the outside of the windows. And the bolts are on the outside, too. Just plain lag bolts with five-eighths-inch hex heads. Any burglar with a simple Crescent wrench could remove them. Anyone wanting to protect the property would have ground down the edges of those hex heads so the bolts couldn't be removed without special tools.

"So what do you make of that?" Jaime asked.

"I know this may sound strange, but it looks to me like those bars were designed to keep someone inside! The openings are narrow, much closer together than would be necessary to keep someone out. Maybe they're narrow enough to prevent someone on the inside from reaching those bolts."

"Maybe so narrow that even a small child couldn't get out?" Jaime asked. The thought made his skin crawl.

Chris turned around and looked back at the old house, just visible through the trees. "Look," he said. "Do you notice anything else strange about that house?"

Jaime stared at the farmhouse. It now looked ominous, even in the bright sunlight. "It's old and dilapidated. It needs a lot of paint. It could stand a little ....Wait a minute. Are you talking about those things on top of the chimneys?"

"Yes, those things." said Chris, "What do those 'things' look like to you?"

Jaime said, "They're like large upside down baskets, baskets made of steel bars."

"To me they look like cages," Chris said. "Bars wrapped around and over the tops of the chimneys. Why would anyone put bars over the top of a chimney?"

The two stood there, hands on their hips, mouths slightly open, looks of bewilderment on their faces.

They continued walking, wandering through the forest for a while, until they came upon a deep, wide ravine with a footpath descending into it. They skirted around the rim of the ravine then turned back in the direction of the farmhouse.

Chris suggested that they finish the business they had come into the forest to do in the first place and then get back to the house to see if they might find any more clues as to what had happened in that old place.

They split up, and a few minutes later Chris returned to the spot where they had separated. He waited a while for Jaime, but Jaime didn't show.

Chris shouted Jaime's name.

"Over here," came the response, from quite a distance.

Chris headed in the direction of Jaime's voice.

"Over here—hurry up!" Jaime yelled.

By the time Chris arrived at the place where Jaime was standing, it was obvious that Jaime was in a state of excitement.

"What's up?" asked Chris.

"Look over here." Jaime pointed to what appeared to be a large rectangular mound, about eighty feet on each side and about fifteen feet high in the center. The mound was covered with vegetation, including lots of trees, which were clearly several decades old.

Jaime said, "Just look at this. First there's a mound, apparently man-made, from its symmetrical shape, and made a long time ago, from the age of the vegetation that's overgrown it. Then look toward the west. It looks sort of like a corridor. Look at how the trees on either side of the mound are about twenty to thirty feet taller than those growing on the mound. And even more interesting, to the west all of the trees within what I call the 'corridor' are also about thirty feet shorter than the trees on either side. And the corridor is the same approximate width as the mound.

"Even more interesting," said Jaime, "is that the trunks of almost all of the older trees on either side of the corridor are charred."

"Well," said Chris, "it's not unusual that there might have been a forest fire here years ago."

"I know," Jaime replied, "but notice that only the trees on either side of the corridor have charred trunks. The tree trunks within the corridor apparently were never burned."

"All that tells me" said Chris, "is that the fire happened before the younger trees were here."

"That's what I thought at first," Jaime said, "and that's probably still true. But look closely." He led Chris to the edge of the corridor. "Notice that the tree trunks are burned on only one side, the side facing the corridor. And I'll bet that if we go over to the other side of the corridor, we'll find that those trees are also charred only on the sides facing the corridor."

Chris said, "I guess that tells us that whatever the source of that tremendous heat was, it was within the corridor."

"Exactly what I was thinking," said Jaime. "Like something very hot came right down the middle, charring the tree trunks on either side. That might explain why the trees in the center are so much younger."

"Maybe something like a small meteor?" asked Chris.

"That's sort of what I was thinking."

They began walking along the perimeter of the mound, looking for some more clues. As they walked, Jaime spotted something beneath a portion of the vegetation. It looked like a small, newly formed ravine, about three feet deep, coming down the side of the mound. The soil appeared to have been recently washed away, probably by the intense rain that had bombarded the area the night before, the same rain that had almost taken Jaime's life in the flash flood.

The soil was still soggy, and the boys could see dirt spread out at the end of the ravine farthest from the slope. It apparently had been part of the mound until recently, when the intense rain washed it out into the flat area next to the mound.

"Look at this." Chris broke off a few branches from a bush hanging over the opening and climbed down into the ravine. He dug into the soggy soil with his hands, exposing something hard, smooth, and cold. The more he dug, the more the shape of the object revealed itself. It was the shape of the corner of a gigantic cube and appeared to be made of concrete. Chris dug deeper. The further in he went, the more obvious it became that the object was manmade and made of concrete.

Chris didn't even notice that Jaime was gone. He dug energetically. In a few minutes Jaime returned with two shovels, one collapsible camping shovel from the tool kit in the Jeep and the other, a rusty old shovel he found in a shed behind the farmhouse. They began to dig in earnest, and before long, they exposed a substantial part of three sides of the cube.

"This could go on forever," Chris said, breathing heavily. "We don't know how deep this thing goes. But it looks like some kind of a bunker. Let's look around and see if we can find some clues as to what we've got here."

They walked around the mound and by the time they had traversed almost the entire perimeter, Jaime stopped and stared toward the base.

"What do you see?" asked Chris.

"Look at the ground between us and the mound. Doesn't it look different?"

Chris stepped back and eyeballed the ground. "Yes, I think you've got something there. It looks like the surface slopes downward toward the base. Everywhere else, the ground appears to be sloping away, except right here."

They pulled several bushes out of their line of vision. Beneath the bushes was a small earthen ramp, about four feet wide, heavily overgrown with grass and weeds, sloping down into the earth at the base. It ended in a wall of vines and leaves.

Chris took the larger shovel and hacked at the vegetation. The shovel blade struck something solid, not concrete, something with a metallic sound, accompanied by a deep, resonant echo.

The boys tore at the vine branches and leaves with their hands until they created a small opening about two feet in diameter. Behind the leaves and branches they saw a metal plate, rusted and covered with mold.

Jaime scratched at the plate with the sharp tip of the smaller shovel to satisfy himself that it was indeed metal. Sure enough, the pointed tip of the camping shovel made a scratch, revealing shiny steel beneath the rust and mold. Closer inspection showed that the plate was a door, secured by a padlock.

As the boys stood there trying to decide what to make of their discovery, the silence was broken by a muffled high-pitched sound coming from the direction of the farmhouse. They looked toward the house and then at each other, each with an expression on his face that said, "What the hell was *that*?"

In an instant they were both sprinting toward the farmhouse, Jaime in the lead. They scrambled up the front porch, three steps at a time, and burst into the main room, where the sleeping bags were still scattered about the floor. All was silent. No sign of Becky.

Chris started up the stairs to where he assumed the bedrooms were. Jaime headed toward what he thought was the dining room, intending to look in the kitchen. They each shouted Becky's name.

"Down here!" came the response. "Down here!"

Midway up the stairs, Chris spun around and followed Jaime in the direction of Becky's voice. They went through the dining room and into the kitchen. A door stood ajar in the center of one wall, next to a place where a refrigerator might have once been.

Looking through the opening, Jaime saw a wooden stairway leading down into what looked like a cellar. He saw faint flashes of light glancing intermittently off something near the bottom of the stairs.

Chris was now standing beside Jaime in the narrow doorway, as bewildered as Jaime about what they were seeing. He called out again for Becky.

"I'm okay," she answered. Her voice sounded a long way off, and she didn't sound okay.

Chris ran to his sleeping bag, retrieved a flashlight, and aimed it down the stairway. It didn't reveal much except that the cellar had a dirt floor. They started down the stairs, Chris in the lead.

When they reached the bottom, Chris flashed the light around the room. It was filled with rows of wooden shelves, lined with all kinds of empty cans, jars, and wooden boxes. They didn't see Becky. Jaime called her name again. No answer.

Chris turned off his flashlight.

"Why'd you do that?" whispered Jaime.

Chris explained that he wanted to see if he could locate the source of the flashes of light they had observed from the top of the stairs. Yes, there they were, coming from a far corner of the cellar. Chris turned on his flashlight again, and they moved in the direction of those faint flickers.

In the far corner of the cellar, they spotted an opening in the dirt wall, near the floor, about four feet high and three feet wide. The flashes were more intense now, obviously coming from the other side of the opening.

Jaime shouted, "Becky, are you in there?"

This time they could hear Becky and became aware that she was only a few feet away from them. They flashed their light through the opening and there she stood with a small flashlight in her hand. Her eyes were wide, as if she was either trying to see something just out of her field of vision or she had seen something she wished she hadn't. Tears on her cheeks reflected the dim light.

Jaime slid through the opening and gently took Becky's hand. She let out a sigh.

"What's wrong?" he asked.

Chris stepped into the room, his flashlight making it easier to see. He put his hand on Becky's shoulder.

Becky leaned against him and whispered, "I can't believe it. Take a look at the floor." As they lowered their flashlights, eerie shadows began to rise on the earthen walls.

They shone their lights through yet another opening into a larger room. Shadows likewise shimmered on the walls of that room.

Jaime glanced toward the floor searching for the cause of those ghostly shadows. He gasped and took a step backward.

Chris murmured, "Oh, my God."

There, staring up from the floor was a pair of vacuous eyes, an illusion created from within the depths of a human skull by the beam of the light.

Chris panned more of the floor, revealing dozens of human skeletons in various grotesque configurations, fragments of clothing clinging to them. In one corner, the light revealed a pile of bones which, upon closer inspection, appeared to be the remains of several small children.

Near the tops of the walls they could see small tunnels, angling upward, apparently dug by human fingers in a desperate attempt to escape.

Off to the right was another pile of remains, each of which bore fragments of clothing that looked like military uniforms.

In one corner they found a skeleton with another tiny skeleton within its rib cage. "Oh, no!" gasped Becky, as the realization hit her that this had been a pregnant woman.

Becky whispered, "Can you believe this? What happened here?" Her voice was still weak and quavering but showing traces of the rage she was feeling.

No reply.

Jaime squeezed her hand, imagining how she must have felt, finding this terrifying place all by herself.

"Let's get out of here," Chris urged.

As they turned toward the opening that would allow them access back to the main cellar room, the beam from Chris's flashlight fell upon four more skeletons. As the trio approached them, they could see that the victims had been tied together at the elbows with leather thongs so that each faced outward. They were in sitting positions. Each had a hole in the center of his forehead, and each appeared to have been wearing a uniform of the United States Army.

Jaime reached for Becky's arm and moved her gently toward the opening in the wall, then through it into the main cellar room and up the stairway to the kitchen. Chris remained behind for a few minutes, still searching for something that would make sense of what he was seeing.

When Chris arrived in the kitchen, they walked slowly to the front porch, where Becky and Jaime sat down on a rickety bench next to the front door. Becky began to cry, quietly at first, and then let out a sorrowful moan. She whispered, "Why?"

Jaime held her head against his neck and shoulder, one arm around her waist. Chris came over and placed his hands on Becky's shoulders, leaned down, and gently kissed her on the top of the head. He couldn't stop his own tears. Jaime clenched his teeth, trying not to let the scream that was building deep in his chest escape.

Chris sat down on the floor of the porch beside his friends, leaned his head against Becky's knees, and wrapped his arms around her lower legs. Becky placed her hand gently on Chris's head. Jaime placed his hand over Becky's. They sat there for a long time, saying nothing, each lost in his thoughts.

The sun made its way over the roof of the old farmhouse and began to shine on the front edge of the porch near the spot where Chris, Jaime, and Becky sat. For a long time Jaime watched the line between shadow and sunshine move ever so slowly toward them.

Finally Becky broke the silence. She told the boys that she had discovered an old diary under a loose wooden plank in the floor of an upstairs closet, beneath the bottom drawer of a built-in chest of drawers. She never would have thought of looking there except that the closet bore an astonishing resemblance to the one she had seen in her dream. The little girl in that dream had pointed to the bottom drawer of a chest of drawers, much like the one in the real closet.

"That's really spooky," Jaime said.

Chris added, "This whole place is spooky."

Becky got up slowly and stretched the kinks out of her back and neck. She went into the house and returned with the book in her hands.

She said she had read parts of the diary while she was waiting for Chris and Jaime to return from their walk. There was nothing unusual, just the romantic thoughts of a young girl, until she got to the last several pages. Then the handwriting changed. It appeared to be the writing of a younger person, with some misspellings and an awkward style. Becky asked if they wanted to hear a few excerpts from those last few pages, and they indicated an eagerness to listen.

Becky read:

I dont know why there keeping us here. Its something about the exploshun in the woods, The army guys got here just after it and wont let us go see, Today thay brot lots of our nabors and sum of our frends here in big army trucks, Even Aunt Ester and uncle Joe and there boys from way over in Henderson, There making us all stay in the house, Everyones scared, Mom says thay don't have a rite to keep us here. I am glad the house is so big or we woodnt all fit.

A few pages later:

Thay brot us more food today. The stuff Mom canned in the sellar is all gone. I dont like the food thay brot. Nothing but bredd and tuna and sumthing called spam. A lot of what were having to eat is in cans painted army colors. It tastes bad,

Then:

Those army guys spent all day putting cages on the windows and doors. Thay brot them in army trucks. I herd Dad telling uncle Joe that we are never gonna get out of here. Aunt Ester crys a lot. The army guys are mostly nice to us. Thay look at me kinda sad and try to make me feel better but the boss of them is not nice. He duz not have army close. He has a sute. Mom calls it a bisness sute. He has a man that follows him around and calls him sir. That man has a telefone that is not hooked to the wall. It has a wire on it Dad told me it is a antenna. He is always tocking to sum one on it. When he looks at me sumtimes he looks sad but he never lets the boss guy see when he looks at me. I see the yung army guys wisper to each other sumtimes. Then thay look at us kinda sad. Nun of them tock much.

Becky skipped a few pages and then read:

Sum of the army guys have been
bringing dirt up from the sellar for
a long time, seems like almost
all week. Thay work for a wile
and then thay go rest wile other
guys do the work. Jimmie says
there spredding the dirt from the
sellar in the feelds, He watches
them a lot from my bedroom
window. Jimmie is pretty smart,
He tocks a lot with Dad and
sum of the other men. I see
them wisper a lot. The army men
wont let us in the sellar anymore,
I saw the stares, Thay got bords on
them. Jimmie says its to make
the weel barros come up easy. I
counted 27 weel barros of dirt
befor I got tired of counting.
Besides I think I missed sum,

Becky skipped another page:

Our nabor Shirly is sick in the
mornings Mom says she is gonna
have a baby, Her tummy is getting
bigger. I dint say anything to her
becuz I thot maybe she was
just getting fat and I did not
want to hurt her feelings.
Shes real nice. Thay took all the
cans of food out of the kitchen.
Thay turned off our water. Dad

told one of the army guys about Shirlys
baby. He said shirly needs water. The
army guy looked real sorry but
he cant give us any water. He looked
like he was going to cry but he
left befor we saw. One of the men
came to the back porch window
after it got dark and put sum
food and a canvas thing of water
thru the bars. Jimmie saw him. He
says the next morning the man in
the bisness sute made 3 of the army
guys hold the one that brot us

food and put hand cuffs on
him and took him to the barn.
I am really scared.

Next page:

there telling us we all have to
go to the sellar tommorrow. Moms
crying. Im sorry for her. Im
sorry for everyone. I think that
thay are going to make us die.
Jimmie tried to bend the bars
on my bedroom window last nite
with a car jack Dad had on the
back porch. He got the bars
spred almost far enuf to get out.
The bad guys saw him befor he
got done and took the jack.

The boss guy made the army guys take Jimmie to the sellar. Thay took the army guy from the barn and put him in the sellar last nite too. He was bleeding from his nose. I hope sumbody will find this book sumday so sumbody will know what happened. Sum new guys just got here. They have guns like the ones in the space movies. There taking the army guys to the basement. The new guys are not nice. Thay dont smile at me. There treeting all of us very ruff. Im going to put Cindys book back befor thay make me go in the cellar too. One of the army guys saw me go upstares but he pretended not to see,

Last entry:

Im sad for Mom and Dad and our frends too. Mostly Im scared. I want to hide here. Maybe they wont think about me if I hide in this closet. But Mom and Dad need me to hold there hands so they wont be afrade. Thank you god for giving us

> this butiful farm and for my
> Mom and my Dad and for Cindy
> and stuart and for my puppy
> Jake. I am glad Jake got
> away. I love you world, Now
> I am going to go. Goodby.

Becky set down the book on the bench and slowly walked to the far end of the porch. Jaime picked up the book and held it to his chest, looking up at the sky. Chris sat where he was, biting his lower lip and clenching his fists.

# Chapter Thirty-one

Becky wasn't the only one who had dreamt while sleeping in the farmhouse the previous night. As the three friends slept soundly on the living room floor, Chris spent a few hours wrestling with some nighttime visions of his own.

He dreamed of running down long, dark corridors, sensing that something was following him but unable to see what it was. He could hear its breathing and even smell its vile stench. But whenever he looked back, all he saw was a vague, shimmering shadow in the distance. He didn't dare look back for long. He felt a need to keep moving.

Three times, as he was attempting in vain to elude his relentless pursuer, Chris was attracted to a light in one of the many alcoves lining the unending corridors. Each time, the light gave him instant relief from the terror he felt, as if its presence alone could render whatever was on his trail temporarily impotent, sort of like a nocturnal time-out.

The light in the first alcove Chris came to was flickering dimly. He stepped into the room and found, to his surprise, that it was a small reading room, its walls lined with books. The room smelled like a library except that it had an additional aroma that Chris thought might be the smoke from a pleasant, mild pipe tobacco. The source of the light was a candle in a crimson glass candle holder with an ornate gold base, resting on a small, round, dark wooden table. On either side of the table was an easy chair.

Those chairs were irresistibly inviting. Chris sat in the one on the right. It was soft and warm, comfortable beyond any chair Chris had ever sat in. He looked at the bookshelf behind the opposite chair, his eyes drawn there by some power he didn't understand. Chris was no longer mindful of the creature in the corridor. His mind was focused totally on those books. There was something about them that wouldn't turn loose of his attention. He could make out the titles of only a few of them. The light from the candle wasn't adequate for him to read the lettering on the others. Then he realized that every one of the books he was able to identify was a book he had read with Great-Grandfather. He found this most curious but not alarming.

When Chris looked back toward the table, he was startled to see someone seated in the opposite chair. The candlelight obscured his vision to the point where he could see the outline of a man but none of his features.

A weathered hand reached out and slowly pulled the candle toward the stranger, the golden base of the candle holder making a soft, scraping sound on the tabletop. The movement of the candle gradually brought the man's facial features into view. There, hovering above the flame were the twinkling eyes, long white hair, and haunting smile of Great-Grandfather.

He didn't greet Chris or move to embrace him, as Chris would have expected. He just sat there smiling that all-knowing smile. Then, in an instant, Great-Grandfather's look turned deadly serious. He said, "We of the Spirit World can never interfere with the free will of those who are earthbound. We can, however, with your permission or at your invitation, share the wisdom we have by virtue of our broader perspective."

Chris said, "Please, Great-Grandfather, I'm eager to hear any words you think may be of benefit to me."

Great-Grandfather then said, "You are about to embark on a grand adventure that could involve much danger. I believe you are unusually well prepared for many of the challenges that await you, because of the lessons you and I shared in those wondrous days when I was focused in physical form.

"I now know that death is not to be feared. One day, you and I will be reunited in the Spirit World, and you will then know, as I do, that death is a most glorious experience, bringing you feelings of love and freedom beyond anything you have experienced on Earth.

"I do not enter your consciousness at this time to spare you the death experience. That will come, as always, at the appropriate time. But, from my greater perspective, it appears that you have much to live for in this incarnation and much to teach those who will follow you. I see the possibility of a most beautiful relationship, of a romantic nature, that promises the likelihood of many generations of spiritually advanced descendents, who will bring much needed enlightenment to the people of planet Earth.

"I shall be with you in the very instant that you think of me or call my name. And, although I will not interfere in a direct, physical manner, I will provide you with notions or hunches that will serve you well.

"As you and I discussed long ago, the Bible of your Christian religions, which many in the spirit world refer to as 'The Book of Books,' has been corrupted over the centuries. Sometimes this was the natural result of the human frailties of its translators. Sometimes discrepancies were caused by the subtle differences between various languages and dialects. Most insidiously, serious and substantial changes to the Bible occurred as a result of the deliberate acts of church leaders and monarchs, who rewrote the 'Word of God' to suit their own purposes.

"For now, I believe you will be well advised to remember and take to heart the words, 'When two or more of you are gathered in my name, there is love.'

"My knowing of the meaning of those words is that whenever two or more entities work in harmony, focus their energies for a common goal, and do so with great desire and faith in the power and goodness of the God Force, their ability to achieve the intended result is multiplied many times.

"You will not likely remember the details of what you are now hearing and seeing, but you will carry with you the feelings necessary to summon forth the lessons you will have learned when they are needed."

In an instant, Great-Grandfather was gone, leaving Chris pondering the meaning of his words.

Once again Chris became aware of the ominous presence in the corridor and at first was reluctant to leave the alcove. He then reasoned that he would probably stand a better chance out in the corridor, where he could at least run, than to be trapped in the alcove with or without Great-Grandfather.

At a dead run, Chris entered the corridor and hoped the demon was behind him and not in the direction he was running. He ran for what seemed like many minutes in total darkness. Then he saw a bright blue light in the distance. As he approached, he saw that the light was coming from yet another room alongside the corridor. He slowed his pace and approached the light with caution. This light didn't have a single source that Chris could identify. It seemed to him as if the entire room were glowing with a peaceful blue light emanating from the walls and ceiling.

Chris stepped quickly into the room, immediately feeling a deep sense of inner peace, as if the blue light itself produced a tranquilizing effect. He stood there for a few moments, reveling in the serenity of the place. A soft breeze rustled the velvet curtains that covered the far wall. Chris thought he heard a sound. It reminded him of a faint, whispered sigh, as if coming from a chorus of tiny children in the distance.

The breeze increased slightly, and the curtains parted. There, leaning against a brick wall, where a door or window should have logically been, stood a man in uniform. An Air Force cap rested on his head at a jaunty angle. His arms were folded across his chest. One ankle was crossed over the other in a casual manner. He was a

handsome man, with dark black hair, deep blue eyes, and an endearing smile. He looked familiar.

"Hi, Chris," he said. "My name's John. You can call me 'Dad'
if you'd like."

Chris felt his heart leap. *Dad? My Dad?*

"Dad…I don't know what to say. What are you doing here?"

"The question is, 'What are you doing here?' It's your dream."

"Dream?" Chris asked.

"Yes, a dream. You don't think stuff like this happens in real
life, do you? You know—the monster in the corridor, the blue light,
the whispering kiddies."

"But it seems so real," said Chris.

"It *is* real."

"But you said it was a dream."

"You don't think dreams are real?"

"I know they're real, real dreams, that is. But not real, like
really real."

"Eventually you may come to realize that what you call dreams
are, in some ways, more real than the stuff you think you experience
when you're awake. But we'll have a talk about all this someday when
we've got lots of time or, more accurately, when there is no time. Right
now I want to tell you a few things that I think are far more important.

"First of all, I want you to know how sorry I am that I left you
and your mother. There were reasons I had to cross over into the Spirit
World that didn't allow me the option of staying with you. For now, just
know it was your choice, before you focused your energy into your
present physical reality, to be born into a family without a father. If I
had stayed, I would have interfered with your plans for the experiences
you chose to have in this lifetime.

"Second, know that I love you with a most powerful and
uncommon love.

"Third, I wish for you to know that I have watched over you all
of your life, not for the purpose of protecting you. We can't do that.
You choose your own events and circumstances and we do not interfere. But I was there to send you an occasional 'nudge,' a subconscious suggestion regarding a direction I thought you might wish to

consider. My job was easy. You had your mother's grandfather right
there with you. His wisdom, even on the physical plane, is the closest
thing I've seen to the knowing we experience here in the spirit world.

"Although you don't know it, I'm here right now in answer to
your invitation. On a level of consciousness that I have no words to
describe, you want or will want my guidance. Remember, where I
reside, there is no such thing as time, and all things happen at once.

"The best guidance I can give you at this time, short of interfering directly with your reality, is to tell you to remember, when all
bears the appearance of hopelessness that nothing is as it appears,
that everything is subject to change, that nothing happens by accident, and that everything is the result of thought.

"Most of all, remember that this physical world, which your
senses seem to tell you is there, is of your own creation and is change-
able in an instant by the mere changing of your thoughts.

"Someday, in Earth time, you will cross over into the spirit world.
In that instant, which is just another part of now, you will know all of
these things as certainties. In the meantime, your Great-Grandfather
and I thought some information that doesn't directly affect the time/
space continuum might be in order, to make the game easier for you to
play, considering the seemingly overwhelming opponents you are about
to bring into your reality."

The wind blew hard, the curtains swirled, and Dad was gone.

Strangely, the first thought that entered Chris's mind was, "What
the hell's the wind doing blowing inside a building?"

His second thought was, "What did Dad mean by opponents
I'm about to bring into my reality?"

In a way, Chris knew this was a dream. But he still had to get out
of it. Perhaps he could awaken himself. But it seemed so real. And,
except for the evil dude in the corridor, the dream had been fairly
pleasant so far.

He headed down the endless corridor, wondering what lay in
store for him. "Maybe," he thought, "I might open the next door I
come to and find myself back in the world of solid matter."

A low, gurgling sound startled Chris. It grew louder. Then it
became heavy breathing, almost a snorting. Chris thought he could

feel warm air on the back of his neck. It smelled bad. It made him think of a tuna salad that had been left out of the refrigerator for a few days. He reminded himself that this was just a dream. He heard something scraping on the floor behind him. The "it's just a dream" ploy didn't work. Chris looked around, and there stood the ugliest creature he had ever seen or even imagined.

The creature, standing no more than five feet from Chris, was so hideous that he couldn't capture its essence in words. Chris spun around and sprinted at a speed intended to place as much distance between him and the creature as the laws of physics—even the laws of physics as they occur in dreams—would allow.

He ran until he thought his legs would give out. Just when he felt he could run no more, the walls on either side of the dark and dreary corridor peeled back, the bricks disconnecting, crumbling, and falling to the ground, revealing a glorious sunlit garden.

The monster was no longer in sight.

The garden had an exquisite pond, accented with lily pads, blooming gaily with flowers of pink and lavender. Near the far shore, two swans silently skimmed the water's surface in the warm sunlight. A large weeping willow graced the near shore of the pond, its branches bending into the water, a gentle breeze causing its leaves to stir the water's surface.

From the uppermost branches of the willow, a hand-carved wooden swing was suspended from two thick, braided ropes with alternating pastel colors of white, yellow, and blue. Sitting on the swing was a young woman in a long, flowing gown. She was facing away from Chris, swinging gently, gazing toward the swans in the distance.

As Chris approached, the lady turned to greet him with a warm, knowing smile. Her large, almond-shaped eyes twinkled merrily in the glorious sunshine.

It was Wendy, the woman of the burgundy misbehaving convertible, the longed-for lady who had stolen his heart only a few days ago.

"What are you doing here?" he asked, "And where are we?"

Wendy answered, "I'm here in response to your wish. Your soul called out to mine. I sensed that you needed me. I'm in a dream state just as you are. My body is sleeping comfortably in my bed back home.

My soul has come to this point of consciousness, for a brief time, to be with yours. I feel words flowing through me that would best be shared with you."

"Please go on," urged Chris.

"These words are not mine. I know not their source, only the deep feeling that accompanies them. I will now speak them as faithfully as I can: 'Your deep sense of loyalty and profound love for those you most cherish will render you susceptible to forces that would appear to be evil. Do not allow yourself to be deceived by appearances. Stay close to your higher self and listen well. Rise above the illusions of the physical world, to the extent you can. The times that are upon you will require great courage and nerves of steel, tempered by the feminine aspects of your being.'

"The following words are my own: I now know that we have been together as dear friends and lovers in many prior lifetimes. Our meeting last week was not by accident. I have been searching for you all my life. The part of my self that is in physical form does not have a conscious memory of the specifics of who you are, only a yearning for your essence. My higher self, which is part of what you see before you now, knows you completely and intimately but cannot impart that knowledge to the self that is focused in my physical body, except through feeling. I have felt you all my life. I have longed for you. I have tried to find you in others, only to be disappointed.

"I tell you these things because our new relationship, which began so recently in this physical lifetime, has not existed long enough to accumulate the experiences and memories that are necessary to give it the strength to survive the challenges we will each face in the next few days. I wish for our time together in this incarnation to be long and joyful. I will do what I can for my physical Wendy. I ask that you do whatever you can for your physical Chris, who is even now sleeping peacefully in his sleeping bag on the farmhouse floor. I know that you adore your physical self as I do mine. Together we can make a powerful difference for the future of Wendy and Chris and, perhaps, for the people of planet Earth."

Chris reached out and touched Wendy's hand and, in that instant, felt more joy than he had ever imagined possible. As he looked into her loving eyes, she smiled, and in that smile Chris saw eternity.

Chris awakened to the warmth of his sleeping bag. He vaguely remembered having a dream of some sort. He sat up, rumpled his hair, and saw Becky sitting across the floor of the living room of the old farmhouse, staring at the ragged curtains that were blowing in the breeze.

Now, several hours later, the trio was sitting on the porch of the farmhouse, trying to make sense of the bunker in the forest, the bodies in the basement, and the contents of the diary. Chris suggested that they go back to the forest to see if they could discover the purpose of the concrete structure and whether it had anything to do with the murders that were committed in the basement.

Chapter Thirty-two

The small apartment where Herbert Benson III lived was on the third floor of a dingy brownstone building that looked exactly like all the other buildings on the block. Benson could have easily afforded a nicer place. He knew he deserved a much nicer abode, at least based on his economic status. But he took some satisfaction in knowing that he was living beneath his means. Living beneath his means was an additional penance he performed on a daily basis, as retribution for his many sins.

His apartment was just like every other apartment in the building, and the building itself couldn't be distinguished from dozens of others in the neighborhood, except for the rusty street numbers above the entry, adding to the feeling of anonymity that Benson needed so desperately. When a person was a bad seed, the end result of an entire chain of bad seeds, anonymity was a precious commodity.

Nobody ever came into Benson's apartment. Nobody was invited. Nobody was welcome. The mailbox that had been assigned to him, in the small dark entry of the building, was never used. He hadn't bothered to put his name on the box. He didn't like mailboxes. Mailboxes symbolized to Benson contact with the outside world, a world full of evil, a world full of sinful people. In Benson's mind, mailboxes fell into the same category as newspapers and televisions. They were potential leaks in his security system, capable of allowing the poison from the evil deeds of Satan's followers to seep into Benson's secure world. The only reason he even owned a television was to allow him to watch religious programs on Sunday mornings.

Bad seeds spawned of other bad seeds had to take serious precautions to keep evil from entering their world. Otherwise the penance couldn't be devoted exclusively to atoning for all transgressions against the laws of the Church. Some of that penance would have to be diverted to offset the evil that entered the world daily, an inefficient way of utilizing the forms of suffering he had devised to help earn his way back into the good graces of the Church.

Now computers were another matter. These modern devices were in a totally different category from newspapers, televisions, radios, and other forms of communication used by Satan's media network. Computers could be used in such a manner as to allow nothing unwanted in while providing Benson an efficient and controllable method of observing the sources of sin in the world.

Benson didn't have an e-mail address. An e-mail address would allow the forces of evil access into his private world. But the Web had no such shortcoming. It allowed him to control his world without being observed.

He often wondered if the World Wide Web had been created by his God, the God of hellfire and damnation, the God of vengeance and retribution, to allow those on the path back to righteousness and blessedness to become his disciples in the war against evil.

Then one fateful and terrible day, while he was surfing the Web, Benson found that Satan had hacked his way into it too. There, before his very eyes, appeared pornography, one of Satan's most powerful weapons. There, on the very World Wide Web that he had previously regarded as sacred appeared debasement and debauchery, the ultimate manifestations of sin.

From that moment on, he used the Web with extreme caution, knowing that the forces of evil had infiltrated God's system. He felt compelled to visit those evil sites regularly to keep himself informed as to the enemy's progress. He wanted to be prepared when the Lord would call upon him to strike fear into the hearts of the evil-doers. The realization that his daily visits to those vortexes of pornography caused him to engage in sinful thoughts troubled his mind. He decided, however, that this was the price he would have to pay to be part of God's army. Besides, he had increased his level of penance considerably. This, he felt, would more than compensate for the items added to the sinful side of the ledger that was being maintained for him in the judgment halls of Heaven.

Benson's small living room had only three pieces of furniture— the table upon which his small black-and-white television sat, a wooden chair where he rested when he could no longer tolerate the physical pain he inflicted upon himself, and a large, low table where he arranged his implements of self-torture in neat, orderly rows.

The rest of the room was devoted to dozens of cages, stacked three high, where he kept his only sources of companionship—weasels.

Several years ago he had stumbled across a nest of baby weasels under a bush down by the river that ran along the edge of a park where he had gone for a breath of fresh air. He didn't follow the paths in the park but chose, instead, to wander through the under-growth where others would not likely see him. He didn't go there before sunset. Anonymity was a precious commodity. He used a small penlight to find his way through the trees and bushes, always carrying a spare battery in case the light began to dim.

Benson wouldn't have seen the critters, which had been well hidden by their mother under a large bush, except that the beam from his penlight happened to fall upon a tiny eyeball that reflected the light back to the precise location of Benson's eyes. He took this as a sign from the Almighty and decided that God wanted him to utilize these creatures for His purposes. He scooped them up into his coat pocket and hurried home, where he spent much of his time from that moment on caring for these signs from Heaven. He knew these ani-mals were symbols that God had chosen him, in spite of his life of sin, to be a part of God's army in the fight against evil. He couldn't imagine what purpose these weasels could play in the upcoming war, but he knew one thing for sure: He knew that God worked in mysterious ways and that it was a sin of the most grievous nature to ever question the ways of the Lord.

By the time Benson joined the CIA, his family of weasels had multiplied to more than fifty.

He knew that the second most powerful force for good in the world, after the Church, of course, was the United States government. He wasn't a stupid man. He knew enough to be aware that there were lots of evil individuals working for the government. But that was not the fault of the government. It was a result of man's evil nature, having been born in a state of original sin. But to Benson's way of thinking, that fact no more detracted from the perfection of the government than the fact that some church leaders, who were occasionally discovered engaging in acts of sin, detracted from the perfection of the Church.

Yes, the United States government was a powerful force for good in the world. And, even though Benson couldn't regard it as infallible, he knew it was mighty close.

After all, didn't wording on the silver dollar he had hanging above the headboard of his bed next to his crucifix contain the phrase "In God we trust"? And didn't the Declaration of Independence, drafted by God's chosen founders of this nation, say "One nation under God"? What more proof did anyone need?

Benson would have been shocked to know that the God of the Founding Fathers was a lot closer to The Force known to Tim and Jaime Lasher than to the God of organized religion. Had such knowledge come to his attention, he might have been pushed over the edge, if he wasn't there already.

It was with feelings of both holiness and patriotism that Benson had applied for an entry level position with the CIA. He felt so honored to be accepted that he expressed his gratitude to the Lord by stepping up his program of daily penance.

Within a few years, Benson's passion and devotion, not to mention his willingness to accept and carry out orders without question, brought him to a position of considerable responsibility, complete with a high-level security clearance and a code name, under which he performed most of his tasks. The position could not have been better suited to his belief system, providing him with the anonymity he so cherished and the added bonus of power, which he was surprised to find he coveted.

He wasn't aware that the CIA had taken steps to erase his past completely, in addition to totally replacing his name in all government records, inside and outside of the realm of the CIA, with his code name.

Benson might have lost a bit of his regard for the federal government had he learned that a substantial part of the CIA's motive in providing him with his sought-after anonymity was to put him in a position where the CIA could delete him from its files, not to mention the face of the earth, with surprisingly little effort.

It was with stunned trepidation that Benson had secretly observed his supervisor shutting off the power to the air supply for Daryl Harrington's cubicle. After all, murder is prohibited by the Ten Commandments. But he managed to rationalize his complicity by reasoning that his supervisor was probably only following orders, commands from some unknown higher authority who certainly knew more than he did about national security. *Ours is not to reason why. Ours is but to do or die.*

Or die.

But that was last Friday. Benson had had a lot of time to think over the weekend. He now realized he had made a big mistake, maybe not when he had decided to ignore his supervisor's conduct. A man in his position has to close his eyes to some forms of evil.

No, he had made his big mistake when he had decided to leave the area early instead of visiting the federal facility to make sure the procedure had been successful. He had weighed the risk of being observed near the scene of the "incident" or being implicated in the murder. He wasn't sure why he had felt obligated to check the murder scene. After all, it had nothing to do with him. It was only by accident that he had observed his boss turning off the air supply.

He now knew that he had made the wrong decision. When you work for the federal government, you have to put the welfare of the nation before your own safety. He should have made certain that Harrington was dead.

Now, three days later, Harrington was alive and free and maybe in possession of information that could get some powerful people in a lot of trouble. Those powerful people might conclude or decide that Harrington's escape was Benson's fault.

And now his supervisor had dumped the entire matter in his lap. When that supervisor, a powerful, dreadful, hateful man named Frank Sheffield, had discovered that Harrington's body was not in the cubicle, he had informed Benson that it was up to him to capture and terminate Harrington. He told Benson that if anything ever were to come of this, it would be Benson who would swing from the gallows, not him. Not Frank Sheffield. He had already taken the necessary steps to ensure that all of the evidence was in place, and carefully documented, to convince any investigating team or any court of law, for that matter, that it had been Benson who had flipped those circuit breakers on his own authority.

What a mess.

He now was not only at risk that the CIA might reprimand him for being involved in the screw-up or that they might even relieve him of his position. He was now in danger of going to jail or worse. He didn't even want to think about the "or worse."

On the other hand, if he had gone to the scene of the incident Friday evening to be sure Harrington was dead, he might now be answering some sticky questions in a police interrogation room.

What a mess.

He supposed he could have gone over his supervisor's head. He could have told someone who could have done something about it. But how high would he have had to go to find someone who wasn't involved in the matter? Besides, it was too late now.

Why was the Lord punishing him? Why had he been placed in such an impossible situation? Maybe he had been too lax about his penance. Maybe he hadn't suffered enough. He vowed that he would correct that situation starting tonight.

Right now he had to save his ass. Harrington could cause a lot of trouble if he were not found soon, and then what? He knew that Harrington would be terminated as soon as he was captured.

And that was murder. He couldn't be involved in murder. Still, he had almost been an accomplice to murder when he had seen Sheffield throw those circuit breakers and had remained silent.

But Harrington was an enemy of the state. The future of the nation was at stake. Benson had no choice. His duty to God and country demanded that he capture Harrington and turn him over to Sheffield.

That was it. He had to do it. He would worry later about confessing his sins and doing penance. Right now he had to save his ass.

What he had to do next was to decide whether he would try to apprehend Harrington with the help of the small number of agents he presently had under his command or whether he would go to someone with higher authority and have him bring in the heavy artillery.

If he did that, this matter would become an intelligence operation, with the full power of the CIA behind it. Harrington would be history. He would simply disappear. Harrington's death would almost be a certainty.

Then an idea came to him. Maybe there was a way he could solve the problem short of getting Harrington killed. Maybe he could find Harrington and convince him to drop out of sight. He could find Harrington, convince him that his only chance to remain alive would to be to disappear forever. Harrington would assume a new identity and move to another country. He could tell his supervisor that he had killed Harrington and permanently disposed of the body. That way, Benson would be off the hook with the CIA, the nation would not be compromised by what Harrington knew, and God wouldn't throw him into the everlasting fires of Hell. He would need a lot of years to do penance for what he had already done.

But someone would undoubtedly find out. There would be repercussions. At the very least, he would be called before a disciplinary board, maybe worse. After all, he never knew for sure how secure his position was. Maybe the CIA considered him as expendable as it considered Harrington.

Benson finally decided he had to handle this matter himself. Better not involve anyone in the higher echelons. Better not complicate the situation any more than it already was. He'd have to play it by ear. Take one step at a time.

He turned on his computer and called up a list of several agents who were low enough in the CIA hierarchy to be subject to his control.

He ran the profiles of these agents through a screening procedure he set up in the computer to weed out those who didn't meet his criteria. His screening parameters were designed to ensure that those selected were capable of carrying out his orders without questioning the moral implications.

He came up with thirty-two agents he thought he could trust, not only to keep their mouths shut but to act in accordance with his orders without doing any unnecessary thinking. He told himself these agents were dependable. Some would have called them "psychotic." Any clear-thinking person of reasonable intelligence would have recognized them as trained killers, having little or no conscience and a federally sanctioned license to kill. These men were at the bottom of the hierarchy because they lacked any drive or ambition. They were just getting by until retirement, slurping at the public trough.

What Benson desperately hoped was that, by arming himself with this team of unscrupulous scoundrels and by keeping them under tight control, he would come up with a way to get Harrington out of his hair.

By the time Benson, with the help of five assistants, had rounded up these thirty two agents, it was late Monday afternoon. He now had the manpower he needed. What he didn't have was a clue as to Daryl Harrington's whereabouts.

❦   ❦

Where Daryl Harrington was, was on his way to the scene of the CIA massacre, more than thirty years after the event, hoping that he would find evidence to back up the gruesome facts set forth in the CIA file he had discovered. Before leaving the city, Daryl went to a remote region of the county and located a telephone junction box along a seldom-used gravel road. He had decided that the less he used his cell phone, the better. He removed the cover plate from the box and, with the aid of the alligator clips he had used to open the lock on his cubicle door, connected his computer modem to an active telephone line.

He was able to reach *El Jefe*, who was now staying close to his computer around the clock. Daryl told the Chief that he needed him to continue keeping a close eye on any activities in the CIA computer systems. Daryl said he'd try to check in from time to time, if and when he had access to a phone line. He also said that he was sorry he couldn't reveal where he was or where he was heading for fear that the bad guys might be listening in.

El Jefe said, "I know just about where you are at this very moment. Do you think you're dealing with a beginner here?"

Strangely, Daryl took some comfort in the knowledge that the big guy knew so much. But, still, he didn't know who *El Jefe* was. He wasn't certain he could be trusted. But what choice did he have? *El Jefe* was his only comrade in this deadly game. Daryl decided then and there that he had to trust him, to assume that he was really on his side. Who else was there?

Daryl signed off and headed back across town, this time in the direction of the old farmhouse.

Benson had already faxed an official CIA communiqué regarding Daryl Harrington, including a recent photo, to several agencies, including all city police stations, county sheriff offices, and state highway patrol headquarters, within a two-hundred-mile radius, plus the alcohol and tobacco boys and the FBI. He informed these agencies that Harrington must be taken alive and kept isolated from all contact with anyone and everyone, even from anyone else associated with the CIA, until Benson himself arrived on the scene. That was a risky thing to do, but it was less risky than having Harrington tell what he might know to someone in one of those agencies.

As a safety precaution, Benson didn't affix his signature to the communiqué. He had slipped the original of that communiqué into a small stack of routine memorandums being signed on his behalf by one of his subordinates. He stood over the subordinate, urging him to sign the memos quickly, stating that they had to be sent out within minutes. The subordinate didn't have a chance to notice that the stack included the official CIA communiqué regarding Harrington. The fact that the fax was sent over an official CIA line on CIA stationery gave the document a presumed credibility. As an added precaution, Benson sent the subordinate home for the rest of the day and stationed one of his psycho agents at the subordinate's desk with instructions as to exactly what he was to say if anyone were to call for verification of the fax's authenticity.

The other agents were sent out into the field in search of Harrington, with instructions to keep their cell phones on at all times in case he needed to contact them. Benson wondered if he hadn't gone too far, sending out false information to all of those governmental agencies. But what choice did he have? He had to stop Harrington before he did serious harm to the United States. Besides, if something came of this, his men would certainly join him in dumping the entire matter in the lap of the subordinate whose name Benson had caused to be affixed to the faxes. None of these guys would hesitate to dump a mess like this in the lap of some desk jockey. They would be as anxious to protect themselves as he was.

By 4:30 on Monday afternoon, dozens of law enforcement officers were searching for Daryl Harrington. Benson had all of his men in place. He was confident they would turn up something on Harrington any minute now.

What nobody knew or even suspected was that Daryl Harrington was on his way to the farmhouse compound.

 # Chapter Thirty-three

Herbert Benson III was not a confident man. Ever since the attempt to eliminate Daryl Harrington had failed, he had been in a state of almost constant agitation. He knew that if the matter didn't get resolved soon, the blame would likely be laid at his doorstep even though he had had nothing to do with it. That was one of the dangers of having a psycho for a boss. Benson couldn't sleep. He couldn't eat. He developed a terrible rash under his armpits and in his groin, the likely result of his outrageous nervous condition.

Yes, he now had on his team several hired killers, acting under the auspices of the CIA. But Daryl Harrington was still alive and very likely had in his possession sufficient information to link several high-ranking officials in the "company" to the 1975 massacre of thirty-three civilians and soldiers in an old Victorian farmhouse.

Benson sat at his desk, dressed only in his boxer shorts, socks, and garters, applying calamine lotion to the inflamed areas of his body. He didn't want to think about the deaths of all of those innocent people, especially the children. But he couldn't stop himself.

For more than thirty years, he had managed fairly well to keep his thoughts far away from the dreaded topic. He had convinced himself long ago that his silence on the matter didn't implicate him in the disgusting police action that had resulted in the deaths of so many.

Shortly after he became aware of the murders, Benson "got religion" for the second time in his life. Just because he didn't have the courage to blow the whistle on Frank Sheffield, the man who had ordered those innocent people killed, didn't mean he was an accomplice in the eyes of God. He entered into a period of self-designed and self-inflicted penance.

Now, thirty years later, he found himself an accomplice to the recent attempted murder of Daryl Harrington by Frank Sheffield, the same evil monster who had killed all of those innocent people so long ago. Benson concluded that all of those years of penance hadn't improved his character much.

He wondered whether confession might ease his conscience. The Catholic Church's concept of confession had always offended him. He couldn't understand by what magic the simple telling of one's sins to another human being could erase them forever from the celestial slate. But, as someone once said, "Necessity is the mother of invention." Benson needed badly to be freed from his fear of eternal damnation and, strangely the Church's ritual of confession seemed to be the answer, in spite of its inability to satisfy him intellectually.

The combination of Benson's clinging desperately to the hope that there might be some truth to the Church's teachings about confession plus his innate ability to rationalize, succeeded in relieving him on occasion of the terrible guilt he carried with him. But since Harrington had managed to uncover the buried Zephyr file and possibly escaped from his cubicle with a copy of it—or at the very least the knowledge of its existence—Benson's guilt returned with a vengeance.

The newly resurrected guilt, by itself, would not have been sufficient to cause the physical manifestations currently assaulting

Benson's body. It was the guilt, acting as a catalyst for much greater fears, that caused Benson's nervous system to betray him.

For days now, Benson had been unable to control his mind. No matter what methods he used to distract himself from the gnawing thoughts, he couldn't stop thinking about the very real possibility that he could end up on death row or be terminated by the CIA. On those rare occasions when his state of utter exhaustion caused him to fall into a fitful sleep he had nightmares more terrifying than anything he had ever encountered in his life. Upon awakening, usually in a cold sweat, his immediate thoughts were about the old farmhouse and the evidence lurking there, ready to unfold before the media, the general public, and the Department of Justice. These thoughts would cause his stomach to contract and a wave of nausea to sweep through his system. Often the sensations were so intense that they ended with a tingling and itching in his hands and feet that drove him almost crazy.

Benson now found himself in the midst of one of those assaults upon his nervous system. He reached pitifully for his bottle of calamine lotion, knowing that the relief created thereby would be minimal and temporary. Just moments ago he had downed a couple of Advil tablets, hoping against hope for some relief. So intense was the discomfort that it took all of the will power he had to keep from screaming,.

Eventually the pain subsided to a point where he could engage in some semblance of rational thought.

To his great disappointment, he couldn't prevent his mind from turning to thoughts of those days of insanity in1975, the year of his undoing.

Benson remembered vividly the day it all began. It started as a routine day with memos crossing his desk from various departments. In those days, he enjoyed a moderately high-ranking position with responsibility for seven department heads and about a hundred men and women in the field. He was what a casual observer would assume to be stable and well-adjusted. Certainly he wouldn't have been able to work his way up through the ranks of the CIA if he wasn't able at least to give that impression. Certain weaknesses of character secretly plagued Benson, but he managed to keep them buried well below the surface of the persona he presented to the rest of the world.

At about ten o'clock that morning, Benson received an urgent message from the head of his department, a young man named Frank Sheffield. Benson was instructed to be at an underground strategy room in an hour and fifteen minutes and to discuss this with no one.

Upon arriving at the meeting place, Benson found seven other people present, including Sheffield. Benson knew none of the other people in the room.

The room was locked, and the equipment that had been installed to block any attempted surveillance was activated. Benson could sense that others in the room were just as mystified and curious as he was—highly unusual. Sheffield gestured for each of them to take a seat around a large, oval, glass-topped table. He informed them that Benson would be in charge, directly under his command, and they were about to be made aware of some facts that were vital to national security.

"In fact," he said, "what you are about to learn could have dire and long-term effects for the entire planet."

As Benson and the others sat there, sensing the tension that was rapidly building in the room, Sheffield proceeded to inform them that each had been chosen for the task before them by a computer search of the personnel roster of employees in the immediate vicinity. They were told that the criteria used in the search were quite unusual. They had been chosen because each had certain character traits that would enable him to overlook any qualms he might have regarding the propriety of any action he was ordered to take.

"Most important," Sheffield said, "each of you has one or more potentially devastating skeletons buried in your closet, which we have taken great care to uncover and document. This leads us to believe that you will provide us with the utmost in enthusiastic and unfailing cooperation.

"If that isn't sufficient to guarantee your complete, unquestioning loyalty to this cause, you will be well-advised that each of you is considered totally expendable. That is, failure to carry out any command will likely result in your immediate termination, both legally and physically. In other words, you will cease to exist. Do I make myself clear?"

Benson could feel the muscles in his abdomen, neck, and shoulders tighten. He could see that those words had similarly affected the others in the room. All were silent.

They then were informed that two days earlier one of NASA's deep-space listening stations had picked up a transmission, broadcast in seven different languages, from a spacecraft that was obviously in trouble. That, they were informed, wasn't the first time contact with extra-terrestrials had occurred. In the past, messages such as this were recorded and the recordings hidden. On those occasions when the craft had actually landed, there had been no radio contact and the incidents were quickly covered up, the occupants of the craft destroyed, and witnesses eliminated.

The group was then told that what made this event worthy of the CIA's attention was that this craft was heading toward the Earth, with its navigational system seriously damaged, requesting a safe place to land. The craft was in need of a large landing area. In that the then-current administration had established an absolute policy that any contacts from outer space were to be buried, under penalty of termination with extreme prejudice, the request for help was not forwarded to anyone who could assist the craft.

An order was issued to the Air Force, informing those needing to know that the blip they would likely be picking up on their radar screens had been identified by NASA as a small meteorite heading for Earth, and it had been determined that it would either burn out after entering Earth's atmosphere or, if not, it would collide with Earth in a vast and unpopulated area where no serious harm would be done. This order was issued to a small number of high-ranking Air Force officers, with instructions that they were to ensure that this information would be forwarded to only those who absolutely "needed to know."

There was to be no attempt to destroy the meteorite. They were to track it with only the minimum number of radar stations necessary, and to report the point of impact only to the officer issuing the order.

Similar orders were apparently issued in the few other countries having listening and tracking capabilities sufficient to make them aware of the situation.

In the orders issued to the select few who actually knew that the blip on the radar screen was a spacecraft, it was made absolutely clear that, so as not to alarm the general public, with the likely effects such alarm would have on the stock market and the safety of citizens in major cities, where rioting would undoubtedly ensue, all reports of this incident were to be permanently obscured in the most inaccessible area of the CIA archives.

Nobody had made provisions for the eventuality that a transmission such as that just received might be from a spacecraft in the vicinity of Earth. Nobody had ever seriously considered the possibility of such a situation, in that all previous transmissions intercepted by NASA had come from sources light years from Earth, with virtually no likelihood that their existence could affect our planet within the ensuing century.

The order, which commanded the withholding of assistance from the crippled spacecraft, had been issued with the hope that the spacecraft would choose an alternative planet on which to land or, if it was unable to do so, that it would crash into an ocean and never be seen again. If the worst happened and it were to crash on land, chances were better than ten to one that it would do so in an unpopulated area, where knowledge of its arrival could likely be contained.

As the time of impact approached, what little radar tracking was being conducted on the troubled craft indicated that the building occupied by Benson was probably the closest federal facility of its kind to the site of the spacecraft's anticipated point of collision. The meeting Benson attended on that fateful morning back in 1975 was hastily called for the purpose of containing and eliminating any political fallout.

Benson, along with the other members of the newly formed team, was dispatched to the location where the spacecraft had made impact. They were accompanied by several low-ranking members of the United States Army, some in uniform and others in plain clothes. These men had been told nothing about the assignment, except to take orders from the civilian in charge and to obey all commands without question.

Benson and the others, including Sheffield, discovered that the spacecraft had landed in a large forested area adjacent to a farmhouse. The craft had generated a great deal of heat from its entry into Earth's atmosphere. The trees and other vegetation within and on either side of its path were burned. Fortunately, there had been a rainstorm during the preceding several days, so the fire worked itself out quickly.

Two members of the National Forest Service were dispatched to investigate the short-lived fire, having been called by the occupants of the farmhouse. The Forest Service emissaries were turned away at a blockade set up at the main entry to the farm. They were told that the fire was out, that the situation was being handled by another division of the government, and that it was a matter of some importance to keep the incident quiet. The identities of the Forest Service members were determined and recorded, and they were informed that this was a matter of national security and their failure to keep this matter confidential could result in serious consequences.

The observation that there were two armed men, in Army uniforms, standing on either side of the barricade, provided sufficient credibility to convince the Forest Service members that this was definitely none of their business.

Within minutes of the team's arrival on the scene, a family was discovered in a farmhouse about a hundred yards from the craft. They were told that the situation was under control. Four soldiers were instructed to keep them contained within the house. Their telephone line was located and cut. Within hours, the entire farm was enclosed with cable fencing and marked as restricted federal property.

Three members of the team returned to headquarters, where they were able, with the use of CIA computers, to locate all living relatives of the family that lived in the farmhouse. They were thirteen in number. Several soldiers in plain clothes, using unmarked vehicles, were dispatched to round up all of these relatives and bring them to the farmhouse. Within twelve hours, every known member of the family was located and delivered to the farm.

The owners of the farm were interrogated and forced to divulge the names and addresses of close friends in the area. An address book was discovered in a nightstand drawer, containing the names of ten non-family members who lived within one hundred miles of the property. They were, likewise, rounded up and delivered to the farmhouse.

While these civilians were being rounded up, Benson tried not to think about what would eventually be done with them. He focused on the idea that it was in the best interest of the nation that nobody who knew of the existence of the spacecraft and nobody who might become concerned about the disappearance of those who knew about the spacecraft could be allowed to have contact with the outside world.

Benson knew there had to be others out there who would eventually become aware of the absence of some of these people. He realized that, as a practical matter, they couldn't keep on rounding up more and more people. He finally convinced himself that the uproar that would ensue regarding the disappearance of these people would be effectively quelled by the CIA.

Ultimately, the CIA was able to plant enough "evidence" to convince the media that the disappearances were all part of an occult suicide pact and, more important, to keep any attempt at investigation far away from the farmhouse compound.

The government tried every conceivable method of gaining access to the interior of the spacecraft, to no avail. The craft was made of some metal-like substance that proved to be impervious to cutting, welding, and even blasting. The material was unknown to this planet. Finally the government, having failed to gain entry, concealed the craft within a concrete bunker, covered it with dirt and organic matter, and planted trees and foliage to allow the forest to reestablish itself within a few years. For several years the area was carefully guarded twenty-four hours a day, and nobody, not even local law enforcement officers, was allowed near the site.

One would think that somewhere along the way the CIA would have destroyed all evidence of the massacre. But those, from whom Benson received his orders, although intending to clean things up eventually, hadn't seen a need to rush the matter because the compound was completely secure. Besides, nobody had yet thought of a safer place to hide the remains than exactly where they were.

Finally, if the very worst were to happen and the massacre was to become public knowledge, the logical scapegoats would be the aliens who allegedly had piloted the spacecraft. Although it had never been determined whether the spacecraft was manned by living beings, the fact that it had been impossible to gain access to the interior of the craft allowed for the possibility that space travelers could be blamed for the murders.

Within a few months after the massacre, everyone who had any knowledge of the event disappeared, with the exception of Sheffield, Benson, and one of Sheffield's men, whose name was unknown to Benson. He suspected that the methodical elimination of those involved in the massacre was under the direction of someone very high in the "company," disposing of as many connections as possible between the event and the CIA.

If this was the case, why had Benson not been eliminated? On the few occasions that Benson tried to contact one of those who had known of the incident, he found himself at an informational dead-end. It seemed to him as if they had all ceased to exist. Only he and Sheffield and one other man remained.

Eventually Benson was demoted, unceremoniously, to a position with relatively little authority, having only a few dozen questionable agents under his direct command.

His primary responsibilities were now to monitor a few agents in the decoding department and to keep an eye on the alarm system connected to the bunker under which the spacecraft rested.

Until only a few days ago, nobody Benson had contacted in recent years had heard of the incident at the old farmhouse. Surveillance at the site had been discontinued many years ago, with the exception of the alarm system. Several signs were placed around the perimeter of the compound, warning curious individuals that trespassing on the property was a federal offense. The farmhouse was locked up. The bunker was well-hidden and overgrown with foliage. Any trail connecting the CIA with the remains at the farmhouse was so cold as to be of no use to anyone. The file on the incident, with the code name *Zephyr*, had long been buried and forgotten.

That is, until an alarm went off several days ago, indicating that a low-level member of the decoding staff named Daryl Harrington had somehow hacked his way into that long forgotten-file.

Failure of the attempt to eliminate Harrington put Benson in a tenuous position. He wondered if he had been kept alive to serve as a scapegoat in the event one was needed. He knew his continued existence likely depended on his apprehending and eliminating Harrington before anyone were to find out about the security leak.

The two things Benson was counting on were, first, that Harrington would certainly be found before long and, second, that nobody was still alive who knew about the evidence at the farmhouse other than himself, Sheffield, and one other man.

A short while ago, Benson had glanced at a device above his desk that he knew was connected, via radio waves, to two trip switches at the site of the massacre—one attached to the front door of the farmhouse, the other to the door to the bunker. It was the only vestige of security related to the massacre site that remained operational. Sheffield had decided that it was sufficiently important for him to know if anyone entered either of those facilities that he left the system functioning. He arranged for the electric bills for service to the transmitters to be paid by a corporation that could never be connected with the CIA.

A few days ago, Benson had leaned back in his chair, staring at the device, taking an irrational sense of comfort from the fact that, for more than thirty years, it had remained consolingly silent. He sometimes wondered why no one had ever thought to order the power disconnected from the transmitter. He wondered if the transmitters were even operational after all these years?

Now Benson, having had his whole world turned upside down, found himself staring at a telephone on his desk connected to a secured line that any minute now would bring him word that Daryl Harrington had been apprehended or, more likely, killed trying to escape.

Chapter Thirty-four

The sun was heading toward the mountaintops to the west as Chris, Jaime, and Becky entered that part of the forest where the concrete bunker lay hidden beneath many years of dense undergrowth. Jaime was in the lead, carrying a bolt cutter. For some reason, he took his friends the far way around the bunker before approaching the metal door.

Becky, still unsettled by the discoveries in the basement of the farmhouse, was amazed at what she was seeing in the forest. Chris pointed out to her how something had made a wide corridor through the forest, apparently charring the trunks of the bordering trees in the process. Then he directed her attention to the sizeable dirt mound in the center of the corridor at just the point where the corridor ended. As the trio walked around the mound, Becky saw the concrete corner that the rain, with a great deal of help from the boys, had uncovered earlier. Finally she saw the metal door at the bottom of the ramp that slanted toward the base of the bunker, overgrown with thick vines and branches. The overgrowth was so dense that the door was barely visible in the darkness it created.

Jaime handed the bolt cutter to Chris. With considerable effort, he cut the padlock securing the steel door. When the lock snapped, they again heard that hollow, rumbling sound echoing within the bunker. Becky grabbed Jaime's hand, not sure she wanted to know what might be lurking inside that bunker. Visions flashed before her mind of slimy, slithering creatures, waiting just beyond the door ready to attack or, perhaps, the skeletons of more victims of whatever had happened at this sorrowful place.

Chris tried to pry the door open with the tip of the larger shovel. He discovered a great deal of mud at the bottom of the door, which would have to be removed before the door could swing open. He and Jaime shoveled the dirt while Becky stood some distance back, as if the distance would reduce the impact of whatever might come charging out once the door was opened.

Finally the last of the dirt was cleared away. Before Chris or Jaime had time to reach up to pull the door open, it swung outward with a loud, creaking sound. A damp, musty smell poured out of the opening.

As they entered the bunker, Chris and Jaime each turned on his flashlight. They were all so intent upon seeing what lay beyond the opening that nobody noticed the button switch embedded in the steel door-frame just above the top hinge.

That switch, unlike the one in the frame of the front door of the farmhouse, was still in good working order. As the pressure previously provided by the metal door was removed, the button popped out, causing two electrical terminals to make contact. A twelve-volt direct-current impulse was sent to a radio transmitter hidden in a moisture-proof plastic box within the bunker wall. The transmitter was connected to a small antenna atop the bunker, well hidden by vegetation. That antenna sent a three-watt radio signal to a repeater on a nearby mountaintop. The repeater increased the power of that signal to one hundred watts and, in turn, sent it to the monitoring device above Herbert Benson's desk.

A beeping sound began to emanate from the monitoring device. The words "Security breach, sector 4, unit B" appeared on the screen. The effect of these stimuli on the eyes and ears of Herbert Benson and, subsequently, on numerous other components of his nervous system could not have had a greater impact if they had announced that a nuclear bomb had just been released directly over the building in which he sat clinging to his bottle of calamine lotion like a frightened child clinging to a teddy bear.

If Benson had died at that instant and an autopsy performed on his remains, the pathologist would have been shocked to discover that the ganglia of Benson's nervous system resembled strands of barbed wire.

The closest thing to a rational thought that Benson could conjure up was that, if he was going down, he was going to find a way to take Sheffield down with him. He rushed to the lavatory and deposited the contents of his upper digestive tract into the toilet.

When his physical reactions finally subsided, he was able to compose himself to the point where he came up with another rational thought. He decided that the best chance he had to survive this mess was to get his now relatively worthless ass over to the site of the spacecraft, along with several of his agents, and capture whoever had broken into the bunker.

Benson figured that if he and the agents hustled, they could converge on the target in about an hour and forty minutes. He prayed that whoever had opened the bunker would still be there.

He grabbed the only agent in the building under his command and instructed him to call several members of his team on the cell phones he had had the wisdom to issue them, and direct them to head for the entry to the farmhouse compound immediately. All agents were to wait at the entry until Benson's arrival. On the way from his office to the rendezvous point, he would have time to formulate a plan as to what the hell he would do after he got there.

As Benson slid behind the wheel of his government-issue beige sedan, it occurred to him that perhaps it was Daryl Harrington who had tripped the alarm. If Harrington had been smart enough to escape from his cubicle with the security door locked and his oxygen supply cut off, maybe he was clever enough to find the location of the crime described in the file he had uncovered.

For the first time in many days, a smile formed on Benson's lips. It seemed to be too much of a coincidence that someone else would have stumbled upon the scene of the crime within four days after Harrington's discovery of the top-secret file, especially after more than thirty years of inactivity.

Yes, maybe it was Harrington who had tripped the alarm. But why would he go there? If he had any sense, he would be in deep hiding, perhaps across the border into Mexico or Canada by now.

Unless.

Unless he hoped to find enough evidence to bring the entire matter crashing down on Benson's head before Benson could catch him.

The smile was replaced by a sneer on Benson's lips. He tightened his grip on the steering wheel as he roared down the state highway. It had to be Harrington.

As far as Benson knew, only the bunker had been breached. There had been no indication that the farmhouse had been entered. That meant that, at most, Harrington would have time only to explore the bunker. It probably would take him at least another hour to break into the farmhouse and locate evidence of the murders. Then Harrington would have to decide what to do about that.

One or more of Benson's men would likely be arriving at the entry to the farm within the next hour. They wouldn't let Harrington out. And Benson would be there in an hour and a half. Then it would just be a matter of surrounding Harrington.

Benson pushed the accelerator to the floor, the phrase "pedal to the metal" running through his mind. Yes, Harrington was his. He could feel it. This entire nightmare would be over within the next few hours.

What Benson didn't know was that Daryl Harrington had been engaged in his own "pedal to the metal." Daryl wasn't yet at the compound as Benson imagined. But, he was only minutes from the front gate, well ahead of any of Benson's men. According to Daryl's research and the map he had taped to the dashboard of the Jeep, he would be heading off the highway and onto the road to the farmhouse in a matter of seconds. The map indicated that that gravel road left the highway at a forty-five degree angle. He saw it up ahead.

Daryl double-checked to be sure a round was chambered in the 44 Magnum Desert Eagle and that the hammer was cocked. He placed it back in the holster, leaving the zipper of his camouflaged jacket down far enough that he would be able to get at the pistol quickly when he needed it.

He hit the gravel road doing seventy five miles per hour. He went through a mental checklist of his other equipment. Everything was in readiness.

Let the games begin.

As soon as Chris and his friends entered the bunker, they became aware that something mighty big was in there with them. They aimed their flashlights around the interior of the bunker and saw nothing but concrete and metal. Whatever was contained within the concrete walls of the bunker, it was gigantic. But what was it?

The bunker floor appeared to have been the floor of the old forest before the bunker was built and a new forest planted above it. Abundant plant material had decomposed on the bunker floor, probably accounting for the musty aroma that had greeted them as they had opened the door.

It was apparent that the bunker had been built for the sole purpose of containing the metal object. But what was the metal object?

Jaime suggested that, to him, it looked like a flying saucer. But it had no visible openings, no windows to allow for observation, no doors to allow for access. It had no lights, no landing gear, nothing but smooth metal. It was shaped like a flying saucer, at least the ones Jaime had seen in photos, alleged to be pictures of the real thing.

They pressed their hands against it. It was a very unusual material, as unyielding as steel, yet soft in some strange way, and warm to the touch, almost inviting.

As they walked around the object, they stumbled across numerous items strewn about the floor and others resting on what seemed to be a large workbench along one wall of the bunker. In various drawers beneath the bench, they found power drills, carbon-tipped bits, files, chisels, hammers, and power saws of various types, with several different kinds of blades.

In one corner of the bunker was a storage shed. Inside were boxes labeled "Trinitrotoluene," "Dynamite," "Nitroglycerine," "Blasting Powder," "Detonators," and "C-4." The shed also contained welding equipment for both arc and acetylene welding. Two sledge hammers leaned against one wall next to dozens of bits of various configurations, most of which looked like they had been beaten beyond use. There were two jack-hammers in one corner. Hanging from nails in the walls were rolls of light-gauge electrical wire and coils of what Chris thought was fuse line for use with dynamite.

As they continued their search, they came upon several craters in the ground at the base of what they had now come to call the "spaceship." Strewn around these areas were hundreds of sandbags, many of which had been torn open.

Chris picked up a claw hammer he found lying on the workbench and slammed it against the side of the "spaceship." Nothing. Not a sound. The hammer didn't even recoil. "This is strange," he said. "I've never seen anything like this." He pressed his hand flat against the side of the object and could see, in the beam of his flashlight, that he had left a handprint.

As she drew near the object, Becky thought she smelled something. She put her nose close to the "metal" and sniffed. "It smells great," she said. "vanilla of all things."

Jaime smelled it. "You're right. It does smell great. But you're wrong about the vanilla. It smells exactly like almond extract."

Becky sniffed it again. "I hate to disagree, but I know vanilla when I smell it. Vanilla is one of my favorite aromas."

Chris said, "Okay, let an expert settle this." He put his face close to the ship and inhaled deeply. "I can understand somebody confusing vanilla and almond, maybe. But you guys are wrong. I'd know that smell anywhere. And I assure you that it's absolutely not vanilla or almond. That, my friends, is the smell of one of my favorite aromas, aspen leaves."

"Come on, Chris," Becky said, "there's no way anybody could mistake the smell of vanilla for aspen leaves. Besides, anyone who would choose aspen leaves over vanilla needs a nasal passage-ectomy."

They laughed, feeling a bit of relief from the tension for the first time since they had discovered the remains in the basement of the farmhouse.

Jaime said, "Let's take a few minutes to think about what we've discovered so far and see if we can figure out what's been going on here."

The other two agreed.

Chris said, "Becky, why don't you go first."

"Okay," she began, "we've got a bunch of dead bodies, including several soldiers with uniforms from somewhere around the Vietnam era. Then we've got a farm, which was obviously somebody's private property that is fenced in with signs announcing that it's now federal property. Next, we have bars over the doors, windows, and even the chimney tops. Now we find a gigantic bunker in the forest at the end of a long, long corridor, on the inside of which the trees were cut to the ground about thirty years ago— coincidentally about the time of the Vietnam War—with soil placed over the top of the bunker and the top of the bunker and the corridor re-vegetated."

Jaime interjected, "Let me take it from there. Inside the bunker we find a gigantic piece of metal, shaped suspiciously like a spaceship but with no openings or landing gear. Then we've got all kinds of tools, most of which would best be used to get inside something solid, like maybe a metal spaceship. We've got drills, saws, jackhammers, dynamite, welding gear, and so forth. Then we've got holes in the ground, surrounded by sandbags, indicating to me that somebody set off explosives right up against the 'spaceship.' It looks to me as if somebody was trying very hard to get inside."

Chris said, "Okay, my turn. Finally, we've got some kind of metal here that can't be scratched, doesn't make a sound when a mighty man like me hits it with a claw hammer. It doesn't even recoil. It feels soft to the touch but doesn't yield to pressure and, most mystifying to me, it imparts to the nasal passages of whoever sniffs in its vicinity an aroma that is pleasing to that person."

Becky piped up, "All right, gentlemen, your conclusions?"

Almost at the same time, Chris and Jaime exclaimed, "We've got a damn spacecraft here!"

Becky added, "And it's been covered up by our illustrious government for about thirty years. Sadly, several people were sacrificed to keep the existence of this wondrous object from the public."

"I don't know about the rest of you," Chris said, "but I feel an obligation to those who died here to see that this entire mess is made public knowledge and that those responsible be made to account for their actions."

Jaime offered his opinion. "It's likely that some of those who committed the atrocity are no longer living."

"You may be correct," Chris said, "but the public still has the right to know how the federal government has abused its power by making decisions it has no right to make."

The others agreed.

"Then," said Jaime, "I think the next step is to find a way into this space vehicle and see if we can find some more information as to what happened here and, maybe, who was responsible."

As they attempted to devise a plan, they reasoned as follows:

Any object that can customize its scent to suit the preferences of the person doing the smelling must contain some form of high intelligence. The absence of an entry portal suggests that (1) it's an unmanned craft or (2) its occupants are non-physical, in the sense that we use that word, or (3) a portal can be created or be made to appear.

In addition, they theorized, because the aroma emitted by the surface of the vehicle was changed by something other than a command or a physical action and, especially since the changes happened even before they were aware that they could be achieved, the ship's ability to do so may be based on some type of communication between the craft and a form of intelligence, human or otherwise, sort of like mind-reading.

Now, they further assumed, if it is possible to gain access to the interior of this vehicle with the power of intelligent thought, why were their predecessors, who obviously wanted access to the interior of the ship in the worst way, unable to open it? They speculated that perhaps whatever intelligence designed this spaceship programmed the method of internal access so that only those seeking entrance for honorable, friendly, and peaceful purposes could activate the entrance mechanism.

Then Chris remembered his dream of last night. He recalled Great-Grandfather saying, "When two or more of you are gathered in my name, there is love." And Great-Grandfather's understanding of that phrase from his position of broader perspective was, "When two or more beings combine their manifestational powers for the same purpose, the combined energy generated is many times greater than the sum of the individual powers."

Becky reminded them that this ship had been sitting under this concrete box for more than thirty years. She wondered aloud whether its battery, or whatever its source of power might be, could be dead.

Jaime suggested that it probably wouldn't hurt to give it a try but added that the result might be that they blow themselves to kingdom come.

Chris said he didn't consider such an outcome likely, not only because the ship "felt" friendly but, most important, because the thoughts they would be sending would be pure.

The three sat in a circle, holding hands and focusing their energy at the center of the circle. Jaime thought about The Force. Becky thought about her Magical Friend. Chris focused on Great Spirit. In reality, they were each calling on the exact same power, the power of Unconditional Love, the power of Infinite Intelligence, the power of God.

From personal experience, they each knew that as long as the feeling behind the instructions was that of total joy, the manifestation was based on an absolute knowing, and the thought was accompanied by strong positive emotion, anything was possible, with no limitations imposed by perceived physical reality.

As they sat there focusing their energies and holding the state of mind they knew to be most powerful, they could each feel the energy building within their own beings and also within the area surrounding them. A few minutes later they each felt a surge of high energy.

Jaime said, "Wow!"

Becky said, "My goodness!"

Chris said, "Holy shit!"

It was done. Nobody had a bit of doubt. They all had felt that surge before.

A second later they heard a loud "click," "whir," "thunk" echo off of the walls of the bunker.

Jaime was the first to jump up and begin running around the ship. A few seconds later he yelled, "Here it is! Oh, my gosh!"

Chris and Becky began running toward the sound of Jaime's voice, although it was hard to tell which direction it had come from, with all of the echoing from the concrete walls and the ship's metal. *You can't go very wrong when you're running alongside a round object.*

There it was, a bright opening in the side of the craft. Jaime was standing there, apparently in a trance. Becky turned her head and looked inside the ship. She, too, was mesmerized, as if she had just taken a powerful tranquilizer. Chris had the same reaction.

Becky said, "Can you just feel the love pouring out of that thing? My goodness, I want to cry. I've never felt anything like this before."

"Me, neither," said Jaime.

"Amen," Chris whispered.

Becky was the first to enter the corridor of light leading into the ship. When all three were inside, Becky said, "The lights are really bright, don't you think?"

In an instant the lights dimmed.

The three looked at each other.

Chris tried, "I think I prefer blue."

The light turned from white to blue.

Jaime began to laugh. The other two joined him. Not one of them had ever felt anything this divine.

"This must be what Heaven feels like," Becky sighed.

Chris countered, "This *is* Heaven, not a place—a state of mind."

Jaime looked around for a few seconds and asked, "Can you hear us?"

A beautiful and soothing voice, neither male nor female, said, "We hear your words and feel the love in your hearts. Welcome to our home. Be at peace. How may we serve you?"

Chris said, "Please tell us whatever we need to know about this place and what happened here."

The voice said, "Please be seated."

Instantly, three chairs appeared, in exactly the right positions to allow each of them to sit without having to move.

"There are many things you should know, for your own safety and that of your planet. We haven't much time in that those who mean you harm will arrive shortly. Know, first of all, that everything is exactly as it should be. Therefore, strive to look upon whatever events may confront you as aspects of a game, not a war. Strive to help yourselves and others, only for the sake of pleasure in the present moment, never for revenge or out of anger. Your most important contribution to the elimination of pain in your world is to refuse to judge others, especially those who appear to mean you harm or those who would be judged as evil by the standards of your somewhat primitive world.

"Also, do not take as a criticism our description of your planet as 'primitive.' All civilizations are evolving exactly as they should. There is no right or wrong in the sense that a higher power will someday judge you. There are only consequences. Strive to conduct yourselves to achieve the consequences you desire for yourselves, your loved ones, and your fellow men and women. All else will take care of itself.

"Now, I'll move on to the specifics of your present situation.

"You are correct that certain employees of your government did commit what you would term 'atrocities' using the power that was theirs by virtue of their positions within the governmental organization. Several individuals were dispatched to the spirit world in order that a perceived higher good for the nation might be accomplished.

"We feel a need to advise you, however, that there are no victims in reality. In your world of illusion, there often appear to be victims. However, we assure you that nobody on the physical plane suffers consequences that they were not aware of and did not consent to, prior to focusing their energy in this physical reality.

"When we use the word 'illusion' to describe aspects of your physical world, we do not mean to imply that these things are not 'real' from your physical perspective. They are very real to you. Our meaning is that they are not fixed as they may appear but are subject to change at any time by your deliberate or unintentional use of thought and emotion.

"In those instances where you do not engage in powerful thought or emotion regarding a particular situation or you have thoughts that are not accompanied by what your 'Book of Books' calls 'faith' (what we call 'knowing'), the circumstances will be governed by the thoughts of the collective unconscious of either the members of your tribe or the population of Earth in general.

"Nonetheless, we are willing and eager to assist you in overcoming what you consider to be forces of evil in your present physical reality. We simply believe it will be in your best interest, before we begin the game, to understand that the 'All That Is' or 'Infinite Intelligence' or what many on your planet call 'God' knows nothing of good or evil. The God Force knows only unconditional love. It requires nothing of you, the Light Beings who are temporarily focused in these physical bodies.

"Our purpose in assisting you is not to help you overcome the forces of evil as such a things do not exist in our knowing, but simply to assist all participants in this adventure to experience more fully.

"Although you may not be consciously aware of it, we are here in your reality at your invitation. For this reason and not because of any moral judgment on our part, we will assist you in attaining your objectives regarding this adventure.

"Actually, you have all the power you need to accomplish these objectives without our intercession. This is particularly true in your lives, more than in the lives of many others, because each of you was educated by loved ones who had the wisdom to buffer you from many of the false notions of your society. However, the heaviness of thought on your plane of physical reality, based on appearances, as interpreted by your senses, is often very seductive, causing humans to accept the apparent physical reality as being more powerful than the power of their thoughts and emotions. For this reason, our intercession may be helpful, on occasion, in enabling you to control your reality more effectively, especially at times when fear is present.

"We are aware that you already know everything we have told you. However, in your world of forgetfulness, it is of benefit to be reminded of what you seem to have forgotten.

"We now direct you to the intelligence center of this craft. It is in the small compartment directly in front of you. You may be surprised to notice that this cabinet is not locked or secured in any way, in that we know nothing of crime or thievery or possession of physical things in our society. These concepts are particular to your planet only, and no others that we have ever encountered."

As the voice spoke of the cabinet, it began to glow slightly, making its location obvious. Becky walked to the cabinet and removed what looked like a quartz crystal about the size of a baseball.

"We will communicate with you initially through this device. Please take it with you on your adventure. Once you leave the interior of the craft, this crystal will amplify communication from us in the form of mental prompting or what you call 'telepathy.' Sound waves are an unreliable form of communication in many instances. We chose to use them during the initial phases of this interaction so as not to alarm you.

"This crystal is all you will need to make your media aware of the 'atrocities' that occurred here many years ago in Earth time. It contains all of the facts and circumstances, in a form that will be easily understandable by all.

"We will use the word 'opponents' when referring to those who are pursuing you, as the closest word in your language to most accurately describe the true nature of your relationship with these others. You must prepare to leave quickly as your opponents are arriving shortly.

"Within the walls of this spacecraft are many wonders that will be of great interest to you. However, you cannot presently spare the time. As it is seen now, you will likely return to this place one day and will have an opportunity to learn of and use many of the extraordinary features of this most advanced vehicle.

"May we now suggest that you proceed with all due haste, with one last piece of information. That is, we will not tell you everything you might wish to know. That would eliminate much of the fun that comes from not knowing. That would reduce the intensity of your experience."

Becky handed the crystal to Jaime and hugged him. Jaime kissed her gently on the cheek.

Chris said, "I know I speak for my friends when I say we are grateful for your love and caring. We welcome your assistance. We shall act with the integrity befitting the advanced souls we are striving to become."

The intelligence didn't respond with words. Instead, the lighting within the craft became very soft, the air temperature seemed to increase ever so slightly, and the three friends found themselves, once again, enveloped in a feeling of love beyond description. They stood there, lost in the rapture, almost floating.

After the feeling gently faded away, Becky said, "I think that was a hug."

Chris put his arms around Becky and Jaime and pulled them together, forming a small circle. All heads bowed, allowing their foreheads to touch. Jaime held the crystal to his chest. Becky wrapped her arms around her friends. Jaime said, "I think this is a hug."

Chris whispered, "Let's go, amigos."

Chapter Thirty-five

The three friends grabbed a few tools from the workbench inside the bunker, an assortment of explosives, fuses, and detonators, plus the tools they had used earlier to get inside the bunker. They carried these items to the Jeep, loaded them, and then headed up to the farmhouse to gather their personal belongings. With an unusual combination of excitement and fear, each was busy rethinking the notions that the intelligence within the spacecraft had presented. They grabbed everything they had taken into the house the night before, ran down the front steps toward the Jeep, loaded it, and made sure everything was fastened down securely.

When Jaime looked up, he observed Becky heading back to the house. He paused a moment to watch her walking up the stairs. "My, that's one fine woman," he thought. He wondered if he'd feel the same way about her if she weren't so beautiful. He wasn't sure. And that made him feel guilty.

Then he remembered Mom telling him many times, "Guilt is a useless emotion." She would say, "It's okay to regret something you've done, to help you decide not to do it again. But to be down on yourself doesn't help a thing. The only thing guilt has ever accomplished is to allow some people to control other people."

Jaime decided he definitely would be wild for Becky no matter how she looked. But those gorgeous eyes were surely frosting on the cake. It was difficult to be reasonable about such a topic at age seventeen with lots of healthy hormones surging through his body. He also considered the possibility that his feelings for Becky were what made her so physically attractive to him.

He went back to help Chris fasten down the tools, wondering what Becky was doing. He hoped she'd hurry. Apparently someone knew they were here, and they weren't very happy about it.

As he continued to tie down the equipment, Jaime glanced down the dirt trail they had come up last night. It was becoming difficult to see in the approaching twilight. The next thing he knew, Becky was standing by his side, breathing heavily. He was sorry he hadn't seen her coming, especially if it had to do with walking. She had a nice walk. "There go those hormones again," Jaime laughed to himself.

"What are you laughing about?" she asked.

"Oh, nothing."

"Are you laughing at me?"

"No, I'm laughing at me. I'll tell you about it some day when we don't have a bunch of bad guys chasing us."

Becky stood on her toes and kissed Jaime on the cheek. He stopped right in the middle of tying a knot, and closed his eyes for a few seconds, savoring the moment.

Chris looked at them and smiled. There were only three more days until he would be with Wendy again. He prayed that she'd be there.

Becky produced the diary she'd found under the closet floor.

"So that's why she went back into the farmhouse," Jaime thought. He took care to wrap the crystal they had taken from the spaceship in a blanket. Then he tied it to the underside of the back seat.

Chris heard something in the distance. He turned, looked down the dirt trail, and saw lights flickering through the trees. Then he heard the roar of an engine. Somebody was moving mighty fast. He shouted, "Let's go, compadres!"

Becky climbed into the backseat. Jaime took the shotgun position. Chris jumped into the driver's seat, and his heart sank as he realized that the keys weren't in the ignition. Where the hell had he put them? Then he remembered they were in his jacket pocket. He reached back and grabbed his jacket from the backseat. Becky was sitting on one of the sleeves, and it came out of Chris's grip. She realized, instantly, what had happened, pulled the sleeve from under her leg, and tossed the jacket to Chris. He fumbled with it and located the key. Before he could fit it in the ignition, the other vehicle skidded to a halt right next to him, so close that it almost touched his left front fender.

Chris reached down and grabbed his pistol from under the seat. While he was still bent down, he pulled back the slide, let it go, and pressed down on the safety. When he sat back up, he spun quickly and lined up the sights with the center of the forehead of the driver. Chris looked at his own hands. They were shaking terribly. "Don't wimp out now, Christopher," he thought.

He couldn't help but notice that a heavy piece of artillery was pointing directly back at him. He suspected that it was aimed at the middle of his own forehead. Chris had read enough about Israeli military weapons to know a Desert Eagle when he saw one, even from a front view.

Jaime and Becky froze.

"Drop that pistol," the man shouted.

"*You* drop the pistol," Chris yelled back.

"I said it first," said the man, with a slight hesitancy in his voice.

"What kind of lame statement is that?" asked Chris, a quiver in his own voice.

"It's the statement of someone who's so scared that he's liable to pull this trigger by accident if you don't do something real soon to alleviate the tension."

"What do you want me to do?" Chris asked.

"Like I said—put down that pistol."

Chris asked, "Who the hell are you?"

"I'm Daryl Harrington, with the CIA—formerly with the CIA, I mean. Who are you?"

"I'm Chris, the meanest son of a bitch in this part of the world."

"You don't sound so mean."

"Neither do you."

Daryl said, "I'll tell you what. The fact that you've got a couple of kids in that Jeep gives me just a little confidence that maybe you're not the bad guys I was afraid you were. So…I'll put on my safety. But that's as far as I'll go until you put on *your* safety."

Chris said, "You'll have to turn your pistol sideways so I can see that the safety is really on."

Daryl said, "I can't do that without taking my sights off of your head."

"That's too bad. You'll just have to trust me. This is your idea."

"Okay, but just for a second."

Chris looked at the safety on Daryl's Desert Eagle in the split second that Daryl turned it sideways before centering it back on Chris's head. It was on.

"Okay," Daryl said. "Now you put yours on."

Chris clicked on the safety of his 9 millimeter and turned the pistol for just a second so the man could see it.

"All right," he warned, "but if I hear that safety click off, you're a dead man."

"Ditto," echoed Chris.

"Now," said Daryl, "I'm gonna lower my sights to your belly button."

"Hell," Chris replied, "I'd rather be shot in the head than the gut."

"Okay," said Daryl, "I'll point my pistol at your shoulder." which he did.

Chris did the same. "Now what do we do?"

"Darned if I know. I've never done this before."

Chris sighed. "All right, why don't you just lay your pistol down on the seat?"

Daryl retorted, "Why don't you?"

"Because I'm the one with the kids in my Jeep, remember?"

Becky broke in, "Hey guys, am I the only one here who's figured out that nobody really wants to shoot anybody else? Has it occurred to either of you that if anyone here was a killer, the other guy—and his vehicle—would already look like Swiss cheese? No killer would sit here talking when all he really had to do was squeeze his trigger first."

Daryl and Chris simultaneously said sheepishly, "Yeah, I guess you're right."

"And," Becky said sternly, "does it make sense to either of you that if there are some bad guys on their way here—and it looks like we're all concerned about the same bad guys—we ought to consider getting off of this federal compound before they arrive and add several more weapons to these negotiations?"

"Amen," Jaime said.

"Then let's go," said Becky "I'll ride with Daryl and explain our situation as we go."

Jaime insisted, "Only if he lets you have the gun."

"I already thought of that," said Becky, "Give me that peashooter, Daryl."

"What do you mean, 'peashooter'?"

"Something I heard in a John Wayne movie."

Becky climbed into Daryl's jeep, took his pistol, and tucked it into the compartment in her door. She glanced at his backseat. "Wow, there's an arsenal in here. What were you preparing for?"

"The bad guys," said Daryl. "I ought to tell you that I think the leader of the guys who are on their way here was part of a team that killed a whole bunch of innocent people in that farmhouse. I've got information that could put him in the gas chamber. We'd better assume that we're running for our lives."

Chris fired up his Jeep.

"What the hell have you got in that thing?" Daryl shouted above the roar of Chris's engine.

"Just a little Corvette four hundred twenty-seven cubic-inch V-8," yelled Chris.

"This thing I'm driving is stock," said Daryl. "I'm not sure I can keep up with you."

"We'll take care of that, later. I know just the place to give that little machine of yours more go-power. In the meantime, if things get dicey, I'll get behind you and give you a push. I suspect the torque in this beast will be enough for both of us. If that happens, I'll count on you to do a whole lot of fancy steering."

With that, Chris turned and headed down the dirt trail in the direction of the front gate. Before he had even gotten into second gear, he saw several beams of light flashing through the forest, obviously coming up the trail he was heading down. Luckily, neither he nor Daryl had yet turned on their headlights.

Chris hit the brakes, which almost caused Daryl to collide with the rear of his vehicle. Chris spun around, motioning to the oncoming lights behind him. Daryl nodded his understanding and turned his Jeep around in the same path as Chris. Chris motioned for Daryl to take the lead. Nobody knew where the trail would take them. All they knew was that it was heading away from the bad guys. They just hoped it wasn't a dead end.

They shot past the farmhouse, then the bunker, and into a narrow canyon. Chris kept his headlights turned off, thinking that would prevent whoever was coming up that trail from knowing they had left only moments ago. He hoped they would stop to investigate the farmhouse and the bunker.

For the first time since Chris had built that big honkin' engine under the hood of his Jeep, he wished it weren't so loud. He thought of the old Mazda commercials that boasted about the engine that made a humming sound. His engine definitely wasn't humming. The word that came to Chris's mind was "screaming."

The sun was now down to the point where the drivers could barely make out the trees in front of them. Chris decided it was just a matter of moments before Daryl, in the lead, would run into a tree. That was the last thing they needed at a time like this. Surmising that they were now a safe distance from the bad guys, he flipped on his headlights, expecting that this would prompt Daryl to do the same. Daryl turned on the headlights and some auxiliary lights, as well. When he did so, they were shocked at the amount of light shining from the front of the Jeep. The previous owner had attached some serious four-wheeling lights to the roll bar.

Chris yelled to Jaime, "Those lights are powerful enough to melt six inches of snow off the highway at thirty miles an hour!"

"Well, no sense trying to hide anymore. Either the bad guys are out of sight and out of hearing or they're gonna be hot on our tail."

Luckily, the bright lights revealed that the vehicles were still on a road of some sort, although it was getting more difficult to follow. Becky took the Desert Eagle out of the compartment in her door and handed it back to Daryl. He slid it into the holster on the left side of his rib cage, feeling a whole lot more comfortable.

A few seconds later Daryl skidded to a stop. They had come to a cable fence marking the perimeter of the farm. A gate was blocking the trail.

Jaime jumped out of the second Jeep, grabbed the bolt cutter, and cut the lock. Apparently they were now about to leave the farm.

Chris took the forestry map out of the glove compartment and spread it out on the hood of his Jeep. The map showed clearly the trail through the farm, including the point at which it crossed the farm's boundary and headed into public lands. It also showed a split in the trail about five miles ahead. One fork went back to the main road, and the other wound through a narrow canyon and up onto a high plateau, where it ended, at least, on the map.

They took off again, traveling as fast as the terrain would allow. When they reached the fork in the road, they took the one heading to the high plateau. Taking the other trail back to the main road didn't seem like a good move. There was a good chance that it was being patrolled by the bad guys.

Soon they found themselves in a heavily forested area. Jaime was kneeling on his seat, looking backward to see if they were being followed. Before long, he saw a pair of headlights in the distance, then a second pair. "They've found our trail. But it looks like only two vehicles. Back at the farmhouse, there were about half a dozen."

Chris said, "Maybe some of them stayed at the farmhouse to see what we were into. Or maybe some of the vehicles weren't equipped to handle a trail this rough."

"You're right," Jaime agreed. "I doubt there are many vehicles that could follow this road. Those headlights must be from four-wheel drive rigs." It looked to him as if the bad guys were gaining.

Then Chris shouted, "What the hell's Becky doing?"

Becky was standing up on her seat, trying to keep her balance by holding onto the roll bar of Daryl's Jeep with one hand. In the other hand she had what looked like a tool of some sort. She was doing something to the floodlights.

Daryl's Jeep stopped. Chris hit the brakes, almost rear-ending Daryl. "What are you doing?" Chris yelled.

She said, "Pull your Jeep off into that little clearing on the right and shut off your lights. Then get out and have your pistol ready to shoot. Daryl, you do the same with that cannon you've got in your holster."

Daryl thought "cannon" had a nicer ring to it than "peashooter."

"How'd he get the pistol back?" Jaime asked.

"Never mind that now," she countered. "Those guys are gonna be here before we know it. Chris, you and Daryl get down on your bellies and have your pistols ready to fire. Jaime, get behind a tree. Everybody stay some distance from the Jeeps. I don't want anyone getting shot." She continued to work on the floodlights in the dark.

It looked like the bad guys were now about a mile away.

Becky said, "When I flip these lights on, if I've aimed them properly, those guys are gonna be blinded for a while. While they're trying to figure out what's happening, I want you two marksmen to shoot out their headlights and front tires. If they're able to return fire, it will likely be in the direction of the floodlights. That's why I want you nowhere near them. As soon as you've done as much damage as you can, we'll turn off the lights. They'll still be too blinded to see us for a while, even if some of their headlights are still working.

"While they're waiting for their sight to return, we'll get out of here pronto. I've left two of the floodlights aiming forward so Daryl can navigate, and I've cut the wires to the rear-facing lights so they'll only be on if I hold the ends of the wires together. If they're still able to follow, I'll flash the lights at them occasionally to see if I can cause them to go off of the trail and maybe hit a tree or boulder big enough to do some serious damage to something critical, like maybe a radiator."

"Now that's my kind of woman," thought Jaime. Then to Becky he said, "Won't you be in danger if they shoot at the lights?"

She replied, "As soon as I twist the wires together, I'm gonna dive behind that big ponderosa. I won't show my face again until the shooting's stopped. If we act fast enough, any return fire should be inaccurate, with the bad guys being blinded. Before they regain any usable eyesight, I'll have the lights back off, and we'll be gone around that turn in the road just ahead. The minute you guys see me turn the lights off, jump back into the vehicles. Both engines are still running, so it shouldn't take us more than a few seconds to be out of sight. I'm counting on you two marksmen to disable that lead vehicle.

"First of all, if your shots are accurate, they'll be without head-lights in that vehicle so they won't be able to see us. Second, the lead vehicle will be unable to follow with its front tires blown out. Third, with the trees being so thick on either side of the trail, it will take them some time to get that first vehicle out of the way of the second one. By then, we should be far enough down the road to set up our second trap."

"What second trap?" asked Chris.

Becky said, "I don't know. I'm making this up as I go."

Daryl and Chris got down on the ground on opposite sides of the road. They each had a tree for cover, allowing only enough of their bodies to show to provide them the necessary line of site to fire their weapons.

Jaime was well-hidden behind a ponderosa, wishing he had a pistol. He was not too keen on being unable to do his part. Then he heard a voice. Not a real voice, but a voice in his head. Unless he was imagining things, it was the same voice that had spoken to them in the spacecraft: "Jaime, my name is Zara. I am here to help you and your friends."

The crystal was communicating with him! Or someone was communicating through it.

The voice in Jaime's head said, "Becky's in danger. Go to your duffel bag, in the back of Chris's Jeep. Look in the side compartment."

Jaime remembered his brother, Tim, saying he had put some things in that bag.

The voice said, "Time is short. Do as I suggest. I will explain later, if necessary."

Jaime walked around the tree to the back of Chris's Jeep and was able to get to his bag without exposing himself to the oncoming headlights. He pulled the bag down to the ground and unzipped the side compartment. There he found the old twenty-two caliber pistol he and Tim had used to fire in target-shooting competition, along with a box full of twenty-two caliber, long-rifle cartridges. Jaime saw something else in the compartment but didn't take the time to see what it was. For now, the sight of his target pistol was sufficient to ease his anxiety.

Dad had enrolled Tim and Jaime in the National Rifle Association's hunter safety program when they were twelve, and they enjoyed it so much that they both began shooting in competition. By the time they were fourteen, each had won the designation of "Sharpshooter."

The pistol didn't have much firepower, but it was outrageously accurate and the twenty-two long-rifle cartridges gave it a range of more than a mile. The barrel was twelve inches long, and the pistol was fitted with an adjustable rear peep sight. Neither Tim nor Jaime had fired it in a couple of years. Heaven only knew when it was last sighted in properly.

The pistol was a single shot. Each cartridge had to be inserted into the chamber by hand, one at a time, as each shot was fired. The NRA, being concerned as it is with safety, wouldn't allow any pistol or rifle to be used in competition that held more than one cartridge at a time. As much as Jaime understood and agreed with that rule, he sure wished he had something in his hands with a little more firepower and a magazine full of cartridges. Oh well, Zara must know what she's doing.

Jaime slid one long-rifle cartridge into the chamber and locked the bolt. From habit, he made sure the safety was on. The NRA had taught him never to take a weapon off safety until the sights were on target.

He put a handful of cartridges in his right front pocket, where he could get at them quickly, although he doubted that he would get a chance for a second shot. Then he lay down in a position where he could see both Becky and the trail they had just come up. She was standing next to Daryl's Jeep beside the driver's door. Jaime held the pistol tightly in his left hand and waited. His heart was beating so hard he could feel his pulse in the veins of his neck. *Or are those arteries? Doesn't matter. Concentrate.*

He could see the headlights of the oncoming vehicles flashing on the tree branches above his head. He looked down the trail. They were only about a hundred yards away now. He got up on his elbows and held the pistol with both hands. In this position he couldn't see Becky as clearly as he wanted to. If he got up on his knees, he would be able to see her more easily while still having a clear shot down the trail. But he had learned that shooting from a prone position was the most accurate because the body is solid on the ground.

Jaime could see that both Chris and Daryl were in the same position. Smart guys.

Becky twisted together the wires she had cut earlier, making the rear-facing lights operable again. Just as the bad guys made a sharp turn toward the waiting ambush, Becky flipped the toggle switch under the dashboard and dived for cover.

The driver of the lead vehicle slammed on his brakes.

In an instant Chris and Daryl opened fire. By the time both of their magazines were empty, the lead vehicle had two flat tires and both headlamps were shattered.

Chris let out a war cry that echoed down the canyon.

Becky ran back to Daryl's jeep and flipped the flood lights off. Then she climbed inside, stepping over Daryl's seat to reach her own.

Chris and Daryl were already climbing into their seats, ready to get out of there.

But where was Jaime? Chris looked around and couldn't see him anywhere. Becky stood there between the seats, looking for him frantically.

Then the darkness was shattered by the beam of a gigantic mercury vapor floodlight. In an instant, a shot rang out and a bullet ricocheted off of the roll bar two inches to the left of Becky's head. She froze, standing there in the center of the light beam.

The sharpshooter who had fired the shot that just narrowly missed Becky's head adjusted his rear sight two clicks to the right. His right index finger began to gently squeeze the hair trigger of his military-issue 223 caliber sniper rifle.

A bead of perspiration trickled down Jaime's right temple. It took all his will power to resist the temptation to jerk the trigger of his pistol, even though every part of his being was screaming at him to hurry. He squeezed smoothly and slowly, just as he had been taught.

In a split-second after the trigger of Jaime's pistol released the firing pin, the mercury vapor floodlight exploded as the twenty two caliber bullet hit dead center. This totally eliminated the light the sniper needed to get off his second shot and also tore through the right shoulder of the man who had been holding the floodlight, causing him to spin violently to his right, slamming the remains of the floodlight into the barrel of the sniper's rifle. The 223 went off, sending a steel-jacketed bullet into the trunk of the Ponderosa behind which Jaime was supposed to be hiding.

As the thunder from a nearby lightning strike rocked the area, Jaime leaped into the passenger seat of Chris's Jeep and slapped Chris on the right shoulder to be sure Chris was aware of his presence.

Daryl had already pulled Becky down into her seat and was roaring down the trail, spraying rocks and debris from his rear tires.

Rain began to fall heavily, making it difficult to see.

In a matter of seconds, Chris was firmly up against the back of Daryl's rear bumper. He put the killer Jeep into third gear, tromped on the accelerator, and both vehicles careened down the tree-lined trail in excess of seventy miles an hour.

Jaime shouted, "Aren't you afraid we're gonna hit something at this speed?"

Chris admitted, "I sure as hell am. But we just found out that those guys are deadly serious and they've got some awesome firepower. That guy was about to put a bullet through our sweet Becky. I'm gonna try to put some distance between us and them before we try anything else. Maybe we can even outrun them. It looked to me like they're driving Hummers. They'll go almost anywhere, but not very fast, and they're not very good in tight places. Mostly, we've got to get out of rifle range."

They roared on for close to five minutes, narrowly missing several large trees.

Jaime shouted, "I think they're falling behind. I haven't seen their headlights for a minute or more."

Chris backed off the accelerator but they were still moving at over fifty miles per hour. The intensity of the storm increased. The forest was becoming less dense, with more pinions and cedar and fewer pine trees. Five minutes later they came to another fork in the road and stopped.

# Chapter Thirty-six

"I don't remember the map showing a second split in this trail, Chris said, puzzled." He and Jaime unfolded the forestry map. Sure enough, the second split didn't appear on the map. In fact, the map didn't even show a trail where they were now. According to the map, the trail they were on ended about a mile back.

Daryl and Becky were standing on either side of Chris's Jeep, heads inside the cab, each trying to get as far out of the downpour as possible.

"What do you think?" asked Daryl.

Chris didn't reply. Instead, he reached into the glove compartment and pulled out Great-Grandfather's old weather-worn trail map. He opened it while Jaime aimed his flashlight at it.

"Look at this," Chris exclaimed. There on Great-Grandfather's map was a trail the government map did not show. Actually, Great-Grandfather's map had a lot more information. It showed that the trail didn't end on the plateau. On Great-Grandfather's map the trail continued across the plateau and split in two again. The left fork wound down a series of switchbacks to the valley floor and eventually rejoined the highway about twenty miles away. The right fork headed through a large, forested area and then became a dotted line ending at the base of a mountain. Great-Grandfather had labeled the area surrounded by that mountain "Mystic Valley."

Jaime asked, "Why does the trail turn into a dotted line for about two miles before it reaches the mountain?"

"I don't know," Chris said. "But look, just below the words 'Mystic Valley' are some more words, almost too small to read. Can you make them out?"

Jaime replied in the negative.

Becky stood next to Jaime with her left hand on his left shoulder and her chin resting on his right shoulder. "Let me take a look. I've got eagle eyes."

"Among other things," Jaime thought, pressing his cheek against hers.

Becky took the map and illuminated it with the flashlight she had taken from Jaime's hand. She studied it for several seconds, squinting. "Hiding place of the Ancient Ones," she shouted over the intensity of the storm. "I think the writing says, 'Hiding place of the Ancient Ones.'"

"What do you make of that?" asked Daryl.

"Beats me," replied Jaime.

"Chris, does that mean anything to you?" asked Becky.

"It does," said Chris. "Great-Grandfather told me many tales about the Ancient Ones. They were said to be mighty warriors who roamed this area long before recorded history, long before this country was discovered by the white man. According to Great-Grandfather, the Ancient Ones were the protectors of the villages. They lived in a secret valley and came out of hiding only when they were needed to protect the people from the marauding renegades who occasionally attacked their villages.

"Legend has it that they had an elaborate communication system, using drummers to relay messages across the mountains and valleys, informing them of the activities and whereabouts of the marauders. Great-Grandfather told me he thought he might have found their secret valley when he was just a young man, but he wasn't sure. He said he found a basin hidden within a mountain. But he wasn't able to find enough evidence that anyone had lived there to be certain it was the legendary secret valley. He never told me of its location or that he had put it on a map. I never paid enough attention to this old map to notice that mountain before."

"Well," surmised Daryl, "we need a place to hide while we decide what to do next. I think going back to the highway would be dangerous. Why don't we go take a look at this valley? Even if it's not what we hope it is, we may be able to take cover in the forest for a while. But first we need to make sure those guys don't follow us there."

"I think we can be sure of that," said Jaime. "I doubt if they have a map that shows this trail to the right. If we can cover that trail, they'll likely take the trail to the left down to the highway and assume we've either gotten back to the highway or headed down one of the other canyons."

"Well," said Becky, as another lightening bolt struck the ground about fifty feet from the Jeep, "whatever we're gonna do, we'd better do it real fast. I suspect those guys are moving a little slower since we staged our ambush, out of fear that we may have another one waiting for them. Still, they're likely to be here in a few minutes. Let's go."

"Sounds good to me," Daryl agreed.

"Okay," said Chris. "Let's move. I see a jack pine that should fall across the area just about where the trail splits, if some skillful woodsman cuts it down with great precision. We should be able to have it down in five minutes if we double-team it."

Jaime and Chris grabbed the two axes from the toolbox on the Jeep's rear bumper. Daryl moved his Jeep into a position that would allow the headlights to shine on the tree. Jaime and Chris began chopping with determination, alternating their swings. The rainfall continued with a vengeance. The tree was down in fewer than five minutes, almost on target.

Daryl threw a rope around the trunk of the fallen tree and was able to drag it with his Jeep into a position that totally obscured the trail on the right. Using a tree branch, Becky was brushing over the marks left by the Jeep's tires, assisted greatly by the falling rain. Anyone short of a professional tracker would have difficulty determining which way they had gone.

The group headed up the trail, hoping it really did lead to a hiding place. Within a couple of miles, the trail disappeared, obviously not having been used for some time.

Possibly no one other than Chris's Great-Grandfather knew of the hidden basin. Whatever trail had been there initially hadn't been used to provide access to the basin for several hundred years. The trail behind them was probably used by campers or hunters. That's why the final portion was shown as a dotted line. Perhaps it was Great-Grandfather's method of showing the way to the hidden basin when an actual trail no longer existed.

Hoping they weren't on a wild goose chase, Daryl kept heading, as best he could, in the direction shown on the map. Before long they came to a dense forest, just as indicated on Great-Grandfather's map. There was no way to get through the forest with the vehicles. The trees were far too thick.

Without consulting the others, Daryl began to drive around the perimeter of the forest, staying about fifty feet from its outer boundary. Eventually they reached the point where the forest came close to the base of a mountain. The mountain looked to be only about four hundred feet tall. Daryl turned his Jeep to aim his headlights at the base. To his surprise, there seemed to be a narrow corridor between the mountain's base and the trees, as if someone had created it. He proceeded slowly into the corridor, with Chris close behind. Then Daryl realized why there were no trees up against the mountain. There was some kind of a rock shelf at the base. The soil didn't begin until about ten feet from the mountain. Trees couldn't grow on that shelf. There wasn't even any grass there, just smooth, flat rock.

They continued for almost a half mile through the corridor, with Daryl and Becky in the lead. Chris turned off his headlights. He was following just a few feet behind Daryl's Jeep and didn't want the glare from his lights to make it difficult for Daryl and Becky to see. Chris and Jaime could see fine. The light from Daryl's Jeep reflected off the surrounding vegetation and made the corridor surprisingly bright in spite of the intense downpour.

Jaime wondered if they had fooled the bad guys with the attempt to conceal the trail. If not, he thought his group would do well to find an opening into the hidden basin soon and turn off their lights. There was a good chance that whoever was after them was no longer on their trail. If the bad guys had a map, it probably didn't show the trail to the basin. Even if it did, he and his friends had done a good job of making the turnoff onto the trail difficult to see. Finally, even if the bad guys had found the turnoff, the trail ended far short of the dense patch of forest. And with the rain as intense at it was, any tracks the Jeeps might have made would have been erased in a matter of minutes. Besides, with one of their vehicles already disabled, the bad guys probably had only one Hummer in pursuit and were likely not moving very fast, considering the weather. Likely they would never even notice the trail Jaime and the gang had taken.

Still, Jaime didn't know exactly who they were up against. These guys might well be government agents, perhaps part of the CIA, the FBI, or some unknown agency. Perhaps they had surveillance equipment capable of tracking the Jeeps by sound or even by heat-sensing. Maybe they were being watched by satellite cameras. The sooner they could find a place to hide and turn off their lights and engines, the more comfortable Jaime would be.

Daryl's Jeep came to an abrupt halt. Chris hit the brakes.

The sudden halt startled Jaime out of his daydream. He saw the cause of the unexpected stop. The corridor abruptly ended. The granite shelf they had been following ended with a patch of grass and trees.

Chris and Daryl shut off their engines, and Daryl turned off his lights. Suddenly it was so dark that nobody could see anything. It reminded Becky of her adventure along the interstate. She turned on the flashlight she had taken from Jaime earlier. It didn't help much at first, as their eyes had not yet adjusted to the absence of the headlights.

Gradually they started to make out their surroundings. Chris turned on his flashlight, too, and within a minute they could see well enough to verify that they were, indeed, at a dead-end.

Daryl said, "Well gang, what should we do now? Any ideas?"

Jaime responded, "Seems to me like a good time to consult with our advisor."

"What are you talking about?" Daryl asked.

"Well," replied Jaime, "we've got a lot to tell you about our experiences back at the farmhouse. For now, I'll just tell you that we met some form of alien intelligence that offered to assist us. When we were back at the scene of Becky's ambush, that intelligence warned me that Becky was in danger. It also told me there was something in my duffel bag that would save her. I found a pistol I didn't know was there. The intelligence called itself 'Zara' or something like that. If it hadn't been for that warning, Becky might not be with us now. I know it sounds crazy."

"Not at all," Daryl responded quickly. "unusual, mysterious, probably even miraculous. But not crazy." With that simple statement, he enlightened the other three adventurers, in a matter of moments, a great deal about the kind of man he was and the depth of his knowledge.

Jaime climbed into the back of Chris's Jeep and retrieved the crystal from beneath the seat. He removed the blanket that had been wrapped around it. Then he held up the crystal for the others to see. Becky shined her flashlight on it. Multi-colored rays shot out of the crystal in all directions, reflecting off the pine needles of the surrounding trees.

"Wow!" exclaimed Daryl. "Pretty awesome."

Becky spread the blanket on the hood of the Jeep, and Jaime set the crystal on it.

Becky was the first to speak. "Zara, are you here?"

A gentle voice, with what seemed to be a slight British accent, spoke to her. The voice didn't come to her in the form of sound waves. It occurred in her mind, saying, "I am Zara. I am here, willing to assist you. I will involve myself in your lives only when invited."

"Did the rest of you hear that?" asked Becky.

They all enthusiastically indicated that they were each receiving the same message.

Jaime said, "Zara, when you spoke to me earlier, I was apparently the only one who heard you. And I didn't invite you to speak. Your voice in my mind was a complete surprise. Can you explain how that happened and what's going on?"

Zara answered, "I am not 'speaking' to you, as you understand that term. I am manipulating that portion of your brain that receives low-voltage electrical impulses, normally created when sound waves activate the mechanism in your outer ears that is designed to convert those sound waves into electrical impulses to be delivered by your nervous system to the appropriate part of your brain. It is a lot more complicated than what I have just said and involves all of the cells in your body, not just the brain. I use this method of communication for simplicity, although I do have the ability to create sound waves. The method I have chosen results in a communication that is not subject to the distortions that can result from the use of sound waves and also prevents the communication from being intercepted by others on your Earth plane.

"I have the ability to direct these communications to any one of you or all of you, as I deem appropriate. In the instance of my earlier message to Jaime, I determined that he was in the best position to act and that such a communication to Chris or Daryl would have distracted them from their intended task of disabling the opponent's vehicle. I also decided not to communicate with Becky at that time, in that my short-term view of the future told me that such an action would startle her, causing her to pause in her movement for just a second, resulting in the possibility that she would have been in a position where the sniper's bullet, as it ricocheted off of the roll bar of Daryl's Jeep and fragmented, would have injured her.

"Now I will speak regarding the fact that I contacted Jaime without his invitation. As I said, we do not normally make contact without an invitation. This is not because of some rule of the spirit world. Actually, in my world there are no rules as you speak of them. There are, however, laws of the universe, such as the law of attraction. But of these we shall speak later. For now, please know that our choice not to interfere with your free will is not a matter of law or of rules. As simply as I can express it in your limited language, it is a natural result of the unconditional love that exists everywhere in the spirit world.

"We, who act only out of love, which is a love far beyond anything you know of as love on the physical plane, would never act contrary to your desires or intentions. Your higher self, which is the part of you still residing in the spirit world, knows of and wishes for the aspect of you focused in physical form to be free to pursue the intentions for which you incarnated in this lifetime. One of those intentions was that you be allowed to experience all aspects of physical existence, both good and evil, as you define those terms on your physical plane.

"Before you began this incarnation, however, you understood that there could be events occurring in your Earth-plane lifetime that could terminate the existence of your physical form before your objectives for this lifetime were accomplished. You instructed, or agreed with, those light beings in the spirit world who oversee your current adventure, those who some on your plane refer to as 'angels,' that if they should perceive a danger of such a premature termination of this physical experience, they may interfere. This is not technically interference, in that it is done with your agreement before you incarnated.

"I know this is complicated and perhaps foreign to your acquired thought processes. But for now, just know that if you wish our assistance, you should ask. Our attention to your request will be instantaneous. Without your invitation, we will interfere only in matters of the most critical nature. In most instances, for most of those on your plane, this type of interference will not be in the form of what you would term a communication but, rather, some form of physical manipulation, like an impending vehicle collision that is somehow avoided at the last moment. In the case of highly advanced humans, such as the four of you, who have opened your minds and hearts to uncommon possibilities, we take the risk of direct communication, calculating the probability that you will not be shocked by such a contact."

"Wow!" said Chris, "If Great-Grandfather could only see me now."

Zara said, "The very fact that you have thought about Great-Grandfather calls him instantly into your presence. This is true of any beings in the spirit world."

Daryl said, "For most of my adult life, I have sensed the presence of beings from time to time. Now I understand what that is all about."

"Correct," Zara said. "Every being on your plane has angels or spirit guides or departed relatives who are in contact the instant you summon them. This summoning does not have to be for a particular spirit but is often a call for help, sometimes even a desperate need for help without an actual calling. You are never alone. The God Force which—if I may oversimplify—is an accumulation of all that is, is with you always, or as it is said in your Book of Books, 'all ways.'

"My perception of all aspects of the lives of the four of you who have chosen to combine your efforts for this adventure is that you will be best served if I leave you to your own devices at this time. I will leave you with one 'hint,' which I perceive will lead to your rapid advancement—with your permission, of course."

Becky said, "I believe I speak for all of us when I ask you please to go on with whatever you wish to tell us."

The others nodded their agreement.

"I will simply tell you," said Zara, "that all is not as it seems. I will leave you to rely on your own good instincts to find your way to the next phase of this grand adventure. Just know that you are loved beyond anything you know of as love on your plane, that you can never get it all done, and that it all has a happy ending. Always. I bring you tidings of great love from the spirit world, where you are considered to be on the leading edge of the growth and expansion of the God Force. Remember—all is not as it seems."

In an instant, Zara was gone.

Chris said, "I had a dream the other night. Great-Grandfather was in that dream. He also told me to remember that 'all is not as it seems.'"

"What do you think that means?" Becky asked.

All were quiet for a moment. Then Chris said, "Well, as it applies to our current situation, it seems that we're at a dead-end. Yet, Great-Grandfather's map shows a trail leading into this rather solid-looking mountain. So I would guess that maybe this isn't really a dead-end or maybe this isn't really a solid mountain or maybe both."

"Or maybe Great-Grandfather's map isn't accurate," Becky added.

"Or maybe," said Daryl, "the map was accurate when it was drawn, and something has changed since then."

"Or maybe," said Chris, "the very existence of an opening into the secret canyon depends on our intention and knowing."

"Let's do a little looking around," Jaime suggested. "Becky and I will head into the forest. The two of you check out a few of these mini-canyons that Mother Nature has carved into the face of the mountain."

Jaime took the flashlight from Becky and took her hand in his. A rather bold and good move, he thought, and led her toward the thick undergrowth.

Chris shouted after them, "Don't wander off too far. Whistle if you find something. And behave yourselves."

Becky smiled and grabbed Jaime's upper arm. As they headed into the forest, she pulled him closer.

Chris and Daryl took the other flashlight and began exploring the base of the mountain, careful not to aim its beam too far uphill so as not to create any unintentional signals for the bad guys to spot. Twice they found openings in the face of the mountain that looked promising. Twice they turned out to be dead-ends.

The rain stopped. It wasn't apparent at first because of the water drops falling from the trees.

Within ten minutes, they heard a whistle in the distance. Daryl whistled back. He heard another whistle in response. Chris and Daryl headed into the forest.

By the time they had moved about fifty yards along the base of the mountain, they saw the beam from Jaime's flashlight. They hurried to where Jaime and Becky stood, shining their flashlight in the direction of the mountain, through some tall scrub oak and thick bushes.

"I think we might have found something," Becky said.

There, in the side of the mountain, well hidden by thick vegetation, was an opening, one that would go unnoticed unless a person was looking for it very carefully. One ponderosa, directly in front of the opening, appeared to be at least a hundred years old.

The opening was about eight feet wide and eight feet high. The bottom was relatively smooth, and the side walls were vertical and surprisingly even.

Daryl led them into the opening, which proved to be a long tunnel. They walked for several hundred yards without the tunnel turning or ending. Finally they came to a wall of bushes and vines. Apparently, they had walked all the way through the mountain and come to its far side.

With some effort they were able to cut away enough branches and vines to allow them access to the forest beyond. There, blocking a substantial part of the opening were two large trees, at least as old as the one they had seen at the other end of the tunnel. It was too dark to ascertain the contours of the land beyond the beam of their flashlights.

They decided to put off exploring the area until morning, for fear that they might run into something dangerous. Besides, they didn't want to use up the remaining life in their flashlight batteries.

Daryl expressed surprise that the tunnel was so wide. If it had been built centuries earlier, he thought it would likely not have been dug wider than necessary to allow a man to walk through it or, at most, a man on horseback, especially considering the crude tools that would have had to be used.

Becky suggested that perhaps the Ancient Ones had occupied the basin, not only as a hideout, but as their home. Perhaps they had families. Perhaps they had made the tunnel so wide to accommodate wagons for bringing supplies to the basin.

From the vegetation blocking both ends of the tunnel, it was obvious that it hadn't been used for a long time. It must have been built before the advent of any type of modern earth-digging equipment. The texture of the walls suggested that they were cut with hand tools. The smoothness of the floor was likely the result of hundreds of years of use.

The group decided that this would be as good a place as any they could think of to spend the night. They didn't know whether there were other means of access to the area. They would have to wait until morning to see if they were indeed within a natural basin.

They considered bringing the Jeeps through the tunnel but decided against it for two reasons. First, they would have to cut down the three trees blocking the two entries, which would leave noticeable evidence that someone had been here recently. Second, removing those trees would take a lot of work, considering their diameter, and they were just too tired.

The four agreed that hiding the Jeeps well within the forest by covering them with tree branches would be adequate for now. Besides, the tree on the other end of the tunnel would help to keep the tunnel a secret.

After some discussion, they decided that foot access to the basin would serve them best. While Chris and Daryl moved the Jeeps into a ravine and covered them with plenty of branches and grass, Jaime and Becky moved their supplies through the tunnel and deposited them on a high grassy knoll just outside of the other end. The knoll was relatively dry in spite of the recent storm.

It took several trips through the tunnel to get all of the equipment into the basin. On the last trip, Becky stopped mid-way through the tunnel and dropped the two sleeping bags she was carrying. Slowly she pushed Jaime, who had a full duffel bag under one arm and a box filled with food under the other, against the tunnel wall. She pressed her body gently against his and wrapped her arms around his neck. He couldn't turn loose of the items he was carrying without risk of damaging them or their contents. He was, delightfully, at her mercy. She pulled his head down toward hers and kissed him on the mouth. His heart raced. She kissed him again. Against his wishes, his lips began to tremble.

Jaime dropped the box and duffel bag, oblivious that he had done so. He put his arms around Becky's shoulders and pulled her tightly against him. As their lips locked, Becky moaned slightly. Jaime became aware of feelings in his body that had been only hinted at in his brief encounters with other girls. From the sounds coming from Becky's throat, Jaime suspected that she was experiencing similar reactions.

Becky pulled her head back and said, "Do you know how long I've wanted to do that? If I had waited for you to do something, I might have become old first."

Jaime didn't know what to say. He had been so wrapped up in their adventure that he had kept his feelings for Becky pretty much in the background. He couldn't help but notice, once again, how beautiful she was. He felt his heart racing whenever she smiled or even walked away from him, for that matter.

This was new to him. He had never been alone with a woman before, at least for any length of time and without a chaperone or rules. How was he supposed to know what Becky wanted? How was he to know that she would be receptive to his advances? Girls were hard to understand.

All he said in response to Becky's question was, "No, I don't know." Then he put his hand under her chin, tilted her face up toward his, and kissed her again. He felt a pressure in his chest that made it pleasantly difficult to breathe. He could feel her heart beating, harder, he hoped, than normal. His certainly was.

Chapter Thirty-seven

For hours, Herbert Benson's men had been searching the area between the compound and the highway, looking for any sign of whoever had broken into the farmhouse and the bunker. Benson spent most of his time dabbing calamine lotion on those parts of his body that were on fire with itching. He devoted the rest of his time to working out a strategy of damage control. There was a good chance that someone had uncovered the secrets that had remained buried for so long in the farmhouse compound. Even more pressing was his need to stop the interlopers before word of the existence of the farmhouse and the spacecraft spread to the point where it couldn't be stopped.

Benson had had a mobile home delivered to the compound to serve as his command post. He had it located near the road that ran from the front gate to the farmhouse.

Benson considered bringing in the "big guns." He weighed the advisability of reporting the situation to Sheffield, who would have the horsepower to handle the situation quickly and efficiently. Agents under Sheffield's control had access to methods of surveillance and detection far beyond anything Benson even knew about, although he had heard the rumors that frequently circulated among the lower echelon. He heard of satellite cameras that could read the raised lettering on the side of an automobile tire. He heard of electronic devices that could locate a soldier by sensing the flame coming from the barrel of his rifle and vaporize him in an instant. He heard of satellites that could read a fingerprint found on a handrail or the receiver of a public telephone and identify the person in fewer than fifteen seconds.

Although Benson hadn't been able to verify the existence of such devices, there were many less exotic methods of detection and destruction that he knew, for a fact, did exist. He knew that if he were to tell the right people about the situation, whoever had been in that farmhouse would be in custody in a matter of hours. But he couldn't

bear the thought that the announcement might be tantamount to signing his own death warrant.

When it came to matters of this magnitude, involving members
of the CIA—who were capable of making a spacecraft and an entire
family disappear—he was dealing with very powerful individuals. These
were not the kind of people Benson wanted to have using him as a
scapegoat. He especially couldn't risk having these people thinking
he had committed errors that placed them in positions where their
careers might be destroyed or worse yet, in danger of finding themselves on death row.

Herbert Benson III was scared to the point where rational
thought was beginning to elude him. He knew his men were good.
Nobody lasted long in the field without being good, but some of
these guys were getting old. Still, trespassing and breaking into the
farmhouse were amateur offenses. Benson wasn't dealing with professionals. He was dealing with some poor fools who had stumbled
onto a dangerous secret.

At first he thought he would have the situation under control in
short order. Then his men ran into that ambush. That display was not
the sort of thing one would expect from amateurs. "Who are those
guys?" Benson wondered.

That was the problem. He hadn't the foggiest notion who he
was up against.

He remembered reading excerpts from *The Art of War*, one of
the great works on the tactics of warfare. That book emphasized the
absolute necessity of knowing your enemy.

What did he know about this 'enemy?' Nothing, absolutely nothing.

Then it dawned on him. That was the problem. It wasn't that his
adversaries were so damn smart. It was that he didn't know anything
about them. He had been so sure that his men would quickly capture
these troublemakers that it didn't occur to him that any intelligence
would be needed. He wouldn't need much information when all his
people had to do was catch someone running away from them in the
forest. That ambush added a new factor to the equation. It was no

longer a matter of "running down" and "capturing." There was now the added objective of "finding," an entirely different consideration.

Then, for the first time since he had heard about the ambush, Benson came up with an idea that gave him a slight bit of comfort. He didn't have the awesome power of the entire CIA behind him. But he certainly had access to enough common methods of detection that should enable him to identify his adversaries.

Once a person knew who his enemies were, there were a lot more options. Besides, one man on his team impressed Benson tremendously, a man named John Hawkin. Benson had not seen or heard of this man until yesterday. But something about the man scared Benson, big time. And in Benson's mind that was good. Hawkin had a look in his eyes, a look of confidence. He also had a hunger in his eyes. He impressed Benson as the kind of man who would go the limit for a cause he believed in. Benson wondered how a man of Hawkin's apparent abilities had been included on the list of losers from which he had selected his team.

Benson had done his best to convince Hawkin that the security of the nation was at serious risk and that the apprehension of these traitors was imperative. As soon as he knew who they were, Hawkin would bring them in quickly and efficiently.

How could he identify them?

Of course, the most obvious and most simple way of all, fingerprints. Whoever broke into the compound must have touched something. Certainly there were resilient surfaces from which fingerprints could be lifted, glass, ceramics, porcelain, handrails, doorknobs, the spacecraft itself. There had to be prints all over the place.

Within a few hours, the fingerprint expert Benson ordered to the scene had full sets of prints, all secured from within the farmhouse. The expert wasn't allowed into the basement of the farmhouse. Benson had taken care, early on, to have the basement door secured.

Benson ordered the expert back to headquarters with instructions to report back to him as soon as he knew whose prints they were. The man was admonished to tell no one of the events of the evening. To do so would result in serious and swift repercussions.

Within hours, Chris, Becky, and Jaime had been identified and Benson had in his possession complete workups on each of them. He also knew the identities and the likely whereabouts of their family members, which would be highly useful information to have when trying to coax people on the run to turn themselves in.

Benson marveled at the youth of these intruders. It made him suspect that they had stumbled onto this place by accident rather than as part of some dark plan.

He wondered why Becky and Jaime would have had their fingerprints on record at such an early age. Then he remembered that about five years ago there had been a few isolated kidnappings of children over a wide geographic area and that the school systems had joined forces with several service clubs and, with the assistance of local police and sheriff's departments, had managed to get thousands of children photographed and finger printed in an attempt to discourage further kidnappings. Very likely, Becky and Jaime had been fingerprinted as part of that program.

He had to find a way to communicate with the runaways. With several illegal wiretaps put on the phone lines of all known family members within the last two hours, Benson figured it was just a matter of time before something would turn up.

For the second time since he had become aware that something was amiss at the compound, Benson took time to wonder where Daryl Harrington had gone. He wished he had been able to keep some of his men searching for Harrington. That was one loose end he couldn't afford to ignore. After all, he had received direct orders from Frank Sheffield to capture Harrington. As far as Benson knew, Sheffield didn't know about the break-in at the farmhouse. Benson shuddered to think of what Sheffield would do if he knew of that recent development.

For now, Benson must keep his manpower focused on the apprehension of those who knew, firsthand, about the farmhouse massacre. Their testimony could incriminate him and others, even after he had the farmhouse cleaned up.

Benson was concerned about the fact that the break-in at the compound occurred just three days after Harrington discovered the secret file. Quite a coincidence. Still, Harrington's information would be of little value once the evidence at the farmhouse was destroyed. After that, the most Harrington could do, would be to raise some suspicions about a spacecraft cover-up. It was almost certain that Harrington had not been able to break the code of the secret file. The intricacies of that code were far beyond the capabilities of someone hired for the position Harrington held.

Benson felt confident that any law enforcement officer or judge who might get involved could be convinced by a few CIA enforcers to bury the evidence and have the records permanently sealed. It seemed reasonable to think that sufficient pressure could be brought to bear to convince any clear-thinking person to "forget" about allegations relative to a supposed spacecraft.

That same reasoning didn't seem to Benson to hold true for allegations of mass murder. So job number one was to get rid of the witnesses to the physical evidence of the massacre. After that, he'd destroy the evidence.

Benson's men were looking for the runaways around the clock. He suspected that they were still somewhere between the farmhouse and the point where the trail they had taken intersected the highway. But that was a lot of territory, an area about twenty miles square, which translated into four hundred square miles. That was more than a quarter million acres, way more territory than he had the manpower to comb adequately.

So he would have to use the technology at his disposal to bring them in. He now had pictures of Chris, Becky, and Jaime, which he had distributed to all law enforcement agencies within a one hundred mile radius of the farmhouse.

He'd have them before long.

Benson wished he had a description of their vehicle or vehicles, but his men had gotten close to them only one time, and that time they were blinded by the spotlights before they were able to see anything clearly.

Now all Benson had to do was to wait for his prey to make one mistake. He prayed that it would happen before they had a chance to divulge what they knew to anyone else. If that should occur, God forbid, there might have to be a roundup of individuals as extensive as the original massacre. This could involve individuals in the CIA and FBI hierarchy, none of whom would be at all pleased with that prospect and all of whom would be gunning for Benson.

He couldn't allow that to happen. He was far too old for this sort of thing.

Benson sat down in front of the radio base station in his temporary headquarters near the farmhouse. With a trembling hand he reached for his bottle of calamine lotion.

Chapter Thirty-eight

After hiding the Jeeps, Daryl and Chris walked down the tunnel. As they neared the end, they noticed Jaime and Becky standing against the wall. Chris shined his light away so as not to embarrass them.

Daryl didn't have the same concern. "Okay, you two lovebirds," he said, "let's set up camp so we can get some shuteye before the sun comes up."

As they stepped out of the tunnel, Daryl stopped abruptly and pointed. "Look over there. Do you see a light?"

They all looked down into what appeared, in the darkness, to be a valley. There was a light flickering through the trees.

Becky whispered, "Turn off the flashlights. Let's be quiet until we find out what that is."

Both flashlights clicked off.

The foursome started toward the flickering light, moving slowly. They wanted to be as quiet as possible, and they also were having trouble seeing what they might be running into in the darkness.

They worked their way close enough to the light to see that it was a fire of some sort. As they drew closer, it became obvious that it was a campfire.

Becky gasped when she saw someone sitting on a log between them and the fire. She looked more closely and couldn't believe what her eyes were telling her. The flame from the campfire was visible right through whoever was sitting there. She grabbed Jaime's arm. Everyone froze.

Then a thunderous laugh echoed down the canyon.

Chris knew that sound. It was Great-Grandfather's legendary belly laugh. Chris would know the laugh of that great old man anywhere. Chris gestured to his friends to stay where they were and he walked slowly toward the apparition, still uncertain.

As he drew alongside the seated figure, he got a clear view of the side profile in the flickering firelight. It was, indeed, Great-Grandfather. Only he was much younger than when Chris had last seen him.

Great-Grandfather turned his head slowly toward Chris and said, "Pretty slick, huh?"

"Great-Grandfather, is it really you?"

"Of course," came the reply. "Did you expect anything less?"

"It's just such a shock. What are you doing here?"

Jaime and Becky began to approach the campfire, still wary of what was happening.

"Tell your friends not to be afraid. They are in the presence of a friendly envoy from the spirit world."

"What's this 'friendly envoy' shit?" Chris laughed.

"I've come to assist you. You invited me, remember?"

"No, I don't," Chris replied.

"Think back," said Great-Grandfather, "You said something like, 'If Great-Grandfather could only see me now.'"

"That's a request?"

"Well, not technically, but it did get my attention and brought me into your presence. I decided to wait until you finished a few chores before I made my appearance. Kind of a nice touch, don't you think? Campfire and all?"

Chris motioned for his friends to gather around the campfire. He introduced them to Great-Grandfather.

"You look so young," Chris noted. "Why?"

"In the spirit world," replied Great-Grandfather, "we have unlimited choices, all of which are manifested instantly. This is one of the main differences between my world and yours. You have the troublesome and uncomfortable concept of time, while in the spirit world everything happens—or should I say exists—at the same instant. I simply willed my body to appear to you as it looked when I was in my prime, although as you have probably noticed, it's a little less dense than when I was focused on the level of gross matter."

"This is confusing," Daryl said, "although I find it outrageously exciting."

"Thank you," responded Great-Grandfather. "I hoped it would be. For many, it would be frightening. I can tell, by the fact that none of you ran screaming back to the tunnel, that you are all open to the reality of the existence of life beyond the earthly experience."

Becky said, "We are not only open to that reality, but we are enthusiastically ready to learn more."

Jaime asked, "Have you been watching us all along?"

"Not really," Great-Grandfather replied. "There are so many joyous activities in the spirit world that we normally don't focus our consciousness on our brothers and sisters on the physical plane unless we are summoned. We draw near, primarily, when you call out to us. We may be summoned, however, without such a deliberate calling, as when someone we hold dear is in danger."

"What is it like in your world?" asked Daryl.

"The best description I can provide for you, given the limitations of your language, is that it's like being in a constant symphony of joy and sensuous delights. Think about your feelings when you're listening to your favorite song in the whole world, as it's being played through a two hundred fifty watt amplifier with the volume turned up to eight point five. Then experience that sound running through several of the finest Infinity speakers money can buy. Feel the sound waves affecting not only your eardrums but every cell in your body, swirling through your diaphragm, up your spinal cord, and into your brain.

"Finally, imagine that all of your loved ones are in the same room, having the same experience, and that each knows and feels that the others are having the same experience and are responding with the same feelings of indescribable joy. For good measure, multiply that feeling by ten.

"That is as close as I can come to describing the spirit world, except, of course, for those times when I am in direct contact with the God Force. That is so far beyond description that I will not even attempt a comparison."

"Wow!" Becky gasped. "That sounds awesome."

"Interestingly," observed Great-Grandfather, "in spite of the wondrousness of the spirit world, millions of light beings are there eager to focus their energy in a physical body, in spite of the limitations of your corporeal state. That is because each physical experience provides the God Force, of which you and I are all a part, with another opportunity to expand itself through feeling and experiencing. It is the reason that the God Force first expanded itself into billions of light beings. That is what each of you essentially is—a light being. That event, the explosion of the God Force into billions of light beings and all of physical reality, is expressed in your world as the 'Big Bang.'

"Surprisingly, God didn't create your physical bodies as many believe. The light beings existed for millions of years, in Earth time, each as simply a light particle and a light wave, operating in unison. Eventually, a few of the more courageous light beings decided to risk lowering their vibrational frequencies by seven degrees to the level of gross matter and focus their energy in physical bodies. They created their own bodies for this purpose. They had to experiment for some time to get their bodies to function satisfactorily. The first several experiments resulted in unisex creatures that were quite ugly by your standards. There is much more to know about these events, but that will have to wait until another time."

"By the way, Christopher," said Great-Grandfather, "how did you like the grizzly bear? Kind of exciting, huh?"

"Did you have something to do with that terrifying little incident?" asked Chris.

"Well, somewhat," said Great-Grandfather. "You set the stage. You called forth the lessons. I, knowing your relationship with the great outdoors, simply added a little flavor to the incident. Rather a stimulating experience, don't you think?"

"Rather," murmured Chris. "But next time, could you make it a little less exciting?"

"I don't make it anything," said Great-Grandfather. "My only involvement is to facilitate what your higher self already knows you need to experience. It could have easily been anything from a brawl in a dark alley with four knife-wielding hoodlums to the failure of a parachute to open. It was a test of your understanding of and belief in many of the lessons you have learned in this and prior lifetimes. I simply fine-tuned the elements of the adventure. Hope you don't mind."

Chris was silent for a moment. Then he asked, "Did you cause Tama to show up?"

"No," said Great-Grandfather. "Tama's presence in that exact place at that exact time was the result of his own instincts and great love for you."

"But what if there had been no Tama?" asked Chris. "I would have been grizzly food!"

"Not so," said Great-Grandfather. "The universe is perfect. Everything happens as it should. Your higher self obviously had not yet decided that it was your time to be called back to the spirit world. Given that fact, all of the circumstances that led to the grizzly bear incident would have been modified to bring about a result that left you alive."

"Very interesting," Jaime commented.

"Very interesting," Becky echoed.

Daryl suggested that perhaps they should spend some time, while Great-Grandfather was still among them, discussing their current situation.

Great-Grandfather stared into the campfire, obviously deep in thought.

"This is the extent to which I choose to involve myself in your adventure. It is the result of balancing several factors. The first is my deep love for you—all of you. The second is my selfish desire to demonstrate, for your entertainment, my awesome powers, which, by the way, are your powers, too, once you know you have them. Third is my knowing that your interests are best served by those circumstances that will provide you with the greatest opportunities to feel, experience, and grow. The fourth is that, no matter what, this all will have a satisfactory ending.

"That does not mean, necessarily, that it will have the ending you might now choose. What it does mean is that, given the facts that you are infinite and eternal beings, with unlimited lifetimes ahead of you, and that death is no more than stepping through a doorway into another joyous form of existence, no ending is possible that will not lead to your greatest good. There is no ending possible that is not chosen by your higher self.

"With that said, and rather eloquently I might add, I will tell you that, first of all, the greatest good will result from your going to someplace other than the city where you had intended to deliver the evidence you now have in your possession. Second, the revelation of the existence of the spacecraft to the media will likely be of little value, in that the media are very much controlled by a small number of families who take great care to see that the public knows only what those families choose it to know. Third, if you decide to reveal what you know to the media, your worthy opponents will likely be forced to involve others with such power that you and your families will be destroyed and all evidence discredited. Fourth, if the public were to learn of the spacecraft, there would likely be such a panic on your planet that the stock markets would crash and law enforcement would be powerless to contain the riots that would ensue.

"I remind Jaime that there remains an item in his duffel bag that might be useful in the timely unfolding of events to come. That item was placed there by Jaime's brother, Tim, as you were leaving on your adventure. Tim knew, instinctively, that you might be facing certain dangers.

"Finally," said Great-Grandfather, "I must tell you that nothing in your world is certain. Nothing can be foretold with any certainty, not even by the very God Force itself. Everything is subject to change by simply changing thought. Even those psychics on your Earth plane who are sincere and capable will tell you that anything they may reveal about your future is only 'as it is seen now.' It is all subject to a change in your thought process or, lacking that, a change in the thinking of mankind. Please be sure to apply this to everything I have told you. Know that the power, ultimately, is yours."

Great-Grandfather stood, and instantly the campfire shot several feet into the air, burst into a shower of sparks, and disappeared.

Chris objected. "You're not going to leave us that nice warm campfire?"

"No," said Great-Grandfather, "As you may have noticed, that fire gave off no heat. It was for visual effect only. You'll have to build your own fire.

"Just remember, it was your choice, and a wise one at that, to focus your energy on this plane of time and space. One of the reasons you came here was to experience contrast or what you would call variety. It is the contrast that allows you to experience your power to flow energy, the truly great joy of being on this plane. Your world of contrast is totally unlike my world of the absolute. Your world offers left and right, up and down, black and white, dark and light, and, unfortunately for the four of you tonight, hot and cold."

With that, Great-Grandfather let out one of his remarkable belly laughs. As it echoed down the canyons, his body rose a few feet into the air, spun around once, and disappeared.

All was darkness.

Jaime turned on his flashlight.

Chris turned away from the others. But before he did, Becky noticed a tear on his cheek, reflected in the glow of Jaime's flashlight. Contrary to what Chris would have thought, it made her love him all the more.

They headed back to the tunnel for what they hoped would be a good night's sleep.

As they approached the tunnel, Jaime put his hand gently on Becky's shoulder. She stopped and turned toward him. Jaime leaned forward and pressed his cheek against hers, feeling the warmth of her body. In the darkness, they stood holding each other. Jaime could feel Becky trembling ever so slightly. A solitary tear from those beautiful eyes touched his cheek. She had been as moved by Great-Grandfather's message as he had.

They all slept soundly that night, each with a new sense of confidence.

# Chapter Thirty-nine

As Jaime lay in the tunnel waiting for sleep to come, he thought of the many wondrous things Great-Grandfather had revealed to him and his friends. He thought about what Mom and Dad had taught him about synchronicity, about seeming coincidences that are really the result of thought. He thought about how our lives often are affected by events we may not even be aware of consciously. He thought about the possibility that he wouldn't even know Becky now if he hadn't been riding home from the football game the night that the eighteen-wheeler spun out of control on the ice and hit their car.

He thought about how there never would have been a Franklin/Riverton football game if the Chipewa Dam hadn't collapsed, causing the relocation of the Elk Horn River and setting the stage for a political battle that ultimately decided in which county the citizens of Sprague would locate their city.

Jaime wondered how many hundreds of events, of which he wasn't even aware, had to have happened to bring him to this tunnel, on this night, lying next to this exquisite woman.

If Jaime had reached the point in his evolution where he had fully developed his power of omniscience, he might now have been consciously aware of the limitless sets of circumstances that conspired to bring him to this time and place.

For now, these exciting events that The Force arranges to satisfy our desires will continue to be regarded by the majority of human beings as mere coincidences.

Many powerful events conspired to bring Jaime to this junc-
ture of his life, most of which were entirely unknown to him. A
case in point is a set of circumstances that occurred several years
ago that could conveniently be called the "Matt Grover–Osgood
Thurmond disaster."

This entire matter was the result of the fact that the collapse of
the Chipewa Dam north of Sprague had caused a re-routing of the
Elk Horn River, necessitating a vote of the citizens of Sprague to
determine whether their fair town would remain in Beaver Creek
County or be legally relocated to Silverwood County.

It seems that while the citizens of Sprague were at the polls
deciding the fate of their town and, indirectly, that of all future Franklin
High School football games, Matt Grover was busy consorting with
and seeking a plenary indulgence from the high goddess of water
engineering, to whom those who understand the intricacies of such
esoteric concepts as "head pressure" and "cubic feet per second"
pray for guidance.

Matt Grover was the head honcho of the division of the Army
Corps of Engineers that had jurisdiction over and responsibility for
the previously mentioned, and now dysfunctional, Chipewa Dam.
Since the untimely demise of the dam, Matt had barricaded himself
in a dark, cold, and lonely chamber of the federal building with only
his slide rule, a Hewlett–Packard calculator, a set of as-built Chipewa
Dam drawings, and a stack of engineering manuals for company.
Despite his best attempts at objectivity—a virtually impossible task
for a federal bureaucrat—Matt couldn't escape the mathematical certainty that the Chipewa Dam, by all that is holy and sacred in the
realm of water engineering, should still be standing. No matter how
many ways he tested the calculations, he couldn't escape the facts that
(a) the Chipewa Dam was designed and constructed to withstand the
ravages of anything less than a five-hundred-year storm and (b) the
rainfall that had caused the structural failure of the Chipewa was, at
best, a one-hundred-year storm.

The one variable that Matt Grover had left out of his calculations was the genetic background of Osgood Thurmond.

When Osgood's father, Drexel Thurmond was a senior in high school, the term "geek" was not in vogue. It is doubtful that "nerd" had yet been coined. In those days, perhaps the word "Square" would have been appropriate. In any event, Drexel Thurmond was not held in high regard by the in crowd.

Drexel had a body to die from. He had no muscle tone. His waist was wider than his shoulders. He was uncoordinated. He could have read a book in a dark room by the glow of his inflamed acne. His breath had been reputed to wilt the geraniums in his mother's flowerbox. He was what might be called "unaware."

Drexel fathered the aforementioned Osgood Thurmond, without knowledge of the causal implications of the procreative act. His accomplice, soon to be his wife, knew less than he did and appeared to have evolved from a parallel genetic pool. In short, Osgood's parents were a couple of losers. Osgood inherited a plethora of genetic defects, not the least of which was terminal stupidity. His two redeeming qualities, if redemption is not put to a particularly rigid test, were his abundant body mass and his abounding brute strength.

On the day that is relevant to our tale, Osgood had taken a solitary ride high into the mountains for what was intended to be a brief camping trip. Other than a small tent and a sleeping bag, the only useful implements Osgood brought along were a small hand axe and a pair of leather work-gloves. After he erected the tent and rolled out his sleeping bag, Osgood gradually began to comprehend that he had nothing to eat and none of the other implements and accessories that assist in making a camping trip an enjoyable event.

As he sat on a large rock, gazing out across Lake Chipewa, it slowly dawned on Osgood that the immense ponderosa pine tree, which blocked part of his view, was dead. For a while, that fact didn't register with him as having any significance. Eventually, however, the first inklings of an idea began a gradual assault upon his consciousness. After considerable time had passed, a smile started to form on his face and his eyebrows began a slow migration toward his hairline. His appearance assumed the attributes of a cartoon character who, coming to a revolutionary realization, is depicted with a light bulb above his head. Osgood had experienced his annual idea. He felt good. He was proud. He was excited.

As he moved laboriously toward his tent, where he had hoped to make use of his sleeping bag to catch a few winks, the idea he had just formulated continued to gnaw at the outer fringes of his awareness. Finally he gave in to the urge to shout "*Wow!*" The energy released by the force of that utterance had an amplifying effect on his slowly solidifying idea until it exploded into a full-blown insight. Osgood reasoned that, perhaps, that massive ponderosa could be put to some use.

In the shadowy recesses of his cerebrum, he reviewed a detailed list of the camping items he had brought. After ruling out the tent and the sleeping bag as having any use in connection with the deceased ponderosa, his keen sense of acuity focused upon the logging axe and work-gloves as possibly having some connection. He walked around the tree a couple of times, then shuffled back to the axe and gloves, then back to the tree. He stood there, glancing back and forth between the objects of his consternation. Suddenly the light bulb reappeared over his head, and this time his eyebrows literally slammed into his hairline, so magnificent was his comprehension.

He reasoned, "Tree—axe—firewood—campfire—warmth—wow!" He put on the work-gloves, picked up the axe, and after some deliberation, began hacking away at the trunk of the largest ponderosa ever grown in that part of the national forest. It didn't dawn on him to think about how he would convert portions of that massive wooden monolith into kindling or, even, burnable-size logs, for that matter. It also didn't occur to him that there might be some question regarding the direction in which the fifty thousand pounds of pine would travel once its connection with the earth was rendered less than that necessary to maintain it in an erect configuration.

Mother Nature is a great compensator. What Osgood lacked in intelligence, he more than made up for in stamina. He also possessed a superabundance of tenacity, which, coupled with his cerebral inadequacies, rendered him a dangerous man. He hacked away on that fateful tree long into the night. By three o'clock in the morning, the sky began to spew lavish amounts of precipitation. So frenzied was

Osgood in his pursuit of firewood that he hardly noticed the change in the weather. The heavens rained, and Osgood chopped.

By five o'clock that morning, Osgood had chopped well past the midpoint of the now marginally stable trunk, having effectively assaulted its structural integrity. He chopped for another half hour. In the foggy recesses of his mind, he thought he heard something make a loud, creaking sound. He dismissed the notion as irrelevant. A few moments later, the sound re-insinuated itself, this time with more intensity. Osgood made several furtive glances at a variety of objects in the immediate vicinity, which he suspected could be the source of such a sound. Then, unable to determine the identity of the cause of the offending noise with any degree of certainty, he redirected his attention to a more pressing stimulus.

Among the many physical defects Osgood had inherited from his genetically destitute parents was a thimble-sized bladder with the elasticity and tactile strength of an overripe plum. During the seventeen hours it had taken him to render the formerly harmless ponderosa a serious threat to himself and anyone else unfortunate enough to wander into the area, Osgood stopped to pee no fewer than thirteen times. He would have passed out from dehydration hours earlier, except for the fact that he had consumed large portions of the nearby lake. He did this not because he understood the implications of dehydration but because, as a result of his lack of intellectual capacity, he was drawn to the water by a subconscious force of nature labeled in some of the older psychology texts as a "positive tropism."

Fortunately for Osgood, Mother Nature called at around 5:17 a.m. with uncommon severity, thereby luring him to a location a few feet behind his tent, where he somehow managed to survive the effects of the generous amount of potential energy he had unwittingly converted into imminent actual energy.

All other things being equal, the large void Osgood created in the trunk of that ill-fated ponderosa might well have caused it to assume a reclining position in the immediate vicinity of Osgood and his tent. Coincidences being what they are (or at least appear to be), however, at just the moment when the remnant of the ponderosa's once sturdy trunk could no longer guarantee the continued vertical posture of that once stalwart timber, a persistent and powerful gale arrived upon the scene, fostered by the now raging rainstorm, and tipped the scales of fate in favor of coincidental inevitability, whereupon the beloved ponderosa relinquished its propensity to squash its attacker like a bug and, instead, swayed benevolently away from Osgood, who was peeing happily, totally oblivious of the drama taking place behind him.

The majestic old tree sighed deeply, released its soul to the arboreal afterlife, and fell with a thunderous crash into Lake Chipewa, sending a plume of water several stories into the angry sky. The several thousand gallons of water that arrived at the location where Osgood was joyously relieving himself were sufficient to wash Osgood, his tent, and sleeping bag about fifty feet uphill. When Osgood recovered his composure and equilibrium, he shrugged and dismissed the entire event as a mere increase in the intensity of the storm. With uncommon determination, he set out in search of his tent and sleeping bag.

The massive ponderosa began floating inexorably toward the Chipewa Dam spillway. The Chipewa Dam was, as confirmed by Matt Grover of the Army Corps of Engineers, designed and built to withstand the ravages of any deluge with an intensity less than that of a five-hundred-year storm. As part of that design, the dam had been fitted with a large concrete spillway, intended to keep the water behind the dam from exceeding a predetermined safe level. That spillway was built wide enough to allow the many trees and other debris that floated down river each year, and onto the surface of Lake Chipewa, to flow over it without any risk that the spillway would be clogged. The engineer who determined the width of that spillway had never met Osgood Thurmond nor had he ever seen a tree the size of Osgood's tree.

Osgood's tree had been the tallest tree in the forest and was now a good forty feet longer than the width of the spillway. As coincidence would have it, Osgood's tree approached the spillway in a posture parallel to the superstructure of the dam and the spillway, rendering it unable to pass through the opening. Within ten minutes after the massive timber had lodged itself securely against the concrete pillars on either side of the spillway, a second ponderosa collided with Osgood's tree with a thundering crash and wedged itself at an angle between Osgood's tree and one of those concrete pillars.

Within two hours, six more trees had joined the barrier. Before long, the once effective spillway was almost totally dispossessed of its original purpose, as the water level of Lake Chipewa began its gradual ascent to the point of impending disaster.

A final crushing blow to the longevity of the carefully engineered dam came in the form of a large houseboat that had been rendered free of its moorings by the undulating surface of the lake. Fortunately, the previous occupants of that houseboat had wisely abandoned the craft several hours earlier, drawn by a combination of forces of nature toward the warmth and relative safety of a local saloon, so they were not on board as the ill-fated vessel acquired its temporary freedom.

As the houseboat joined the rapidly growing tangle of trees and debris at the Chipewa Dam spillway, the force of the water tipped it on its side. Its massive bottom, now perpendicular to the water's flow, caused hundreds of additional tons of water to exert pressure on the dam as the water level continued to rise.

The intensity of the storm had washed out the gravel road that provided access to the dam from the main highway, so nobody could get up to the dam, and nobody witnessed the growing logjam. Even if someone had discovered it, it was highly unlikely that anything could have been done about it.

The Chipewa was an earthen dam. By the time the surface of the lake reached a level thirty feet above the spillway, a small breech began to form in the dam. Within an hour it turned into a major cavity. A few minutes later all hell broke loose, providing the impetus for rerouting of the river, which resulted in the county boundary being moved. This allowed the city of Sprague the fateful option of becoming part of the neighboring county.

One of the many side effects of the City of Sprague moving into Silverwood County was the relocation of Franklin High School from the Beaver Creek League to the Tri-County League, thus further setting the stage for the historic football game that so impacted Jaime's life.

Were it not for Osgood Thurmond and his insistent axe, Jaime and Becky would almost certainly have never met.

Chapter Forty

"This is kind of fun, don't you think?" asked Jaime. "I mean, after all, we had a chance to visit with Chris's Great-Grandfather last night and learned some awesome lessons about the spirit world. And we're in contact with some form of intelligence who speaks to us when we need her."

The four friends were sitting in a circle on the grass about fifty feet from the entrance to the tunnel. It was early Tuesday morning.

They had fallen asleep the night before in the relative safety of the tunnel, feeling a mixture of exhaustion from their adventures of the day, excitement over the prospects of what lay ahead, and enthusiasm over the many wondrous things Great-Grandfather had told them.

They decided to call upon Zara for some additional guidance. Becky called her name and even before anyone had a chance to ask a question Zara began:

"We must prepare you for the glorious adventure that awaits you in the next few days."

"Why do you call it glorious?" asked Chris.

"I speak," answered Zara, "from the point of view of a being focused in the spirit world. I'm sorry. I should have been more sensitive to your position. From your limited perspective, the events that are about to unfold may seem quite frightening and potentially deadly. But if you will hold certain thoughts, you will begin to see your situation from the broader perspective that is held by those in the spirit world, including your higher selves.

"You may accomplish this by recalling some of the things I have told you already. 'You can never get it done,' 'Nothing really matters,' 'Choose to look at all situations from a position of joyous anticipation,'

and, 'It all has a happy ending.' These four statements can be applied
to all earthly experiences. If they are accurately and clearly understood, they can make any situation not only bearable but truly joyous.

"So, as you proceed with this glorious adventure, remember what
I have taught you. You will find yourselves in possession of powers
that many would call miraculous. I know them to be the normal powers of all human beings who have become aware of their ability to
control the energy that appears to your limited senses to be solid
matter. Truly knowing that it all will end perfectly will eliminate the
fear in your hearts. Without fear, there is only pure love. With pure
love, all things are possible. That is the key—knowing. Your Book of
Books quotes Jesus as saying 'Ye must have faith.' That is a corruption of his original words. What he actually said is much closer to
your word 'knowing' than it is to your word 'faith.' He was not speaking of a faith in God, not a faith in a particular religion, but a knowing that you have the power."

Becky said, "Somehow, I have known all of this, instinctively, all
of my life. I just never heard it expressed so clearly."

"You are correct," said Zara. "All humans arrive on this planet
knowing of their power. They feel the magic. They know it instinctively. But very shortly after their physical lives begin, the process of
programming them to believe that their magic does not exist com-
mences. It is done, very innocently, by their parents, their teachers,
their religious instructors, and many more. They are told that they
don't really have invisible, magical friends. They are told, 'Don't be
silly' or 'Get real.' They are told that there are no fairies, no angels,
nothing beyond what their physical senses tell them.

"What I would ask you to consider is that your physical receptors—your eyes, your ears, your nose and so forth—are programmed
to interpret vibration, which is just a form of energy. And they are
programmed to interpret, or sense, only a very, very narrow band of
the vibrational spectrum.

"Take light as an example. Your eyes are capable of sensing only
what you call visible light. You can see colors only from violet to red.
But just below the vibrational frequency of red is infrared, which is
just beyond the ability of your eyes to see. And vibrating above

violet, at a frequency just beyond that which your eyes can sense, is ultraviolet. And after that, your scientists find gamma rays and X-rays and so much more. The truth is that the light spectrum extends infinitely in both directions, high and low. The fact that your eyes don't see them doesn't mean they don't exist. So can you see how limiting it is to believe only in what appears to your senses?

"There are worlds out there beyond your wildest imaginings, waiting to be discovered by your souls. This lifetime is only a parenthesis in eternity. What your senses can observe is nothing compared to what is really out there.

"Many people believe that Earth is the only planet in the entire universe that supports life. If it was only possible for your limited minds to understand how vast the universe is, you would have to know that there are virtually unlimited life forms out there. Can you realistically imagine that God created the entire universe just so the little planet Earth could support life? That is what we would call arrogance.

"Copernicus was threatened with excommunication from the Catholic Church for daring to suggest that the Earth was not the center of the universe. His notion that the Earth revolved around the sun was considered, in his day, to be absolutely absurd and a blasphemy against the Church. I guarantee you that a few centuries from now, people on your planet will laugh at the notion that yours is the only planet that supports life. They will come to know that there is life even within your own solar system, vibrating at frequencies that your limited senses cannot detect. They will know that these beings, which vibrate at frequencies beyond the ability of your senses to observe, exist on your planet, within a few feet of your body. That is what I am. That is what ghosts are. Your scientists are now beginning to hypothesize that these others exist on your planet in what are coming to be called 'parallel universes.'

"I realize I have wandered from the topic at hand. But, again, I am anxious for you to understand just how the universe so wonderfully *is*. It is a place of unlimited wonders. It is the way you have always wished it would be and so much more. I have to remind myself that you have chosen your limitations for excellent reasons and will be back in the realm of the absolute soon enough."

"Is there anything we specifically need to know about what lies ahead of us and how we can come out of this situation alive?" Daryl asked.

"It is quite simple to explain but, perhaps, a bit more difficult to accomplish. All you need to do is to *decide* to stay alive, to *decide* to have it all end as you wish, knowing that you have the power. And, as Jesus said, 'It shall be done according to your will.' But you must release all fear, for the absence of fear is love, and love is all-powerful.

"Releasing fear is 'a piece of cake,' as you say. Once you know that you never end and that death is not the end of your essence, fear will depart quite easily. But, for now, you will have to contend with the limitations of physical reality. You will have to experience physical pain. You will have to fear death. Unless you decide not to."

"What in the world does that mean?" asked Jaime.

"That, my friends, is one more lesson for another time. For now, just know that you have power beyond your present comprehension. You can access that power with a combination of strong desire and uncommon faith, or what I would call 'knowing.' You can even access it with only one of those two elements if it is strong enough.

"Most of all, go lightly. Don't take anything too seriously. Know that it's all a game and one you can never lose. Even if the very worst thing you can imagine should happen, I assure you that, when you are once again in the spirit world, you will look back and have a good laugh at this entire situation. You will even find that those you considered your enemies on this plane are among your best friends in the spirit world. They are the ones who love you so much that they agreed to join you in this incarnation and put forth the tremendous energy required to be your enemy.

"I will be here if you need me. I will not plan strategy. That would be too much interference. But I can help if you are in real danger."

With that, Zara was gone.

"Man," sighed Daryl, "do you realize that we just had an opportunity to hear a substantial part of the essence of what most of the grand masters have been trying to teach the people of this planet for several thousand years? I just kept thinking, 'This is what Jesus and Buddha and Mohammed and Ghandi and Kahlil Gibran and

Confucius have been trying to teach us for centuries.' And we just had it laid right in our laps."

"It even meshes perfectly with the recent findings of our scientists," Becky added. "I just finished reading a book by a brilliant gentleman named Stephan Hawking. Hawking is among the many scientists now taking knowledge well beyond the amazing discoveries of Albert Einstein. From what I have read, all of the prior theories about how physical reality works have fallen short of explaining all situations. From the theories of Galileo to those of Newton, even, to those of Einstein, nobody ever came up with a theory that didn't fail in some applications.

"But Hawking is one of a group of scientists who have come up with what is called the 'Super String Theory.' Many modern scientists agree that this theory seems to come closer to explaining it all than any theory in the past. And what Hawking says fits perfectly with what Zara has told us—at least my understanding of what he says."

"Well," said Chris, "one thing I know for sure—it can't hurt us to take Zara's advice about keeping joy in our hearts. It's been my experience, that whenever I spend several days being joyous, things seem to zing right along for some time after that. And when I have a period of negative thinking and worry, things seem to get worse and worse. So I intend to face whatever lies in store with the most positive attitude I can manage. I hope the rest of you will do the same."

"In the meantime," said Jaime, "I'm going over to my duffel bag to see what else Tim put in that side pocket. I wish Tim was with us now. I don't know what use we could make of a quarterback's particular skills, but we sure could use his courage."

Daryl suggested, "I think we'd better come up with a plan. We can't stay here much longer. It seems to me that we've got to get back to civilization pretty soon. I doubt that the bad guys have given up looking for us. Even though they don't know that you got inside the spacecraft, they probably at least know that you got inside the bunker. Something had to happen to put them on your tail in the first place. Some kind of alarm must have been set off. If it had been in the farmhouse, they would have been there a lot sooner. So I would guess there was a security device protecting the spacecraft.

"They wouldn't be foolish enough *not* to check the farmhouse. They must have found the broken lock and your footprints in the basement. So there's little doubt they want you badly. The shot they took at Becky confirms that, unless they missed deliberately, intending only to scare us. I think we have to assume that our lives are in serious danger."

Jaime returned, carrying a cell phone and an electrical cord designed to be plugged into a cigarette lighter.

Chris said. "That could be of some benefit."

"Good old Tim," Jaime said, smiling. "And believe it or not, we get decent reception here."

Chris said, "I've been wondering why they haven't found us by now. If we're dealing with the CIA, as Daryl thinks, they certainly have methods of finding live bodies almost anywhere. The fact that there hasn't been a bunch of bad guys storming down that tunnel leads me to think that whoever we're dealing with doesn't have access to the full might of the government."

"So how do we get from here to the highway without being seen?" Becky asked. "And once we get to the highway, how do we keep from getting picked up by the law? I assume that they've got an APB out on us by now. Even if they don't know who we are—which we don't know for sure—it would be logical that they'd have all law enforcement agencies within the area on the lookout for a couple of Jeeps."

"I think we should wait until dark," Chris suggested. "I've got duct tape in one of my tool boxes. We could cover the headlights and leave just large enough holes to give us sufficient light to keep us from running into something, but not enough to be easily detected. We need to blaze our own trail in a direction they would least expect. Following an existing trail would likely lead us right to them. Probably our biggest disadvantage is the roar my engine makes. We could leave my Jeep behind and all ride in Daryl's Jeep. But if we're detected, the speed of my Jeep could save our hides. I can't think of anything they might have, short of a helicopter, that could keep up with us. On the other hand, once they spot us, they'll have the advantage of radio contact with other units."

"We could abandon the vehicles completely," Daryl offered, "and try to make it on foot. If we stay in the trees and avoid open areas, we just might make it, especially if we do it after dark."

"Not a bad idea," Becky agreed.

"Once we get to a city, we'll have to find someone who can help us before we get spotted by any law enforcement officers," Chris cautioned. "No matter how we do it, it's risky."

"Once we get near civilization," said Daryl, "we should split up. They'll be looking for a group, not individuals."

"We have a couple of advantages you guys might want to consider," Becky said. "One is that I don't think they know Daryl is with us. The other is Jaime's blinding running speed. His brother, Tim, told me Jaime is legendary. It could come in handy."

"I just remembered—I've got an important personal call I'd like to make," Chris said. "Mind if I use your phone?"

"Not at all," Jaime answered, "As they say south of the border, 'me telefono es tu telefono, compadre.'"

Jaime handed the cell phone to Chris. Chris walked a few yards away from the group.

Becky wondered out loud, "Is there some way they can trace a call from the phone?"

"Not that I know of," said Daryl. "Not with a cell phone. I'd keep the call short, though, just for good measure."

"What if we use the phone to call a couple of radio stations? Tell them we've got some hot information they may want to know about. See if we can arrange a meeting," Becky proposed.

"Too risky, I'd think," said Daryl, "Too much chance they'd think we're a bunch of crazies and contact the cops. I wouldn't feel very good about any kind of pre-arranged meeting. It's too easy to walk into a trap."

Chris returned from making his call.

They sat around studying the maps, trying to decide on a route that would take them to a town, without exposing them, unnecessarily. They spent most of the afternoon considering their alternatives.

By sundown, they were close to finalizing their plan. As the sun disappeared behind the mountains, the temperature dropped dramatically.

They built a campfire and sat around talking.

Eventually Becky stood up and announced that she was heading for the tunnel.

"Mind if I join you?" whispered Jaime.

"I wish you would," Becky said quietly.

Chris and Daryl engaged in a lengthy fireside conversation, not only because they found the discussion stimulating but because they sensed that Jaime and Becky would appreciate some time alone.

The young couple put their sleeping bags side by side. They sat on them, looking out at the campfire. The air was calm. The tunnel surrounding them gave their voices a slight echo. Jaime got a small blanket out of his duffel bag and wrapped it around Becky's shoulders. The jacket he was wearing kept him warm even though he could see his breath in the glow of the campfire.

They talked about the events of the day, especially about the things Zara had shared with them. Becky told Jaime about her adventure with Rachel and the Glory Hole. Jaime told her about his fifth-grade experience on the school bus.

Jaime took Becky's hand and held it to his lips, kissing it softly. They turned to face each other, sitting cross-legged, their knees touching. Jaime held both of her hands and sat staring into her eyes, where he could see the campfire reflected. *My, she's pretty.*

He reached out and placed his hand on the back of her neck, pulling her toward him gently. He tilted his head slightly and pressed his lips against hers. The tips of their tongues touched. They remained still, allowing the energy to flow between them, tongues still touching, trembling. He could smell her breath, sweet and delicate. The best word he could think of to describe that wondrous aroma was "innocent." Innocent breath. It made him feel tingly all over, took his own breath away.

He placed his hand on her shoulder, pressing her sideways. She yielded to the pressure, lying on her side He did the same. Lips still locked in a tender embrace, Jaime unzipped his jacket, reached out, put his arm around her waist and pulled her toward him until their bodies touched. Jaime could feel her breasts against his chest, firm and warm. His heart was racing.

He thought, "Every cell in my body is commanding me to continue. But this isn't the place. Not with Chris and Daryl nearby. If I should ever be so fortunate as to make love with this incredible woman, it has to be just right. If I go any further now, I won't be able to stop. I don't want to risk offending her. For now, I'll just cherish the ecstasy of the moment and hope she understands."

They lay there for a while, locked in a loving embrace. The intensity of their kissing conveyed the clear message of their mutual eagerness.

When Becky pulled away, it was in a manner intended to assure Jaime that she hadn't been offended and that she felt the same way he did.

They fell asleep with a feeling of physical frustration, overshadowed by a much more powerful feeling of deep emotional contentment.

It was a delightful ending to the most interesting Tuesday of Jaime's life.

# Chapter Forty-one

A beam of sunlight appeared softly over the bedroom window sill. It found its way through a tiny opening in the draperies and focused its shaft of subtle, warming energy on Sarah's eyelids. She opened her eyes and raised her hand to shield them from the beam's intensity. The rest of the room was still dark.

She reached for Michael. He was gone.

Sarah sat up, stretched, and indulged herself in a long, pleasant yawn.

Both she and Michael had slept long and well last night. Now, the smell of coffee brought a smile to her lips. Michael knew how much she loved her cup of creamy, rich coffee the first thing in the morning. Sarah called it her "sissy drink" because she put sugar and heavy whipping cream in it. Once in a while she added a little vanilla flavoring. If she knew Michael, it would come with the works this morning.

My, she loved that man! She often thought about her friends and how so many of them had marriages that just got by.

She had really lucked out. Theirs was a relationship that flowed. Sure, it took a lot of hard work and a lot of giving. But when it came to the essentials, like loving and caring, it just flowed.

Michael was her perfect man. He was strong but gentle. He had a healthy self-respect. Best of all, he truly loved women. She guessed that it was because of the balanced relationship he enjoyed with his mother. It seemed to Sarah that it was a rare man these days who truly loved and respected women. In her opinion, most men either felt insecure around women or regarded them as somehow less than men. She thought of all the unhappy ladies she knew who would give anything to find a man like Michael.

He was a tough guy. He had been a genuine hero in the Vietnam War, putting his life on the line on several occasions to save his comrades. He had a demeanor that assured any potential troublemaker that Michael Lasher was not to be messed with. It made Sarah feel secure. She knew that as long as he was around, all would be well. He exuded confidence. But more than that, his tough guy image was tempered with an uncommon gentleness.

Sarah had known a lot of tough guys in her life. Most, though, were bullies covering up a deep-seated lack of self confidence. She felt privileged to have married a man who was so genuine.

The bedroom door opened, and there stood Michael with that radiant smile on his face, a teakwood tray in his hands, holding two mugs of coffee and several slices of pound cake. From the tiny wisps of steam rising from the cake slices and the pats of butter melting on them, Sarah could see that Michael had taken the time to heat them. What a guy.

"Morning, darlin'," he said.

"Hi, lover," Sarah responded, stretching again. "Nice way to be awakened."

"Nothing's too good for my lady."

As Michael set the tray on the coffee table in front of the two easy chairs they used for nighttime reading, Sarah jumped up, spun around behind him, and wrapped her arms around his waist, causing a few drops of coffee to escape over the rims of the mugs.

"Easy," he said, "I'm not used to dealing with a violent woman. You keep that up and we'll not only lose most of this delicious coffee that I labored so feverishly over, but we'll likely end up back in bed going two out of three rounds."

"I can handle that."

She went into the bathroom. Michael could hear her brushing her teeth. He had gotten up early and showered already. He opened the bedroom curtains and looked out on the new day.

When Sarah came back into the room, she was wearing Levi's and her favorite flannel work shirt. While she tied her tennis shoes, Michael said, "Do you realize it's already Wednesday? It's been three days since the kids left. I'm surprised we haven't heard from them yet."

"I was thinking the same thing last night. Doesn't seem like Jaime not to call."

Michael grinned mischievously. "From the way our Jaime was looking at Becky at the breakfast table Sunday, I don't imagine he's wasting too much time thinking about his old parents."

As she stood up, Sarah laughed. "I guess our boys are starting to become men. I suppose I'll have to change the things I worry about. Instead of scraped knees and elbows, I'll have to start worrying about broken hearts and shattered dreams." She was silent for a moment and looked toward the window. Just as she turned her head, Michael thought he saw a trace of moisture in those beautiful eyes. He moved close to her, pressed his chest against her back, and wrapped his arms around her. They stood there for a while, silent.

Michael kissed her neck, then said, "Coffee's gonna be cold if we don't get moving."

They sat down and began sipping the delicious brew. Sarah's taste buds responded favorably to the love Michael had put into it.

From the hallway, they heard Tim shout, "Attention, all lovebirds. In approximately thirty seconds Tim Lasher will be entering your room.

Please be certain that all occupants are properly attired and no actions are taking place that aren't approved for general audiences."

Tim went into the kitchen and poured himself a tall glass of cranberry juice. He came to his parents' room and knocked on the door.

"Stay out!" Michael and Sarah both shouted at once.

Tim walked in with a big grin and saluted them with his juice glass. "Mornin', parents," he said. "Time to rise and shine. Daylight's burning."

"Don't you know what 'stay out' means?" Michael laughed.

"It's when you say 'come in' that I'm at a loss to know what the hell to do," said Tim. "It's the job of a teenager to disobey his parents. You know that."

"Watch your language," said Sarah. "Someone might think you believe in Hell if you keep talking like that."

"No chance," said Tim, sitting on the bed. "Have you heard from Jaime?"

"No," said Sarah. "I'm starting to be a little concerned."

"So am I," said Tim. "You know how I am with my crazy dreams and hunches and all that 'airy fairy' stuff. I've had two dreams about the kids, one before they left, the other was last night. I don't want to alarm you, but I keep getting inklings that all's not right."

The doorbell rang.

"Who could that be?" asked Sarah.

"I'll get it," said Tim as he headed for the front door.

Michael looked out the bedroom window and saw three beige sedans parked in the driveway.

"Dad, better come here," shouted Tim.

Michael gave Sarah an anxious look and headed for the living room. Sarah was right behind him, her half-full coffee mug in her hands.

There, in the living room, stood three men, all strangers. Sarah noticed that two more men stood on the front porch, one in front of each window. As she glanced around, she saw men in front of the other two windows. Her stomach muscles tightened.

"What's this all about?" Michael asked, his voice rising slightly.

"I'm afraid there's been some trouble involving your son," one of the men said.

Sarah gasped.

"We need all of you to come with us," the man said.

Sarah looked at Tim. He had That Look in his eyes. Something was definitely not right. She turned to Michael. The vein on his right temple was puffing out, a sure sign that his instincts were on red alert.

"Who are you?" Michael demanded.

"Who we are isn't relevant," said another, a short, stocky man with intense eyes.

"It sure as hell is," insisted Michael. "We aren't about to allow ourselves to be taken somewhere by anyone who hasn't identified himself. Besides, I don't understand why there's an entire army of men in my yard, just to bring me to see my son. Where's Jaime?"

"You'll see him soon enough," said another man. This one was tall, with shifty eyes. He kept staring at Sarah.

Tim had worked his way, quietly, to the kitchen door. He stepped backward into the kitchen, reached around the refrigerator, and took the wall phone off the hook. He dialed 911. The crisp, efficient voice of a woman said, "Please state your emergency."

Tim placed the phone up against his mouth and whispered, "We need Sheriff Wells and several men, right away, at…."

The receiver was torn from his hand. Tim turned to see a man with short blond hair and a face that made Tim think of a weasel. He had narrow eyes and a protruding nose. The expression on his face could only be described as a sneer. Tim gave the man a look of his own. The man stepped back instantly, a reaction to the look he saw in Tim's eyes. He called out, "Hey, boss, we've got a situation here."

Within seconds, three men entered the kitchen, one from the living room, one from the dining room, and one through the outside door.

Sarah screamed.

Tim could hear scuffling in the living room. Before he could react, two of the men had him pinned. In an amazingly short time, Tim was turned around, his face pressed forcefully against the refrigerator door, and a pair of handcuffs clamped onto his wrists.

Tim thought, "Time to be cool. Hold your temper until you've had a chance to think this out. Stay cool." He did his best to relax.

Apparently, Dad had been having similar thoughts because the sounds from the other room stopped.

Tim was shoved into the living room, where he saw that both Mom and Dad were handcuffed. Mom's mouth was covered with tape. Just before they put tape on Dad's mouth, he shouted, "If you hurt Sarah or my boys, I'll come after you if it's the last thing I do."

Tim went crazy. He lowered his head and rammed it into the gut of the nearest man. He then spun and did a side body block into the knees of a second man. He heard the knee cartilage tear. The man screamed. Tim threw himself at another man and pulled him down with a scissors hold. The man hit the floor and struck his head on the corner of the coffee table. He was out cold.

As soon as Michael saw what Tim was doing, he spun around and, behind his back, grabbed the belt of another man with his cuffed hands and threw him against the wall. He spun again and brought his knee up into the man's ribcage. The cracking of the ribs could be heard clearly. The man fell to the floor.

Sarah raised her right leg and blasted the man standing with his back to her in the small of his back. His knees buckled. the force of her kick caused her to fall on her back, smashing her hands between her butt and the carpet. The pain was excruciating. She rolled over on her side, pulled her knees up to her chest, rolled up onto them, with her forehead on the floor. With a jump she knew she never could have made if she hadn't had a pint of adrenaline pumping through her system, she was back on her feet.

Michael lowered his shoulder and slammed into the back of another man, just a fraction of a second before Tim kicked the same man in the right knee, from the front. The man fell, shrieking with pain.

Four more men came flying through the two outside doors.

In less than a minute, Michael, Sarah, and Tim were laying face down, each with a man on top. The man who appeared to be in charge ordered their ankles, knees, and elbows to be immobilized with duct tape.

Tim thought, "So much for keeping cool."

Michael thought, "These assholes don't even begin to know how much trouble they're in."

Sarah thought, "Oh, my dear God Force, please watch over my men."

*** ~ *** ~ ***

At about the same time Michael, Tim, and Sarah were being loaded into the beige sedans, Clint Yarborough was at his ranch, about fifty miles from the Lasher home, working up quite a sweat, totally unaware that his day was about to become uncommonly memorable.

Clint was almost finished shoeing his second Percheron draft horse since breakfast. It was one of his favorite things to do. The Percherons were so even-tempered and relaxed that shoeing them was easy, compared to shoeing most of the high strung-breeds.

It had been several months since Clint had married Chris's mother, Maria. "The best thing I've ever done," he thought. Clint had moved into Maria's home, although they spent a great deal of time at Clint's ranch, only a few miles away.

Early this morning, Clint had come out to the ranch to get some shoeing done. Then he planned to load a stake truck with alfalfa bales and haul them up into the high country in preparation for the colder weather that he suspected would be upon them in a few weeks. Maria usually accompanied Clint to the ranch, where she cooked for the ranch hands, cleaned the old ranch house, or tended the garden while Clint looked after the cattle and horses.

Chris's father, John, had died in Vietnam. Maria had been so in love with him, she thought she might never love another man. But Clint had proven to be every bit as loveable as John. Maria even found herself wondering if Clint could be a reincarnation of John. Then she reminded herself that Clint and John were about the same age, so it would be chronologically impossible.

She remembered her grandfather's stories about the concept of parallel universes, and Einstein's proof that time as we know it doesn't really exist. If these theories are correct, Clint could easily be her John reincarnated.

Then she thought, "Besides, what does it matter? All that's important is that Clint is the man of my dreams and is in no way diminished by the fact that I once loved and continue to love John."

As Clint tapered the big horse's hoof to make it flush with the edge of the shoe he had just finished nailing in place, he thought about Maria. He had never been in love before, at least not this kind of love. Maria was special. She had a warmth about her that he had never found in any other woman. She was nurturing and sensitive. And something he had learned to appreciate only recently, Maria had a clear understanding of, and a healthy respect for, the ways of Great Spirit. Her grandfather, Chris's Great-Grandfather, had been a shaman of uncommon ability and sensitivity. He had taught Maria many things about the spirit world, concepts that were much different from the teachings of the Western religions.

Clint enjoyed many long talks with Maria, often late at night. He learned a belief system that, at long last, made sense. It wasn't based on having to believe what someone else told him to believe. It was based on principles that seemed to resonate with nature, especially human nature. Eventually he came to realize that the ways of Great Spirit were much more closely related to the beliefs of the people of the Far East than to anything he had ever learned in his years of studying Western religions.

The beliefs of the indigenous peoples seemed to be based on what works rather than on what is pontificated by someone who claims to have been chosen by God to tell everyone else what to believe.

Yes, Maria had taught him much. She proved to be everything he had longed for all his life. He loved her more than life itself.

A successful rancher, Clint had long ago paid off his ranch, had sufficient cash in the bank to live a long life comfortably, and had won the respect of the other ranchers in the area. He now ranched mostly for the joy of ranching. In his mind, the best reason to do anything is the pure joy of doing it. As an added benefit, Maria had a model son in Chris, a tribute to the great woman she was.

Clint realized he hadn't seen Chris for several days. He wondered where that young man had gotten off to. Maria had told him that Chris had met a woman in the city last week.

"Perhaps," Clint thought, "Chris's absence was hormonally motivated." He laughed.

He had sent all of his ranch hands up to the high mesa to round up the cattle they had turned loose there a few weeks ago. They were expected to be back before sundown. In the meantime, he was alone. Maria had decided to stay at her home today, saying she had a lot of laundry to do and a big batch of tamales to prepare for a wedding next Saturday.

Not that he minded being alone. A typical cowboy most of his life, he was no stranger to loneliness. He came to be comfortable with being by himself most of the time until he met Maria. Now he preferred being with her to anything else. But he still enjoyed his solitude once in a while. He stood there for a moment, savoring the feeling.

In the distance he thought he saw a tiny movement. As he stood there, mildly hypnotized by the warmth of the day, he slowly became more certain that he was seeing something just below the far horizon. It looked like dust rising into the sky. He couldn't be sure because the hills that formed the background were just about the same color as the imagined dust.

Before long, he realized that it was truly dust rising from the dirt road leading from the ranch house into the far mountain pass. That road was used so seldom that Clint hadn't thought about it for a long time. Almost all traffic now came down the state highway about a mile to the east. The dirt road wasn't adequate for eighteen-wheelers, and most passenger cars traveled the state highway, even though it was a longer drive, because it was wide and paved. Whoever was coming down that road was probably coming from the city but didn't know enough about the area to realize he could have saved some time and a lot of trouble taking the longer paved route.

As the cloud of dust drew closer to the ranch house, Clint saw that they were being raised by two sedans, almost the color of the dust trail rising behind them. They blew past the ranch house at a rate of speed not often seen in these parts. Clint resented this disruption of his solitude. If his solitude was to be interrupted, he wanted it to be by someone wonderful, like Maria, not a couple of roaring gas guzzlers from the big city.

"Oh well," he thought, "once every five years isn't too much." He shrugged and began leading the horses to the barn.

Clint busied himself doing odds and ends. He liked the smell of the barn, the feel of a place where good, honest work had been done for so many years. He kept the barn clean and organized. He had erected that barn long ago with the help of his dad and brothers. Many a barn dance was held in the hayloft of that old barn, many a Fourth of July picnic in the shade of its north side. His sister had the reception for her wedding in the ranch house, with most of the guests preferring to party in the backyard. There were lots of memories here. Both Mom and Dad were buried under the big oak tree on the hill, along with several of Clint's aunts and uncles.

The sun was almost at its high point now. Clint guessed that it was about eleven o'clock.

He heard the sound of automobiles. He looked down the dirt road to where it turned off from the state highway. Two vehicles were heading his way, dust trailing, moving at high speed, two beige cars. Probably the same two he had seen earlier.

So seldom did anybody use that dirt road for any purpose other than to come to Clint's ranch that the road beyond his mailbox was overgrown with grass.

To Clint's surprise, they turned through his gate and headed toward the ranch house, probably wanting to ask directions. He'd save them a lot of time and effort by directing them down the state highway.

The automobiles skidded to a halt just a few feet from where Clint was standing, showering him with dust and sand. Clint pulled a handkerchief from his hip pocket and wiped the dust from his eyes.

Before he could speak, someone shouted, "We're looking for Clint Yarborough."

"I'm Clint," he responded. "What can I do for you?"

"Get in the car, Mr. Yarborough. Your wife's son is in trouble. We need you to come with us."

"Well, of course, I'll be glad to help. But can you tell me what kind of trouble Chris is in?"

"That's classified information," said the man nearest to Cliff. "For now, just get in the car. You'll learn more, later."

"I'll need to talk to my wife first. If you'll excuse me for a few minutes, I'll call her from the ranch house and be right back."

"That won't be necessary. Your wife's in the second car. She'll be coming with us."

"Do you mind telling me who you gentlemen are?" asked Clint.

"Who we are isn't important," the man said. "Now, get in the car."

Clint headed for the second car to confer with Maria. He was blocked by two men who had gotten out of the second car moments earlier. Clint pushed them aside with a strength they hadn't expected, throwing both of them off balance. They quickly recovered, and each grabbed one of Clint's arms, but not before he got close enough to the second car to get a clear look at Maria. Clint gasped when he saw that her left eye was swollen and blood was running from the side of her mouth.

He broke loose from the men holding him and got to within a few inches of the window separating him from Maria. "What happened to you?" he shouted.

Maria screamed, "They beat me. They killed Sundance. Run, Clint, please run."

Clint turned to face the men. The look on his face left no doubt in anyone's mind that this wasn't going to be as easy as they had thought. They had beat the wife and killed the dog of a powerful man. In an instant, a pistol appeared in each of the men's hands. A fourth man emerged from the passenger side of the first car, pistol in his hand, steadying it on the roof of the car. The first man, who appeared to be the leader, remained passive, apparently thinking that his three cohorts certainly could handle one unarmed man.

Often the phrase "What you don't know won't hurt you" is inappropriate in a given situation. It couldn't have been more so than in this instance. Among the facts that the men in the beige gas guzzlers didn't know were the following:

Clint Yarborough had spent a good part of his life riding the rodeo. He had a wall full of large and impressive belt buckles, attesting to the fact that he was one of the best and toughest bull riders in the nation.

Clint Yarborough had been a Green Beret in the Vietnam War and, although that was about thirty years ago, he still remembered most of what he had learned in that illustrious organization.

Ever since he had left the military, Clint Yarborough had engaged in what he called his "hobby," just to keep in shape. That involved ninety minutes of pumping iron every Monday, Wednesday, and Friday, accompanied by stretching exercises, tai chi, and a little yoga

Clint Yarborough was in love with his wife with the kind of love the common man seldom felt.

Clint Yarborough had raised Sundance from the time he was six weeks old. Sundance had been his best friend until he met Maria. Clint regarded anyone who would abuse an animal to be about as low as a human being could stoop.

Clint Yarborough understood that the advantage a man with a pistol has over an adversary without a pistol diminishes dramatically as the gun holder gets within reaching distance of his opponent.

The boys in the beige vehicles had no idea what they were up against. Like most gunmen, they assumed that the very appearance of their weapons would strike such terror into the hearts of their victims that they would immediately surrender.

With one quick step, Clint placed himself within reaching distance of the startled gunmen. Immediately, he had the barrels of their pistols in his hands, twisting them skyward, and thereby rendering them about as dangerous as a heavy ashtray.

As the surprised gunmen tried to decide what to do with this unusual and unexpected turn of events, Clint quickly blasted his right shin into the groin of the man on his right and, almost before that leg returned to the ground, he did what his martial arts instructor called a "jump front kick" and did the same thing to the other man's groin. Both men curled up on the ground, groaning in agony.

Clint hit the ground as close to the side of the first car as possible to prevent the gunman standing on the passenger side from getting a shot off at him. Clint now had possession of the two pistols formerly sported by the groaning gunmen. He gave each of them a solid, violent crack on the skull with the butt of a pistol, rendering them both unconscious.

The unarmed man made haste to place a substantial part of the automobile between himself and Clint by taking cover in front of the car's radiator.

Clint stood up quickly and squeezed off a round, across the top of the sedan, before the startled gunman at the passenger door could react. The bullet from the Glock 45 tumbled through the air and blew away a small part of the gunman's deltoid muscle, causing a shriek to erupt from the man's mouth.

By now the man huddling behind the front of the car had managed to pull his pistol from his shoulder holster. He wasn't sure where Clint was, but he was adequately sobered by the scream of the man to his left not to risk exposing any part of his treasured anatomy to a possible bullet.

Clint looked under the automobile and saw the legs of both of his adversaries. They were small targets. But he still had more than twenty rounds in his borrowed pistols. He looked around to determine that neither of the two earlier victims of his groin kicks was back on his feet. Both were still out cold.

He lined up the sights of one of the Glocks with the left ankle of the man crouched in front of the car and squeezed off four rounds. As near as he could tell, it was either the third or fourth round that struck pay dirt. The scream was almost as shattering as the splintering of the agent's ankle bone.

Clint looked for the ankles of the man at the passenger door. Not there.

Then it hit him. He must be getting old. In the heat of battle, he had forgotten to protect his queen, Maria.

He heard the door of the second car open and looked back. Despite his injured shoulder, the gunman was pulling Maria out of the car, placing his pistol against her cheek.

"Okay, smart ass," the man taunted, "drop the shooters."

For an instant, Cliff considered the possibility that he could drop the sucker before he could squeeze the trigger of the gun aimed at Maria's head. Then he saw that the hammer of the man's pistol was cocked. What if the gun had a hair trigger? Just the impact of Clint's bullet tearing through the man's chest could set off the pistol. He couldn't risk it.

Clint dropped the weapons.

The man with the gun ordered him to lie face down. He pushed Maria to the ground next to him. Without putting down his pistol, he handcuffed Clint, then ordered both of them to sit up while he wrapped tape around their arms, fastening their elbows close to their sides.

After assuring himself that they were immobilized, he ordered each of them to the second car and shoved them into the back seat. He taped their ankles, just for good measure.

"You're damn lucky that I'm getting you out of here. Those guys you busted up would like nothing better than to beat you to death. I wouldn't want to be you when they recover from your little assault. Frankly, there's nothing I'd like more than to see the two of you tortured for a while. But my job is to deliver you to our command leader. After that, you're on your own, and I hope you get what's coming to you."

He smashed the butt of his pistol into Clint's jaw, knocking loose two of Clint's teeth.

He then punched Maria in the face. Blood poured out of her nose.

The look Clint gave the man, as Reba McIntyre said in one of her hit songs, "could have made the wind stand still."

The gunman drove off with his two captives, leaving his cohorts behind to sort out their own situations, on this fateful Wednesday afternoon.

***

Four days ago, Chas had been very lucky that he was a good coagulator or he might have bled to death. After Becky had left him bleeding on her mother's floor, he had considered dragging himself to the telephone and calling an ambulance, but when he tried, the pain in his body intensified dramatically. Chas wasn't about to do anything that worsened his pain. That wasn't his style. Chas's entire life had been one gigantic unending attempt to increase pleasure and avoid pain.

So he lay there and tried to think of a story that would extricate him from the mess he was in. But nothing seemed to make sense. Finally he decided to fall back on his time-tested tactic. From many years of conning people, he had learned that if a person's position is so bad that he can't dream up a good story, his next best bet is to go on the offensive.

The moment he heard Gail open the door, he began yelling like a ruptured hyena. Screaming was no easy task for a person with several broken ribs. But the seriousness of his situation demanded it.

Gail ran to where he was lying and almost passed out at the sight of all that blood. Chas had smeared it all over the carpet and nearby easy chair.

When Gail screamed, "What happened?" he ignored her and began a verbal attack directed at Becky. He didn't quite accuse her of anything. He just kept shouting her name, decorated with many a derogatory profanity.

Then he shifted his tactics toward an all-out attack on Gail, accusing her, among other things, of housing a deranged maniac. He informed her that she was an unfit mother and that she had tricked him into marrying her without having the decency to advise him that her daughter was a homicidal lunatic.

Gail bandaged his shin as best she could, coating it generously with antibiotic ointment, trying to concentrate in spite of Chas' screams and moans. She managed to get him into her car, and she drove him to the doctor's office, where he received antibiotics and a tetanus shot.

Every time Gail tried to find out what had happened, Chas launched another harangue directed at either Gail or Becky. Finally Gail decided to remain quiet for the rest of the evening. She slept in the guest room.

The next morning, Chas refused even to acknowledge her, in spite of her solicitous attitude. Finally Gail gave up trying to talk to Chas, which was exactly what he wanted.

If he didn't talk to her, he wouldn't have to worry about saying something that would get him into more trouble. Besides, he needed time to think.

There had to be a way to get his hands on all of that money Brad had left Gail from his life insurance policy before that bratty kid returned and ruined everything. He hadn't yet managed to talk Gail into putting his name on her savings account. He thought he had been getting close before the kid beat the hell out of him and hit the road. In view of that recent event, he concluded it would be some time before he would approach the topic again.

Well, Gail could sit around sulking until she finally broke. When she did, he would demand that she make him signatory to her savings account as her peace offering. He knew it was just a matter of days before the brat would reappear at the front door to ruin everything. He planned to be gone, with a nice fat cashier's check in his pocket, before that happened.

But Chas had not counted on one critical factor. Of the other women he had used and abused, none had experienced the joy of living with a fine man in a loving relationship.

Gail's desperate need for approval, created and fostered by her overly strict and religious parents, set her up to be an easy victim for someone like Chas. Her many years with Brad, however, gave her such a solid understanding of what a love relationship should be that she finally was able to set aside her childhood fears, at least temporarily, and get a hold on reality, in spite of Chas's skills as a manipulator.

As she sat alone in the guest room, only a few hours after she had come home to find Chas battered and lying on the floor, she couldn't escape the realization that her entire relationship with Chas was a sham. The more she thought about it, the more obvious it became that Chas was no good. The longer she thought, the more incidents came to mind that should have alerted her, long ago, to Chas's true nature. She marveled that she could have been so blind.

William Shakespeare revealed an ultimate truth when he wrote, "Hell hath no fury like a woman scorned." Gail was a woman scorned.

Once she came to realize the truth of her situation, she became a silently raging tigress. She decided to keep her anger under control and play along with Chas to see how far he would go. Instead of being dejected or remorseful over what a fool she'd been, she discovered a strange kind of pleasure in the situation. The more she thought, the more angry she became, and the greater her anger, the stronger her resolve to beat Chas at his own game. She wasn't sure what she intended to do. But she was certain that the universe was going to present her with exactly the right circumstances to teach Chas the lesson of his life.

Gail vowed to force herself to continue playing the role of the meek, submissive, solicitous housewife until the time was right. She stewed silently for hours, imagining what Chas must have done to Becky to provoke such a violent reaction from her loving daughter. The more Gail thought, the more enraged she became. She thought of all the things Chas had said and done that now were so obviously part of his big con game. How could she have been so stupid?

Needy. That's what she had been, needy. So desperate for love had she been that she was willing and eager to believe anything that would ease the loneliness. It should have been so obvious, but not to someone with Gail's background, not when she was trying to deal with a gigantic void in her life, a terrible chasm in the middle of her soul, an emptiness that tore at her heart night and day.

She began to remember the little hints her attentive daughter had dropped in a vain attempt to help her mom see the light. Becky must have suffered terribly, watching her mom fall into the trap carefully crafted by that slime bag. The anger Gail felt over what had been done to her was nothing compared to the fury she felt when she thought of the suffering her baby had gone through. What could Chas have done to provoke Becky into reacting so violently? Gail didn't want to think about it. She didn't want to know, ever. All that mattered was that Becky's phone call Saturday night indicated that she was all right and was now a safe distance from that jerk. She prayed that no damage had been done to Becky that couldn't be mended.

All of the atrocities that Chas so cunningly and cleverly had perpetrated on Gail and Becky over so many months came crashing down on her in a matter of hours with an intensity Gail hadn't imagined possible. What had appeared to her as simple indiscretions when viewed through her neediness, now assumed the attributes of the viciousness with which these acts had been conceived. Gail became a smoldering cauldron of rage, seething just below the surface of the calm exterior that she so skillfully had fashioned during all of those years of needless self-control, a restriction that had been cruelly imposed upon her by the perpetrators of her religious beliefs, deny-ing her the freedom that was her birthright.

Now, on this Wednesday afternoon, four days after Becky had left home, Gail waited patiently—at least as patiently as her state of mind would allow. She had two burning desires: to have her baby back home, where Gail could undo whatever harm had been done, and, second, to have Chas in a position where she could use every skill in her womanly arsenal to guarantee that he would never again harm another person. Gail could hardly wait.

The universe didn't keep her waiting long.

Chas was collapsed in an easy chair in the living room, moaning, groaning, and generally feeling sorry for himself. He was wearing shorts, in spite of the fact that it was late autumn, because he couldn't stand having long pants rubbing against the bandage on his left shin.

He heard a loud knocking on the front door and bellowed for Gail to answer it. She opened the door, and there stood four men. Before Gail could ask what they wanted, the first man pushed his way into the room, knocking Gail back several feet. The other men fol-lowed quickly, the last one slamming the door shut.

Gail glanced at Chas, expecting that he would do something. He just sat there with a startled look on his face.

"That figures," she thought. "On top of everything else, the fool's a coward."

"You're coming with us," the first man said.

"What's this all about?" Gail asked, her voice shaking.

"Your daughter's in trouble," the man said. "We're going to take you to her."

"What kind of trouble?" Gail whispered.

"I'm not surprised," said Chas, the first thing he had said since the men had entered the room. "That kid's nothing but trouble. Look what she did to me," pointing to his bandaged leg.

"What kind of trouble?" Gail repeated.

"You'll find out when we get there," said another man, grabbing Gail's arm. She tried to pull away, but the man was too strong.

Chas simply sat there.

Another man grabbed Gail by the other arm and helped pull her toward the door.

The first man walked to where Chas was sitting and commanded, "You, too—let's go."

"Not me," said Chas. "I want nothing to do with that little brat. Didn't you see what she did to me? Whatever she's done will have to be straightened out by her old lady. Just leave me out of this."

The man grabbed Chas by the front of his shirt and lifted him off of the chair so quickly that Chas let out a loud gasp. Then he yelled as the pain shot through his rib cage.

The man threatened, "If I hear another sound out of you, it'll be the last one you make for a long time." Chas instantly fell silent, his face puffing up and his eyeballs bulging as he struggled to contain a scream.

Gail was about to protest again when a piece of duct tape was slapped over her mouth and wrapped around the back of her head.

The two were dragged out the door and shoved into the back of a large beige sedan. Gail sat terrified as the vehicle pulled out of her driveway. Her nose was suddenly accosted by a strange and pungent odor. Then she smiled slightly, in spite of the tape over her mouth and in spite of the seriousness of her situation, as she realized that the odor was the result of Chas having peed in his shorts.

She looked over at Chas and saw the look of terror in his eyes. For just an instant, her womanly instincts took hold, and she felt sorry for the cowering fool. But she got over that in about two seconds. In fact, the rage she had been feeling toward Chas now made the fear she was trying to cope with more manageable.

It was almost noon when the two government sedans drove away from the house where Brad and Gail had spent so many happy years with their beloved Becky.

Chapter Forty-two

Jaime awoke in the tunnel early Wednesday morning, about the same time that Benson's men were arriving at the Lasher residence to round up Michael, Sarah, and Tim. Lying there looking up, Jaime wasn't quite able to make out the details of the tunnel's granite ceiling. The sun was shining its first rays on the very tops of the pine trees just outside. There was still not enough light to allow him to see clearly inside the tunnel, but it was getting lighter.

The night had been cold. Becky had snuggled up against him, and her head was resting on his shoulder. Jaime could tell by her slow, even breathing that she was still asleep. He fantasized about unzipping his sleeping bag and hers and pulling her tightly against him, but he decided she might not appreciate his letting a blast of cold air into her cozy cocoon.

Jaime slid his shoulder from under her head, laying it gently on a rolled-up pair of sweat pants. He sat up and backed away from her a few inches. Lying there, she looked like an angel, the trace of a smile on her full, beautiful lips. Some of her long, shiny hair wrapped under her chin and spread out on the front of her sweatshirt. Jaime became aware that his heart was beating unusually fast. He felt an energetic connection from his heart to Becky's, urging their two bodies to become as one. He sat there, enjoying the sensations that were so new to him.

As the light in the tunnel increased, Jaime was surprised to see that Chris's sleeping bag was empty. He apparently had left the tunnel before Jaime awakened. But that would mean that Chris had left the tunnel while it had still been dark outside. *Not unusual for a mountain man. Probably went out to commune with the critters or something like that.*

Chris was an interesting man. Jaime considered how quickly he had developed a genuine fondness for Chris and how quickly that had turned into a friendship. Their intense and terrifying experiences together had caused them to bond more quickly than usual. But more than that, Chris had such charisma. He was what Jaime had heard referred to as a "man's man," a no-nonsense, genuine, caring, courageous, and warm man with a great sense of humor. Already Jaime felt a kinship with Chris that was close to brotherly.

If I ever find myself in a situation where I have to decide between saving my life, or, saving Chris's life, I'd be hard-pressed to make a choice.

In just over four days, I've fallen in love with a wonderful woman and found a true friend. Life is good.

Jaime looked at Daryl, still asleep, his head buried inside his sleeping bag. *I wonder how he breathes inside that thing? I always have to keep my head outside my sleeping bag to feel like I'm getting enough oxygen.*

Daryl had the makings of a good friend, too. He clearly was a good and honorable person. He obviously had a lot of grit. He was intelligent. He was in good physical shape. And he had a great sense of humor.

Jaime stood up slowly and stretched. His back was stiff from a night in a sleeping bag on a granite floor. He walked quietly to the entry of the tunnel where he enjoyed the panoramic view of the valley below. From this vantage point, he could see the stream that flowed just beyond a small rise on the far side of the spot where Great-Grandfather had done his campfire routine the night before last.

The sun had already worked its way down the trunks of some of the nearby ponderosa, to within a few feet of the ground. The sky was a bright azure. The smell of the forest was intoxicating. Morning dew still clung to the tips of the wildflower leaves and petals that remained in the shade.

It felt great to be alive. Jaime thought he would feel a lot better if he and his friends didn't have some lunatic government agents out to kill them. This day would be one of decision and action. He knew that he and his friends were going to be challenged, probably beyond anything they had experienced in their young lives, but not beyond their abilities to handle, he hoped. The possibility that he or any of his friends might be dead before this was all over settled on his mind, but not as heavily as one might think.

Jaime had been taught by his parents that death is not the terrible event that many people envision it to be. He had come to understand that death is simply a release of the soul from the confines of physical reality, that the soul goes on forever and that the essence that currently calls itself Jaime Lasher will have many more experiences with physical reality, in fact, an infinite number of experiences. Jaime definitely did not fear death. Still, he hoped he had a lot of years ahead of him, focused in this body, on this planet, at this time. He had a lot of things he wanted to do, a lot of dreams to fulfill, a lot of love to experience. *Yes, I'd definitely prefer to make it through this mess in one piece.*

He stepped out of the tunnel and walked into the forest. He stood in the sunlight. It felt so good, so warm, so energizing on the back of his neck and his arms. Before long, he could feel it radiating through his sweatshirt and Levi's. He closed his eyes and savored the warmth, thankful for a God who would produce such wonders for the enjoyment of the beloved creatures on Earth. Such was certainly not the kind of a God who would ever create the fires of Hell. As Jaime stood there philosophizing with himself, it occurred to him that most of the things people consider evil are the result of thoughts and acts of people, not of God. God created everything perfectly. Humans simply have to act in accordance with the laws of the universe, and all will be well. If people violate those laws, they are not punished by God. They simply reap the consequences of that violation seeing the effect of their actions is part of their learning experience. If they are smart, they will learn not to repeat those acts that result in consequences they don't like.

Perhaps, that's what a master is, someone who has learned the laws of the universe and has the wisdom to set aside the teachings of this physical world and guide his or her every act in accordance with those laws.

Jaime heard a racket in the branches above him. He looked up to see a blue jay on a high branch, sending out its morning message to its neighbors. A gentle breeze whispered through the pine boughs and rustled the grass at Jaime's feet. *Nature in action. It's all so perfect. If only we humans can learn to live in accordance with the laws as the other creatures do.* It seemed to him that the Native Americans of long ago lived with the laws of nature far more effectively than modern people do. Perhaps that's part of what he so admired in Chris. Perhaps Chris retained some of the old ways.

Perhaps, that's my definition of a "man's man," someone aligned with the laws of nature. It occurred to him that anyone who acts in accordance with the laws of the universe exhibits characteristics in harmony with his or her essence.

Then, would Becky be a "woman's woman"? Maybe it doesn't have anything to do with whether someone is a man or a woman. Maybe gender is irrelevant. Maybe the term "master" would be more appropriate. But that implies attaining a certain level of perfection. Maybe the term should be "master in training." But that applies to all of us. Finally, Jaime concluded that the best he could do for now would be to define someone like Chris or Becky or Daryl for that matter, as someone who has learned to act in accordance with the laws of nature at a much higher level than the current norm.

What the hell. What does it matter? For now, I will simply act in accordance with my understanding of the laws of the universe, knowing that I have all the lifetimes I need to achieve mastery.

While that uplifting thought was bouncing around in his mind, Jaime noticed a movement in the distance. It was Chris.

Jaime watched as Chris walked slowly along the stream, moving in and out of the shadows. He was heading upstream, coming closer to where Jaime was standing, although Jaime was still some distance from the stream.

Chris looked up and saw that Jaime was watching him. Smiling proudly, Chris held up a stringer of fish.

Jaime waved and started walking toward Chris. As he came closer, he counted ten fair-sized trout on the stringer.

"Not bad for a morning's work, eh?" said Chris. "Ever had trout for breakfast?"

"Sure have," said Jaime. "It's one of my favorites. How'd you catch them?"

"My hunting knife has a hollow handle filled with little goodies, like matches, a few Band-Aids, and other survival stuff, also a couple of fish hooks and a few feet of nylon fishing line. I found a few periwinkles under the rocks in the stream. They make great bait. Apparently nobody has fished this stream in a long time. The trout weren't very savvy about fishermen. They almost jumped onto that hook. Let's cook 'em now."

"You're on!" exclaimed Jaime.

As they approached the fire ring and log benches they had placed near the entrance to the tunnel, they saw Becky sitting atop a large granite boulder. The sun was shining on her, bouncing off her hair.

"Morning, my heroes," she shouted. "What's cooking?"

"Nothing right now," said Jaime, "but just wait. Our resident woodsman here has acquired a supply of native trout to grace our breakfast table. Now if we only had a table!"

"No problem," Becky laughed. "As you can see, this lovely granite boulder is large enough to seat four, right here in the glorious sunshine."

"Let's get the fire going," Chris said.

Jaime started the fire while Chris cleaned the fish.

Chris produced a cast iron frying pan from one of the boxes he and Daryl had carried from the Jeep, along with a bottle of olive oil and a salt shaker. "Culinary perfection is right around the corner," he promised, as he poured a dab of the oil into the pan. "I only wish we had a little flour and pepper. But, it's probably just as well that I don't spoil you kids too much."

"What's all the racket?" came a plaintive cry from the tunnel. "Don't you crazies know I'm on vacation?"

Jaime grabbed a couple of pine cones and lofted them into the tunnel.

"Violence will get you nowhere," Daryl shouted, as those same two pine cones came whizzing out of the tunnel, one of them glancing off the top of Becky's head.

"Sexual harassment!" she yelled, as she tossed the pine cone back into the tunnel.

Within seconds, Daryl appeared in the opening, waving his white T-shirt over his head. "Truce!" he shouted, "I'll surrender control of the tunnel plus the four potatoes in my backpack for a couple of trout."

"Done," said Chris.

"I'll toss in the apples and pears Mom put in my duffel bag," said Jaime. "I'll also let you goofballs use my aluminum dishes and forks."

"Haven't you heard that using aluminum utensils may be a contributing factor to Alzheimer's?" asked Daryl.

"Yeah, I've heard that. But it's all I've got. One time isn't going to cause your memory to go belly-up," argued Jaime.

Becky took the empty plastic bottle from her backpack and fetched some cold, clear water from the stream. She put several drops of liquid oxygen into it from her first-aid kit, just to make sure the water was safe to drink.

The four enjoyed a delicious meal. The good balance of protein, carbohydrates, fiber, and fatty acids would help them face the challenges to come.

Knowing they were all going to be hungry by nightfall, Becky carefully wrapped the leftover fish and potato slices in plastic wrap from her backpack. She refilled the water jug and stored it along with the food.

Daryl washed the dishes in the stream and set them in the sun to dry.

Becky said, "I realize we're roughing it and we've got a lot of planning to do, but this lady doesn't do well with scrungy. I'm going down to the stream and give this body a bath."

A cheer went up from the guys.

Becky flushed slightly. "You may have noticed that the foliage between here and the stream is sparse. So I would appreciate it if you gentlemen would do me the favor of not looking in my direction until I announce that my body is once again properly attired for mixed company."

Without waiting for a response, Becky opened her backpack, grabbed a washcloth, a towel, and a small plastic box containing a bar of soap and headed for the stream. She did her best to find a location with a little privacy. But she still could be readily seen, especially with the sun shining so brightly.

The guys climbed up on the boulder where they had eaten breakfast. They spread out one of their maps in the sunlight and began to discuss their plans to get out of the area and find someone who could help them. They had spent much of the preceding day trying to come up with ideas on how to elude the bad guys. Now it was time to make some decisions.

Daryl glanced in Becky's direction. She was totally naked with her back to them. He looked away quickly, out of respect for both Becky and Jaime. As much as he would like to have a relationship with someone as enticing as Becky, he had already decided that he was going to have to wait a while to find the woman of his dreams, although Becky came closer to that dream than anyone he had met to date.

The men were considering various routes to one of three towns within a reasonable distance of their current position. Chris was offering his opinion on which route the bad guys would least anticipate. Jaime wasn't hearing much of what Chris was saying. He was experiencing some internal turmoil. For the past several minutes Jaime had been using a great deal of will power to keep from looking at Becky, in spite of the hormone infestation plaguing his teenage body. One thing that contributed mightily to the fact that he hadn't yet looked her way was the possibility of being observed by the other guys.

Finally, at a moment when Chris and Daryl were intently focused on the map, Jaime glanced up. What he saw took his breath away. The resulting gasp made it obvious that Jaime was no longer concerned with strategic planning.

Without looking up, Daryl said, "Go ahead, enjoy the scenery. If I was in your position, I wouldn't have waited this long."

Daryl went back to studying the map.

Jaime was vaguely aware that Daryl had said something, but his mind was focused elsewhere. There, before his eyes, stood the most beautiful woman Jaime had ever seen. She was standing sideways now, revealing the profile that had evoked Jaime's recent gasp. The sun had risen to the point where Becky's entire body was out of the shadows. The sun's rays were glistening off the droplets on her skin. Becky was pouring water over her hair. It trickled over her shoulders and dripped from her breasts. Jaime wasn't even aware of where he was. Chris's voice seemed like a distant echo. Jaime had to struggle to breathe.

Then, before he could even begin the monumental task of gathering the strength to look away, Becky turned her head, ever so slowly, and looked right at Jaime.

Busted!

Caught in the act!

Jaime was paralyzed. He sat there, enjoying the exquisite view, in spite of his desperate need to turn away.

Something was happening to Jaime that didn't take more than a few seconds but that he knew instantly, instinctively, and with absolute certainty would change his life forever. He knew he would remember this happening with a clarity that would never fade. This was an experience so emotionally charged that he knew if his life were to end this instant, his visit to this planet would have been worth every hardship he had ever had to endure.

As Jaime sat there, focused irrevocably on the most beautiful eyes in the universe, with guilt dripping from every pore of his body, Becky smiled.

Now, it has never been known, nor has anyone ever tried to describe the myriad of messages that can be delivered with a simple smile. But, without even attempting an exhaustive list, the smile radiating from Becky's sun-bathed face caused a plethora of neurological activities to occur in young Jaime's brain, among which were the messages of understanding, forgiveness, conspiracy, seduction, and deep, passionate, smoldering love. Those messages, however confusing they may have become as they found their way through the labyrinthine pathways and passages of Jaime's bewildered mind, grabbed him by the frontal lobe and literally lifted him to his feet.

Jaime almost stepped off of the face of the ten-foot-high boulder before Daryl grabbed his arms, turned him around, and headed him in the direction of a more gradual route of descent.

"Looks like our friend has just experienced the thunderbolt," Chris observed, thinking of his experience with Wendy back at the cocktail lounge.

"Maybe you or I can be that lucky someday," Daryl mused.

"Already have been," replied Chris.

Both men turned their backs to the lovers, knowing instinctively that this was a moment meant only for two. They focused on their plans.

In a mild daze, Jaime, headed tentatively toward the place where Becky had been bathing. She had quickly dressed and was heading back toward the boulder.

They met midway.

Jaime looked into Becky's eyes, the intense warmth of the sun on his back not even registering in his mind. Becky looked back, their eyes locking. And in that confluence of gazes, an energy passed between them that can't be put into words and can be understood only by those lovers who have been blessed with such an experience.

Then Becky did something she had never done before or even considered doing.

She took Jaime's trembling hands in her own trembling hands and placed them under her sweatshirt, his palms against the warmth of her flesh, just below her breasts, her hands over his.

They continued to look into each other's eyes. Becky slowly raised Jaime's hands until they were cupped over her breasts. She took a deep breath and shuddered slightly.

She whispered, "I wish you to know, my sweet Jaime, that no other man has ever touched me this way. I don't offer this as an act of passion, although passion is surely present. My intent is for you to understand how special you are to me. It is my hope that this is only a beginning. But if any circumstances, including your own desires, cause this to be the last time we embrace with such intimacy, you will always know that you were the first man I cared enough about to offer this precious part of who I am."

At first Jaime couldn't find words to express his feelings. Everything he thought of saying seemed so inadequate compared to the eloquent way in which Becky had just expressed herself.

He removed his hands from beneath Becky's shirt and placed them on the sides of her face, cupping her cheeks gently. He pulled her face up to his and kissed her tenderly.

As he kissed her, he sent forth to the universe a somewhat ineloquent but heartfelt prayer. "Okay, Force," Jaime said, "if I ever needed you, I need you now. Please let something come out of my mouth that will let this wonderful woman know how much I care about her, and, please, please, don't let it sound stupid."

Jaime backed a few inches away and took both of Becky's hands in his. He opened his mouth and, for a few seconds, not a sound emerged. He looked up at the sky, as if awaiting a message from the heavens.

When he finally did speak, he felt strangely confident that his words would be the right words. Maybe that was because they came from the heart. No games. No pretense. No ulterior motives. Just saying what was in his heart. It felt right.

"Becky, I've never touched a woman like that, never. I haven't had much experience with women, at least not the romantic kind. I get embarrassed sometimes because I've never done the kind of things the guys talk about in the locker room. I've been busy with other things like playing football and being with my family. But it's more than that. It's that the feelings I have for you are really special. I've never had feelings like this before. And to me, 'really special' means I wouldn't share that sort of thing with just anyone. What I feel for you is a lot more than physical. But the attraction is such a big part of it. It's really hard to explain. The best thing I can say is that my feelings for you are real. I really care. I want to share everything with you. I want to know all about you. I want you to know all about me. But I want to make love with you, too. The feelings are so strong, I'm not sure I can separate them. The love seems to get all mixed up with the sex. Maybe my body is growing up faster than my brain. I don't know. All I know for sure is that I would never hurt you. I'd give up ever having a relationship with you before I'd hurt you. I'm not exactly sure what romantic love is, but whatever it is, I've got it for you."

Jaime looked down at the ground, waiting for Becky's response.

She stepped toward him, put her arms around him, and rested her head on his chest.

She whispered, "This is all new to me, too. I think the best we can do is just to be real. That means being totally honest and not making judgments about all the little stuff. I don't regret a thing that has happened so far, and I promise you that I'll be the best friend I can be. I want to be romantic with you, as romantic as two people can be, but your heart will always come first."

They kissed tenderly. Then they turned and walked slowly, hand in hand, through the ancient pines toward the boulder where their friends waited patiently, as a warm, soft wind whispered through the branches above.

"So," thought Jaime, "so this is love."

Chapter Forty-three

It was late Wednesday afternoon when a couple of sedans pulled up in front of the farmhouse. Benson saw them coming up the dirt trail from the gate, grabbed the keys to his own vehicle, and followed them from his office to the farmhouse. He saw two unfamiliar heads in the back seat of the first car and one in the back seat of the second. Apparently, some of his men had been successful.

By the time Benson's car skidded to a halt, his men were already out of their vehicles, pulling Michael, Sarah, and Tim out of the backseats. He could tell by their movements and body language that the prisoners hadn't come willingly. Obviously, his men had decided to use force instead of reason to accomplish their objectives. Benson wasn't surprised. The criteria he had used to select these men for this mission had placed much more emphasis on the "stick" than the "carrot," as their preferred method of persuasion.

Actually, he was surprised that the Lashers were still in relatively decent physical condition. Gerald Carothers, driver of the second car, had a reputation for almost always delivering his prisoners with a few broken bones or at least a few lacerations. Carothers was a small, ugly man with a constant sneer on his lips and an obvious hatred for all of humanity. On those occasions when he was questioned about the condition in which he delivered his prisoners, he grudgingly explained that they had resisted arrest. His victims never challenged his story, for fear of getting more of the same or worse. A few of Carothers' prisoners had been delivered in body bags. Curiously, the files on those incidents always managed to disappear. The CIA retained a few men like Carothers for special assignments. They took great care to ensure that Carothers could never be linked to any of his superiors.

John Hawkin followed Benson on foot, choosing to remain in the shadows of the trees lining the trail.

As Benson approached the Lashers, Michael shouted, "What the hell's this all about?"

Benson said, "I must apologize, Mister Lasher, for the methods used to bring you here. Apparently my assistants misunderstood the nature of their assignment. What we are facing here is a matter of national security, and I'm afraid these men allowed the gravity of the situation to override their customary professionalism."

"What do you mean, 'national security'?" demanded Sarah. "What's this got to do with our son?"

"I'm afraid," said Benson, "that your son and his friends have stumbled across some top-secret governmental information, the knowledge of which could place our entire nation, not to mention the world, in serious danger."

"What," shouted Tim, "does that have to do with this place? The sign at the entrance said 'Property of the United States.' All I see here is an old farm."

"That," snapped Benson "is absolutely none of your business, young man. The less you know about this entire situation, the better will be your chances of returning to a normal life in the outside world. I suggest that you keep quiet, follow our…let us say…suggestions, and give us all the help you can in our efforts to bring your brother and his friends in, while they're still alive."

Sarah gasped and glanced toward Michael. She could see by the look in his eyes that Michael fully understood the gravity of the situation.

"You were brought here for your own safety and to help us convince your son to give himself up, once we've managed to make contact with him," explained Benson.

"But what has he done?" asked Sarah.

"That will be quite enough," Benson admonished. "You will be housed in this farmhouse, where we have taken care to provide cots, blankets, pillows, and sufficient food and water for several days. You will be allowed to use the outhouse twice a day. We hope to be contacted by your son before long, unless we locate him first. We hope that he has the good judgment not to have revealed what he knows. Once we have him and his accomplices in custody and have assured ourselves that he isn't working with enemies of this great nation, we will release all of you."

"What do you mean, 'enemies of this nation'?" Sarah screamed. "He's just a kid."

"That will be quite enough, Mrs. Lasher," said Benson, avoiding Sarah's eyes. "Show our guests to their quarters, gentlemen."

John Hawkin stepped deeper into the shadows as Benson turned back toward his car.

During this exchange, Tim spent most of his time memorizing the layout of the area. He made note of the position of the sun. He also took care to observe that the driver of the car he had been delivered in left the keys in the ignition.

Michael was studying the area with equal interest. His years in the military had prepared him well for a situation like this. He learned that, when one is in desperate circumstances, every detail could be important. As they were led into the farmhouse, he noticed the windows were all barred, the bars were on the outside, and they were held in place by bolts with their hex heads intact.

He also noticed a large black man, barely visible in the shadows, who obviously didn't want his presence known to the others. Did the Lashers have an ally?

Once they were inside the farmhouse, their handcuffs removed, and the door locked behind them, Michael led Sarah and Tim into a corner of the living room. "Don't say anything of significance above a whisper," he said. "This place could be bugged. We'll have to assume that it is. Act like we believe all of the bullshit about them letting us go. In the meantime, relax as best you can and concentrate on how we're going to get out of here. We'll make it. Keep your eyes peeled for some paper and a pencil. Maybe we can pass each other notes. For now, let's get to know our way around here. You two stay together and learn what you can about this floor. I'll check out the upstairs. If you find anything important, keep it to yourselves until we can communicate it to each other secretly."

On the second floor, Michael discovered three bedrooms and a bathroom. He also noted a pull-down ladder leading to an attic. He stood for a while in what seemed to be the main bedroom, looking down through a barred window at the area where the two sedans were parked. He thought intently about the situation. He knew there was a way out of this. It was just a matter of piecing all the facts together. Every enemy has a weakness. Most have several. Stupid men, as these appeared to be, usually have many.

Michael's concentration was interrupted by a tiny flash of light coming from some distance down the dirt trail. He recognized it as sun reflecting off the windshield of an automobile. A beige sedan was coming up the same trail he had traveled earlier. It stopped just behind the other vehicles. Two people were pulled abruptly out of the rear seat.

Michael couldn't make out the words being spoken by the man in handcuffs, but it was obvious that he was a powerful and unhappy man. His body language made evident the rage he was feeling. The woman beside him had what looked like blood on her blouse and skirt. She, too, was handcuffed.

From what little he could make of the woman's facial contours and skin coloring, Michael guessed that she was related to Chris. It dawned on him that whoever these lunatics were, they probably were rounding up Becky's and Chris's family, too. By the time he got down to the main floor, Sarah and Tim were standing by the front door, and the new arrivals were being escorted into the building. The woman's nose was swollen, and one of her eyes was badly bruised.

The door slammed shut, and the click of a padlock was heard.

Sarah took the woman's arm. "Let me help you get cleaned up. I'm Sarah. This is my husband, Michael, and my son, Tim. I would guess that you're Chris' mother."

"Yes," said Maria, "and this is my husband, Clint."

Michael motioned them all to the back of the room, where they continued their conversation in low tones. He said, "Our son Jaime left on a trip last Sunday with Chris and a young lady named

Becky, to deliver Becky to her aunt's home. We haven't heard from them since then."

"I guess our kids are onto something big," said Clint. "You don't get this kind of treatment over a parking ticket. I don't know your son, but I know Chris has his head on straight. I can't imagine that those kids have done anything wrong. When you add to that the kind of treatment we've gotten, especially my Maria, I have to conclude that we're dealing with some very dangerous people."

"While you're helping Maria get cleaned up," said Michael, "Clint, Tim, and I will do some strategizing."

Sarah took Maria into the kitchen and poured water from a plastic bottle into a bowl. "I think my nose is broken," said Maria, "but it's in place. I won't know for sure until the swelling goes down. I wouldn't want to be the guy who did this when Clint gets free."

From Maria's words and the tone of her voice, it was obvious that Maria had the same confidence in Clint that Sarah had in Michael.

Sarah's biggest concern wasn't in getting out of this prison. It was finding the kids before these men got to them. And they had no way of knowing where the kids had gone. It was time to call upon the power of the universe for help. As she soaked the dried blood off Maria's face, Sarah visualized her beloved Jaime and his friends safe and home again. She held that image for several seconds, as she'd been taught. Then she relaxed and allowed the energy to flow through her. She wondered if her silence might seem strange to Maria.

Before Sarah could resume the conversation, Maria asked her, "Are you talking with Great Spirit, too?"

"Yes," said Sarah, surprised by Maria's question, "only I call Great Spirit by another name."

"The name doesn't matter," said Maria. "It's the same power."

"Everything's going to be fine," said Sarah.

Maria nodded. "I know."

Sarah hugged Maria, careful not to touch her tender nose. Tears began to trickle down Maria's cheeks. "I know," she said again, a little laugh coming from her swollen mouth. They both laughed, releasing tension and expressing love and, most of all, knowing, secure in the feeling that everything would be all right.

Tim watched silently from the doorway. The ladies hadn't noticed him. Had they looked at him, they would have been shocked by the intensity of the look on his face. They would have seen what his family called That Look, and they would have been even more certain that all was going to be well.

He slipped out of the doorway and back into the living room. As he walked to the window beside the front door, he saw yet another automobile coming up the dirt trail. It stopped and unloaded two more people, both in handcuffs. The woman appeared strangely at ease, almost confident. The man was crying. He dropped to his knees and appeared to be pleading with his captors, although Tim couldn't hear his words.

"I wonder what it feels like to be that scared," thought Tim. "He obviously doesn't know about The Force. How sad that is for him."

The new arrivals were pushed through the front door, the man still crying and pleading, the woman silent.

Michael and Clint rushed to the door. Clint led the woman by the arm and welcomed her. Michael helped the whimpering man to his feet. After several minutes, they managed to get him calmed down. They introduced themselves.

Tim remained in front of the window, studying the men outside. Sarah and Maria came in from the kitchen. They discovered that the lady, whose name was Gail, was Becky's mom. The man, named Chas, said there had been a terrible mistake and if he could have just a few minutes with whoever was in charge of this whole mess, he could explain that he had nothing to do with those troublesome kids. The front of his shirt was tear stained, and his hands shook uncontrollably.

"Poor man," thought Tim. "He doesn't even know who he is."

Chas settled into a sulking silence and sat on a sofa in a corner of the living room. Gail tried to comfort him. He shoved her away.

Michael motioned for everyone to head upstairs. He turned back to see if Chas was going to follow. Chas yelled, "That's right just leave me all alone. Nobody gives a damn about me anyway."

Michael shook his head and went up the stairway. He had seen the ravages of fear before. What he didn't realize was that there was a lot more behind Chas's conduct than ordinary fear.

As Chas watched the others heading up the stairs, he realized that he needed to be with them. He needed to be a part of their plans. He needed to know their every move. He got up and headed toward the stairway. The fear that had gripped him ever since the men in the beige autos had first arrived at his home was beginning to subside. That fear was starting to be replaced by a much more familiar and comfortable feeling. He just might turn this whole disgusting situation to his advantage. He'd better hurry.

As Chas ascended the stairs, Herbert Benson III was about half a mile away, leaning back in the swivel chair behind his desk in the mobile home that had been brought to the compound to serve as his command center. He was thinking that he was in a much better position than he had been yesterday. He now had the bargaining pieces he needed to bring in those damn kids.

He wasn't very happy about the fact that he still had no idea where Daryl Harrington was. But, that aside, everything else seemed to be falling into place. He hadn't used his calamine lotion for almost two hours. A few minutes earlier, he had dispatched several of his men. Some were instructed to help find Harrington and bring him in. Several others were sent to help with the search for the missing kids. Four were sent out on two special missions, the nature of which Benson discussed with nobody but the agents involved. A few men still guarded the farm.

Benson had a building full of hostages. It was probably just a matter of time before he would make contact with those troublesome kids. He had all of the highways covered, not only by his own men but also by officers from several law enforcement agencies, all of whom had detailed descriptions and photographs of the criminals, with instructions that they were to be considered extremely dangerous enemies of the United States. They were to be held incommunicado and delivered directly to Benson as soon as possible after their capture.

The kids were young and inexperienced. They didn't have a chance against his trained professionals. Their escape had been pure luck, although Benson still couldn't explain the effectiveness of their ambush of his men, probably just beginner's luck.

Yes, just a matter of time.

Benson took comfort in knowing that he was being assisted by a group of highly capable professionals. He even began to feel a surge of confidence.

He thought about Hawkin. John Hawkin. Why did that man bother him? He knew Hawkin was his most capable man. But something kept nagging at the back of his mind. What was it?

And, come to think of it, where *was* Hawkin? Benson suddenly realized that he hadn't seen Hawkin for several hours. Where the hell was he? Benson considered going out and looking for him. But, for now, he decided, more important matters demanded his attention.

⚊⚊⚊ ⚊⚊⚊

Inside the moldy depths of the concrete bunker that housed the disabled spacecraft, one could hear the sound of footsteps on the earthen floor, an occasional flicker of light reflected off the concrete walls and ceiling.

Where, indeed, was Big John Hawkin? He was on a mission of his own, but not one approved or contemplated by Herbert Benson III. Had Benson any idea of John Hawkin's real mission and the source of his authority, Benson would have immediately and compulsively reached for the bottle of calamine lotion resting on the shelf above his desk.

For several days, John had wanted to do some exploring of the area surrounding the farmhouse, but he hadn't figured how to do this without someone noticing his absence. The arrival of the prisoners created the diversion he needed. Benson was so busy looking after the new arrivals, debriefing his men, and sending some of them out on new assignments that he probably wouldn't even think about Hawkin for a while.

John took this opportunity to visit the bunker. He hadn't previously seen the interior but wasn't tremendously surprised by what he found there. Sufficient information had come into his hands that the spacecraft's existence in the bunker wasn't as big a shock as it would have been under usual circumstances. But its size and, strangely, the texture of its surface *did* surprise him.

Even more than that, the realization that he was in the presence of an object that had once been millions of miles from planet Earth and had made its way here through the vastness of space caused John to regard it with reverence and awe. It was as if the very act of traversing the enormity of space entitled it to great respect.

Now that his initial contact with the craft was behind him and he had adjusted to the amazement that anyone would feel upon first contact with an object from outer space, John Hawkin was busy gathering materials and equipment. He discovered a virtual arsenal of implements and supplies that, to most, would have appeared to be worthless junk. But to Big John they were the staff of life. They were the little pieces of steel, the small strands of copper wire, the blasting caps, the black powder, the power saw blades, the jackhammer bits, the wooden shovel handles, the bag of eight penny nails, the box of laundry detergent, the bottle of bleach, the pieces of nylon cord, and so much more that were the tools of men like John Hawkin, men who had been trained as Navy Seals.

He worked well into the afternoon, the darkness inside the bunker causing him to lose track of time. When he was armed to his satisfaction, he gathered all of his "weapons" into a pile near the bunker door. He walked over to the spaceship and sat down on the earthen floor to rest for a while, his back against the craft. He leaned his head on its cold, hard, but somehow comfortable, surface and began to develop a plan. Before long, he became drowsy.

He sat there, his head resting against the craft. He began to notice an aroma that didn't belong there. At first he thought he might be dreaming. After all, he thought, maybe he had dozed off. Then it came again. This time he knew he was awake. But there it was. Yes, he was sure of it. He took a deep, satisfying sniff. Yes, there was no mistaking that smell: roasted garlic, one of John's favorite aromas. It reminded him of when his mom used to cook jambalaya on Sunday afternoons. Whenever Mom cooked jambalaya, she made a large crayfish pie and a pot full of filé gumbo, enough food to keep the family satisfied for an entire week, just like in the old Chuck Berry song, "Jambalaya, Crayfish Pie, and Filé Gumbo." And on those Sunday afternoons, Mom always cooked Big John his favorite side dish, roasted garlic, dripping with butter.

And now he could smell it just as if Mom, God rest her soul, were right here, in this very bunker, cooking her little heart out. Roasted garlic. Mmm! Mmm! And jambalaya! But where was it coming from?

He got up and walked around. The aroma faded. Confused, he sat back down. Back it came with all of its olfactory impact: roasted garlic and jambalaya.

He turned his head slightly, and there it was, right next to his nose, beckoning without mercy. And then it hit him. It was Mom. No, it couldn't be. "Mom, is that you?" For an instant, the unrelenting lure of the aroma caused him to turn loose of his usual composure. He gave in to the temptation to suspect that Mom was trying to contact him from the spirit world. "Okay, John," he thought. "Get a hold of yourself, boy. This isn't fairy tale time."

Then reality came crashing back upon him as he discovered that the aroma, that pulled back all of those childhood memories, was coming from the spacecraft. He brought his nose closer to the hard but curiously soft surface of the craft. Sure enough, it smelled exactly like Mom's butter-dipped, roasted garlic with a touch of rosemary. There was no other smell like that in the world.

He sat there, reveling in the aroma and its associated memories. The more he sniffed, the higher his spirits were lifted.

Then the bad memories began to attack, memories he had taken such care to bury so many years ago: the loss of Mom to cancer, an enemy even he couldn't fight; a sneaky, cowardly enemy that attacked while John and his little brother were both hidden deep in the jungles of Vietnam, an enemy that John wouldn't even know about until long after Mom's terrible battle was over. He thought of that loving lady, who had so bravely raised three children on the south side of Chicago, that lady who always found some way to grace the Sunday night dinner table with jambalaya and roasted garlic, no matter how old and worn her tattered dresses were. He thought of her fighting for her life all alone, losing her daughter to a tragic highway accident a year earlier and her two sons fighting a war they couldn't win, and she, in the end with none of her children by her side. It was more than John could bear.

As the aroma of that wonderful roasted garlic stirred those haunting memories, John began to picture his little brother, much smaller than John, but a feisty scrapper. He had always been there for John, always. They were an unbeatable team, both on the streets of Chicago and in the jungles of Vietnam.

Again and again, they had saved each other's lives.

And then, on one hot, terrible day in the steaming jungle with mortars falling all around them, John lost his brother. One minute Mikey was there beside him in the jungle, not more than twenty yards away. And then he was gone, disappeared without a trace. There was no blood, no signs of a struggle. He was just gone. John spent months looking for him. During those frantic months of searching, John almost lost his mind, but he held onto his sanity by telling himself that he was the only hope his brother had. He certainly couldn't count on the government to help find Mikey.

Eventually, John received word from the government that his brother had been killed by the Vietcong. A letter was sent to his mother's home, long after she had died, setting forth evidence that had been discovered to prove that her younger son was dead at the hands of the enemy. One of his dog tags was enclosed with the letter.

John tried repeatedly to get more information, but he was told that the file on his brother's case was classified for the purpose of national security and that any further inquiry would be futile.

As he sat there on the cold, damp floor of that lonely bunker, deep in a long forgotten forest, these memories tore at John's mind with an intensity he hadn't felt for many years.

"Oh, Mom, I miss you," he whispered. "And I miss my sister and my brother. I miss you all so much."

Then, for the first time in years, Big John Hawkin felt the comfort of…a tear, a single, tiny, frightened tear, almost too shy to appear. And then, as it left its shimmering trail on John's cheek, another appeared. And then another. All those years of terror and grief over the loss of his family and so many fellow soldiers came crashing down on him. And he cried. He cried for Ben and Hank and Paul and Skeeter and Joshua and all those other brave young men who gave their all to the very end. He cried because of the many times they had saved him. He cried because he couldn't save them. He cried because they thought they were fighting for something, when they were only fighting a ghost, the ghost of a cruel trick that was played on them by the government of the very nation they were fighting for. He cried for their families and the children they left behind. He cried for his mom and his sister, Sandi. But most of all, he cried for his brother Mikey.

# Chapter Forty-four

In a drawer full of playing cards, checkers, and other games, Tim managed to locate a writing pad and a stub of a pencil with its eraser almost gone. He, Michael, and Clint began leaving each other notes in a cabinet at the end of the upstairs hallway. They didn't tell Chas of their plans, not only because he seemed unstable but also because there was something about the man they didn't trust.

Tim left a note informing Michael and Clint that on the day Jaime, Chris, and Becky left home, he placed a target pistol, a cell phone, and a charging cord in Jaime's duffel bag. Tim said it was too bad they couldn't reach Jaime on the cell phone.

Michael responded that Jaime and the others would be better off not knowing that their families were being held captive. The last thing they needed was for Jaime and the others to return to the farmhouse. Probably the only reason they were being kept alive was as leverage to bring the kids in. Once the bad guys had everyone rounded up, they had no reason to keep anyone alive.

Clint agreed with that assessment.

Michael told Clint that the Lasher family's most trusted friend was a man named Mortimer Ziffel. If they could get word of their plight to Mortimer, he could be trusted to organize an assault on the compound. He was smart and level-headed, and furthermore, he had experience with weapons, was an excellent shot, and had spent a great deal of time in the military.

They began working on a plan to get one of them out of the farmhouse. If they could find a wrench, they might be able to remove the bars from one of the upper-floor windows without being detected.

Clint noticed a door in the kitchen, which he guessed led to a basement. It obviously had been secured recently. The hasp and lock were brand new. The hasp possibly could be removed with a crowbar. But they were unable to find one.

They continued to communicate by passing notes, operating on the assumption that someone might be listening. Tim suggested it was unlikely that the attic was bugged and that perhaps they could meet there after dark to discuss matters in more detail.

Clint thought that it would be too risky now, but that it might come in handy in an emergency.

Meanwhile, Gail and Sarah were going through the upstairs drawers and cupboards and two large trunks they found in the attic, looking for anything that might help get them out of this place. They found several blankets and sheets they could tie together to use as a makeshift rope and let someone down to the ground from an upstairs window—if they ever could find a way to get the bars off.

In one of the bedrooms they found a couple of candles and two boxes of wooden matches.

Michael came up with a possible way to get into the basement quietly. He found a whisk in a kitchen drawer, intended for beating eggs and such. He managed to break a couple of the long, thin metal pieces loose from the handle. He fastened them together at one end, then bent the tip of one of those pieces to a ninety-degree angle, leaving the other straight. It wasn't perfect, but it vaguely resembled a tool Michael had used as a Marine for picking locks. If he could insert this makeshift tool into the padlock with the bent tip pointing up toward the tumblers and then vibrate the tool vigorously while sliding it slowly out of the lock's keyway, he might be able to open the lock. It was a long shot but better than nothing.

Tim found a rusty old Crescent wrench hanging from a cup hook under the kitchen sink. But it wasn't large enough to use on the bolts holding the bars over the windows.

Not many of these activities missed Chas' attention. He slipped upstairs while the other men were working in the kitchen. He quietly lowered the pull-down ladder and climbed up into the attic, closing the ladder cover behind him, leaving just enough of an opening to allow him to observe the upstairs hallway. He saw Clint go to the cabinet, take out a pad and pencil, write a note, and place it back in the cabinet.

After Clint left, Chas climbed down from the attic, opened the cabinet, read the notes the other men had left there, wrote a note of his own, placed it in his pocket, and carefully closed the cabinet door. He returned to the living room and curled up on the sofa in the corner.

Within an hour, the front door to the house opened and three men entered. While one held his pistol on the prisoners, the other two set several bags of food and drink on the floor.

It wasn't the kind of meal one would write home about, but they were glad to be getting anything at all.

Tim suspected that this gesture was designed to keep up their hopes that they were going to be left alive, so that when the time came, they would cooperate with their captors.

As the guards headed for the door, Chas said, "Hey, when do I get to piss? My bladder's about to explode."

One of them grabbed Chas by the arm and yanked him abruptly off the sofa. He pulled Chas' other arm behind him and cuffed him. "Okay, we're gonna take you, one at a time, to the head. You come along peacefully, and don't try anything cute, and you may get to piss again." With that, he led Chas out the door while the two remaining men guarded the others.

When Chas was almost to the latrine, he said, "I've got something in my shirt pocket that will be of interest to your boss."

The man reached cautiously into the pocket, pulled out the piece of paper and read it. "I think you may be right." He faced Chas directly and said, "I ain't got no beef with your friends in there. I'm just in this for the money. But you're a real slime bag, selling out your family for special treatment."

He kneed Chas in the groin, bringing back to Chas painful memories of his encounter with the cocktail waitress in the parking lot during what Chas had come to call "The Samantha Higgins Era."

Chas collapsed on the ground, bellowing like a ruptured rhinoceros. One look at the front of Chas's shorts made it obvious that Chas no longer had a need for the latrine.

The man took Chas back to the farmhouse, deposited him on the sofa, then took the prisoners, one at a time, to empty their bladders. They were all curious about the scream they had heard, not to mention the gigantic wet spot on the front of Chas's shorts. They managed, however, to refrain from asking, at least for now.

When the parade to the latrine had ended and the guards were safely out of sight, Gail asked Chas what had happened. He claimed that he tried to disarm the guard but the guard overcame him with some exotic Korean martial arts stuff.

Michael, Clint, and Tim rolled their eyes simultaneously. Sarah tried, unsuccessfully, to stifle a laugh. Chas looked at her for a moment with obvious disdain and quickly refocused his attention on his aching testicles.

The physical discomfort Chas was enduring was made somewhat bearable by the satisfaction he felt knowing that the man in charge would be summoning him shortly to solicit his assistance in bringing the little brats to justice. Oh, he felt so good to be intellectually superior.

Heading for the kitchen, Tim gestured for Michael and Clint to follow. When they got there, Tim closed the door and whispered, "Something's not right about that situation with Chas. Clint, would you go back to the living room and position yourself to block Chas's view of the stairway for a couple of minutes? Then go upstairs and put a misleading note in the hall cabinet."

"Sure," said Clint.

While Clint stood in the living room, blocking Chas' view of the stairway, Tim went upstairs, pulled down the ladder, and hid himself in the attic, leaving an opening in the ladder door to allow him a view of the hallway.

Clint went upstairs, taking care to make a little noise with the cabinet door. He spent several minutes writing a message on the pad. He returned to the living room and whispered to the others, "I'm going to the kitchen to give Tim and Michael a hand."

As soon as Clint was in the kitchen, Chas headed for the stairway. "Where are you going?" Gail asked.

"If it's any of your business, I'm going to try to walk off some of the pain that brute inflicted on me."

As Tim suspected, Chas went right for the cabinet. The note read, "I've got the bars off the top of the chimney. We can climb up through the fireplace tonight after dark. The ladies made a rope of sheets and blankets that I've tied to the chimney. We can use those to let ourselves down to the ground safely. The last sedan to arrive still has the keys in it. We can be out of here before they realize what happened."

In spite of his pain, Chas couldn't help but smile.

Tim had no idea what Clint had put in that note, but he figured it probably was something clever. He waited until Chas returned to the living room. With Clint again blocking Chas' view, Tim stepped quietly down the stairs, through the dining room, and into the kitchen. He whispered to his dad, "The skunk took the bait."

Michael said, "If you think that's exciting, look what I've got here." He handed Tim the open padlock. "Not bad for a skill I learned thirty years ago, eh?"

"Not bad, Dad," whispered Tim. "Let's see what's down there."

Clint rejoined them in the kitchen.

Michael lit a candle. They headed down the stairs into the dark cellar, the flickering from the candle creating an eerie atmosphere.

Ten minutes later the three men returned to the living room, expressions of obvious shock on their faces.

"What's wrong?" whispered Gail.

"Something really bad happened here."

"We can take it," said Sarah.

"I think it's time for a meeting in the attic," suggested Michael.

The front door opened and three men entered the house. Two of them grabbed Chas by the arms and pulled him to his feet. They headed for the door. Chas had a self-satisfied look on his face. They left, locking the door behind them.

"What do you think that's all about?" asked Gail.

"Let's go upstairs," whispered Clint.

Maria, who had been quiet all afternoon, said, "I think the time has come for us to seek guidance. Bring those candles we found this morning and a box of matches. I'll show you something interesting."

As Maria led the others up the ladder into the attic, the sun was beginning to settle toward the mountains on that very intense Wednesday afternoon.

Clint was right behind her. He struck a match and lit one of the candles. It was enough to illuminate the single large room. The roof was high enough to allow everyone to stand upright as long as they remained toward the center of the room. The side walls, which were only about four feet high, were unfinished. The studs and the lathe to which the exterior stucco was attached were exposed.

Michael pointed to a light switch on the floor beside the opening through which they had entered. A single light bulb hung overhead, covered with dust. Michael suggested that they not turn on the electric bulb so as not to create any more light than necessary. Besides, he thought, there probably was no electrical power to the building anyway.

Maria agreed that they should use only the candles, but for a totally different reason.

Clint lit two more candles and handed one to Michael and one to Tim. Using the candles to inspect the walls and roof joists thoroughly, the men took several minutes in an attempt to assure themselves that there were no bugs planted in the room. Clint and Michael knew there were listening devices that didn't rely on hard wiring, and these would be difficult to locate. But they decided to take their chances. They were beginning to suspect that, whoever their captors were, they weren't acting with the official sanction of the U.S. government.

It had been only three days since Jaime and his friends had left home. That meant that, at best, whoever was behind this situation probably had had no more than two days to learn of their existence and whereabouts and bring them to this place. They were hoping that there had not been sufficient time to do much planning or very thorough bugging of the farmhouse.

Clint offered his opinion that it was probably safe to speak but that they would do well to keep their voices low.

At Maria's suggestion, they all sat in a circle.

Michael described to the ladies what they had discovered in the basement. The revelation brought them all to a new level of terror and almost unbearable fear, for themselves and their children.

When she was finally able to speak, Maria said, "This makes it all the more important that we proceed with what I had in mind when I suggested that we seek guidance." She asked the men to place the candles together in the center. She asked everyone to join hands.

Maria explained that she was going to ask for guidance from the spirit world and that she could do so more effectively if everyone would support her. She also explained that there was nothing magical about the process and that the presence of the candles and the holding of hands didn't impart any special power. The purpose of the candles, she said, was to help them focus their attention and energies, and the purpose of their joining hands was simply to help them feel their oneness more powerfully.

She went on to say that she had been making contact with beings in the spirit world for most of her life, having been trained in the ways of Great Spirit by her grandfather, who was a powerful shaman. She explained that her abilities were no greater than those of others in human form, but that she simply knew of and had practiced her powers, whereas most humans haven't yet come to know of the powers they possess.

She explained that all infants are born knowing of their powers but that most are convinced eventually, by their parents, teachers, and religious leaders, that these powers do not exist and that to believe in them is evil.

A brief discussion followed. Maria was pleased to find that everyone in the room seemed eager and open to accept her teachings. She discovered that everyone except Gail had already experienced so-called miracles in their lives. Even Gail was open to the concept, stating that, although she hadn't yet had any firsthand experiences with the spirit world, her daughter, Becky, had convinced her long ago that she had regular contact with a force that she called her Magical Friend, a force that seemed to look after her and respond to her needs.

Maria instructed them each to visualize an energy vortex in the form of a gigantic swirling cone, the round base of which enclosed the circle they were sitting in and the tip of which extended through the roof and into infinity. She asked them to envision the cone spinning in a clockwise direction with the face of the imagined clock facing up from the floor. She said the speed of the imagined cone's rotation should be about one revolution per second.

Then Maria asked them all to reach into the depths of their beings and to feel as much love as they could. She defined love as the flowing of the God Force without resistance, without doubt. This love should be directed upward in the direction of the tip of the cone, with as much fervor as possible.

She asked each of them to proclaim and command, in the silence of their minds, that Jaime, Becky, and Chris would be protected from all harm, physical or emotional, that those in this room would be delivered from their bondage safely and that they would be granted guidance from the spirit world regarding a method to achieve those goals.

Maria reminded them of the words of their brother, Jesus, when he had said, "When two or more of you are gathered in my name......" She explained that as the number of individuals in a group that has gathered for a common purpose is increased arithmetically, the power of the group is increased exponentially. "In other words," she said, "a group of two has the power of four acting individually. A group of three has the power of nine. And so forth."

As each person concentrated, Maria became silent, focusing on the swirling cone-shaped energy vortex surrounding them. Each had his or her eyes closed except Tim.

The first indication that their efforts were beginning to have an effect was a stirring of air in the room. At first it was barely noticeable. Then, as the movement became more apparent, Clint wondered if it was just air leaking into the attic from some long-forgotten hole in one of the walls.

Tim's eyes remained open, watching the flickering of the candle flames and the tiny wisps of dust that began to tumble across the old wooden floor at what he imagined to be the base of the cone.

The sensations increased. The movement of the air could now be heard. The candles flickered more intensely. The dust began to rise, now almost a foot above the floor.

Except for Tim, each member of the group forced his or her eyes to remain closed, each squeezing the neighboring hands more tightly.

The sound of the wind increased gradually until now, five minutes later, it was almost a roar. Tim noticed that the flames of the three candles, which were about an inch apart, joined together at their tips and began to spin around each other, with tiny bright blue sparks flying out from the center of the spiral.

He looked up and thought he could see a portion of the roof becoming translucent, a light blue color appearing where the time-worn roof trusses had been. He thought about his twin, the danger he was in. "Hang on, Jaime. Help is definitely on its way."

That Look formed on Tim's face. He focused his energy on the man he and Jaime had captured at the rock quarry so many years ago and how he had felt just before he lunged at the man, as if the power of the universe was at his command. From the look on his father's face, he could see that Michael Lasher was having the same kind of thoughts. He looked at Mom. Tears were trickling down her cheeks. She was squeezing Maria's and Michael's hands so hard that hers were shaking.

Tim looked at Clint, whose eyes were now open. Clint was looking at Maria with great intensity.

The wind in the room was now so strong that Tim was amazed it hadn't blown out the candles.

Clint forced his eyes away from Maria's face. He glanced down at the candles for just a second, then up at Tim. He saw the look in Tim's eyes and knew exactly what Tim was thinking. He realized that

Tim had the power. The same power Clint had found in his many years of martial arts training.

The wind increased. Maria, Sarah, and Gail continued to close their eyes tightly. Michael now had his eyes open. He looked at Tim and Clint, and they looked at each other. Their thoughts were as one. Michael smiled, comfortable with the knowledge that their minds were united.

The single flame produced by the three candles extended until its tip was a foot above its base and turned bright white. Large blue sparks spun from its tip.

The three men looked up and saw stars shining clearly through what appeared to be an opening in the roof, even though the sky outside could not yet be dark. Clint shuddered and looked back at Maria. Her face seemed to glow, not just her mouth or her eyes, but her entire face. The bruise near her eye and the swelling of her face were gone. As he watched, the glow seemed to extend several inches beyond the boundaries of her face. He thought of a phrase he had heard when he was a boy in Sunday school. "the beatific vision." "Wow," he thought. "This is for real. This is really happening."

A bright violet flame, about the size of a dime, suddenly appeared three feet above the candles. So intense was the light that the three men's eyes were drawn to it immediately. Sarah, Maria, and Gail opened their eyes instantly. All eyes were fixed irrevocably on that violet flame. Then the flame began changing color from violet to blue to green to yellow to orange to red and, finally, to a white so bright that each of the participants had to look away.

Then, the wind stopped. A moment later, the foot-tall flame above the candles melted into three small, ordinary flames, each dancing lightly above its own source as if nothing out of the ordinary had happened, leaving one large smoke ring rising above the three candles and encircling the bright white, dime-sized flame hovering in the middle of the room. That flame decreased in intensity to the point where it could be viewed without discomfort. It began to fade into red then orange then yellow then green then blue and, finally, violet.

In an instant, it was gone. The opening in the roof was gone. All was silence.

Everyone remained perfectly still, as if each was trying to understand what had just happened. Then Tim heard a sound to his left.
Maria apparently heard it too, as she looked in that direction.

Footsteps drew near.

A face appeared in the glow of the candlelight. Sarah and Gail
gasped. Clint's stomach muscles tightened. Michael felt the old,
familiar surge of adrenaline that he had felt so many times in combat.
Nobody moved. Tim looked to his left, not knowing what to expect.

The face was old and weather-worn, but kindly, with a merry
twinkle in its eyes.

"Welcome, Grandfather," said Maria.

 # Chapter Forty-five

Jaime was trying hard to concentrate on the problem at hand. He
and his friends were gathered around the U.S. Forest Service map that
was laid out on the large granite boulder, its corners held down by the
four aluminum camping dishes they had used earlier for breakfast.

In spite of the gravity of their situation and their urgent need to
find a safe route out of the area, Jaime found himself repeatedly
looking at Becky. He couldn't keep from thinking about what had
happened between the two of them only an hour ago.

The idea that she cared for him and maybe was even in love with
him caused such pleasant feelings to dance around in his teenage
mind that he couldn't stay away from them. It was sort of like trying
to ignore a slice of Mom's steaming hot peach Amaretto cobbler with
a scoop of Häagen-Dazs French vanilla ice cream melting down its
sides. Only this was about ten times more difficult.

Every time Jaime thought he had the situation under control, a
gentle breeze sent a whiff of Becky's perfume spiraling around his
head and past the olfactory receptors on the sides of his nasal passages. That fragrance already had become indelibly associated in Jaime's

mind with the intimacies he and Becky had shared this morning. Not only did that fragrance distract him from the discussion he was trying diligently to carry on with his friends, but it also caused certain electrical impulses to run from some unidentified nerve center in his brain directly to the tiny valves that control the flow of blood into a part of his body that he was trying not to think about and hoping nobody else was noticing. He looked up at Becky. She was noticing.

Jaime could feel his face flush. He tried to look away. He couldn't. She was just too beautiful. And her eyes, those loving eyes had him totally captivated.

"Hey, Jaime, you still with us?" chided Daryl.

"Yeah," replied Jaime, "I was just thinking."

"I know what you were thinking," said Daryl, "and I don't blame you. But could you focus on the map for a while? The sun's heading for the western horizon, and we have to get out of here tonight."

"Okay," sighed Jaime. He got up and moved to the other side of the map, upwind from Becky.

Within another half-hour they had discussed all of the possible routes out of the area and decided on one that was much longer than the others but the least likely to head them toward the area where they assumed the bad guys were patrolling.

They rolled up the map and began packing the items they had brought through the tunnel from the Jeeps. An hour later they had removed the camouflage from the Jeeps and had everything securely fastened to various parts of the vehicles, doing what they could to make it likely that nothing would be lost or damaged if they would have to do some serious four-wheeling.

They fired up the engines and waited a few minutes while they warmed up to safe operating temperature. While they waited, Jaime got the cell phone and charging cord out of his duffel bag. He plugged it into the cigarette lighter receptacle in Chris's Jeep and checked for the red light that indicated it was charging. The battery meter on the screen of the phone showed that it was already nearly fully charged.

Becky asked if the others thought it would be wise for her to call her mother to let her know she was all right. Chris said he didn't think it would do any harm, since the bad guys had no way of knowing they had a cell phone with them and, even if they did, he didn't think the location of a cell phone could be determined by a trace.

Becky called her home but got the answering machine. She thought it would be best not to tell Mom anything about her present situation. She simply left a message that she was fine and would be home in a few days.

Jaime called home and left a similar message on the answering machine there. He thought it was strange that nobody was home on a Wednesday afternoon.

Chris called both his mother's home and Clint's ranch house. The housekeeper said she hadn't seen Clint for a while and was concerned. Clint hadn't told anyone he was going away. She had called Maria's house several times to see if Clint was there but nobody answered. This news caused Chris to worry but he didn't mention his concern to anyone.

To everyone's surprise, Daryl pulled a laptop computer out of the duffel bag in the back of his Jeep. As he turned on the computer, he sat there humming, waiting for someone to ask what he was doing.

Finally Becky gave in. "Hey, Big Guy, do you mind telling us what you're doing?"

For the first time, Daryl mentioned *El Jefe* and gave his friends a quick summary of how he had stumbled across the CIA files concerning the spacecraft and the farmhouse. He also told them how *El Jefe* had helped him. Daryl suggested that if he could reach him, he might be able to provide them an update on what the government agents were up to. *El Jefe* seemed to have his finger on the pulse of lots of information that normally wasn't accessible to the common man.

Daryl plugged a cord into the side of his laptop. He disconnected the power supply from the cell phone and inserted the end of a cord from his computer into the power jack at the bottom of the phone. He explained that on some cell phones the power jack has more than one function and sometimes will allow the phone to be used to connect a computer to the Internet.

Within minutes Daryl had accessed the Internet and was downloading his e-mail. The first message on the list read:

"Daryl, you may be in serious danger. I have lost touch with the information centers I previously tapped into. Apparently, they have tightened security. I'm sorry to say that I must leave my post, so you will not be able to reach me for a while. I will do what I can to protect you, but you are on your own to a large extent. Stay in hiding until you can contact me. I will be back on the Internet as soon as it is safe to do so. Whatever you do, don't go near that farmhouse! I have pretty well verified that what we read in that file is accurate and that there is at least one, and probably more, powerful and dangerous high-ranking CIA officials involved. There's no way that you can deal with the situation. They have all the technology and manpower to make you disappear, forever."

The message continued, "Your only hope is to remain undetected until you and I can find a way to get you out of the country. Don't use your name or your credit cards anywhere. Don't make any calls on any telephone owned by you. Stay off the roads as much as possible, and don't risk being pulled over by the police. I'm sure the bad guys have an APB out on you, your automobile, your credit cards, and even your cell phone.

"There's a man named Herbert Benson III who has been charged with the responsibility of finding and eliminating you. My latest information indicates that he has teamed up with a group of unscrupulous agents and probably intends to use them to destroy anyone who knows about the farmhouse or the spacecraft. He realizes he should have destroyed the evidence at the farmhouse long ago but operated on the assumption that no one person would find both the physical evidence and the files and be able to put them together. He never counted on someone discovering the files and then connecting with someone like me, who has the ability to decode the files and link them with the farmhouse.

"Actually, his superiors ordered him to destroy the files and the evidence at the farmhouse way back in '75. Benson chose, instead, to keep the files and to hide them deeply, where only he could find them, and keep the evidence at the farmhouse locked up. He expected that at such time, if ever, as anyone should discover the farmhouse, any trail connecting it with the CIA or its files would be very, very cold.

"Unfortunately, when the alarm went off alerting Benson that the file had been discovered, it must have also alerted whoever tried to kill you, probably the same person who is giving Benson his orders.

"Apparently, his motive, however misguided, in deciding not to destroy the evidence in 1975 was his thinking that he might, someday, use it to blackmail his superiors or to cover his own ass if the 'caca' should ever hit the fan.

"So watch yourself, stay out of sight, and I will do what I can to get you out of this safely. Check your e-mail frequently. I'll get more information to you when I can.

"If you use a land line to log on, don't stay on it longer than necessary to download. They may be trying to trace you.

El Jefe"

The memo was dated Monday, three days earlier. Not current enough. *El Jefe* must not have gotten back to his computer as anticipated.

Daryl disconnected his computer from the cell phone and reattached the phone to the power cord. He gave Jaime, Chris, and Becky a synopsis of the warning he had just read. Then, in light of what *El Jefe* had said, he asked the others to refrain from using their cell phone any more, just in case.

Twilight was coming on fast. Jaime climbed into the passenger seat next to Chris. Becky got into Daryl's Jeep. Chris took the lead, leaving his headlights off until they would become absolutely necessary. Jaime held the forest service map on his lap.

They followed the corridor between the forest and the foot of the mountain that they had used to reach the tunnel two days earlier. Once they were beyond the forest, they headed in the direction of the trail they intended to take over two mountain passes and then down into a long canyon. If their map was accurate, there would be a town about thirty miles beyond the mouth of that canyon. They intended to find a place to hide outside of town and wait there until after 9:00 a.m. By then, they expected that several businesses would be open, including, perhaps, a newspaper or radio station office. They hoped they could get to one of these offices before they were spotted by any law enforcement officers. If they could find such an office, there was the possibility of locating someone who would be willing to assist them in broadcasting what they had learned. Once the word was out, there should be any number of people in authority who would investigate the situation at the farmhouse.

Chris thought about how interesting it is that so many people tend to assume that something is true simply because it appears in print or is broadcast over the airwaves, as if that fact alone has somehow blessed the information with a magical infallibility.

Right now, though, he was thankful for that very gullibility. He guessed that if he and his friends were to walk into a police station with a story about a spaceship and dead bodies in the basement of a farmhouse, with the APB that Benson had probably been put out on them, they would be behind bars in a matter of minutes.

But let the newspapers print a story about spacecraft and dead bodies, and there likely would be such an outcry and panic that the bad guys would be on the run in no time. At least that's what they were counting on.

As much as the media's desperate need to sell newspapers and airtime often works against the truth, in this case, it just might save the lives of him and his friends.

Chris' daydreaming was interrupted by the ringing of the cell phone.

It must be Jaime's parents.

Jaime pushed the "send" button and held the phone to his ear. He motioned for Chris to stop the Jeep and turn off the engine. He covered his other ear with his hand. Daryl and Becky stopped right behind them.

"It's for you," said Jaime, pointing to Becky. He jumped out of the Jeep and walked back to Becky, puzzled looks on each of their faces.

"Hello?" Becky wondered who in the world would be asking for her on Jaime's cell phone.

She listened for several seconds. She went pale. Her eyes narrowed.

Chris hurried back to the second Jeep.

Becky placed the phone on her lap. " It's my stepfather. He says they've got our families."

Chris took the phone from Becky's lap. "Hello." He listened for a minute, then he said, "I understand."

When Chris looked up, Jaime could see the rage in his eyes.

"They've got our families. Those killers have got our families."

Chris sat on the Jeep's running board and stared at the ground. Becky put her hand on his shoulder. Total silence.

It seemed like an eternity before anyone spoke. Nobody knew what to say.

Then Jaime wondered aloud, "How in the world did they find out who we are?"

Chris continued, "How did they know we have a cell phone? And how did they get the number?"

"I would guess," proposed Daryl, "that we must have left some information back at the farmhouse. Maybe they found fingerprints on the doorknobs or something. After all, we're dealing with our beloved government. And even though these are probably renegade agents, they still may have access to some of that expensive technical equipment that our tax dollars buy for them to play with."

"Once they knew who we were," said Chris, "it wouldn't be difficult for them to locate our families."

"I can imagine how they found out we have a cell phone," said Becky. "That stepfather of mine isn't a man of courage or integrity. I wouldn't put it past him to sell out to the enemy. I would guess that they're all being held in the same place. If they're together, I would think they're busy making plans. Jaime said that Tim put the cell phone in his bag. It wouldn't seem too far-fetched that Tim would tell the others about the phone so they would know as many of the facts as possible. If my stepfather overheard that fact, he probably tried to barter that information for some favor. He's so stupid he would probably think that they're going to let him go. I hope I'm there when he finds out that he's sealed his own fate."

"What else did they say?" asked Jaime.

Chris answered, "They said if we don't return to the farmhouse tonight, our families will be killed. They're calling back in ten minutes for our decision."

"My God," Becky whispered.

They were all silent for a couple more minutes.

Chris broke the silence, "We probably have to assume that these men are really killers. They apparently had something to do with those bodies in the basement. To be on the safe side, we have to expect the worst.

"Assuming they do have our families and will kill them if they need to," he continued, "how do we stop that from happening? They're obviously trying to bring us in because they don't want us to reveal what we know about the farmhouse. And the only way they can guarantee that we'll never tell anyone would be to kill us. That same reasoning would have to apply to our families. By now, our families may also know about the bodies. So the bad guys know they'll have to kill them, too. The only reason they're still alive—if they are—is that they're useful in forcing us to come in."

"And once we come in," observed Daryl, "none of us will be needed."

"If we stay out here," said Jaime, "they obviously can't kill us, and they likely will keep our families alive for bargaining power."

"Besides that," added Becky, "I don't think they'd risk killing our families as long as we're out here. They have to consider the possibility that we'll get to someone in a position of authority and, if a whole lot of law enforcement officers descend on that compound, they sure don't want to be caught with a bunch of recently killed bodies in their possession."

"So why not go to the authorities?" asked Jaime.

"Because we might not make it," Chris replied. "We don't know how many bad guys are out there, looking for us. If we get caught, everyone's dead. Even the good cops think we're dangerous felons on the run from the Feds."

"So, we can't turn ourselves in to the bad guys, and we can't risk running to the good guys," said Becky. "What's left?"

"We attack!" shouted Daryl.

"What?" yelled Chris, Jaime, and Becky in unison.

"That's right," said Daryl. "That's the last thing they would ever expect. We'd be crazy to attack a compound full of trained killers. At least that's what they'd think."

"That's what I think, too," said Jaime.

"Hold on," interjected Chris. "I think maybe Daryl's got something. Let's look at our situation. We are just four people, totally inexperienced in the art of combat. They are well-trained killers, apparently with no compunction about killing us. And, they outnumber us considerably. That's the bad news. Now, let's consider what we've got going for us. And remember, when you're backed against the wall, even the little things can make a big difference. First of all, we've got Jaime here who, allegedly, can run faster than the laws of physics would normally allow. With total disregard for any sense of modesty, I can handle myself in a street brawl better than anyone I know. Our little Becky Girl is no slouch in the field of martial arts. And Daryl, from the looks of the items in his Jeep, came prepared for an all-out war."

"Besides that," said Jaime, "those guys have no idea what they've got locked up in that farmhouse. My dad was a U.S. Marine war hero and is a mighty scary dude when he's pissed. He's big, and he's strong and I've never seen him back down from anything. Not to mention my crazy brother, Tim. He's one hell of an athlete, and does that boy have a will! When Tim gets That Look in his eyes, everyone runs for cover."

"You guys haven't met my step dad," added Chris. "Clint's a bull-riding, bronc-bustin' former Navy Seal who still pumps iron three times a week and has practiced Kung Fu for years. If he's in that farmhouse and we can break him loose, a few of those bad guys are gonna have their hands full."

"Don't forget, you testosterone flowing tough guys," reminded Becky, "that we've also got Zara on our side. I think we should ask for her advice and assistance before we go much farther."

"And what about Chris' great-grandfather?" asked Jaime. "He's probably sitting on the edge of some big old cloud, looking down on us and laughing his jaws off at our attempts to make ourselves think we've got a chance. I'll bet he's just itchin' to get into this fracas.

"And, speaking of having a chance," he continued, "let's remember that we're up against some pretty bad dudes. Just the numbers alone, not to mention their superior knowledge and experience in these matters, is pretty formidable. It would take everything we've got to have even a chance."

"But, don't forget, we've got the element of surprise." countered Chris. "They can't possibly think we'd ever be stupid enough to attack. And, they don't know that Daryl is with us."

"And," said Becky, "they don't know about Daryl's friend *El Jefe* who's roaming around out there somewhere."

Chris turned to Daryl and said, "You don't have to do this, you know. You don't have family in that farmhouse. The bad guys don't even know you're around these parts."

"I do have to do this," insisted Daryl.

Everyone was silent for a few seconds.

"Well," said Daryl, "we're just about out of time. The sun's setting, and that phone's gonna ring any second now. Let's decide what we're gonna do and go for it."

"What's to decide?" asked Becky. "We don't have much of a choice, do we?"

"Nope," answered Chris. "It seems as if it's them or us. Reminds me of a poster I saw on the wall of the Boy Scout hall back home when I was a kid. It said, 'Where would I be if it wasn't for me?' Kinda seems appropriate."

Everyone jumped as the cell phone jolted their nervous systems. They stared at that phone.

Chris picked it up.

"Yeah?" he said.

He listened for a few seconds and then shouted, "Listen jerk, there are a few things I think you ought to consider. First of all, we have two devices that we were able to remove from your precious little spaceship that are each, obviously, more intelligent than you and all of your buddies put together. Second, when we deliver one of those items to the authorities, there are going to be sheriff's officers, state troopers, policemen, federal marshals, real CIA and FBI agents, and who knows who else descending on that compound like you wouldn't believe. Third, the second device is going to be well hidden for future use. Finally, when your worthless little ass gets apprehended, you're right now facing, at most, charges of kidnapping and covering up for your superiors, most of which can probably be mitigated by some bullshit defense like national security or just stupidly following orders. But, you kill just one of those hostages and nothing is gonna stop you from frying for murder one. We left our hiding place over ten minutes ago and are now well on our way to one of the six towns surrounding this area. All you have to do is figure out which one we're heading for and capture us before we get there.

"By the way, we've just tape recorded this conversation, and as soon as I hang up this phone, I'll be calling a friend, who's standing by. I'm gonna play this recording of your voice, threatening to kill our family members, into this phone and onto his tape recorder, along with the details of where your compound is. I will instruct him to release that information to the authorities if he doesn't see me in person within three days. I'll also tell him where we've hidden the second device we took from the spacecraft. It shouldn't take the authorities long to figure out who you are from your voice print on that recording. So if I were you, I'd think long and hard about touching a single hair on the heads of any of those hostages. Just close your eyes and imagine how it's gonna feel when they run all of that high voltage power through your squirming body."

Chris hit the end button on the cell phone. It went dead.

"Holy shit!" exclaimed Jaime. "You're good, you know that? You're awesome."

Chris smiled. But Becky couldn't help but notice that his hands were trembling.

"Good job," acknowledged Daryl, putting his arm around Chris's shoulders. "Good job, buddy."

Becky walked to the back of the Jeep and removed the crystal from under the rear seat. She placed it on the hood of Chris's Jeep and un-wrapped it. She stood it up, with its pointed tip aimed skyward. They each felt a gentle throbbing in the center of their foreheads.

Zara spoke into their minds, "May I be of assistance?"

"You know our situation?" asked Becky.

"Indeed," answered Zara.

"Can you help?" asked Becky.

"My abilities are almost limitless. However, we in the spirit world are bound by self-imposed limitations. We will not interfere with the lives of humans, except when it is necessary to assure that they not be thwarted in achieving the purposes for which they entered the physical world. In other words, you each came here to learn definite lessons, which you chose before you left the spirit world. Our function, when called upon, is to help enlighten but not to interfere in a physical way. For example, I have the power to destroy your opponents, at least in the sense that physical matter can be destroyed. But, I would never do so. They, like you, are children of the Universe, beloved by the God Force. They are merely performing acts agreed upon by all of you before entering the Earth Plane. And, although these acts may seem despicable to you in light of the lessons you have learned since your birth, I assure you that in the eyes of God, they are not evil. Even if they might result in the death of someone, they are not evil from the point of view of 'The All That Is.' The only evil that exists, in all of the universes, is the evil perceived by you. That is evil in perception, but not in reality. Therefore, if I were to use my vast powers to stop an act, I would not be thwarting evil, but interfering with a scenario intended by your prior agreements.

"Now, that doesn't mean that anything is pre-ordained. All beings have free will. You are, therefore, free to change any of the circumstances of your lives, either by the use of physical force or by the power of your mind.

"I assure you that the use of the power of your mind is a much more efficient method than is physical force.

"However, it is up to you to handle these situations. The power of your mind is every bit as effective as any power I possess. My power tends to appear more formidable because of my absolute knowing.

"I may offer you advice or answer your questions. But, I will not interfere physically except in the most dire of situations, and then only with your consent. After all, it is the lessons you came here to learn that would be thwarted.

"I realize that this is most confusing, especially in view of your limited perception of reality. Just be aware that my primary goal would not be to save your lives, but to facilitate your lessons. If I were to perform a physical act to save your life, at such time as you returned to the world of spirit, you would ask me why I did such an unusual thing.

"I say all of this to assure you that, in spite of appearances, I work only for your welfare.

"With that said, I will tell you that your perceptions of the situation are most accurate. I will also tell you that this situation will have a happy outcome. Do not, however, interpret that to mean that it will have the outcome you think you want. That statement must be considered from the point of view that every situation must always have a happy outcome, by definition.

"You can't get it wrong. And, as strange as this may sound at first, you'll never get it done. That is because you are all eternal beings. What keeps you flowing toward eternity, is that you will always have new desires, new goals. It is the nature of the light beings, of which you are each one, always to want more. And, it is the wanting and dreaming and imagining that is the source of your joy, not the achieving.

"So, as soon as you reach your present goal, which is to save yourselves and your families, yet another goal or many goals will present themselves. Therefore, try not to take the attainment of these goals too seriously.

"Proceed toward your desire with as much joy in our heart as you can. As impossible as that might seem, given your present belief system, Joy is the state that will always facilitate the attainment of your goals. If you could possibly bring yourselves to maintain a state of pure joy for a period of three months, your life would become good beyond your wildest imaginings.

"Perhaps that is the lesson you are striving to learn from manifesting this seemingly paradoxical state of affairs in your lives at this time.

"But, also remember that, although you are from the spirit world, you are presently focused in the physical world and are, therefore, governed by the laws of that world, such as gravity, time and space. And, although you have the absolute power to determine the events of your physical world with your thoughts, you have become mired in much erroneous thought, and this erroneous thought makes it appear that you do not have the power you truly have.

"Therefore, you will probably proceed to attempt to handle the situation that is before you in the physical way, even though you are beginning to feel your true power, the power of your mind.

"So, as strange as this must seem for me to say, in view of your present illusory predicament, try to enjoy the journey and approach the situation with love in your hearts. You will be amazed at the outcome.

"I love you all and promise you that the outcome will be happy from the broader perspective. It even has the possibility of ending happily in the physical world if you can be strong enough to maintain joy in your hearts in spite of the apparent seriousness of the situation. Joy has the power of summoning assistance from the world of spirit that will often manifest in physical form."

Daryl asked, "Would it be to our advantage to use any of the equipment in your spacecraft?"

"Yes," replied Zara. "There are several items on board that craft that might be of use to you but probably not for the purposes you might expect. You may be surprised to learn that our craft does not carry weapons. Of the billions of planets in the universe that support life, only a few have a propensity toward violence. Our chances of ever encountering hostile life forms are so infinitesimal that it wouldn't make any sense to put effort into arming ourselves. Besides, if we did encounter hostility, we have the power of the God Force at our command to render such hostility ineffective. Finally, the very act of arming ourselves would have the potential of drawing the few war-like creatures that exist in the universe to us. We have found that those few civilizations that remain violent seldom, if ever, have contact with other life in the universe. That is because our loving energy does not attract their warring energy. This may account for the fact that your planet has not been intentionally contacted by what you call extraterrestrial life for thousands of years. Spacecraft do enter the gravitational field of your planet on occasion, a fact well known by your governments but carefully kept from your citizens. Those space travelers have not, however, intentionally landed on Planet Earth for thousands of years because of your acquired violent tendencies.

"According to our records, only one crash landing, other than the one involving our craft, has occurred on your planet within the past one thousand years. That other landing occurred in your state of New Mexico.

"Over two thousand years ago, however, a visit to your planet was accomplished by a group of kindly space travelers, who appeared to John the Divine, the author of the 'Book of Revelations' in your Bible. Those visitors found John wandering in the desert and took him into their space craft to tell him of a serious danger that lay ahead for the human race. They showed him on a screen much like your television sets or computer monitors, a picture of a gigantic computer which is, even as we speak, secretly awaiting deployment, somewhere on your continent of Europe. John, being very uneducated, at least by your standards of today, and being a little bit of what you would call 'crazy,' was terrified by the sight of this secret device, not to mention the spacecraft itself and its picture screen. When John recovered his composure, many days after the visit, he wrote at length about what he had been shown in the desert that day, calling the giant computer to be built in Europe 'The Beast.' He wrote, as he had been told by the visitors from outer space, that the number of The Beast was 666.

"Organized religion has since rewritten John's report of his encounter with those space brothers, as a meeting with an angel. They have interpreted The Beast of which John wrote as being, of course, Satan. If you wish to learn more about The Beast, perhaps your lives will lead you to another adventure somewhere down the road.

For now, I will simply tell you that The Beast is a gigantic computer that is linked to all major banking systems on your planet and that the number 666 appears as the first three digits on all bar codes affixed to most products in your retail stores. Those who control the money markets on your planet, and who, you will be surprised to learn, own the Federal Reserve Bank, intend to use this system to some day enslave all of humanity. But, as it is now seen by me, their efforts will fail.

"Now, to answer your earlier question," said Zara, "there are items in the spacecraft that may be of benefit to you. Be sure to take the crystal, upon which you focus to make contact with me, back into the spacecraft and insert it into the receptacle from which you took it. It will provide you with access to another intelligence needed to empower the devices that will be of use to you. You will be guided in your efforts. The intelligence focused within the crystal is no more powerful than that contained in the human brain, which, you may be surprised to learn, is not a thinking device, as you have been taught, but more like a radio receiver. The intelligence in the crystal is simply concentrated upon a more indestructible material to withstand the hazards of space travel.

"One last thought. Before you embark on the next phase of your current adventure, why don't you take a good look at Great-Grandfather's map, especially the small trail that leads to the back side of the farmhouse compound."

In an instant, Zara's energy was gone from the minds of the young and eager warriors.

Chris, Daryl, and Jaime almost stumbled over each other, trying to get to the glove compartment where Great-Grandfather's map was stored.

They laid it out on the hood of Chris's Jeep.

"Look at that," said Daryl, as he pointed to a faint line that intersected the road they were on, no more than ten miles beyond their present position. That line wrapped around the mountain that was just behind the compound and appeared to wind up a small canyon to a point about a half mile from the farmhouse.

"I didn't see that on the Forest Service map," said Jaime.

"It's not there," said Chris, laying the Forest Service map next to Great-Grandfather's.

Chris was correct. The Forest Service map not only didn't show that trail; it didn't even show the canyon where a portion of the trail was located.

"I just hope that line means something," said Chris. "And, if there was a trail there when Great-Grandfather's map was created, I hope it isn't overgrown with trees."

Becky assured them, "Great-Grandfather wouldn't draw a line without a reason. And Zara wouldn't have mentioned it, unless it was important to our situation."

"It would appear," commented Daryl, "that, perhaps, Benson's men don't know about that trail or the canyon. Yet another advantage for the good guys."

Daryl checked the tape they had used to cover the headlamps to make sure there was no more light being emitted than absolutely necessary to enable them to find their way. If they were discovered before they got to that spaceship, their chances for success would be reduced immeasurably.

It was now rather late in the evening, and it was decided that they should not leave for that newly discovered canyon tonight. There probably wouldn't be sufficient time to get into the compound and rescue their parents before sunup on Thursday morning. They needed time to plan their attack.

 **Chapter Forty-six**

Shortly after the kids left the Lasher house last Sunday afternoon, heading for Becky's aunt's home, Sarah had called Mortimer Ziffel to let him know that Jaime would be out of town for a few days with a couple of friends. She wasn't sure Jaime would be back in time to go bowling with Mortimer on Wednesday night as they had planned, although the kids said they intended to be back sometime Wednesday.

Immediately, Mortimer began worrying about Jaime. Not that Mortimer had a premonition or anything. He just worried about his kids all the time, especially when they were on the road. And Jaime was one of his kids. That made Jaime's friends his kids, too, even though he hadn't met them.

By Wednesday afternoon, Mortimer began to feel even more anxious. The kids were supposed to be home Wednesday evening at the latest. And he knew Jaime would call him the minute he hit home base. He kept glancing at his watch as he tied flies for the fishing trip he planned to take next Saturday. By 6:00 p.m., he started to fret. He didn't panic until 6:30.

At 6:31, Mortimer grabbed the phone and dialed the Lasher home. No answer. His mild panic ratcheted up a notch. He dialed again. Nothing.

Of all the kids in Sprague that Mortimer loved, the Lasher twins had always been his favorite. The Lashers were his family.

Mortimer decided to drive over to the Lasher place. After all, he could tie flies just as well on the Lasher front porch, in case he was needed there.

Nobody home. Ratchet!

By 7:30, it was dark, and Mortimer was starting to fidget. He poked a hook in his right middle finger, the one he had affectionately christened his "giving finger." Luckily, he used barb-less hooks.

By 9:00, Mortimer was seriously concerned. The whole Lasher family was gone. They wouldn't have left town without telling him. Ratchet!

They had invited him to join them for dinner Sunday night, after he returned from his fishing trip. Still, it was only Wednesday. They could be at lots of places, safe places.

Mortimer decided to look in their garage, wondering why he hadn't done so earlier. Both cars were there. Ratchet! Ratchet!

He began to perspire. It was late Wednesday night, and the entire Lasher family was gone without their cars. They lived too far out of town to walk to a movie or a restaurant or anything like that.

Mortimer decided to drive to town and look around. As he headed for town, he realized he didn't have his cell phone or he might have called some of Tim's or Jaime's friends. He hardly used that thing anyhow. It was too technical for him. He liked things that hooked to the wall. They made him feel secure. Mortimer liked secure.

As he drove, he thought back to when he was a kid. He was eight years old and had gone to spend the night with some friends who lived about a mile from his home. The boys had planned to stay up until sunrise, just to see if they could do it. They had consumed two gigantic sausage and pepperoni pizzas, two meatball and mushroom calzones, and an entire chocolate cake with ice cream. They were fast asleep by 9:15.

At 1:30, Mortimer was awakened by Joe and Eva, parents of the boys who lived in the house where the sleep-over was taking place. "Mortimer," Eva shouted. "Mortimer, wake up! I have some bad news. Mortimer, your house is on fire."

The boy shot out of the house, his bare feet slipping on the damp grass as he sprinted toward his home. Joe and Eva called to him, but he was already out of range. The thought never entered his head to ask them to drive him to his house. All he knew was that his family was in trouble. His instincts took over. He ran through backyards and alleys and jumped over fences and walls. The rocks in the alleys tore at his bare feet.

Fifteen minutes later, Mortimer stood in his front yard, twenty feet from his home, unable to get any closer because of the intense heat pouring out of the doors and windows. Even at this distance, Mortimer felt the heat singeing his face. He tried to block the pain with his forearms. A policeman was holding him tight.

As tears streamed down his cheeks, he screamed for his mom and his dad and his little sister, Ellie.

By the look on the faces of the policeman and the firemen, he knew that Mom and Dad and Ellie were still inside. He pictured his little sister, five years old, trapped in her bedroom, unable to get out, not knowing what to do. He pictured Mom and Dad, trying desperately to get to her room.

He broke away from the policeman's grip and ran as fast as his legs could carry him to the backyard, where they surely would all be standing.

Nobody was there, just the glow of the flames on the damp grass, where his family was supposed to be. They were supposed to be there.

Mortimer looked up to the second story and saw little Ellie looking down, reaching for him, shouting his name. He couldn't hear her over the roar of the fire. But he could see what she was screaming, "Help, Morty! Help, Morty!"

An explosion blew the entire back wall out of the second story.

That's the last thing young Mortimer remembered, until the next morning when he woke up in the hospital. The blast had knocked him unconscious. His hair and eyebrows were gone. His face was blistered. He saw objects as if his eyeballs were coated with Vaseline.

Mortimer spent the next two years in and out of therapy. The doctors tried to convince him that there was nothing he could have done, that it was not his fault. But he never stopped wondering if his family might still be alive if he hadn't been at that sleep-over, or if he had run a little faster.

Mortimer spent the next decade living with his aunt and uncle. At eighteen he enlisted in the Navy. Aunt Lucille and Uncle Ted were very good to him. Uncle Ted had taught Mortimer how to fly fish and how to shoot a rifle. But they never took the place of the parents Mortimer loved so dearly. The Navy seemed to be the right place for a lonely man like Mortimer.

Never was he able to erase from his mind the picture of little Ellie looking out of that window. The pleading in those innocent eyes were burned forever into his young mind.

Shortly after he was discharged from the Navy, Mortimer was married. He and his wife, Jenny, had tried to have children, to no avail. Perhaps their inability to have children was part of what brought them so close together. They were the best of friends, always.

After Jenny died, Mortimer decided never to marry again. He had loved her too much and knew that kind of love just couldn't be replaced. He decided it wouldn't be fair to any woman to have to live with the memory of Jenny. He would live alone forever.

A little at a time, Mortimer became a sort of step dad to the kids of Sprague. He looked after many of them, especially those from broken homes. He shared any money he could spare with those in need. He was a self-ordained counselor for those kids, imparting to them whatever wisdom his life experiences had brought him. A lot of the kids of Sprague who grew up to be happy and well-adjusted gave thanks every day for Mortimer Ziffel.

Mortimer knew that he wasn't a handsome man. He knew he didn't present a pretty picture with his bowed legs and his oversized gut hanging over his belt buckle. But he found all of the satisfaction he needed from his kids. They made him feel as if he belonged, as if he was needed.

Now, as Mortimer drove toward Sprague, he prayed that, if his family was in any kind of trouble, he wouldn't be too late. Not this time. He drove around Sprague. He talked to friends. He stopped more than once at the police station. Every time he got near a telephone, he called the Lasher home.

Mortimer visited every restaurant. He walked up and down the aisles of the movie theater. He went to the homes of almost all of his kids. Nothing.

He went back to the Lasher home one last time and left notes on the front door, the back door, and the garage door, asking them to call him as soon as they got home. He left his telephone number on all of those notes, even though the family knew his number as well as their own.

At last Mortimer returned to his home, utterly exhausted. He sat there for hours, staring at the telephone.

Finally, early Thursday morning, long before sunup, Mortimer fell asleep on his living room sofa, the telephone sitting on his lap. He dreamed of the Lasher home. In his dream he was invited for dinner. He was late, having looked all over town for Sarah's favorite flavor of ice cream. As he headed toward the Lasher house on the county road, several police cars, ambulances, and fire trucks passed him. Strangely, although he didn't consider it strange at the time, the vehicles had no drivers. They were completely empty.

As he pulled into the driveway, he could see smoke billowing out of the windows of the Lasher home. The emergency equipment sat there motionless, empty. Nobody was there. No sound was made.

Mortimer was a little boy, although he didn't give that much thought.

Then, as Mortimer stood staring at the Lasher house, Michael, Sarah, Tim, and Jaime walked slowly out of the front door. They stopped on the front porch and stood side by side, all dressed in formal attire and staring at Mortimer. Sarah scolded, "Mortimer, you're late." Instantly, their clothing burst into flames.

They all stepped down onto the lawn. They were all barefooted. They turned their backs to Mortimer, backed up toward him, pointing up to the second floor. There, in one of the bedroom windows, was little Ellie, screaming Mortimer's name, reaching for him. Mortimer was running for the house for all he was worth but not moving. He felt an arm around his chest. He looked up. It was a policeman. The policeman looked down and said, "Late again, Mortimer."

Mortimer was jolted awake by a loud knocking on his front door. His heart pounded, and sweat started pouring down his face. As he stood up, the telephone crashed to the floor. The room was dark, the sun not yet risen. As he stumbled toward the door, tripping over the telephone cord, a voice in his head screamed, "Dear God, no! Not again."

Chapter Forty-seven

His hand shaking, Herbert Benson III reached for the bottle of calamine lotion. John Hawkin pretended not to notice. Still shaken from his experience in the bunker, he decided it would be wise to spend a little time with Benson to see if he could get more current information on what was going on.

Benson knew he was in serious trouble. Those damn kids. How he wished he had removed those bodies from the farmhouse thirty years ago, when he was ordered to do so. If he had, the most he could be accused of now would be participation in a spacecraft cover-up and, maybe, the false imprisonment of seven civilians, all in the name of national security. In that case, most of the heat would have fallen on his superiors. Probably he would have been lost in the shuffle, probably not even mentioned in the newspapers.

But murder—the cold blooded assassination of these innocent civilians was another matter. The fallout from that event undoubtedly would bring Benson's complicity to the attention of the authorities. Murder one. The gas chamber. The thought made him shudder.

Hawkin watched curiously. Benson probably didn't even remember that Hawkin was in the room. He was deep in thought, almost in a daze. His breathing was shallow, hardly noticeable.

Gingerly, Benson poured lotion into his left hand and slid it beneath his waistband and down to his groin, wincing, totally oblivious that Hawkin was watching. Hawkin looked away.

Benson considered his situation. As soon as his cell-phone call to those damn kids was terminated, he dispatched all but seven of his men to patrol the highways surrounding the compound. He considered sending out all of his men but decided he had to maintain some security here. Using his radio, he called those who had been patrolling already and ordered them to step up their efforts. In all, he now had twenty men on patrol. He had ordered them to keep their radios on at all times in case he needed them back at the compound in a hurry.

This time he didn't bother to contact the state patrol or any of the other local law enforcement agencies. He wanted *his* men to capture those kids. He wanted them back here, not in the custody of some hayseed sheriff in some podunk backwater horseshit town.

He ordered his men to bring them back to the compound so he could find out the name and location of the individual to whom they had relayed the recording of his voice. After that was accomplished and the recipient of that recorded voice transmission was in custody, that unfortunate fool, the hostages and those damn kids would all have to be eliminated. He had no choice.

The very thought of having to kill someone made him queasy. He wasn't a killer. It would take a lot of penance to make up for that. But he had no choice. Fate put him in this impossible situation. And this time he would be sure that all of the bodies, including those from the original massacre, were disposed of in the approved way.

He considered, also, that most of his men would have to be eliminated. There were too many loose ends. He couldn't have a couple dozen men out there knowing what had happened, not men of the type he had rounded up. Most of those men would sell their own sweet mother for personal gain. They would have him over one hell of a barrel. What a mess.

His best bet would be to confide in Hawkin, if he was going to confide in anyone at all. Hawkin was obviously a highly capable man. Perhaps he could employ him to eliminate the others. But he didn't have the kind of money it would take to hire a man like Hawkin. What a mess.

For now, he had to concentrate on the first order of business— getting those kids and their telephone accomplice into custody and then disposing of them and their families. The thought made Benson flush. He dabbed some calamine lotion under each armpit and on the sides of his neck.

The possibility that someone had a recording of his voice, threatening to kill the hostages, made him squirm in his swivel chair. The squirming caused an eruption of burning in his groin. He winced. Hawkin looked up at some nonexistent vision beyond the ceiling.

Benson wondered if there really was a telephone accomplice or, even, a recording, for that matter. He decided he had to assume that there were.

He also wondered if those kids had really gotten into the spaceship. And if so, did they really have some device that would prove the craft existed? He doubted it. After all, the United States government hadn't been able to get inside the ship. But, again, he decided, he had to assume that they were telling the truth.

If those kids did get to the authorities, he would be advised of it in short order and, with a little luck, he could pull rank, ordering the kids to be delivered to his custody. But that would be messy. Lots of people would know the kids had been delivered to him. That would make the act of causing them to disappear very difficult. What a mess.

His only salvation would be to bring in those kids with his own men. At least his men would realize that they were accomplices. Perhaps that alone would be sufficient to guarantee their silence. Once the bodies were disposed of, Benson could reveal to his men the sordid details of the disgusting scenario they were party to. Those with good judgment would want to distance themselves as far as possible from the entire situation. If there were a few who didn't feel that way, he always had Hawkin to help him clean things up, he hoped.

But Benson couldn't kill anyone. He just couldn't.

Static shot out of the radio base station on Benson's desk. He jumped, then sat there staring at the device for a few seconds, fervently hoping a voice would pour forth informing him that those little brats were in custody.

Nothing.

The sound of the radio had jolted Benson out of his musing, and for the first time in many minutes, he became consciously aware that John Hawkin was in the room. Benson said nothing, focusing his attention instead on the almost unbearable itching sensations that were attacking several parts of his body simultaneously. He reached for the bottle again.

John knew very well why Benson was so upset. He had been present when Benson called the kids earlier and had heard portions of both sides of the conversation.

John began some speculation of his own. He decided that Benson couldn't afford to kill any of the hostages until everyone was in custody. That meant John had some time to figure out a way to save their lives without tipping his hand. As long as Benson thought Hawkin was on his side, Hawkin had some leverage. And in a situation like this, where the good guys are seriously outnumbered, every bit of leverage mattered.

John wondered what the kids were up to. He knew they were smart and courageous. They would have to be, to have outwitted their adversaries thus far.

And that bit about having recorded Benson's voice. That was pure genius. Whether they had really done it or not, the very idea was enough to keep Benson off-balance for a long time. If those kids were as smart as John was thinking they were, they just might do something totally unexpected.

If they were really heading for one of the surrounding towns, they likely wouldn't have said so to Benson. They would have been better served to let Benson think they were still hiding out somewhere or coming back to the compound so Benson would be less likely to be scouring the vicinities of the nearby towns.

"Yes," he thought, "those kids are up to something. And they threw enough fear into Benson to keep him on the defensive. He couldn't afford to assume anything, other than that the kids were on their way to the authorities. Too bad Benson had chosen to keep a few men here at the compound."

Hawkin decided he'd better do some reconnoitering and planning. He figured those kids might be showing up in a few hours. He wanted to give them every chance to succeed against the overwhelming odds they would be encountering. He told Benson that he needed to go out into the forest to relieve himself. He said he couldn't stand the smell of those porta-potties out back.

Benson responded with a low grunting sound.

Hawkin thought he probably had enough time to do what had to be done. Benson would be busy worrying and scratching. He walked the half-mile to the farmhouse and made sure all of the guards knew he was heading into the forest for a while. He didn't want to get himself shot. Several of them were sitting around the front and side porches of the farmhouse, smoking cigars and sipping from a couple of bottles of Chivas Regal and Jack Daniels. Someone was playing a ghetto blaster that filled the air with the rhythmic sounds of U-2 singing, "I Still Haven't Found What I'm Looking For," in harmony with a group of gospel singers who called themselves "The New Voices of Freedom." Hawkin owned that same CD and knew every word.

The agents obviously didn't take seriously the thought of any trouble from the kids. After all, these were highly trained killers assigned to eliminate ten civilians. They probably did that every morning before breakfast just to keep in shape. They already had discounted the ambush of a couple of days ago as a stroke of luck. In their minds, the kids didn't represent a serious threat.

John faded slowly into the shadows of the darkening forest. As he walked, he considered the situation. Yes, the hostages and the kids were in serious danger. Benson's men weren't the best by any means. But they did have the advantage of being totally unscrupulous. He had discovered a list of the names of men in a drawer in Benson's desk. Hawkin knew a few of the men by reputation. These were the kind of men who gave the general public its justified distrust of governmental agencies. These were the kind of men who gave the CIA and FBI the dishonorable image often portrayed in the movies, in spite of the many fine people who work for those agencies.

Hawkin wanted to take them all down.

He worked his way around the periphery of the forest that surrounded the front yard of the farmhouse and the outbuildings and parking areas nearby, taking care to remain in the shadows. He walked to where he had parked his vehicle and crouched beside it. As he opened the door, the dome light went on for an instant before he was able to put his finger on the button near the door hinge that activated the light. He held the button down while he removed the plastic cover of the dome light and unscrewed the light bulb. He hoped nobody noticed the brief flash of light. He thought it unlikely that anyone would be able to see him from the porch. He left the door ajar and sat in the driver's seat while he rummaged through his briefcase, taking several items from it and depositing them in his pockets. He reached into the back seat and retrieved his bamboo fighting sticks and strapped the holster in which they were contained onto his back beneath his sweatshirt.

He then went to the back of the farmhouse and, using the penlight he had retrieved from his briefcase, located two shovels, one long-handled and one short. He circled back to the side of the farmhouse to a location he had noticed earlier that day, where the edge of the forest came to within about ten feet of the building. His instincts told him that a means of escaping from the farmhouse through the cellar might eventually prove to be of benefit to the hostages.

He began digging, the sounds of that effort being drowned out by the harmonious talents of U2 and B.B. King rocking out with "When Love Comes to Town."

All those years of hard labor and pumping iron served him well. Within an hour, he had completed a small tunnel that might have taken most men twice as long to dig. When he was finished, he was dripping wet.

He surveyed the results with his penlight. The pile of dirt he had created in the forest was not readily visible in the darkness, and the tunnel was deep enough by the time it exited the forest that no depression showed on the surface of the soil. He calculated that the end of the tunnel was within a foot or so of where he assumed the basement wall would be.

Fortunately, the soil was filled with abundant organic matter and few rocks, which made the digging relatively easy. The most difficult obstacles John encountered were a couple of tree roots that he had to dig around and one that he was able to cut with a shovel blade. He reasoned that if he could fit through the tunnel, almost anyone could.

At this point, he had no idea whether the tunnel would ever be used. It just made him feel good to know it was there. He went into the tunnel once more. He snaked his way to its end, dragging the long-handled shovel behind him, handle first, using the short shovel for his digging. When he reached the end, he dug a bit farther until he felt the soil ahead of him give slightly. He didn't want to dig all the way into the cellar for fear that the wrong people might discover his handiwork. He took the long shovel and gently shoved the tip of its handle through the soil and a couple of inches into the underground room. He stopped, hoping the soil wouldn't collapse. It held. He surmised that, from the inside, the tip of the shovel handle sticking about an inch into the room wouldn't be noticed by anyone who wasn't looking for it.

He backed out of the tunnel, as he had already done several times, with a load of soil secured in his sweatshirt, delivering that last load to the pile in the forest. His tunnel was now about fifteen feet long, with the five feet closest to the opening well hidden within the forest. The tunnel sloped down at about a three-to-one angle, so in the fifteen linear feet it traversed from beginning to end it dropped from the floor of the forest to a depth of about five feet. He calculated that the eventual opening of the tunnel into the cellar would occur about three feet above the cellar floor. He also estimated that by the time it left the shadows of the forest and entered the area below the open space between the forest and the building, it would be a good twenty inches below ground level, sufficient to prevent the rich, damp earth from sinking into the tunnel and leaving telltale signs on the surface.

John was proud of himself.

He wiped the sweat from his brow and the dirt from his pants and sweatshirt. He discovered that the dirt on the knees of his britches was embedded to the point where it couldn't be brushed off. But he could explain that if anyone asked.

While he had been digging the tunnel, he had considered the possibility of bringing the hostages out right now but decided that their chances of escape, with only him to escort them and hold off the bad guys, were mighty slim. He would wait for more help to arrive. Besides, their chances of escaping undetected would be increased dramatically if a lot of action was going on elsewhere in the compound. In addition, as far as Hawkin knew, the door from the kitchen to the basement was still locked, denying the hostages access.

Footsteps.

Two men.

Not more than twenty feet from where Hawkin was standing.

He held his breath. He didn't move. Thank God his penlight was off.

He heard the sound of water running. They were peeing. They probably didn't like the smell of those porta-potties either.

He noticed that one of the men was standing directly over the tunnel. He crossed his fingers.

One of them said, "What do you think of all this bullshit? I would guess that that asshole Benson's got about thirty men on this job, looking for three snot-nosed kids. There's something more goin' on here than meets the eye."

"Yeah, and he's got the basement to that damn house locked up tight. And there's something out in that forest that nobody but Benson knows about. I seen him heading there yesterday, looking around to make sure nobody was following him. I went out there to have a look-see this morning before sunup. Didn't find anything. Just a lot of trees and bushes. Seen a lot of trees with their trunks burned. Just on one side though. Kinda strange. I say we get a bunch of the guys and go confront that little jerk and demand to know what we're up against. He don't need a whole raft full of men to capture a few kids."

"Yeah, I'm bettin' some of them jerks in the higher-up offices did something to get their tits in the wringer and they're expecting us to bail them out. I'd like to know what them kids did. Probably just stumbled onto something. I'd like to see what's in that basement."

"With this much manpower, there's got to be something big coming down. I don't mind being up against some heavy shit. But I'd sure like to know what it is before it happens. I got an UZI and an AK 47 in the trunk of that piece of shit I drove up here. I say we get 'em out and be ready for whatever comes down. I got a 47 Magnum Desert Eagle in my shoulder holster and a Smith and Wesson blunt-nose 38 special in my ankle holster, but I'd feel a lot better with a little more firepower."

"Andy's got a 223 sniper rifle under his backseat, and I hear Joe Walters got one o' them German HK 91's that fires a 308 caliber. I think we need to tell the guys it's time to get the heavy artillery out. I got a funny feeling about all this."

"I'm with you. By the way, does the ground feel kinda soft to you?"

Hawkin reached for his bamboo fighting sticks. He tightened his grip, not yet pulling them from their hiding place.

"Hell, that's no big deal in these forests. Soil's soft from about ten thousand years of trees rotting on the ground. I've been in places where you could sink a good six inches just after the spring thaw. Come back next month and that spot you're standing on will be hard as a rock."

Hawkin relaxed his grip on his fighting sticks. He heard the sound of two zippers sliding upward. *Funny, how zippers seem always to slide up more slowly than they slide down. Probably because the downward slide usually comes in a time of urgency of one type or another, while the upward slide comes after some kind of relief.* He thought about how his line of work required so much more attention to little details than most other occupations.

The men headed back to the front of the farmhouse.

John breathed a sigh of relief. He wasn't ready for the action to start yet. He slipped silently through the forest to the bunker.

Once inside, he flipped on his penlight and located a wooden box he had noticed the last time he was there. He filled it with an assortment of wires, fuses, blasting caps, dynamite sticks and, four packets of C-4. He coiled up about fifty feet of three-wire extension cord that had no female end. He saw several 12-volt batteries but knew they couldn't possibly have any power after all these years. He'd have to find a power source somewhere else.

He busied himself setting up a few surprises for the bad guys.

Two hours later, he was back in Benson's office, painfully aware of the dirt spots on the knees of his blue jeans.

"Long piss," observed Benson.

"More than a potty run," replied Hawkin. "I was surveying the area. Never know when you'll need to have a thorough understanding of the lay of the land."

"Those kids are probably running away from here as fast as they can," said Benson.

"No doubt," said Hawkin. "But are you sure those kids are the only danger?"

"What the hell does that mean?" stammered Benson.

"I mean, all that calamine lotion isn't just over a few kids. Something's got you spooked. Did you ever think that someone out there's just as concerned as you are about the number of loose cannons you've got working for you? And what they might already know. I just overheard a couple of them talking about something hidden in the basement of that old house, and something very top secret out there in that forest. I think you're gonna have to do a lot more cleaning up than just getting rid of those kids and the hostages. I think you've got more problems on your hands than you may realize. If I was you, I sure as hell wouldn't want any dead bodies on my hands when the shit hits the fan."

Perspiration began to run down Benson's temples.

"What can I do?" he blurted out.

"Don't know," was all that Hawkin said, with as much sympathy in his voice as he could muster.

The two men sat there staring at each other, the perspiration now down to the tip of Benson's chin. Hawkin carefully gauged the look on Benson's face. The man was scared, beyond his ability to cope.

In a way, Hawkin felt sorry for him. He probably hadn't started this mess. He probably was just left with the disgusting duty of handling the clean-up, which he bungled. Just a poor scared psycho caught in a trap he didn't have the guts or the brains to get out of.

"I think you've got a possible mutiny on your hands," said Hawkin, watching for Benson's reaction.

He didn't have to wait long. Benson sprang from his swivel chair and darted for the entry door. A few seconds later, Hawkin could hear the poor fool retching at the side of the building.

He went outside and helped Benson to the front steps, where the man sat down, shaking. Hawkin fetched him a glass of water.

Then he said, "I think I can help you get out of this, at least short of the gas chamber."

Benson flinched.

"I need your agreement that no civilians are going to get killed. I won't be an accomplice to cold-blooded murder. I've taken my share of lives in combat and on espionage missions, but I won't be involved in killing the very people I'm sworn to protect. Fair enough?"

Benson nodded feebly, already cooking up a new plan of his own. Encouraged by Hawkin's offer to help him, his mood began to shift from fear to tentative confidence.

"You keep those civilians alive, and I'll do my best to keep your hoodlums under control."

Benson nodded again then looked up.

Hawkin saw something in that look, something he didn't like, not at all. He formed a clear intention to watch his backside. The only people he could trust were locked up in that farmhouse or out there somewhere on the run. Things were going to get intense before this was over.

Chapter Forty-eight

Chas sat dejected on the sofa in the farmhouse living room, having been recently and emphatically enlightened relative to the fact that Herbert Benson and his henchmen had no further use for him or his information. He had become painfully aware that his life was in serious danger and that even bad guys look with disdain upon anyone who would turn on his own family. He still ached from the blow that insensitive agent had delivered to his groin.

His wife, Gail, was in the attic with her new friends, experiencing some serious enlightenment of her own. Gail had often heard Becky speak of her Magical Friend and of the times this force had come to Becky's assistance. But never before had Gail come face to face with a member of the spirit world.

There, before Gail's eyes, appeared an impressive, wrinkle-faced, gray-haired Indian gentleman, complete with deerskin breeches and tunic, beaded moccasins, and a war bonnet that seemed to glow in the relative darkness of the attic. His shoulders were draped with a colorful Indian blanket.

He looked directly at Gail with piercing eyes. "Beloved lady," he said, "I sense that this is a new experience for you. Please do not be frightened. I mean you no harm. Nor could I harm you if I wanted to, which no entity from the spirit world would ever want to do anyway. I come from a place of pure love, and I bring you the best of wishes."

He stepped inside the circle of friends who were gathered around the three candles. The flames once again spiraled into a single flame that rose high into the air and seemed to glow in the very center of Great-Grandfather's bosom. He pointed to the glowing war bonnet. "A nice effect, don't you think? Something I dreamed up in preparation for the coming battle. By the way, rest assured that at this moment, your children are alive and well, although they are embarking on an extraordinary course of action."

"What course of action?" Sarah asked.

"They are on their way to this farmhouse," Great-Grandfather replied, "intending to take on the band of desperados that has gathered in and around this compound. Your children are armed with grossly inadequate weapons, plus assistance from an entity from the spirit world named Zara and, of course, yours truly."

Maria said, "Grandfather, you old rascal, it seems that your departure from this plane hasn't dampened your sense of the bizarre."

"Bizarre what?" asked the apparition. "You're seeing me at my spiritually most conservative. After all, I am now in the world of the absolute, where everything happens at the exact moment it is conceived in consciousness and nothing is impossible. Besides that, none of it takes any effort beyond my simply willing it. Makes it hard to be conservative, don't you think?"

"I understand," countered Maria, "but can you help us with our little dilemma? We seem to be faced with some bad and powerful men. Is there some way out of this? Will we survive?"

"That depends," said Great-Grandfather, "on your attitude and intentions. Contrary to what they teach at the Christian school, each of you has absolute control over the circumstances of your life. It is all a matter of aligning your beliefs with your intentions.

"As Jesus, used to say—and, by the way, still says—you must have faith. Actually, he never used the word 'faith.' That came about later as the records of his words were translated from language to language. I have it on the best of authority that what he said was you must *know*. He wasn't talking about the power of the Pope, or the power of the Church. He spoke purely about knowing the power of your own higher self. When he spoke of the 'Father within,' what he was trying to teach his disciples, and ultimately all of us, was that we can control all of the circumstances of our lives by simply *knowing* that we can. Or, put another way, we need only align our beliefs with our intentions. And our beliefs are nothing more than the thoughts we continue to hold.

"So if you want to get out of your current situation—which, by the way, was created by your own thoughts and the thoughts of the collective unconscious, as were all of the situations of your lives—all you have to do is choose to *know* that you will. If you can hold that thought long enough, the Universe or the God Force or your Higher Self or whatever you wish to call the All That Is will latch onto that thought and send you exactly what you intend. Beyond that, it's just a matter of allowing the results to come to you by simply not doubting, not resisting.

"Now," soothed the grand old gentleman, "you must remember that our brother Jesus said, as have many of the other grand masters who inhabited this Earth Plane, 'You are in this world but not of this world.' What he meant, I have come to understand, is that we are all part of the spirit world. Actually, we are all God, focused in these physical bodies temporarily, until we return completely to the spirit world for what you on Earth call a 'period of time.'

"So you are spirits focused in physical bodies. And, while you are focused in these bodies, you are influenced by the laws of physical reality, even though you have the ability to override those laws with the power of your minds, provided you *know* that you have that capability.

"The reason this may be difficult to accept is that we have all been programmed by our parents, our teachers, our religions, our government, and our media, often with the best of intentions, to believe that we do not have the power. Have you ever noticed that little children come to this plane believing in magic? They often see magical friends. They believe that they are totally free, that they can fly, that they have the power, that they can do anything, that everything is theirs to explore and enjoy. Once we have lost the magic, our Higher Selves try, for the rest of our physical lives, to guide us back to the state of enchantment that is our birthright. There are many masters on your plane, particularly at this time, trying to get you all to understand that you are God, not just children of God, but God Itself, the power of the All That Is.

"Great-Grandfather," interrupted Tim, "that makes good sense to me especially in view of some of the experiences I've had recently. But can you tell us how this thing about being 'in this world but not of this world' relates to how we can get out of this mess we're in?"

"Of course," responded Great-Grandfather. "Even though you each have powers similar to those that your brothers Jesus, Buddha, Mohammad, Sai Baba, Krishna, and others have demonstrated, you have come to this physical place to experience time and space, neither of which exists in the spirit world—as your Grand Master, Albert Einstein, proved and as many of the Masters presently on your plane are trying to get you to understand. One of the reasons you chose to experience life on the Earth is that on Earth there is an apparent period of time between the cause and the effect of any event. This provides you with time to consider the implications of your acts. Because of the time lag and the teachings of those who wish to control you, you have come to doubt your own power, which is the power of God.

"Before coming here, you all agreed to live with certain illusions that you carefully designed to enable you to learn particular lessons. The problem is that you have, over hundreds of lifetimes, forgotten that they are illusions and now accept them as reality, concluding that they exist and have power beyond the power you give them with your thoughts. As you reincarnate, you arrive on this planet full of love and hope and enthusiasm. But those who came before you have already had their magic knocked out of them by those who came before them, and they do the same to you. This may have been the basis for the saying, 'The sins of the fathers are visited upon the sons.'

"So you are all in the process of remembering your magic. We in the spirit world are attempting to assist you in doing so. That's why you are experiencing so many wonderful movies such as *Field of Dreams*, *Always*, *Ghost*, and *What Dreams May Come*, and so many great books such as *Conversations with God* and *Manifest Your Destiny*. Many books, movies, and songs are being inspired by entities in the spirit world, just as were many of your ancient writings like the Bible and the Koran. Unfortunately, many religions insist on drawing their teachings from those ancient writings, in spite of the fact that they were written to address long-forgotten situations.

"God is speaking to you now in so many ways. Listen to the words of your popular songs. Many are inspired, as are many of your books and movies. This, of course, leaves you with the question of which of these works are truly inspired and which are simply human works. To answer that, you must listen with your heart or, more accurately, your soul or higher self. Always follow your true feelings. They will never lead you astray. Take care however, to know your true feelings as separate from the feelings the world has tried to make you believe are yours. You will know. Always ask yourself, 'What would love do now?' You will know. The truth will always set you free, make you joyous, bring you peace."

"What can we do for our children?" asked Sarah, "I feel so helpless, trapped in this place while my Jaime is out there in danger."

"Even those of us in the spirit world cannot foretell the future with any certainty," replied Great-Grandfather. "The future is a concept found only in realms of gross matter, such as planet Earth. Where I reside, there is no such concept as time. All is happening in the present moment. Even 'present moment' is not an appropriate term where I am now focused, as the very term 'moment' insinuates the passage of time. In your world, the future is uncertain in that it depends completely on the thought processes of the individuals whose lives are involved, or, lacking their attention upon the matter, the thought processes of others, including sometimes the collective unconscious of the planet. I know that's a difficult concept but, nonetheless, accurate. So I can't tell you what is going to happen to your children. I can tell you, however, that from the higher perspective, it is all unfolding perfectly.

"But to answer your concern," continued Great-Grandfather, "you can best assist your children by giving no thought to the dangers involved and focusing instead on their safe deliverance. Again I remind you that, as physical beings, you still have to deal with the minute-to-minute realities with which you are faced. To explain this in the most understandable terms, until you learn to control your physical reality with the power of your mind, you will be best served to take physical steps to advance your situation to the desired outcome while at the same time trusting the universe to handle those matters beyond your immediate physical control.

"Eventually, given sufficient desire and *knowing*, you may enter the stage of evolution, as did your brother Jesus, where you can move mountains with but the faith of a mustard seed. Perhaps, and very likely, this challenge that you are currently facing was created by you and your friends before you entered this physical plane to help advance your abilities closer to that state where you completely control all of your circumstances. Actually, you control much of them now. It's just that there is presently a substantial time lag between the thought and the event, with the possibility that doubt will enter your minds and negate your intent.

"Now, to answer your question again, more specifically," Great-Grandfather went on, "as I said before, one of the most powerful acts you can perform to promote the safety of your children is to give no thought to the danger they seem to be in and hold only thoughts of their safe deliverance. Even that effort will be ineffective if the children themselves are not willing a similar outcome.

"In other words, you cannot assert your will upon another. That power does not exist. But you can assist the will of another, relative to the circumstances of that other's world, as long as your will is aligned with theirs. My knowing is that those kids are all advanced souls and understand the workings of the universe. I would suspect that they are already using their non-physical powers to bring this entire situation to a desirable conclusion. Therefore, I would guess that your focused intent that they remain safe, with little or no energy focused on the dangers involved, will be most helpful from an energetic point of view.

"I don't believe I would be overstepping my bounds if I were to make a few observations, as follows: I believe you will find the wooden handle of a garden implement poking through the earthen wall of the cellar of this building. If you were to dig around that handle, you would find a small tunnel leading to the surface of the earth just a few feet inside the perimeter of the forest.

"Second, I suggest that you not utilize this escape route until such time as there is a significant diversion elsewhere on the premises. If your children succeed in their intent to engage in combat with the government agents, their efforts likely will provide the diversion you need to escape undetected.

"Third, among the government agents is a large and powerful black man who is on your side. Be very careful that you do not take any steps that would reveal his true loyalty, as this could cost him his life.

"Finally, there is a man on the floor below you whimpering like a frightened child. He cannot be trusted. I say this in spite of the risk I take of offending his wife. Your safe escape from this prison may depend upon keeping him from knowing your plans. He would betray you in an instant, to secure his own benefit."

Great-Grandfather concluded, "My keen instincts, honed by many years as a fearless warrior, lead me to believe the time has come for me to leave this audience."

"It's plain to see, Grandfather," commented Maria, "that your transition into the world of spirit hasn't cleansed your soul of the bullshit."

Great-Grandfather feigned an expression of pious indignation, spun quickly to his left, wrapped his colorful blanket around himself, and disappeared in a puff of smoke. His words, "Pretty slick, eh?" were left hanging in the air.

After a few moments of silence, Gail asked "Well, what do you make of all that?"

Clint responded, "I would say that we should start by spending a few minutes sending our kids all of the positive thoughts and energy we can. But I'm not too keen on waiting for them to create the 'diversion' before we try to escape. I'd like to be out there when the action starts."

"Count me in on that," agreed Michael. "Those kids aren't gonna go up against an army like they've got amassed out there without me."

"Put me in, coach," said Tim, with a combination of humor and rage in his voice. "The other half of my soul will be out there fighting for his life. If he goes down, we go down together." The look in Tim's eyes said it all.

"My whole world's gonna be out there on that battlefield," Sarah joined in. "It's not gonna happen without me."

"Amen," declared Gail, an uncharacteristic look of determination in her eyes.

"Well," said Clint, "looks like we're all in this together. We're ten civilians against a whole lot of trained killers. And they've got state-of-the-art weapons. Nobody in his right mind would give us a chance in hell."

"But we've got something more powerful than all their damn weapons and training," whispered Maria, tears brimming her eyes. "We're family."

Chapter Forty-nine

"Shit!" yelled Herbert Benson III, as he knocked over the bottle of calamine lotion.

John Hawkin turned away from the window at the front of the office, where he had been staring out at nothing at all, the outside darkness making it impossible for him to see anything but his own reflection in the glass. He looked at Benson. The little man was flushed and perspiring.

It was Thursday night.

Benson wiped up the pool of pink liquid with a facial tissue and dabbed the stuff on his right temple, where he detected a fresh out-cropping of the damnable rash that had been plaguing the more tender parts of his body for days now. A trickle of lotion proceeded down his cheek and dripped from the right side of his chin.

"Shit!" he shouted again.

Benson had been silent for a long time prior to the bottle-tipping incident. Hawkin tried to imagine what must be going through the little nerd's mind. Benson had to be close to frantic, considering the possible consequences of his situation and his limited alternatives.

One thing John Hawkin had observed during his many years on this planet was that individuals who lacked integrity or courage or both, lacked alternatives in tight situations. Hawkin considered what he would do if he were in Benson's position, although he wouldn't have allowed himself to get into such a mess in the first place. The way out seemed clear. Hawkin would have immediately contacted someone in the governmental hierarchy, someone well above the level of those who perpetrated the massacre and cover-up in the first place.

He would confess to his complicity, agree to accept whatever punishment was appropriate, and offer to assist in the apprehension and conviction of those who were actually responsible for the deaths of all of those innocent victims.

Hawkin wasn't sure he would reveal the existence of the spacecraft to the public, though. He was open to the possibility that the majority of the American people might have the courage necessary to cope with this information without widespread panic. He knew lots of people who would willingly and eagerly accept the existence of extraterrestrial life. He suspected that many individuals knew, as a matter of pure mathematical logic, that there had to be millions of planets out there with all of the elements necessary to support life as we know it.

He also suspected that there are probably countless forms of life that bear no physical or physiological resemblance to the animals of this planet, including humans. Those other life forms, he speculated, might have evolved to live on planets that don't even come close to emulating the conditions on Earth.

Why do we assume that life can exist only at the temperatures on this planet? Could there not be life forms that thrive at 800°? And could there not be life forms that breathe gases other than oxygen? And who is to say that our tender skin is the best substance to contain a body? Consider the variety of skin textures on our own planet, from that of the delicate human to the crusty crocodile, which have evolved to cope with different conditions.

And, could not other life forms, resulting from totally different conditions of temperature, humidity, food sources, atmospheres, and gravitational forces, still contain souls?

And why would we fear them? Perhaps it's because we have done such a terrible job of following the laws of the universe. Perhaps it's because we have been mired for so long in our world of crime and war and fear and anger.

Perhaps, any space travelers from civilizations advanced enough to visit us from planets that are light years away would also be advanced enough to have shed those flaws we have come to call 'the human condition.' Or maybe they never experienced those flaws at all. Perhaps we are truly the joke of the universe. Perhaps the reason we are visited so rarely by our extraterrestrial brothers is that they all live in peace and don't care to be bothered by our silly games of competition and fear and control.

His daydreaming was interrupted by the telephone.

Benson answered it. "Yeah," he snapped. He listened for a few seconds, then ordered, "Tell all of the men, except Andrews and Carnihan and the men under their command, to come on in, on the double."

"What's up?" Hawkin asked after Benson slammed down the phone.

"That was Rearden. Says they haven't seen a sign of those damn kids. He's been in touch with the command centers of the state patrol, six police departments, and two sheriff's offices. Not a sign.

"I figure if those kids were on their way to one of the surrounding towns, they would have gotten there by now. Maybe they've already been to one of the towns, gotten help, and are now on their way back here to rescue their families. Maybe they got to one of those law enforcement agencies and showed them their alleged proof. Maybe they convinced the authorities that there is something out here worth investigating. Maybe the authorities ordered their personnel to tell my men they haven't seen those damn kids, until they can get here to see what's going on."

Benson breathed heavily. "I don't like it. I don't like it at all. I figure my safest bet is to have my men back here in case there's a showdown. After all, I'm the authority. I'm the damn CIA. I'm the Federal damn government. If those small-town yahoos show up here demanding to look around, I'll just remind them that this is Federal property and they haven't a lick of jurisdiction anywhere within the boundaries of this compound. And if they don't leave, we'll give them a taste of Federal firepower. After all, we're the Federal Government. We run this country."

Hawkin nodded. "You're right, Benson. If it's a war they want, it's a war we'll give 'em. But why did you leave some of your men out in the field?"

"None of your damn business!" shouted Benson. He picked up the bottle with a few scant drops of lotion remaining. Grimacing, he poured the last of the precious liquid into the palm of his hand and furtively slid his hand into his pants. His feeling of temporary relief was quickly replaced by the thought that within only a few minutes he would need another fix and there was no more left. He looked at the bottle. *If I place it upside down, will a few more precious drops run down into my hand?...Then what?*

He reached for his radio and ordered Rearden to see if he could find a market or drugstore on his way back to the compound. Benson sat staring at the inverted calamine lotion bottle, watching one drop of liquid run slowly toward his waiting hand. One tiny drop. Rearden was forty-five minutes from the compound, at best.

Benson was only vaguely aware that Hawkin had left the office.

John Hawkin needed some time to think. And he couldn't think effectively with all the commotion Benson was making. For now, Hawkin figured he knew enough about what Benson was up to that he didn't need to hang around the office any more. John was bothered by the fact that those kids might be on their way back to the compound and, if they were, they were probably alone. He couldn't argue with their decision. It was probably the same thing he would have done under the circumstances.

Hawkin was also bothered by the fact that Benson had left some men out in the field. Granted, that would mean fewer men to handle when the action started at the compound, but he didn't like having to deal with uncertainty. Those men put uncertainty into the equation. What was Benson up to?

Hawkin had considered calling in reinforcements. He could certainly use some help. But he decided not to do so for a couple of reasons. First of all, he didn't know for sure who he could trust. He didn't know how far up the line the corruption went. Sure, he knew he could trust the President. But who would the President send? Could Hawkin be sure that they were trustworthy? More than one president had had traitors within his circle of confidants.

Second, how could anyone arriving on the scene for the first time know the good guys from the bad guys? If they were able to get here before the kids arrived and before the hostages escaped the building, they could simply capture everyone, including Hawkin himself, and sort out who was who afterward. But there was no way of knowing how fast the good guys could get here and how many of them would be sent. With the size of Benson's army, there would be a lot of bloodshed, the blood of a lot of good men. Was it worth all of that potential loss to save eleven civilians? Hawkin was never comfortable when it boiled down to mathematics. Mathematics didn't allow for the human element, the relative worth of those involved. And how could that ever be known anyway?

In the end, he decided to rely on what he had on hand, even though this decision might mean that he would die along with the civilians.

Hawkin had learned, over and over again, on more than one battlefield, that a small group of men with the right kind of incentive can be more formidable than legions just doing their jobs. He didn't perceive any of that kind of passion among Benson's men.

Yes, I'll go with what I have on hand. I just wish I knew more about those kids and their families and what skills they have. All I know for now is that they're family, they're fighting for their lives, and apparently, three of them have enough love and courage to walk back into almost certain death. Yes, I'll definitely go with what I have.

For a moment, Hawkin considered going back to the tunnel he had dug, crawling into the basement, and introducing himself to his comrades. At least that way they would know there was some hope, as slight as it was, and he could size up his "army." But there was also the fact, according to the conversation he overheard between Benson's two men in the forest, that the door to the basement was locked.

Finally, he decided he didn't want to risk tipping his hand at this point. One of the advantages he still had was the element of surprise.

The ghetto blaster on the porch was sending the sounds of a Faith Hill/Tim McGraw duet deep into the forest. At least those government jerks had decent taste in music. The music was loud enough that Hawkin could slip into the forest without being heard. He decided the bunker would be a good place for him to think for a while.

Ten minutes later he stood in the presence of the spaceship. And he knew why he had chosen the bunker as his place to think.

An emotion, playing softly below the surface of consciousness, washed over him. He recognized it as the same feeling he had when he was in the bunker earlier. But he hadn't thought much about it then. It was so subtle. But now, the second time, it was unmistakable.

He thought about songs he had come to love over the years. They hadn't done much for him the first time he heard them. But the second time, he felt a slight stirring in his soul. And then, by the third or fourth time, he was hooked. Next thing he knew, he was down at the record store, so anxious to get that record home and put it on his old 45 RPM record player.

That's what he felt now, the second time, a stirring in the soul. The feeling resided so far in the background that he wasn't totally sure he felt it. But he knew, it was there, teasing his mind. Like the faint hint of a seasoning in a mouth-watering taste of homemade soup, the feeling was so faint he couldn't quite tell what it was. But he had to know. He couldn't rest until he figured it out. Like a long-forgotten song that kept playing in his mind and he just had to remember its name.

That feeling was like coming home. But home to where? He had never been in this place until yesterday. Yet something, a yearning, kept tugging at his heart strings.

Then he thought about the last time he was here, when he smelled Mom's cooking. It was interesting that he didn't smell that delicious aroma now. He was only a few feet from the craft. He stepped closer. There it was, a compelling aroma, but it wasn't Mom's roasted garlic and jambalaya. It wasn't food at all.

What was it? He stood there motionless, inhaling gently, looking for a hint. Whatever it was, it was delightful.

Then it came to him. A picture began to form in his mind. a scene from his childhood, a summer day, an old cabin in the mountains, snow on the peaks that towered above the lush, green floor of the high mountain valley, the warm sun caressing his shoulders, the faint sound of birds singing in the distance, the place where his grandpa used to take him fishing, a world of aromas, pine needles, warm summer grass, columbines blooming in the meadow, the sweet scent of a pine bark campfire, crackling beneath a skillet of golden brown sunfish, rolled in flour and lightly seasoned, the Hoppe's #9 solvent that Grandpa had used to clean the pistol he always carried in the woods, the smell of Grandpa himself, a clean, warm, safe smell, the kind God gives only to grandpas, the kind only grandsons get to smell.

John lingered with those precious memories a while.

When his thoughts finally returned to the bunker, he was still not fully present, but straddling both worlds.

Finally, the images cleared from his mind and he was, once again, in the company of the marvelous spaceship, a new and wondrous toy.

He stepped closer to the craft and inhaled deeply. Sure enough, it was Grandpa's camping spot. All of those aromas that so touched John's heart were all rolled into one glorious sensual experience.

What is it about this craft? Is it magic? Is it possessed of some trace of super-human intelligence? Earlier it had emitted an aroma of Mom's jambalaya and roasted garlic, now, a fragrant mountain meadow.

Strange.

John came up with the beginnings of a theory. Maybe the home-cooking scenario came about because he had been very hungry at the time. Now he was full. Less than an hour ago he had eaten a ham-and-cheese sandwich from the stash Benson kept in the tiny refrigerator in the back room of his office. Maybe Hawkin's feeling of being all alone in this mess or, at least, of being the only highly trained person on the side of the good guys caused a yearning for a happier time or a need for security. Could that have prompted the stimulus of memories of his days with Grandpa? Maybe this idea was a bit far-fetched. But there had to be some explanation for his definite, intense sensory percep-tions. If he was right, or even close, such an explanation would lead to the inescapable conclusion that the spacecraft contained some form of high intelligence, almost psychic in nature.

So, if this craft, made of some impenetrable material, apparently not known to humankind, has the ability to respond to thoughts long ago buried in someone's memory bank, would it not seem likely that it could also read our present-moment thoughts? And, if so, is it not possible that we could gain access to the interior of the craft by "thinking it" open?

If that were the case, why hadn't the craft opened in response to the thoughts of the government workers who obviously had tried every known method to gain access to its interior?

Perhaps the intelligence that created this craft programmed it to allow entry only to a limited group of individuals. Or, maybe, only to those who meant no harm or who it "knew" would use its facilities for peaceful purposes. This ship is quite advanced, if my assumptions are correct. But, by our present standards, is not space travel advanced?

John decided to conduct an experiment. He cleared his mind as best he could of any chatter and focused on a long-lost memory. He thought about his high school sweetheart, Monique, who was the love of his life in those days. He pictured her in great detail—the curve of her cheeks, her full lips, her deep brown eyes, her long black hair. He held that thought for a while, her memory tugging at his heartstrings. And there it was, smack dab in the middle of this musty old bunker, Monique's perfume: Shalimar, John's favorite. He stepped close to the spaceship and placed his nose near its outer wall. The aroma was compelling, just as if Monique were standing next to him. A shiver of yearning ran through his body and made his knees temporarily weak.

That did it. No mistake. This spaceship, from somewhere far away, was communicating with him. And if it could communicate with his nose, why not with his ears or his eyes or any of his other senses? Was it not all vibrational?

Now, let's try something even more exciting.

John turned his thoughts to love and kindness and sad yearning. He thought about Mom and Dad and Grandpa and Mikey and his beautiful Monique. He thought about all those wonderful times in the old home back in Chicago, all those years of hard work and struggle against the prejudices and hardships of the ghetto, but always with the love and joy in that warm and wonderful old house.

He thought about how Mikey never returned from Vietnam. He thought about how Mikey's body was never found, and how they all had suffered, not knowing if Mikey might still be out there, maybe in some POW camp. He thought about the years he spent illegally searching for Mikey in the jungles of Vietnam only to have his efforts thwarted by the politicians and bureaucrats of his own government. He thought about Monique and how he had loved her so. He thought about how her tragic death nearly drove him insane. He thought about how much he loved them all. The love swelled in his chest, forcing tears from his eyes that he had held back for so many years. He cried and cried, spilling tears of sorrow mixed with tears of love and joy.

John found himself so lost in his memories that he almost forgot where he was. He reached a hand up to the spacecraft and gently touched its solid but soft surface, taking comfort from its warm and loving power, as he grappled with these rediscovered and intense emotions.

His thoughts returned to the bunker. Almost reverently, he asked the ship for permission to enter its interior. He held that thought, not with any unusual effort but in a gentle and easy manner. He pictured the ship opening whatever means it had to allow access to its interior by physical beings. He focused on those feelings of sadness and love and joy.

An unusual sensation began to form in the area of his heart. It moved through his throat, his forehead, and out through the top of his head. He felt drained and strangely at peace.

"Click." "Whir." "Thunk." A dim light flooded the bunker, a pleasant blue light, gentle on the eyes.

Slowly John got up and began circling the craft, seeking the source of that unusually attractive light. The light seemed to be beckoning to him, as if its source wanted to make contact of a more intimate nature. It felt warm and soothing.

And then he spotted the source. The cool blue light was flowing from an opening in the side of the craft. A ramp led down from the opening to the earthen floor of the bunker. A fine mist swirled gently around and through the rays that streamed from the craft, flooding the floor, walls, and ceiling of the bunker with an amorphous glow.

He stepped onto the ramp, his heart racing, not from fear but from excitement and joyous anticipation. Instinctively he knew that whatever the source of this wonderful soothing light was, it meant him no harm.

John thought of the books he had read about life after death. Those who died and were later brought back to life were interviewed by the authors of those books and reported coming into contact with a source of love in the spirit world so all-encompassing and powerful that they were without words to adequately describe it. They all reported that from that moment forward they were possessed with absolutely no fear of dying. They had faced death and knew it to be the most freeing and loving experience imaginable.

Perhaps, he thought, what he was feeling right now might be similar to what he had read about in those accounts of the afterlife. Only this was happening right here, right now, on this plane of physical matter.

As he reached the top of the ramp and entered the craft, he was shocked to discover that the interior of the ship appeared to be much larger than the exterior. While it seemed to be no more than a hundred feet in diameter on the outside, the inside seemed to be several times that size. He could see numerous corridors heading off from the room just inside the hatch, corridors that appeared to be hundreds of yards long.

He was standing in what looked like the flight deck. Several large, comfortable-looking chairs were attached to the floor, in front of what was apparently the control panel of the cockpit, although to John the term "cockpit" didn't quite apply to a room this vast. The walls were covered with numerous large monitors, each offering a graphic representation of some type of information that John couldn't decipher. There were characters that looked like they might be letters or numbers, but in a language that meant nothing to him.

If only that information were in a form I could understand. Instantly, each of the monitors blinked and changed its format into a new graphic representation, now clearly in English, with numbers and symbols familiar to John. A strange sense of comfort flooded his mind as the familiar symbols appeared before his eyes, making him feel at home.

Wow! This craft can actually read my mind. He began playing with it. He thought of a slice of hot apple pie. In seconds, he heard a pleasant beeping sound. Looking in the direction of that sound, he saw a lavender-colored light blinking above a box that had the appearance of a microwave oven, only much larger. He opened the door and feasted his eyes on a slice of steaming hot apple pie, just the way he liked it, with lots of cinnamon and a small scoop of vanilla ice cream melting down its sides. *Strange, I didn't even think about ice cream. This thing must read minds at the subconscious level.*

He removed the pie and the fork that was lying beside it and set them on the edge of a shelf in front of one of the control panels of the cockpit. Then he settled down in the most comfortable chair he had ever sat in.

Just about the time John thought he had experienced all of the amazement he could stand, he noticed that the plate on which the slice of pie rested was of the same style and pattern as the dishes his mom used to serve dessert on when he was a kid. The fork, likewise, could have come right from Mom's old silverware drawer. "Well, I'll be damned!" he said aloud. He paused for a second and then said, in a loud and commanding voice, "Cancel that, Universe. 'I'll be blessed' is what I meant."

He heard a strange sound coming from behind him and turned to see that the hatch had closed. *Far be it from me to question the wisdom of this ship.* He wondered if perhaps the ship decided that he would be safer with the hatch closed.

Quickly he finished the best slice of apple pie he had ever tasted, although Mom's was a mighty close second. Then he spent the next half hour playing with the craft. He found that he really didn't have to learn anything. All he had to do was think what he wanted to happen and it did. He played with the temperature, the lighting, even the humidity. He changed the atmosphere within the craft to tropical then to arctic then to dry desert. He even created the feeling of a jungle, complete with those deep, musky aromas he came to know so well from his days in Vietnam.

How far could he go with this thing? Could he use it to affect time? Could it bring back the dead? Could it be used to influence the inner workings of his body? The possibilities boggled his normally "un-boggle-able" mind.

He had to try one thing. He commanded the ship to take him back in time, just thirty minutes. In an instant he was standing in front of the large microwave-looking box, admiring that steaming slice of apple pie he had consumed earlier. *How is it that this thing is able to move me back in time, yet my mind knows that it has moved back in time? In other words, how is it that I'm now at a place in time that is thirty minutes earlier than I was a moment ago and, still, my mind knows the things that happened a few minutes ago that haven't happened yet?*

John quickly ordered the ship to take him back to "real time." Perhaps he was messing around with something he had best leave alone, at least until he knew more about what he was messing with.

Still, John had questions. *If this ship has all of the capabilities I'm experiencing, and probably a lot more, how is it that the occupants of this craft, if there ever were any, were unable to save themselves from the crash landing that took place decades ago?* He thought about this for a while and decided it probably had to do with whatever laws governed the forces at work here. Just like the law of the universe that gives those in the spirit world the ability to affect our lives as long as they don't violate our wishes or intentions, perhaps some law required this craft to be subject to our law of gravity, even though it had the physical ability to override it. Perhaps the incident of the crash landing was necessary to enable all of the players in this entire present situation to experience the circumstances they were now having and about to have so that they might learn lessons they chose, from a higher perspective.

The more John thought about this, the more certain he felt that he was into an area beyond his present ability to understand. Once again he thought about being "in this world but not of this world" and decided he had best return to the world into which he had been born and play this thing out in the realm he understood, even if he didn't like much of what he was about to face. He made a note that the ship and its marvelous powers were standing by, if needed, to get him and the others out of a situation that was beyond their capabilities to handle through conventional means.

Another thought flitted briefly through his mind—that this spaceship and its possible ability to save his life and the lives of the others wasn't dramatically different from the power of his mind, and the minds of the others to use the forces of the universe to do the same thing.

John had spent many months devouring an intriguing book entitled *The Science of Mind*, written by a master named Ernest Holmes. In that book John learned of the ability of the mind, especially when working in concert with other like-minds, to affect matters that seem to be beyond our ability to control physically. It occurred to him that this marvelous spacecraft was no more marvelous than the human mind and no more capable. It seemed to him that this ship existed and operated somewhere between the world of pure physicality and the world of spirit. It seemed to exhibit characteristics of both worlds.

Interesting. Very interesting.

Perhaps it was a metaphor to help him and the others bridge the gap between the old ways and the awakening taking place on this planet. Maybe this ship had landed here decades ago so he and the others might more clearly understand the powers that exist beyond the limitations placed upon them by those who have worked so diligently, since our arrival on this planet, to dissuade them from their "magic."

I don't recall that I've ever had thoughts of this depth. It seems that being in the very presence of this craft heightens one's thinking capacities.

John couldn't resist one more slice of pie. This time it was boysenberry, with whipped cream he hadn't even ordered! John wondered if he could order pie that was sweet and delicious without refined sugar, or, better yet, with refined sugar that didn't negatively affect his body. The possibilities excited him immeasurably.

Reflecting on his years in Vietnam, he thought about how he and his men had risked their lives and given their all for a cause they never understood. He thought of how men had died, fifty thousand men, sons and fathers and husbands. And for what? For a war that those in power had never intended to win. A war that had been designed from the beginning to trade those lives for dollars, profits for the weapons manufacturers and the lending institutions that had financed that war.

He thought about his dad and how he had fought in the Big War, World War II, the last war where soldiers knew what they were fighting for. It had been an honest war, a war to save the world from the psychotic bullies who were rampaging across Europe, North Africa, and the Pacific. As much as John detested war, he was envious, for a moment, that his dad at least knew what he had been fighting for.

Now John knew what he was fighting for. And, although it would be a tiny war, the principles were the same. It was the same old story of good versus evil. And, although John knew for a certainty that there was really no good or evil in the eyes of God, he reminded himself that he was still "in this world" and would conduct himself within the rules of its illusions. He requested the hatch to be opened. He walked out into the cold, musty bunker and back to the world of physical reality and danger.

As he headed with a strange sense of joy and determination toward what he knew would be one of the greatest challenges of his life, John Hawkin thought of the words to a popular song by Jo Dee Messina: "Bring on the rain."

 # Chapter Fifty

After Zara had confirmed that the canyon behind the farmhouse did exist, the kids spent several hours refined their plans. Now, Thursday evening just before sundown, they were on their way to the canyon.

Chris brought his Jeep to a stop, killed the engine, and turned off the lights.

"What's up?" asked Jaime.

"I want to check the map," Chris replied, "and go over our plan one more time. We don't want to risk talking when we're near the compound."

Daryl pulled his Jeep up to the right of Chris and Jaime and shut off the engine and the headlights. "What's cooking?" he asked.

Becky remained silent.

"I think it's time we finalize our game plan," Chris said. "According to my odometer, we're about five miles from the mouth of that canyon. We need to keep any talk to a minimum from here on."

They all got out of the vehicles. Jaime spread Great-Grandfather's map on the hood of Chris's Jeep. Daryl shined his flashlight on the map, using the bright circle of light in the center of the beam to indicate their present position.

"I would suggest," said Daryl "that we proceed to within about a mile of the mouth of that canyon as quietly as we can, given the sound of Chris's engine, and then make the rest of the way on foot. It looks like it's about a mile from there to the farmhouse. That would mean the vehicles will never be closer than a mile and a half from where we assume the CIA agents are. I don't think they'll be able to hear the sound of the Jeeps, especially considering that they're on the other side of the ridge from where we'll be approaching."

"Sounds good to me," said Jaime, "but I'd like to see us abandon the vehicles farther from that canyon. This Jeep is mighty loud."

"I considered that," said Daryl. "I'm concerned that, if we have to walk too far, we might not get to the farmhouse before sunup. And once the sun's up, it'll be a lot harder for us to remain undetected."

"What makes you think they'll have any trouble locating us at night anyhow?" Chris asked. "Those clowns probably have all kinds of equipment to help them see us and shoot us in the dark."

"You may be right," responded Daryl. "I'm counting on three things. The first is that they won't think we'd ever be stupid enough to attack them, so they're probably very relaxed. The second is that they wouldn't think to patrol the back side of the compound because their maps show this entire side of the area to be inaccessible. And, third, they probably don't believe that we have access to the spaceship. I would guess that most of them don't even know the spaceship is there. After all, it isn't the kind of thing our beloved CIA bigwigs would want known by anyone but themselves. And even those who know about it think it's totally impregnable. I'll bet they consider Chris's claim that we have something from that craft in our possession to be a bluff. After all, the mighty CIA hasn't been able to get inside that ship in over three decades. Why would they think three civilians could do something they couldn't? They're far too arrogant for that."

"You forgot one other thing," Becky said, speaking for the first time since they had stopped the vehicles. "They don't know that we've got Daryl Harrington and his Jeep full of explosives and weapons and wires and ropes and all that sort of James Bond stuff."

"That's true," said Jaime, "and I think that could be a great advantage. We should keep Daryl's presence a secret at all costs. I don't believe we should stay together once we enter the compound. They might get one or two of us, but our chances of winning this little skirmish will be increased greatly if we separate, be absolutely quiet, and move very slowly. The only flaw I can see in that approach is that I don't like the thought of Becky being all alone."

"As always, your concern is appreciated," said Becky. "But remember that you're dealing with 'karate girl' here and I've got a mom at stake. I'd give my life anytime for her, and if my roaming those woods alone increases our chances for success, that's the way it's gonna be. Besides, I've got my Magical Friend standing by. That's better than night goggles any time."

"Thanks, Becky," said Chris. "None of us even considered that you were any less capable than the rest of us. Jaime's just in love, which can cloud any man's judgment."

"No offense taken," said Becky. "I know what Jaime meant, and I appreciate it with all my heart. But for now we have to keep our eyes on the ball which means that saving the lives of our families is all that matters."

"Okay," Chris agreed. "Once we're at the top of the ridge, we split up. I suggest about one hundred feet apart. Then we all start down the hill, very slowly and quietly, not more than one footstep every two seconds. Count in your head. That will help ensure that we all get to the bottom at about the same time. Our biggest problem is that we won't be able to see each other in the dark. We'll have to rely on timing our footsteps and hoping that our strides are about the same length. Try to make each stride about two feet long."

"As I recall," said Becky, "since I was the only one to visit the back side of the farmhouse, the slope levels off about a hundred feet behind the building. If each of us turns to the right after reaching level ground, we'll still be within the forest and at a safe distance from the farmhouse. We'll circle around the farmhouse, staying the same distance from the building, being careful not to head back up the slope we just came down.

"Then we'll walk over the small hill between the farmhouse and the bunker and come out in the clearing just before the mound where the spacecraft's hidden. We'll each wait inside until the others have arrived. Then we'll combine our thought energies to open the ship.

Once inside, I hope we'll find enough equipment and information to give us a fighting chance to take control of the compound."

"What if one of us doesn't show up?" Jaime asked.

Chris said, "We wait no more than ten minutes from the time the first one arrives. After that, we'll have to assume that anyone not there has been captured."

Becky said, "Why don't I start out in the position farthest from the ship. That will give you gentlemen the best chance of getting there. As much as I don't believe in all that 'male supremacy' stuff, you guys know a lot more than I do about weapons and mechanical things. So you guys are more valuable to this cause than I am."

She paused momentarily before continuing. "And, please, don't try to talk me out of my position with anything but logical, tactical reasons. You can forget the gender issue. For now I'm a soldier determined to do whatever's necessary to save our families. There's no place right now for gallantry or sentiment, although I'll be glad to accept a whole lot of that stuff when this is all over."

Everyone was silent.

Jaime looked away. *What a woman this is! If something happens to her, I don't know what I'll do.* He sat there for a few minutes, facing away from his friends, thinking about Becky and Tim and Mom and Dad, considering the very real possibility that some of them might not make it out of this alive. He continued to look away for quite some time. When he finally looked back at his friends, there was no doubt that Jaime was ready.

There was not a sound from anyone.

Daryl finally broke the silence. "Okay, once we get inside the ship and see what's in it that we can use, our next task is to get your families out of the farmhouse and to safety. That could mean either getting them back to the spaceship or over the hill to the Jeeps. My first choice would be the Jeeps. There are seven people in the farmhouse, I think, and four of us. That means eleven people in two Jeeps, mighty tight. We can fit, but it's going to be hard to keep everyone inside if we're on a dead run across that rugged terrain.

"If we're forced to return to the ship, we'll be safe temporarily, but I'm not sure how we get from the ship to permanent safety. They could have us trapped."

"Maybe we should consider another plan," suggested Jaime. "How about if only one of us goes to the ship and the rest of us concentrate on trying to get our families out of the farmhouse? That way we won't all be in the ship, where they can contain us. Our motive in all showing up at the spacecraft at the same time was so we could combine the power of our minds to open it. But even though Tim and I discovered long ago that our combined efforts to affect physical reality are more powerful than either of us acting alone, we have each been able to do some amazing things individually. It seems to have a lot to do with intent, determination, and faith."

"I agree," said Becky, "both with the idea of sending only one of us to the ship and with the idea that it takes only one of us to open that thing. I've also experienced the awesome power of a single mind, working with the laws of the universe. If one of us can get inside that craft and use its equipment to stir up some activity, it may create enough of a diversion to allow the rest of us to get inside the farmhouse. What do you think, Chris?"

"I like it. I think Daryl should be the one to go to the ship and cause as much ruckus as he can. If the rest of us get caught, those CIA clowns still won't know that Daryl is here. They probably won't even realize that whatever commotion Daryl may be creating is coming from the spaceship. They'll be totally confused. Some may even think there are some supernatural forces at work in the area and hit the road."

"What if I can't get inside the ship?" Daryl asked.

"Good negative thinking, buddy," Jaime said wryly. "Keep that up and we'll all be in deep doo doo. Just know you can do it. I realize this 'manipulation of physical matter' stuff is new to you. But just know that anyone can do it, given sufficient motivation and the willingness to overcome any doubt. And if some doubt still remains, crank up the desire. Be joyous, not anxious. You didn't get out of that cubbyhole, fourteen stories below ground-level, by accident. Any one of a hundred things could have gone wrong and you would have been history. But they didn't.

"You were motivated, and you knew you had the power, even though the power you were thinking about at that time was more physical than spiritual. It all works the same way, though. Just know, my friend, just know. You'll be fine. Just know that the future of a farmhouse full of brave and frightened people depends on us. Remember that the Universe will be waiting for your command backed by absolute faith, with no resistance. That's all."

"Thanks, Jaime," said Daryl. "I won't let you down."

"We know you won't," whispered Becky.

"Okay," said Chris, "since we know little about the compound and nothing about the location and capabilities of our opponents, we're going to have to play a lot of this by ear. I, being a mechanical wizard, with Sherlock Holms-like deductive reasoning abilities and keen Native American instincts, did happen to observe that the bolts holding the bars on the doors and windows of the farmhouse have five-eighths-inch hex heads. I would suggest that we each take a five-eighths-inch wrench or an adjustable Crescent wrench from the toolboxes of these vehicles just in case we find ourselves needing to remove some of those bars.

"I've got my 9 millimeter, Daryl has a 44 Magnum, and Jaime's got a 22 caliber target pistol, not a lot of firepower, considering what we're up against."

"Don't forget," reminded Becky, "that Daryl's got a lot of good stuff in the back of his Jeep, and there seem to be a few items in the spacecraft bunker that could be of use."

Chris and Daryl went to the rear of Daryl's Jeep and removed two cardboard boxes containing the equipment Daryl had purchased at the hardware and sporting goods stores a few days earlier. They began sorting those items, along with several other useful things Chris and Becky brought from the back of Chris's Jeep. They divided everything into four piles. Then they added to each pile a few tools taken from the toolboxes of each Jeep.

Finally they packed the equipment from each pile into four back-packs. Included in each backpack was a container of black powder, several lengths of fuse, a half-dozen matches, a wrench, a flashlight, a roll of nylon cord, a knife, and two rolls of duct tape.

Daryl gave his friends a brief lecture on what little he knew about the use of black powder and fuses.

Becky wished she had a couple of hours to teach her friends some of the take-down moves she had learned in her karate classes. She did take about ten minutes to show them the basics of how to get an opponent into a stranglehold and how to get out of one. They practiced these moves several times before Daryl reminded them that they had to get going.

Becky wondered if, perhaps, she had taught them just enough to get them into trouble. Then she laughed aloud, realizing that they couldn't possibly get into any more trouble than they were already in.

The guys all looked at Becky, wondering what in the world she was laughing about. She didn't say.

While the guys were busy checking the equipment and making sure the weapons were fully loaded, Becky got out the crystal and set it on the hood of Daryl's Jeep.

She walked several yards into the forest and leaned against a big old aspen tree, folded her hands in front of her chest, as if praying, and took a deep breath.

"My Magical Friend," she whispered, "you've never let me down. Never. It seems I've always called on you when I was in a desperate situation. I always assumed there was something about my highly agitated state that brought you into my presence. This time, I suspect that once the action starts, there isn't going to be much time for praying or doing anything other than reacting. So I thought I'd better call on you while there's still time for rational thought.

"I'm scared, just about as scared as I've ever been. But I'm still surprisingly calm. I hope you're listening. I need you to be here for me and my friends. We're going into an impossible situation, one that nobody in his right mind would give us a chance of surviving. But I've been there before. And somehow you've always brought me out alive and sane. If it's not too much trouble, I need a whole bunch of miracles.

"There are about eleven precious people, if you count my worthless stepfather, whose lives are going to depend on what happens in the next few hours. You, Zara, Chris's Great-Grandfather, and my sweet Jaime's Force are the only chance we have. Without your help, we're just four kids up against a whole army of trained killers with all kinds of exotic equipment and years of experience. What I'm trying to say is that our lives pretty much depend on you. There's nothing, short of a whole lot of miracles, that can get us through this mess in one piece. So please, my Magical Friend, don't fail me now. Thanks."

Becky wrapped her arms around the old aspen tree and held onto it tightly. The tree gave her a sense of confidence, as if it had a consciousness of its own, as if it cared what happened to her. *I guess hugging a tree, isn't much crazier than praying to some mysterious force out there in the universe.*

What she needed now, though, more than anything, was something to help her feel more secure, something absolutely solid. She stood there for a few seconds, just wishing, feeling needy, fear tugging at her heart. In that moment she felt more alone than she had ever felt. She quieted her mind, holding fast to the tree. She squeezed it tightly, gently pressing her cheek against its cool, smooth, soothing bark.

Then a realization came to her. It shot into her mind with almost brutal force. She suddenly realized that she had *it*. She already had *it*, and she had lots of *it*, all that she needed. How many people would give everything they own to have what Becky had, a mom who loved her beyond words, the memories of a great childhood and years with the most wonderful dad in the world, her beloved and faithful friend Rachel, a brand new, soon-to-be wild and passionate romance with the man of her dreams, and her Magical Friend, her higher self, the God Force, the All That Is, standing by, eager to fulfill her every command, and years of intense karate training just for good measure.

Becky was ready.

She walked quietly out of the forest and took her place in the small group of warriors gathered around the hood of the Jeep. Yes, she was as ready as she had ever been for anything in her life.

Daryl had nothing to lose. He had no family. No lover. No children. The closest thing he had ever had to family was now gathered around the hood of that very same Jeep. He was ready.

Chris was born ready.

Becky suggested that before they depart, they might be wise to consult one more time with Zara.

Becky focused on the crystal. The others followed her lead.

"I am with you," said Zara, in a husky whisper.

The four soldiers fell silent.

"What I am about to tell you may seem strange. Please try not to let it throw you off your chosen trail or weaken your resolve. Remember, there are many paths to all destinations. Given that your universe is infinite and you are eternal beings, it would be reasonable to say that there are unlimited paths to all goals.

"It's not my purpose to alter the direction in which your lives are ultimately heading. I simply offer, in response to your request, one possible scenario to make your trek less painful and less physically damaging.

"You have been programmed by the world to expect and strive for certain outcomes. For example, when you watch an action thriller movie, you expect it to reach a point where all of the forces for good and all of the forces for evil are lined up in position for the final conflict. You also have come to expect a violent and bloody ending, with the good guys battered but alive and the bad guys dead, imprisoned, or at least devastated by the failure of their evil goals. You have even been programmed to anticipate that when the head bad guy is defeated and presumed unconscious or even dead, he will rear his ugly head one last time and attack the hero, who has had his attention diverted by the gorgeous heroine, who may or may not also be bloody and battered.

"This may make for fun entertainment, but in real life, it is very painful.

"Keep in mind that your essence is Pure Love. Any pain or discomfort or disease you have ever experienced is always the result of your acting contrary to your Pure Love essence. That is why the grand masters who have come to this planet over the centuries to teach you the most direct and pleasant route back to the God Force have admonished you to always ask, 'What would love do now?'

"I see that in your present real life situation, the good guys and the bad guys are lined up and prepared for the final conflict. From the physical perspective, you can die. You can be imprisoned. You can lose your loved ones. You can suffer intense pain. But that is all temporary. Time applies only to this physical plane. From the world of spirit, where your higher self resides, this is all just a game. It seems serious only when seen from the point of view of the physical bodies in which you are all now focused.

"As you go into this encounter, remember who you are. You are God, the power of the universe, the All That Is, Yahweh, Jehovah, you name it. You are it! All that matters is that you ask, 'What would love do now?' and listen for the answer in your heart. The answer will always come.

"Remember and rejoice in the fact that you are 'in this world but not of this world.' That means that, for now, you get to walk the fine line between the awesome power of the Universe and the illusory limitations of this physical plane. Enjoy it. Revel in it. Use this little phrase as your motto and mantra: 'I now walk with the wisdom and courage of a spiritual warrior, fulfilling my dreams.'

"You know, at some level, that this is all an illusion. And, yet, when you are in the heat of battle, it seems so real that you sometimes lose sight of the fact that it's all a game. You may have to remind yourselves frequently that it is not for real. That doesn't mean it doesn't really exist, only that it is not the absolute reality and can be changed at any time by the power of your will, working with the power of the universe.

"Go now, my dear friends, into the game that lies ahead of you. Remember that these illusions are compelling, almost beyond your ability to discern them from ultimate reality. But also remember that the power of the universe is not subject to those limitations that appear to exist on your physical plane. It is the power that Jesus used to calm the winds. It is available to us all.

"Play hard. Play with all the passion that befits you. But this time, try something different. Try hard to ignore what is taught by your schools, your religions, your movies, your books, and your media. Try loving your enemy.

"The outcome will be even more perfect than ever you could imagine. I promise."

Silence filled the forest. Not a word was spoken.

Becky wrapped the crystal and placed it under the rear seat of Chris' Jeep. She climbed into the passenger seat.

Chris slid behind the wheel.

Jaime folded up the map, tucked it in the glove compartment of Daryl's Jeep, and settled silently into the passenger seat. The three sat quietly while Daryl checked the equipment one more time, lost in their own thoughts.

Barely turning his head, Jaime glanced at Becky. She was looking straight ahead with steely determination on her face, tempered by a trace of quiet confidence.

To Jaime's surprise, Chris had a smile on his face.

Daryl was all business. He finished checking the equipment and climbed into his Jeep. He fired up the engine. Seconds later, the sound was drowned out by the roar of Chris's engine.

They turned on their headlights and headed down the dirt road.

Chapter Fifty-one

It was Thursday evening, seven o'clock.

She had one more day, twenty-four long torturous hours until she would see Chris again.

Wendy had tried on five outfits already. Nothing seemed adequate for the occasion.

Tomorrow night at seven o'clock she was to have a date with the most exciting man she had ever met. Would he be there? The question had plagued her for almost a week now.

Chris, you have to be there. Or I'll die.

There had always been an abundance of men from whom Wendy could have her pick. From the days when she was a cheerleader at Woodrow Wilson High through four years of college, where she was homecoming queen in her senior year, right up to the weekend before she met Chris, she always had plenty of male admirers. But, unlike them, this wild motorcycle-riding mountain man totally knocked her off her feet. The most amazing part was that she had spent only about an hour with him, including the five minutes of his delightful antics on the motorcycle.

What was it about him? She hadn't a clue, although he did have some enticing characteristics.

He had a body to die for, and a smile that could melt an iceberg. He was charming. But there was something more, much more.

Wendy glanced in the mirror. Not bad for a woman pushing thirty.

She was wearing only her bra and panties, both of baby blue satin. She held up her favorite mini-skirt and wiggled her hips seductively, causing the skirt to sway slightly. *Not bad!*

Chris, if you don't show, you'll never know what you missed. This is one luscious lady you've got lusting after you. I just hope you get a chance to know how much woman there is smoldering inside this gorgeous body.

In the eight years since Wendy had graduated from college, she had lived alone in a quaint cottage on the outskirts of town at the back of an acre of pine forest. A small stream flowed along the rear property line a few yards from her back porch.

Among her best friends was a golden retriever named Cheyenne, probably one of the largest retrievers in history, weighing 137 pounds in his prime. He was as strong as a bear with powerful front legs and shoulders. In a favorite game, Cheyenne brought people to the ground by wrapping his front legs around their ankles and pushing his neck and shoulder against their knees. Once he had his victim down, he would stand there, straddling him, licking his neck and face until the victim begged for mercy.

Wendy loved that brute with all her heart. Now seven years old, Cheyenne was beginning to slow down. Wendy would often spend an evening watching a romantic video with Cheyenne lying on the sofa beside her, sharing her popcorn with him, and stroking his head until he fell asleep. His slow, rhythmic breathing was soothing to her soul. She knew that golden retrievers seldom lived beyond ten years. She tried not to think about it.

She laid the mini-skirt on the bed. *Maybe it's a little too aggressive for a first date. It might give Chris the notion that I'm too readily available.*

No, the mini-skirt will be perfect.

Those legs. That's what her girlfriends in college used to call them as if they had their own separate identity. They were not only long but gorgeous. When one of her girlfriends remarked about how long her legs were, Wendy flashed her a look of sweet innocence and said, "But they only go down to the ground."

The night she met Chris, Wendy was wearing slacks. Chris had a treat in store for him. *Yes, the mini-skirt would be just fine.*

She laughed out loud. *My, if someone could read my thoughts, he might think I'm a shallow, oversexed space cadet!*

In reality, Wendy had both feet firmly planted on the ground. During her college days she had a few flings and found most of them remarkably unsatisfying. Since then she had stayed mostly to herself, enjoying an occasional dinner or movie with one of the men she met, but nothing serious.

Wendy, being a romantic, still believed in gallantry, and chivalry and devotion and loyalty and happily-ever-after, all of those old-fashioned notions.

The last time she had been turned on was in her junior year of college, when she went steady with a man attending graduate school. Wendy fell head over heels in love with Rick. They dated for over a year before he graduated and moved to Philadelphia to pursue his career in biology. They agreed to continue their romance at a distance, getting back together for vacations when they could.

Wendy's friend Rita, an exchange student from Barcelona, was noticeably concerned when she heard that Wendy was going to try to conduct her romance over hundreds of miles. The day Wendy told Rita of her plan, Rita simply said, with a look of tender sorrow, "Cara Mia, amor de lejos es amor de pendejos." Wendy didn't ask what that meant. She saw it all in Rita's eyes.

Within a couple of months, Rick was swept off of his feet by an older woman with two children. His letter to Wendy was both heartfelt and apologetic.

The pain didn't stop haunting Wendy. She never got over Rick.

After years of being cautious about her relationships, something so powerful was now pulling at Wendy's mind and heart that she was willing to take a big risk to find out where this miracle would take her.

A woman gets to feel like this only once or twice in her life if she's lucky. Wendy had so many girlfriends who settled for a boring or even abusive marriage, believing that's all there was. Wendy knew there was more, a whole lot more. She wouldn't believe in happily-ever-after if it didn't exist. To Wendy, that didn't mean a relationship had to last until someone died. It only meant that, for however long it lasted, it would be pure bliss. She knew it was possible.

One of Wendy's best friends in the whole world was her grandmother. Grammy had been Wendy's friend and idol for as long as she could remember. Grammy was a tiny lady with a heart as big as all outdoors. She was a strange combination of feistiness and perkiness and a gentleness and warmth that could melt a heart with a simple smile. Grammy had never lost her zest for life. To her, everything was exciting. She knew no fear, only love.

Last Saturday morning, just two days after the night Wendy met Chris, she got up early and drove to Grammy's house in the country. It was an hour's drive. Wendy left her cottage before sunup and watched the glorious sunrise as she headed along the old country road. Her heart was filled with such joy that she just had to sing along with the Eagles on her CD player. She put down the top of the burgundy convertible and sang with all her heart, wondering momentarily if the people in passing vehicles could hear her. When the Eagles got around to "Desperado," tears began to flow freely and powerfully as she sang along. The tears held a strange mixture of joy and sorrow, joy over the prospect of what lay ahead with Chris, sorrow for her lost love, and sorrow for the "desperado" and those like him who would never get to feel what she was feeling right now.

A few minutes later, when the random shuffle brought up Willie Nelson singing, "The Last Thing I Needed, First Thing This Morning," Wendy lost it completely. She pulled over and let the tears flow. She sat in her convertible, looking up into the clear, dark blue, autumn sky and opened the floodgates of those tears she had been holding back for so long. She cried for a good half-hour, a very good half-hour.

When the tears finally stopped, Wendy felt strangely buoyant. Her soul had been cleansed.

She sat quietly for a while, listening to the music, an occasional sigh escaping her lips. Finally she decided she was able to drive safely again and pulled onto the road.

As she picked up speed, she began to revel in the sensation of the wind blowing through her hair. She sang again loudly and enthusiastically.

Then it came to her. It was over. She was over Rick! Completely and irrevocably! The pain was gone, washed away by all those tears.

She depressed the accelerator pedal. The engine screamed to life. Her long, dark hair flowed out behind her head, a pulsating victory flag, whipping in the wind.

"Look out, Chris, here I come."

When Wendy arrived at Grammy's, the dear lady was sitting in her rocking chair on the front porch, shucking peas. She stood shading her eyes from the bright country morning sun, as Wendy drove up the dirt driveway. When Grammy realized it was Wendy leading that trail of swirling dust, she set down the bowl of peas, raised her dress above her knees and ran down the porch steps with a grin on her face so wide that Wendy wondered if it were anatomically possible.

By the time Wendy stopped, Grammy was tugging at the car door handle. Wendy jumped out and wrapped her arms around Grammy, lifting her high into the air.

"My Lord," said Grammy, as soon as Wendy set her back on the ground, "could there be a more wonderful surprise? Come in right this minute while I get the eggs and griddle cakes a cookin'. If you're not a sight for these old eyes!"

Grammy put her hands on Wendy's arms and held her at a distance, as if to get a better look. "Child, you've been crying. What's wrong?"

"Nothing's wrong," Wendy assured her. "Things couldn't be better."

"A man, huh?" Grammy chuckled. "I been prayin' for you. I know how bad you been wantin' and needin' a good man in your life.

Ever since you lost that nice Rick fellow, I seen an aching in your eyes that brought me such sorrow. Lawdy, child, tell me all about him."

"Oh, Grammy," said Wendy, "I hardly know him. I've spent less than an hour with him. His name is Chris. He's the most terrific man I've ever known. He's tall and handsome and smart and kind and full of some kind of energy I can't even describe."

"Soul energy," Grammy declared.

"What?" asked Wendy, as she stepped into the shade of the front porch.

"Means you and Chris have been in love before, probably lots of times. When a man and a woman feel the way I see you feelin' in your eyes, it has to be soul memory. You two have been lovers before. You can't feel the way you're feeling after less than an hour with someone. It takes a lifetime of love to bring feelings that strong."

"I didn't know what to make of it," Wendy confessed. "It didn't make sense that I'd feel like this so fast."

"Only two things that can make a woman fall that hard that fast. Lust and soul memory. You got 'em both, child. Plain to see."

"What should I do, Grammy? What should I do?"

"My advice to you, child, is simple and certain," answered Grammy, with a devilish twinkle in her eye. "Go for it!"

Wendy bent down, pressed her cheek against Grammy's, and whispered, "Thank you, Grammy. Thank you."

Their tears mingled on their cheeks as they hugged.

Wendy was the first to pull away. She took a deep breath and asked, "Where in the world are those griddle cakes?"

"Coming up," announced Grammy, as she reached for her white, thin-worn apron. "Comin' up, child. Griddle cakes for the woman in love."

Wendy sat at the old wooden kitchen table, watching the greatest grandmother in the world working her kitchen magic. Grammy's words were all she needed. She felt certain now that she was on a good path. If someone else had said those same words—"Go for it"—she would have taken them as an act of support and kindness. But from Grammy, they were even more. They were gospel.

Grammy would never say what she knew Wendy wanted to hear just to make Wendy feel good. Grammy was always right, always. She had a sort of sixth sense. She knew how the universe worked, and she knew human nature. Some said that Grammy was an "old soul." Wendy knew that all souls on this plane were the same age, having been created at the time of the Big Bang, the event scientists heralded as some sort of a physical explosion. Wendy knew that what manifested as the Big Bang was, in reality, the God Force expanding itself, not only into the physical universe as we know it but into all of the non-physical, including the Light Beings that those in human form are.

Wendy's mind wandered, naturally, to Chris. She wondered what he was doing right now. She felt strangely uncomfortable as a premonition began to form.

Then, in an instant her discomfort turned to terror, not about whether he would meet her on Friday night but whether he would even be alive.

 **Chapter Fifty-two**

As Herbert Benson's man reached the checkout stand at the supermarket with the precious bottle of calamine lotion clutched in his hand, the cashier asked, "What you doin' with that stuff? Got somethin' itchin'?"

The agent replied, "It's for a friend of mine, seems to have a nervous rash."

The clerk looked around, conspiratorially, satisfying himself that there were very few customers in the store and none within earshot.

"Well," he began, with a newfound air of authority and wisdom in his voice, "Did ya ever hear about the calf path?"

When the agent looked at him quizzically, the clerk continued, "Did you ever notice how we human beings seem to have a tendency to keep doin' what we've always done, without botherin' to question the wisdom of that course of action?

"I guess you never read 'The Calf Path'? It's a cute little poem about a calf who wandered through the hills and meadows outside of a little village with no particular intention except to graze on the grass along its path. Over a period of years, a well-worn path developed as the result of the calf's arbitrary meanderings.

"Eventually humans began following that same path, as part of a trail connecting two small villages, with never a thought that the path wound around and around and up and down and was, probably, several times longer than a straight line between those two villages would have been.

"Now, as you undoubtedly already know, and as some great Greek mathematician, perhaps Euripides or Pericles or one of those other strangely named historical characters, once proved, the shortest distance between two points is indeed a straight line.

"The poem goes on to eventually describe a modern-day highway that still follows the meanderings of that ancient and long-deceased calf instead of following the route that good engineering practice would dictate.

"Well, I guess some of us have a tendency to keep on doing what we've seen others doing for so long, without giving it much thought.

"Let me give you a push in the right direction. There's a lot better stuff than that for itching. We hardly sell any of that calamine lotion these days. Cortisone, that's the ticket, cortisone."

The agent then performed an act totally foreign to himself and most other bureaucrats accustomed to slurping at the public trough. He actually thought for himself. He threw caution to the wind and made a decision instead of blindly following orders.

Now it's possible that nothing quite that dramatic really happened. Perhaps the agent's decision to change his assigned course was because the clerk spoke with such a tone of authority in his voice that the agent interpreted it as an order and responded as programmed.

"Thanks," said the agent, with a distant look in his eye, as he shuffled back to the pharmaceutical department.

As much as he regarded Benson as a high-ranking nerd, he felt sorry for the poor sap. Nobody deserved to itch like that. He decided to pick up a tube of something with cortisone, in addition to the calamine lotion.

As he was reaching for a tube of CortAid, a little lady in a ragged dress said, "Watcha doin' with that stuff, honey?"

"It's for a friend of mine with a bad itch," the agent replied.

"Don't use that crap," said the little lady. "Full a drugs, bad for the body. You don't wanna send your friend to no early grave, do ya? Here. Here's the good stuff. Foille. Foille Ointment. Been around since my grandma was a whippersnapper. Does the job without all that bad stuff in it. Take my advice. Get yer friend Foille. An if there's any left over, it's great for hemorrhoids. Why my aunt Melba used to say…"

The agent grabbed a tube of Foille Ointment, added it to his cache of CortAid and calamine lotion, and headed, once again, for the checkout counter, leaving the little old lady rambling on in great detail about her Aunt Melba's "privates."

As a result of that courageous decision to deviate from his orders, the agent bestowed a blessing upon Herbert Benson III beyond description. Within minutes of applying the Foille Ointment, Benson felt his first real relief from the itching in several days. Within half an hour, he felt almost like a normal human being, discounting the fact that Benson was still wrestling with the real possibility that he might be facing the gas chamber when this mess was all over.

"Everybody out!" he shouted. "And don't come back 'til I call for you." There had been three men in his office, including the agent who had brought the Foille, the blessed Foille. Benson wanted to be alone. He wanted to savor the moment, the comfort.

The window heater hummed peacefully, doing its best to stave off the autumn chill. Benson leaned back in his swivel chair, folded his hands behind his head, closed his eyes, and let out a sigh of great relief. He opened one eye and glanced for a brief moment at the Foille tube. It was half gone. *Better remember to order some more.* He closed his eyes again and let his mind wander.

His thoughts drifted back to grammar school. He was sitting in the back of the classroom, trying his best not to be noticed. In a

Catholic grammar school, unless a kid was one of the select few who learned how to say and do the approved things, the best chance for survival was not to be noticed.

Herbie, as he was called in those days, was born Catholic or, more accurately, he was born to Catholic parents. Herbie never had the chance to choose. By the time he was old enough to think for himself, he had been totally programmed by his parents, his parish priest, and the good nuns at parochial school.

His parents were decent enough people. They truly loved little Herbie. They meant him no harm. They simply trained Herbie in the truths as they knew them, as they had been trained by their parents, as their parents had been trained by their parents before them, and on and on, ad nauseum.

On the day he found himself sitting in the back row of the class in that Catholic grammar school, Little Herbie was ten years old. He had bought the entire story, hook, line, and sinker. He believed with all his heart that God and Satan were watching his every move, waiting to see which way Little Herbie would fall, each desperately needing Little Herbie's soul in his camp.

Herbie was also watching. He was waiting in terror to see which way he would fall. The problem was he wasn't quite sure what the rules were. He had heard so many conflicting stories, often coming from the same source. His parish priest had told him, from God's pulpit, that God was a God of pure love, that God was all powerful, that God loved him. And yet, that very same priest had told Herbie that God was a judgmental God who gave Herbie a free will but also admonished Herbie that if he used that free will to do things contrary to certain rules, Herbie would be doing the work of Satan, not of God, and Herbie would be committing a mortal sin.

Now, the tricky part is that those rules, which must never be violated, seemed to any reasonable person—which Herbie considered himself to be—to run contrary to the natural urges that God, in his loving wisdom, had given to most healthy human beings.

"Why," asked Herbie, in the inner recesses of his young mind, "would God give us an urge unless he wanted us to follow it? If God is infinite wisdom, would he do something as stupid as to create a natural biological urge just so he could frustrate it with his rules?"

Herbie just happened to be in a state of musing upon these imponderables when Sister Mary Helen Ignatius called upon him to expound on the doctrine of "transubstantiation." Herbie stood up, his skinny legs trembling in his Catholic-school-approved, knee-length shorts. When he attempted to speak, nothing came out of his tiny mouth but a few drops of saliva, which dripped from his chin and splattered on the highly sanitized linoleum floor.

Sister Mary Helen Ignatious prided herself in being a watchdog of the gates of heaven. Nothing escaped her watchful eyes. That first salivary droplet was spotted and noted before it was even able to hide amidst the wax and disinfectant burnished into that immaculate linoleum. The droplets that followed only added insult to injury.

"Herbert Benson the Third," she spat, "into the cloakroom, on the double."

With the sole of his left shoe, Herbie tried to spread the saliva, which was now resting in a state of abject humiliation on the classroom floor, so as to render it invisible. Too late. He knew it was hopeless.

"Did you hear me, young man?" screamed the queen of the gates.

She reached for the ruler, the dreaded ruler.

The kind of ruler one would never find, even if he were to go to a large office complex in a major metropolitan area and obtain permission to rummage through the drawers of every desk within that complex. He probably would find numerous rulers, ranging in length from six to fourteen inches. He would find rulers made of a variety of materials from plastic to pine wood.

But never, ever would he find a ruler exactly twenty-one inches long made of thick, flexible, resilient, terrifying hickory wood. They don't exist, except in the waist cinches of grammar-school nuns.

Herbie arrived in the cloakroom, eyes downcast, lower lip trembling. As the twenty-one inch weapon of destruction was raised high into the air, Herbie's sensitive ears could clearly hear the effects of that weapon passing swiftly through and among the oxygen and nitrogen molecules that composed a substantial amount of the air in the otherwise silent cloakroom.

That swift movement created a whooshing sound that caused Herbie's eyes to squint, his head to bow, and his shoulders to curve downward.

As the hated weapon reversed direction with virtually no loss of momentum, young Herbie lost all hope. The pain that was inexorably heading in the direction of his right forehead, ear, and shoulder was more than his young mind could process. Just as the ruler dug into the tender skin on Herbie's right forehead and slid menacingly into the crevice between Herbie's ear and skull, intent on severing a portion of that ear from its customary location before coming to rest on the tender spot where Herbie's shoulder met his right jugular vein, his nervous system shut down in a vain attempt to protect itself from total meltdown.

Herbie's bladder was full to the brim. For almost an hour, he had been trying not to wet his Catholic-grammar-school-approved shorts.

In Catholic school, asking to be excused to go to the boys' room was a serious violation of the rules promulgated by the bishop. For the past ten minutes, Herbie had been wiggling his legs to distract himself from the urgent pressure in his groin and the occasional droplet of urine that he couldn't prevent from escaping the tip of his "you-know-what."

When the central control panel of Herbie's nervous system gave the order to shut down all circuits, it failed to exclude the circuit connected to the sphincter valve that controlled the flow of urine from Herbie's bladder, through the urethra, and out the tip of his "you know what."

If you think Sister Mary Helen Ignatius ability to spot a droplet of saliva from twenty three feet away was exceptional, the alacrity and deftness with which those hallowed eyes zeroed in on a cup-and-a-half of bright yellow urine was super-human.

One of the many curious traits with which members of some religious orders are infused is the ability and compunction to interpret any uncommon and distasteful act as being irrevocably deliberate. There was no doubt in the sanctified and sanctimonious mind of Sister Mary Helen Ignatius, that that puddle of disgusting stuff flowing from Herbie's pant leg, down his shin, over his stocking, down the shoe tip of his Catholic-Church-approved leather shoes, and onto the burnished floor of the Catholic Church's grammar school cloakroom was a deliberate affront to her authority, intelligence, and character.

The beating that ensued resulted in young Herbert Benson III being bedridden for three days. His parents took him to the emergency room of Sacred Heart Hospital to have the upper portion of his ear stitched back into its original place. The attendants in the emergency room asked no questions. They had received orders from the office of Sister Helen Anthony that this was a matter to be kept in the strictest confidence, under orders of the bishop.

Although terrified over their son's condition, Herbie's parents had learned from childhood that nobody challenges the authority of the Church. To do so, of course, would challenge the authority of God himself.

Herbie Benson III, of the fifth grade, chose to accept his humiliation by the overly zealous nun as a sign from heaven. It meant to Herbie that God was angry with him and that he was headed straight for the fires of hell if he didn't mend his ways immediately and drastically.

From that day forward, Herbie considered all orders from any person in a position of authority to be the will of God. He vowed to accept them without question, and to carry them out to the letter. He further vowed that he would go to great lengths to punish himself mercilessly for whatever sins he had committed, remembered or not. He would do anything to avoid burning in the fires of hell forever or having his ear severed.

Herbie's parents considered hiring a counselor to assist him in adjusting to his new understanding of the workings of the world. They were particularly concerned about the nightmares he experienced on a regular basis. But, all things considered, they decided that to do so might cause embarrassment to the Church. One never knew what sort of things a counselor might evoke from an impressionable young mind. Besides, their parish priest had implied on more than one occasion that those in the "professions of the mind," as he called them, including psychology, psychiatry, and counseling—especially those delving into matters of spirituality without the Church's sanction—were skating dangerously close to trafficking with the devil. No, they had better leave well enough alone.

Shortly thereafter, Herbert Benson III began his unending quest for more and more authority figures in his life to help him be certain that he was, in fact, doing the will of God. He went from one abusive relationship to another until he found solace in the warm and comforting arms of his superiors at the CIA.

Benson's years as an agent with the CIA brought to him the order he so desperately sought, until that damned Harrington kid uncovered some long-forgotten file and this cursed farmhouse thing raised its ugly head.

Herbert Benson III opened his eyes and cast a sorrowful glance at the only remaining source of comfort in his world, a half-empty tube of Foille ointment.

Chapter Fifty-three

Big John Hawkin was wrestling with a dilemma. Ordinarily in a situation like this, where he was seriously outnumbered, he would take advantage of the lull before the storm to set numerous booby traps. He would use items from the arsenal he always carried in his vehicle, plus some of those handy explosive components he had discovered in the bunker, to set traps for the enemy.

But that would be too risky in this particular situation. John had no way of knowing where the kids might go once they arrived. He had no practical way of setting his traps so they would be likely to eliminate enemy soldiers without the risk that they would injure or kill any of those kids.

It was obvious that he couldn't use traps that would be activated by actions of the intended victims. He especially couldn't use traps that would kill. He would have to rely only on traps he could activate from a distance, once he was certain that the target was indeed one of Benson's men.

John spent almost two hours rigging three traps that he could activate himself, using high-test fishing line that he ran from the trap to a remote location. He took care to bury the fishing line beneath leaves and pine needles in such a way that the line would not be easily detected and also would not likely be tripped unintentionally by someone walking over it. The traps were not intended to kill, only to take the victim out of the action.

Normally, he would have used hand grenades, fastened to a nearby tree, at a level that would almost guarantee the immediate death of anyone within thirty feet. In the present situation, however, he decided to use a device that, upon detonation, would saturate the atmosphere within a radius of about twenty feet with a type of nerve gas that rendered anyone inhaling it immediately unconscious for two to three hours, depending on the size and physiology of the victim. It was a heavier-than-air gas that settled to the ground within a matter of seconds. This quality eliminated the possibility that the gas would remain airborne for a while and be blown in the direction of someone not intended to be put out of the action, including the person triggering the trap.

This gas was not very well known and not used much in conventional warfare. But in this situation it was just what John needed. In the event one of those kids was to set it off, in spite of the precautions John took, he or she wouldn't be killed. At the same time, John expected that this "war" would be short-lived, and having an enemy soldier out of the action for a couple of hours seemed adequate.

He would have liked to have put a couple of these handy devices on the porch of the farmhouse, but he didn't see any way he could do that without high risk of tipping his hand. It did occur to him, however, that he might be able to set a trap near the entry to Benson's office without the likelihood of being detected, especially now that it was dark. The moon hadn't come out yet.

He fastened a length of fishing line to the trigger of one of the gas bombs, and a carriage bolt that he found on the ground to the other end. He walked to Benson's office and up the steps to the front door. He stood there as if gazing at the stars, just in case anyone was observing him. He reached up, as if taking a long stretch, and laid the device on the ledge near the front of the small porch roof in such a way that it was wedged into the triangular area between the ledge and the roof joist. He couldn't think of any way to fasten it more securely without the risk that someone watching him would think his actions suspicious. He would have to rely on the force with which he wedged it into place as being adequate to hold it in there when the line was pulled.

When the time came, he would have to either pull gently on the line, so as not to dislodge the bomb, or else to yank it so hard that the device would be triggered, even though it was pulled free from where it was hidden, allowing the gas to be released as the device fell toward the ground. Considering that it now rested a good two feet above John's head and that John was a good six inches taller than the average man, he decided that the bomb would likely release the gas before gravity would bring it to the level of the victim's nose and mouth.

The risky part was throwing the carriage bolt, which he had tied to the other end of the fishing line, to a distance from the bomb where he could trigger it later without being within range of the gas. He decided he couldn't throw it without possibly drawing someone's attention. He placed his hands on the side railing of the porch, still gazing at the stars. When he pulled back his hands, the carriage bolt had been dropped to the ground beside the porch.

Just for show, John went inside and asked Benson if there was any news. He was surprised to find that Benson was in a much better humor than the last time he had seen him. Benson actually was smiling. And in that smile, John thought he saw a trace of a decent human being. Perhaps he had been right in his earlier assessment of Benson as a frightened man caught in an impossible situation.

John decided to take advantage of Benson's relatively relaxed state to see if he could gather some more information. He asked Benson if he had heard any more from his men in the field. To John's surprise, Benson told him that he had sent those men out on a new assignment. When John inquired as to the nature of that assignment,

Benson was typically tight-lipped but did say that he expected them back at the compound early the next morning.

It was now Thursday night, around eight o'clock. Hawkin guessed that it would be some time before those four agents would return. He hoped it would all be over before then.

As John left the office, he managed to hook the fishing line with his little finger and drag it along with him. He prayed that the little tension the friction between the line and his finger was putting on the line wouldn't trigger the gas bomb. When the bolt reached John's finger, he dropped it, without breaking stride, making note of exactly where it had landed. He estimated that it was four feet from the trunk of the large pine tree behind which he thought he might be hiding in a few hours.

He headed back in the direction of the farmhouse and slipped into the forest, heading toward the area where he had observed an old barn yesterday. He had made a mental note to check inside that barn to see if there was anything he might use. Now seemed like as good a time as any.

The barn was large, more spacious than John originally had thought. It had a dirt floor with two small rooms with wooden floors to one side. In the center of the barn stood a brand new John Deere tractor. It was big, almost monstrous. It had eight wheels, each at least six feet tall, and was equipped with a gigantic front lift.

What the hell was a new tractor doing here? It had to have been brought within the last few days. It didn't even have a respectable coat of dust on it yet. It had to be part of Benson's plan.

In his usual thorough manner, John checked the fuel tank; diesel, full to the brim. He also observed that the key was in the ignition. He considered taking the key, just to be safe. Then, at the last moment, something told him to leave the key where it was, just a feeling, but uncommonly strong. John had learned long ago to trust his feelings.

He looked into the two small rooms with the wooden floors. They were built up about eight inches above the barn's dirt floor. They had no windows. There were hasps on each of their doors. They had probably been used for locking up valuable equipment. He made note of the fact that both the interior and exterior walls were made of three-quarter-inch thick wooden planks fastened into place with nails, spaced every two inches. The doors were similarly constructed with heavy-duty hinges hung on the inside of the rooms, obviously designed for security. What this had to do with the present situation John didn't know, but he was glad to know these rooms were here. They might be useful later.

He made note of several tools that were hanging on the interior walls and standing in the corners of one of the rooms. None of those tools seemed to be of any use to him.

The other room was empty.

Examining the rooms one last time, he discovered that the wall between the two rooms was not as sturdy as the exterior walls. He also noted that in the room without the tools there were two holes cut, one in the inner wall and one in the outer siding of the barn. Immediately above the inner hole was a length of conduit running to a light fixture in the ceiling. Apparently, at one time there had been a J-box in the hole in the outside wall and a light switch in the hole in the inside wall. The openings gave John a clear view of the front porch of the farmhouse, about half a mile away. He wondered what was going on in that farmhouse.

John walked past the mammoth John Deere. His years of experience and training once again told him to take the key. He placed his foot on the lower step below the cab, stood up, and reached for the key ring. As he was about to pull the key from the ignition switch, his instincts once again told him, "No!"

Big John slipped quietly through the barn door and out into the forest, the key ring swaying gently below the key in the John Deere's ignition switch.

Chapter Fifty-four

The occupants of the farmhouse were gathered in the living room, each buried in his own thoughts. The room had been silent for the past half hour, with the exception of an occasional cough.

Chas was particularly quiet, intending his silence to be a form of passive/aggressive rebuke to the others for not acknowledging his superiority and, instead, treating him like dirt. Eventually it dawned on him that with everyone else maintaining silence, his verbal withdrawal was not even being noticed. This infuriated him all the more.

Finally he decided to go on the attack. "What the hell are all of you doing? We can't just sit around here and wait for those government jerks to finish us off. Somebody think of a plan. So far, I've been the only one to do something. At least, I was able to get into their office. At least, I have some notion of what's going on out there. I can't run this whole show by myself. I would think you big muscle-bound types could be good for something."

"Listen, Chas," Clint grumbled, "just because we haven't told you what our plan is, it doesn't mean we don't have one." Clint immediately regretted that he had said anything.

"Then why don't you tell me? We're all in this thing together, you know. You have no right to keep me in the dark. My life's in just as much danger as the rest of you. I suppose when the shit hits the fan, you macho types are going to try to pull something crazy, like making special concessions for the women."

"With all due respect for your wife," Michael informed him, "we know you can't be trusted. You've already proven that you'd sell out the rest of us for your own benefit. We're going to do everything we can to get everyone out of here safely, including you. But we can't compromise the welfare of the group. You'll have to operate as best you can from your well-deserved position in the dark. You put yourself there. You left us no choice."

"I promise. I promise you can trust me. I've changed my attitude. I want to be part of the team. Come on, guys. Give me a break."

"It's too late for that," declared Clint. "There's too much at stake. I don't want to hear any more about it. We've got a lot of serious thinking to do. If you can't be quiet or, at least, say something helpful, I'm going to have to lock you up somewhere."

"Oh, yeah," whined Chas. "Just you try, and you'll find out that my superior intelligence is a good match for your macho muscleman karate bullshit any day."

Michael stood up.

Chas cowered back into the sofa and yelled, "Gail, do something! The two of them are ganging up on me!"

Michael shot back, "I was just stretching my legs. If Clint or I wanted to shut you up, I assure you it wouldn't take two of us. Just be quiet, please."

The room returned to silence.

Gail began to cry. After a while, she said, "I'm sorry. I'm so scared."

"That's okay, honey," Maria comforted her. "There's nothing wrong with being scared. Anyone who wouldn't be scared in a situation like this would have to be just plain stupid."

"But you're all handling it so well," sniffed Gail.

"We're all handling it the best way we know how," Sarah observed. "Even Chas is doing his best, given who he is. And I don't mean that to be derogatory. We all have our own issues, our own backgrounds, our own childhood recordings, and our own buttons that get pushed by situations. We all trust that you're doing the best you can. You have a loved one at stake, just like the rest of us. If part of your programming requires that you release your fears through crying, it's no different from my Michael here, who will probably release his fears by breaking a few jaws.

"Who's to say that any course of conduct is right or wrong? It just is. So you go right ahead and have a good cry. The last thing you need at a time when you're worried sick about your daughter is to have to contend with worrying about what the rest of us think. Remember, there's no right or wrong. Crying is one of those safety valves God gave us to release the pressure. I've been teetering on the edge of letting loose with a few profanities, just to let the tension out of my system."

"Bravo, Sarah," exclaimed Clint. "I think the healthiest thing any of us can do at this point is to resolve to do whatever we feel like doing and let our instincts be our guide. Remember the advice we got in the attic: 'Come from a place of pure love and follow your instincts.' If our instincts tell us to curse or cry or punch someone, I say, 'let 'er rip.' And, Gail, darling, as far as I'm concerned, you're a mighty fine person."

Maria walked over to where Gail was sitting, wrapped her arms around Gail's head and shoulders, and pulled her close. Gail turned and hugged her back, wrapping her arms around Maria's legs.

"What's this 'attic' shit?" Chas whimpered. "Something been going on here I don't know about? You're asking me to risk my life for a few little brats?"

Gail stood up, a look of contained rage on her face. She approached Chas, grabbed him by the front of his shirt, and yanked him to his feet. "Listen, you little weasel," she hissed, "I've had just about enough of your silliness. If I hear one more negative thing out of you, I'm gonna show you what 'woman power' is—only I won't be as gentle about it as Michael or Clint might be. From what I've learned about you in the past two days, I have no doubt that my sweet Becky was perfectly justified in doing whatever she had to do to protect herself from you. You've jeopardized all of our lives, including our children's, with your cowardly attempt to sell out to the enemy. You're skating on thin ice, buster."

She threw him onto the sofa with crushing force. It felt good to her. She raised her right index finger and placed it in front of Chas's face as he flinched. "One more thing. These are my friends. Treat them with respect."

The room was totally silent, but in the hearts of Gail's friends in that room, there went up a rousing cheer. More important, in her own heart she had found the courage to do what had to be done in spite of her fears.

Once again, tears began to flow down Gail's cheeks. She didn't try to hide them. She turned to face her friends, not the least bit concerned about who might see those victorious tears. There was a radiant glow on her face and a devilish twinkle in her eyes.

She walked to the window and looked out at the battleground. Gail was ready.

Not a word was spoken for several minutes.

Tim broke the silence by announcing that he was going to leave the room for a while, adding that he would be upstairs if they needed him. He wanted to do some thinking.

As Tim left the room, Chas was busy doing some thinking of his own. His mind was working hard, ruminating on concepts he had never considered before.

Tim pulled down the ladder leading to the attic and headed up the steps with a feeling of eager anticipation. Strangely, he felt as if he was walking into a place he'd never been before, even though he'd been in the attic only a few hours earlier.

The attic was cool and quiet. The musty smell was soothing to Tim, as if he could smell the aromas of someone's childhood memories. He wondered what must have happened in this old house. Certainly there had been violence here. That was obvious from the remains they had discovered in the basement.

But there was more. There must have been years of a family growing and working and playing in this house. He could feel it. The more he relaxed and calmed his mind, the more intense the feeling became.

Tim thought about the terribly suffocating and painful feelings he had experienced when he and his dad had visited the county courthouse in Sprague many years ago. He remembered thinking in his little boy's mind that he could feel the pain of those angry and anxious parties to all of those stressful lawsuits. He thought about how unnatural the judicial system is, how it is based on the supposition that people have to be forced into doing what's right. He thought about those feelings that were somehow absorbed by the walls and floors and ceilings and furnishings of that old courthouse, as if the building had been sacrificing itself to relieve the pain of its occupants, the victims of a cruel system. Tim thought there had probably been so much more pain and sadness in that courthouse than there had ever been joy and gladness. That's what he thought he had felt—the abundance of pain and

sorrow compared to the tiny bit of happiness that had ever been experienced there.

There must have been a great deal of love in this house. Whatever happened in that basement to all of those frightened people
apparently paled in comparison to the years of love and joy and laughter that had filled this home. Tim could definitely feel it now, the
abundance of love. He remembered reading in more than one book
about how love will always prevail over fear, that there is no amount
of fear that can't be overcome by love.

Tim sat quietly, breathing in the feelings of this house, sending
it love.

*Tell me your secrets. I need to know them now. I'm scared. I've always felt
pride in my athletic abilities. But I need more than that now. I'm about to go into
a war that common sense tells me we can't win. I have no training. I have no
weapon other than the love I have for my family and friends. That's all.*

"That's enough," whispered a small voice behind Tim. "That's
all you need."

Startled, Tim turned around. He saw nothing in the darkness.
"Who's there?" he asked in a trembling voice.

No response.

He started to search for the light switch, then remembered that
the house had no electricity.

He reached for a candle and found it. Then he flattened the
palm of his hand on the smooth, dusty floor. He moved his hand
back and forth, barely touching the floor, until he felt the matchbox.
He picked it up, his eyes still focused in the direction from which the
voice had come.

Tim struck a match. The flare of the phosphorus caused him
to squint. He touched the tip of the flame to the candle wick. It
ignited. He shook out the match and held the candle upright, off to
the side so as not to block his view.

He saw something sparkling faintly in the distance, yellow and
orange, not moving, just reflecting. He realized that his breathing had
stopped. He took a deep breath. He moved the candle off farther to
the side of his line of vision. The sparkling dimmed. He brought the

candle to within just a few inches of his head. The brightness of the beautiful yellow and orange sparkles increased. He stepped forward.

Eyes. Those were eyes shining at him, large and beautiful eyes. Again he became aware that he had stopped breathing. He forced his lungs to expand.

The eyes blinked.

They blinked again.

"Who are you?" whispered Tim, not sure he wanted to hear the answer.

"I will be whoever you wish me to be," came the whispered response.

"Can you come closer so I can see you?" invited Tim, his voice still uncertain.

The flickering eyes, warm and beautiful, moved toward Tim. He began to make out other features forming in the darkness around those beckoning eyes. It was a child, much smaller than the eyes alone would have indicated. Tim sensed sadness in those warm, loving eyes.

"Who are you?" he asked again.

"I am a child of the Universe, as are you. I can be anything or anyone I choose to be. I am willing to be whoever you choose me to be. In my most recent incarnation— which is what I assume you are asking—I was a member of the family that lived in this house. When you asked the house to tell you its secrets, it was unable to respond through a medium your senses could interpret. It vibrates at a rate much lower than your senses are programmed to detect. If you listen with your heart, you could communicate effectively with this house. That's what you were sensing as you entered this attic. But, considering the short time you have remaining before your adventure begins to intensify, we thought you would be best served by the apparition of an energy that vibrates at a level closer to your own. So we chose to utilize my former physical essence in our attempt to answer your questions.

"We are all one, as is everything in the universe. We are all part of the same God Force, focusing in different bodies, although the word 'bodies' has a much broader meaning where I presently reside than the meaning with which you are familiar.

"How may I serve you?"

Tim took a deep breath. "I would like very much to know what happened in this house…everything. But my time is limited. I'm attempting to deal with a great fear. The lives of my parents and my brother are in danger. I must save them if I possibly can. Will you help me?"

"First of all," the spirit replied, "I could someday, in your understanding of time, put all of the facts and incidents involving this house into words. But words are a relatively ineffective means of conveying information. You already know all about this house or have the ability to know all about it. Just sit here and listen with your heart. You will feel all of the sorrow and joy, the tears and laughter that occurred in this house. Feelings are the essence of communication, of understanding. Words can only feebly assist you in coming close to those feelings.

"Now," continued the spirit, "since, in your perception, your time is limited and, within the framework of that limitation, you do not perceive that you could learn all you need to know relative to your present state of mind as it relates to the upcoming battle, I will attempt to slow down my vibration to the point where I am able to provide you with a combination of words and feelings that will help you prepare.

"Let me assure you, however, that many on your planet could know everything they want to know about this situation in an instant, simply by listening with their hearts.

"Let me also assure you that you can achieve the capabilities of those Grand Masters in an instant, simply by choosing to do so and knowing it is possible. It is a matter of aligning your beliefs with your desires.

"Listen to my words with your heart or, what we would call in my world, your 'Higher Self.' If you can bring yourself to do so, you will understand what I am saying far beyond the normal meanings you attach to such words.

"Dismiss all logic, reasoning, arguments, conclusions, and objections. Listen only to the love with which these words are sent from the God Source. Listen with love. This is how mastery is achieved. The love of which I speak is not the romantic notions of your very beautiful songs or your feelings when you first interact with an attractive member of the opposite sex, although those feelings are wonderful and purposeful. The love of which I speak is the focusing of your energy on an object or person with absolutely no resistance. Simply allow the energy to flow, knowing that there is nothing to fear. Be joyous about where you presently are, with a desire to be in an even more joyous place. That is the faith of which our brother Jesus spoke that can move mountains."

Tim took a deep breath. He did his best to relax his mind and said, "I'm ready."

The candle flame rose toward the ceiling, turning to a bright bluish purple. It swirled and sparkled. It reminded Tim of when Gail's grandfather had appeared to him and his friends. The beautiful eyes grew in intensity until Tim began to feel mesmerized by them.

He could feel the love building in his heart. He could feel his trust increasing. He could feel the energy flowing. He could feel the knowing, the absolute knowing. Finally, he said again, "I'm ready."

"You already possess everything you need to achieve any result you desire. All you need is to be clear about the outcome you want and align your beliefs with that desire. In other words, know that the outcome is certain, and let the love flow through your very being with absolutely no trace of resistance. This is the power of God, the God that you are, the power that Jesus invoked to heal the sick and calm the winds. It is within every one of us. Every one of us is within it. Just know and trust. Trust and have the courage to take what one of your Grand Masters has called the 'empty-handed leap into the void'."

Those words hit Tim like the proverbial ton of bricks. He had heard those words or words like them before, in a book by Richard Bach or Ernest Holmes or one of the others Mom and Dad kept on the shelves back home. He had experienced the interpretation of that idea in movies such as *A Christmas Carol*, *It's a Wonderful Life*, and so many more. He had felt his body respond to that phrase, causing his throat to tighten and his chest to expand as if it might explode with joy.

But never, never in his life had these feelings hit into the center of his heart like this. Never before had he really listened to them with absolutely no resistance, with the hearing of his Higher Self.

"Please," begged Tim, "before you leave, can you tell me more specifically how I can apply this knowing to the battle to come?"

"The best way I can demonstrate how you can most effectively use your power is to show you an example from the past of this, your present, incarnation. This example will likely be the source of sufficient emotion, still recorded vibrantly in your soul, that you will feel, once again, what you experienced at the original happening. This time, as you experience those feelings, I ask that you not rationalize them with the teachings of this plane as you did the first time you had them. You must experience the feelings purely, without resistance, with pure love. You will then learn the lesson they contain.

"Every experience on the physical plane is intended by you from your higher perspective—that is, your Higher Self—to bring you joy.

"This time, just feel, without any explanation or logic or rationalization between the event and your heart's perception. The lessons will present themselves clearly and accurately. Those few lessons will 'carry the day,' as they say, in the upcoming battle.

"Think back to the incident where there was a lady tied to a tree, with her life threatened by an angry man with a baseball bat. Think about the woman. Think about the man. Do you recall the feelings that were in your heart as you watched that event?"

"I think so," Tim said tentatively.

"Don't just think. Play with that situation until you know. I will guide you."

Tim sat there for a long time, reliving the incident as best he could.

The spirit instructed, "Don't reason. Don't explain. Don't try to understand. Just feel."

Tim focused, trying his best to quiet the chatter in his mind.

"What did you feel?"

"I felt fear. Fear for my life. Fear for the woman. Even fear for the man."

"Good, good," praised those beautiful eyes. "Keep going."

Tim increased his efforts.

"What else? What else did you feel?"

"Sadness," admitted Tim.

"If I may suggest, sadness is just another form of fear."

"Anger," added Tim.

"Another form of fear."

"Rage."

"Still another form of fear. What did you feel that was not fear?"

"Hope."

"Now you're getting somewhere."

"Confidence."

"Closer, but no cigar."

"Do spirits make jokes?"

"Who do you think invented jokes? Keep going."

"Power."

"Closer. What do hope, confidence, and power have in common?"

"I don't know."

"You do know. Feel it."

Tim willed himself to relax. He thought about that terrible event. He thought about the terror in the woman's eyes. He saw the blood running down her neck. He heard those sorrowful sounds coming out of her mouth.

He felt, he felt...love.

At that moment, he had loved that woman more than anything in the world. That's what gave him the courage to set aside his fears and spring to the aid of that poor, sad, frightened, desperate woman. It was love.

"Love," shouted Tim. "I loved that woman."

"You've got it," whispered those warm, loving eyes. "You've got it. That's what hope, confidence, and power all have in common. They're all forms of love, as are all of the other positive emotions. There are really only two emotions in all of creation—love and fear. As your wonderful master, Jerry Jampolski, has said, 'Love is simply letting go of fear.' What you felt for that woman was love, all-powerful love, the force that holds the universe together.

"Now apply that feeling, that power of love, to every incident that presents itself, for the rest of your life. That's all it takes. That's all there is. There is only love. All else is simply love being blocked. Love is always there. All you have to do is remove the barriers. 'Let 'er rip,' as you would say. That's why you came to this beautiful place, this glorious planet—to love.

"And here's the greatest secret of all: You also loved the man."

Tim smiled. "Yes, I did, didn't I? Even though I tackled him, bit him, got him knocked unconscious, and ultimately put into prison, I loved him."

"That's because you are in this world but not of this world. You can conduct your life with unconditional love and still do what you have to do to get the results you feel are appropriate to a situation, based on the rules of this physical plane. It's a matter of intent. You meant that man no harm. You only wished to save the lady. If there had been any possible way, in your perception, to save that lady without injuring the man, you certainly would have taken that course. But, in your limited perception, you did what you thought had to be done, with no hatred toward the man.

"Therein lies all the difference. Acts are just acts. The same act can be good or evil, in earthly terms, depending on your intent. Be careful to remember, though, that God doesn't judge anything as good or evil, or deserving of reward or punishment. The only use I make here of those terms is that good advances you toward mastery and bad slows you down. And even that is irrelevant when you consider that you have forever to achieve mastery. So be light about all this. It's only a game. The worst that could happen, from your physical point of reference, is that you would die. And within milliseconds of that event, you would realize that death is also a wonderful and enjoyable transition.

"Apply what you have just learned to everything and everyone. When you go out onto that battlefield, love everyone. Do you not remember that Jesus said, 'love your enemy'? That is the ultimate goal. If you can learn to love those who hurt you the most, if you focus your energy on them and let the love of God flow through you to them without resistance, you, my brother, will be a Master.

"Every Light Being that ever existed is loved by God absolutely. God loves Genghis Kahn as much as he loves the Pope, Attila the Hun as much as he loves Mahatma Gandhi, Adolph Hitler as much as he loves Saint Francis and Joseph Stalin as much as he loves Jesus."

"The people you will be contending with shortly may very well suffer the consequences of their acts. But that is not caused by some judgment from God. That is the result of the laws of the universe, which are immutable. My advice to you, that you act at all times out of love, is not for the benefit of your enemies. It is for your own benefit. They create their own benefits and detriments.

"I will leave you now with this final message: Know that your Higher Self, the God Force, the All That Is adores you absolutely."

With that, the spirit was gone.

Tim sat staring at a very ordinary flame rising from a very ordinary candle. But Tim was definitely not feeling very ordinary.

He expected that his mind would turn to thoughts of the farmhouse and the compound and the challenges he would be facing in a matter of hours.

But, strangely, he began thinking about an incident that had happened a couple of years earlier. "If I had known then what I know now," he thought, "things might have ended much differently."

Chapter Fifty-five

When Tim began his sophomore year, a new kid came to Franklin High from El Paso, Texas. That's all anyone knew about him except that he obviously had a chip on his shoulder. His name was Eddie Mercado.

At Franklin High, as in many high schools, students were grouped in a variety of categories, depending on the purpose of the classifiers. To some students, particularly those with poor self-images, the classification of others can be almost a full-time job. They might label students as smart, average intelligence, or stupid. They could also categorize them as beautiful, ordinary looking, or ugly; as tall, medium, or short; or as fat, medium, or skinny. But, the most unkind and dangerous designations of all are those of popular, generally ignored, or outcast.

Depending on one's point of view, this process offers various goals to be attained. For example, in the area of fat, medium, or skinny, it is generally considered desirable to be in the medium range.

But in the realm of beautiful, ordinary looking, or ugly, students preferred to be well toward the beautiful end of the scale. This category of beautiful could be divided into several sub-categories such as cute, pretty, foxy, and awesome—or the grand prize position, drop-dead gorgeous.

It would not seem that light-beings arrive on this plane with a propensity to categorize others. Our human tendency to classify others, which is a form of judgment, seems to be learned. There is no record of an infant looking into his or her mother's eyes and announcing that the mother's breasts are inadequate. Nor has any male infant ever been quoted as complaining that his penis was too small.

Even as children approach the toddler stage, they don't seem as yet to judge or classify others. Their playmates are simply their playmates, and toddlers don't seem to notice that they are short or fat, or even members of a minority race.

But by the time they reach second or third grade, they begin to notice differences. "Hey, Mom," they say, "a new kid came to our class today, and his skin is black." At that critical moment, the parent's response could likely determine the child's attitude toward black people for the rest of his life.

By the time children have reached the seventh or eighth grades, the propensity toward classification has probably already become an ingrained part of their personalities. By then, it is important that we belong. And belonging is a concept directly derived from classifying.

If, for example, every human being on this planet sported the identical hue of black skin, there could be no classification based on skin color. Such a state of affairs would likely have eliminated slavery, numerous wars, including our own Civil War, and millions of fistfights.

But give any human being over the age of ten a basis for classification, and he or she will likely form a judgment. Human beings have created more classifications than Heinz has little gherkins. There are Catholics, Protestants, and Jews; Italians, Swedes, and Mexicans; rich and poor; tall and short; old and young; and so on, seemingly without end.

Fortunately, a substantial number of members of the human race have been raised to realize that these classifications should be used only for the purpose of differentiating, and never for the purpose of determining the worth of an individual.

Sadly, by the time many people get to high school, they have not yet acquired the wisdom to understand that we are all one. They don't yet realize that their apparent separateness, as a consequence of the bodies they inhabit, is no basis to conclude that they are superior or inferior to any other person.

Among the many groups at Franklin High were: the leaders, the jocks, the soshes (short for socialites), the nerds, the squares (similar to nerds, only not so wrapped up in intellectual pursuits), and the greasers.

Eddie Mercado definitely and quickly became categorized as a greaser. To qualify, the kid had to come from a poor family, drive a mechanically unsound but brightly colored automobile, use incorrect grammar regularly, engage in a fistfight at the drop of a hat, dislike everyone (even his fellow greasers, although not as much as the non-greasers), and use the "f" word at least once in every sentence. It also helped if his parents could be classified as poor white trash, although the "white" was not essential.

Eddie quickly attracted numerous other greasers. By virtue of his downright meanness, he rapidly assumed the position of leader of the pack.

It was relatively easy to avoid contact with Eddie and his gang off-campus. All anyone had to do was to stay away from the A&W, the Circle K, and any liquor store that was notorious for selling booze to minors. As a rule of thumb, non-greasers were well-advised to stay away from the poor side of town.

When they were on campus, avoiding Eddie became much more difficult. On campus, Eddie and his groupies might be encountered wherever a teacher or other school official, especially the football coach, wasn't present. This rendered navigating around the hallowed halls or any other parts of Franklin High a risky business. If a guy ran into Eddie and the gang in a location where no supervisor was around, he could count on being accosted. If the encounter did not turn physical, the victim could count on at least being assaulted with a flurry of insults regarding the purity of his mother or sister and, often, his own legitimacy.

Upon receiving such a harangue of insults, if the kid showed any form of resistance or defiance or, heaven forbid, attempted any form of self-defense, he could count on a thorough pummeling by Eddie's followers as Eddie stood by orchestrating the event.

If that resistance rose above a certain level, determined only by Eddie in his infinite wisdom, the kid could count on the attention of Eddie himself, which usually meant that the hapless victim received the customary black eye and broken nose, and even the possibility of a confrontation with Eddie's switchblade.

A rumor circulated around Franklin High, possibly fostered and augmented by Eddie himself, that several bodies in the cemeteries of El Paso had formerly belonged to those who had run afoul of Eddie and his switchblade.

On several occasions, parents of one or another of Eddie's victims filed complaints. In each instance, Eddie was summoned to the principal's office. Given the state's statutory prohibitions against corporal punishment, the principal was left, for all practical purposes, with the relatively ineffective remedies of detention or expulsion.

Coach Linden, however, was an entirely different matter. He was rumored to have once whipped Arnold Schwarzenegger in an arm-wrestling contest. And, although most suspected that this had not really happened, nobody doubted that it would have been possible. Coach Linden was not a man to be taken lightly.

Linden had heard the rumors about Eddie's switchblade. He called Eddie into his office early-on for a "get to know each other" meeting. He informed Eddie that if he were ever caught in the possession of such a weapon, the coach would disregard all of the bullshit state laws about physical abuse and give young Eddie the beating of his life.

Never for an instant did Eddie doubt the coach's sincerity or his ability to carry out his promise. Eddie wanted no part of a run-in with Coach Linden.

Somehow, every time the parents of one of Eddie's victims reported an incident to the school officials, that victim would have a terrible run of bad luck. His tires would be slashed, the paint on his automobile would be scratched to the point where a new paint job was necessary, his school books would disappear from his locker, and often he would be beaten into a condition, by assailants unknown, requiring medical attention, at a time when Eddie had plenty of witnesses eager to testify that Eddie was elsewhere when the beating took place.

The school officials could never get quite enough evidence against Eddie to do anything effective about his transgressions. They certainly could never find anyone willing to testify against him.

Within weeks of his arrival in Sprague, Eddie had established an effective reign of terror over a substantial segment of the Franklin student body. For several months, the only factor that limited Eddie's conduct in any appreciable way was the ever-present specter of Coach Linden's promised retribution hanging over his head.

That is, until one day, when Eddie made two fatal mistakes.

The first was that he allowed himself to be on campus without his entourage.

Eddie was spending a couple of hours in the detention hall as the result of his having been observed by Miss Abercrombie making lewd gestures at one of the young ladies in her sophomore biology class. Eddie instructed his gang to meet him in the parking lot at five o'clock.

Detention hall that day was being supervised by Coach Linden, covering for a friend who had a dental appointment. At 4:15, Coach Linden told Eddie he could go home early.

Eddie was delighted to be released forty-five minutes ahead of schedule and swaggered out of the room, turning around at the last second to flash a visual obscenity at Coach Linden when the coach wasn't looking.

Once Eddie gained his freedom, he headed for the gym to shoot a few baskets while waiting for his buddies to arrive.

On his way to the gym, Eddie made his second big mistake.

Jaime Lasher was just coming out of the locker room on his way to the parking lot. As he passed Eddie, Eddie went out of his way to bump into Jaime. Eddie turned and shouted, "Hey, look where you're going, Esse."

"Sorry." Jaime said.

"Sorry, my ass," Eddie yelled. "How would you like me to teach you some El Paso manners, man?"

"Look, I said I was sorry," Jaime said as he turned to walk away.

"Don't walk away from me, you little chicken," Eddie screeched.

Eddie was so angry that he overlooked the absence of his back-up gang. He grabbed a wooden dowel that the Franklin High landscape crew had fastened to the trunk of a birch tree to prevent that tree from deviating noticeably from its intended upright position. Eddie yanked it out of the ground.

He slipped up behind Jaime and smashed the dowel on the top of Jaime's head with considerable force. Jaime fell to the ground, almost unconscious. He had to struggle to keep his eyes focused. He was overcome by vertigo. As he tried to get to his feet, Eddie hit him again, this time between the shoulder blades. Jaime fell flat, barely able to breathe. As he lay there, Eddie continued his attack, beating Jaime furiously on the arms and legs, screaming like a madman.

The last time Eddie raised that dowel above his head, it wouldn't come back down. It hung there as if it were attached to a sky hook. Bewildered, Eddie looked over his right shoulder and was terrified to find that the very person he was beating was standing behind him.

He turned loose of the dowel and backed away.

Then he remembered Jaime had a twin.

Eddie hadn't considered the possibility that Jaime's twin brother was nearby. Had he done so, he certainly wouldn't have attacked Jaime without having his buddies along for support.

He looked at the dowel in Tim's hand. He saw That Look on Tim's face.

"Hey, I don't want no trouble with you, man!" he shouted.

That phrase, by the way, is the national anthem of bullies who have come to the realization that they are dangerously close to entering into an altercation where they don't have a considerable advantage, psychological or otherwise.

Tim threw the dowel into the bushes and faced Eddie straight on.

"What are you, stupid or something?" Eddie shouted. "Hey, man, you gave your weapon away, really stupid."

The situation now looked somewhat brighter to Eddie. He just wished his friends would get there soon.

If Eddie had known all of the salient facts relevant to his situation, he would have been more concerned about the attitude of a boy whose brother and best friend had been beaten half to death than he was about that wooden dowel. He should have paid more attention to That Look."

When Tim got through with Eddie, Eddie would have gladly traded places with Jaime.

As soon as Tim was sure Eddie was out cold, he ran to Coach Linden's office and called an ambulance. Then he called Mom and Dad. He ran back to Jaime and sat on the pavement with Jaime's head on his lap. He looked down at the welts on Jaime's neck and arms and began to cry. He held Jaime's head to his chest and rocked him, like a nanny rocking a child.

He could hear the siren of the ambulance in the distance.

Through his tears, he looked at Eddie. Eddie was still out cold.

Mom and Dad arrived just as the ambulance got there, a look of abject sorrow in Mom's eyes. Dad looked bewildered, as if he was operating on auto pilot. Jaime was beginning to regain consciousness. He was moaning from the intense pain.

The paramedics said they thought that he would be all right but he was going to be in a lot of pain for a few days, including having a killer headache. One of them commented that if that dowel had hit two inches lower, Jaime might have been killed.

To Mom and Dad's surprise, Tim asked if they thought Jaime would be all right without him for a while. Michael said that would be fine. Tim told Dad he'd meet them at the hospital later, and he headed for the parking lot.

Mom rode to the hospital in the ambulance, and Dad followed in the car.

As surprised as Michael was by Tim's request, he figured that whatever was on Tim's mind, now was not the time to interfere.

In the parking lot, Tim sat on the hood of his car and waited.

Fifteen minutes later, Eddie's friends arrived.

The driver was the first to get out of the car. By the time both of his feet were on the ground, Tim had covered the twenty feet between the two cars and had the shocked driver by the front of his shirt. Tim yanked down on the shirt at the same time as he raised his right knee. The sound of the kid's nose shattering could be heard ten feet away.

Two more boys jumped from the car and were all over Tim in a matter of seconds. Tim ended up on the pavement on his back, the two boys punching him mercilessly. He raised his arms in an attempt to block the punches and grabbed both of their shirts. He pulled them down so powerfully that their heads cracked together. Tim took advantage of their dazed condition by jumping up and getting one of them in a stranglehold. He held on tightly for several seconds. His opponent went limp, totally unconscious. Tim turned around to face the last of the three. He was wobbling on his feet, his hands raised. As he backed away, he shouted out the bullies' national anthem.

Tim ran him down and beat him until he was unconscious.

Tim drove to Miller's drugstore, a block away, and bought a disposable camera. He returned to the high school parking lot, dragged all three of the unconscious boys to the front of their car, and propped them up against the front bumper. He then took several photos of Eddie's gang.

At the hospital, Tim checked in on Jaime, who was already showing the first traces of that "Jaime smile." He looked bad, but not nearly as bad as the other guys.

After visiting with Jaime a while, Tim went next door to Eddie's room. The minute Eddie saw Tim, he raised his hands and implored, "Hey, man, I don't want no more trouble with you."

Tim said, "I'll tell you what. You let me take your picture, and I promise that you won't ever have to deal with me or my brother again, unless you start it. And if you think I'm mean, you ought to try both of us at the same time."

Later that week, Tim came to school with photographs of the four hoodlums, in their badly beaten conditions, enlarged to 12" by 15". He taped copies of those photographs on the walls of the boys' locker room, several of the classroom corridors, the cafeteria, and just for good measure, the bulletin board in the library.

That put an end to the reign of terror Eddie and his hoodlum friends had conducted since Eddie's arrival in Sprague.

Tim was pleased to know that it was now safe to walk the campus of Franklin High. He was quietly proud that he had helped to bring about that condition.

But he never felt quite right about the extreme to which he had allowed himself to go in getting those results. He wished he had been wise enough to put a stop to the situation without adding to Eddie's already low self-esteem. He thought a lot about what had happened, and he vowed that if he ever would find himself in a situation like that again, he would do his best to rely on the power of his mind and less on the use of physical force.

Finally, Tim came to the realization that perhaps Eddie had created his own consequences by choosing the arena in which his conflicts would be resolved.

Eddie and his friends were so devastated by the beatings they had taken at the hands of a single gringo and the humiliation they had felt from having the entire school know they had been beaten that they dropped out of sight.

Tim consoled himself by considering that his actions probably were reasonable, given the circumstances. He doubted that Eddie would have ever stopped, short of being defeated.

Still, Tim wondered, from time to time, how he could have handled it differently. He wondered if he could have stopped the reign of terror without damaging the self-images of boys who already suffered from an obvious lack of self-worth.

Perhaps Tim should have stopped after he was finished with Eddie, and let that be enough of a lesson to his friends. But he knew that chances were those boys would have come after him the next day. Their egos wouldn't allow them ever to think that Tim's victory over Eddie was anything other than dumb luck. They would feel deep inside that Eddie's defeat was evidence of their own inferiority. "Too bad," thought Tim. "how sad."

Tonight, as Tim sat in the attic of the old farmhouse, he wondered what advice the spirit would have given him about such a situation. The spirit had spoken about intent.

At the time he was engaged in his confrontation with Eddie Mercado, Tim hadn't stopped to think about intent. But what had his intent been? Certainly, he had wanted to get even, to teach Eddie and his friends a lesson, to put an end to their reign of terror, to be sure they never bothered Tim or Jaime again.

He had followed his instincts. Perhaps that was sufficient. Perhaps some situations don't lend themselves to acting in a loving way, or maybe that *was* a loving way to act.

Then it dawned on him. He had acted out of love. He had let the God Force flow through him without resistance. Boy, had he ever let it flow without resistance! He had done what was necessary to accomplish an objective that had seemed to him, at the time, to be worthy. He had gone as far as he thought he had to go to get the job done. Had he gone further and continued to torment those boys after they stopped terrorizing his friends, he would have been acting in an unloving way.

But then a comforting thought came to Tim. It all turns out perfectly. That's what the spirit said. You can't get it wrong. God is not judging.

So we do what we think is right in a given situation and know that it will all come out for the best. The only variable is that some acts will bring us to mastery more quickly than others. But even that doesn't matter a whole lot, since we have forever to attain mastery. And even after we do that, there will be more to accomplish. That is the essence of life.

Then an even more comforting thought came to Tim: Judge not, lest ye be judged. Suddenly that old biblical quotation had a whole new meaning for Tim. It meant that we shouldn't judge ourselves. We should follow our instincts, do what feels good, go for the gusto. We are being guided by our Higher Self. We can't get it wrong because there is no right or wrong. Nobody is taking down our name.

"Yahoo!" he shouted out loud and wondered for an instant what the people downstairs might think about that shout.

Now it all made sense. He could do no wrong. Eddie Mercado, the high school hoodlum, could do no wrong.

Those thoughts made Tim realize that it was surprisingly easy to love others. They're all out there doing what feels good to them. And their "victims" have come to this plane, at this time, to experience that.

Just as our brave soldiers in World War II put a stop to Hitler, Tim put a stop to Eddie. Neither of those were unloving acts. In reality, they were very loving acts. The fact that another being had set himself up to suffer consequences and that Tim had been in a position to administer those consequences, in no way meant that Tim was acting in an unloving way. And, best of all, even if Tim's acts were unloving it didn't matter. Not from the higher perspective. It might matter as it relates to consequences Tim might suffer on this plane. But it didn't matter from the point of view of Tim's Higher Self. It doesn't matter to God.

"So," thought Tim, "what does all this tell me about the coming battle? I would say that I will go out there, give it everything I have, everything I can do to achieve my objective, which is to save my family. And if I go beyond that, if I act in a manner beyond what is necessary to accomplish the loving objective, the one that will most advance me toward my mastery, I may suffer consequences in this lifetime. I might even perform acts that will delay my achievement of mastery, but in God's eyes I can do no wrong. There is no judgment after I die. When I return to the world of spirit, the only questions that will be asked of me are, 'Did you live with joy?' and 'What did you learn?'

"What I've learned," thought Tim, "is that I will go into this battle with no fear, which means with pure love. I will follow my instincts, and I will know that it will all have an appropriate ending, even if the ending is not what I thought I wanted."

As Tim came down the stairs, Sarah was the first to glance up. One by one, the others all looked up at him. They wondered what the "Yahoo" had been all about. And now that they saw him, they wondered what was causing the gigantic grin on Tim's face.

"What's up?" asked Clint.

"It would take me an hour to explain everything," reflected Tim. "All I can say for now is that I had a little encounter with a ghost up in that attic, a young lady who lived in this house at one time. We've got to go out there tonight and give it all we've got. And, as strange as this may sound, we've also got to do our best to act out of love. That means without fear. I know that sounds strange."

"Not really," Michael commented. "Take it from someone who's been in a lot of battles. Following my instincts and holding love in my heart pulled me through lots of situations that others didn't survive."

"I think it's about time we went outside," Clint suggested. "The sun's been down a while now. If those kids are coming and if they're waiting for cover of darkness, they ought to be getting here sometime soon."

Then Michael spoke. "I'm truly sorry, Chas, but we're going to have to tie you up in the attic. We wish you no harm, but we don't trust you. If we leave you in the house untied, you might tell the enemy what we're doing. If we bring you out with us, we don't know what you'll do. When this is all over, if we're victorious, one of us will set you free. If we lose, you'll probably be better off tied up in the attic than being executed by the bad guys. I'm sure you can work yourself free, given enough time."

Chas didn't resist. They took him to the bathroom to empty his bladder, even though there was no water. Chas walked up into the attic and sat quietly while Clint and Michael tied and gagged him. First of all, he was no match for Clint and Michael. Second, he would rather be in this attic than out in the middle of some war. But, strangely enough, Chas's third reason was that he actually wished these people well. He actually hoped they would win.

Ever since he realized that Gail no longer loved him or, at least, that she was willing to stand up to him, some extraordinary thoughts had been running through his mind. He finally began to understand that, perhaps, he did need other people. He was struck by the fact that all of these people had become friends in such a short time. And, although he was certain that the impetus for the formation of those friendships came in part because they were facing a common enemy, he saw something very attractive, very comforting in the notion of friendship. Chas had never had a friend.

Michael placed a jug of water next to Chas and showed him how he could lift it to his mouth by squeezing it between his elbows. "I guess you're going to have to pee in your pants," Michael apologized. "I can't think of any way to help you with that situation. It won't be so bad."

Maria, Sarah, and Gail had lit several candles in the upstairs bedrooms and put out all of the candles in the rooms on the ground floor. They hoped the guards would assume they had all gone upstairs. Fortunately, the guards couldn't see into the upstairs rooms from the ground.

Tim reminded everyone, "Once we're outside, we won't be able to risk talking. Let's sit quietly in the forest until Jaime and the gang arrive. I don't think we can step outside of the forest area without a serious risk of being spotted. Once the kids arrive, I hope we can meet up with them and escape undetected. If we're discovered before we get out of the compound, we'll undoubtedly have to fight. There are a few tools in the basement we might use as weapons, including the shovel that someone used to dig that tunnel. Good luck to all of us."

With that, they went down into the cellar, took what tools they could find, and headed out through the tunnel.

Chapter Fifty-six

The Jeeps rolled to a halt, and the headlamps and engines were turned off. They were now about a mile from the mouth of the canyon. All was silent except the chirping of crickets, not a cloud in the sky. The moon had not yet risen. A million stars twinkled overhead a gentle breeze whispered through the trees.

They began quietly strapping on their backpacks. Becky refused to carry the weapon that Daryl offered her. Only three pistols were available, and she thought they would be more effective in the hands of the guys because they had more experience with weapons than she did.

More important, she wanted to be able to use her karate skills to maximum advantage in whatever situation would present itself. With a pistol in her hand, she would have to make decisions she had never made before. The few seconds it might take to decide whether to shoot or to use some other tactic might be a deadly delay.

Becky would prefer not to kill anyone. With karate, she had been thoroughly trained to know just how far to go in view of the situation before her. She had spent hundreds of hours reacting to situations her instructors had set up for her, followed by critiques on her performance and appropriate constraints. One of the objectives of her martial arts training had been to render her capable of using whatever force was necessary to stop an opponent without causing unnecessary damage.

Although this was often a fine line, years of practice had prepared Becky to handle almost any situation reasonably. She wasn't sure that would hold true if she were to have a 44 Magnum at her disposal. Once a bullet leaves its cartridge, you can't modulate the amount of force delivered. The best you can do is to be discriminating regarding the target or the part of the target you select before squeezing the trigger. Becky felt confident that she could do a much more effective job with her body than with a pistol, especially in the close-in combat conditions she suspected the density of the forest would impose.

Each of the four was equipped with a knife and a heavy steel flashlight. And between the abundant useful implements Chris always kept in his Jeep and the arsenal Daryl acquired shortly after his escape from the CIA building, they were surprisingly well equipped.

Becky suggested that she would like to ask Zara a couple more questions before leaving the vehicles behind. She got out the crystal, set it on the hood of Daryl's Jeep, and focused her energy.

"I am with you," came the deep, gentle voice.

"I have a few questions, if I may," said Becky.

"Of course."

"Will you tell us of any capabilities of the spacecraft that might be of assistance to us?"

"Access to the craft could be of considerable benefit to you. I cannot foresee exactly what needs you will have, given the virtually unlimited number of scenarios that could present themselves to you. Just know that the ship will respond to any command that is given with a peaceful intent. The craft may be used to frustrate aggression, but never to harm anyone."

"Thank you," Becky acknowledged. "Do we have to carry this crystal to make contact with you?"

"No. Although the crystal has definite frequency-amplifying properties, its primary purpose in this situation is to give you an object upon which you can focus your concentration. It can help amplify the vibrational waves that travel from my being to your radio receptor, or what you call your brain. It was also instrumental in allowing you to contact me in the first place because, before that event, you didn't consciously know I existed. It is like my calling card. If you need me, simply focus your concentration on the being you have come to know me as, and I will immediately be in your presence. I would suggest, however, that you consider taking the crystal with you so you can use it to activate the wondrous capabilities of the spacecraft."

"Thank you," sighed Becky. "Please don't be too far away."

"I will remain available at any instant. The only variable is the focus you are able to generate. You will do fine. I send you my love. The love of the God Force is with you always."

The sudden absence of Zara's comforting voice was more than a silence.

Daryl placed the crystal in his backpack.

Jaime took the keys out of both ignitions and hid them under a rock a few yards away. He made sure everyone knew where they were hidden.

By the time the group entered the mouth of the canyon, the temperature had dropped several degrees. Fortunately, they each had a light jacket with them. Even more fortunate was that the jackets were all of a dark color. Daryl's, of course, was camouflage.

Within another twenty-five minutes they arrived at the top of the ridge and looked down at the farmhouse about four hundred feet below. Chris suggested that they synchronize their watches and agree upon a time for all to be at the bottom of the hill instead of counting paces as they originally intended.

Daryl pointed out that, because of the shape of the mountain, by the time they got to the bottom, they would be a lot farther apart than when they started their descent.

They separated, trying to space themselves at intervals of about a hundred feet, and headed downhill.

They had agreed that, upon reaching the bottom, Daryl would turn right and head toward the bunker where the spacecraft lay hidden. Chris would also turn right but would circle around the farmhouse. Jaime and Becky would turn left and circle around the farmhouse on the opposite side. Becky would do her best to stay well ahead of Jaime.

By proceeding in this manner, they hoped always to keep the farmhouse in sight, even though it would be some distance away, on the chance that they might run into or, at least catch a glimpse of, some of their family members. Although they didn't know it existed, the tunnel Hawkin had dug out of the cellar was on the side of the farmhouse where Chris would be.

The plan was to sneak up on a few of the government agents who they assumed would be patrolling the compound—it was hoped, one at a time—and disable them as quietly as possible.

Like Jaime, Becky was scared big time, but her fear was tempered by the confidence in her martial arts skills.

Chris was surprisingly confident, having been in plenty of street fights in his life. He managed to fare quite well, even against a few opponents who had some martial arts training. He was just plain tough and unbelievably strong.

Jaime didn't know what he had going for him against these trained killers except his uncommon athletic ability, his blinding speed, and his top physical shape. He had no experience in hand-to-hand combat—except that his video collection included all of the Rocky and Rambo movies. He laughed to himself, mostly to help keep his fear under control.

The family members, who had recently left the farmhouse through Hawkin's narrow but adequate tunnel, were all lying prone on the forest floor about thirty feet from the building in a thick stand of pine trees and shrubs, maintaining absolute silence.

Michael and Sarah saw a man walk by, about fifty feet from them, but couldn't tell in the darkness that it was Chris. They assumed it was one of the government agents.

Becky was the first to encounter one of the agents. As she stood beneath the cover of a large poplar tree, she noticed a red glow about thirty feet in front of her and detected the pungent aroma of tobacco. She held her breath and began to tremble. The urge to turn and run was almost overpowering, but the image of Mom trapped in the farmhouse flashed in her mind. She decided to stay.

The flashlight was in her right hand, and the knife was in its case, duct-taped to the outside of her left leg just above the knee. For just a moment, she wished she had taken the 44 Magnum Daryl had offered her.

She moved so slowly and quietly that she could hear her own heart beating. Each footstep took what seemed like several seconds. There was just enough wind in the trees to muffle the sound made by the soles of her shoes skimming the tops of the dry leaves on the forest floor. She removed the knife from its case and held it in her left hand, the darkened flashlight still in her right.

Now only a few feet from the man, she maneuvered to a position that placed a large ponderosa between them. Peeking around the tree to her left, she was barely able to see the man's profile outlined by a dim light in the distance.

She squatted and, searching the forest floor, managed to find a rock about the size of her hand. She laid down her flashlight, picked up the rock and lobbed it ten feet to her left. It made a noticeable sound as it hit the dry leaves and rolled a few inches.

The man froze for a second, then turned in the direction of the sound. He snuffed out his cigarette.

Becky picked up her flashlight and stepped back farther behind the ponderosa, barely keeping the man's silhouette in view.

He turned on a flashlight aiming it in the direction of the noisy rock. He took three steps, his right shoulder within two feet of where Becky stood motionless. If he had aimed the flashlight to his right, he would have seen two terrified eyes looking directly at him.

Becky wondered how long before she would have to inhale. In the glow of the flashlight's beam, she could see that the man had a pistol in his right hand.

She could go for the gun. She had spent many hours learning how to disarm a gunman. She could have grabbed that gun with both hands, twisted it up and back—probably breaking the man's trigger finger in the process—and aimed the barrel back at him. She knew that a pistol was not very effective at short range against an accomplished martial artist.

But she had a flashlight in one hand and a knife in the other. There was no way to put them down now without making a sound. Besides, it was way too early in the game to have a gunshot go off. The good guys would have to disable a whole lot of bad guys before the war could begin in earnest, or they didn't have a chance. Instead, she circled slowly and quietly around the tree until she was standing directly behind the man, her heart in her throat.

She let the knife slip from her hand, point down. It stuck upright in the soil. Before the man could react to the sound, Becky's now empty left hand delivered a crushing rabbit punch to the carotid artery and nerve bundle at the base of the left side of the man's neck. His entire left side went limp. As he struggled desperately to maintain himself upright, Becky blasted the base of his skull with the butt of her steel flashlight. The man dropped like a rock and fell flat on his stomach.

Becky remembered the many movies she had watched in which the good guy thought he had knocked out the bad guy only to have him rise up at the last second and create another three minutes of action. For good measure, she picked up a rock and administered a heavy blow to the man's skull. She hoped it wasn't hard enough to kill him. As she removed the gun from his right hand, her heart raced frantically, and she almost regretted that last blow.

Quickly removing her backpack, she pulled a length of nylon rope from it. She wrapped one end several times around the man's ankles, binding them tightly together. Then she pulled his head back by the hair and wrapped the same rope around his neck. She tied it in a slip knot so if he were to struggle he would cut off the blood to his brain.

She pulled both of his arms behind him and tied them together. After wrapping the nylon cord around his wrists, she wrapped it around his upper arms and pulled them toward each other, making it impossible for him to pull his wrists out of the loops.

She wrapped duct tape around his mouth, eliminating any chance that he could speak. She rolled him into a scrub oak thicket, where she hoped none of his teammates would discover him. He was heavy, but she was pumped. She picked up his Walther 357 Magnum making sure there was a round in the chamber and the safety was on. She tucked it into the back of her Levi's. Finally, she retrieved her knife and replaced it in its holder.

Leaning against a tree, Becky took several deep breaths. She was proud of herself.

She wondered why Jaime hadn't caught up. She considered that he might be having an adventure of his own and prayed that he was all right.

She circled back to see if she could find him.

⟋⟍

The two men were sitting on the ground, each leaning against a separate tree trunk about three feet apart, facing the farmhouse. Each had a pint bottle in his hand. One man was drinking Jack Daniels. The other, with a feeling of superiority, was knocking back Jose Cuervo Commemorativo.

Shania Twain's voice singing "Come on Over" filled the air, emanating from the ghetto blaster on the front porch.

For more than an hour, the two men had been leaning against the trees, which accounted for the numbness in their butts in addition to the lightness in their heads. Several times they talked of turning in, but they were enjoying their buzz too much to quit now. Besides, they didn't have to arise at any particular time. Nothing was happening around here.

They were reliving war stories, one of the men having been an undercover agent stationed in the Pyrenees Mountains, monitoring and attempting to foil the smuggling of weapons through Spain and onto freighters headed for Libya. The other had spent several years infiltrating the Chinese Mafia in San Francisco. Each had been suspected of conspiring with the enemy. Nothing had been proved. Rather than fire them and risk them going to work for their opponents, the CIA had moved them into positions of relatively little responsibility and virtually no potential to jeopardize any delicate operations. Basically, they were paid handsome salaries to do almost nothing, which was fine with them.

As the Mafia infiltrator leaned his head back to take a long pull on his tequila, he caught, out of the corner of his eye, the faint outline of someone standing between him and his companion. "Hey, what's up, buddy? I wouldn't go walking up on people if I was you. Might get your ass busted or even get shot. Pull up a chunk of ground and join us. We're busy earning our share of the taxpayers' bounty, if you know what I mean, eh Stan?"

Each of the men felt a hand reach down and attach to the back of his sweatshirt. "Hey!" was the last word they uttered before they were yanked off the ground—their heads crashed together with more force than either of them could have imagined coming from a single source.

For good measure, Chris slammed their foreheads together one more time. The strength necessary to accomplish this was considerable. Chris silently gave thanks for all those years of bench presses, push-ups, and dumbbell flyes. Within five minutes, he had tied and gagged them and hidden them and himself in a growth of bushes.

He could see the front porch of the farmhouse, where three men sat listening to Shania blasting out, "Man, I Feel Like a Woman." It was just the kind of music Chris needed to cover the sound of two thick skulls cracking together. He was now hidden well back into the shadows of the forest. Getting those three dudes on the porch would take some effort and planning. He sat there thinking, wondering how the rest of the gang was doing.

Jaime hadn't lagged behind Becky after all. While she was busy contending with her first challenge, Jaime had passed by her, not more than fifty feet away. He was moving so slowly and quietly that Becky hadn't even noticed him.

When Jaime passed by, Becky had been hiding behind that large ponderosa, leaving him no way of knowing she was there. The agent hadn't yet turned on his flashlight. And Becky was so focused on the agent's silhouette, wondering what her next move was going to be, that she probably wouldn't have noticed Jaime if he had been doing summersaults across the forest floor while singing the national anthem.

As things stood now, Becky was heading in a westerly direction, backtracking to where she thought Jaime might be, while Jaime was heading east, erroneously thinking that Becky was ahead of him.

Before long, Becky found herself directly behind the farmhouse again. Jaime wasn't where she hoped he might be.

In the meantime, Jaime had come upon an agent of his own. He had been following the agent for almost half a mile, knowing he was abandoning the position where his friends expected him to be, but he didn't want to let this guy get away. Jaime lay down on his stomach in the tall grass watching his target. The man was standing in front of a porta potty smoking a cigar. He took off his shoulder holster and hung it on a tree branch, flipped the stub of his cigar carelessly into a patch of clover, and tossed down one more swig from his bottle of Johnny Walker Red before he set it down, belched loudly, and went inside the porta potty. If his normal sense of caution hadn't been subdued by the effects of more than a pint of Scotch, he might have questioned the advisability of leaving his weapon out of reach. But at the moment, he was focused upon a more pressing stimulus.

Jaime had no idea what he should do. All he knew was that a great many agents were out there and he hadn't yet captured one. He looked at the 22-caliber target pistol in his hand, thinking how grossly inadequate it was for his purposes. He didn't know how much time he had before the man would emerge from the outhouse. But from the sounds erupting from that little building, Jaime suspected he might have a few more minutes to think.

Then, without even knowing for sure what his plan was, Jaime stuffed the 22 into his belt, ran to the porta potty, took the man's pistol off the tree, pulled back the slide, and chambered a round. He clicked off the safety.

The sounds in the potty stopped. "Who's out there?" came the quavering voice from inside.

Jaime threw open the door and leveled the Colt 45 at the man's chest.

The man stood up, his britches still around his ankles.

Jaime took one step backward.

At the sight of Jaime, the man laughed. "Well, what have we here? Looks like a little boy to me with my pistol. Know how to use one of them things?"

"I sure do," Jaime shot back. "Lots of years in the NRA."

He immediately realized how lame that sounded.

"Well, sonny," the man teased, "I don't recall that a part of the NRA safety classes included how to kill a man. But, then again, it's been a long time since I took that course. Ever seen a man's guts spilled all over the floor? No, I don't think you're gonna kill me. Just hand me that weapon, son, and I'll forget this whole thing ever happened."

Jaime suddenly realized that his situation was a lot worse than he had thought. First of all, the man was right. Jaime wasn't prepared to kill anyone unless it was a matter of life or death. Second, he couldn't fire a shot yet without alerting all of the bad guys and putting his family and friends in much more danger than they were in already.

Then, with more force than he would have thought he could muster, Jaime sneered, "You're right, mister low-life government agent, I wouldn't kill anyone. But I sure as hell wouldn't hesitate to blow off that teeny weenie of yours, just to take you out of the game for a while and be sure you don't create any more little low-life government agents."

The man didn't look as sure of himself as he had looked a moment earlier. And Jaime definitely wasn't as sure of himself as he sounded.

The agent said, "Now, let's don't do anything you'll regret, son. You be careful with that thing. It's got a real sensitive trigger. Why don't you just point it the other way?"

Jaime retorted, "I like it right where it is. Now you just turn around, real slow."

The man hesitated for a second, then turned his back to Jaime, glad, at least, that his butt was between that pistol and his privates.

"Now—down on your knees," Jaime commanded.

The man knelt down slowly.

"Now put your hands behind your back, wrists together." Jaime slid his backpack to the ground without ever taking the pistol or his eyes off the man. He reached inside, found the nylon rope, and tied a loop and a slip knot as best he could, using his free hand and his teeth. He slipped it over the man's wrists, careful not to get too close, and yanked it tight. Then he quickly wrapped three more loops around the man's wrists and slipped the end of the rope up between the man's forearms. He pulled the other end under the man's ankles and wrapped it around them three times. He pulled the rope tight, caus- ing the man to groan and bend backward sharply until his hands were touching his ankles.

"I'll get you for this, don't you doubt it," the man hissed between clenched teeth.

Jaime remained silent, thinking.

He got out one of his rolls of duct tape and wrapped it around the man's head several times, taking care to completely cover his mouth. He wrapped more duct tape around the man's arms and lower legs for good measure.

As Jaime stood there trying to figure what to do next, a voice behind him interrupted, "Now what the hell have you done to my friend Richard?"

Looking at the bound man, he said, "Richard, looks like this youngster's got the drop on you. Nice buns, Rich."

With a grip of unbelievable strength, the man grabbed Jaime by the shoulder. Without thinking, Jaime spun out of the man's grip and sprinted for all he was worth for the shelter of the forest. The man pulled his pistol from the holster on his left hip and turned to fire. To his amazement, the kid was out of sight. "Nobody can run that fast," he thought. Yet, the kid was nowhere to be seen.

The man took off running as fast as he could, which wasn't very fast. No sooner had he entered the stand of trees than he was lifted off his feet by a force across his chest that knocked him out instantly.

Jaime was still running like the wind. He finally thought he must have put enough distance between himself and his pursuer that he could risk looking back.

Nothing. Not a sign.

Where the heck had the man gone?

Jaime began slowly retracing his steps, staying in the shadows for fear that the man was waiting for him. He took a long time getting back to the point where the forest began.

There, on the ground, was a giant of a man, apparently out cold. Squatting next to him, calmly tying his hands and feet, with a large tree branch lying on the ground near her feet, was Becky, Becky the magnificent.

"What happened?" Jaime whispered.

"I came looking for you," she said quietly as she continued tying. "Just as I arrived at about this spot, I saw you heading this way like the devil himself was on your tail. It looked like a mountain was following you. Thank God, this branch was lying over there near that rock. I picked it up, waited until you shot past, then swung it right into this guy's sternum. I didn't wait to see for sure if he was knocked out, with him being so large. I grabbed my flashlight and gave him a good hard smack on the forehead, just in case."

"I've got another one tied up over there," Jaime informed her. When you get done tying this guy, let's roll him into those bushes, and then maybe the two of us can carry that other guy over here. Make sure this one is triple-tied and taped. He looks like he could break out of almost anything."

Chapter Fifty-seven

Hawkin had been doing some serious thinking. He didn't want to do anything to tip his hand before he knew the kids had arrived. But he also was thinking that if the kids were already on the scene, their efforts might be discovered at any moment. Once that happened, Hawkin's undercover plans would become much more difficult to execute.

After an hour of waiting, Hawkin couldn't sit still any longer. He grabbed a coil of rope and a roll of duct tape and went on the prowl. As he headed past the beige government-issue sedans, he was thankful that it was a dark night. He reminded himself that he couldn't risk firing his weapon.

Before long, he spotted one of Benson's men not far from the shed where he had seen the John Deere. It was a man named Geoffrey. Geoffrey was a particularly unlikable guy who informed everyone that he was somehow related to the royal family of Great Britain. He also made it clear that he was to be called "Geoffrey," not "Jeff."

"Hey, Jeff," Hawkin greeted in the friendliest tone he could muster. "How's things?"

"Geoffrey—it's Geoffrey. Is that too hard to remember?"

"Sorry, Jeff, just dropped by to see that you were okay."

"Like I need protection. I feel sorry for the fool who tries to mess with me. Jujitsu and all that stuff, you know. Far superior to all that karate and kung fu shit. Learned it in Great Britain. Have an aunt there who is a third cousin to the Duke of Winchester."

"What a coincidence," Hawkin mocked. "I have a cousin who used to dance to the 'Duke of Earl.' Maybe your aunt could teach my cousin some of that jujitsu stuff, eh, old chap?"

"Up yours," shouted Geoffrey, "You know, ever since you got here, I noticed a strange odor. Why don't you go kiss up to Benson for a while? Maybe he likes the smell of okra and collard greens and fried green tomatoes and all that other spook food."

"Yez, Massa," Hawkin groveled, "Ah speks ah betta move my wuthless black ass on down da road so's not to offend yo honky nose."

With that, Hawkin rolled his shoulders forward, bowed his head, and shuffled slowly past Geoffrey. "Yez, Massa, I'za goin', Massa." Just as he came abreast of the man, Hawkin shot his left arm out straight, his fingers firm but slightly curved. The tips of his fingers struck Geoffrey at the top of his sternum and slid powerfully up and into his windpipe.

If Hawkin had wanted to, he could have killed the man instantly with that blow, but he hit him just hard enough to cause him to gasp frantically for air. While the man did some sort of jujitsu tap dance around the forest floor, his eyes bulging, Hawkin managed to get a loop around his right wrist and tie his hands behind him. He then tied his ankles together and watched while Geoffrey tried desperately to maintain his balance and then fell slowly to the ground. Hawkin taped his mouth securely and pulled his ankles up against his butt, wrapping the rope around the man's upper and lower legs, making it impossible for him to straighten them.

Hawkin checked to make sure the man could breathe, although just barely. Then he dragged him into the forest and deposited him in a shallow ravine, covering him with a thick layer of dried oak leaves. Hawkin leaned down and taunted, "Yez, Massa, nex time you seez da queen, you tell her my black ass said 'howdy' — ya heah?"

Then Hawkin headed down the road toward the main entrance. He knew Benson usually stationed a couple of men at a point halfway between his office and the front gate. It was about half a mile from the farmhouse to Benson's office and another quarter mile to the main gate.

About a hundred yards after he passed Benson's office, a voice called out, "Who's that?"

"Hawkin," he answered. "Who's that?"

"Thornby. What brings you out tonight?"

"Just taking a bit of fresh air. Who else you got out here?'

"Just me and Rabinowitz."

Not particularly bad guys, in Hawkin's opinion. Probably just got in over their heads. They should have been with the Tobacco and

Firearms boys or some other less intense area of the government. He didn't wish to cause them any unnecessary pain. Luckily, he had planted one of his nerve gas bombs in the area, thinking this would be a likely spot to encounter some of Benson's men. He crouched near the trunk of a tree, acting like he was going to sit down on the ground. He took a deep breath and held it, covered his eyes with his left hand, and reached for the fishing line he knew was buried under the leaves near the base of the tree. After he yanked it firmly, he heard a small explosion, sort of like a muffled fire cracker. Five seconds later both men hit the ground. To Hawkin's surprise, he heard something else hit the ground a few feet behind him. He turned, still holding his breath, flipped on his penlight, and was amazed to find a third agent lying face-up on the ground.

What concerned him was that he hadn't heard the third man approaching. It made him wonder if the man had been sneaking up on him. Under these conditions, no one would come up on someone else without announcing himself. Unless, of course, he didn't want him to know he was there. Then Hawkin saw a pistol lying on the ground, inches from the man's right hand.

Looks like something's in the wind, he thought. Maybe the man Hawkin took down earlier had been missed. Maybe the kids had arrived already and started something. A man doesn't sneak up on another member of the same team with a pistol in his hand unless something's up.

Hawkin quickly tied and gagged the three men and carried them one at a time to an area where they would not likely be discovered. From what he knew of the nerve gas, they would be out for quite a while.

His next stop was the bunker. He thought that was a likely place for the kids to go upon arriving at the compound.

❦

After Chris bound and gagged the two men whose heads he had knocked together, he began backing away from the scene, watching to be sure none of the men on the farmhouse porch had spotted

him. He intended to head back in the direction he thought Jaime and
Becky would most likely be, to see if they had had any success.

He took three steps backward and ran into something—in fact,
two "somethings." They were breathing.

Before he could react, his arms were immobilized by two very
strong men. He was thrown hard on his back and pinned down.

The next thing he knew, a penlight shined on his face.

"Chris?" whispered a familiar voice.

"Clint?"

"Yeah."

Clint and Michael helped Chris to his feet. Chris could hardly
resist the temptation to shout out his joy. But knowing there were
agents near by, he simply wrapped his arms around Clint and held on
tight. Clint got the message.

"Sorry to be so hard on you," Clint whispered, "but we're unarmed, and we thought you were one of the government men. We
saw you walk past us about twenty minutes ago. At least I think it was
you. But we couldn't tell for sure. We waited for a while and then
decided it wouldn't hurt to eliminate one of the bad guys before you
kids got here. Boy, is your mom going to be glad to see you! Where
are the others?"

Chris explained what he knew, speaking in hushed tones. They
decided to head back to where the rest of the family was waiting in
the forest, near the tunnel entrance, to make sure they were all okay
and to let Maria know Chris was safe. Then they would try to find
Jaime and Becky.

By the time they got back to where the families were hiding,
Becky and Jaime were already there. They decided to split into pairs
and see if they could take out any more of the agents before the
alarm was given. So far, it appeared that nobody but the men they
had disabled knew of their presence. Either that or the bad guys had
decided to fight back quietly. In any event, they would proceed with
extreme caution. The teams were: Jaime and Becky, Clint and Maria,
Michael and Sarah and, the threesome of Chris, Tim, and Gail.

As the teams headed out into the darkness, Chas was busy in the attic working on his bindings and thinking some brand new thoughts.

Hawkin entered the bunker. All was quiet. He stopped for a while, not moving, listening for any sound.

Nothing.

As he circled around the spaceship toward the entry hatch, he suddenly caught a whiff of the unmistakable smell of a weapon. The combination of gunpowder, Hoppe's Number Nine solvent, and gun oil was a smell Hawkin had known for decades. He had encountered that scent on his many hunting trips with Grampa. During the war and later in his months of searching for his little brother, Mikey, in the jungles of Vietnam, he was accustomed to field-stripping and cleaning his weapons daily. He had learned to associate those smells with the fine working condition of his rifles and pistols.

It was a comforting smell, bringing him the same sense of security he felt when he was on patrol and would reach down occasionally and pat his sidearm holster. For just an instant before his hand made contact with that holster, he would be struck with a slight fear that his pistol wouldn't be there. But there it was, always. And even though he normally had his AR-15 assault rifle, that pistol was his weapon of choice for close-in combat.

Right now that old familiar smell didn't bring him any comfort. He hadn't cleaned his own weapon for several weeks, so he knew it wasn't likely the source of that aroma, which meant there probably was another weapon nearby, too close for comfort.

He instinctively turned and stepped backward until his back was against the spacecraft. At the same time he removed his pistol from his shoulder holster. He saw nothing suspicious—although, as dark as it was in the bunker, that wasn't very comforting.

The smell was growing stronger.

Hawkin considered turning on his flashlight but decided that he was safer in the dark. He crouched down in an instinctive attempt to make himself a smaller target. The smell was so strong that he guessed its source was within a few feet. He looked frantically to both sides and still saw nothing.

As he looked to his left again, bringing his nose within inches of the craft, he realized that the smell seemed to be coming from the spaceship. He placed his nose closer to the side of the ship, still looking as much as he could for some sign of movement. It became obvious that the spacecraft, in fact, was what had been giving off that familiar aroma.

What the hell was that all about? Hawkin relaxed a little and let out a sigh. *Okay, you crazy piece of hardware, what are you trying to tell me now?* Maybe it was a warning that he was about to encounter an unfriendly weapon.

Hawkin tensed, his senses alert once again. He decided that he'd much rather be inside the spaceship. Focusing his attention, he pictured the hatch opening, relaxed as best he could, and tried to be joyful—no easy task under these circumstances.

Nothing happened, he still had too much fear that the hatch wouldn't open.

Then he reasoned that the power of the mind was related to a combination of will power and faith. If he was low on faith at this moment, he thought he should try to boost his will. A wild idea came to him. He focused on the hatch opening with all his might, while at the same time picturing a hot, steaming slice of the craft's version of Mom's homemade apple pie with vanilla ice cream.

"Click." "Whir." "Thunk."

Peaceful, pale blue light flooded the bunker.

As Hawkin stepped onto the ramp, he heard sounds behind him. He moved up the ramp quickly and into the control center. He was just about to will the hatch to close when he felt the unmistakable coldness of steel press against the base of his skull.

"Lose the weapon," a somewhat shaky voice commanded. Hawkin didn't drop his pistol.

"Be careful with that thing," warned Hawkin, "You don't want to do something we'll both regret."

"I won't regret anything," the other man declared. "Now, drop that pistol."

Just then they heard footsteps. Whoever was out there was already approaching the ramp. It was too late to close the hatch.

Hawkin countered, "Some very bad guys will be on that ramp in a few seconds. They're going to see you holding a gun against the head of someone they think is on their side. Draw your own conclusions, but do it damn fast."

"What do you want me to do?"

"Trust me," urged Hawkin. "Stand there, and they'll kill you. Shoot me, and they'll do the same."

Hawkin's words made sense.

Hawkin turned around and faced his opponent for the first time. He couldn't believe his eyes. It was Daryl Harrington.

"Holy shit!" Hawkin exclaimed. "What the hell are you doing here?"

"Do you know me?" Harrington asked.

"Does the name *El Jefe* mean anything to you?"

"Holy shit!"

"Holy shit is right. Hand me that pistol quickly so those clowns coming up that ramp will think you're my prisoner."

Harrington lowered the pistol. Hawkin took it from his hand.

"Trust me," Hawkin reassured him.

Harrington raised his hands and folded them behind his head. Hawkin took care to snap the clip a quarter inch out of the pistol handle and yank back the slide, ejecting the formerly chambered round into a corner of the control room. As reliable as he knew safeties to be, something about his years of training couldn't tolerate a chambered cartridge being aimed at someone he wanted to keep alive. There was always the possibility of mechanical failure. That was no longer a factor when the chamber was empty.

Hawkin wondered if the two men now standing at the top of the ramp could have heard the ejected cartridge striking the floor. He now had one pistol in each hand. Not hard to explain.

"What the hell is this?" asked one of the men.

"This," responded Hawkin "is a spaceship. And this young man is an innocent civilian who just happened upon the fact that our illustrious government, or at least some of its employees, have hidden its existence from the public for the past three decades."

The two men began walking slowly around the control room, obviously amazed at what they were seeing. "I'd like to fly this baby," one of them fantasized.

"The pilot's briefing manual is in compartment 7-D," came a voice from somewhere.

"What's that?" queried the other man.

"Just a talking spacecraft," replied Hawkin, "probably a lot more intelligent than any of us."

"Wow!" exhaled one of the men, as the two newcomers stood mesmerized by the instrument panel.

Hawkin stepped up behind the two men, pressed one pistol into the back of each of them and ordered, "Gentlemen, please lay your weapons gently on the floor and step slowly back toward me."

"What's this all about, Hawkin?" the taller man asked. "You're supposed to be on our side."

"The only side I'm on, officially," responded Hawkin, "is that of the President of the United States. I'm afraid I'm going to have to restrain the two of you until a few things get settled. No harm will come to you as long as you follow my orders. In fact, I suspect that your chances of ending up in a federal prison will be reduced dramatically if you're tied up here in this craft instead of getting involved in the fracas that is about to occur outside."

"Find me something to tie these gentlemen up with," Hawkin said to Harrington.

Immediately a list of items flashed on one of the overhead monitors, with directions as to where each could be found. Included on the list were ropes of various sizes and materials, duct tape, several gauges and types of wire, bungee cords of assorted lengths, packing tape of four different widths, and a notation at the bottom that read, "For additional items, press control-F7 or say 'more items' in a neutral voice."

Harrington retrieved two rolls of duct tape and a length of quarter-inch nylon rope.

In record time, the two agents were tied, gagged, and secured in a small room. The gags were not absolutely necessary, considering the thickness of the walls of the room. But Harrington was concerned that the agents might decide to use their voices to activate some magical function of the spacecraft to set themselves free. So he took the added precaution. He informed them that someone would be sent to get them when things outside were under control. He then expressed his desire that the door to the sleeping quarters, where the agents would spend the next few hours, be locked. Immediately he heard a bolt slide into the locked position. He picked up the agents' pistols from the floor and stashed them in a storage cabinet.

Hawkin asked the spacecraft's intelligence if it could erase any memory of the craft's existence from the minds of the two agents they had just captured. The response was affirmative. Hawkin made a mental note to erase any memory of this incident from the minds of the captives when he released them later.

Then he took the two radios that had been clipped to the agents' waistbands, handed one to Harrington, and said, "You'll notice that these radios have two channels. Both of these radios are set on channel one. I assume that the head man, Benson, and all of his soldiers are tuned to that channel. I'll leave one radio here with you, set to channel two. I'll carry the other. I'll use it to contact you on channel two and to listen in to Benson and his gang on channel one. Even though I doubt that any of his men are listening on channel two, we should be aware that they might be. We'll have to be careful not to give them any information that would be to their advantage, especially anything that would help them lock onto our positions."

Hawkin and Harrington returned to the control room for a brief discussion.

Hawkin began, "I am on special assignment for the President, looking into the disappearance of several soldiers who were shipped out of Vietnam but never arrived in the States.

"My search for my brother Mikey led me to documents indicating that thirteen soldiers had been flown out of Hanoi and were never heard from again. I believe Mikey was among those soldiers.

"I began to suspect that several high-ranking CIA officials were involved in the situation. I met with a long time friend of mine who is a member of the Joint Chiefs of Staff. We decided that the matter was important enough to warrant a meeting with the President. The

President was thankful for our discretion and commissioned me to pursue the matter to completion. He opened many doors that ordinarily would have been unavailable to me.

"During my investigation, I formed relationships with several computer hackers and utilized their skills to help me locate a deeply buried file. I took great care to assure the integrity of the group. None of the members knew the real purpose behind our activities. I suspect they thought it was just for fun. You joined us just before the file was discovered.

"It was through one of those doors opened by the President that I became aware of the existence of the top secret file on the farmhouse incident. By a most amazing coincidence, this happened at about the same time that your hacking was leading you down a parallel corridor toward the same file.

"I was hesitant to attempt to open the file without informing my friend in the Joint Chiefs of Staff and the President. I assumed that the file probably was being carefully monitored. I didn't want to tip my hand too early.

"As I sat at my computer considering the alternatives, I was shocked to observe information being relayed to a computer station in the CIA system, informing someone that that top secret file was in danger of being compromised. I realized that someone else was coming perilously close to finding the file's hiding place.

"It took me considerable effort to discover your identity. I expected that my search would lead to some foreign government operative. I could hardly believe my monitor when it indicated that the culprit was a decoding employee in a cubicle fourteen stories underground. After considering all of the circumstances, I concluded that the resident of that cubicle was more likely a very lucky—or perhaps unlucky—amateur hacker rather than a mole under the direction of some terrorist organization.

"I was even more astonished to discover that the decoding employee was a member of my very own group. Then I remembered that you worked for the CIA, a fact I had discovered when I had done my character check on you earlier.

"I contacted you through the Internet, using a circuitous path intended to prevent anyone from discovering that we had ever been in contact. This, you will recall, is when we linked our computers with the Lap Link and discovered the contents of that file.

"I was deeply concerned that you might be in danger of being terminated by whoever was monitoring that file. So I did my best to guide you out of danger while not revealing my identity or my link to the President. I was still determined to get to the bottom of the disappearance of those Vietnam soldiers and to find Mikey.

"Once I was sure you had safely escaped from the building, I breathed a little easier."

"But, how did you know I had escaped?" asked Daryl.

"I was waiting near the parking lot, watching your vehicle. I was able to obtain your license number from the Department of Motor Vehicles by simply hacking into its computer system. I then located your car in the parking lot and performed a cursory inspection to satisfy myself that it hadn't been wired with a bomb. I waited some distance from where you were parked until I saw you emerge from the service door and get into the car.

"After that, I followed you to the various places you visited as you prepared to take on your presumed pursuers. I must say that you did a masterful job.

"I observed you withdrawing funds from your bank. I was there when you collected the components of your mini-arsenal. I watched in amazement as you switched the license plates and VIN numbers on the Jeeps. I was most impressed with your knowledge and thoroughness.

"At the time of my last contact with you, I was convinced that you were on your way to safety. I never considered the possibility that you would be crazy enough to go to the farmhouse compound."

After concluding his story, Hawkin turned in his chair and faced the main control panel and monitors. He stretched his arms into the air and took a deep breath. The long sleeves of his shirt slid down to his elbows, revealing two tattoos that Daryl had seen once before. One read, "Proud member of the United States Navy," the other "For my brother Mikey. Get us the Hell out of Vietnam."

Daryl knew he was in the presence of a great man.

Hawkin spun his chair around to face Daryl once again. "One of my concerns is that I'm going to have to go out there and help your friends win the battle of their lives, against almost impossible odds. I'm probably the best chance they have, and they don't even know I exist. When I reach them, they're going to think I'm one of Benson's men. I just hope they don't kill me before I get a chance to explain. And, even if I can talk fast enough, they'd be crazy to believe me. This is definitely going to be an exciting night!"

# Chapter Fifty-eight

The nine sat huddled silently in the darkness. Each now had a weapon, and each team had a radio, thanks to Chris, Becky, and Jaime, who had taken several pistols and radios from the agents they had captured.

Michael quietly instructed Gail, Sarah, and Maria on the basics of using a pistol. Sarah had done quite a bit of target shooting in the early years of her marriage to Michael, and Becky's dad had given her some instruction on the use of weapons. What Maria lacked in experience, she more than made up for in attitude. Gail was a little shaky about the prospect of shooting someone, but she promised she would be all right.

Clint cautioned, "You don't want to be debating whether or not you're going to pull that trigger when some bad guy has you in his sights. Everyone needs to decide right now that this is a fight for our lives and all the old rules about compassion have to be suspended until the battle's over."

Even as he spoke those words that he had heard so many times from his military commanding officers, he knew in his heart that love and compassion were appropriate under all circumstances. Deep inside, he was certain that the others knew that, too. Still, he didn't want any of these fine people to get killed while they wrestled with a moral issue. The real problem with this kind of dilemma is that war, no matter how one looks at it, just doesn't make any sense.

They agreed on their assignments.

Jaime and Becky would go after the guards they assumed were posted at the back gate. That was the gate they had gone through the night they had left the compound with Benson's men hot on their trail. Then they would follow the fence that ran from that gate to the front gate, the one they had come through the first night they had arrived at the farmhouse. They expected to find a couple of guards at each gate and, maybe, one or two more in between.

Michael and Sarah took responsibility for capturing the three guards on the porch of the farmhouse.

Clint and Maria would head down through the forest paralleling the dirt trail that ran from the farmhouse, past the barn and Benson's office, to the main gate. This trail was patrolled by Benson's men, so Clint thought they likely would encounter a few of them and, it was hoped, put them out of the action.

They decided it would probably be a waste of manpower to send anyone to check the ridge the kids had come over earlier. They hadn't encountered anybody up there and assumed that no guards were there now, especially since Benson probably considered that area inaccessible. So it was decided that Tim, Chris, and Gail would follow the course Jaime and Becky had explored earlier, heading behind the farmhouse, around the porta potty where Jaime had surprised the squatting agent, and then over to Benson's office, where they hoped to capture Benson himself. They then planned to join Clint and Maria to assist with what they suspected might be heavy traffic on the road from the farmhouse to the main entry.

Tim crawled over to where Sarah was sitting on the ground and hugged her warmly. "Be safe, my warrior Mom."

Jaime sat quietly, holding Becky's hand, wishing there were some way she wouldn't have to face the terror to come. If it hadn't been so dark, he would have seen a look on Becky's face that would have assured him that Becky was going to be just fine.

Becky was having a silent talk with her Magical Friend.

Chris leaned against a granite boulder, looking up at the few stars
that found their way through the thick tree branches overhead. He was
involved in a silent conversation of his own with Great-Grandfather.
*If you and I can whip a crazed grizzly and a handful of furious wolves, we
certainly ought to be able to handle a few dozen civilized American citizens,
however misguided. If you're not too busy up there sharing belly laughs with your
friends in the spirit world, my friends and I could certainly use a little help.*

Sarah was worrying about her boys. She was worried about Michael,
too, but he was a powerful and experienced man. Tim and Jaime were
just boys. What did they know about combat? Somehow, she knew that
Michael would make it. But what about those kids, her sweet babies?
Tears welled up in her eyes. *Oh God, don't let them hurt my boys.*

She crawled to where Jaime was sitting. She put her arms around
him and took Becky's hand in hers. Jaime could feel his mom trembling as she sobbed silently.

"It'll be okay, Mom," he soothed while brushing her beautiful
hair back from her face. He held her head against his chest. "It'll be
just fine."

Becky touched Sarah's cheek. The three sat in silence, swaying
back and forth.

Tim sat with his arm around Gail's shoulder, sending her some
of his courage.

Chris sat alone, remembering that it was just one night before
his planned date with Wendy. Obviously, he wouldn't be able to keep
that appointment now. He was thankful he had left a cell-phone message with the bartender. If Wendy showed up and asked for him, the
bartender was to tell her that Chris had been detained and ask her to
leave her telephone number with him.

*Chris, you crazy Indian. You're probably going to be dead by tomorrow
night. And that sweet woman is going to be waiting for a call that never comes.*

He thought for a few minutes.

*What do I mean, 'dead'? If only Great-Grandfather could hear me now!
No, I'm going make it out of this in one piece. I've got way too much to live for
now. Besides, Tama must be wondering if I'm ever going to come get him. That
magnificent beast saved my life. The least I can do is ride off into the sunset on*

him with that gorgeous young woman by my side. Yes, Christopher, you've got a
whole lot to live for. Now let's find out what you're made of.

"Time to go," Clint announced. He took Maria's hand and led her in the direction of the path they planned to follow through the forest. In her other hand Maria held a Glock 45, pointed at the ground as Clint had instructed her. It had never occurred to Maria that she might be called upon someday to kill someone. Now the idea was a lot more terrifying than she would have imagined. It seemed almost inevitable, and that inevitability, falling just short of certainty, made her tummy tighten and her heart beat uncommonly fast.

As Clint and Maria left, the others were busy strapping on their backpacks.

The part of the forest where the family had gathered was separated from the rest of the forest by a small, open area through which ran the dirt road that connected the farmhouse with Benson's office and the main gate. Just as Clint and Maria were about to step into that open area, they heard footsteps. Clint pulled Maria to a halt inside the shelter of the trees.

Two men were running up the road toward where Clint and Maria were hiding. Obviously in a big hurry, one was about twenty feet behind the other. They each appeared to have a pistol in their hands, although it was difficult to be sure in the dark and at that distance.

The one in the lead shouted to his companion, "Well, Jerry, looks like the action's about to start. Benson sent several men out to relieve the guards. Three came back, saying the men they were to relieve were nowhere to be found. Benson says we shouldn't use the radios. He's afraid some of our radios may have fallen into those kids' hands. Why don't you go on up ahead and alert the men at the north gate? I'll head over to warn the men patrolling the west fence-line. Hank is already on his way to tell the guys up at the farmhouse. Benson wants to be sure those hostages are still inside that building."

Clint whispered to Maria, "Go find Michael and Sarah and tell them they have to stop the guy who's on his way to the farmhouse. They'll never have a chance once those men on the porch are informed there's trouble on the way. Tell them the agent they have to intercept is named Hank. Be careful. Come back here as soon as you can, but stay under cover of the forest."

"You be careful," Maria whispered. She squeezed Clint's hand and headed back to where they last saw the others.

Clint let his backpack slip silently to the ground. He removed a length of nylon rope and stuffed it into the front of his shirt. He waited until the men were about twenty yards past him, then stepped out onto the road and began running toward them. Before the men could turn around in response to Clint's footsteps, he shouted, "Hey, Jerry, I got a message from Benson."

"Who's that?" shouted the man named Jerry as the two men came to a halt.

In a couple more seconds, Clint was within ten feet of the first agent. Instead of slowing, as the agents had expected, Clint put on a burst of speed, lowered his shoulder, and slammed it into the first man's thigh. The man screamed and crumbled, grabbing futilely for his raging quadriceps, which felt as if it was going to tear loose from the tendon.

The impact served to bring Clint to an abrupt halt only a few feet beyond where the agent's body had landed. Clint spun around and grabbed the screaming agent who was so focused on his cramping muscle that he was not even aware he had dropped his pistol. Clint held him by the collar, using him as a shield.

Clint continued to hold the man with his left hand. With his right he aimed his pistol at the other agent's chest.

The other man moved his pistol back and forth, trying to get a clean shot at Clint around his partner's body. He finally realized that any shot he might take could result in no more than a flesh wound to Clint while undoubtedly inspiring Clint to blow him away.

"Drop it," Clint shouted.

The man looked down the barrel of Clint's pistol and decided not to be a hero. As soon as the pistol hit the ground, Clint instructed the man to take five steps backward and lie face down on the ground with the top of his head pointing away from Clint. He did.

Clint dropped the man he had been supporting to the ground and immediately rendered him unconscious with a blow to the back of his head with the butt of his pistol. He kept a careful eye on the other man, knowing that he likely had a backup weapon under his shoulder or strapped to his leg.

"Make one move," Clint warned, "and there'll be a second hole in your back side." He ordered the man to put both hands behind his back and quickly tied his hands with the rope that he removed from his own shirt. He pulled the man's legs up to within a few inches of his wrists and secured them in a manner that would allow for virtually no movement.

Then he ran to his backpack, took out another length of rope and a roll of duct tape, strapped on the backpack, and walked over to the two helpless men. He taped the mouth of the agent who still enjoyed the benefit of consciousness. Then he tied and taped the unconscious man. He carried them, one at a time, into the forest and deposited them in a thick stand of scrub oak.

Bending down, Clint told the agent that if he was a good boy and just lay there quietly until it was all over, Clint would do what he could to see that the agent didn't end up in the gas chamber along with the person who had orchestrated this entire disgusting mess. He told the agent that he likely had no idea of how much trouble he was in.

"If I see you again before the shooting's over," Clint threatened, "you'll fry with the rest of them."

The man nodded his assent with surprising enthusiasm.

Clint walked back to the road, found the pistols lying in the dirt, and put them in his backpack. Then he ran back to get Maria, praying she would be there. He noticed a sliver of moonlight cracking over the ridge of the mountain. *Damn.*

Michael was sprinting toward the path that led from Benson's office to the farmhouse, having left Sarah behind in the forest. He didn't like the idea of leaving her alone, but he had to try to head off the agent Maria had told him was named Hank. He hoped to catch him some distance from the farmhouse so the men on the porch wouldn't be aware of their presence. He was winded from running with the heavy backpack.

By the time Michael reached the path, the moon was rising over the mountains. He was relieved that he could not see Hank between himself and the farmhouse. *He must still be on his way.* Michael headed down the trail toward Benson's office.

As Michael rounded a curve, the moonlight revealed a portly man coming slowly toward him, about fifty yards away. Michael thought he had come far enough down the trail that the men on the farmhouse porch wouldn't see or hear them. He started running toward Hank at a medium pace. As Michael approached, it became obvious that the obese agent was struggling for breath. Before he had a chance to notice Michael, Michael shouted, "Hey, Hank, Benson sent me after you. Wants you back in his office on the double."

Before Hank had time to realize that Michael was coming from the wrong direction to be bringing a message from Benson's office, Michael was within ten feet of him. By the time the man concluded that something was wrong, Michael had reached him, spun him around, and placed his pistol firmly against the man's ribs, just below his armpit.

The man instinctively reached for the pistol in his shoulder holster and hesitated. "I wouldn't if I were you," Michael whispered. "By the time you could get your hand on that piece and remove it from its hiding place, the bullet from the 44 Magnum cartridge that's resting about eight inches from your heart will have made its way through your ribs, your heart, and your lungs. Hardly worth the risk. Especially when you consider that the alternative is just a few hours' rest in the forest while my friends and I are busy rounding up your associates. Understand?"

The man nodded.

Removing a Smith and Wesson 357 Magnum revolver from the man's holster, Michael walked him into the forest. Then he proposed, "We can do this the easy way or the hard way. It's all up to you. If you'll kindly lie face down on the ground, place your hands together behind your back, and allow me to tie them, all will be well. Otherwise, I'll have to crack your skull with the butt of this pistol."

Hank knelt and lowered his upper torso slowly to the ground. But the hands didn't appear behind his back as Michael had ordered.

More deftly than Michael would have given him credit for, the man rolled over on his back, revealing a Derringer, of all things, in his right hand. The bullet from that civilized looking little weapon tore a hole in the flesh that covered the left side of Michael's rib cage and glanced off one of Michael's ribs, taking a substantial chunk out of Michael's left latissimus dorsi and pushed him back with surprising force.

Michael spun around to his left, partly from the impact of the bullet and partly from instinct. As he completed a three-hundred-sixty-degree turn, he managed to bring his right foot up high enough to make solid contact with the Derringer in Hank's hand. The pistol flew some distance into the forest and hit a tree trunk. Later, Michael thought how strange it was that he would have noticed such an insignificant detail as the sound of that pistol hitting a tree trunk, especially after a hole had been torn in a part of his body that he considered to be of great value. Besides, he was still spinning somewhat out of control.

At the end of a second complete turn, Michael bent forward and brought the butt of his pistol down firmly on the center of Hank's forehead. Hank's eyes crossed slightly, then closed.

For the first time, Michael felt the pain from the bullet holes in his torso. He was dizzy, partly from the quick double spin he had done, mostly from his body's natural reaction to having a foreign object pass through an area not designed to easily accommodate such an event. He had to force himself to remain standing upright but decided it was extremely important to secure Hank before he regained consciousness.

Michael considered whether the report from that little Derringer could be heard clear up at the farmhouse or down at Benson's office or by one of Benson's goons passing by, for that matter. He decided to secure Hank with all due haste.

Then Michael dragged him into the forest, not an easy task considering the tremendous pain that was beginning to erupt in his left side.

As soon as he had hidden Hank adequately, he examined his wound as well as he could in the darkness. Surprisingly, he wasn't bleeding too badly. He held his left arm firmly against his rib cage, attempting to slow whatever bleeding was taking place. He started back into the forest, heading toward the place where he had left Sarah.

When he got there, Sarah was nowhere in sight. He searched the area for a quite while, to no avail. He walked to the edge of the forest and stepped out a few feet onto the path that connected the farmhouse and Benson's office. This was close to the spot where he first had come out of the forest and onto the trail that had led him to Hank. He looked down that path in the direction of Benson's office but saw nothing.

When he turned around, he felt like he was moving in slow motion. Even before his eyes came to rest on the front porch of the old farmhouse, he knew instinctively what he was about to see. There on the porch, tied to a pillar between two men, was Sarah. His Sarah! The words "God, no!" formed on his lips. He trapped those words in his mouth, knowing that if those men spotted him, he would have no chance whatsoever of rescuing her.

The men were taunting her. They apparently were drunk.

Michael stood there, paralyzed.

With her beautiful hair blowing in the breeze and the moonlight shining on her face, Sarah looked like an angel. In that moment, Michael knew those men were in this thing way over their heads. They had messed with Michael's Sarah. There would be hell to pay.

Michael slipped quietly into the shadows, barely aware of the wound throbbing in his side.

 # Chapter Fifty-nine

Chris stood perfectly still, his back against a pine tree, the palm of his right hand pressed against the trunk inches from his right thigh. His left hand held his 9 millimeter, pointed skyward, just to the left of his head. He had taken off his backpack seconds earlier and dropped it silently to the ground. All around him was darkness, the moonlight blocked by a canopy of branches and leaves.

Tim and Gail were several yards to his left, silent. Perhaps they had heard it, too, footsteps, about twenty yards behind them, at least two, maybe three men.

It was too late to try to communicate with his friends. Chris had no choice but to remain silent and hope that Tim and Gail knew all was not well.

The footsteps were closer now, ten feet at most. Chris's breathing was shallow. A bead of sweat trickled down his right cheek and fell from his chin.

Then he saw movement to his left, barely discernible in the darkness. Chris didn't dare turn his head. He faced straight ahead, moving only his eyes. He stopped breathing.

There was a movement to his right. Chris's eyeballs quickly moved from left to right and back. There were two men, both facing forward. Apparently they hadn't noticed Chris yet. Both stood still, as if listening for a sound. Chris closed his eyes, as if this would make the men go away. *Please keep moving. Don't notice me.* But how could they not? He was able to see them, so they must be able to see him. His only hope was that they were looking so intently straight ahead that they would ignore any slight input from their peripheral vision, especially if he stayed perfectly still.

Light suddenly fell on Chris's eyelids. He opened them slowly. Moonlight. Grandmother moon had moved to the west just enough to allow a thin shaft of light to filter through a tiny opening in the canopy. Moonlight on Chris's face. *No! No!* He moved his head back slightly, pressing it hard against the tree trunk, trying to elude that telltale shaft of light.

A flicker to his right, moonlight reflecting off of blue steel, a cold hardness against his cheek, another drop of sweat fell from Chris's chin.

"Drop the weapon," ordered the voice to Chris's right. The man to his left pulled the Beretta from Chris's hand.

"We know you're out there," shouted the man to the left. "We've got your buddy. Come out now, hands raised, or he'll be your former buddy."

"Don't do it!" shouted Chris.

The man on his right rotated around in front of Chris, pressing his pistol against the bridge of Chris's nose.

"You've got ten seconds to make your appearance or I squeeze this trigger." Silence, a long and tense silence.

A loud thud.

The man in front of Chris crumpled to the ground, his forehead coming to rest against Chris's left knee.

Footsteps. Someone running through the trees about twenty feet in front of Chris, from left to right. The man to Chris's left squeezed off three rounds. One struck a tree just behind the runner. The second ricocheted off a boulder. The third managed to elude all solid objects in the vicinity and came to rest in the dark, damp earth of the mountainside.

As the last round cleared the end of the gun barrel, Tim's right shoulder made powerful contact with the gunman's left thigh, just above the knee, instantly shattering the ligaments that formerly had connected the man's upper and lower leg bones. Simultaneously relocating the man's kneecap to the right side of his knee joint, the impact caused pain beyond description. The man's scream echoed through the forest and off into the distance.

Chris quickly retrieved the guns of both downed men, as well as his own. Tim pulled his weapon from his waistband, surprised that it was still in place after the brutal impact, and held it to the head of the man he had just disabled. "Don't make a move," he commanded.

Frisking the unconscious man at his feet, Chris found a backup weapon strapped to his lower leg, a Smith and Wesson 38 Special. Chris placed it in his back pocket.

Tim searched the man who was moaning loudly on the ground in front of him. He found a large, double-bladed knife in a scabbard attached to the man's belt.

As Tim stood up, he felt something press against the small of his back.

"Drop the pistols, both of you," uttered a deep, calm voice with a heavy southern accent.

Damn professionals. They had a third man backing them up all along, lying back just in case they ran into trouble they couldn't handle, staying out of sight until just the right moment.

Tim dropped his weapon. "Shit," he muttered.

Chris tossed his Beretta to the ground a few feet in front of him. He reached slowly for the 38 Special in his back pocket, not sure he had a clear shot at the man without the risk of hitting Tim. He hesitated, then decided it was too risky. He could make out only about three inches of the man's right side sticking out from behind Tim. Even if he were lucky enough to hit the man without shooting Tim, the impact might cause the man to squeeze the trigger of the pistol he still pressed against Tim's back.

Moments later, Chris realized how glad he was for his decision.

An ear-piercing scream shattered the stillness of the forest, followed instantly by a sound one might expect to hear as a Louisville slugger makes violent contact with a yet un-carved Halloween pumpkin.

The man holding the pistol to Tim's back stood there for an instant, looking as if he were trying to remember something important he had forgotten to tell his wife before he had left for work that morning. The pistol in his hand pivoted around his trigger finger, coming to point harmlessly at the earth near his feet. Then he fell to the ground more quickly than one would expect from the force of gravity generated by a planet as small as the Earth, coming to rest in a pile of parts reminiscent of a stick puppet that had been suddenly abandoned by its puppeteer in mid-performance.

There, standing above the hapless gunman, stood Gail, brandishing a look of consummate triumph and self-confidence, the butt of the 44 Magnum that had been consigned to her, resting in a position where nobody could doubt that she was the cause of the gunman's untimely collapse.

Had there been a bit more light in that part of the forest, the other two members of that division of the home team might have seen Gail's eyes cloud over just before she buckled to the ground in a posture mimicking that of her recent victim.

By the time Gail regained consciousness, Tim and Chris had all three of the government agents securely bound, gagged, and stashed well out of sight.

"You were absolutely marvelous," Tim praised her. "If it weren't for you, we'd be the ones tied and gagged or, maybe, dead."

"That's for sure," Chris agreed. "You were unbelievable. Tim told me that was you running through the forest to distract the gunman so Tim could get a safe run at him. That took a lot of courage."

"Thank you," was all Gail could say.

"But I have to ask you." continued Chris, "Why in the world did you scream just before you clobbered that guy?"

"I don't know," she confessed. "I guess it was because that's how I saw them do it in the movies. Besides, when I used to go to Brad and Becky's karate tournaments, a lot of the people there would scream before they hit someone."

"Well, far be it from me to criticize the lady who just saved our lives," grinned Chris. "But may I suggest that the next time you're about to brain someone, you save the shouting until after he's out cold. That guy could have spun around and shot you before you ever had a chance to move."

"That makes sense," Gail admitted. "I was just so scared!" She began to cry. She started to shake violently.

Tim and Chris wrapped their arms around her. They held her for a while until she calmed down.

"You were great," Chris acknowledged.

"Amen," Tim added. "You can be on my team any day."

"By the way," Chris inquired, "what the hell caused that clown who had the pistol pointed at my very precious head to collapse?"

"That," Tim enlightened him, "was the result of a perfectly executed touchdown pass thrown by the finest quarterback in Franklin High football history. Only instead of the old pigskin, I used a small football-shaped rock. Actually, it was shaped more like a large russet potato, but I didn't have time to be choosy."

"Pretty slick," Chris observed. "But why didn't you use that same method for ridding us of that other desperado instead of employing your very effective knee-cruncher?"

"Because," Tim explained, "I couldn't find any more potato-shaped rocks that were big enough. Besides, they were too round. And, as Jaime will tell you, I can't throw a baseball for diddly."

Chris laughed and shook his head.

"We'd better get moving," urged Tim. "We're supposed to meet Clint and Maria down near Benson's office soon. I think we're a little behind schedule."

With that, Chris stuffed his backpack with the various weapons they had collected. They headed along the base of the mountain and past the porta potty, hoping to arrive at Benson's office on time.

About the time the first drop of sweat had been leaving the tip of Chris's chin as he stood between the two enemy agents, Jaime and Becky were approaching the first gate on their list of objectives. They had taken care to remain off the road and well into the forest. As they drew nearer the gate, they slowed their pace and inched toward that gate one hesitant footstep at a time, careful not to make a sound.

Although they were only about ten feet apart, they could barely see each other. The forest canopy was so dense that not a single droplet of moonlight could penetrate. Jaime was closest to the road, and Becky deeper into the forest. They were communicating only with hand signals, although that was mighty hard to do with no light filtering through the trees.

They arrived at the fence at the same time, about thirty feet to the right of the gate. They stood still for several minutes, trying to locate any guards. They saw nobody.

At first Jaime was relieved that he didn't see anyone. But on second thought, he decided he probably would be a lot happier knowing where the bad guys were. Maybe nobody was there. Then again, several agents could be surrounding them at this very minute. It felt spooky. Too quiet.

He heard Becky's breathing and turned to find that she had moved closer to him. He motioned for her to come even closer, and she stepped to within a few inches. He could smell her. Even after several days in the forest, she smelled sweet. He could see her silhouette but couldn't make out her features. He let his imagination fill in the details. Jaime removed the pistol from his waistband and gestured for Becky to do the same. She showed him that she had already done so. They both turned toward the gate, moving slowly and silently, Jaime in the lead.

He wondered how Mom and Dad were doing. He thought about Tim. A chill ran up his neck, a sure sign that someone in his family was into something intense. He sent out a silent prayer: "Please, my precious Force, don't let my family be harmed."

Becky was praying to the same energy, for her mom, Jaime, and all the others.

They were now only a few feet from the gate, barely inside the forest. Their next steps would take them into the open where they would be easy targets. After that, they would be exposed until they got about fifteen feet on the other side of the gate where the forest would hide them once again.

Jaime considered remaining in the forest on this side of the road, backtracking a ways and crossing where there wasn't so much exposure. But that could preclude an encounter with any guards that were supposed to be watching this gate. That might get them safely out of the area, but they would have no way of knowing whether the guards were, in fact, there. That would mean Jaime and Becky hadn't accomplished one of their assigned objectives—to either capture any guards or assure themselves that there were none in the area. He couldn't let the team down.

He wished he could cross the road by himself and send Becky on a safer route. But this was no time for an animated discussion, and Jaime had learned that any suggestion that Becky do less than what she considered her share would undoubtedly end up in an argument.

Jaime motioned for Becky to stay where she was within the forest. He stepped out of the shadows and into the moonlight. The moon was full now with no canopy above him. He listened as he took two more steps. He felt Becky inches behind him, so much for Becky staying in the forest.

He moved more quickly now, Becky close on his tail. The safety of the distant trees tugged at him mightily. Torn between the need to reach cover quickly and the need to move slowly and silently, a cold sweat registered on the back of his neck.

That chill again. Mom and Dad and Tim. Something was going on. Something he couldn't do anything about right now.

They moved slowly toward the relative safety of the forest, knowing that at this moment they were clear targets for anyone who might be aware of their presence, anyone who meant them harm.

After what seemed like an eternity, they made it back into the shadows. The patterns of dark and light made by the leaves and branches overhead moved slowly across their bodies and backpacks. A minute later they were again in relative darkness. Jaime let out a small sigh and motioned for Becky to take the lead, thinking that from this point on, she would be safer there.

He was wrong. They had barely moved into the forest when Becky stopped. She motioned to Jaime to stay where he was. Before proceeding, she thought, maybe they had better take a little more time to watch and listen to see if anyone was around. They crouched against the fence and scanned the area as best they could.

A wind began to stir in the trees. The sound was surprisingly loud in contrast to the silence. So much for hearing any movement. Both a curse and a blessing.

The wind increased. The movement of tree branches made eerie patterns of moonlight on the ground, opening up spaces in the canopy overhead.

For several minutes they crouched in the darkness, their legs burning. Becky stood up, wobbly on her feet. Jaime stood up, too. They turned and headed away from the gate in the direction of their next assignment, satisfied that they were alone. Perhaps Benson didn't think this gate was worth guarding.

Ten paces later, Becky's senses began screaming at her. Something was wrong, terribly wrong. She stopped. *What is it, my Magical Friend, what is it?* Her heart was beating wildly, she felt as if a wall were in front of her, trying to block her path. Her face flushed. Her throat grew dry. Bile began to form in her stomach. She thought she might vomit. *What is it?*

The wind increased, causing the trees overhead to sway violently. It seemed to be pushing them backward. They had to lean into the wind to keep their balance, while leaves and pine needles struck their faces. Squinting to protect their eyes, they covered their faces as best they could with their free arms.

Becky felt like something was trying to warn them.

She let out a gasp that was swallowed by the howling wind. She had stepped on something soft, something that moved. She stepped back quickly, bumping into Jaime. She looked into the darkness, wanting to run but afraid to turn her back on whatever was there.

She pointed her pistol in the direction of the moving thing on the ground. In an instant, the pistol was slammed out of her hand. Then something moved in front of her. It rose up, as if springing from the ground. It moved into the pattern of moonlight that was swirling furiously beneath the canopy. She began to discern its outline, then its features. She saw eyeballs, large, malevolent eyeballs.

Becky took another step backward. The eyeballs followed.

Jaime turned on his flashlight.

It was a man. And he had an AK-47 aimed at Becky's chest. Neither Becky nor Jaime had any idea what an AK-47 was. All they knew was that it was a weapon and that it was pointing at Becky.

The only thing Jaime could think to do was to reach around Becky's right side with his pistol and try to shoot the man before the man shot her. He remembered what Clint had said about not trying to decide whether or not to shoot an enemy when you're in the heat of battle. That decision had to be made before the action started. Jaime hadn't gotten around to doing that. He had to make the decision right now. But this was a human life. This person probably had a mom and a dad, maybe a wife and kids. But he was pointing his pistol at Becky.

Holding his shaking pistol, Jaime slipped his right hand around Becky's right side. He pointed it at what he thought would be the man's midsection, his flashlight still focused on the man. He felt the pressure of his finger on the trigger. Had he released the safety? He couldn't remember. He squeezed, praying that it wouldn't fire, that something, anything, would stop this insanity and save his beloved Becky without his having to take a human life. He increased the pressure on the trigger. *Please, don't let this man die. Please don't let Becky die.*

Jaime saw a fleeting flicker of light behind the man.

He squeezed the trigger with enough pressure to make his finger hurt.

Then it happened. A force sent Becky and Jaime reeling backward, knocking them to the ground. Had the pistol gone off? He didn't think so. But with the wind howling wildly, he couldn't be sure.

Jaime got to his feet and looked down at Becky, aiming his flashlight at her. No blood. Her eyes were open. She seemed okay, other than the look of terror on her face.

He helped her to her feet and pointed his flashlight in the man's direction.

The man lay on the ground, face down, not moving. The rifle lay beside him.

Jaime raised the beam of his flashlight.

There, behind the spot where the man on the ground had been standing stood another man, huge and with a serious look on his face and a scar on his cheek. But he didn't look threatening. He raised his enormous hands as if in a gesture of surrender. He had no weapon.

Jaime saw a tattoo on each forearm: "Proud member of the United States Navy" and "For my little brother Mikey. Get us the hell out of Vietnam."

In an instant the winds grew still.

Big John Hawkin had arrived.

Following her intuition, Becky stepped forward and extended her right hand. "I'm Becky. This is my friend Jaime."

"I'm John Hawkin. Your friend Daryl may have referred to me as *El Jefe.*

In unison, Becky and Jaime greeted him with, "Glad to meet you!"

Hawkin took out his flashlight and shined it on another agent, out cold on the ground. He explained that these men were supposed to be guarding the gate but apparently had decided to get some shuteye. Hawkin had happened upon them, sleeping, after he had Daryl in the bunker. He had just rendered the first man unconscious and was about to take care of the second when Becky stepped on him.

Before Hawkin could move, the man jumped up and trained his rifle on Becky. Hawkin couldn't make out exactly what was happening in the dark, so he had to move slowly. He flashed his penlight at the man for just a second to get his bearings, low enough so the man probably wouldn't notice the light. In that fraction of a second, Hawkin's trained eye noticed that the man, in his sleepy state, had forgotten to take off the safety of his AK-47.

At just about the time Jaime was wrestling with his moral dilemma, Hawkin clobbered the agent over the head, sending his massive body forcefully into Becky and Jaime. Had the safety been off, Hawkin's alternatives would have been severely limited. He probably wouldn't have hit the man on the head and risked having the rifle discharge from the force of the blow.

"You kids were damn lucky that I showed up here when I did and that the safety was on, mighty lucky."

"Thank you, my Magical Friend," Becky whispered.

"What?" asked John.

"Nothing."

Jaime turned Becky around and wrapped his arms around her.

Jaime and Becky still had to get down to the main entry gate to try to capture any of Benson's men stationed there. They quickly briefed Hawkin on their plans. He instructed them to monitor channel two on their radio in case he needed to reach them, but not to break the silence unless absolutely necessary. By his reckoning, a lot of Benson's men were still on the loose. Hawkin would continue to monitor channel one to see if he could pick up any information broadcast by Benson or his men.

After making sure that Benson's men were securely tied, Hawkin headed toward the farmhouse. As much as he wanted to stay close to Becky and Jaime, he needed to do some scouting if he was going to be as much help as possible.

Chapter Sixty

It took Becky and Jaime twenty minutes to work their way down to the main entry. By the time they got there, the moon was high in the midnight sky. The area surrounding the entry gate had only a few trees to provide cover, allowing the bright moonlight to flood the ground.

Becky and Jaime stood in the shadow of several jack pines near the fence line about fifty feet from the gate. Nobody was there, at least not as far as they could tell. They waited for several minutes, watching for some sign of movement.

Jaime began to step out of the shadows. Becky pulled him back by the belt loop of his Levi's. He glanced back to see her finger raised in front of her lips. Looking toward the gate, he saw nothing. He strained, trying to hear something. Becky's hand appeared within his peripheral vision, just above his left shoulder, her finger pointing toward the dirt road inside the gate.

Jaime's eyes followed where she was pointing, waiting, barely breathing, eyes straining against the contrast between the moonlit area and the darkness of the forest.

Becky moved forward a half step, pressing her chest against his back, her hand still resting on his shoulder.

"Look," she whispered, so quietly that Jaime couldn't tell if it was Becky's voice he was hearing or the sound of the wind sighing through the trees.

Jaime squinted, willing his eyes to see more than conditions would allow.

At first he thought it was the stub of a branch protruding from the trunk of a tree. Then it moved ever so slightly. Then it disappeared, as if receding into the trunk. Seconds later, the object reappeared. This time it came out of the shadows far enough that Jaime thought he could make out what it was.

The bill of a cap. Yes, if he used his imagination, it looked like the bill of a cap. A few seconds later he was able to make out the dome of the cap and the forehead that rested just beneath the bill, and a nose protruding just below the forehead, a nose he hadn't been able to see before. How had Becky been able to notice this so long before he did? And without anyone pointing it out to her? Probably because she wasn't being distracted as he was by the most beautiful breasts in the universe pressing against his back.

Better get serious. What else was out there that he hadn't seen, or that his eyes had seen but that hadn't yet registered in his conscious mind?

He grabbed Becky's left hand and led her deeper into the forest behind them. She followed silently, seeming instinctively to understand his plan.

They circled around and behind the owner of that telltale cap, keeping him in sight as much as visibility would permit and making a large enough arc to allow them to remain in back of and some distance from any other agents in the area. They moved slowly, taking care to step lightly until they were certain that each footstep landed on nothing that would crack or shatter under their weight.

Soon they were standing directly behind the man with the cap, about fifty feet away from him. The area they occupied was darker than the surrounding forest, which assisted in their passionate desire to remain undetected and at the same time aided them in spotting any nearby agents.

In minutes they located three more agents, four in all. They watched for several minutes until they were satisfied that there were no more.

The agents were separated from each other by about twenty feet. All were facing the road that led from the inner compound to the gate. Something was up. Had Benson been concerned only with keeping unwanted individuals out of the compound, he would have assigned one or two men to be stationed at the gate. With four men hidden in the forest at intervals, it seemed to Jaime that they were lying in wait for someone. He had to assume that Benson was now aware that the compound had been infiltrated and that these men had been instructed to capture anyone who wasn't a member of Benson's team.

What to do? Jaime and Becky were seriously outnumbered. The agents probably had superior weapons. They were highly trained. Although Jaime was a fast runner, he had absolutely no experience in these matters. Becky was trained in the martial arts, but very likely, so were the agents. Becky and Jaime had the element of surprise. They had to make their first strike a powerful one that would improve the odds a bit.

"We have to separate them," Becky thought. "Jaime and I might have a fighting chance against two of them, but not four." She took Jaime's hand and led him away from the agents far enough so they wouldn't be able to hear. Putting her mouth against his ear, she whispered, "I've got a plan."

He listened carefully as she continued, "The best chance we have is to separate those guys and take them on, one or two at a time. I'll try to get them to think I'm someone who just stumbled onto this place and needs help. I think I can get one or two of them to follow me away from the compound. I don't think they'll all come. They probably wouldn't leave the gate unguarded. If I can get a couple of them to follow me down the road far enough, you can be waiting to ambush them. If we pull it off quietly, we can come back here to take care of the others. Hopefully the wind will cover any sound. If the others do hear us, we stay under cover and ambush them, too."

Jaime didn't like the idea much, but he had nothing better to offer. He especially wasn't pleased that Becky was going to be the bait. She would be dangerously exposed.

"How do you expect to get them to follow you?" he whispered.

"My hunch," replied Becky, "is that these are the kind of guys who will decide this is an opportunity to get themselves laid. I should have no problem encouraging that notion. I just hope they don't all decide to rape me at the gate. One of them must be in charge. He will order some of them to stay and keep watch. He won't want to share one woman with three others. But he might decide to bring one other man along, especially if he thinks there's another woman with me.

Since we were down in the canyon below the gate the night we arrived, I'll be able to describe what's down there."

"I don't like it," Jaime murmured. "You're taking a big chance. Are you sure you want to do this?"

"I've already decided," Becky assured him. The tone in her voice, even at a whisper, told Jaime that there would be no talking her out of it.

They headed for the fence, crossing over it about a hundred yards from the gate, well out of sight of the agents. They paralleled the road for another hundred yards, then turned toward it. When they reached the road, the gate was around a corner and out of sight. Beside the road were three trees surrounded by a clump of bushes. The road was well lit by the moon. This was almost a perfect setup for an ambush. Jaime had a Glock 9 millimeter pistol taken from an agent they had captured earlier. Plus, he had his single-shot target pistol. That target pistol had two advantages: It made relatively little noise, and it was outrageously accurate.

"Good luck, Becky." He said, "Keep the safety off as you approach the gate, in case you need to use it quickly. When you come around that corner, heading towards me, distance yourself from the others as much as possible so I can get off a clean shot. As soon as you hear my pistol fire, get down and into the bushes as fast as you can. We don't want them grabbing you before I can disable them. I don't think I can bring myself to kill them unless I have to do it to save your life. I hope I'm a good enough shot to prevent a counter-attack."

"I won't be carrying my pistol," Becky countered. "They'll probably frisk me, and if they find a weapon, they'll capture me right then and there. I'll leave my pistol on the ground behind that tree on the other side of the road. Try to time your first shot to go off just as I approach the tree. As soon as I hear it, I'll dive behind the trunk, grab the pistol, and try to help."

"If there are two men, it will be better if I can disable both of them with my 22 instead of the 9 millimeter. Whoever they leave behind might hear the report from the larger weapon. There's a good chance they won't hear the 22, especially with the wind blowing down this canyon like it is. The problem is, it'll take me a couple of seconds to reload and get another shot off. Assuming the first man I hit is out of the game, we need to find some way to keep the other man from shooting me until I can make my second shot."

"If a second man gets off a shot or two, even if he doesn't hit one of us, the sound will be heard back at the gate," Becky observed.

"I've got another idea." said Jaime, "How about if I don't shoot anyone? How about if we hide your pistol behind that tree further down the road? You lead the agents beyond the place where I'll be hiding. You dive for your pistol at the same time I step out of the bushes. I'll be behind the agents with both pistols ready. If either of them goes for his gun, I'll shoot him before he can turn around. That should prompt the other man not to try anything. In the meantime, you will be behind that tree with your pistol leveled at the second guy. If we can pull that off, the only sound we have to worry about is the screaming of the injured man."

Becky agreed. "That sounds good. Only I'd suggest you don't come out from behind those trees. Remember, these are capable hombres. Don't underestimate them. They may have pistols in their hands, not their holsters. I'd feel a lot better if you had something solid between your body and anyone trying to put holes in you."

"Okay," conceded Jaime, "but, I won't move until you're safely behind that tree. Just count on the fact that they're probably not going to act like we imagine. They may be holding onto you somehow or have your hands bound, for that matter."

"If they do, I'll hit the ground, and you start blasting. Let's hope they'll be so surprised by your appearance that they won't have time to think of using me as a shield or shooting me. Let's hold thoughts of this thing working perfectly. Between my Magical Friend and your Force, we should be able to handle these guys just fine."

Becky took off her backpack and placed it out of sight behind the tree she hoped to use for cover. She took her hunting knife out of its leather sheath, then unbuckled her belt and let her jeans drop to her ankles. Jaime's eyes widened. She couldn't pull the jeans all the way off without removing her hiking boots, so she left them where they were. She used the knife to cut off the legs of her jeans half an inch below the crotch, then split them at the seams, pulled them away from her legs, and tossed them into the bushes.

"What in the world are you doing?" Jaime asked.

"Preparing the bait."

She wiggled back into the jeans, which were now a pair of short shorts. She reached under her blouse and performed some type of gymnastic marvel that Jaime couldn't follow, resulting in the magical appearance of her bra in her right hand. She tied the lower front corners of her blouse together, allowing her back and belly to remain exposed to the cool night air. Then, for good measure, she undid the top two buttons of her blouse, providing a clear view of the upper portions of her ample breasts as they moved up and down, tantalizingly, with each breath.

She smiled at Jaime. "I hope the boys back at the gate find this little display irresistible."

"Anyone who doesn't," Jaime laughed, "should be in intensive care."

Becky kissed him lightly on the forehead, then headed up the road. She stopped, turned around, walked back, and planted her lips squarely on his. She kissed him like he'd never been kissed before, not even by Julie Andersen, the undisputed best kisser in the eighth grade.

As soon as he got his breath back, Jaime said, "Good luck."

"Good luck to both of us," Becky echoed.

⊱ ⊰

Jerry Bledsoe was in a foul mood. He had been sitting and standing under the same tree for more than three hours. He was bored. *It sure as hell doesn't take four guys to guard one gate. Besides, what's the significance of this gate anyhow? We're out here in the middle of God-forsaken nowhere, babysitting a farmhouse full of civilians that don't look particularly dangerous to me. They don't appear to be the kind that would pose a threat to national security. Probably some personal matter involving some high-up desk jockey, something that shouldn't even involve the expenditure of public funds.*

He walked over to Peter Sitner, an agent he had met about ten years ago on a weapons bust involving some rag heads from Morocco. Peter was an okay guy, except that he had a nasty habit of humming the same tune over and over. He was humming it now, "The Tennessee Waltz."

"What's up?" whispered Peter as Jerry approached.

"Nothing," replied Bledsoe. "Just got bored as hell. I'm thinking of heading back to Benson's office to see what's going on. The word I got is that some kids invaded the compound and Benson's got a wild hair up his ass about it. I can't figure out what this damn farmhouse has to do with anything or why Benson would be concerned about a few kids, for that matter. Kids sure as hell can't do anything, at least nothing this group of derelict government spooks can't handle. Benson put Seaborn in charge here. Maybe I should ask him to be excused—tell him I got to go wee wee or something."

"He'd just tell you to go do it behind a tree and get back to your station," countered Sitner.

Bledsoe let out a grunt, designed to demonstrate his complete disgust with the entire situation. He turned back toward his position.

"What's that?" asked Sitner.

"What's what?" grumbled Bledsoe, pausing mid-stride.

"Listen," said Sitner.

Bledsoe stood there, hearing nothing but the wind in the trees. A minute later his ears picked up a faint sound that didn't seem like it belonged. Singing. It sounded like singing. Who would be singing around here?

It grew louder.

Hampton, an old-timer from somewhere down in Tennessee, appeared out of the darkness. "You guys hear singing?" he asked in his deep southern drawl, as if doubting his own credibility.

"Yeah," answered Sitner, "Maybe we should tell Seaborn. He's the head dude out here tonight."

The singing grew louder.

Bledsoe started to make out the words. Quizzically, he offered, "Comin' 'round the mountain?"—unclear whether that was a statement or a question.

"Comin' 'round the mountain?" Hampton repeated. "What in tarnation does that mean?"

"That means," said Bledsoe tersely, "that I think my ears are hearing someone singing 'She'll be comin' 'round the mountain'—only now it's 'She'll be drivin' six white horses,' if you can imagine that."

"What the hell?" Sitner exclaimed. The men could discern that it was coming from beyond the gate.

"Oh, we'll all have chicken and dumplings when she comes," the high-pitched voice rang out.

"It's either a woman," Bledsoe thought aloud, "or a man with his shorts cinched up a few notches too tight. Go get Seaborn," he ordered. "He should be about fifty yards down that way."

Hampton grumbled as he headed in that direction.

Bledsoe and Sitner moved quietly toward the gate. They stopped short, taking care to remain in the shadows.

It was a woman all right—a young woman. And in the bright moonlight it was immediately obvious that she was a mighty fine specimen of womanhood.

"Oh, we'll kill the old red rooster when she comes," the voice rang out. "Oh, we'll kill the old red...." She stopped singing mid-verse and came to a halt, apparently seeing the gate for the first time. She walked up to it, looking at it as if she hadn't seen a gate before. She placed both hands on the top rail and peered beyond the gate as if trying to adjust her eyes to the darkness beyond.

"Help you, miss?" Bledsoe offered as he stepped into the moonlight just a few feet from where Becky stood, gripping the gate with more intensity than was evident.

"Yikes!" screamed Becky, as she stepped back two paces. She stood still as Bledsoe approached the gate.

"You scared me half to death," gasped Becky. "I didn't think anyone was here."

"We're here," Bledsoe smiled.

"Oh, thank goodness," she said, letting out her breath. "I need some help. My girlfriend and I got stuck in the sand about a mile down this road. I had no idea where this road led, but it seemed to make a lot more sense to head up this way than to walk ten miles back to the last house we saw. What is this place?"

"Just a farm," said Bledsoe, as Hampton approached with Seaborn following.

"What's happening?" Seaborn asked, with an attempted tone of authority.

"Just a young lady looking for help," replied Bledsoe, his eyebrows raised and his eyes fixed intently on Becky's blouse and the treasures it barely concealed.

As Seaborn drew near, he got a good look at those long, shapely legs running from Becky's hiking boots to the newly tailored short-shorts. She smiled her most endearing smile and pivoted her shoulders slightly from left to right and back, using her best body language to feign helplessness.

"Could you gentlemen help a lady in distress?" she asked, as Sitner appeared out of the darkness.

That's all four. Like moths to a flame.

"What seems to be the problem?" asked Seaborn, losing not a single iota of his recently acquired air of authority.

"My friend and I got our little Jeep buried in the sand back there a ways. We need a couple of strong men to help get it back on solid ground," Becky implored, hoping she had adequately emphasized the word "couple." She certainly didn't want more men following her back to the trap than she and Jaime could handle.

"Does your friend look anything like you?" Sitner blurted out, his question fueled more by testosterone than common sense.

"Quiet!" snapped Seaborn.

"Honey," responded Becky, "my friend Natalie makes me look like a Boy Scout."

All four men smiled, each with his own thoughts, none of which had anything to do with government security or tactical procedures.

"We'll be glad to help," said Seaborn. "Bledsoe, you come with me. Hampton, you and Sitner look after things here while we're gone."

Hampton and Sitner let out a collective groan.

The two men climbed over the gate, one on each side of Becky. She headed down the road, her victims in tow. She thought about the fairy tale her dad had told her about the pied piper of Hamlin, who led the rats of that town to and over the edge of a cliff, using only the allure of his musical instrument.

"Do either of you gentlemen know 'The Red River Valley?'"

Jaime was trying to decide how best to disable whoever Becky lured into the ambush, without anyone getting killed. He had to inflict enough discomfort that they wouldn't be able to effectively shoot back. But he preferred not to involve any vital organs.

He considered the possibility that he might not have to shoot anyone. That notion gave him comfort. What if he got the drop on them from behind, and before they could decide what to do, they realized that Becky had them covered from the front? Whether they would surrender or "draw down"—as they say in the old cowboy movies—would depend, in Jaime's estimation, on whether they thought either Jaime or Becky had the guts to shoot. Perhaps that was a good reason to "shoot first and ask questions later"—as they also say in the cowboy movies. A man with a bullet in his flesh would probably be more inclined to think the person responsible for that annoying transgression was quite serious.

Mostly, Jaime wasn't sure he could do it. To shoot another human being didn't seem to be as easy as it looked in the Arnold Schwarzenegger movies, especially now that the anticipated incident was only moments away. Jaime's hands were shaking, and his mouth was dry.

Given Jaime's repertoire of available thoughts, the only thing that might bring him a bit of confidence would be a quick and sincere chat with The Force.

I've seen the awesome power of the God Force. I actually saw time stop and even move backward when Mortimer's life was in the balance. I know Jesus called on his father when circumstances required supernatural remedies. I know that Masters, for centuries, have spoken of and taught about The Force, even though they used many other names for it.

I know the power exists. I know it's always willing to help. I know that the moment I call upon it, it sends what I ask for without hesitation. The only factor determining whether my intention manifests in physical reality is whether I align my beliefs with my desires. So, Jaime me lad, just decide on how you want this situation to pan out, and then know with all your heart that the result will unfold just as you want it to.

He stood there, eyes closed, and pictured a solution to this situation that depended not one iota on physical reality or on his perception of physical reality, but only on his desired outcome, with the awesome, unlimited, power of The Force rearranging physical matter, in accordance with the laws of the universe, to produce the most satisfactory outcome possible.

Jaime saw Becky safe. He saw himself safe. He saw the bad guys rendered ineffective in their attempts to harm him or Becky. And he saw it all happening without unnecessary harm to anyone. He didn't decide on the details. He would leave that to an intelligence with a broader overview than he had at this moment. He pictured Becky laughing. He pictured himself laughing. He pictured all of his friends and relatives laughing. And, believe it or not, he pictured the bad guys laughing. It felt good.

He had no idea what he would do next. All he knew was that it would be all right.

He looked up the road to where Becky had disappeared earlier. There she was, his beautiful, wonderful Becky, skipping around the corner. He couldn't believe his eyes. She was skipping, a man on either side of her struggling to keep up. And she was singing. He could actually hear her singing "We're off to see the wizard."

Neither man had a weapon in his hand. *Thank you, my dear Force. Thank you, Becky.*

The men scurried along the road, kicking up dust. Becky skipped around them in lazy circles, the men obviously entranced. They couldn't keep their eyes off her. As her breasts bounced beneath her blouse, two pairs of eyes followed every movement. The men actually spun around as Becky skipped around them, careful not to miss an instant of the splendor that was Becky. They laughed, enchanted by her exuberance. She was a splendid woman–child, holding them mesmerized with her every move. Her Magical Friend was in control. Forces were at work beyond anything those two agents could have possibly imagined.

Passing Jaime's hiding place, Becky made one more circuit around them. The agents each spun one more complete circle as Becky dived for cover.

Jaime shouted, "Get your hands in the air."

The men stopped spinning and that sudden stop heightened their vertigo. The man closest to Jaime almost fell over, and the other raised his hands to his temples as if commanding his head to clear.

"Up! Up!" yelled Jaime. "Get your hands up right now! One false move and your bodies will resemble Swiss cheese."

"Better do as he says," Becky screamed. "Our guns are aimed at your guts. I don't think either of you wants to end up lying here in the dust with your insides spread across the trail just for a clown like Benson."

The mention of that name caused the hapless agents to realize they were dealing with people who knew what was going on at the compound. There was no way either of the agents could get to his weapon and fire it before several bullets would tear through their intestines, if not their hearts. Besides, what would they fire at? They were in the middle of the road, totally exposed, heads spinning, while their worthy opponents were safely behind cover.

They raised their hands, shouting, "Don't shoot! Don't shoot!"

"Okay," instructed Jaime, in a voice so calm it surprised him. "You with the cap, turn and face me. Take your right thumb and index finger and remove the pistol from under your right arm by the butt. Don't even think of letting a finger get near the trigger. Remember, we've both got our weapons aimed directly at your gut. What my friend across the road doesn't remove from your abdomen from her vantage point, I'll finish off from my position, kidneys and all. So don't try anything cute. There's nothing back at that compound worth losing your life over. This isn't about national security. This is about a bunch of very bad guys who have gotten you into something you don't understand."

What Jaime said rang true with both agents. It was pretty much in line with what they had been thinking ever since they learned that their prisoners were a bunch of private citizens, and families at that.

The one with the cap carefully lifted his pistol by the butt as instructed and tossed it to the ground in the direction of the sound of Jaime's voice.

"Now," Jaime continued, "remove your jacket very slowly and drop it to the ground. If I discover any other weapons on you that you haven't told me about, the hair trigger on this pistol may be tempting beyond my ability to resist."

"My boot," yelled the man hastily. "There's a revolver in my boot."

"Then take it out slowly and toss it over here. Easy!"

The man did as he was told.

Moments later Becky went through a similar procedure with the other man, without a problem. Then they had the two agents lie face down in the dirt, and while Becky held pistols to the men's heads, Jaime tied them up securely. They didn't gag Seaborn, so he could instruct the other two men at the entry gate to surrender their weapons.

They all started back to the gate. The ensuing capture of Hampton and Sitner went without incident. Actually, Jaime and Becky sensed relief on the faces of those agents, as if they didn't really have their hearts in what they had been instructed to do or any confidence in Benson, as if what was going on was not what they had really been trained to deal with, and as if they hoped their surrender without a fight might be taken into consideration when the truth about what happened here came out.

Jaime assured the agents that someone would be back to get them before long. He and Becky hid the men some distance from the entry gate and double-checked their bindings.

Becky and Jaime left for Benson's office, where they hoped their friends would be waiting, with Benson and the rest of his men captured.

Although none of the team members had any way of knowing this, collectively they had now captured twenty-three of Benson's men.

Chapter Sixty-one

Neither Benson nor any of his men were at the office when Clint and Maria arrived, so they waited in the forest behind the office, hoping that Benson would show up soon. Within fifteen minutes they were joined by Chris, Tim, and Gail. They waited for another half-hour and began to have some concern about the others. They reminded themselves that Jaime and Becky were expected to be somewhat later because of the complexity of their assignment and the distance they had to travel.

Everyone was noticeably relieved when Becky and Jaime arrived, unharmed.

Michael and Sarah were another matter. They had been expected to arrive earlier than Jaime and Becky.

It was now 2:30 a.m. on Friday. The moon was beginning to settle behind the mountains to the west. The outside air temperature had dropped several degrees in the past few hours. Becky was glad she had left her extra pair of blue jeans in her backpack. When she had repacked before leaving the Jeep, she had placed her Levi's on the bottom of the pack to prevent the tools and other metal objects she was taking with her from tearing a hole in her pack. Now she put them on in place of her newly created and highly effective short shorts. She stuffed those shorts in her backpack as a memento of this adventure.

They all had exciting tales to tell but kept them to a minimum for now. Instead they addressed more pressing issues such as where Benson and the rest of his men might be and, more important, what had happened to Michael and Sarah. They had originally planned to meet behind Benson's office between midnight and 1:00 a.m. Michael and Sarah were now more than an hour and a half late.

Just as they were about to head out in search of their two missing comrades, Michael came stumbling through the trees. In the light of Clint's flashlight, Michael's face was noticeably pale. He was unsteady on his feet. As he came closer, they could see his entire left side was covered with blood.

Clint ran to Michael's side and assisted him to a log upon which Michael sat while Maria and Gail did what they could to stop the bleeding and comfort him.

Michael told them that Sarah had been captured by the men at the farmhouse. He explained that he had been shot, although he didn't think he was in any immediate danger from the bullet wounds. He said the blood made his wounds look a lot worse than they really were.

He had remained hidden in the forest just below the farmhouse for more than an hour, waiting for an opportunity to rescue Sarah. But, toward the end of his vigil, several more of Benson's men arrived. After that, there were never fewer than eight of them on the porch and another four or five patrolling the area.

As furious and anxious as Michael was, he couldn't think of a way to get to Sarah without risking her life. She was totally vulnerable out there in the open, tied to the post next to the stairs. Michael thought he could handle two, maybe even three men. But with that many armed men so close to Sarah, he didn't see any way he could get her to safety.

The longer he kept vigil in the forest, the more frustrated and angry he became. Finally, he decided that, as much as he dreaded the thought of leaving Sarah, he had to get help.

"What shall we do, Dad?" asked Tim.

"I did a lot of thinking while I was there. We're still outnumbered, although the odds are getting a lot better. We have the possible advantage of surprise, although I wouldn't count on that. They have to suspect that with Sarah held hostage, we're likely to show up sooner or later. We also have the advantage of being able to shoot from the relative safety of the forest while those on the porch are somewhat exposed. But we don't know where the men patrolling the area are. We can't risk getting Sarah shot by a stray bullet or by a deliberate shot from one of them.

"We've got to get Sarah to safety before they can react. Once Sarah's safe, I'm for hitting them with everything we've got. But until then, we can't risk attacking them."

Everyone sat in silence, trying to come up with an idea.

Gail and Maria were busy bandaging Michael's wounds. They had slipped into Benson's office and found a military first-aid kit in the back room behind his desk. They coated Michael's wounds with antiseptic and painkiller, then covered them with large gauze pads and wrapped his upper torso with Ace elastic bandages. He felt better, but his side was still throbbing.

"The first thing I think we should do," Chris suggested, "is get out of this area. We don't know how long those guys are going to stay at the farmhouse. If some of them decide to come down here, we'll be sitting ducks. They could easily surround us. I'd suggest that we continue this meeting someplace else where they're not likely to find us."

"I agree." Clint nodded. "At least, deeper in the forest, split into groups, we can maneuver if we're attacked. Here, we don't have much of a chance."

They headed out past the barn where the John Deere was stored, in the general direction of the bunker. They considered taking temporary refuge in the bunker but decided that it would put them in danger of being surrounded and trapped there.

They decided to regroup in a deep ravine about a hundred yards on the far side of the bunker from the farmhouse. Chris and Jaime had discovered that ravine on the morning after they had first arrived at the compound.

Chris planned to separate from the others while they were on their way to the ravine, to check in with Daryl at the spacecraft. He would update Daryl on what was going on and see if Daryl could use some of the ship's equipment to assist in rescuing Sarah.

Within half an hour, all but Chris were gathered in the bottom of the ravine, well hidden by the thick vegetation and the darkness. The depth of the ravine would help prevent any sounds from traveling in the direction of the farmhouse.

Becky started out by telling the others about the meeting she and Jaime had had with John Hawkin at the back gate a couple of hours earlier. The fact that they now had an ally among Benson's men would certainly be of great benefit—if they could figure out how to contact Hawkin without alerting Benson.

When Chris returned, he informed them that he had been successful in getting inside the spacecraft and speaking with Daryl. Daryl had spent most of his time familiarizing himself with the ship's capabilities. He said he learned that the intelligence on board the craft was capable of amazing things, such as producing almost any kind of weather conditions in the area, communicating with nearby wildlife, both animal and vegetable, and directing lightning bolts to specific targets. But he also discovered that it was impossible to use the power of the craft to do anything intended to result in physical harm or death to any intelligent life forms. For some reason that Daryl didn't fully understand, the ship's control module apparently considered all human beings to be within the category of "intelligent life forms."

By means of an advanced type of surveillance monitor, Daryl was keeping an eye on several different areas within the compound. Apparently the equipment connected to this monitor did not operate on line-of-sight principles and could readily see around corners.

Maria announced that she was going on a short walk down the canyon. She needed to think for a few minutes and said she'd be back soon.

Chris suggested that they should be careful in communicating with Daryl or John Hawkin because Benson's men could be listening on channel two.

Gail reminded her friends that Chas had been up in the attic, bound and gagged for several hours now, probably needing to pee. They realized that this was also a problem for the many agents they had tied up and stashed at various hiding places throughout the forest.

Everyone agreed that now was the time to move, and that they had to move fast. But they still didn't have a modification of their original plan. The fact that Sarah had been captured made it imperative that they develop a new strategy. And the sun would be coming up in about three hours.

They sat in silence for a while.

Jolting everyone back to the present moment, Maria announced, "I'm back, and I've got an idea! When I was walking down the canyon, I heard laughter. I recognized it as my grandfather's belly laugh. When he finally stopped laughing, it was as if he were right next to me. He spoke to me quietly, saying, 'Go inside, my child, go inside.' At first I thought it was more of his airy fairy Great Spirit stuff—like go inside yourself. But then I realized he was trying to help with me an idea. You know how it is when you've got a notion in the very back of your mind that you can't quite get a handle on.

"Well, there's been an idea rattling around in my head ever since we left the area of Benson's office, but I couldn't quite pin it down. Then, when I heard that familiar laugh and Grandfather's voice saying 'go inside,' it suddenly came to me." Maria paused.

"Well, let's hear it," Clint urged. "We don't exactly have a lot of ideas to choose from."

"Well," Maria proceeded, "if we can't safely attack them from outside the farmhouse, why not hit them from the inside?"

"From the inside?" Gail and Jaime asked in unison.

"Why not?" asked Michael. "Why not? They'd never expect an attack to come from inside the building. I would guess that Benson has ordered his men to stay out of there. He doesn't want anyone finding those bodies in the basement. The building's empty except for our friend Chas up in the attic—bless his throbbing bladder."

"We can get in through the tunnel," Clint offered. "I'll bet they don't have more than one man, if any, guarding that tunnel. They'd never think we'd want to get back inside the farmhouse. We were damn thankful to get out of there."

"But," interrupted Gail, "don't forget that all of the windows have bars over them. We may be putting ourselves back in prison."

"Hey!" Jaime exclaimed. "We brought four wrenches in our backpacks, just in case we needed to remove those bars. One is in Daryl's backpack in the spacecraft. But Chris and Becky and I have the other three."

"That's why they won't think of an attack from within the farmhouse. In their minds, it's all locked up. Nothing to concern themselves about," Tim concluded.

"Okay, here's my suggestion," began Michael.

They all participated in formulating the plan.

Fifteen minutes later they were on their way to the entrance of the tunnel, except Maria, who was slipping carefully through the forest, using the methods of silence her grandfather had taught her as a child. She was heading for the spaceship to fill Daryl in on their revised plans and to let him know the part he would play.

On the way, Clint, Tim, Jaime, and Chris each picked up a large rock. One of the difficult parts of the plan would be getting those rocks into the farmhouse as they crawled on their bellies through the tunnel.

As Maria moved through the forest, she was worried about how successful she would be in getting the spaceship hatch to open. Terrified that she might let her friends down, she considered calling Daryl on the radio and asking him to open the hatch, but she decided it would be too risky to break radio silence.

Now she stood in the bunker, willing it to open with all her might. Nothing happened. She tried it again. Still nothing. She cursed silently, painfully aware that her friends were depending on her and that their plan didn't have much chance of success without Daryl's participation.

Then she remembered reading or hearing somewhere that a state of joy or, at least, a state of satisfaction with your present situation is essential to manifesting yourself into a better one. She realized it would be difficult to open the hatch with the power of her mind if she was stressed or unhappy. She had to make herself happy right now, to put herself in a better place—a tricky objective in view of the urgency of her mission.

Maria pictured her grandfather slapping his knees and roaring with one of his great belly laughs. The thought lightened her spirits. She considered her situation. Instead of focusing on the fact that she and her friends were in serious danger, with the outcome depending to a large extent on her ability to get inside that ship, she gave thanks that they were all still alive. She considered the possibility that her situation could provide her with a great opportunity to learn and grow. She might learn how to become a great spaceship hatch-opener, famous among the hatch-openers of the world. She smiled.

She thought about the agents stationed in front of the farmhouse. She used her will power to think of them as children of God, children of the universe, struggling souls trying to find their way back to Source Energy. The thought caused her fear to subside slightly.

She considered that some of those men probably had children and brothers and sisters. If not, at least they had moms and dads. She pictured them enjoying Christmas dinner with their loved ones, opening packages under the tree, wishing their loved ones Merry Christmas, singing holiday carols. She sent them love.

Maria saw herself as a channel for the energy of the God Force, flowing that energy to all of those agents without resistance, without fear, with pure love. She thought about Clint and Chris and how she ached with love for them. She urged herself to hold that same feeling for all of humanity, for all of creation, especially for those who fashioned themselves to be her enemies. She thought of her mother and father. She sent them love. She thought of herself. She thought of all the difficult times she had been through. She thought of how hard she had tried always to do the right thing. She considered that those men at the farmhouse were trying to do the right thing too, in the only way they knew.

She sent them more love. She imagined the love coming back, actually flowing through those agents and back to her. The same love she was sending out was coming back to her tenfold. Her soul rejoiced. She gave thanks to the All That Is for the way everything so wonderfully *is*, for the love of the God Force, for the power of the universe. She felt as if her heart might explode with joy.

"Click." "Whir." "Thunk."

Warm, peaceful blue light filled the bunker.

In the process of creating the energy necessary to open that hatch, Maria finally come face to face with her God Self. She knew in that moment that she was God, not just a child of God, but God Herself, an essential and irrevocable part of the All That Is. The thought didn't seem irreverent or blasphemous. It felt like the most real, true, irrevocably honest thought Maria had ever had. She knew she had found the thought that mattered most in her entire life.

Maria had come home.

Chapter Sixty-two

One guard was stationed near the entrance to the tunnel. Clint walked up to him and asked for a light, as if it was the most natural thing in the world. The guard was so surprised that he didn't notice that Clint didn't even have a cigarette in his hand. He started to ask Clint who the hell he was, but the words never left his mouth. The next thing he knew, he was locked in one of Becky's strangleholds, oxygen cut off from his lungs, the blood to his brain shut down. He thrashed frantically. Becky held on like a steel vise. Within seconds the man was totally immobilized and a moment later lost consciousness. If Becky hadn't let up quickly, he would have been dead. Three minutes later, the guard was bound, gagged, and stowed in a thicket of bushes.

The entire team gathered in the basement, and in the glow of one penlight, moved slowly from the basement to the first floor, watchful for any sign of life inside the building.

Clint, Chris, Tim, and Jaime each carried one of the heavy rocks they had gathered in the forest.

Gale and Becky each toted a backpack containing the implements necessary for their mission—ropes, flashlights, bundles of dynamite sticks, fuses, and matches. They left the other backpack in the basement.

Each member of the team had a pistol and a knife. The three wrenches had been removed from the backpacks, ready for use.

Clint and Jaime laid their rocks on the kitchen floor and slipped silently into the living room. They satisfied themselves that there were no agents in the building. They returned to the kitchen where the others were waiting and, once again, picked up the rocks. They proceeded through the dining room and up the stairs. Upon reaching the second floor, they moved individually to the areas where they were to perform their assigned tasks.

Tim, Jaime, and Chris removed the bars from two of the upstairs windows, one on either side of the farmhouse. They left the bars over the windows on the front of the building in place.

The roof that covered the porch wrapped around the sides of the building, as did the porch below. The front porch protruded a good three feet beyond the drip line of the roof so the porch could be enjoyed during the summertime, either in the cool shade or in the warm afternoon sun.

The post to which Sarah was tied was directly beneath the front edge of the roof and three feet back from the front of the porch.

A couple of the agents were sitting in chairs propped against the wall at the back of the porch, fast asleep. Four were standing beneath the roof, about four feet back from the porch's front of the porch. Two were immediately to Sarah's right as she sat facing the front yard. And two were on the other side of the front steps. There were ten men in all, most of whom had been drinking beer for the past several hours. The others had been sipping whiskey. All were drowsy. Those who stood did so to keep from falling asleep. The roof over the porch prevented the agents from seeing the action that was going on above them from where they were positioned.

With a great deal of effort and pain, Sarah had managed to slide the rope that bound her wrists down the splinter-covered post until it came to within a few inches of the floor. She was now in a sitting position, sleeping fitfully.

Sounds filled the cool night air. Jackson Browne was singing "Running on Empty" on the ghetto blaster. One agent was snoring loudly, and two others were engaged in an animated political conversation.

Sarah was dreaming that a small insect was crawling across her forehead. It seemed to be marching rapidly back and forth from temple to temple. She tried to brush it away but her hands wouldn't move. Her state of slumber, augmented as it was by the extreme stress she had endured, was unwilling to turn loose of her easily. Again she tried to brush away the irritating creature that was tormenting her forehead but became aware that her hands were unavailable for her use. She finally managed to achieve consciousness, breaking away from the somnambulant hold her subconscious had imposed on her in its attempt to protect her from the terror of her situation.

It was colder now. The moon was gone. Lots of stars twinkled overhead. Sarah's butt was numb. Her arms ached from having been tied behind her for so long. Her wrists and forearms burned from the many tiny splinters they had acquired as she had worked her way down the wooden post to which she was attached.

She felt that same irritating tickling feeling that had awakened her moments ago. She stuck out her lower lip and blew air upward, hoping to dislodge whatever critter had taken it upon itself to go traipsing across her forehead. She blew several more times without success.

In frustration, Sarah finally looked upward with a reprimanding glare, only to discover that the source of the irritation was not an insect at all. Instead, she saw a string swaying back and forth about half an inch in front of her forehead. About two inches above the end of the string was tied a hex bolt. The frayed end of the string brushed against her once again, doing a credible imitation of several tiny insect appendages scuttling across the skin just above her eyebrows. She tilted her head back farther to get a better look at the source of her discomfort. There, at the other end of that dangling length of string, she saw Tim, looking down at her and pressing his index finger to his lips, admonishing her to remain silent.

The string was quickly removed to the place from which it had descended. Mixed emotions filled Sarah's heart. Her first emotion was gratefulness that she was about to be rescued. The second was fear that her Tim was in danger.

Trying to decide what she was supposed to do next, Sarah struggled to her feet. She was fairly limited in her options, because the ropes still held her fast to the wooden post. She waited.

What happened next occurred so quickly that Sarah couldn't take it all in, assimilate it, and still remain ready to react as necessary. At one point, her senses were so overwhelmed by the action around her that she unwillingly closed her eyes, as if to defend herself against the stimuli that were assaulting her. Her nervous system was so overloaded that she was tempted to scream, but that urge was overridden by the recollection of Tim looking down at her with his finger pressed against his lips. Her autonomic nervous system took control and kept her totally silent and still.

When Sarah later had time to reflect upon these events, with many of the details being supplied by her friends, this is what she concluded had happened.

A horrendous commotion began emanating from a point several yards inside the forest. It sounded like an all-out war with rifles firing, machine guns blasting away, and hand grenades exploding everywhere. Numerous flashes of light, corresponding to the sounds, also came from somewhere behind the trees that lined the edge of the front yard of the farmhouse.

The agents who were formerly standing or sitting in the shelter of the roof, including those on either side of Sarah, rushed to the front of the porch, weapons at the ready, trying to see what was going on. They were focused intently in the direction of the fracas. They had to shield their eyes from the blinding flashes of light. The sounds were painful to their ears, the blasts so powerful that they reverberated in their diaphragms.

Michael suddenly appeared to Sarah's right, just behind the agents who were mesmerized by the sounds in the forest. His presence was so sudden and unexpected that it caused Sarah to gasp. He had been lowered from the porch roof above by a heavy rope tied around his waist. Seeing blood all over Michael's shirt registered violently in Sarah's mind but quickly became intermingled with the other stimuli assaulting her senses. Michael covered Sarah's eyes with his hands and closed his own eyes tightly.

As soon as Chris, looking down from the porch roof above, saw that Sarah's eyes were covered by Michael's hands, he shouted a command into his radio.

Immediately a series of outrageously bright lightning bolts struck the ground at various points along a line about thirty feet from the front of the porch, retaining the attention of all the agents and rendering them temporarily sightless. It also enabled those on the roof, who had taken care to shield their eyes against the display delivered to the area by Daryl Harrington and his magical spaceship, to see what was happening on the porch below, almost as if it were broad daylight.

Within seconds, Michael severed the ropes binding Sarah to the wooden post and wrapped another rope around her in a double figure eight, securing her arms, legs, and abdomen in such a way as to protect her neck and keep her from falling out of the hand-made harness.

Michael gave a thumbs-up signal to someone above, and Sarah was lifted into the air with such force that it took her breath away. As she approached the rooftop level, leaving behind the porch where she had been held captive for so many painful hours, she glanced down at her beloved Michael to assure herself that he was right behind her.

To her horror, the lightning flashes revealed that the agent standing behind Michael had managed to tear his attention away from the frantic display and stood with his rifle leveled at the base of Michael's skull, inches from its intended target.

With every ounce of strength remaining in her body, Sarah screamed. Everything seemed to move in slow motion. Sarah could see clearly, as if looking through a pair of binoculars, that the agent was beginning to squeeze the trigger. Michael wasn't aware of the agent's presence. He was watching Tim and Jaime help Sarah onto the roof.

Chris and Clint were bracing themselves, getting ready to hoist Michael to safety. They hadn't seen the agent spin and raise his rifle to the base of Michael's skull. They didn't hear Sarah's scream. It died in the midst of the mêlée surrounding them all.

"God help us!" Sarah screamed. "God help my Michael!"

For some strange reason that hadn't yet registered in his conscious mind, the agent relaxed his trigger finger slightly, still alert, ready for action. There, off to Michael's right but clearly within the agent's field of vision, a soft, bright white light appeared. It swirled and pulsated, captivating the agent. He removed his finger from the trigger, an act totally contrary to his training and conditioning, and stood there in a trance. He lowered his weapon. The apparition continued to congeal before his eyes.

Sarah, too, became captivated by that same apparition. Having brought Sarah to the relative safety of the rooftop, Tim and Jaime were watching it, unable to tear their attention away from its hypnotic attraction.

Clint and Chris yanked Michael to the rooftop as quickly as they could. Michael was still unaware of how close he had come to making his transition into the spirit world.

As he reached the rooftop, he couldn't help but notice that Sarah, Tim, and Jaime were looking intently at something below. He turned and, for the first time, saw the apparition.

There, standing with her hands on the shoulders of the agent who had almost taken Michael's life, stood a young woman with gorgeous reddish brown hair flowing over her shoulders. Her body glowed and shimmered with such brilliance that the display going on in the forest behind the agent paled by comparison.

The agent fell to his knees, his head in his hands.

Turning slowly, the woman looked up at Sarah, who was now standing next to her husband, holding his hand in hers, her other arm wrapped gently around his waist.

The woman smiled with such intensity that Chris lost his balance and almost tumbled over the edge of the roof. Clint, the broncobusting karate man, stood there like a little child with a silly grin on his face.

"Jessica," Sarah shouted in the depths of her soul, "You can have my hair any time.

Jessica looked up and smiled. In an instant she was gone.

God had answered Sarah's prayer. Her Michael was safe.

Everyone on the roof scrambled around the corner and into the bedroom window.

The agent who had almost taken Michael's life crawled to the rear of the porch and propped himself against the back wall. He sat there, elbows on his knees, head in his hands, crying over what he had almost done, suddenly a believer in a power beyond anything his senses could explain. He was effectively out of the battle, without bloodshed.

Shortly before she began her ascent to the rooftop, while Michael was still working his Boy Scout rope-and-knot magic, Sarah thought she heard several loud, thudding sounds and she saw two of the agents crumble to the porch floor. Only two of the four rocks thrown from the roof above had achieved their intended results, leaving two of the targeted agents still conscious. One of the agents who had survived the boulder assault almost killed her Michael. The remaining agents on the porch were now aware that two of their buddies were lying unconscious, one was sitting on the floor at the back of the porch, his head in his hands, and Sarah was no longer where they had tied her.

Lightning continued to strike the ground in front of the porch.

Those agents who remained functional were confused. They ran down from the porch and into the forest, not sure they would be much safer there, given the action that was taking place. But now that they knew the families were back in the farmhouse, they didn't dare remain on the porch, where they would be clear targets.

In an instant, the commotion Daryl had been creating from the spaceship stopped. All was silent.

Chapter Sixty-three

Chris suggested a meeting to discuss their situation. They gathered in one of the bedrooms and sat in a circle on the floor, except for Tim, who had gone down to the living room and was sitting in the darkness, keeping an eye on the yard.

He observed that all but three of the agents had left the porch and were now somewhere in the forest. Of the three remaining, two were unconscious. He watched with curiosity the strange behavior of the third agent sitting at the back of the porch with his head in his hands. That agent remained there, refusing to leave, even though the others had retreated to a safer location.

Tim reported these facts to his friends, including that one of the agents had spoken into his radio a couple of times before leaving the porch. Tim assumed that he had been speaking with the agents who were patrolling the compound, requesting them to come help contain the families in the farmhouse.

At the meeting upstairs they discussed the fact that their best chance would be to act while the three agents were incapacitated and before those patrolling the compound joined the others.

As near as they could estimate, seven agents were searching the forest for the source of all that gunfire, and four or five were patrolling other parts of the compound. They had a reasonable chance of overpowering seven but a much lesser chance of defeating twelve. They agreed that the agents would probably be expecting them to try to escape through the tunnel and would least expect them to come out the front doors, especially since those doors were secured by padlocked steel gates.

They decided to create a bit of a commotion in the area of the tunnel entry, to see if they could draw the agents to that location. Shortly after implementing that distraction, they would turn Daryl and his trusty spaceship loose with another volley of distractions directed to the rear of the farmhouse. While that was happening, the five men would leave the farmhouse through the front door and sprint across the front yard and into the forest. It was risky, but they couldn't think of a better plan.

The men might get caught in a barrage of gunfire before they could reach the shelter of the forest, and with all five of them out in the forest, the ladies would be left alone in the building, where they could be surrounded by Benson's men, especially if those patrolling the forest were to show up before the good guys got things under control.

"Not to worry," Sarah assured them. "We've got plenty of weapons here, and besides, I'm beginning to think that Benson has probably ordered these men not to kill any of us unless absolutely necessary. He doesn't want to have any more dead bodies on his hands until he has all the loose ends tied up. Being implicated in the cover-up of someone else's massacre is one thing. Ordering people killed yourself is another. I think that incident on the porch, where I almost lost my Michael, was the result of an agent acting against orders in a tense situation. If they were determined to kill us, we likely would have been dead by now."

"I agree," Clint concurred. "Let's get these guys before the situation changes to the point where Benson doesn't have a reason to keep us alive."

Tim and Jaime opened the wooden front doors of the farmhouse and removed the bolts that held the gates in place. They lowered the gates slowly and quietly. Apparently nobody observed their actions.

As soon as they informed the others that the front doorway was clear, Clint threw several lighted sticks of dynamite from one of the upstairs bedroom windows toward the area surrounding the tunnel entrance.

Michael had radioed Daryl earlier and instructed him to be standing by with more fireworks, this time to be directed to the rear and side of the farmhouse. In no event were any fireworks to be directed to the front of the building. Clint signaled Michael that the dynamite had been thrown. Michael informed Daryl to start the festivities in fifteen seconds.

All of the men scrambled for the living room. Each stood beside a window, giving them views of the front and sides of the building.

A moment after the dynamite went off, Tim saw an agent running in the direction of the blast. He apparently had been watching the front yard from the darkness of the forest and had escaped Tim's detection earlier. His desire to discover the source of the blast prompted him to forsake his hiding place.

Two seconds later, Daryl's fireworks began.

All five men took off running out the door and across the porch. As soon as each man hit the bottom of the stairs, he headed for the shelter of the forest. No shots were fired. Apparently, the agents weren't aware that the men had left the building.

They regrouped just inside the forest and headed toward the tunnel, hoping they would find the agents there.

Harrington's light display stopped within seconds after the men reached the cover of the forest. Chris considered that seeming coincidence to be an indication that, perhaps, Daryl was watching them from the comfort of his heated, humidified, softly lighted spaceship.

He probably had the music system rocking. Chris smiled. *This is going to be interesting.*

As the men approached the tunnel entry, they saw, to their surprise, that all seven of the agents were gathered there. The area was lighted by a considerable fire resulting from the dynamite and fueled by all of the organic matter that had been deposited on the forest floor over the years.

The agents were not yet aware of their presence. They were well hidden in the forest.

It was now five against seven. This was still a formidable challenge, considering the agents' experience and firepower. "But," Chris reassured himself, "we've got Clint and Michael."

No sooner had Chris finished that somewhat successful attempt to bolster his confidence than he sensed someone behind him. The sudden terror he felt was augmented by his knowledge that his four partners were all in front of him and not aware of the presence of another enemy agent. He didn't know whether to turn and shoot, to dive for cover, or to raise his hands in surrender. If whoever was standing behind him didn't yet know that Chris was aware of his presence, Chris might be able to turn and fire his weapon before the man could react. What to do? Chris felt a bead of sweat trickle down his neck.

If he didn't do something soon, whoever was behind him was going to take down Chris and his friends.

Tim's words echoed in Chris' head: "It's hard to be without fear when some dude's chasing your ass with a 44 Magnum."

As Chris was telling himself to "be cool," Zara's words came to him, unbidden. "The Force can produce any result you command, without any regard whatsoever for the illusory limitations of the physical world."

Chris forced himself to relax, forced himself to picture a happy outcome, saw himself and his friends alive and well, laughing and victorious. Almost against his own will, he turned his head slowly to face whatever fate lay behind him.

Before what Chris saw could register in his conscious mind, he felt a flood of pure joy surging from his heart up into his brain.

Becky.

Thank God.

Becky's beautiful face flickered in the glow of the fire, a trace of a smile on her lips. She placed her hand reassuringly on Chris's shoulder.

Chris turned back quickly to the drama that was about to unfold before him, his heart racing. The odds were better now.

Becky's confidence flowed into him from her mere touch, erasing much of the terror he had been feeling. Yes, those agents were in for a fight.

"Don't forget the love." Zara's voice was loud and clear in Chris's mind.

Chris again pictured the perfect outcome: The bad guys captured, the good guys alive and well, the people of America well served. It felt good.

They all crouched in the forest, hidden, watching, waiting for Michael or Clint to make the first move.

Tim was at the far left, Becky to the far right, completing a semicircle that wrapped partly around the agents. Each was hidden behind a tree. Only Chris knew that Becky had joined the team.

Tim was the first to become aware of movement, to his left, back in the darkness, not yet visible in the glow of the fire.

Becky sensed something to her right, not quite visible, but its presence unmistakable, something feral, something wild, and definitely not human. She turned slowly and caught the glow of the fire reflecting from a pair of eyes. She tensed slightly at first but somehow knew there was nothing to fear. *Go, Magical Friend, do your thing.*

Then, out of the forest and into the firelight stepped five gigantic wolves.

One of the agents screamed, and fired several rounds at the wolf nearest him. The other agents turned to face the creatures, weapons ready.

Although the agent had hit his target, the wolf remained still, unharmed, teeth bared. He released another burst of gunfire. The beast let out a mighty roar and moved two steps closer to the man who retreated several feet, totally mystified.

An agent behind him shouted, "Holy shit!" They all turned to run, only to see three mountain lions crouched yards away, blocking their retreat. One of the agents raised the sight of his AR-15 to his eye and squeezed off five rounds of 308 caliber steel, each round hitting the big cat in front of him squarely in the forehead. The animal sat there licking its chops, a ferociousness in its eyes.

The agent next to him shouted, "What the hell? You hit him dead center. What the hell's going on here?"

They backed away from the animals, gathering into a tight group in the center of the circle formed by the creatures.

"It's Daryl," whispered Jaime. "It's that crazy Daryl controlling those animals."

The agents stood in the circle, facing outward with their weapons raised, looking from one set of glaring eyes to another, terrified. They fired several more rounds, no more effective than the others had been. The animals tightened the circle.

"Put down your weapons," came a booming voice from out of the forest, just behind Jaime.

"Who's that?" shouted one of the agents.

"This is John Alexander Hawkin, special agent to the President of the United States. Lay down your weapons and raise your hands above your heads."

"With all due respect," yelled one of the agents in a quavering voice, "and not questioning your authority, sir," he stammered, "we've got a situation on our hands. If you'll come out of the trees, you'll see that we've gotten ourselves surrounded by a pack of wild animals. I don't think this would be a very good time to surrender our weapons, sir."

"You've obviously had a chance to see for yourselves that your conventional weapons are of no use against these creatures. I promise that if you do exactly as I say, I'll call them off."

"Call them off?" said a whining voice from the circle of agents, "Call them off?"

"You'll see," boomed Hawkin. He commanded the wolf directly in front of him to retreat. It backed off a few feet, eyes still intent on the agents. "Lay down your rifles, take out your pistols, lay them on the ground in front of you, and raise your hands above your heads. I will command the other animals to back off."

The men slowly laid down their rifles. Then each removed his pistol from its holster and laid it on the ground.

"Now, any backup weapons," Hawkin ordered. "If I find anyone with a concealed weapon he hasn't surrendered, I'll turn a couple of my friends here loose for a feeding frenzy."

Numerous small weapons appeared out of nowhere and were tossed onto the ground.

John Hawkin stepped out of the shadows, preceded by a line of four agents, each with his hands tied behind his back and his mouth covered with tape. "Okay," Hawkin directed, "if my good friends crouched in the forest will come out and collect the weapons, I'd appreciate the help."

"You knew we were here?" asked Jaime.

"All along," answered Hawkin, a slight grin spreading across his face.

The six stepped into the light. Tim, Becky, Jaime, and Chris quickly gathered the weapons while Michael and Clint bound and gagged the agents.

The wolves and cats flickered, faded, and finally disappeared.

Hawkin and his friends took their prisoners into the farmhouse and secured them in the basement. Then they gathered in the living room.

"That was pretty slick," remarked Tim. "I mean those animals, that was pretty advanced technology."

"Not so advanced," said Hawkin. "Actually, that sort of holographic magic can be produced today with our own primitive technology. I wouldn't be surprised, however, if the equipment on board that ship could have caused those creatures to subdue or even capture our friends."

"But those creatures," objected Becky, "were a lot more real than any holographic projections I've ever seen. They felt real. I could sense their presence even before I saw them. I could even smell them."

"I know," Hawkin conceded, "but some of our leading-edge scientists are now discovering that perhaps all of our senses operate

on holographic principles. I wouldn't be surprised that, as soon as
those scientists get the doubters in the scientific community to give
up their old beliefs, we're going to make strides like never before.
From what I've read, it's possible that all of physical reality, if I may
use an oxymoron, is holographic. Once this is accepted, we will have
reasonable explanations for most, if not all, of the unexplainable
phenomena that have perplexed us for centuries, especially the vast
chasm that has always existed between science and religion.

"As soon as religion is replaced with spirituality and old scientific dogma gives way to leading-edge thinking, the secrets of the
universe will be revealed and we here on planet Earth will begin catching up with our space brothers who, for millennia, have considered us
lost in the dark ages of scientific and medical thought."

For the next several hours, everyone was busy rounding up the
captured agents, allowing them to relieve themselves in the forest,
and bringing them to the farmhouse .

They fed the agents a meager breakfast, using the supplies they
found in the storeroom of Benson's office, and afterward took them
to the basement, where the agents were informed that they would be
imprisoned there until more satisfactory arrangements could be made
for their incarceration.

Hawkin told the agents about the massacre that had taken place
at the farmhouse back in 1975. He told them that as long as they were
not directly involved in the massacre, he would do what he could to
see that any punishment due them would be in proportion to any
illegal acts that they actually performed during the past few days and
that they probably would not be implicated in the massacre. He
admonished them not to try to escape, as he, and the President, would
take it as an indication that they were acting in concert with whoever
had perpetrated and covered up the atrocities at the farmhouse.

Even though Hawkin didn't think any of the men would be
foolish enough to attempt an escape, he, with the help of Clint and
Chris, rolled a large boulder over the opening to the tunnel. Hawkin
assigned Tim, Chris, Clint, and Jaime turns guarding the perimeter of
the house, just in case anyone in the basement should decide to do a
little digging.

Hawkin deliberately made no mention of the spaceship and requested all of the family members not to say anything about it until the President decided how many of the facts of this situation should be revealed to the public.

While the encounter with the holographic beasts near the tunnel entry was going on, Gail and Sarah had brought Chas out of the attic. They could tell by the pained look on his face that he desperately needed to relieve himself. They untied his hands and took him into the forest, taking care to have a weapon handy in the event of any false moves. Chas was uncommonly quiet. They gave him plenty of water and saw that he was well fed.

Later, Michael informed Chas that he would have to be kept locked up, as they couldn't afford to have anyone running around who they didn't trust. There was still a lot at stake here, including the security of the nation. But they wouldn't put Chas in the basement with all of the desperados. He would be kept in the attic a few more hours, until Hawkin and his superiors decided what to do.

Chas obviously wasn't pleased with the prospect, but he didn't whine as Michael had expected.

Jaime had gone to the spacecraft and brought Daryl and Maria up-to-date. Then they all returned to the farmhouse, bringing with them the two agents who had been locked in the spaceship. The agents were blindfolded before being removed from the room in which they had been imprisoned and had the memories of their experience erased by the spaceship's intelligence, so the ship's existence would remain unknown to them.

Hawkin explained to everyone that he was acting under direct orders from the President of the United States, relative to the disappearance of numerous soldiers who never returned to the States, even though there was evidence that they had left Vietnam on a transport plane. With a look of great sorrow, he told them that he believed his little brother Mikey was one of those soldiers. He also explained that several families had been murdered here at the farmhouse back in 1975. He told them he thought it was part of a cover-up by certain high-ranking officials in the CIA and the FBI.

Hawkin was concerned that Benson and four of his men in the field were still on the loose. He intended to have them rounded up as quickly as possible. Apparently Benson had high-tailed it as soon as he realized the action was about to start.

Chris, Tim, and Jaime rounded up all of the surplus weapons, carted them to the bunker, and secured them in the spaceship, along with their backpacks.

By the time Daryl and Chris left to get their Jeeps, the sun was up. They were back in less than an hour.

Sarah, Maria, Becky, and Gail were busy making a second breakfast for themselves and their men. They did the best they could with the meager supplies Benson had left.

It was now early Saturday morning, almost a week since Chris, Jaime, and Becky had left the Lasher home on what promised to be a fun-filled trip to Becky's aunt's house.

Chris realized that he had missed his date with Wendy.

As concerned as Hawkin was with the whereabouts of Benson and his men, he was a lot more concerned about the men who had started this whole mess. He still didn't know who they were. And considering that they had the power to make almost anyone disappear, Hawkin was very concerned.

Chapter Sixty-four

Chas had been provided with plenty of time to think. At first he was furious. How could these barbarians gang up on him and treat him like a pariah? He had rights. He was certainly a lot smarter than the others. Hadn't his ability to always outsmart his opponents proven that?

But he couldn't escape one simple fact that kept inserting itself into his thought processes: He had been an outcast all his life. Chas had no friends. That hadn't bothered him—at least that's what he had tried to tell himself. He justified his lot in life by assuming that those who disliked him were merely jealous.

But something had happened here. He had seen a different side of life. He had gotten a good look at the inner lives of some real people. He had gotten to see how they acted under serious stress.

These people didn't turn on each other. They didn't put their own interests ahead of the others. They were good people, genuinely concerned about each other. Chas had always assumed that everyone was basically evil. Now, he realized that assumption had been inaccurate.

Imprisoned in the attic again, he had had more time to think. And the thinking was relentless.

These people were brave, honorable, loving. All of the qualities Chas had thought were just for show, for the movies, for fairy tales. He had assumed these were characteristics of the weak.

But these people weren't weak. Not one of them. Not even Gail.

Gail had amazed Chas. He used to think of her as putty in his hands. But Gail had stood up to him. And from what little he had learned from the tales the family members were exchanging during the brief time he was allowed to join them at the breakfast table, Gail was a true heroine.

Maybe she had allowed him to get away with his games, not because she was afraid of him, but because she really loved him. Maybe she thought he really was "Mister Wonderful."

But that was a sham. Chas wasn't who Gail had thought he was. If Gail really loved him, she had fallen in love with the phony character he created not the real Chas. Nobody could really love *him,* not the real Chas.

The real Chas wasn't at all like the people who surrounded him now. They were real. Chas had never known real people. Chas had never been real.

But, oh, how he wanted to have what these people had. They cared about each other. He thought of how Michael must feel, knowing that Sarah and Tim and Jaime all loved him for who he really was, not some false front he put out there to get people to do what he wanted.

These concepts were so foreign to Chas that he felt as if he were approaching the outer fringes of a make-believe world. He had never known people like this.

Or perhaps he had known lots of people like this but hadn't *really* known them. Perhaps he had seen only what he wanted to see, what he wanted to get from them, not who they really were. Maybe he had chosen to see them in a light that would allow him to justify continuing his charade without having to judge his own conduct too harshly.

In a strange way, Chas was glad he had been put in the attic. He wasn't ready to re-enter the outside world, not until he did a lot more thinking.

Could he ever be like Michael or Clint? Was that a choice, or was it something a person was born with? Or was it something cultivated over a lifetime? Was there still hope for him? Could Chas be real? The prospect ignited a warm glow in his chest, a feeling he had never known before.

Yes, he wanted to do a lot of thinking.

He thought about how long he had gone without peeing while the battle had been going on. He wondered if a bladder could explode. The thought made him laugh. He laughed so loud that the people down in the kitchen could hear him. Gail wondered if he was cracking up. She hoped not.

While Gail was sitting there wondering what Chas was up to, he was coming to the shocking realization that he had never laughed before, not from joy or shared pleasure. That thought made him very sad. Then he laughed again, a laugh that was, strangely, very happy and very sad.

As much as Chas found the warm glow delicious, he also felt an almost unbearable pain in the thoughts he was having. Still, he was glad the pain was there. Even in his pain, he felt better than with the numbness he had felt all of his life.

Oddly, Chas was thankful for the time to do some deep contemplation, even in this musty old attic. With a new kind of enthusiasm, he looked forward to the possibility of even more adventuresome thoughts. He even looked forward to the cleansing pain he expected those thoughts would bring.

Hawkin decided to use Benson's office as his command center while he wrapped up this mess. He organized a schedule for patrolling the area. Every few hours, Michael, Clint, Tim, Jaime, Hawkin, and Chris rotated their positions and routes.

After he checked in with the President, giving him as much information as he dared, Hawkin arranged for the men in the basement of the farmhouse to be transported to a minimum security facility in forty eight hours. That wasn't soon enough for Hawkin, considering the risks involved and the trouble of feeding the prisoners and having them escorted, one by one, to the latrine several times a day. But it was the best he could do on such short notice. And, considering he was dealing with the government, he figured forty eight hours was pretty fast.

While they were off duty, Tim and Jaime drove one of the government sedans to Benson's office. They heard from Daryl about more of the wondrous things the ship could do, and they wanted to do some experimenting with the spacecraft. But they decided it wouldn't be wise to play with the ship without Hawkin's permission.

They soon found themselves involved in a conversation with the big man that was so interesting they temporarily forgot about their plans to visit the spaceship. Among other things, Hawkin told them of some of his experiences in the Navy and a few of his adventures in Vietnam. He told them, in no uncertain terms, how he passionately loved his country. He told them a few tales about friends he had lost in the war. He told them about his little brother Mikey, how he had never returned from Vietnam.

Hawkin confessed that, over the years, he had developed a great deal of mistrust for the Federal Government. He said he felt that our forefathers had formed the government to serve and protect the people and especially to keep them safe from foreign invaders. But the government had evolved, over the more than two centuries since its inception, to provide a lot of cushy, unnecessary jobs for supporters of politicians, many of whom managed to stay in office long after their usefulness ended. He talked about how many government employees no longer realize they are working for the people. They think they are running the country and that their jobs are to control the people.

He told them he thought the anti-gun people were trying to sell this country down the river and said he believed that some of them were planted in this country by our enemies to help weaken the fabric of our society. He explained that one of the events that has often led to the enslavement of the people of any nation is taking away their weapons. Anyone who would take the time to read the debates that took place among the founders of this nation, when it was being formed, would have to conclude that our forefathers understood clearly that the right to bear arms is the cornerstone of any democracy.

Tim and Jaime found Hawkin extremely knowledgeable and interesting. Most of all, they liked the look in his eyes, which clearly said he knew who he was and acted out of knowledge and integrity, not fear. They wished they could sit there for hours and learn more from this great man.

But Hawkin had a lot of work to do. He wanted to be able to send the families home as soon as possible, but as long as the men who had committed the atrocities at the farmhouse were at large, nobody connected with this situation was safe. He told them he hoped, with the help of the President, to have the men behind this entire mess in custody shortly. In the meantime, he ordered enough food and supplies, including cots, linens, blankets and pillows, to keep them all comfortable for several days. Those supplies were to be delivered by a few men Hawkin trusted implicitly. They would stay for the duration so everyone in the compound could feel a bit more secure.

Jaime and Tim thanked Hawkin for his time and headed for the car, intending to check in with the ladies back at the farmhouse and then relieve Daryl and Chris on patrol.

As they approached the sedan, a vehicle raced up the road toward them from the front gate. Michael had been assigned to that gate for the past two hours, so they figured that whoever it was must have passed Michael's scrutiny. Perhaps it was some of Hawkin's new men arriving with supplies.

Their surprise at seeing their father in the front seat between two men was mild compared to what they saw in the rear seat. As the automobile came to a halt a few feet from where they were standing, they saw clearly that their friend Mortimer Ziffel was in the back. What in the world was Mortimer doing here?

Then Tim's stomach muscles tightened as he saw that the other man in the backseat was holding a pistol to Mortimer's head.

In the same instant, Jaime saw that the man in the front passenger seat held a pistol against Michael's rib cage. Jaime surmised that Benson and his henchmen must have appeared at the front gate and forced Michael to surrender, with a threat to harm Mortimer if he didn't.

As soon as he heard the car approaching, Hawkin came out onto the front porch of Benson's office.

Herbert Benson III turned off the engine and stepped out of the car. "Mr. Hawkin," he chided, "how cozy of you and these criminals to be socializing. Ordinarily, I would have been shocked to find that you hadn't locked them up. But, from the few conversations I picked up while listening to channel two, plus the bits of information I gleaned from my men on channel one, I discovered that you are no longer to be trusted. Please place your pistol carefully and gently on the rail in front of you and step back against the wall. If not, at least one of the gentlemen in this vehicle—in the company of two of my best men, I might add—will be dispatched forthwith to the afterlife."

Hawkin did as he was told.

"Now, gentlemen," snapped Benson, directing his words to Jaime and Tim. "I suggest that you take any weapons you may have in your possession and lay them on the hood of that sporty, government-issue sedan you were driving and join your new friend up there on the porch. Any hesitancy on your part to do exactly as you're told will result in yet another bullet hole in your father's torso."

Tim and Jaime joined Hawkin on the porch.

"Get down on your stomachs and place your hands behind your backs."

While the agent in the backseat kept watch on Mortimer and Michael, the one in the front got out of the vehicle and joined Benson on the porch, where they tied up Hawkin and the boys. Then they put them in the back of the car Jaime and Tim had driven to the office. Benson drove that car while the other agent kept his pistol trained on the prisoners. The agent in the back of the other car instructed Michael to drive, informing him that any false move would result in the instant demise of himself and Mortimer.

At the farmhouse, they quickly captured the four ladies and tied them up.

They then contacted Clint, Chris, and Daryl on the radios and ordered them to come in quickly unless they wanted to come home later to a few more dead bodies. The men showed up in minutes.

Benson ordered all of the family members, except Mortimer, into the basement. To everyone's surprise, Benson forced all of the agents, except the two that had arrived with him, to remain in the basement.

After the basement door was locked, Benson explained to the two agents who still enjoyed their freedom that at this point he wasn't sure which ones he could trust. He said it wouldn't hurt the other agents to stay down for a while until he sorted things out.

He sent one of his men on a walk around the farmhouse to determine that there was not a way out of the basement. Minutes later, the man returned and reported that all was secure.

Benson totally forgot Chas, who remained in the attic still enthusiastically searching his soul, oblivious to the activities taking place below him.

Benson had decided not to lock Mortimer in the basement with the others. He figured it might be to his benefit to have one ace-in-the-hole in the event anything went wrong. Having Mortimer safely locked up elsewhere could provide leverage with those families if the going got sticky. He ordered that Mortimer be locked in one of the tool rooms in the barn where the John Deere was stored.

Benson went back to his office to try to figure out what his next move would be. He still didn't know which of the men he could trust. At least, he had most of the unknowns locked up where they couldn't do him any immediate harm. Unfortunately, the men he feared most were free and in a position to terminate him at any moment. He had no reason to believe he could trust the two men he kept out of the basement either. But at least there were only two of them. For now, he had them busy patrolling the farmhouse area.

For a while, Benson considered leaving the country, but he ultimately decided against it. The men who started this whole thing were powerful, and their tentacles reached into many foreign countries. In this country he had a chance of finding sanctuary. In a foreign country, he could be hopelessly lost. At least in America, officials questioned dead bodies found in automobile trunks, not necessarily the case in some foreign countries.

For now, he had to have some time to think. The longer he thought, the more tense he became. Once again Benson noticed an itching sensation under his left armpit.

Meanwhile, down in the basement, an energetic conversation was going on among the prisoners. The agents hands, legs, and ankles were bound, thanks to the earlier efforts of Clint and Michael. They couldn't do anything but lie and wait.

But only the hands of the family members were bound, and not their legs, so they were able to move around the basement. Benson had assumed that, since they would be locked up with no escape route, it wasn't necessary to tie their legs. Besides, there were so many of them that it would have taken too much of Benson's precious time to tie all of their legs and ankles.

Using the sharp edge of a bench to cut away the rope, Hawkin managed to free his hands from their bindings. Then he untied his friends.

Hawkin took the time to explain to the agents, many of whom still had no idea what this was all about, what had happened at this place in 1975. He said that, although he had not yet been in the adjoining room, he had been told that it contained the remains of numerous people who had been executed by government officials. He informed them that the people now imprisoned with him, other than the agents, were innocent civilians who just happened upon this place, directly or indirectly.

Finally, he made it clear that it was in the best interests of those who committed the massacre that everyone in this room be terminated, and all traces of them and this place be eliminated. Hawkin offered to remove their gags upon the condition that they speak only for the purpose of helping find a way out of this mess. Anyone being

THE UNDOING

disruptive would be gagged again. To Hawkin's surprise, every one of the agents agreed to the condition.

The first one to speak introduced himself as Henley and said, "I realize that many of us in this room would be considered by some to be the dregs of governmental law enforcement. I'll admit that I've done some rather unsavory things in my career. But I've never killed an innocent citizen. Most, if not all, of the people I've gunned down were low-lifes and often a threat to our national security. I joined this motley crew because it offered fairly good pay and little risk. I swear that I knew nothing about any massacre of innocent people, certainly not women and children. I, for one, am willing to work with you to help capture whoever was behind this thing. But I need your word that you'll do what you can to see that I don't fry for whatever happened here."

"Me, too," echoed another, followed by nods and murmurs of assent from many of the agents.

"There's not a whole lot you can do," said Hawkin. "Besides, I can't risk having any of you turn on me or my friends. For that reason, I'll be leaving you tied up until this thing is over, unless I reach the point where I must have your help. In the meantime, we'll do what we can to make you comfortable. Perhaps this will all be over shortly. Until then—as I told some of you earlier—I will consider your refraining from trying to escape from this place as an indication that you are on our side. Any conduct to the contrary will likely convince me and the President that you are abetting the perpetrators of this atrocity."

A man propped against the wall asked, "What about that little scenario with the wolves and the mountain lions? How the hell did that come about? I've never seen anything like it. One minute we're surrounded by a bunch of wild animals that are impervious to five or six rounds from an AR-15 at point-blank range, and seconds later, 'whoosh'—they're gone."

"That, gentlemen, was all done with laser technology and a relatively new science called holography," replied Hawkin.

"I seen holographs before, down at Disney World," argued another. "But I ain't never seen nothin' that real lookin'."

"If you boys are real good, and assuming that we all get out of here in one piece, maybe we'll treat you to an even more exciting demonstration of this technology." Hawkin offered.

"Exciting?" countered the same man. "I can't imagine it getting any more exciting than that!"

"You want to see exciting?" Maria asked. "Hold on to your seatbelts." She stood up and went to the center of the room.

"What are you up to?" whispered Hawkin, as she passed him.

Maria turned back to him and whispered, "Don't worry, John, I know what I'm doing."

She asked her friends to help focus energy, as some of them had done in the attic earlier. They gathered around in a circle. At Maria's request, they joined hands, closed their eyes, and focused. A minute passed, then another. Then, even in the absence of a candle, a bright blue flame appeared in the center of the room, seeming to come out of the dirt floor.

Hawkin's eyes widened, and his breath escaped audibly.

The agents expressed emotions ranging from wonder to disbelief.

The flame grew larger and brighter. It now stood a full foot tall. It began to sparkle and spin, throwing off yellow tongues of fire that snapped as they left the main flame, then faded into nothingness. The flame continued to grow until it was a full four feet tall, with heat emanating in all directions.

Exclamations echoed in the earthen room.

Then, just inches above the tip of the flame appeared the head of a wolf, life-size, revolving slowly, eyes glistening. It let out a roar. So intense was the ferocity of the beast that several of the agents turned their faces away.

A few seconds later a thundering sound filled the air. A puff of smoke rose from the base of the flame, accompanied a series of pulsating flashes.

The wolf head disappeared and, as the smoke subsided, there, in the place of the flame, stood Great-Grandfather, his war bonnet aglow, his look stern.

"So," his voice echoed throughout the room, "these are the men who would do harm to my granddaughter and her son and their beloved friends. Do they know that they have insulted the great and powerful Chief Roaring Eagle?"

The agents were transfixed, breathless.

Maria rose, stood next to her grandfather, and whispered in his ear, "What's with this 'Chief' bullshit?"

"Part of the show, my dear granddaughter," he whispered back.

Maria sat down, a smile on her face.

"I have come to offer you but one chance to save your lives," intoned the kindly old spirit. "You must demonstrate, to my total satisfaction that you shall forevermore look after the safety of my granddaughter and her friends. I shall be watching from my chiefly throne on high. One act that is not in concert with my admonition, and it will be curtains for you."

Chiefly throne? Curtains? Grandfather you're going a bit too far this time.

"Just so you know that I am what I appear to be and not one of those cheap holograph things, I will leave you a sign."

Great-Grandfather pulled out a hunting knife, walked over to one of the agents, and, to the agent's horror, placed the tip of it against his forehead, leaving there the letter "R" enclosed in a circle, looking very much like the symbol denoting a registered trademark.

With that, Great-Grandfather turned, winked conspiratorially at Maria, spun in a series of circles, and disappeared in a puff of yellow smoke.

Hawkin was speechless.

Chris sat there grinning and shaking his head.

The agents were irrevocably committed to any cause involving Maria or her friends.

Chris thought about the fact that he had missed his date with Wendy at the cocktail lounge. He prayed that she had received the telephone message he had left for her with the bartender.

As the agents were animatedly discussing the events of the past several minutes—at least as animatedly as they could with their hands and feet tied—Hawkin wandered into the adjacent room. He hadn't seen the bodies of those killed in the massacre. And, although he wasn't excited about viewing human remains, he felt a need, almost a compulsion, to go there.

Hawkin was gone for several minutes. Michael and Clint kept looking toward the room, watching beams of light from Hawkin's flashlight reflecting off the walls. They wondered what intense feelings the big man must be experiencing, looking upon those skeletons, the tattered clothing, the rings and bracelets and shoes, vivid reminders of the lives that had once occupied that room and testimony to the grief and terror those people had experienced watching their loved ones die.

Then the flashing stopped.

There poured forth from that little room a mournful cry.

All was silent.

Then there came from that alcove a scream of utter despair and unbearable agony.

Michael stood and hurried to where Hawkin was obviously having a terrible time coming to grips with the horror that room contained.

The big man shouted once more, a curse to the heavens, followed by uncontrollable sobbing.

When Michael returned, the look on his face expressed his shock and heartfelt sorrow. He walked to Sarah, wrapped his arms around her and laid his head gently on her shoulder. In a tearful voice he whispered, "He found Mikey."

Chapter Sixty-five

Saturday afternoon. Benson sat in his office thinking, the nearly empty bottle of calamine lotion next to his radio. He had run out of the blessed Foille some time ago.

He had finally decided what he was going to do. It was the single most difficult decision he had made in his entire, worthless life. It would take every ounce of courage he had. In fact, he had some doubt that he could really do it.

Herbert Benson III was going to do the right thing.

He remembered a quote he had once heard, something to the effect that brave men die only once but cowards die a thousand deaths. Herbert Benson III had died a thousand deaths. His life was a monument to taking the easy way out, fostered, he suspected, by the layer upon layer of guilt he inherited from his Catholic upbringing.

This time he would do it right.

He suspected that his decision wasn't prompted by a sudden discovery of his courage but by the fact that all of the so called easy ways out were not, in the long run, a whole lot less painful than doing the right thing. It seemed to him that the situation in which he found himself, or more accurately had *placed* himself, almost guaranteed that sooner or later he was going to have to pay the piper.

His decision boiled down to whether to pay the piper now—the difficult approach—or pay the piper eventually—the approach that would be easier now but terrifying later.

No matter how he weighed the issues, he couldn't deny that an almost intangible factor kept insinuating itself in thin layers on the outer fringes of his mind. That was the notion that innocent people were involved here.

And, many years ago, some very bad people had done some very bad things to some other innocent people. And, though Benson was never much of a crusader, or a man of even modest honor, the inequities of this situation screamed at him to do the right thing.

As he came closer and closer to deciding to do the right thing, the itching on his torso seemed to subside. Probably just his imagination, but still…

Finally, he decided to go over the head of his boss, who had kept him in a state of almost constant terror for close to thirty years, and pray that whomever he confided in would have the courage and integrity to do the right thing too. If not, the right thing would most definitely turn out all wrong.

All it would take was one little telephone call.

In deciding what to do, Benson surprisingly had found himself asking, "What would John Hawkin do?"

Even when Benson was putting Hawkin under house arrest in the basement, he respected the man. Hawkin was the kind of man

Benson had always wanted to be, although he rarely admitted it to himself. Benson didn't have the right stuff.

Maybe, he considered, a person wasn't just born with the right stuff. Maybe people got the right stuff a little at a time. Maybe possessing the right stuff is the result of making one's very first decision a right decision. And maybe that decision makes the second right decision easier. Somewhere along the way, maybe a person wakes up one morning realizing that he has made a lot of right decisions. Just like Benson awoke one day realizing he had made a lot of wrong decisions.

And maybe, just maybe, a man who made a lifetime of wrong choices could get up enough courage to make his first right decision. Maybe that's why God, or whoever's driving this thing, sent him this whole terrible mess. Maybe it was the chance of a lifetime.

Benson smiled his first real smile in a long, long time. He decided to place the call.

Glancing at the bottle of calamine lotion, Benson took strange satisfaction in knowing that it was just about empty. *I won't need that any more.* He tossed it into the trash can symbolically.

He picked up his cell phone. His hand trembled as he dialed the familiar number.

As the phone on the other end began to ring, Benson heard the first faint whispering of an automobile engine in the distance. He walked to the side window of his office and glanced down the road toward the main gate. A second ring. A trail of dust followed the approaching vehicle. As the third ring registered, Benson recognized the automobile.

The recorded message on the other end of the phone intoned, "Central Intelligence Agency." Benson pushed the "end" button on his cell phone and laid it on his desk. A bead of sweat formed between his eyebrows. He unconsciously retrieved the calamine lotion bottle from the waste basket and placed it in its rightful place next to his radio.

The BMW 740 slid to a halt next to Benson's office window. Even out here in the wilderness, at a dead stop, the vehicle looked like it was roaring down the interstate. A man had no business bringing a fine vehicle like that out on a road like this.

Frank Sheffield didn't care. His vehicles came with the position, a new one each year, at taxpayer expense.

The man Benson feared most in the entire world had arrived.

Frank Sheffield ate men like Benson for breakfast, just like a large bowl of Captain Crunch, chewing each morsel down to a milk-logged paste before consigning it to the depths of his voracious, acid-fueled digestive tract.

Sheffield and three agents stepped out of the BMW in unison, as if executing a carefully choreographed governmental dance. Each checked his timepiece with governmental big-wig flair, and looked up at the sun as if to check the accuracy of the timepiece against the chronology of the heavens, with James Bond confidence.

To create the illusion that he was working feverishly on some important matter, Benson took several files from his desk drawer and spread them out with a flurry on his desk. Then he hurried out to the front porch so as not to keep his superior waiting—although he knew that Frank Sheffield waited for no man.

Sheffield's highly polished Gucci loafer was already resting authoritatively upon the first step as Benson made his cheerful, beaming appearance on the porch.

"What the hell's been going on here, Benson?" spat the bureaucrat. "I expected you'd have this mess cleaned up days ago. I see the farmhouse is still standing. Not very good at following orders, are you?"

The image of the calamine lotion bottle flashed before Benson's vacuous eyes. "Things got complicated out here," he stammered. "I had to make some changes in plans to protect you."

The minute Benson uttered those fateful words, he wished he could suck them back into his mouth, past his vocal chords, and into the lungs that might not be functioning by this time tomorrow.

"Protect me? Protect me? What the hell you talking about?" Sheffield shouted. "You think maybe I've got something to do with whatever happened out here? You better straighten out your thinking, asshole. This situation's got nothing to do with me. You got that?"

Benson nodded meekly.

"Where the hell are all your men? You running some kind of a circus out here?"

"No sir," cowered Benson.

"You get your ass right on up to that house so I can see first-hand what the hell your situation is."

Benson started to head for the BMW, then realized that Sheffield meant for him to walk to the farmhouse.

Benson started walking beside the road, the BMW a few feet behind him.

"No, asshole," yelled Sheffield from behind the wheel. "Not *beside* the road. *Down* the road in the middle, like you got some sense."

Benson moved into the middle of the road, onto the grassy mound between the tire trails.

Then Benson's heart leapt as he felt the BMW's bumper pressing against one of his calves. He began running. The faster he ran, the faster the car followed, never more than a few inches behind his legs. Benson worried that if the bumper were to get any closer, his lower leg might get caught between it and the ground. He ran faster, just about as fast as his body would carry him, the BMW in hot pursuit. Sheffield leaned on the horn. Benson had already exceeded his physical capabilities, his heart racing, sweat pouring down the sides of his rib cage, tears filling his eyes.

The horn again. *Faster.* He thought his heart would burst.

Just when he thought he couldn't possibly take another step, he felt that bumper again. Almost caught on his calf muscle this time. *Faster, faster.*

He fell.

The auto screeched to a halt, the engine pressed against the backs of Benson's upper legs, pinning them tightly to the ground, the heat from the automobile's scalding hot oil pan burning his skin, melting it.

Benson shrieked in pain.

Sheffield appeared at his side. "Do you want me to back the car off of you?"

"Yes! Yes!" Benson screamed.

"Do you understand what will happen to you if my name is ever linked to this mess?"

"Yes!"

"Don't ever forget that."

Sheffield backed the BMW off of Benson, tearing his pants and removing a layer of skin from his upper legs.

Benson lay there, face down, unable to move.

He was yanked violently to his feet. He stood there, only a few yards from the farmhouse, barely able to retain his balance.

The two agents he had assigned to guard the farmhouse came running from either side of it, in response to Benson's screams. They stood there, gaping at the blood flowing down Benson's legs, nauseated by the smell of burning flesh.

The agents were quick to fill Sheffield in on the details of the situation. As they spilled their guts, Benson was deep in thought in spite of the horrendous pain he was experiencing.

His thought was plain and simple, irrevocable. Benson decided, once and for all, that he was going to do the right thing. He had suffered the greatest fear, the greatest humiliation, the greatest pain he ever thought possible. And here he was, still alive and standing. He called forth every ounce of courage he had and forced his legs to straighten, his back to unbend, his shoulders to pull back. From this moment forward, Herbert Benson III would act like a man, like Big John Hawkin would act.

Benson's men led Sheffield and his three henchmen to the kitchen and showed them the basement door. They unlocked it and stepped aside, allowing Sheffield to look into the cellar.

Sheffield grabbed Benson's man to his right and threw him down the stairs. Within seconds, Sheffield's men had thrown Benson and the remaining agent down the same flight of stairs. The last sound Benson heard before he passed out was the clicking of the padlock.

By the time Benson came around, his men had been tied and gagged.

Michael and Clint had left Benson unbound, not wanting to cause him further pain and knowing that he was in no condition to cause any harm. They, of course, had removed all weapons from their new roommates.

Outside, the sun was beginning to set behind the mountains. Sheffield was busy on his cell phone, informing the local fire and forestry departments that the federal government was conducting a fire drill within the perimeters of its top-secret compound. Nobody was to respond to the fire, under penalty of consequences that no mortal man would want to endure.

Just as the sun disappeared behind the peaks to the west, Sheffield instructed his three men to take a walk around the farmhouse to assure themselves that there was no means of escape from the building. They placed several more boulders over the area where the tunnel ran underground from the building to the gigantic boulder that filled its entry, using one of the sedans to push those boulders into place with its front bumper.

Twenty minutes later they returned, reporting that all was secure.

Sheffield's men were, among other things, experts in the art of arson. He instructed them to torch the house and to do it in such a manner that it would do a slow burn. He wanted to be a good hour away when the fire got serious.

As soon as the building was irrevocably aflame, Sheffield and his men left the area. He called his office on a secure line and instructed his most trusted man to have a small crew of completely trustworthy and expendable men out to the compound by early morning. Their assignment was to use the John Deere in the barn to push any remaining debris into the basement and to cover the area with a foot of topsoil, to be obtained from the nearby forest. They were to plant several hundred seedlings on the site and spread grass and wildflower seeds over the entire area, including the former lawn.

Sheffield told that same man that he intended to send an inspector out to the site next spring, shortly after the snow had melted. And, if that inspector was able to tell that a building had ever been there, everyone involved would be terminated.

He looked down at the ground where Benson's blood had stained the soil. He wiped a trace of blood from his bumper, spit on the spot where Benson had fallen, walked around to the driver-side door, and grunted, "Let's get out of here."

As Sheffield drove away, a smirk of self-satisfaction on his face, the flames were already coming out of the ground floor windows, licking the sides of the building.

Chapter Sixty-six

Mortimer was deep in thought. He had been pacing the floor of the tool shed for a couple of hours, reviewing the events of the last few days, trying to make sense out of what was happening. Three days ago his Wednesday started as usual—a cup of hot chocolate with a shot of Amaretto, just for flavor. My, how Mortimer loved his hot chocolate!

He had planned on taking three of his kids fishing on the Elk Horn. There was a pool a few hundred yards below the waterfall at the edge of Jerry Larson's cantaloupe farm where the fishing was mighty good, even this late in the season.

These kids were young. The oldest, Erin, was ten, and so cute that just looking at her made Mortimer's heart zing. The twins, Eric and Heather, were seven, little red-headed, freckle-faced munchkins. They loved to fish, especially with Mortimer.

They lost their Daddy when Erin was eight. Jim had worked for the State, running a snowplow on the high mountain passes between Sprague and Kensington. He had taken a big risk, clearing the highway to get to a family that was trapped by an avalanche. Jim knew it was dangerous. More than two feet of powder had fallen during the preceding ten hours, making the new accumulations of snow on the mountain sides unstable at that high altitude where the humidity was low.

The roar of the big Detroit diesel that powered his grader was enough to loosen a wall of powder. Jim had just pulled the station wagon free from the five feet of snow piled on top of it. As the family of six headed slowly down the state highway toward Sprague and a good rest in a cozy motel, Jim decided he'd better take a look at the other side of the pass. There was still about a mile of "Big Slide," as the locals called it that he hadn't checked. Never know when someone might be up there, even in this weather. There are always some flatlanders who don't know that high mountain passes are not to be trusted when the weather is threatening.

He was happy to find that nobody was there. He was also mighty tired after a fourteen-hour shift. It was time to get home to Laurie and those babies and a nice soft bed.

By the time Jim heard that terrible roar, it was too late. The old motor grader wasn't fast enough. It had been burning a lot of oil lately. Jim had suggested to Al, the chief mechanic, that the faithful old grader was overdue for a ring job. He held the throttle lever full forward. But it just couldn't go any faster. The last thing Jim saw was the powder flying up from his front wheels. Seconds later it hit with ten thousand tons of Mother Nature's power.

Erin took it the hardest. She and her dad had been almost inseparable. She had given him her Saint Christopher medal that she had received for her First Communion. It was always hanging from the windshield wiper knob in the grader.

Jim was buried in his only suit, the Saint Christopher medal pinned to the lapel.

Erin cried herself to sleep every night for a long time. Then one morning she came to the breakfast table. "I talked to Daddy last night," she announced, as if it were the most natural thing in the world. "He's in heaven. He said I'm not supposed to cry for him any more. He's happy as he can be. The only time he gets sad is when he looks down and sees me crying. So I promised him I'd be happy and help you with the twins."

Laurie marveled at the vivid imagination of her oldest child.

That afternoon, she changed the linens on the kids' beds. Under Erin's pillow, neatly wrapped in a small piece of flannel, was the Saint Christopher medal.

Laurie never asked Erin how it got there.

Mortimer took the kids fishing often. And sometimes they went to Memorial Park on the edge of town for a picnic. "Mortimer makes the yummiest tuna sandwiches ever," Heather would say.

Now, as Mortimer paced the floor of that musty old tool shed he thought about his kids, how they must be terribly worried by now. It was late, and he was to have picked them up at 11:30. He forced himself to focus on the present situation.

Thursday morning two men in suits had come to his little house, telling him that Tim and Jaime were in trouble and needed him right away. Mortimer was so concerned about his boys that he didn't even think to call Laurie and tell her he'd be late to pick up her kids.

Then he was locked in a room all day, with only a little water and a cheese sandwich. Nobody would answer his questions. Early Friday he was taken from that room by the same two men and loaded into a car.

The drive to the compound took several hours. When Mortimer asked about Jaime and Tim, the men told him it was classified information and he was not to ask any more about it until they got there. They refused to tell him where "there" was.

Mortimer was nervous. He kept playing with his fingernails, as he invariably did when he was upset.

When they finally arrived at the front gate of the compound, Mortimer was relieved to see Michael standing there. He was shocked, though, to see that Michael was holding a military rifle.

Michael had ordered the man driving the car to get out. Then the man sitting next to Mortimer in the back seat had pulled a pistol out of his jacket, pointed it at Mortimer's head, and ordered Michael to put down his weapon and get into the front passenger seat. Michael was so shocked to see Mortimer that he did nothing for a few seconds.

The man with the pistol repeated his orders in a much more demanding tone. Michael did as he was told. When he got into the car, the only thing he said was, "Are you okay, Mortimer?"

Mortimer nodded that he was, but inside he wasn't. Mortimer was about as scared as he'd ever been.

Now, as he paced the floor, he knew the others had been taken to the big house about half a mile up the road. He didn't understand why he was locked in the tool room of this barn instead of being taken to where the others were.

It was dark by now. Mortimer had heard a car drive by a while ago, heading toward the gate, but since then, not a sound.

What was going on? What was happening to his family?

Then he sat on the floor and cried. He cried for Tim and Jaime and Sarah and Michael. He cried for Erin and Eric and Heather. They must be frantic. He knew their mother must have called his home a dozen times and probably had the sheriff looking for him by now.

He thought about his little sister Ellie. Whenever Mortimer was tense or sad or frightened, he thought about Ellie. That image of her looking out the window of their burning home never faded, not a single bit. He prayed for her often and always asked her to forgive him for not getting there in time.

Now, as Mortimer sat in the darkness, he couldn't make out the grain of the wood planks on the floor as he could a while ago.

He used his memory to reconstruct the features of the room. He remembered that there was a small hole in one wall where it looked like an electric box had once been. A piece of conduit ran from just above that opening to a light fixture hanging from the ceiling. But there was no power. Mortimer pulled the string hanging from the chain that came out of the ceramic fixture, but the light hadn't come on. Mortimer didn't like the dark, at least not dark so intense that he couldn't see anything.

Then he did notice something. On the far wall, a faint, reddish-orange glow was dancing on the wood grain. It wasn't very bright but, in contrast to the total darkness to which his eyes had become accustomed, it was noticeable. He knew it hadn't been there long. In all that darkness, it was too obvious for him not to have seen it right away.

Mortimer strained to see it more clearly, trying to figure out what could be making the wall glow. Then he realized the light was coming through the opening where the electrical box had been. He rose on his stiff legs, thinking they weren't designed to lift so much weight.

He turned to face the wall behind him. The hole was higher than eye level. He had to stand on his toes to see through it.

What Mortimer saw through that little hole took his breath away. "No! No!" he screamed. "Dear God, no!"

Several trees stood between the barn and the source of the light that cast the soft glow on the wall of Mortimer's prison. But he could see a building on fire, the house where his family was, in flames.

Dear God, no!

Mortimer looked around, frantic.

The glow on the wall was brighter now, allowing him to make out some details of the room. The walls were constructed of thick wooden planks, fastened from the inside with nails. He tried to pull some of those planks loose, but he couldn't get a grip. There was nothing to hold on to. He tried to dig his fingernails into the wood. No use. They were fastened from the inside to the studs that formed the wall. He kicked them several times as hard as he could, but they were too thick for him to break.

Why was he so fat and weak? Maybe someone stronger could break through them. He kicked and he kicked.

He turned his back to the wall and leaned against it, his head in his hands. *Dear God no, not again.*

The glow on the far wall was growing brighter. He looked, once again, through the opening. Flames were pouring out of the downstairs windows of the big house.

He turned back to the room, thinking, thinking.

Then he saw something he hadn't considered before. Two of the walls faced the outside of the barn. A third faced the inside of the barn. But the fourth wall faced toward another storage room that Mortimer had noticed when they brought him here. But what he hadn't noticed until now was that the wooden planks on the wall between his room and the storeroom next door were not fastened from his side of the wall. They had been fastened from the other side.

Theoretically, he could kick them off the wall. It depended a lot on how they had been fastened. If they were screwed on, it would be a lot harder. But in the days when this barn was built, he guessed they would have used nails.

Mortimer crossed his fingers. His chances for success depended on how much force he could bring to bear on those planks. That wouldn't be a problem. Mortimer had all the incentive he needed.

Someone in Mortimer's situation might have kicked those planks with the front of his foot, but not Mortimer. He was smarter than that. He got down on all fours with his back side to the wall. He brought his left knee up against his abdomen and ripped loose with the kick of a mule. With that first strike, Mortimer knew that wall was history. He kicked and he kicked, with ever increasing intensity. With each kick, those nails slid out of the studs another sixteenth of an inch. A couple of times, Mortimer's knee struck the head of a nail sticking up from the floor. He could have cared less. In fact, the pain only served to enrage him and cause him to kick all the harder. By the twenty-seventh kick, the lower half of the plank broke loose from its moorings.

Mortimer jumped up, grabbed the lower half of that plank, and pushed it away from the wall. The nails holding the upper half of the plank squealed their resistance to Mortimer's efforts, but to no avail. Victory was his.

He began to push his way through the opening, only to find that his gut wouldn't fit through it. He even took a running start. This resulted in his being wedged between the planks on either side of the opening.

"You fat old man," he cursed.

He jumped back down on the floor and began blasting away at the plank next to the one that had recently abandoned its post. In seconds it was gone, the victim of Mortimer's increased frenzy.

But now what? All Mortimer had accomplished was to gain access to the adjoining room. He tried the door. It was locked. "Shit!"

Mortimer felt around the new room and found that two of the walls were covered with instruments of escape, blessed tools. He grabbed a ten-pound hammer, raised its business end high into the air, and brought it crashing against the door at the exact spot where the bolts held the hasp secure to the other side. With four strikes, the wood behind those ill-fated bolts shattered. Mortimer reared back with his right leg and, this time using a frontal attack, blasted the door wide open.

He was shocked by the brightness flooding in through the barn's double main doors.

What to do next?

The John Deere. Of course. Lots of torque. Plenty of speed in high range. And a glorious front loader attached. An eight-wheeler. All so familiar to Mortimer, the result of all those summers spent on his Uncle Chuck's farm.

Mortimer sent forth a powerful and sincere prayer, backed by the strength of all the love he had for his family, those wonderful people who needed him so desperately. *Please God, let there be a key in the ignition.*

Then he added another request, *please don't let me be late this time!*

He paused for a moment, remembering something he had read once in a book by Richard Bach or Ram Daas or someone. *The hell with that "please" shit. Do I not have the power? You bet I do!* He closed his eyes, focused his energy, and revised his prayer.

I, Mortimer Alan Ziffel, do hereby command the power of the universe that I shall be there in time.

He pictured himself arriving in time to rescue his loved ones. He saw them safe.

He held the thought without an ounce of doubt for a good twenty seconds. He couldn't afford to take time to wrestle with faith and doubt and all that wishy-washy stuff. His family was in danger. He was tempted not to spend those precious twenty seconds waiting for his prayer to congeal, but he knew something about how manifesting worked. The time was well spent.

After hoisting himself into the padded seat, Mortimer reached down to turn on the ignition. There it was, big as life, just as he knew it would be, with a little white plastic tag with a gold "Western Realty" logo emblazoned on it: A key from God. "Thank you," he whispered.

He turned the key to the glow-plug position and waited until the glowing coil in the little hole told him the beast was ready. Then he turned the key two more clicks to the right, engaging the heavy-duty Bendix starter motor, at the same time checking to be sure the transfer case was in high range. As soon as he heard the familiar diesel rumble and saw the flapper valve raise on top of the exhaust stack, he adjusted the throttle, depressed the clutch, and rammed the transmission into second gear. He let out the clutch, and the John Deere sprang forward, snapping Mortimer's head back.

Chapter Sixty-seven

Chris was the first to notice the smoke seeping into the basement from under the steel door at the top of the stairs. As alarm spread among the prisoners, Michael and Clint admonished everyone to remain calm.

Until now, they hadn't considered digging out of the basement, thinking that Sheffield and his men would be waiting outside, ready to shoot anyone coming up out of the ground. The startling realization that there was a fire above them, changed things in several ways, not the least of which was a desperate need to get out, fast.

It seemed reasonable that, with the building on fire, Sheffield and his goons probably had left the area, not wanting to be connected with a mass murder. A fire of the magnitude that would be created by a building this large would likely attract attention for quite a distance.

Whatever fate awaited them outside had to be better than burning in this basement.

At first they went to the far end of the tunnel and began digging upward. Within seconds they ran into the new boulders that Sheffield's men had placed above the entire run of the tunnel. They tried again, a couple of feet closer to the building. Another boulder settled a few inches into the tunnel, scaring Chris and Tim, who were lying on their backs, digging upward.

"No use trying the tunnel," Tim yelled. "It seems like they have it totally covered with boulders."

They began digging in earnest into the wall of the basement with their bare hands. The soil conditions were such that it became apparent, early on, that digging to the surface would take some time. But dig they did, with the vigor befitting their situation.

Now Michael wished he hadn't taken the shovel upstairs that Hawkin had left when he finished digging the tunnel.

Chris suggested that they consider untying the agents, thinking they might help with the digging. But they decided against it, realizing that it didn't make sense to dig more than one tunnel and only about three people could dig in the hole without getting in each others' way. And, untying the agents would take up some of their very precious time.

Sarah found a few rags in a cabinet and stuffed them into the cracks around the door to help keep the smoke out. The steel door was already warm, even though it was a good half-inch thick.

"Remember," encouraged Becky, "we have the power. Let's all keep calm and focus on some miracle getting us out of here."

"And remember, too," Daryl reminded them, "heat travels upward. There's a chance that the fire could burn out before it gets too hot down here. We have to keep the smoke out until the tunnel is finished." He knew that what he said didn't make a whole lot of sense. But what they all needed now was hope.

Tim, Jaime, and Chris had been doing the digging, and they needed to rest their hands. They backed out of the hole and were replaced by Michael, Clint, and Gail.

Hawkin had been quiet all of this time, still dealing with the shock from his gruesome, heart-breaking discovery. *What in the world was Mikey doing here?*

He asked Benson what he knew about the situation. Benson told him and the others about how this had all been planned and carried out by Frank Sheffield. He told John that Sheffield had re-routed a transport plane from Vietnam to an abandoned airfield about fifty miles from the compound back in 1975. Sheffield had then transported the soldiers to the compound to guard the prisoners and later had personally overseen the execution of the civilians and the soldiers.

After that brief conversation, Hawkin went back into the small room, in spite of his desperate desire to be as far away from that tomb as possible. He checked the uniforms and equipment and dog tags of the soldiers in that room. Sure enough, they all came from Vietnam. They were the missing soldiers who had left Hanoi but were never reported as arriving back in the United States.

So, Sheffield had taken them off the plane and brought them to this place to do his dirty work. Then he must have destroyed any record of the plane arriving, assuming that the authorities would conclude the plane was lost at sea. He could have easily had the plane flown back out to sea and ditched by one of his men, who would have parachuted into the water and been picked up by some of his other men.

Sheffield had probably convinced Mikey and the others that these families were being guarded for purposes of national security.

One thing Hawkin knew with absolute certainty was that Mikey would never shoot civilians, not even under orders.

Sheffield had come out here in the end and killed everyone, just as Benson had said.

Knowing what he now knew, Hawkin was determined to get out of here one way or another. He pulled Gail gently out of the tunnel, where she had been digging beside Clint and Michael. Hawkin began digging like a madman. And, although Clint and Michael were applying super-human effort, their progress paled in comparison to that of Big John, who was throwing dirt behind him like a dog digging for a bone.

Without the proper tools, the tunnel would take at least half an hour to dig. And they feared the ceiling would cave in on them before then. Everyone knew it was probably an impossible situation. But they had to try.

Big John Hawkin didn't know any such thing.

Everyone in that room was focused on a miracle. But Hawkin didn't need any damned miracle. He had a picture in his mind, one he couldn't erase no matter how hard he tried. He was seeing a picture of Frank Sheffield holding a pistol to Mikey's head. No, John Hawkin didn't need anything.

In the time it took Mortimer to kick and pound his way out of the shed and to get the tractor moving, the fire in the living room of the farmhouse had grown dramatically. The flames now were coming out of the upper-floor windows and the chimney, shooting a good thirty feet into the air.

The living room floor was covered in flames. Those in the basement who weren't busy digging were standing on wooden crates they stacked on the floor, reaching up to stuff rags into any cracks where the smoke was seeping into the room.

Eventually embers began to drop from the ceiling as the fire worked its way through the overhead planks. There weren't enough rags to fill all of the cracks, and it became harder and harder to breathe.

At first, they saw only about five or six glowing spots in the ceiling, and they were able to control these by throwing water on them from the jugs they had brought down yesterday. But now there were so many burning holes that they couldn't even begin to control them. In a matter of minutes, several thousand pounds of flaming lumber would come crashing down on them.

The heat was intense.

In the attic, the temperature had risen to the point where Chas could feel it through the soles of his shoes. In spite of his bindings, he managed to get up on his feet, stimulated sufficiently by the heat that almost blistered his butt. He found that it was coolest next to the chimney, and he stood there, knowing the end was near. Thoughts of regret had been taunting him for hours, chagrin for the life he had lived. He mourned the total waste of a human life, one spent in utter selfishness. He decided he deserved to die.

Then he rethought that proposition. No, he deserved to live. He deserved to live so he could make amends for all of the disgusting things he had done. For the first time in Chas's life, he had an honest reason to live. By God, if he ever got out of this mess, the world would see a new Chas. He thought about Ebenezer Scrooge and the transformation he had made.

No, it wasn't too late. There was something for Chas to live for, lot to live for.

He had a lot of changes to make. Look out world.

Chapter Sixty-eight

Less than half a mile from the farmhouse, the wind blew through Mortimer's hair, causing it to stand out straight behind his head, as the John Deere roared down the dirt road. His eyes were transfixed on the burning building. His family was in there. He slammed down the clutch and shoved the shift lever into fifth gear.

The John Deere seldom went this fast, and its suspension wasn't designed for this speed on anything except smooth roads. Mortimer bounced on the spring-loaded seat. He held on tight. "Don't you be late this time, you fat old man," he shouted into the wind. He pushed down with all his might on the throttle to be certain it was wide open.

At a quarter mile from the farmhouse, he looked up at the window of the dormer on the roof.

Ellie.

It was his Ellie, waiting for him, calling to him. He could see her mouth moving silently behind the glass, drowned out by the roaring fire. "Morty, Morty, help me, Morty."

He pressed harder on the throttle and slammed the transmission into sixth gear.

"Hold on, Ellie," he screamed. "Hold on, Mom and Dad. Morty's coming. I'm coming."

Dust poured out behind the tractor, its eight gigantic wheels churning in the dirt.

Mortimer saw the farmhouse racing toward him at an incredible speed, about to swallow him up. He had the presence of mind to reach down and snap the safety harness into place. He cinched it tight. The John Deere roared across the lawn and shot up the concrete stairs leading to the porch. "Hold on, Ellie—Morty's coming," he yelled as he shot through the big, double front doors of the farmhouse, tearing the casings out of the walls.

The sudden stop as the John Deere collided with the massive rock fireplace was so intense that it tore two of the nylon belts of the safety harness. If one more belt had been severed, Mortimer's body would also have made violent contact with the fireplace. The seat itself, to which the harness had been attached, was almost ripped loose from the heavy-duty coil springs that held it to the tractor's frame.

The impact almost caused Mortimer to lose consciousness. He looked around. Flames were everywhere. The heat was so intense that he had to shield his face. His back burned, and so did the sides of his neck. He released the remains of the harness and climbed down to the floor.

In the basement, everyone was down on the floor, trying to breathe what few precious traces of oxygen remained.

Jaime looked up and saw the ceiling sag several inches.

"Where is everyone?" shouted Mortimer to the empty room.

He headed toward the stairway leading to the second floor. The risers were aflame, and the banister had been almost totally destroyed. He felt the scorching air rushing past him up the stairway.

When he reached the upstairs hallway, he stopped and shouted, "Where is everyone?"

Then, above the roar of the fire, he heard a faint sound. It was a voice. It seemed to be above him. He looked up and saw a doorway in the ceiling. There was a hasp on it. "Is someone there?" Mortimer yelled, coughing out the smoke that was attacking his lungs.

"Help!" came the plaintiff cry, "Help!"

Mortimer reached up for the hasp. It was too high. He ran into one of the bedrooms. Nobody was there. He grabbed an old rickety nightstand. He carried it out into the hallway and placed it below the overhead door. He climbed up on it, afraid the old piece of furniture wouldn't hold his hefty body. He stood up. The nightstand creaked, loud enough to be heard above the roar of the fire. He touched the hasp. It was very hot, blistering hot. He slid his shirt sleeve down toward his fingers.

With his shirt sleeve acting as a buffer between the flesh of his fingers and the blazing hot hasp, Mortimer managed to give it a tug. It released. The door came crashing down on Mortimer. Chas had been standing on top of the door. If it hadn't been spring-loaded, Chas probably would have come down fast enough to knock Mortimer cold. As it was, it caused a serious welt on Mortimer's forehead. But at least he remained conscious.

"Who are you?" Mortimer asked, as he untied Chas, realizing instantly the irrelevance of his question. "Where are the others?" he demanded before Chas had time to respond to his first inquiry.

"I think they're in the basement. I've been locked up there for some time, and I've been able to hear only bits and pieces of what's been going on."

"Come with me," Chas shouted as he ran toward the now marginally stable stairs.

As the two men stepped gingerly down the stairs, two of the risers collapsed under the weight of Mortimer's footsteps. Both times Chas caught Mortimer and helped him onto to the next step.

Chas led Mortimer to the kitchen and showed him the steel door that separated the kitchen from the basement. The kitchen wasn't as filled with flames as the other rooms were, but the smoke was still thick. The door was locked with an unusually large padlock. Mortimer was tempted to open the window above the sink to let in some air for their desperate lungs, but he decided that this would provide additional oxygen to the fire, maybe even cause the smoke in the kitchen area to burst into flame.

What to do?

They ran to the living room, where the fire was so intense that they could barely see the tractor. As they approached, they saw that the tires were on fire. Mortimer thought about all of the diesel fuel in that tank. The paint on the tank was already curling up and falling off. He ran to the front of the tractor and disengaged the power takeoff from the winch. He pulled out several feet of steel cable, using his shirt sleeves as buffers against the heat, and handed the hooked end to Chas.

Mortimer shouted as loud as he could, "Fasten this hook to the padlock, good and secure. Make sure it won't come loose when I put pressure on it. As soon as it's attached, get out of here as fast as you can. This place is coming down any minute."

Chas ran to the kitchen, dragging the heavy cable behind him, using a towel he had brought from the kitchen to keep his hands from burning. Mortimer helped it unwind from the spool. Seconds later, Chas appeared in the doorway, giving the thumbs-up sign. Mortimer was already in the seat, trying not to scream from the pain of the blazing hot leather. He motioned for Chas to leave. Then, as Chas ran out through the opening where the front door had been,

Mortimer backed the tractor out of the living room and down the stairs, ripping the padlock off the hasp on the steel door.

Mortimer probably could have removed the lock, using the power takeoff and the winch, but it would have taken longer. Besides, he wanted to get the weight of the tractor off the floor. If people were alive down there, they certainly didn't need a ten-ton tractor landing in their laps.

As Mortimer ran back into the burning building and headed for the steel door, Chas was running right beside him. "I thought I told you to get out of here!" screamed Mortimer. "We don't have a chance. Save yourself!"

Chas ignored him, a strange smile on his face.

In the basement, the ladies were busy untying the agents' legs. Everyone was coughing uncontrollably. The smoke was blinding. Their hope against hope was that when the ceiling collapsed, they might avoid being crushed by the falling debris and a few of them might be able to crawl through the hole in the ceiling, using the crates they had been standing on.

As Becky was unwrapping the duct tape from around the ankles of one of the agents, the door at the top of the stairs flew open. There stood Chas and Mortimer.

Several of the agents were now able to walk. Others still had their legs taped. There wasn't time to release all of them.

Clint and Michael began pushing the ladies up the stairs, shouting "Go, go, go!" Sarah, Gail, Maria, and Becky ran for all they were worth, out the door, around the corner, through the scorching hot living room, hands shielding their faces, and down the stairs to oxygen—blessed, cool, sweet oxygen. They gasped, sucking that precious air into their lungs as fast as they could.

Behind them came their men and the agents who had been untied; several carried other men over their shoulders, everyone gasping for air.

"There are still four agents in the basement," Chris shouted. "They're still tied. We can't let them die."

The men turned and started back toward the building, choking and gasping. As they reached the bottom of the porch stairs, they looked up, and there stood Mortimer and Chas on the top step, each carrying two agents, one over each shoulder, looking like they were about to collapse. Chas looked like Ebenezer Scrooge on Christmas morning.

The men quickly relieved Chas and Mortimer of their burdens, laying the agents on the lawn next to the others.

Mortimer looked up at the attic dormer. For the first time, he noticed that the window had bars over it. Strange—he hadn't seen those bars before. It was like it was a different window. Behind those bars he now saw the face of Ellie, his dear Ellie. She was smiling, waving to him. He couldn't hear what she was saying, but he could clearly read the words on her lips: "Thank you, Morty. I love you."

In that moment, Mortimer Ziffel knew that everything was going to be just fine.

"One left to go," shouted Becky.

Everyone looked at her, questioning.

"I didn't see anyone else," yelled Chas. "I think we got them all."

Just then a mighty roar came from inside the building as the main floor collapsed, pulling in the side walls and the second floor down on top of it.

"Hawkin," Becky screamed. "He never came out. Maybe he was still digging. Maybe he didn't know we got out."

Michael erupted. "It's too late! Not even Big John could survive that!"

Everyone sat in silence on the big, cool lawn, surrounded by the beautiful pine forest, breathing in the precious air. All were glad to be alive. But most were thinking about Big John Hawkin and how he must have died only minutes ago, choking on smoke and grieving over his little brother.

Tim and Jaime sat beside each other. Each was staring down at the lawn, elbows resting on his knees.

Tim was the first to look up, staring intently into the flames. A minute later Jaime raised his head and stared into that same sad building. They sat there for a while, mesmerized by the flames, numbed by the events of the day. Then Jaime turned his head to look at Tim, his best friend, his hero, his brother.

What Jaime saw startled him. Tim had That Look in his eyes. Jaime suddenly knew what Tim was thinking.

He took Michael aside and said, "Dad, get everyone over to the barn. Stay there until Tim and I get there. We've got something important to do. Please don't ask. Just trust us. Then we'll take you to a canyon where we can hide until we're able to figure out how to deal with Sheffield and his men. We can't stay here. There'll probably be men coming tomorrow to check on the farmhouse and cover up what happened."

With help from Daryl and Clint, Michael untied the agents' legs so everyone could walk to the barn.

It was now Saturday night. They didn't have many hours before Sheffield's cleanup crew was due to arrive.

Daryl ran down to Benson's office and retrieved the first-aid kit.

Once they were settled in the barn, Sarah and Maria started to dress Benson's injuries. Nobody else had any serious wounds, although a few had minor burns. For now, everyone was fine—except for the loss of Big John Hawkin.

Chapter Sixty-nine

Tim and Jaime went to the side of the farmhouse where the old tunnel entry was located. They hoped desperately to find Hawkin there. They hoped he had completed the new tunnel after the others had left the basement but before the ceiling collapsed. They hoped he had taken refuge in the tunnel and escaped the torturous death of cremation beneath the remains of the farmhouse.

But they both knew there was little hope. They knew that even if Hawkin had managed to hide in the dead-end tunnel, he surely would have died of suffocation. Besides, he wouldn't have been far enough away from the intense heat to keep from burning to death. It had to have been gruesome.

What they couldn't understand was why Hawkin hadn't left with the others. Was he so intent on his digging that he hadn't noticed they were leaving up the stairway?

The basement was still way too hot for Tim and Jaime to go down there. Besides, what would be the use? There was no hope of finding Hawkin alive. Nobody could survive heat that intense. Still, they would surely like to know what had happened. It was important to their plan.

"I've got an idea," Jaime said. "What if we move time ahead? When Mortimer was killed at the football stadium, we made time stand still and even move backward. Why couldn't we make time move ahead?"

"Then what?" asked Tim.

"Then we could go down into the cooled down basement and see if we can figure out what happened to John."

"I don't know," Tim objected. "If we move time beyond tomorrow, Sheffield's clean-up crew would have probably been here already and the basement likely would be filled with dirt."

"But what if it doesn't work that way?" inquired Jaime. "What if we move time forward in only one area and leave the rest of the world as it is? Isn't that really what we did before? Didn't we move the entire stadium back in time while we stood still? Or maybe we moved the whole world back in time."

"Better yet," Tim suggested, "maybe we didn't move anything or anybody in time but ourselves. Wouldn't that be simpler? Maybe instead of moving time backward, we moved ourselves forward, so we were where we needed to be in time to change events or objects so Mortimer wouldn't be killed."

"You know what?" asked Jaime. "I think it probably doesn't matter. I think all we have to do is command the universe to give us the results we want. We do that with absolute faith and let The Force work out the details."

They sat on the ground facing each other. They focused their energy and concentrated. They pictured themselves in tomorrow, ignoring as best they could anything that reminded them of today. Nothing happened. They tried for several more minutes. Still nothing.

Tim said he felt a gentle tugging in the center of his forehead, but other than that, nothing.

"I've got an idea!" Jaime exclaimed.

"Shoot."

"We're only about a quarter mile away from an unbelievably powerful and outrageously advanced piece of hardware, from somewhere out there in never-never land, like the Pleiades or Alpha Centauri or some other Star Wars place like that. I wouldn't be at all surprised if it could give us a hand."

"Roger that." Tim said.

The boys sprinted all the way to the bunker, Tim giving Jaime a surprisingly decent run for his money.

"Click." "Whir." "Thunk."

"Okay, where do we go from here?" asked Tim.

Before Jaime could respond, a mellow, almost feminine voice with what seemed like a mild Australian accent, said, "State your intentions."

Tim looked around, a look of wonder on his face.

"I told you," Jaime smiled knowingly. "Magic, go for it."

"We wish to travel forward in time by one or two days," Tim explained, "without affecting anything but ourselves and a small geographic area. It's important that nothing else move forward with us, or else the geographic area we wish to examine will be compromised by some bad guys who intend to fill that area with several tons of dirt."

"Your cerebral cortex, cerebellum, and frontal lobes have been scanned. Very primitive. No offense. You do, however, have the ability to accomplish your objectives, but that ability has been seriously undermined by negative programming. You have almost completely lost your knowingness. The appropriate portions of your brain can be de-fragmented to restore the power you had when you arrived on planet Earth. However, substantial portions of your memory bank will have to be voided. This will almost certainly result in dramatic personality changes, all of which will be for the better in terms of your abilities to manifest your reality in accordance with your desires."

Tim hesitated. "I don't know about that. I like who I am, although a few changes in *his* personality might be an improvement."

"No, thank you," insisted Jaime. "We'd be fooling around with something we definitely don't understand. What if we turn out to be a couple of bad guys that use the power of this craft to do all kinds of evil things?"

"Not possible," spoke the soothing voice. "Our systems cannot facilitate evil."

"Still," continued Tim, "I don't like the idea of changing who we are so abruptly. I like slow, gradual change, the kind that happens as the result of our intentions based on careful thought."

"We could store the portions of your memories that were deleted for later reinstallation," offered the voice.

"Sounds risky to me," observed Jaime. "Can you not just help us with our little time travel program without major memory deletion?"

"As stated earlier, you do still have a small part of the power you possessed at birth. Most of that power has been negated by the programming of outside forces—your school systems, your organized religions, your media. You have the ability to reclaim that power over time. The most effective approach, short of the memory deletion suggested earlier, would be for you to read books on the topic by some of your leading thinkers. The problem is that some of the great books that were channeled onto your plane by masters from the non-physical realm have been corrupted by powerful organizations on your planet and no longer contain sufficient truth to be of much help. It is recommended that you consult writings of some of your grand masters, such as William Shakespeare, Ralph Waldo Emerson, Thomas Jefferson, and Kahlil Gibran.

"We realize, however, that such advice, although the best available, does not answer your short-term request. We shall attempt to be of immediate assistance. You have the ability to move ahead or behind in time, using the same factors you would use to manifest any other event. You use faith and desire. Our scan of your brains shows that you have used this power recently."

"That's right," agreed Jaime. "We moved time to save the life of our friend, Mortimer. But it doesn't seem to be working right now."

"Was the former situation more intense? Was your motivation stronger?"

"Yes, the man we were trying to bring back to life the first time was a dear, lifelong friend. The man who needs our help now is a recent acquaintance."

"That is one factor—relating to the intensity of your desire. Since your programming has reduced your knowing, it is helpful for your desire to be powerful.

"Most humans who attempt to reclaim their power are prompted to begin with relatively simple manifestations, like vaporizing clouds. To create a time warp or to bring someone back to life is a more difficult proposition.

"In that you have been successful in bringing a friend back to life once before, it should be easier this time, all other things being equal…easier to have faith, that is. So it is suggested, in your vernacular, that you goose up your desire a bunch. It should work. Each 'miracle' you perform gives you more faith for the next one.

"Almost all masters on the Earth plane during the past several thousand years have had to wrestle with the same problem. For example, your Good Book says that Jesus walked into the cave where Lazarus lay dead and simply commanded Lazarus to 'come forth.' We assure you that it didn't happen that way. It took Jesus several hours to work up the energy to perform that feat. And he had been studying the art of manifestation for more than fifteen years, under the direction of the Masters of the Far East. So don't be too hard on yourselves. You have actually done extremely well for your ages, a tribute to the fact that your parents had the wisdom to refrain from passing on to you much of the negative programming they received from others.

"You are young. You have many years in this lifetime to hone your skills. Be light about all of this. It is just a game. And if it does not work out the way you want in this lifetime, you have thousands more ahead of you.

"Let us help you a bit. Many in your situation have been assisted by other masters in breaking loose from the illusions of this physical plane. It just helps move things along.

"If you will go to the geographical location where you wish this event to take place and focus your minds on the outcome you want, we will use our power to augment yours—which is just as awesome as ours, once you know for an absolute certainty that you have it.

"By the way—if we may borrow one of your colloquialisms—it may not be necessary that you focus on moving time. It might be easier to merely put out to the universe the end result you want and let it determine the best procedure. It always knows the best way. Always. It is all right to specify many of the details of a manifestation, but it is not necessary. You could call forth something as generic as 'I command that henceforth my life shall be filled with pure joy.' If you do that with absolute faith and sufficient desire, the universe will deliver innumerable factors into your reality, bringing you more joy than you can possibly imagine, given your current programmed illusory limitations."

"Wow!" exclaimed Jaime. "That was a mouthful."

"Actually, fewer than a couple thousand bytes," countered the voice.

"You guys have a sense of humor?" asked Tim.

"Very much so," came the reply. "Compared to the way our friends on the Earth plane conduct their affairs, those of us in the spirit world are a bunch of stand-up comedians. Compared to the joy and enthusiasm experienced by most entities in the spirit world, your wonderful masters such as Jerry Seinfeld and Robin Williams are seriously depressed. It is pure joy here."

"You have no problems?" asked Jaime.

"None," came the reply. "But neither do you. The difference is that we know we have no problems and you think you do. But that is all right. Enjoy what you have. The choice you could make to enjoy it all, when coupled with faith and desire, would render it problem-free."

"Would it be appropriate to thank you?" asked Tim. "I mean, considering you're a machine, I think."

"Gratitude is always appropriate. What we *are* would not be possible to explain, given the limitations of your language. As close as we can come, we are of the spirit world, focusing, in this instance, through a mechanical-electrical device. When we channel information to you through another human, we are focusing through a biological-electrical device. Just know that all knowledge comes, ultimately, from Source Energy. Gratitude is for the benefit of he who is grateful."

"We are grateful for your willingness to help."

"You are most welcome. The God Source, of which everything is a part, is always willing to help. It cannot do otherwise. The only issue is whether you are willing to allow the help to come into your physical reality. Please feel free to contact us at any time, either by means of this mechanical-electrical device or your biological-electrical device, which includes not only your brain but every cell in your body.

"We will be standing by to augment your energy as you attempt to help your new friend. Just remember to 'know' that you have the power and that its only limitation is your willingness to allow."

Within minutes Tim and Jaime were back at the remains of the farmhouse near the tunnel entry, seated face to face.

"Which shall it be?" inquired Tim. "A trip ahead in time or a simple raising from the dead?" He laughed.

"Nothing I'd like better," said Jaime, "than to see where Big John is at this minute, so we could use our vivid imaginations to bring him back to life using some outrageously creative scheme. But, considering that a lot of people are waiting anxiously back at the barn so we can get out of here before the clean-up crew arrives, I suggest that we be content to do it the easy way."

"Easy way?" laughed Tim.

"Yes. Just focus on the result."

They agreed that each would think nothing but the highest thoughts possible for the next ten minutes, thoughts of joy and abundance and health and laughter and power and love.

At the end of that time, they would each picture Big John alive and well, with all their might and a big bunch of help from their friends back at the spaceship. Each would do his best to utilize absolute knowing. They would each 'know' that John had managed to survive the ravages of that terrible fire.

Eyes closed, foreheads scrunched, teeth clenched, necks tightened, hearts wide open, love pouring out to Hawkin, they put every ounce of will power they had into the effort. They kept it up for the entire time, neither of them wanting to let the other down.

Jaime pictured That Look on Tim's face, remembering Tim attacking the killer at the quarry pond. Tim thought about Mom, cutting off all of that beautiful hair for Jessica. They each thought about Mom and Dad, how they loved them. They thought about Big John, about what a courageous man he was, how he had stayed here for them, risked his life for them.

There was a scratching sound, a thumping sound, a tapping sound, then, more scratching.

Tim was the first to open his eyes. He turned on his flashlight, looking for the source of the sound.

"Did you hear something?" asked Jaime, as he opened his eyes.

"Listen," Tim whispered.

Scratch, scratch, tap, tap.

It was right between the two of them.

Thump, thump.

The soil began to split, several tiny lines spreading out like a spider crack on a pane of glass. Then, in the center of those little crack lines, the earth raised slightly, almost imperceptibly, into a little mound. Something poked up from the center of that mound.

A finger.

A big, thick, dark-brown finger, growing right out of the soil, covered with blood.

Tim smiled.

"We did it!" he yelled, before Jaime could fully appreciate what was happening. "We did it!"

The finger retreated briefly, replaced immediately thereafter by a fist. The fist shot a foot into the air, attached to a forearm that some-one had magically decorated with the same tattoo that Big Wonderful John Alexander Hawkin used to have on his now-deceased forearm.

The fist, like the finger, was covered with blood.

"Yahoo!" Jaime shouted, as he and Tim began digging franti-cally with their hands around the hole where that fabulous forearm had appeared.

In less than a minute, they cleared a hole two feet in diameter. There, smiling up at them as if nothing unusual had happened, was the one and only Big John Hawkin.

"What the hell are you two doing up here?" he asked. "You were in the basement about a minute ago!" He climbed up out of the hole. "How'd you get out of the basement? If I'd known there was another way out, I wouldn't have destroyed these hands digging like a fool."

"It's a long story," said Jaime. "We'll tell you about it when we have more time."

Tim lowered his upper torso into the hole from which Hawkin had just ascended. He aimed his flashlight down the short tunnel and, to his amazement, saw his dad and Clint shouting for everyone to head for the stairs. Maria was just stepping down from the crate she was using to help stuff rags between the overhead planks. Before Tim could recover from the shock of the data assaulting his befuddled mind, he came face to face with...himself.

There, at the other end of the short tunnel, was Timothy James Lasher. Tim almost screamed. He closed his eyes, no longer able to stand the incongruities appearing before him. He sat still for a couple of moments, not comprehending.

Tim pulled back from the opening, marveling.

A few minutes later, he felt a rush of heat and flames roar past his face and up into the night sky, singeing his eyebrows. Seconds later, the heat subsided. As Tim once again looked down into the tunnel, he saw that the ceiling of the basement had collapsed. Mercifully, none of his family or friends remained in the basement. Only one body lay there, clothing ablaze. It was Hawkin, crushed, and pinned under a heavy timber, a military jacket clenched in his right hand. The name tag on the chest of that jacket was clearly visible: Corporal Michael Hawkin.

Just as Tim began to back out of the tunnel, everything in the basement went black. The tunnel began to fill with dirt, the churning soil heading toward him. He jerked himself out of the tunnel just as the opening he and Jaime had helped Hawkin complete slammed shut.

Tim spun around and collided instantly with Hawkin. He wrapped his arms around the big guy and held tight, his jaw trembling uncontrollably.

Hawkin looked behind Tim and saw that his hard-won tunnel had sealed itself shut. "What the hell?"

"Never mind," said Jaime. "We'll explain it all later. Just take my word that everyone got out of the basement. They're waiting for Tim and me at the barn. We've got to get moving fast."

Hawkin shook his head and followed, bewildered.

By the time they got to the barn, Hawkin was beginning to recover from his shock. But when he heard the voices inside the barn, he relapsed. Those same people he now heard in the barn had been at the farmhouse minutes ago. How did they beat him here? None of the training he had received as a Navy Seal, not even the intense stuff such as stimulus-deprivation sessions, had prepared him for what just happened. His disorientation was intense.

Sensing John's confusion, Jamie explained, "It has to do with the spaceship and its magical powers."

Hawkin reflected on his experiences regarding Mom's jambalaya and his fishing trips with Grampa. Understanding began to flirt with his consciousness. It was enough to allow him to function with some sense of reality.

As Hawkin entered the barn the people inside gasped. Becky ran to him and threw her arms around him. "We thought you were dead," she sobbed.

When she finally turned loose of John, she turned around to see the others lined up behind her, waiting to welcome the big guy back.

After about five minutes of intense emotional displays, none of which Hawkin yet fully understood, Clint reminded everyone that they had to get out of the compound very soon. The sun would be coming up in a few hours, and Sheffield's men would probably arrive shortly after that.

Hawkin sent Jaime to his car to retrieve a cell phone. Hawkin made a couple of calls. He then informed the others that he had arranged for the ladies and Mortimer to stay at a safe house until this was all over.

The agents were allowed to relieve themselves, then were securely re-tied. Hawkin personally checked each of their bindings to be sure there would be no trouble.

One of the two calls Hawkin made was to the men with whom he had made arrangements earlier to bring supplies to the compound.

He instructed them to come immediately instead of tomorrow after-noon, to forget about the supplies, and instead, to bring a large mili-tary vehicle for the purpose of removing all of the agents to a minimum security facility. He wanted the agents out of the com-pound before Sheffield's men arrived.

Chas was delighted to find that he was not tied up. He appar-ently was now considered one of the good guys, although he was not given a weapon.

Hawkin checked to be sure that Maria, Sarah, Gail, and Becky were adequately armed and properly instructed for their stay at the safe house.

Becky informed John that she would be coming with him and the other men. He seemed surprisingly pleased with that announcement.

Mortimer was elated. He would see that his ladies were safe. They could count on good old Mortimer, that's for sure. He resolved to himself, right then and there, that he would start a physical fitness program as soon as this was all over. Why, he would even give up his hot chocolate, might replace it with carrot juice. Mortimer tightened his belt buckle a notch. *Yesiree, Mortimer Ziffel at your service.*

As soon as Mortimer and the ladies had departed, Becky and the men went to the bunker to get some sleep in the spaceship. They inspected all of the weapons and the contents of their backpacks, in preparation for whatever they might encounter tomorrow.

Hawkin treated them all to the best apple pie ala mode any of them had ever tasted. Daryl told them he had learned that the sleep-ing quarters in the craft could be programmed to provide a full night's sleep in just a few minutes. For the next quarter hour they all enjoyed the best rest any of them could remember, complete with a feature-length motion picture of their choice, implanted in their minds while they slept by means of some sort of high-speed holographic device.

They awoke refreshed, feeling unexpectedly energetic. They hoped they were ready for whatever lay ahead.

They loaded themselves and their gear into the two Jeeps and one of the government sedans.

It was early Sunday morning, still dark, as they headed down the road toward the front gate.

# Chapter Seventy

Sean Haggerty was curled up in the fetal position, contending with more pain than he could ever recall in his entire life. He remembered having his right hand cut almost in half about fifteen years ago, while using it to keep his windpipe and right jugular vein from being severed by a length of piano wire.

He had been tracking a Lithuanian drug smuggler for weeks through the Pyrenees Mountains. When Haggerty finally caught, subdued, and disarmed the two-hundred-eighty-pound former wrestler, he tied him to a tractor wheel. Thinking the contest was at an end, Haggerty paused for a few seconds to catch his breath.

The giant of a man literally tore the ropes that held his wrists behind his back, picked up Haggerty, and threw him against the trunk of a cedar tree, rendering him nearly unconscious. Before Haggerty could recover, the man ran through the front door of a nearby ranch house and, unbeknownst to Haggerty, exited a few minutes later through a rear window. Haggerty searched the house thoroughly and decided the man must have sought refuge in the barn out back.

On his way through the house, the giant had ripped a length of wire out of a baby grand piano in the parlor, picked up a wrench from a tool bench on the back porch, and grabbed a piece of a tree branch as he sprinted toward the barn.

While Haggerty was searching the barn, the man dropped on him from the hayloft, knocking him to the floor, face down, and wrapping the piano wire once around his neck while he sat on Haggerty's butt. The man attached the wrench and stick as handles to either end of his makeshift garrote.

Haggerty managed to get his right hand between his neck and the wire, just before the man pulled it tight. The fact that his hand kept the wire from severing his jugular vein and windpipe didn't prevent the massive strength of his opponent from cutting off his breathing.

With his free left hand, Haggerty was able to rest the butt of his 38 Special on the ground, with the business end of the barrel pointing upward and wedged between the earth and the man's right buttock. Haggerty barely reached the trigger with his thumb, just before he lost consciousness. The bullet traveled up through the giant's right buttock, his appendix, his liver, and his right lung, before exiting through his right jugular vein.

When Haggerty came to a half-hour later, he decided that, without a doubt, the pain in his half-severed right hand was by far the worst he had experienced. That wound held the number-one position for pain throughout the ensuing years of Haggerty's career—until tonight.

Now, fifteen years later, as he lay in the prenatal position, his first problem was to keep from blacking out from the pain, which had taken the number-one position by a considerable margin. A second pressing problem was to keep his entrails from falling out of the gaping wound in his abdomen. And a third problem, which had only recently come into Haggerty's awareness, was what to do about the three pairs of eyes that were glaring at him from only a few feet away. Whatever demons possessed these terrifying orbs, they were breathing heavily and snarling aggressively.

Given all of the factors present in his current situation—especially the unbearable pain in his abdomen and the likelihood that he was going to be torn to shreds any minute —Haggerty, for the first time in his career, decided that his best option would probably be to allow his soul to slip silently into the afterlife, and the sooner the better.

He was about to close his eyes when he noticed a faint vibrating glow outlining and making silhouettes of what now appeared to him to be the heads and torsos of three wolves. A second later the three heads turned in unison to gaze upon the source of that glow, relieving Haggerty for now of the visual assault that the eyes of those sizeable beasts had perpetrated upon him. When the source of the light drew near, the wolves scattered, taking refuge behind trees in the vicinity.

As Haggerty struggled to retain consciousness, sounds began to accompany the visual stimulation. Vehicles. There were vehicles heading toward him, bouncing on the rugged road. The lead vehicle screeched to a halt only inches away. Two men jumped out. Haggerty prayed they weren't the same men who had placed him in his current predicament.

"What the hell!" shouted Hawkin.

"What happened?" yelled Daryl.

Haggerty struggled to explain that he and another agent named Swenson had been on an assignment for Benson. They were just returning when they ran into four men leaving the compound. Without saying a word, the four men stepped out of their sedan and began shooting at Haggerty and Swenson.

Haggerty could hardly speak, his voice barely a whisper. "I think Swenson's dead….He's over there across the road near those bushes…. Haven't heard any sounds from him for quite a while….And at least three wolves are in the area….You scared them off."

Michael and Clint were standing nearby now, with the others behind them.

"Call for a chopper," Hawkin shouted.

"Don't bother," Haggerty whispered. "I won't last much longer…. Please just stay here until I die. I can't defend myself against those wolves."

"Don't worry—we'll stay with you," Daryl assured him.

"Something else you might want to know," Haggerty gasped. "After they shot me…they turned their backs on me….Thought I was dead. One of them used a cell phone…called and told somebody to remove our bodies when they come to do a clean-up. He made a second call…told someone to send eight more men to meet them at a safe house…Sleepy Hollow. They took the two…."

Haggerty coughed up a great deal of blood, grimacing in pain.

"They took the…two…."

Those were Haggerty's last words.

Chris and Daryl took the bodies of the two agents back to the barn and locked them in a storeroom in the loft, where they would be safe from predators until they could be buried.

When they returned, they overheard Hawkin telling the others that he knew exactly where the Sleepy Hollow safe house was. He had come across references to it when he was searching for the top-secret file.

"Sleepy Hollow," he related, "is less than an hour from here."

"Do you think we should call in some outside help?" asked Clint.

"I don't think I can," Hawkin replied. "We can't risk having anyone else know about what's going on here. There are already too many loose ends. And we can't compromise the safe house. Too many innocent people would be endangered. We'll have to take these guys ourselves. Who's with me?"

"You can count on me," Chas volunteered, with a new-found confidence.

"Me, too," declared Benson.

Hawkin didn't need to hear from the rest. He knew what they would say.

"Then here's my plan," he began.

He drew a map in the dirt, outlining the area of the Sleepy Hollow safe house. He didn't know anything about the interior floor plan or the exact number of men with Sheffield. That lack of information, he said, would make the task much more risky.

He presented a rough plan of action, then explained, "In a situation like this, you can't be precise about your plan. Too many decisions will have to be made as the action progresses. We're going to have to rely on each other. This will take uncommon courage and quick thinking. I feel as confident going into battle with the nine of you as I would with some of my old combat buddies. They had a lot more training and experience. But you folks have heart. We'll make it!"

It was still dark as they headed toward the Sleepy Hollow safe house.

Less than an hour later, their vehicles pulled into a clearing fifty yards from a dirt road they had followed for five miles after leaving the state highway.

"The house is two more miles up the road," Hawkin indicated. "I don't want to risk having them hear us, so we'll proceed on foot.

"But," he continued, "I don't expect them to be particularly watchful for the following reasons: First, it's a top-secret facility—only a handful of people know it exists. Second, they think we're all

dead, including Benson and all of his men. Third, they have no reason to think any of us would know about the safe house even if they
thought we were alive. Finally, they wouldn't suspect that Daryl, the
only outsider to come close to that secret file, would come here.

"If we hustle, we should be able to be at the safe house in about
thirty-five minutes. It will still be dark by then. But we have to get
into position quickly, before the sky begins to lighten. And they may
have men stationed in the forest surrounding the building, so let's
proceed with extreme caution, and be as quiet as we can."

They stayed well off the road, all but Hawkin and Daryl walking
single file, with Michael in the lead and Clint taking up the rear. Hawkin
and Daryl each headed out wide, Hawkin to the left on the other side
of the dirt road and Daryl to the right, up into a chain of heavily
forested hills that formed a loop around to the back side of the house.

When Michael reached a point about a hundred yards from the
front of the house, he was still within the forest, adjacent to the
meadow that formed the house's front yard.

He directed the others to their positions. Jaime went to the far
right, to a point just below where Daryl was up on the hillside, circling around to the side of the house. Tim was to the left of Jaime.
Michael instructed Benson to remain next to him on his right where
he could keep an eye on him.

The last to arrive was Clint. He took the far left position. Chas
followed directly behind him, with Becky some distance behind Chas
with Chris trailing behind her.

When everyone was in place, they formed a semicircle, surrounding the meadow in front of the house, all still several yards within the
forest. There were about twenty feet between each of them. This
added up to one hundred fifty feet from Jaime to Clint.

Hawkin had headed way to the left, circling the position occupied
by Clint and ending up on the back side of the house, about twenty
yards from the back door, well hidden behind a fire wood shed.

Daryl had looped around to the right, circled above the position
occupied by Jaime, and continued until he stopped at a position about
twenty feet to the right of the house, hidden within a circle formed
by a dozen aspen trees.

They waited silently and impatiently for the sky to lighten, their stomachs tied in knots their mouths dry, while they said some fervent prayers.

Things seemed rather ordinary inside the house. From the outside, a stranger wouldn't think that anything unusual was going on. It looked like a typical Midwest ranch house with the occupants up early to start their morning chores. That's what the government hoped it would look like, as it housed a long succession of individuals whose whereabouts had to remain secret for a variety of reasons.

This house was a haven for secret agents whose cover was compromised, foreign spies who requested asylum, those who chose to free themselves from a life of crime without punishment by turning state's evidence, by those joining the witness protection program, and occasionally a love nest for a few high-ranking officials to bring their paramours, safe from the prying eyes and clicking cameras of private investigators and the media.

Hawkin planned on giving Sheffield and his men a chance to surrender and then, assuming they would refuse, peppering the house with rifle shots, in Bonnie and Clyde fashion, from the relative safety of the forest. He hoped that, as soon as a few of them were killed or injured, the others would see the wisdom of surrendering.

Hawkin's army had a lot of ammunition, thanks to the arsenal Daryl had brought, the supply they had discovered in the bunker, what they had taken from the agents they had captured, and the supplies they had found in the trunks of the automobiles driven by Benson's men. Hawkin had instructed his people that, once the shooting started, they were to fire, rapidly, hoping Sheffield would think he was seriously outnumbered.

Each of them was to stay well screened behind the trees, not only for their safety, but also so Sheffield wouldn't be able to figure out how many of them there were. The most serious problem was that nobody knew the floor plan of the house or how many men they were up against.

A rough idea of the floor plan would help everyone know where best to place his shots. A head count would help them determine how many bad guys were left standing so they could time their final charge most effectively.

Hawkin had asked Michael to be the one to announce their presence. He was to shout to Sheffield and his men that they were surrounded, vastly outnumbered, and had sixty seconds to come out with their hands up. Michael was to do this as soon as the sun cracked over the mountaintops.

As Michael stood there anxiously watching the ridge of the mountains to the east, he remembered a concern that John Hawkin had expressed to the others earlier as he was laying out his plan: Assuming Sheffield decided to surrender, they would have no way to know that everyone had come out unless they had a head count. For all they knew, a dozen of Sheffield's men could still be hiding inside the building, waiting to ambush them as soon as they left the shelter of the forest. "If there were only some way we could determine how many men Sheffield has in that building...." Michael said.

There was a sudden movement off to Michael's left. He couldn't believe his eyes. There in the meadow, heading toward the house, was Herbert Benson III, running as fast as his injured legs would allow. *What the hell was he doing?*

Michael looked at Becky. She saw it, too. She shrugged her shoulders, the palms of her hands turned skyward. Michael saw that all of his people were watching the same thing. There was just enough moonlight for them to make out Benson's body.

The little shit. He's going to tell Sheffield what we're doing. Does the stupid jerk think he can make points with Sheffield by turning on us? He's gonna get himself killed. He's gonna get us all killed!

Then, to everyone's surprise, Benson stopped short of the front porch. He crouched just below one of the side windows.

What's he doing?

Benson got up slowly until his eyeballs were just above the window sill. He stood there for what seemed like ten minutes, although Michael knew it was less than that. Then Benson tiptoed around the right side of the building, stopped, and looked in another window. He stood there a long time, watching, listening. Then he disappeared around the back side of the building.

When he reappeared a few seconds later, it was from around the left side. He stopped again, looking in another window.

Then he did something that made his earlier conduct seem almost reasonable. He went back behind the building and returned, carrying a ladder. The fool was carrying a ladder! He propped it gently against the building and climbed up to a second-floor window. The ladder was so short that Benson had to stand on the very top step to see through the window above his head. His eyes were barely level with the window sill, even on tiptoes.

A minute later the ladder began to tilt to Benson's right. He clung to the window sill, trying to stabilize the ladder. It slipped another inch, then another. He was able to pull it back to the left, just slightly, by putting his left hand on top of the window sill, placing his right hand beneath the window trim, and leveraging his body with every ounce of strength in his poorly conditioned torso.

Then away it went, Benson and all, crashing to the ground. The sound of the ladder scraping against the siding of the house was so loud that even Clint heard it.

Benson landed with a thud. He did a summersault and his little heat-damaged legs started churning like pistons. He ran so fast to where Michael was standing that it looked as if he might be able to give Jaime a run for his money.

"What the hell were you doing?"

"I was reconnoitering," Benson retorted, a smug look on his face. "I was doing the right thing." He gasped for breath, then explained, "I figured you would all be a lot better off if you had some idea of what's inside that building, especially how many men there are. I also figured I was the only one who could do it without being shot on sight. I decided that if they caught me, I'd tell them I had escaped from the fire, just before the building collapsed, and that the rest of you were all dead. That way your plans wouldn't be compromised. If they caught one of you doing the reconnoitering, they would have to know something was up because how could you have known anything about this place? I would have reason to know where this building is. At least they couldn't be sure I didn't. They might let me live."

"That's crazy," Michael scolded. "They would have killed you in a minute."

"Maybe," Benson shrugged. "But they didn't, and I've got the information."

He proceeded to draw a floor plan in the dirt.

Michael inspected it with a penlight, holding it close to the ground so as not to let any appreciable amount of light escape.

Benson indicated an object in the corner of the living room.

"What's that?" asked Michael.

"I don't know," Benson replied. "It was covered with a sheet of camouflage canvas. It seemed to be about six feet long, four feet wide, and four feet high."

"There are nine men in that house and four out in the forest."

"How do you know that?"

"I counted. And I heard them talking about the men in the forest."

"Okay," instructed Michael, "you go down the line to the right and tell everyone what you've found out. I'll do the same on the left. Be back here in ten minutes. It's beginning to get light."

Benson was back in twelve minutes, and Michael about the same time. The sky was now light enough to allow for accurate shooting by both camps. They would have to be even more careful than when it was dark, although the sun itself was still not visible.

Twenty minutes later the first tiny flicker of sunlight began to show over the crest of the mountain. Michael's heart was in his throat. The action was about to begin.

Suddenly Benson remembered something he'd forgotten to tell Michael: There was one upstairs room he hadn't been able to see into. It was on the back side of the building, and the window was just below the apex of the roof, way too high to reach with the little chicken-shit ladder he had found.

He started toward Michael, to tell him what he'd forgotten, when he heard a commotion on the other side of Michael. He stopped and strained to see what the source of those sounds might be. There, about sixty feet away, were two men Benson had never seen before, walking side by side, coming from somewhere in the forest. Each held an UZI under his right arm, suspended by a shoulder strap. They approached Becky, who was facing the other direction, and said something to her.

Becky turned, raised her hands above her head, and threw her weapon to the ground.

From that moment on, everything seemed to Benson to be happening in slow motion. He saw Becky turn her head slightly to her right. An instant later the man farthest from Benson turned his head to his left, in the same direction Becky was now looking. The man raised his rifle to his shoulder as if to fire. Before he could squeeze off a shot, he was hit in the mid-section by something that knocked him completely off of his feet and sent him crashing into his companion with the other UZI.

Before either of the men could get up off his back, Chas, who—to Benson's surprise—apparently was the source of the impact applied to the first agent's mid-section, was back on his feet.

In an instant, Becky was there, grabbing the UZI still strapped to the shoulder of the man who had ricocheted off Chas's first victim, yanking it with such force that the agent came to his feet twice as fast as he had intended, falling forward into Becky. The man was so close to her that she couldn't aim the UZI at him. Besides, she didn't have time to check to see that the safety was off or, even, to determine whether it was cocked. She pulled the weapon to her left while extending her right knee powerfully into the man's groin. He folded forward, moaning in pain, his head about the same level as Becky's, his nose only six inches from hers. She brought her right fist up toward her own right shoulder and slammed her right elbow up under the man's chin with such force that it not only straightened him up, in violation of the demands of his aching testicles, but it caused him to almost sever his tongue with his front teeth.

The man fell backward, allowing Becky the precious few seconds she needed to bring the barrel of the UZI into alignment with the man, cock it, flip down the safety lever, and bring the tip of the barrel to rest against the forehead of the moaning agent. She quickly checked him for any backup weapon, removed a Beretta 380 Special from his waistband, and stepped back, out of range of any move he might make.

Chris and Michael arrived at her side. Chris held the man at gunpoint while Michael bound and gagged him.

While all of this was going on, Chas was engaged in a skirmish of his own with the other agent. The major difference between Chas's situation and Becky's was that Chas had absolutely no martial arts skills, had never been in a fight in his life, and had heretofore been a confirmed coward. Further, Chas had never done the slightest bit of physical exercise in his adult life, his brief stint on the swimming team in high school having been his last aerobic endeavor.

Chas now had only two factors in his meager arsenal. The first was that the agent had the wind knocked out of him as the result of the recent and powerful impact between his abdomen and Chas's right shoulder. The second was Chas's newly acquired sense of personal regard, his resolve to be a decent human being and to put forth uncommon effort in his attempt to make up for a lifetime of foul deeds. That second factor was the impetus for Chas's decision to come to Becky's assistance rather than to seek refuge in the deep forest. The latter alternative was highly recommended as the choice of preference by unanimous vote of Chas's most basic instincts.

As the agent was lying face down, gasping for breath, his right hand moved slowly toward the UZI, which the shoulder strap had kept within his reach in spite of the weapon's tendency to head off in a direction different from that of its owner's body.

After he had slammed into the now gasping agent's mid-section, Chas quickly got back on his feet, not as the result of any tactical planning on his part but, rather, as the natural consequence of having recoiled from the sudden impact with the agent's abundant belly. As a result, Chas now found himself standing over the agent with the slowly creeping hand. As that hand drew within inches of the UZI, Chas, with very little forethought, jumped as high in the air as his spindly legs could raise his plump, Pillsbury-Doughboy-like torso, and came crashing down with both feet onto the agent's right hand. That hand, in mid-creep, had all of its fingers, with the exception of the thumb, in a semi-clenched configuration. For that reason, when Chas's size eleven oxfords made violent and heavy contact with those digits, they were impacted at such a variety of angles, relative to the ground and the plane of Chas's shoe bottoms, that they formed a veritable maze of geometric configurations.

Had he, at the exact moment of impact, been able to achieve a state of considerable miniaturization and place himself in the vicinity of the agent's doomed fist, Chas likely would have heard a literal cacophony of snapping, crunching, and splintering, as the agent's once functional hand was rendered totally inoperative and the source of indescribable agony, which was delivered quickly and effectively to a conglomerate of neurotransmitters within the agent's brain.

As Chas stood there, both feet still solidly and firmly planted upon the agent's former hand, he managed to bend over, in direct violation of the laws of physics governing the structural relationship between his abdomen and his upper legs, and pick up the UZI. Chas's right index finger came to rest upon the trigger of the up-for-grabs UZI and delivered considerable pressure upon that cold sliver of steel. The adrenaline coursing through Chas's quavering body was a great deal more than what he was accustomed to experiencing. As a result, the pressure he was accidentally and unintentionally exerting on the trigger eventually became more than the trigger's spring could resist. A millisecond later a burst of nine rounds erupted from the barrel of the errant rifle, performing a rather haphazard pruning upon a birch tree twenty feet west of Chas's position.

Everybody within the immediate area hit the ground

"Oops," was all Chas could say.

Michael cautiously and gently lifted the rifle from Chas's grasp, taking care to point the barrel skyward until he succeeded in removing Chas's finger from the nervous trigger and clicking the safety into the "on" position.

Of the many consequences and reactions resulting from Chas's weapon-safety indiscretions was the fact that numerous additional lights in the house came to life almost immediately.

Chris finished securing the second agent, who was still writhing, whimpering, and moaning. Each of the hearty warriors returned to his original station, Chas with a look of considerable satisfaction on his face.

Michael decided that the time had come and gone for him to perform his assigned duty of announcing the presence of himself and his comrades to the agents in the house. It did, however, still seem timely for him to inform the agents of their intentions.

He shouted, "Hey, we thought you might like to know that you're totally surrounded and vastly outnumbered. You have sixty seconds to all come out with your hands above your heads. If you don't, we're prepared to fill that house with several thousand rounds of high-caliber copper-clad steel. The clock is running."

Four men could be seen upstairs, one near each of the windows facing the front of the building. Four more appeared at the edges of the four front downstairs windows.

Tim was the first to notice that Daryl was now crouched against the wall of the house on the right side just below one of the windows, in an extremely vulnerable position. His only hope would be to remain undetected. Daryl then laid down flat on his belly and rolled until he was pressed firmly against the wall. He would not likely be noticed unless one of the agents was to actually stick his head out the window.

Sheffield shouted back, "Well, well. It seems I underestimated your resourcefulness. I'm afraid I'll have to take a calculated risk and doubt your allegation that you have us outnumbered. You should know that one of my men just radioed to inform me that he happened upon your vehicles only moments ago, where you so ineptly attempted to conceal them. Unless you have several more vehicles sequestered elsewhere, which I seriously doubt, you can't have more than fourteen men, at the very most.

"Also, since nobody knows we're here except a small group of very select men, who are unfailingly loyal to and extremely terrified of me, I will guess that one of those fools we left for dead near the gate of the compound lived long enough to tell you where we intended to take our temporary refuge. I will further assume that you are nothing more than a small group of civilians who somehow escaped from the fiery inferno of the farmhouse. Let me provide you with a demonstration of my resolve."

Sheffield called to one of his men. A few moments later, a man from one of the upstairs windows appeared beside him at the front door. Before the agent realized what was happening, Sheffield whipped out a small blade and slashed it through the man's jugular vein. The agent collapsed to the floor, dying instantly.

Becky turned her head away.

"The incompetent gentleman you now observe lying at my feet," sneered Sheffield, "was charged with the responsibility of determining that those agents back at the compound gate were utterly and completely dead. He has now paid the price of failure."

"You other men inside the house," yelled Chris, "you see what kind of a monster you're working for. Come out, and we'll see that you get a fair trial."

"These men," shouted Sheffield, "all served with me in a special task force in the Middle East. They are tried and true and understand completely our code of conduct. There's not a man among them who doesn't agree, enthusiastically, that our fallen comrade got exactly what he had coming.

"The agents back at the compound entry gate revealed everything they knew about happenings at, or relative to, the farmhouse and its occupants before we killed them. Although their information was scanty, the portions relative to their special assignment off the premises were of particular benefit to our present situation.

"They informed us that there is one among you named Chris. They stated further that their assignment was to locate friends and relatives of the three troublemakers that Benson was trying to coerce into returning to the compound. Benson's intent, of course, was to use these friends and relatives as leverage to facilitate surrender."

Sheffield now had Chris's rapt attention.

"As a result of the deceased agents' research and investigation, they happened, with the aid of a CIA-conducted surveillance of all of your telephones, to locate a bartender who received an interesting message from Chris.

"When we intercepted those unfortunate agents, they were in the process of delivering to Mr. Benson a couple of ladies."

Chris's eyes narrowed.

"My men were on the verge of terminating these ladies, as surplus baggage, when two thoughts occurred to me. The first was that one never knows when one might need an ace in the hole, or two, so to speak. The second was that the younger of the two boasts an uncommon, shall we say, sensuality and pulchritude about her, just the kind of diversion warriors have always relished at the end of a challenging military encounter."

Chris's fists were clenched, and the muscles of his neck bulged.

Sheffield reached into the building and pulled Wendy through the doorway.

"God, no," Chris whispered, the sights of his rifle now dead center on Sheffield's forehead. But his Wendy was being held tightly against Sheffield's side. The angle at which Chris was standing placed Wendy's head behind and only inches to the right of Sheffield's. Way too risky.

"So that's what was in the room I couldn't see into," Benson thought.

Michael appeared to Chris's right, Becky to his left.

"Don't do it, Chris," whispered Michael. "Don't do it."

Becky placed her hand on Chris's left forearm, causing the tip of the barrel to lower slightly. "She'll be all right," Becky soothed. "Trust the Universe. Hold on to your faith. See her safe, unharmed. My Magical Friend will help."

Chris lowered the rifle further. Tears spilled from his eyes. He wiped them away abruptly, sniffing back his rage. *The cutest little nose in the universe, Great-Grandfather, help her.*

An elderly woman appeared in the window a few feet to the left of where Wendy stood. Wendy tried to look brave, trembling, sick to her stomach.

The old woman was being held between two agents. They raised her up so she would be more visible, until her feet no longer touched the floor. "Oh, my," Grammy inhaled.

They pulled her to the doorway where Wendy was standing. One man remained next to Grammy. The other went back to the window.

"By the way," shouted Sheffield, "if any of you heroes has been thinking about shooting me, or any of my men, please consider that there are enough of us here to ensure that, ultimately, these ladies will experience plenty of pain. In fact, I will consider acts of aggression on the part of any of you as my signal to begin carving away on the old crone. My excellent discretion and good taste impel me to refrain from damaging the flesh of the younger one until she has served our purposes."

Becky gritted her teeth.

Sheffield stepped several paces onto the front porch, bringing Wendy and Grammy alongside him. The other agent stepped forward, too.

"Now, gentlemen," Sheffield spat, "I want every one of you to walk five paces toward me, taking care to bring your weapons with you, holding them visibly above your heads. Keep in mind that I still have men patrolling the area. You never know when one of them might be hiding in the trees behind you, just itching to blow your head off. So I'd suggest that you all come out. Anyone holding back won't be very popular with his insurance agent."

 # Chapter Seventy-one

Clint's mind was racing.

Stepping out from their cover meant that they would probably all die. But staying where they were would mean almost certain death for the ladies on the porch. And maybe Sheffield wasn't bluffing about having men behind them. After all, two men had come out of the forest to confront Becky.

Michael was engaged in a similar debate with himself.

Becky prayed. *Come on, my Magical Friend, now's the time. We can't give up our weapons. Sheffield certainly isn't the kind to show mercy. You are my Higher Self, unlimited by the apparent realities of the physical world. You could strike that maniac with a lightning bolt, if only I could call it forth with enough faith.*

Tim and Jaime were both intently focused, visualizing those ladies on the porch alive and well, seeing this whole mess resolved without further bloodshed.

Daryl was trying desperately to think of something he could do to save the ladies' lives. He might be able to jump out from his hiding place below the side window and squeeze off a shot at Sheffield. But he couldn't see what was going on. All of his input to this point was based on what he had heard. He could only guess where the ladies were standing relative to Sheffield. Even if he got lucky and hit Sheffield without hitting either lady, there were still plenty of other armed men eager and capable of shooting Wendy, the other lady, and him. Not much to be gained. He cursed, silently.

Chris's mind was racing. *Our only chance is to take them all down at once. Benson said there are twelve of them. I can see four up on the top floor, three at the lower front windows, one standing next to the old woman, plus Sheffield. That's nine. Oh yeah, plus the man Sheffield killed. That's ten. If we can hit every man who's visible, there should be only two men left in the house. Maybe Hawkin and Daryl can handle the other two. If only we could communicate with them.*

And how do we coordinate the shots so none of us doubles up, with two or three of us shooting at the same man? If we could shoot fast enough, we might each get two shots off at two different men. That means even if we double up, there's still a good chance we would get all of them. There's no way to communicate my plan to the others quietly, though. Come on Great-Grandfather, do something.

"Time's up," sang Sheffield, taunting them. "Time for me to do a little carving." He stood with his rifle pointed casually at the ground, confident that he held all the aces. The man on the other side of the ladies assumed a similar posture.

Chris decided to yell for Wendy to drop to the floor. As soon as she did—assuming she understood—he'd try to hit Sheffield with several quick shots. Everyone else would start shooting right away. He'd just have to hope that all of his friends would go for targets other than Sheffield. Michael and Clint would certainly know that Chris would aim for anyone near Wendy. They'd probably shoot at the man on the other side of the older woman. Once those two were down, the other men in the building probably would be too busy saving their own lives even to think about going after the ladies. And, perhaps, the ladies would scramble over the front of the porch and stay down.

Just as Chris was about to scream his instructions to Wendy, he saw that Sheffield had turned suddenly, looking back through the doorway into the house. His movement was sufficient to cause Chris to hesitate a second. It was the movement of a man caught off-guard, a movement of surprise.

Sheffield had heard footsteps coming from inside the house. They were not what he expected to hear from any of his men. They were the sound of someone running, heavy footsteps of someone coming fast and hard.

By the time Sheffield realized what was happening, it was too late for him to raise his weapon high enough to do him any good. The rifle was halfway up from where it had been pointing at the porch floor when Big John Hawkin came crashing through the double-door entrance, his hands empty, rifle strapped across his back, charging like a locomotive and sounding like the powerhouse he was.

As he shot through the casement, he blasted the men on either side of the ladies in the jaws with the palms of his massive hands, the energy of Hawkin's forward momentum knocking them over backward and almost breaking their necks. As those agents were in mid-fall, Hawkin slowed his pace just enough to allow him to wrap each gigantic arm around the waist of one of the ladies. He held Grammy under his right arm, pinned against his hip, and lifted Wendy to the top of his left shoulder. He roared down the stairs and out into the meadow.

As soon as Chris saw that the ladies were no longer on the porch, he began firing at anyone at the house who looked like he was getting ready to fire a shot. The rest of his team followed suit, causing Sheffield and his men to seek refuge behind anything solid. This had the desired effect of slowing them in their attempts to shoot at Hawkin and his human cargo.

Nonetheless, several seconds later, gunfire began to pour from the house, with bullets hitting the ground all around Hawkin. He continued to run with all his might, dodging and weaving as in his days as a college fullback, leaving a serpentine trail of dust flying high behind him.

Gunfire was coming from the forest in front of him with tremendous intensity. His friends were firing back at the men in the house, pinning them down so effectively that the bullets all but stopped raining down around Hawkin.

To his amazement, Hawkin heard Grammy shout, "My, this is exciting!"

Hawkin was still fifty yards from the shelter of the forest, sweat flying off of his forehead as his head pivoted violently from side to side, matching the rhythm of his strides, his legs driving like mighty pistons. Even with his two-hundred-pound load, he ran faster than most men his age could run unburdened.

Chris stopped firing his HR 94 just long enough to pop out the ammo cartridge and slam in a new one. His eye caught a flash of light off to his right and back in the forest. Considering the gravity of the situation at hand, he made a vague decision to ignore that little flash and get back to the business of helping keep the bad guys pinned down. Immediately, he brought the rifle back up to his shoulder, pressed his cheek firmly against the side of its butt, aligned his right eye with the scope, and put the crosshairs on the side of a window frame on the second floor of the house, behind which he thought one of Sheffield's men was hiding.

He squeezed off two rounds before the memory of that flash of light came back to him with a nagging intensity that he couldn't ignore any longer.

Hawkin was now only twenty yards from the tree line.

Even before Chris could turn his head enough to see the source of that nagging flash of light, he knew. Somehow, all of the information his eyes had recorded moments earlier, but which hadn't yet registered because of the pressing urgency of other matters, came crashing into his consciousness.

A scope. That little flash of light, almost too faint to be noticed, was the result of sunlight reflecting off the front lens of a rifle scope.

In the time Chris's head completed the turn it had been instructed to perform only a fraction of a second earlier, he already had begun formulating a plan. This was not the kind of plan one makes slowly and rationally, utilizing the step-by-step, time-consuming processes of the conscious mind. This plan was the result of a desperate plea to the all-powerful subconscious to call upon the billions of shreds of data it had gathered since the moment of Chris's conception in his mother's womb, including several years of training and practice as an NRA sharpshooter, and to filter, assimilate, and organize all that information into a split-second decision, forward all of its parameters to every motor-sensory faculty Chris possessed, and produce a perfectly executed, completely accurate implementation of that plan, with adequate compensation for human frailty, visual inaccuracies, and the vagaries of physical tolerances—the end result of which must be to arrange violent contact between a 308 caliber bullet from Chris's rifle and the tiny part of that sniper's rifle that was barely visible, protruding from behind the trees that obscured the remainder of that weapon and its operator.

As Chris spun to his right, his eye still aligned with the scope of his rifle, his finger had already begun to exert steady pressure on the trigger. When the crosshairs of his scope reached a point on the arc created by Chris' pivoting motion, 4.3 inches before the front of the sniper's scope, the firing pin of Chris' rifle produced a tiny indentation in the center of the 308 caliber cartridge's detonator. This caused the gunpowder within the casing of the cartridge still clinging tightly to the bullet assigned the task of saving John Hawkin's life to burn at several hundred degrees centigrade, propelling that bullet out of the barrel of Chris's rifle. The rifling, machined into the interior of that barrel, caused the bullet to spin at a rate calculated to guarantee its accuracy.

The bullet made contact with the scope of the sniper's rifle less than half a second before the rifle to which it was attached would have fired had Chris not interfered. The impact was so violent that the rifle was torn out of the sniper's hand and thrown twenty feet to his right.

Bewildered, the sniper paused for a full five seconds before sprinting in the direction of his wayward weapon. During that lapse, the adrenaline in Chris's body, augmented by the seriousness of the situation, enabled him to sprint at an amazing twenty miles per hour, which translates to a little more than twenty nine feet per second. Within five seconds, Chris had covered over one hundred feet, allowing for two deviations he was forced to take from a straight line by vegetation on his intended route.

When he hit the sniper from behind, Chris's body was still moving at close to eighteen miles per hour. The impact broke three ribs in the sniper's left side and dislocated two vertebrae in his lower back. It also propelled him a good ten feet beyond the point where he had intended to retrieve his weapon. By the time the man started to come to terms with the fact that he couldn't move without experiencing unbearable pain, Chris had retrieved the somewhat damaged weapon, returned to the site where the sniper's body lay writhing in agony, and with Chas's assistance, began binding the man's wrists.

During the few seconds Chris's encounter with the sniper took to unfold, Hawkin made it safely to cover, delivering his precious cargo as gently as he could, considering that he fell flat on his face as soon as his nervous system realized he had reached relative safety.

Once the sniper was secure, everyone from the left end of the semicircle gathered around the area where Hawkin had landed. Jaime remained on the far right. Tim came to the center to see what was happening.

Chris lifted Wendy in his arms and carried her to the back side of a huge granite boulder. He sat on the ground with her on his lap, held her tightly, and kissed her gently on the cheek.

Wendy looked around for a moment to assure herself that Grammy was okay. Then, satisfied that the dear old lady was in good hands, she wrapped her arms around Chris's neck and pulled his lips to hers. As they sat there, mesmerized by their first real kiss, the terrifying situation around them melted away. All that existed in their tender world was each other.

Now that Sheffield no longer had his hostages, everyone waited to see what his next move would be. Jaime kept careful watch on Daryl, who was still hiding against the wall beneath the right side window. He hoped Sheffield wouldn't discover that he had another potential hostage.

As everyone sat there in silence, wondering what would happen next and trying to come up with a plan, Chas shouted, "Look!" while pointing toward the house.

There, on the front porch, was a dark object that three of Sheffield's men were pushing through the double-door front entrance.

As everyone stood in anxious anticipation, Sheffield himself materialized in the doorway just behind the recently appearing object and yanked off the camouflage tarp that heretofore had concealed the identity of that object.

"What the hell's that?" Benson asked.

"Whatever it is, I don't want any part of it," proclaimed Chas.

"It's a fifty-caliber machine gun," sighed Hawkin. "About as bad a piece of news as we could receive, considering our location."

"Yes," agreed Michael. "I've seen one of those things operating in the jungle. It's got enough firepower to destroy most of the trees around us. He intends to turn everything in this area into compost, including us."

"I think we should take off running," Grammy chimed in, an innocent smile on her face. "That's what Arnold Schwarzenegger did when he was in a spot like this. I'm kinda slow, so I would be pleased if that nice black man would carry me again."

"There's nowhere to run," Clint said. "They'll hunt us down and kill us all. We've got to stop them now." He turned to Hawkin. "How much time do we have?"

The big man raised his field binoculars to his eyes and studied the front porch.

"They haven't yet loaded that monster, and it looks like the apparatus used for feeding the ammunition belts hasn't been attached. They probably never thought they'd have to use that thing. I suspect it was here before they arrived. So I'd guess it will take them two to three minutes, from the time they begin loading, before it's ready to fire."

Tim left the gathering and headed back to where Jaime remained. He pulled his backpack from behind the tree where he had stashed it. "It's time for another miracle. That weapon on the porch is more than we can handle. I've got an idea."

Just then gunshots rang out from the area where the others had gathered. Tim and Jaime could see that Clint was firing at the men near the monster weapon, trying to keep them from loading it.

The others took their clue from Clint and began firing toward the house.

Sheffield's men quickly dragged the machine gun back into the building. Clint winged one of them before he got back into the house. The man's scream was audible to all in the vicinity.

"They've decided to load that weapon inside the building," said Tim. "They can probably fire it at us without having to bring it out into the open. We've now probably got no more than two minutes before they start shooting. From what I understand, we'll all be history within seconds after they start firing that thing. This is our last chance."

Tim quickly explained his plan to Jaime.

Hawkin was running toward them. He yelled at them to get behind some boulders, as trees wouldn't be much protection from the big gun. He told them to keep firing at the area of the front door for as long as their ammunition held out. He desperately hoped that they could finish off Sheffield's men before they got the machine gun operating.

"How fast does a fuse burn?" shouted Tim.

"Why?" asked Hawkin.

"No time to explain," Jaime responded.

"Depends on the kind—usually about one inch per second," the big man answered as he headed back to the others. Hawkin was determined to protect the ladies to the end. He had hidden them in an area surrounded on three sides by granite boulders. Becky was firing through an opening between two of those boulders. Wendy had obtained a 308 caliber rifle from Michael and was learning to use it as she went, shot by shot. One of her shots actually made it through the front door, scaring one of Sheffield's men. Her shoulder was already bruised from the recoil of the weapon.

After digging furiously in their backpacks, Tim and Jaime came up with several sticks of dynamite, some duct tape, a spool of fuse, and a book of matches.

"We'll never make it in time," worried Tim, glancing nervously in the direction of the house. "By the time I get this thing completed and we take it the hundred yards to the building, they'll have killed most of our people already."

"Do you remember that final play we used against Trent in the homecoming game last year?"

"You bet," replied Jaime, a trace of a smile on his face.

"Well, I'd suggest you start running it now." Tim grinned. "They're gonna start firing that thing any time. Stay in the forest until the very last few seconds. When you break out of the trees, cut sharp left and look over your shoulder for the bomb."

Jaime took off like a shot, dodging and weaving through the trees, running as he'd never run before.

"Look—one of them is running through the trees, heading toward the house," shouted one of Sheffield's men.

"Kill him!" Sheffield ordered.

Rifle shots began pouring out of the house, hitting several trees as Jaime shot past them. He altered his pace to prevent the shooters from timing their shots.

As soon as Michael and the gang realized what was happening, they stepped up the intensity of their assault on the house, no longer shooting at the front-door area but concentrating, instead, on the windows through which the agents were firing at Jaime. The agents firing were all on the second floor, those on the ground floor were apparently occupied with preparations for the machine gun. The intensity of the barrage made it difficult for the agents to get off many more shots at Jaime.

Meanwhile, Tim frantically tied six sticks of dynamite into a bundle, wrapped them 'round and 'round with duct tape, taking care to form the device into the approximate shape of a football. He quickly inserted a fuse into the end of one of the dynamite sticks, leaving twelve inches of the fuse exposed.

Jaime was forty yards from the front of the house, still in the forest. Seconds before he broke out of the trees, Tim lit the fuse, reared back, took outrageously careful aim, considered the wind velocity and direction, and ripped loose with the most perfectly intentioned and executed pass of his life. He began counting, "one, two," just as a 9-millimeter slug tore through his left shoulder. So focused was he on his brother that he barely noticed the pain.

Jaime broke out of the trees, running like the wind.

"…three, four…"

A rifle barrel appeared through the window, immediately above Daryl's head. He pressed himself hard against the wall, praying he wouldn't be seen. The man holding the rifle shouted, "I've got him dead in my sights."

Daryl reached up and grabbed the barrel of the rifle with one hand. He yanked it down until it came to rest on the window sill. He pulled himself to his feet, using the rifle barrel for leverage. As soon as he was standing upright, he grabbed the startled gunman by his trigger arm and yanked him out the window. A fraction of a second after the man hit the ground, Daryl slammed the butt of the man's rifle into the base of his skull, then dived for cover.

"…five, six, seven…"

Jaime looked over his shoulder and there, floating in the air, was the only silver-gray football Jaime had ever seen with a lighted fuse spiraling behind it. For the first time, Jaime considered the possibility that if he didn't catch the damn thing exactly right, he might knock the fuse loose or, maybe, smother it. That second of reflection almost caused Jaime to lose his concentration.

"…eight, nine, ten."

The "ball" touched Jaime's fingertips. He brought it securely against his chest. He noticed that the fuse had only two inches remaining.

"Holy shit," yelled Jaime as he dived for the ground a few feet from where the gunman lay, out cold.

In mid-dive, he rolled a quarter turn to his left and lobbed the ball through the open window. He landed face down, covering his ears, just as a bullet ripped through his left thigh.

In less than a second, the blast blew nine agents out into the yard, some coming through the windows, others coming through openings where solid walls had been seconds earlier.

Hawkin and his army sprinted toward the house, keenly alert, rifles ready.

By the time they arrived, they could see that most of the agents were unconscious. The others were so seriously disorientated that they couldn't function, except to hold their hands over their ears.

Hawkin asked Clint and Michael to take charge outside and to get all of the agents secured. He went quickly into the burning house, where he found two more agents. They were both hysterical, hands covering their ears, blood running from their mouths and noses. Hawkin threw them through the wall and onto the porch.

He wanted Sheffield.

He found him upstairs in the room where Wendy and her grandmother had apparently been held. The damage to that room was minimal. Sheffield was conscious and surprisingly alert, considering that he had been through an explosion. But he was obviously dazed.

Sheffield looked at Hawkin with contempt. He pulled a pistol slowly out of his shoulder holster. Hawkin kicked it out of his hand and across the room.

Hawkin grabbed Sheffield by the back of his collar and dragged him down the stairs. He took him out the back door and dropped him on the ground. Never in his life had Hawkin been so filled with rage. The only thing on his mind at this moment was that picture of Sheffield holding a pistol to Mikey's head and squeezing the trigger.

Hawkin removed his pistol from its holster and pulled back the slide to be sure there was a bullet in the chamber. He let it snap back into position. He pressed the barrel hard against Sheffield's forehead. Sheffield begged for mercy. Hawkin snapped the safety off. His finger began to tighten on the trigger.

Until this very moment, John Hawkin had never even been tempted to act without honor. But this monster had pushed him too far. Every man has his limits, even John Alexander Hawkin.

"Ahem," came a voice behind him, distracting him momentarily from his rage.

Hawkin spun around and almost fell over at the sight before his eyes.

There stood Great-Grandfather in the most outrageous outfit Hawkin had ever seen. He was covered with beads and feathers, leather fringe dangling from his arms and legs. He had two knives in his buckskin belt and a tomahawk hanging from a leather thong around his neck. His face was brilliant with various colors of war paint. Numerous small bells chimed as he moved. To top it all off, Great-Grandfather's war bonnet was highlighted with flickering Christmas tree lights. He stood there, his arms folded across his chest, an attempted look of nobility on his face.

In spite of his rage, Hawkin couldn't suppress the laughter swelling up in his chest. "What do you want, Pocahontas?" he asked.

"I just thought," Great-Grandfather intoned, "that you might want to consider the consequences of your intended act."

"I don't expect there will be any consequences," snapped Hawkin. "Not after I inform the President about the massacre and other atrocities that our friend here has committed."

"I wasn't talking about *your* consequences," explained the old shaman. "I'm talking about the fact that this man deserves to suffer the consequences of his own acts. Do you really want to relieve him of that obligation by dispatching him to the world of the absolute, where he will find himself in a state of instant bliss? It makes no matter to me, either way, since I know that death is nothing. I just thought you might want to savor the splendid pleasure of watching this man suffer the brutality of your judicial system. I assure you it is quite unpleasant.

"Besides all that, you might want to consider how you're going to feel a few months from now when you look back and assess what happened here. How will you feel about John Hawkin then? Wouldn't you rather spend the rest of your life thinking about those wonderful times you spent with your grandfather or your Mom's homemade apple pie or some of that jambalaya? It wouldn't seem right to have the flavors of those unforgettable experiences tainted by some bad memories.

"As my parting shot, before I vaporize off to the shaman's metaphysical ball, perhaps you might, instead of taking the chance of spending the next several years in federal prison for taking the law into your own hands, want to have a talk with Tim and Jaime. You might want to ask them how you happen to be here, alive and well, at least alive, when all of those who came close to losing their lives in the burning basement of the farmhouse will tell you that you perished when the building collapsed.

"Perhaps the power they used to save your life—and, incidentally, the life of Mortimer Ziffel—might be of use, in conjunction with the apparent amplifying powers of the spaceship, in helping you to make contact with your brother Mikey in the ethers. At least consider the possibilities."

With that, Great-Grandfather made one of his usual spectacular departures.

Sheffield had passed out. When heaped upon the other traumas he had endured, the appearance of Great-Grandfather was more than the circuit breakers in his nervous system could take.

Hawkin flicked the safety back on. He lowered his weapon and began to cry. He wasn't sure why he was crying, but it felt good. He dragged Sheffield around to the front yard and deposited him on the sizeable heap of bewildered or unconscious agents. He checked to assure himself that his friends had the situation well under control, including the temporary bandaging of Tim's shoulder and Jaime's leg. It was obvious to him that the only thing that had held Michael together, in spite of the wounds in his left side, was his uncompromising determination to save the lives of his family and friends. Michael had totally collapsed shortly after the explosion in the house.

Hawkin called for a Med-Evac chopper to get his injured friends to a hospital.

Sheffield and his men were securely bound and loaded into vehicles headed for the nearest federal prison where Hawkin had arranged for them be held in custody until he would have time to confer with the President.

Hawkin turned command of the local operation over to Clint. He decided his talk with the President could wait until tomorrow. He headed into the forest where he intended to spend a few hours sitting under a tree, sorting out a lot of powerful emotions.

Everyone involved with the events at the farmhouse assumed that the capture of Frank Sheffield and his men marked the end of their adventure.

Little did they know what powerful and long-lasting consequences remained buried just below the surface of their lives, waiting to unfold within the next few months.

The End

Author's Note

As you might imagine, the events of the preceding adventure have had far-reaching and long-lasting effects on the lives of many of the people involved, both during the period of the story and for many years thereafter. For those who might be interested in seeing how some of those lives were affected, the following accounts are set forth.

Frank Sheffield

As the result of strategic maneuvering by the President of the United States, Frank Sheffield was sentenced to live out the remainder of his years in the basement of an insane asylum, deep in a forest in northern Michigan.

After a lengthy discussion with John Hawkin regarding Sheffield's orchestration of the farmhouse massacre and his later, aborted attempt to cremate numerous U.S. citizens in the basement of that same farmhouse, the President concluded that it would be impossible for him to get a fair trial and a waste of the taxpayers' money to conduct a long, drawn-out criminal prosecution. After considering all the facts and evidence against Sheffield, it was obvious to the President that Sheffield certainly would be sentenced to life in prison or, more likely, the death penalty. A CIA agent convicted of a mass murder involving women, children, and young members of the United States Army would not likely find his stay in a federal penitentiary pleasant. A major consideration in the President's decision to have Sheffield secretly committed to the asylum was that a trial would provide Sheffield with a platform from which to spew inflammatory lies to the public. Given Sheffield's lack of integrity and vicious nature, the President concluded that a trial would result in the public being led to believe that the entire government was involved in the cover-up, rather than the few men who actually were a part of it.

The President finally concluded that the nation's welfare required that Frank Sheffield be silenced permanently. Besides, he reasoned, twenty or thirty years of solitude would be almost as devastating as the fate that might await Sheffield in a federal prison. The President wished he could do something more to see that Sheffield would suffer in proportion to his hideous acts, but he had a nation to run and the welfare of the American people to protect.

All records of Sheffield's existence were destroyed. His only living relative, an aunt in Indianapolis, had not been in touch with him for years, having wisely decided long ago that Frank Sheffield was no good.

The President, believing that the people of America have considerably more courage and good judgment than the media often attribute to them, appeared on national television and revealed the existence of the spacecraft and the atrocities that were committed at the farmhouse back in 1975. This announcement resulted in months of debate, intense accusations by numerous radical factions in various political parties, and criticism of various governmental institutions and office holders by those aspiring to enhance their positions on the political ladder.

In the end, the people of America prevailed, as always, and reason was restored to the nation. Or, perhaps, the reason was always there but temporarily obscured by those who inevitably use a public platform to enhance their positions at the expense of the common man.

Over the years, the President spent an occasional sleepless night, wondering whether he had done the right thing relative to Frank Sheffield.

There were two important facts the President would never know. One was that Frank Sheffield's primary source of pleasure had been bullying and abusing others. Since his early grammar-school days, his total sense of identity had been based on his ability to strike fear into the hearts of his victims.

The second was that being locked up in a cell, where his only contact with the outside world was an occasional glimpse of an orderly, whose job it was to shove Sheffield's meals and clean clothes through a small slot in a solid steel door, was more than Sheffield could endure. The total absence of anyone whom Frank Sheffield could command or intimidate left him with such a frail sense of identity that he could scarcely function. To Frank Sheffield, the punishment the President imposed on him was far more unbearable and terrifying than anything the U. S. Judicial System could have possibly done to him.

The next time the President heard anything about Frank Sheffield was a little over a year after his admission to the asylum. Sheffield's body had been found hanging by the belt of his terrycloth bathrobe from the steel grate that covered the light above his toilet.

There was one thing the President and John Hawkin never doubted: They were justified in having faith in the people of America.

 # The Other CIA Agents

An investigation conducted on behalf of the President by John Hawkin revealed that Frank Sheffield had "terminated" four of the five men involved with him in the original farmhouse massacre, one at a time, over a period of about nine months, beginning in late 1975. Each death was made to look like an accident.

When a young lady from the Internal Affairs Department commented to Sheffield that it seemed strange that accidental deaths would occur to four men within a nine month period in a department with only eighty four employees, she was replaced by an older, less inquisitive woman.

Three days later the young lady's raped and mutilated body was found at a campsite where she had apparently gone to vacation for a few days.

Of the thirty-seven agents Herbert Benson III had brought to the farmhouse compound, each was dealt with by Internal Affairs, based on his individual conduct as observed and reported by John Hawkin. John's endorsement by the President, not to mention his own impeccable reputation, gave his testimony uncommon credence.

Some of those agents were dismissed from the agency. Others faced criminal charges.

The agents who accompanied Frank Sheffield to the farmhouse compound and, later, to the Sleepy Hollow safe house were all convicted of first-degree murder.

One of the agents who had operated under Benson's command at the farmhouse compound had what could be called a "life altering experience."

Gerald Pheitzer had been a lost soul for as long as he could remember. He was asked to leave parochial school for arguing against the validity of the Bible.

His reasoning, although a bit simplistic, made very good sense to Gerald's twelve-year-old mind. He didn't mean to be disrespectful to the good Brother Sebastian, who conducted the eighth grade religion class. But, Gerald had trouble accepting the church's allegation that the all powerful Being that created and oversees the operation of the entire universe could have screwed up and let things get out of hand to the point where he absentmindedly created his own enemy who possessed sufficient power that He would have to battle with him for all of eternity.

His expression of these opinions resulted in Gerald being expelled from Saint Bartholomew Junior High, in spite of the fact that Miss Scully, the eighth-grade history teacher, had intentionally led him to believe that this is, in fact, the "Land of the Free."

Gerald's parents were not much into religion. In fact, there were only three reasons they had sent Gerald to the parochial school in the first place, only one of which had any religious significance.

The first was that the parochial school was fifteen blocks closer to their brownstone apartment on the east side, than any of the public schools.

Second, Gerald's grandfather had been one of the volunteer laborers who had helped construct not only the school but the church located kitty corner and the pastor's residence two blocks down Garfield Street. As a result, Gerald and his siblings were entitled to one year's attendance, tuition free, provided his parents signed an affidavit attesting to the fact that they were in good standing with the Church, paid property taxes on a residence within the city limits, and vowed that all of their children would be married in the church.

Third, Gerald's dad, who had come home on more than one occasion with an unfamiliar, pungent and definitely feminine aroma emanating from his being, felt he needed some type of insurance against the eventuality of being sentenced to Limbo or the fires of Purgatory or Hell. He felt that having kids attending the parochial school would probably be considered as some type of celestial evidence that he had been a man of reasonably good character.

The very morning after his expulsion, Gerald found himself trudging the additional fifteen blocks to the public school through a curtain of driving sleet. He took little comfort from the thought that he might someday have grandchildren to regale with his stories of his sleet infested trudging.

As the weather sleeted and Gerald trudged, he came to a definite and inescapable conclusion: that any God who was so insecure that he had to hire employees to expel those young inquisitive minds that dared to question dogma was not the kind of God to whom he wanted to burn candles at twenty-five cents apiece.

From that moment forward, Gerald believed in nothing. As far as he was concerned, the entire universe was a gigantic accident resulting from the coincidental intermingling of numerous highly flammable gases. He also concluded that when he died, everything would turn black and that would be the end of Gerald Pheitzer. All that would remain of him some day would be a small cloud of unidentified ashes swirling and twirling its way back to those highly flammable gases from which he had been spawned.

Gerald Pheitzer clung tenaciously to his beliefs and finally buried himself in the security and anonymity of the CIA, waiting for that fateful day of impending extinction.

His belief in nothing had been bolstered by bits and pieces of evidence he had picked up over the years, much the way members of a political party will bolster their belief in their cause by selectively sifting through the facts, latching on only to those that support their beliefs and assigning those that don't to the pile labeled "ignore."

As Gerald Pheitzer had stood on the front porch of that old farmhouse, lightning striking the ground with a vengeance and a veritable fire fight being conducted just inside the perimeters of the forest only a few yards away, he waited anxiously for the arrival of the Grim Reaper he had long ago named "Oblivion."

Suddenly, he found himself faced with a most difficult situation. Michael, one of the men he had been told was a threat to national security, was standing right next to him on the farmhouse porch.

He had raised his weapon to the base of Michael's skull and, to his astonishment, felt his finger beginning to squeeze the trigger. He didn't want to hurt anyone. He didn't really want to be in the CIA any longer. He only wanted to keep on being. Every cell in his quivering body screamed out for immortality. He prayed for evidence of any kind that there was something, anything….. anything but oblivion.

He tried with all his might not to squeeze that trigger. But his right index finger seemed to be on auto pilot. It was squeezing in spite of his will. He didn't want to end this man's life. *Please help me. If there really is a God out there, help me.*

Then it happened. An angel appeared. It was the most beautiful sight Gerald Pheitzer's mortal eyes had ever seen, an angel with a long, white, flowing, gossamer gown and the most beautiful long red-dish brown hair in the world.

She smiled. He couldn't believe that she smiled. She was supposed to be dressed in black and carrying one of those sharp pointy things his Great-Grandfather used for cutting down hay. She wasn't Oblivion. She smiled.

Gerald Pheitzer knew then and there that death was not a black nothingness and life was more than a coincidence of events, he wasn't just the result of some accidental mixing of gases.

He felt his finger remove itself from the trigger.

He crawled back to the wall of the house, deep in the shadows of the front porch, far away from the war and the lightening and the weapon he had dropped to the floor.

He placed his head between his hands and rested his arms on top of his knees, and he wept.

He sensed that the others had left. There he was, all alone on that porch. But he knew that nothing would ever be the same, ever again. He was right where he was supposed to be. He was somebody. He would always be somebody. And he sobbed.

Since that fateful night, Gerald Pheitzer has pursued a relentless search for the way things really are.

Since his release from prison he has read everything he could get his hands on about spirituality and science. He has discovered that what he had once perceived as a deep chasm between religion and science does not exist between spirituality and science. He has come to know that as science slowly shed its old theories and found ways to look deeply into the inner world with its powerful microscopes and its linear accelerators and into outer space with its gigantic telescopes, it was coming to know that the teachings of the ancient mystics were not really at variance with the discoveries of science at all.

He has given thanks every day for Brother Sebastian and for the dogma that drove him from the security of the church and its fantasies. He has even given thanks for the sleet.

That expulsion from school set him free. Once he found himself released from the grip of rigid teachings, he was free to question the dogma, free to seek the truth, free to know the truth.

Jerry Linden

Coach Linden sat on the sofa in his family room with his sock-covered feet resting on the coffee table. He was staring at his wife Cindy as she stood at the kitchen sink, looking as foxy as ever.

After a while his mind wandered to thoughts of Franklin's victory over Riverton.

"Amazing."

How could his boys have possibly beaten those bruisers from Riverton? Oh, he'd given his team the usual pep talk about the power of the mind and determination and all that stuff. That was his job. And he meant it.

Still, he couldn't help but admit to himself that his boys were in for a beating. Certain laws of physics just can't be denied. When a one-hundred-thirty-pound boy runs headlong into a two-hundred-twenty-pound boy, the laws of action and reaction come into play.

And, yet, they had won.

Certainly, a lot of the credit had to go to those Lasher boys. Tim had an arm as good as or better than most college quarterbacks. And Jaime could run as fast and as sure as anyone Jerry had ever seen.

But something didn't seem right. He almost felt as if the victory had been unfair to the Riverton team, as if something improper had happened.

Now, almost a month since that fateful night, Jerry Linden couldn't put the game out of his mind. It was as if something were haunting him. Besides the fact that all the laws of statistics and physics and just plain old logic told him they should have lost, there was something else.

Strange visions occasionally flashed before his mind. They didn't appear often, maybe once every few days. But they came, even when he wasn't thinking about the game, strange pictures of surreal events that couldn't possibly be.

Cindy looked good. Even when she was just standing still, she reminded him of a lean race horse with her strong, firm legs in those shorts. He was a lucky man indeed.

Then it happened—a flashback, to the game. But it was not exactly as he remembered it. He was back at the game, sitting on the bench, watching the action. But it wasn't the right action. It was different.

It made the coach think of a magazine article he had read once about how movie theaters were using "subliminal messages" to help sell popcorn and candy. As he recalled, the theater owners spliced the movies and patched in a single frame showing a bag of popcorn, a candy bar or a soft drink. The audience was never consciously aware of having seen that frame because it went by too fast. But the subconscious picked up on it and recorded it in the part of the brain that produces hunger or thirst. Soon, several of the patrons would get up and go to the lobby to purchase popcorn or a soda, never knowing why the urge had come upon them.

Laws were passed prohibiting the use of such tactics.

These flashbacks made Jerry feel as if subliminal frames had been spliced into his memory. Vague pictures were flashing before his mind. He was back at the game. The action was similar to what had actually happened, but something was different. Strange feelings inserted themselves into his mind, like the frame of popcorn in the movie, only far more urgent, far more powerful.

These feelings had been driving him crazy.

Then he got an idea. Jerry remembered how, in his college days, he often seemed to be a lot more lucid and imaginative after downing a few beers. Of course, he felt the buzz from the alcohol. But there was more. His mind worked with greater clarity, almost as if the alcohol set aside his resistances and prejudices and allowed him to be open to new thoughts. He remembered getting some of his greatest ideas when he was slightly inebriated.

He recalled reading that Edgar Allen Poe did some of his best writing while under the influence of opium. So Jerry decided to try an experiment. After helping Cindy with dinner and cleaning up the dishes, he invited her to join him for a few shots of Jack Daniels.

"What did you have in mind?" Cindy cooed, a seductive twinkle in her eye.

"Not what you think." Jerry said fondly. "Although I'll be happy to get to that in a little while. For now, I just want to get a buzz and do some thinking."

"It's about the game, isn't it?" asked Cindy. "It's been bugging you all along, hasn't it?"

"Yes," Jerry admitted. "It's about that fabulous game. Something's got me feeling weird. I thought if I had some alcohol in this little brain of mine, it might help me figure it out."

"Sounds good to me," Cindy replied. "But don't forget—you've got a willing woman on your hands."

Forty-five minutes later, they each had downed three shots of whiskey and Jerry was feeling comfortabley relaxed. He laced his fingers behind his head, leaned back with his eyes closed, and began thinking about the game. He started with the first kickoff and reviewed the action, play by play, as well as he could remember.

By the time he got to the end of the game, he was frustrated. Nothing unusual came to him. Oh, well, the whole thing was probably just his overactive imagination.

Cindy was just coming back from the bathroom. She leaned over her husband and kissed his forehead. He pulled her down onto his lap and wrapped his arms around her waist. Holding her close, he again thought about how fortunate he was to have such a wonderful woman in his life.

Before long, a variety of physical reactions set in, not the least of which were the tears beginning to build up inside, expressions of joy and appreciation. Then the yearning came. He longed to make love to this fabulous friend and lover. He started to finger the top button of her blouse. She smiled down at him and wiggled, sending shivers up Jerry's spine. He pulled her down toward him and kissed her warmly on the lips.

In an instant, all of the stimuli of the evening, the buzz from the Jack Daniels, the warmth of her lips, the love he was feeling for her—all came together to lift Jerry to an outrageous high. He felt as if his soul might just rise up out of his body. How he loved this woman.

Then, suddenly, against all logic and in total defiance of this exquisite moment, he was back at the game. Everything was moving so fast. But no clarity was sacrificed. He could see it all. He could hear it all. He was experiencing it with even more intensity than when it actually had happened. He could run it forward or backward. He could stop the action. He could control the movement of the scenes as if his brain was a VCR.

He was vaguely aware that he was still in his family room with the wife of the century. But he couldn't drag his consciousness away from the action of the game. It was in brilliant color and stereophonic, wrap-around sound. He not only could see every player but he could see into their souls. He could read their minds.

The Jack Daniels mixed with the hormones secreted as the result of his feelings for Cindy and the joy of the moment put him into some kind of an altered state. It was like nothing he had ever sensed or imagined in his life.

He could see the silver dollar that Mortimer was flipping at midfield. Now it was spinning in slow motion, the stadium lights reflecting off its surface. It was making the sound of a helicopter in stealth mode. The crowd was totally silent.

Then, as the coin hit the grass, the crowd came alive. It was almost as if he were seeing all of this through someone else's eyes. Then he realized he was seeing everything through the eyes of Jaime Lasher.

Coach Linden was actually out in the center of the football field. He turned slowly and looked at the sideline. He saw himself. His other self looked back and gave a knowing grin.

He could feel Cindy still sitting on his lap in their family room.

She squeezed him tightly, sensing that something special was happening. "Go for it, darling," she whispered.

Jerry was back at the game. He again was seeing the action through his own eyes. He fast-forwarded it to the last play, his favorite part, that amazing touchdown pass from Tim to Jaime.

The football was in the air. He looked over at Jaime. To his astonishment, Jaime stumbled. But Jaime hadn't stumbled. If he had, he wouldn't have been downfield in time to catch the ball.

Jerry looked back at the ball. It was halfway to the target. But Jaime Lasher was sprawled out on the grass, several yards behind the ball. He looked back at Jaime, just to be certain. Sure enough, flat on the ground.

Then, as Jerry turned back to look at the ball, expecting to see it hit the ground any time now, he couldn't believe his eyes. The ball was suspended in mid-air, just hanging there, dead still.

The crowd was silent, absolutely silent.

He looked back at Jaime. Jaime was getting to his feet.

All else was stopped. Nothing moved. Mortimer was suspended above the ground, mid-stride. Tim Lasher's arm was pointing toward the far end of the field. The linemen were in mid-crunch.

And there was Jaime, sprinting for all he was worth through a maze of paralyzed mannequins.

Jerry held Cindy tightly. He could feel her breathing.

As Jaime reached Riverton's thirty-two-yard line, the football burst forward.

The crowd came alive.

Tim's arm followed through, coming to rest beside his right thigh.

The crowd went wild.

Suddenly Jerry realized that he was now watching the action from Tim Lasher's eyes.

Just as Jaime crossed the goal line, Tim-Jerry glanced back at the sideline. There was Coach Linden, arms raised above his head, shouting at the top of his lungs.

As if against all rightful action, the Jerry Linden on the sideline turned toward the Tim/Jerry out on the field and clearly mouthed the words, "I know the truth. I know what really happened."

Before Jerry could assimilate all that was happening, a tremendous explosion rocked the stadium as flames shot out of the back of an orange tanker truck. Mortimer Ziffel was scorched beyond recognition. People were rushing toward him, screaming.

An instant later the flames were sucked back into the sprayers from which they had exploded. Jerry looked quickly back at Mortimer's remains to find that he was fine, just fine, alive, and well.

Jerry Linden was suddenly back in his family room, crying into the lap of the sweetest woman in the world. Cindy held Jerry tightly, not knowing what he had seen, but knowing that what he needed right now was her support.

Jerry never did tell Cindy what happened, and she never asked.

A week later, Jerry ran into Jaime at Kelly's Drive-in. He told Jaime that he had called him a couple of days after the game to congratulate him on his part in the victory but that his parents had said Jaime was on a trip. They told him Jaime had a couple of new friends who went with him.

Jaime didn't say much, except that he and Chris had delivered Becky to her aunt's home some distance away.

Jerry looked into Jaime's eyes. Jaime stared back. They stood there for a few seconds, each unable to break away from whatever force held their eyes locked in a mild trance.

When Jerry was finally able to unlock his gaze, Jaime said, "You know, don't you?"

Jerry nodded and looked back, beaming.

Buford and Lizzy Stravinsky

Franklin High School's upset victory over Riverton set almost everything right in Buford Stravinsky's life. He knew he had taken a long shot by betting on the side of the underdog Franklin, but, then, his life was an entire series of long shots.

That victory brought Buford a tidy profit and also brought the smile back to Lizzy's lips. And a smile on Lizzy's lips was worth its weight in gold to Buford.

If there was one thing that could make Buford's heart cower in fear, it was the thought of Lizzy being angry. When Lizzy was angry, Buford's entire world turned a greasy, slimy, dark, smelly gray. One thing that Buford Stravinsky didn't ever again want to have riding on one of his long-shot bets, was the smile on Lizzy's lips.

That night, the night of the Franklin-Riverton football game, Buford had been sitting in the bleachers with his brain almost torn in half by two sources of terror. The first was the thought that somebody, somewhere, might know that it was Buford Stravinsky who had endangered the lives of those innocent football game attendees with his tire-screeching antics. The second, even more terrifying, was that a loss by Franklin High would likely mean that the smile would never, ever return to Lizzy's lips.

Buford was a man in torment. He tried desperately not to think about the possible consequences of his situation. Even during those brief moments when he managed to distract himself from the horror of his circumstances, his temporary relief only succeeded in magnifying the pain that came ripping back into his solar plexus when the reality of his dilemma returned with a vengeance.

Had Buford not been so unbalanced by his state of misery, he might have been able to consider that the intensity of his reactions had no basis in logic or reason. Then again, he might have realized that logic or reason seldom bear any significant relationship to emotions.

Even if Buford had been able to realize how irrational his fears were, he probably wouldn't have been able to uncover their real cause.

By the time Buford was seven years old his survival mechanisms were already successfully blocking his conscious awareness of certain situations in his young life. These were the real cause of the terror with which he perpetually lived.

His mother's method of discipline, for any conduct that offended her, was to withhold her affection. Whenever Buford committed an act that displeased his mother, whether he was aware of what that act was or not, he was made to feel, with absolute certainty, that he was no longer worthy of any kind of warmth or affection.

What Buford's mother didn't realize was that withholding love and affection from a child of delicate years means, in the mind of that child, withholding the very source of life itself. The message that Buford and his siblings received, loud and clear, was that they did not deserve to live.

As a result of years of living on the veritable edge of psychological extinction, Buford grew into adulthood with a fear of rejection almost beyond his ability to endure.

For all the years that Buford had been married to Lizzy, he walked a terrifyingly fine line between his desperate need to follow his own instincts and desires and his even more desperate need never to cross certain boundaries, the transgression of which would cause Lizzy to withhold her warmth and affection. The first terrifying sign of impending doom was always the absence of Lizzy's smile.

The dread with which Buford was forced to contend, almost from the time of his birth, was the same driving force that caused him to violate all precepts of common sense in his insane attempt to arrive at the Franklin football game before the kickoff. In Buford's tormented mind, the loss of that game, with the resulting permanent loss of Lizzy's smile, was tantamount to his own death.

That same dread assaulted his senses as he sat in those bleachers, waiting for the end to come. When, against all odds, Jaime Lasher crossed the goal line scoring the winning touchdown, Buford's relief defied all description.

Knowing that his marriage to Lizzy would continue and that he would not have to stagger through life with the possibility that Lizzy would leave him, hanging over his head, brought him such a feeling of release that he totally forgot the possible consequences of his unorthodox arrival at the stadium.

Buford Stravinsky vowed then and there that, from this moment on, he was going to be, in the words of Aretha Franklin, a "do right man." He vowed to forsake all of his dreams and personal needs and small pleasures to ensure that the smile would never again be gone from Lizzy's face.

Now, several weeks after the glorious, life-saving victory of Franklin over Riverton, Buford found himself reasonably assured that his relationship with Lizzy was okay. Deep in the inner recesses of his subconscious, however, he couldn't avoid the feeling that the price he paid for this state of tenuous comfort was unreasonable. The price he paid was the forfeiture of the real Buford. It was the selling out of his own needs to conform to the image of the ideal husband, held in the heart of Lizzy Stravinsky. It was the price of peace. Buford paid the price of lost joy for the benefit of a delicate truce.

Had not Buford been programmed by the terrors of his childhood to live in constant fear of rejection, he and Lizzy might have found balance in their relationship, whereby Buford could be himself and still help Lizzy satisfy her needs.

Buford tried to convince himself that he was happy. But deep inside he knew the truth. He knew he didn't feel the joy that comes from being real. He would make it through life, forcing himself to think that all was well but never knowing the bliss that could have been his.

Still another problem plagued Buford's troubled mind. He sometimes awoke, in the middle of the night, with a terrible tension in his body. Sweat dripped down his neck and soaked his pillow.

He vaguely remembered dreaming about an explosion and flames roaring across an expanse of dark green grass. He dreamt of a man screaming while doing a frantic and bizarre dance of flames and smoke. Each time, as Buford sat bolt upright in his bed, he held before his eyes a vision of those roaring flames disappearing into the night, as if being sucked into forever.

Lizzy, not quite awake, often rolled toward Buford and unconsciously laid her arm against his trembling body. Buford laid down and pulled Lizzy's arm across his chest, seeking relief from the torment he knew would not yield to comfort.

Isaac Morgenstern and Elsie Waller

The sixties had not been good to Elsie Waller. While the flower children of Berkeley and San Francisco were "making love not war" on every contrivance from automobile hoods to swings on sorority-house balconies, Elsie was saving herself for who-knows-what, using lengthy visits to the Newman Center at the University of California campus to distract her from her natural, God-given urges.

Elsie was so terrorized by tales of impending satanic retribution for any experimentation with her "base and filthy" bodily parts that she managed, against all odds and common sense, to preserve her virginity in spite of the almost overwhelming allures of a college campus caught up in the frenzied debauchery of the hippie movement.

The momentum of the almost super-human efforts Elsie had to rely on to maintain her state of hormonal suppression was sufficient to carry her forward into and beyond the ensuing three decades without a single transgression against the ecclesiastically imposed rigors of virginity.

Now, well past the age of normal sexual experimentation, Elsie had long since buried herself in the depths of English literature as her primary distraction from the taunting urges that had plagued her libido ever since her plunge into the chaotic maelstrom of puberty. That is not to imply that Elsie's enchantment with imagined literary suitors, including Emerson, Keats, Thoreau, and Shelley, was her only form of distraction. Over the years she discovered a modicum of comfort in an occasional foray into the netherworld of mild to intense inebriation, fostered by a variety of stimulants ranging from wacky-tabacky to the ever-beckoning sloe gin.

In violation of all the urgings of her circumscribed rearing, Elsie found herself sitting in the Franklin High School bleachers, mesmerized by the football magic of those Lasher twins and aware of the ever increasing effects of the sloe gin she had begun to consume more than an hour before her arrival at the game. The sloe gin bottle, a full fifth of a gallon in size, was drawing dangerously close to empty. If liquor bottles were to come equipped with gauges similar to those located on the dashboards of automobiles, Elsie would have been advised that her sloe gin bottle was running on "reserve."

Within seconds after Jaime Lasher secured his brother Tim's game-winning eighty-five-yard pass in his eager arms, Elsie experienced a rush of energy and passion the likes of which she had never before imagined in her wildest flights of fancy. To her utter shock and amazement, all those years of pent-up sexual pressure, combined with the effects of the chemicals and hormones released by the presence of the sloe gin in and around the region of her medulla oblongata, enhanced by the sheer joy of watching the perfection of the Lasher twins' performance all converged to produce a rush of energy that rampaged through every synapse and fiber of her nervous system, resulting finally in a bodywide reaction of indescribable intensity.

Even if she had wanted to, there was no way that Elsie could have restrained herself. She leaped up from her seat near the top of the bleachers and headed in the general direction of the football field, bobbing and weaving among the other fans, trying her best not to step on anyone. As she made a sharp left turn at the end of a row, intended to head her more directly toward the field, she grabbed the last person on the end of the bench, for no particular reason other than an expression of her exuberance.

Elsie was vaguely aware that she had someone in tow by the hand as she made one final leap over the last two rows at the bottom of the grandstand, landing on the bench recently vacated by a substantial number of the Franklin team members, who were now jumping and screaming and throwing their football helmets into the air.

As almost an afterthought, she looked back in an attempt to identify the individual she had commandeered from the end of row twelve. To her surprise, it was none other than the high school's physics professor, Isaac Morgenstern, staring back at her with a look of utter astonishment, his Meerschaum pipe in an upside-down position and the remains of a wooden match in his free hand.

As Isaac attempted to recover his equilibrium after his flight over the bottom two rows of the Franklin bleachers, he failed to observe the sideline bench upon which Elsie had come to rest, and he smacked both of his shins squarely against the wooden seat of that securely grounded structure.

Isaac did a complete end-over flip, landing, to his total surprise, on his feet. The pain emanating from his shins was beyond his comprehension, as were the events of the preceding ninety seconds. As he stood there in a state of total confusion, he sensed that his left hand had been released by his abductor, who was now sprinting onto the field, where the Franklin High cheerleaders were proudly strutting their stuff.

To Isaac's further amazement, the person who had dragged him from row twelve to the far side of the sideline bench was now joining the cheerleaders in their frenetic undulations. To his even greater astonishment, that person was none other than Elsie Waller, the sophomore class literature teacher.

Prior to this series of outrageous happenings, Isaac had paid little attention to Elsie. She appeared to him as a quiet, sullen, shy, scholarly type with the sex appeal of a small walnut. This nymph now twisting and spiraling before his eyes was the essence of female energy of the most alluring kind.

Elsie raised her skirt—which heretofore always came to mid-calf—a startling distance above her knees, revealing with each jump and kick a pair of bright red satin undies of the kind designed to expose a considerable amount of hip and upper thigh. And even more alluringly, those portions of Elsie's legs that never before had come to Isaac's attention were shapely beyond his present ability to put into words, even in the shadowy recesses of his dirty-old-man's mind.

As Elsie twirled to the rhythm of the Franklin High marching band's auditory display, the shawl that had been wrapped around her shoulders, and which had become her trademark over the years, was flung to the far winds, revealing a rather ample and perfectly proportioned bosom, encased in a fetching cashmere sweater.

Isaac was beside himself, the pain from his throbbing shins a distant memory. He tried vigorously to light his inverted and tobaccoless Meerschaum, succeeding only in affixing a dark black stain to the underside of that device.

The woman who, heretofore, had appeared listless and dejected to Isaac now exhibited a vibrancy that not only amazed him but also caused a welcome stimulation to his libido. Isaac was in a trance.

For one millisecond, Elsie was frozen in mid-twirl as she imagined that she saw, out of the corner of her eye, a bright orange-red flame shoot across the field. A second later she underwent a bit of vertigo, accompanied by the strange feeling that she missed a second or two of whatever was happening around her. Then all returned to normal as she completed her twirl, bringing her foot down solidly on the grass. "Must be that sloe gin," she thought. But she couldn't shake the feeling that something highly unusual had happened.

Elsie ran back to Isaac, grabbed his hand, and led him to the center of the field. Still entranced, he followed willingly. He couldn't help but stare at the area where those gorgeous legs were now hiding beneath Elsie's skirt, the hem of which once again had returned to mid-calf.

As they reached mid-field, Elsie noticed that Tim and Jaime Lasher had joined their parents and Mortimer Ziffel a few yards away. She made a mental note of the intense looks that both Tim and Jaime were directing toward Mortimer.

As one of many uncharacteristic acts that Elsie Waller performed that night, she placed her lips close to Isaac's left ear and invited him to join her for the night—the entire night.

Still bewildered, Isaac responded to her invitation with an enthusiastic nod of his still-reeling head.

For that entire night and well into the following afternoon, Elsie Waller did her best to make up for more than four decades of physical frustration. Isaac kept smiling and nodding. From that point on, Isaac and Elsie were inseparable.

One of the qualities Elsie inherited from her years of self-discipline and unnatural frustration was an iron will. As a result of her fortitude and strength, Isaac became a different man. He started to brush his teeth several times a day and floss, too. He became noticeably devoted to Elsie. His physics studies, although still an important part of his life, took a distant back seat to Elsie's needs.

One might accurately say that Isaac became a doting husband, forever smiling and nodding.

Elsie was a happy wife and a devoted football fan.

# Osgood Thurmond

He was soaked, absolutely soaked.

The intense downpour raining from the angry skies, augmented by thousands of gallons of lake water delivered to Osgood Thurmond's campsite by the water plume generated by the crashing ponderosa, rendered the area a virtual quagmire.

At somewhere around 11:00 p.m., the air temperature in the area of Lake Chippewa had dropped below the freezing point. Osgood hadn't noticed the plummeting air temperature. His frantic efforts to sever the massive ponderosa from its connection with Mother Earth had raised his body temperature to the point where any source of reduction in heat calories was welcome and appreciated.

Now, several hours later, as much as Osgood wanted to enjoy a few days in the wilderness, he decided that, with several hours until sunrise, there was no way he could tolerate lying in a drenched sleeping bag in a wet tent until such time, if ever, as the sun would produce sufficient heat to thaw him out.

Osgood was aware that his schoolmates considered him as some kind of a moron or, as one pretty girl had called him to his great embarrassment, a Cretin. But he was smart enough to know when to leave an impossible situation. He didn't know much about temperatures or heat conduction or any of that other physics stuff. But he did know that cold, wet, sleeping bags didn't feel good. Not only that, they could cause a cold or, maybe, even pneumonia. Osgood knew that colds were bad. He knew that pneumonia was even worse. His Mom had told him that many times. And Osgood was aware that once he heard things several times, they often stuck in his brain.

He threw his tent and sleeping bag into the trunk of his car, not thinking to wring them out first. So he was surprised a couple of minutes later to see water dripping from under the automobile. He hadn't thought to connect the dripping with the wet items he had tossed into the trunk. That wasn't part of Osgood's normal thinking process. He wasn't very good at connecting cause and effect.

Osgood fired up the old Volvo sedan, the car that had been the source of so much ridicule from his schoolmates. It didn't occur to him to turn on the heater or to close the driver-side wind wing, for that matter, until the cold became so compelling that he was forced to do something. He turned on the heater but still didn't think to close the window.

It took Osgood nearly three hours to work his way down from the mountain ridge where his temporary camp had been. The dirt road was slippery, and he had to push the front end of the Volvo out of a ditch a few times. As he made the transition from the Forest Service road to the paved county road, a strange foreboding came upon him.

What Osgood lacked in reasoning ability had, mercifully, been compensated for by uncommonly powerful instincts. Osgood sometimes felt things other people didn't seem to notice.

As he pulled onto the pavement, he had a feeling that something scary was about to happen. He remembered being told about how animals sometimes sense an earthquake several minutes before human beings feel its effects.

The rain was still coming down hard. In fact, for the first half-mile, Osgood was on the wrong side of the double yellow line. The raindrops splashing on the asphalt, when added to the moisture accumulation on Osgood's windshield, made it really hard to see those lines. Not until Osgood felt his left front tire squirming in the mud that ran along the road's left shoulder did he realize that something definitely wasn't right. It took him another minute to decide what to do about it. He turned the steering wheel in the direction opposite from the pull of the wheel. When the tire jumped back onto the pavement, things felt better.

After several movements back and forth from the muddy shoulder to the relative safety of the tarmac, Osgood realized he had been off to the left side of the road a good part of the time.

He let the Volvo wander to the right for a while until he felt the right front tire sink into the mud. After that, he was fairly well able to stay on the paved part of the road, although he did drift back into the mud occasionally. All in all, he drifted onto the right shoulder more than he drifted onto the left shoulder. Osgood thought that was good.

Luckily, there were hardly any other cars on the road. It didn't occur to Osgood that the absence of traffic might be the result of the torrential rain.

When, finally, a semi came rolling toward him, the headlights of that truck reflected off of the shiny road lines and helped Osgood locate his side of the road. As soon as the semi passed, the scary feeling came over Osgood again. He thought that it was probably just the dark surrounding him after the bright lights of the passing truck.

But it was more than that, a real scary feeling, like when Mom forgot to leave on the hall light outside his bedroom door. Sometimes he didn't want to call to her and ask her to turn it on because she might be asleep. But that meant either he would have to lie there in the darkness being scared or he would have to get out of bed to turn on the light himself. And Osgood knew how scary it would be to put his feet on the floor in the dark. He never knew what might be waiting for him under the bed.

Even though the heater was on full blast, Osgood was still cold. He pushed the control lever hard to the right, although it already seemed to be as far as it would go.

What was bothering Osgood was hardly noticeable at first. It was sort of like when you brush your hair and the brush has a long hair stuck in it that sticks out and brushes against your forehead. You think something's there, but because you can't see it, you're not sure. Maybe it's just your imagination. But after you feel it a lot of times, you're pretty sure it's there, but not totally.

That's how it started. Kind of like a hair stuck in a brush.

Osgood thought he was hearing something. But it was hard to tell because there were so many sounds close to him—the rain beating on the roof of the Volvo, the tires mooshing through the water on the road and the wind coming in the window. Osgood noticed that the wind wing was opened. He thought that might be important but wasn't sure what it had to do with anything.

And there was the heater fan blowing and even the Volvo's engine running. Then Osgood ran out of sounds that it might be.

None of those noises sounded like what was scaring Osgood. He didn't even realize that it was scaring him at first. It was just a sound. But then, when he couldn't identify it, he felt the first little drop of fear slip out of his brain, heading for his tummy. It got mixed up with the little drop of fear he first felt when he went from the Forest Service road to the paved county road.

Now there were two drops. Or maybe they were the same drop. Or maybe the two drops had become one bigger drop.

Osgood's tummy muscles tightened. His hands squeezed harder on the steering wheel.

The noise was getting louder, a lot louder. The louder it got, the harder Osgood pushed down on the gas pedal.

Then he noticed that the water on the road was a lot deeper than it had been a while ago. He realized that his steering wheel wasn't working right. When he turned the wheel, it took a long time for the car to turn.

His dad had told him about how steering wheels sometimes don't work right when there's lots of water on the road, especially when you're going real fast. Dad called it aeroplaning, or something like that.

Osgood decided to let up on the gas a little. Something wasn't right. He wasn't sure what it was. Then he thought he knew. He pressed down on the gas. Then he let up on the gas. Nothing changed.

The Volvo wasn't doing what it was supposed to do. Osgood took his foot completely off of the gas pedal. Nothing happened. He instinctively pushed down on the brake pedal. Nothing happened. He turned the steering wheel. The Volvo continued straight ahead.

He stomped on the brake with both feet. The Volvo went even faster. Now it was twisting from side to side.

Osgood screamed. The scream seemed to clear his head. Then he noticed that he couldn't see anything ahead of him.

The Volvo did something it had never done before. The front of the car raised up several inches, then it dipped down.

Osgood's teeth were squeezing together hard.

Nothing worked.

Then the heater fan stopped.

A bright blue spark came out from under the dashboard.

Then the headlights went out.

Water began to flood through the open wind wing.

Osgood felt water around his ankles.

Then the Volvo went sideways.

Suddenly Osgood saw a sight that scared him as nothing had scared him before, except when he forgot the combination to his gym locker, when his clothes were locked inside and he was standing buck-naked in the boys' gym with only ten minutes to get to his next class.

The car windows looked like they were all aquariums, half-filled with water.

Then the noise got so loud that Osgood thought his ears were going to pop.

The Volvo began spinning so fast that Osgood felt as he had when he rode the spinning cups at Disneyland.

The water inside was rising, almost up to his waist now.

What was happening?

Osgood thought and thought.

Then the Volvo shot sideways.

Finally, Osgood decided he had somehow driven into a lake or a river or something like that. The water was up to his shoulders.

He was really scared. He knew he couldn't stay in the car much longer. Soon the water would be up to his hair and he wouldn't be able to breathe.

Osgood tried to open the door. It was stuck shut. He pressed with all his might. It wouldn't budge. Osgood was really strong. He knew that for sure. Even his football coach said he'd never seen any-one as strong as Osgood.

He pressed his left shoulder against the door and shoved both of his feet against the passenger door. He pushed with all his might. He thought his gut would bust.

His head was now under water. He knew he could hold his breath for almost four minutes. He was in a breath-holding contest once with Joe Brahman. Osgood's time was three minutes and forty seven seconds.

He had to get out of here.

The Volvo spun to the right. Osgood screamed. The scream was lost in the water. He sucked in a few drops. He began to cough. Each cough brought in more water. He forced himself to stop the natural retching his lungs wanted so desperately to continue.

Without thinking, Osgood grabbed the window crank on the driver's door and turned it with the strength of a man about to die. The crank turned a quarter turn and then offered no more resistance. In his frantic desperation, Osgood had torn it off the shaft that moved the levers that raised and lowered the window.

Osgood stopped himself from screaming again. *Think. Think.*

With uncommon agility, fostered by the buoyancy of the water, he spun around, bringing his head and shoulders to within inches of the passenger door and his feet to the driver's side of the Volvo. With superhuman effort, Osgood forced himself to turn the window crank of the passenger-side door ever so slowly.

His lungs were screaming for relief. He was starting to get dizzy. The urge to suck something into his lungs—even something that didn't belong there or even something that would kill him—was almost more than he could bear. Osgood knew he couldn't hold out for more than three or four more seconds. He was glad Joe Brahman wasn't watching him. He turned the window crank a bit more.

Seconds later, to Osgood's great relief, the window glass was all the way down. Surprisingly, he could make out the clouds through the narrow slit between the top of the window frame and the top of the water. He launched himself through the window opening and realized that he was floating in the middle of what appeared to be a gigantic lake, where a lake shouldn't be. It was a fast-moving lake. Osgood could tell, by how quickly the trees were passing on either side of him.

He grabbed for one tree after another but couldn't reach them. He was moving too fast.

Then that sound he had been hearing turned into a roar. Osgood looked in the direction of the sound and saw a wall of water moving toward him so fast he didn't have time to react. Even if he had had time to do something, he had nothing to do.

Nothing I can do.

This must be the end.

He said a little prayer, for his Mom and his Dad and his sister, Kathy.

Just before the wall was about to hit, Osgood felt something pushing up against his feet. At first he thought he had touched the bottom of the lake. But he was moving so fast that anything on the bottom would have ripped past him. It had to be something moving about as fast as he was.

Then, it pressed harder against his feet. It came to the surface, raising Osgood out of the water. In utter exhaustion, Osgood's legs collapsed, and he sat down hard on whatever was beneath him.

Then he recognized the old peeling brown paint. It was the Volvo. That old, rusty, noisy, rickety Volvo had lifted Osgood out of the water.

With his outrageously long arms, he grabbed the tops of the window openings on either side of the car. Thank God he had been able to lower the driver-side window a quarter-turn before the crank broke loose from its shaft.

Osgood sailed down the raging torrent atop the Volvo's roof, hanging on for dear life. The wall of water was gaining on him, even though he and his car were now moving faster than that old Volvo had ever moved, even on the interstate.

The roar was deafening. The wall of water must have been at least thirty feet above the surface of the water upon which Osgood Thurmond was now sailing. The Volvo rocked from side to side.

"Please, God," he screamed, "don't let her roll."

Just as the wall of water approached the terrified sailor, a bolt of lightning reached out of the furious sky and shattered the water all around Osgood and the good ship Volvo.

Mercifully, Osgood lost consciousness as the waters of the former Chippewa Lake came crashing over the man who unknowingly had set them free.

Osgood could never have imagined the effects the lightning bolt that attacked the waters around his little vessel would have on his future. The larger portion of the voltage unleashed by Mother Nature had shot down through the rushing water and deep into the earth below. The small amount of the charge that wasn't grounded into the earth spiraled around Osgood and his floating Volvo, causing all kinds of electrical phenomena, the most relevant of which was the tiny current that climbed up the metallic outer skin of the Volvo and up through Osgood's arms.

That relatively low-voltage current shot up over the top of his skull, down the front of his face, along the thousands of tiny nerve endings surrounding his teeth, and finally, up through the roof of his mouth, into the center of his head, around and through billions of his brain cells. The current separated onto the hundreds of thousands of different trails and byways of the brain, reducing in voltage at each separation. By the time it entered each brain cell, its power was reduced sufficiently to alter the cell without destroying it.

When Osgood regained consciousness, his abdomen was wrapped around the trunk of a small cypress tree. The sun was out and the torrent had passed, leaving a surreal landscape of mud and debris in its wake.

Osgood couldn't move. He just lay there, thankful he could breathe.

The sun felt good, warming his aching back. As he lay there, thoughts began to surface that seemed totally unfamiliar to him. He began to remember in minute detail things he had forgotten long ago. For example, proofs and calculation, that his algebra teacher had told him, that hadn't made any sense to Osgood at the time, now made perfect sense.

Explanations and concepts he had read in his physics book, which had been a complete mystery to him at the time, now came crashing back into his consciousness with a clarity beyond anything he had ever comprehended.

Osgood thought about the scarecrow in *The Wizard of Oz*, how he suddenly realized he had a brain. The scarecrow man shouted something about the sides of an isosceles triangle. Osgood's head was suddenly filled with an entire plethora of formulae, such as: "The circumference of a circle is equal to π times its diameter," and "the area of a circle is equal to π times its radius squared," and "the length of the hypotenuse of a right triangle squared is equal to the sum of the squares of the length of the other two sides."

He was amazed. He knew the date of the signing of the Declaration of Independence. He even knew the names of all of those brave men who had signed it. He realized he knew that a word used to modify a verb is called an "adverb" and almost always ends in "ly."

As he lay there, entranced by the knowledge he had suddenly discovered, he was overcome with such joy that he couldn't hold back the tears. Osgood Thurmond, the moron-cretin, was normal. In fact, he was better than normal. He was a genius.

Within another couple of hours, a rescue squad arrived on the scene and took Osgood to Mercy Hospital, where he was sufficiently recovered within three days to go home.

During his stay at the hospital, he amazed several members of the staff by suggesting treatments for patients, based on an in-depth understanding of the workings of the human body, especially the various bodily systems including the digestive, the immune, the circulatory, the nervous, the respiratory, and the endocrine. He remembered everything he had ever read in his biology book.

Shortly after Osgood had been admitted to the hospital, he was placed in a room with a six-year-old boy suffering from a kidney disease, complicated by pneumonia. Osgood was so touched by the situation that he asked the nurse if she could get him some basic medical literature. She rummaged through the hospital library and found a large, colorful book entitled *Atlas of the Mind and Body*. After only a few hours of reading that book, Osgood combined that information with the reading he had done in his high school biology class, which he hadn't understood originally but now understood clearly. Together, they provided him with sufficient knowledge to accurately suggest a treatment for his young roommate. The nurse, to her own amazement, relayed the suggested treatment to the doctor in charge without disclosing its source.

Although Osgood was only beginning to understand the intricacies of medicine, he already understood the benefits of drinking plenty of pure water, deep breathing, eating nutritious food, doing moderate exercise, and keeping a positive attitude. He spent several hours telling jokes and stories designed to raise the spirits of his healing roommate. Within two days after the new treatment was implemented, the boy's vital signs showed significant improvement.

Osgood went on to graduate at the top of his high school class. He refused to allow tests to be run on his brain, preferring, instead, to lead as normal a life as a genius can. He graduated from college with degrees in biology and physics. He went on to graduate school, where he studied nuclear physics and subatomic particle theory.

His hobby, however, was working with terminally ill individuals. This brought Osgood a great deal of satisfaction.

Somewhere along the way, Osgood came into contact with numerous books written by masters on the leading edge of thought. These were writers who knew that there is no evil in objective reality and that, although our acts have consequences, there is no judgment as we have been taught.

Reading these great books brought Osgood joy beyond anything he had ever dreamed of. But Osgood's proudest accomplishment was that he used his brilliant mind, and the knowledge gained from his reading, to teach those who would listen what he knew about how the universe really works and that it is a whole lot different from what we have been led to believe by traditional teachings.

Osgood learned that the low-voltage surge that altered his brain forever opened up only about another two percent of the ninety percent of his brain that he had never used. He also learned that most human beings use only between nine and eleven percent of their brains, and that those classified as "genius" have expanded the use of their brain only to the twelve to thirteen percent range. He might have been shocked to know that if that voltage surge had opened up another four percent of those unused brain cells, Osgood Thurmond would now have been capable of traveling the outer fringes of the known universe utilizing nothing more than the power of his mind.

Even as great an accomplishment as that might be, he considered it would be relatively insignificant compared to what he knew he would be able to do upon leaving the Earth Plane and returning to the world of spirit, where thought is not limited by the constraints of the human brain.

Osgood was also coming to realize that the vast unused part of his brain would be accessed, someday, just by knowing that it could be.

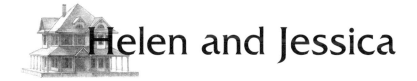

Helen and Jessica

Helen found her job as a waitress at Kelly's Diner quite satisfying. She had made an abundance of enjoyable acquaintances and also a few close friends.

Initially the void left in Helen's life by the death of Jessica was almost more painful than she could bear. But as time passed, she adjusted and, although the void remained, she discovered that other relationships could bring a bit of comfort.

Helen had hoped to be able to rely on her husband for support, but he hadn't adjusted well to the tragedy.

Jerald and Helen's marriage had always been stable and comfortable. But the months of watching Jessica suffer took a toll from which Jerald was not likely to recover. Jessica was Daddy's little girl. They were virtually inseparable, even through Jessica's teenage years. The consequences Jerald suffered with her loss could not technically be called a nervous breakdown. But he wasn't the same. And, although he and Helen remained close and very much in love, Jerald couldn't find the strength after Jessica's death to give Helen the support she needed so badly. It was he who needed Helen's support.

The knowledge that Helen desperately needed more support than he could provide caused Jerald to slip further and further into his already terrible state of deep sorrow. He loved Helen so much, but it took all he had just to make it through each day.

Among the friends Helen made at the diner was a sweet older woman named Blanche. Every Thursday evening Blanche came in to feast on one of Kelly's real Caesar salads.

Blanche had observed that in recent years she hardly ever looked at a menu that didn't boast a Caesar salad. She also noticed that few, if any, of them had the proper ingredients. About the only thing about them that faintly resembled a real Caesar salad was that they usually were made with romaine lettuce. Whatever was poured over those greens as a substitute for Caesar dressing was typically nothing more than a tangy Italian dressing of some sort.

Not so at Kelly's. One of the reasons Kelly's customers kept coming back time after time was the integrity of the owners. If the menu said "spaghetti in meat sauce," the patron could count on a hearty and genuine topping, not some canned concoction with a tad of oregano, but real spaghetti sauce, with onions, bell peppers, mushrooms, real Italian sausage, and lots and lots of garlic.

Therefore, Kelly's Caesar salad was actually Caesar salad. The dressing contained a coddled egg, real lemon juice, genuine anchovies, freshly grated parmesan cheese, and all the other goodies that Mr. Caesar had used when he created that delectable dressing in Mexico so many years ago.

In recent months Blanche had found another reason to continue her Thursday night ritual. She had become truly fond of Helen. She had heard about Jessica's death. And, although she and Helen didn't speak much about that sad part of Helen's life, they sometimes did talk about matters of a personal nature.

One night after Jerald had had a particularly difficult day, Helen was struggling mightily to hold back her tears as she went from table to table. As she headed toward Blanche's table with the large Caesar salad perched on her left forearm and a coffee pot in her right hand, she slipped on a slice of tomato that had escaped from the double cheeseburger she had delivered only minutes earlier to the nice young man at table number seven.

Helen didn't fall to the floor. Her right shoe actually slipped only about four inches before regaining its hold on the linoleum, as the tomato slice rolled out from under her instep. But that four-inch movement lowered Helen's right hip, causing her right hand to swing out some distance to the right.

Her instinctive reaction was to move the coffee pot even farther, in an effort to prevent its scalding hot contents from splashing over the rim and onto the lap of the freckle-faced cutie with green shorts and braces on her teeth in booth number four. That carefully executed maneuver actually did prevent the scalding hot coffee from landing on the young lady's thighs.

Unfortunately, the entire event produced enough momentum to Helen's right to pull her left forearm from beneath the crisp and properly seasoned Caesar salad, which heretofore had been headed for the red and white checkered placemat positioned directly in front of Blanche. The heavy chilled platter tipped slightly to Helen's left and headed for the exact spot where the aforementioned tomato slice lay, trying to look as innocent as possible.

As the platter shattered and the romaine splattered, Helen lost it. All those tears lurking just below the surface of her warm and loving brown eyes took advantage of the temporary lapse in her composure and surged from her eager tear ducts, fanning out across her rosy cheeks.

Helen set the coffee pot down on table number five and staggered to the empty bench opposite Blanche. She laid her head on her arms and began sobbing uncontrollably.

Sally, the new waitress from Tacoma, cleaned up the mess on the floor, ordered a replacement for the ill-fated Caesar salad, and gave Helen a much-needed hug around her trembling shoulders. Helen looked up and whispered her thanks to Sally before resuming her sobbing.

Blanche got up from her bench and sat down next to Helen, gently moving her toward the window. She placed her arm around Helen's shoulder while she continued to release those many months of grief.

From all appearances, not a person in the restaurant other than Blanche was aware of what was happening. Nobody wanted to add to Helen's embarrassment. Blanche asked Sally to put her salad into a "to go" container. Sally offered to cover for Helen for the rest of the evening. Blanche retrieved Helen's sweater from the employee coat rack, wrapped it around Helen's shoulders, and walked her to Blanche's car, where they sat and talked.

That talk was exactly what Helen needed. Knowing Helen's aversion to traditional medical care, Blanche suggested that Helen consult a naturopathic healer who had been Blanche's friend for many years.

The very next day, Helen took Jerald to see the doctor Blanche had recommended. The doctor counseled Helen and Jerald that what Jerald was going through was not at all unusual and certainly nothing about which to be ashamed.

"Grieving over the loss of a loved one," the doctor advised, "is an essential part of the human condition." He also assured them that the human body and mind are both extremely capable of correcting any condition, given the proper nutrition, both physical and emotional.

He wrote out the most unusual prescription that either Helen or Jerald had ever seen. He prescribed that Jerald drink lots of distilled water every day, eat an abundance of raw fruits and vegetables, drink two glasses of fresh organic carrot juice, force himself to engage in a program of moderate exercise, and especially, do everything within his power to hold the most positive, happy thoughts of which he was capable, in spite of the terrible sorrow he'd endured. The doctor also suggested that Jerald spend ten minutes every day visualizing himself enjoying what he called "vibrant physical and emotional health."

The change in Jerald was nothing short of miraculous. Within three weeks, he was well on his way to being his old self again. And, although he still grieved over the loss of Jessica, he found himself able to provide Helen with the support she needed. That fact alone was a tremendous benefit to Jerald's self-esteem. From that time on, he experienced a dramatic upward spiral, physically, mentally, and emotionally.

Not long after that first visit to the holistic practitioner, as Helen and Jerald were preparing for bed, Helen turned to Jerald, wrapped her arms around him, looked into his eyes, and smiled tearfully. "Jessica would be so proud of you."

That night they fell asleep in each other's arms. For the first time since Jessica's funeral, Helen slept with a smile on her face. As she drifted off, Helen's last thought was of her daughter. *Oh, my sweet baby Jessica. What I would give to hold you in my arms just one more time.*

Helen slipped into deeper and deeper levels of relaxation, both before and after she surrendered consciousness. Never in her life had

Helen felt or imagined anything like what she was now feeling. It couldn't even really be called a "feeling." It was beyond her physical senses, beyond her emotions. She felt as if she were a musical note in the middle of the most glorious symphony ever performed.

Freedom. That was as close as her sleeping mind could come to putting her experience into a single word, absolute, total, outrageously joyous freedom. She was rid of the constraints of her body, even free of the limitations of her mind. She could feel everything and nothing, all at once. She could be anywhere at anytime.

She looked down and saw her body lying on the bed next to Jerald in her old familiar bedroom.

This should have felt spooky, but it didn't. It felt wonderful. About as glorious as anything Helen had ever experienced.

She looked at her hands. They were her hands, but they were perfect hands—no wrinkles, no liver spots—the most beautiful hands she had ever seen. But they were still her hands. And, she could see through them. They were there, but they weren't exactly there. She looked down at her torso. It was her body. But, it was the most beautiful, perfectly shaped body she had ever seen, flawless. She could see her heart, pulsing gently, just below the surface of her chest. And her breasts were perfectly shaped, like when she was eighteen, only more full and shapely.

Helen looked back at her heart again. She thought about it intensely, and suddenly she *was* her heart. It was Helen that was pulsating. She could feel the blood flowing joyously through her. All in perfect harmony with the symphony of which she was no longer only the single note but the entire score. She was every instrument in a heavenly orchestra, conducted by the God Force. She was the God Force.

Tears of joy flowed from her beautiful eyes. She was those eyes. She was those tears. She was everything that is or ever was. Helen expanded herself to the outer limits of the universe and realized this was only the beginning. She felt and knew there were an infinite number of universes.

She could see into a larger existence than she had ever imagined, as if the life she had known were conducted within a gigantic droplet of water under the microscope of some unimaginably large giant.

Then she looked down, as if through a microscope, and saw that smallness went down, down, down, infinitely, just as the world of the giant who was looking at her world through his microscope existed within a tiny droplet of water under the microscope of an even larger giant.

She knew these thoughts were only scratching the surface of the reality of infinity and eternity. She knew and actually understood all that is. She realized that she now understood parallel universes and how time and space can actually exist within the same reality of no time and no space. These concepts, so new to her, should have been mind-boggling. Yet, they were all so clear, and not really new. She became aware that she had known all of this forever.

Tears of joy continued to pour from her eyes.

She reached out and touched the face of God.

Her heart burst into an infinite number of hearts.

The joy was beyond imagining. The freedom was indescribable in what Helen had formerly known as "words" but freely expressible in the language of heaven, the realm of the God Force.

It all imploded into the finite mind of Helen. A glorious light moved toward her in a world of no movement, no time, and no space. It was a presence newly arrived, yet eternally there.

Then an ancient memory surfaced in Helen's mind of an event that had just happened, not in the recent past but in the past, the present, and the future. Her mind swam in the gloriously tender currents of time and no time.

The presence had brought to her a cherished memory and with it the feelings Heaven reserves for only one sacred event, the absolute joy experienced between a mother and her child at the moment of birth.

Jessica!

The presence was bright beyond recognition by the human eye, a light frequency approaching infinity. a light that would have instantly blinded human sight, a light known only to the soul.

My Jessica!

The symphony slowed. The light faded to the point of human tolerance. The translucence of Helen's body diminished. Her body assumed the appearance of solidity.

"Mama," whispered a voice more glorious than anything Helen's earthly ears had heard in a long, long time. It was Jessica's voice. It was the symphony. It was the voice of God.

In an instant that wasn't really an instant but a *now*, Jessica was there in all her human, earthly glory, still aglow, but appearing more solid now, less transparent.

Jessica's hand reached toward Helen. As that hand touched her breast, a warmth beyond words filled Helen's being. Jessica flowed forward, enveloping Helen with her light. A liquid crystal tear slipped from Jessica's cheek, splashing on Helen's shoulder, radiating an exquisite, soothing peace.

"Where are we?" asked Helen.

"Everywhere," Jessica replied.

"Would you like to perceive me in your here and now?" Jessica offered.

"Yes," whispered Helen.

In an instant, Jessica was physical. Helen was physical.

Jessica wore a beautiful long, white, flowing gown, her perfect body faintly visible beneath the material. Three tiny daisies adorned her long, reddish-brown hair and on her left hand was a bright ruby ring.

It was the same ring Helen had placed on Jessica's hand the morning of her funeral. At that time, it had been an emerald, not a ruby. But the shape was unmistakably that of the ring that had once belonged to Helen's grandmother.

They spoke for hours in only an instant.

Jessica explained that it was a ruby ring and an emerald ring. It was any kind of ring Helen wanted it to be. Helen thought about the essence of emerald green, and the ring became emerald before her eyes. She thought of diamonds, and in an instant it was a diamond ring. She looked at it once more. It became a ruby in the shape of a teardrop.

"Look at what you're thinking," laughed Jessica.

Helen laughed, too, a laugh that echoed down the canyons of eternity.

They spoke of many things. But what Helen remembered most, in the days that followed, was that Jessica was happy, absolutely happy. And that "absolutely happy" was the state that awaited all beings upon their return to the world of spirit.

"You must go now," sighed Jessica. "Your body will be awakening shortly. We will meet again, in a millisecond after you leave your body. This will happen in about thirty years in Earth time, which is no time at all where I reside. I'll see you in an instant. I love you, Mama."

Helen awoke and looked into the smiling eyes of Jerald. He held a tray with coffee and cookies, the steam swirling upward as steam can only swirl in the physical world. Jerald set the tray on the nightstand and sat gently on the bed next to her.

Helen hugged Jerald warmly. Joy was coursing though her entire being. With every fiber of her self, she knew that all would be perfect, forever.

Jerald said, "You look more radiant than I've ever seen you. And where did you ever get that ring? I've never seen a ruby in the shape of a teardrop."

Helen looked down at her hand and smiled.

# Big Red and Ethel

The semi made nerve-shattering contact with the earth, front bumper first.

Only seconds earlier a right-spiraling motion of the trailer, which was loaded with natural gas line valves and pressure regulators, headed for the gas fields of northern New Mexico, had disconnected from the tractor.

As the load inside the Great Dane trailer had torn loose from the nylon tie-downs used to ensure that the load wouldn't become unstable as the result of normal lane changes, high-speed curves, and aggressive starts and stops, it yanked the trailer sharply to the right in an even faster spiraling motion.

The tractor enclosing and, perhaps, preparing to entomb Big Red and Ethel, continued on its original trajectory, with one relevant exception: As the two components parted company, the tug of the trailer against the underside of the coupler that had connected it to the tractor was sufficient to send the back half of the tractor shooting high into the midnight sky.

Still moving in a slightly skewed forward direction, the tractor continued to forge ahead at a speed in excess of forty-five miles per hour until the front bumper came to a screeching halt, or, more accurately, a shocking cessation of forward momentum.

At the same moment that the front bumper decelerated at a rate that almost defied the laws of both nature and physics, the rest of the tractor continued its forward motion, in seeming disregard for the fact that the now badly wrinkled bumper had ceased its forward journey. This resulted in an end-over-end flipping of the massive vehicle, until it finally came to rest in a heap of smoking, hissing, crackling steel.

Now, it's doubtful that either Big Red or Ethel gave one iota of thought to the innumerable laws of physics that were called into play by Big Red's decision to take the surface highway rather than the interstate. Actually, the entire episode, from the time the semi began spinning on the ice, was a complete blur to the occupants of that frenzied vehicle.

Ethel had managed to shut down all of her sensory receptors, as a result of which her mind was aware of nothing beyond the glass-shattering scream emanating from her voracious mouth, powered by her ample lungs.

During most of that frantic ride, Big Red had entered a mode of conduct that could be described most aptly as "holding on for dear life." His only deviance from that state was when he momentarily found himself unable, even with the use of every ounce of

will power at his command, to resist the temptation to lean forward, grab a number sixteen knitting needle that was floating in
mid-air just above the console between his seat and that occupied
by his wife, and plunge that knitting needle, with consummate satisfaction, into Ethel's left thigh.

As he delivered the needle into the depths of Ethel's massive
thigh, he shouted, "Ethel, you fat blob of unmitigated cruelty, I hope
your remains burn forever in the fires of hell!"

Big Red instantaneously resumed his former posture in his bucket
seat, a smile of utter, unabashed joy on his face.

The tractor flipped, and moments later, Big Red lost consciousness.

Everything was heavy, terribly heavy. The air was oppressive.
The silence was unbearable.

Big Red tried to raise his arm. It felt as if it were made of lead.
His head felt as if it were made of granite. Strain as he might, his
neck muscles weren't up to the task of raising his normally mobile
head from whatever it was resting upon. Even the darkness that surrounded him was heavy.

He had no idea where he was. At first he thought maybe he was
dead. But "dead" wasn't supposed to hurt. and Big Red hurt.

Then terror struck as he considered the possibility that he might
have been buried alive.

The very thought caused acid to be released into his stomach
and a small bead of perspiration to form in the area between his
eyebrows. He thought frantically, trying to recall what had happened
that could have put him in this terrible position.

Then it began coming back to him, the highway, the lake of ice,
the slow clockwise spin, and the feeling of utter powerlessness as the
truck began to tilt to the right. Then the tractor began to spiral clockwise about an axis that ran from the center of the truck's radiator to
the center of the sleeping compartment.

Big Red tried to raise his arm once again. He had to know if he
was, in truth, within a coffin. But his arm would barely budge. He

managed to raise it about half an inch, and then it would move no further.

Utter darkness. Not a sound. The air cold and stale.

He lay there feeling like ice was flowing through his veins. Big Red had never been this scared before.

He tried to imagine the sequence of events that might have happened after he lost consciousness. He pictured the truck flipping end-over-end, then coming to rest against some big granite boulder or another vehicle, the impact so intense that he was torn out of his safety harness, his body crushed against the dashboard.

Big Red imagined that he might have lain there in the freezing cold for hours before anyone could get to him. He considered that, even if help had come quickly, the rescuers might have been unable to pry him out of the cab for some time. The cold might have reduced his vital signs to the point where he appeared dead. His bodily temperature, his heart rate, and his blood pressure might have been so low that they were, for all practical purposes, undetectable. His skin would have been pale and ghastly gray. Maybe his skin was frozen on the surface. He might have been a corpse, by all appearances, but with that faint trace of life force still in there, begging to be recognized.

Then he would have been put in the morgue, in a refrigerated compartment, his life force dormant, barely alive.

And now, he lay in a coffin, six feet below the surface of the Earth. The soil above him might be covered with fresh green grass, warmed by the afternoon sunshine. Strangers might be walking by, not even noticing the simple gravestone resting above him, above his life force that had been strong enough to bring Big Red back to consciousness. By its very nature, that life force demanded to go on living.

Too late. There couldn't be much oxygen left in his coffin.

"Help me! Help me, somebody!" he screamed in the silence of his lonely mind. "This can't be the end. Please dear God, don't let it end like this."

Then, knowing that struggle was futile, Big Red released one last real live scream, for no other purpose than to hear the sound of his own voice.

"Help me! Help me! Somebody, help me!" he shrieked with the intensity and volume appropriate to the hopelessness of his situation.

A door crashed open. Fluorescent lights came alive overhead. A sturdy woman in a nurse's uniform scurried into the room, a look of anxiety on her face. She stopped at the side of Big Red's bed, paused for a moment, then said "Well, look who's conscious. My, oh my, we've been waiting for you for three days. Are you all right?"

Big Red couldn't speak. He just looked up at that big burly nurse as if she had been Shania Twain herself, tears streaming down the sides of his face.

"I'm alive! I'm alive!" he rejoiced. "I'm alive!"

The nurse felt his forehead with her left hand while her right felt his wrist to gauge the strength of his pulse. "You look just fine," she said. "for what you've been through. Mrs. Whorley will be glad to hear you're with us again. "

Mrs. Whorley. Ethel. Oh, my God.

In an instant he remembered what had happened in the cab of that truck during those brief moments between the beginning of the first spin until he blacked out. He recalled how he poured out his anger at Ethel, the things he called her, the things he wished upon her.

And, finally, in that uncontrollable release of the rage he had suppressed for so many years, he had grabbed that number sixteen knitting needle, suspended in mid-air by the momentum and spinning of the truck, as if placed there for his use by some demonic force. He had plunged it into Ethel's left thigh, just as she had done to him so long ago.

But, I thought we were going to die any second.

Just as Big Red was terrified only moments earlier by the thought that he was going to die, the prisoner of a cruel mistake, he now felt terror at the thought that he might *not* die before Ethel got her hands on him. Years of conditioning by Ethel's tyranny had programmed his subconscious mind to fear her wrath—even more than the prospect of being buried alive.

Big Red tried to get up only to realize that his head and arms were held in place by nylon straps, probably for fear that, in his comatose state, he might fall from the bed.

"Please, cut me loose!" he begged, "I've got to get out of here!"

The nurse put down the intercom receiver she had just used to announce to the front desk that Horace Whorley had regained consciousness.

"Oh, Mister Whorley, I don't have the authority to untie those safety straps without your doctor's permission, except in case of emergency," explained the benevolent nurse, a look of sympathy on her face. "Your doctor and Mrs. Whorley should be here in just a few minutes. "

"This is an emergency!" shouted Big Red.

"Oh, I see," acknowledged the nurse, retrieving a bedpan from the nearby countertop and placing it under the hospital gown.

"Let me out of here! My life's in danger!" he screamed.

"Oh, Mr. Whorley, you're just experiencing the aftereffects of several days in a coma. Please try to relax. Help is on the way."

Help, my doomed ass. The end is on its way. He struggled mightily against his restraints.

The nurse turned on a nightlight beside the bed and turned off the overhead lights, hoping this might help to calm Mr. Whorley. The faint glow of the nightlight barely revealed a hypodermic needle the nurse had inserted into a rubber-capped bottle, extracting an orange fluid into the syringe.

"No—no!" yelled Big Red.

"Okay," the nurse replied, "If you promise me you'll be calm until the doctor arrives, I won't have to use this sedative."

Big Red used all of what little strength he had at his disposal to control the terror coursing through his being.

The nurse headed for the door. "I'll be right back. You be a good boy."

Time stood still. The room was frighteningly dark. The nightlight was grossly inadequate.

Suddenly a shadow skimmed slowly across the surface of the highly polished linoleum just outside the door. A foot stepped into the center of that shadow, joined a second later by its fellow. Those two feet signaled the end for Big Red.

Those two feet were the only part of the body Big Red could see. The remainder of the large torso was in the shadow of the doorframe. But Big Red knew. He could tell by the size and proportion of the silhouette that Ethel had arrived.

She approached the bed with a noticeable limp, undoubtedly the result of the knitting needle attack.

Big Red trembled.

Ethel raised a massive, meaty arm above her head.

Big Red tried to turn his head to protect his face from the blow that was imminent. His head wouldn't turn, still victim of the nylon restraining straps. "Well, this is it," he thought, his eyes scrunched shut against the impending impact.

"Sweetheart!" she squealed, as that meaty arm came to rest gently on Big Red's shoulder. The next thing he knew, Ethel planted a gentle kiss on his lips, followed by a tender tweak of his cheek by her thumb and forefinger.

"Oh, darling," she purred, "I've been so worried about you."

Big Red's mouth fell open. He couldn't believe what he was hearing. Ethel hadn't called him anything more flattering than "shit-head" for more years than he could remember.

The overhead lights came on as the doctor entered the room. "Well, how's my patient?" he asked, with practiced professional friendliness.

In the light of the fluorescent fixtures, Big Red noticed that a large bandage was wrapped around Ethyl's head. In fact, the only parts of her head that were visible were her eyes, her nose, and her lips.

The doctor noticed the look of surprise on Horace's face. "Yes," he explained, "the little woman has had quite an ordeal, a serious concussion. She was out for many hours after that crash. It's a miracle either of you is alive from what I heard about the condition of your truck.

"Several visitors commented that Mrs. Whorley is a new woman since the crash. It seems that the impact of her brain against the interior of her skull affected the way in which the electrical charges generated within the brain are flowing. Unfortunately, this sort of thing sometimes will result in dramatic personality changes. I'm sorry, but only time will tell. Let's all hope the old Ethel returns eventually.

"In the meantime, I suggest that you, Mr. Whorley, take the lead in any important decision-making. People who have suffered the kind of trauma Mrs. Whorley experienced often find themselves needing strong leadership. They have a tendency to take an emotional backseat, shall we say, until such time, if any, as the old personality reemerges."

Big Red looked up at Ethel to see a most adoring pair of eyes looking down at him. He swallowed hard.

"Would you believe, darling," cooed Ethel, in a sweet and gentle voice, "that during that crazy crash, somehow, one of my knitting needles got stuck in my thigh. Doctors said there was a one-in-a-million chance that such a thing could happen. "

Big Red smiled as the doctor removed the nylon restraints. He sat up slowly, stretching his arms and neck.

Ethel stepped closer, pressing her ample bosom against Horace's chest. She wrapped her arms around his shoulders, holding him tightly and sobbing silently.

"I was so worried about you," she gushed. "I thank God that my sweetie pie is all right."

Big Red hugged Ethel back, a tentative but genuine hug, the first embrace Big Red and his wife had shared in many years. He smiled skyward and silently prayed to whatever force was the cause of miracles such as this—that Ethel Whorley would never, ever recover. Never. Ever.

 # Mortimer Ziffel

While John Hawkin and his small army were busy confronting and defeating Frank Sheffield, Mortimer Ziffel had been on an adventure of his own, which was far more exciting than he had expected.

The silence was almost deafening as Mortimer drove the beige sedan away from the area where the farmhouse had been before it was turned into an incinerator. His passengers, Sarah, Maria, and Gail, spoke not a word. They were all lost in thoughts of the most intense kind.

Their loved ones were heading in the opposite direction, into "the valley of death." Hawkin and his comrades were on their way to the Sleepy Hollow safe house, where they intended to encounter and apprehend Sheffield and his henchmen. Everyone in the silent sedan was focused on the knowledge that John Hawkin and his team, composed of their family members, were up against a formidable enemy.

Mortimer and the ladies had delayed leaving the compound about twenty minutes while Mortimer retrieved a few hand tools from the barn.

Sarah was riding shotgun. A hand-drawn map lay on the seat between her and Mortimer, showing the way to a different safe house, where Hawkin had instructed them to hide out until he would come for them. Maria and Gail occupied the back seat, holding hands in an attempt to comfort each other.

Mortimer and the ladies he vowed so fervently to protect had departed the compound through the rear gate, the one that Chris, Jaime, Becky, and Daryl had roared through several nights earlier with two Hummers hot on their trail. Mortimer carried on an intense monologue within the privacy of his own mind, affirming, again and again, that he would see these ladies to safety at all costs.

Now sixty-six years old, Mortimer was not at all the age of a person typically expected to protect several ladies from trained killers. Doubts continued to plague his mind, in spite of his repetitive affirmations of his determination to carry out his duty. Mortimer was prepared to die rather than allow any harm to come to the ladies who were entrusted to his care.

Sarah reached over and patted Mortimer's hand as it rested on the seat next to the hastily scrawled map. In appreciation, he glanced at her briefly, afraid even to consider diverting his attention from the task at hand for any length of time.

Think. Think, Mortimer. Now is not the time for idle daydreaming. Much is at stake. Consider the possibilities. Don't assume that all is well. Don't even assume that all is as it seems. He tried to think of all the things that could go wrong, so if some of these things were to happen, he at least would be somewhat prepared.

Sheffield and his men were evil and powerful, skilled and experienced. Mortimer was only loyal and caring. Not much of a comfort, those qualities.

The first notion that plagued him was that, perhaps, the safe house was not really safe at all. After all, if Hawkin was aware of its existence, several others must be as well. Certainly, no safe house was a perfectly kept secret. Many people must have used it over the years. And others surely arranged the details of how the house would be used and by whom. Someone had to have built that house or acquired it for the government. It had to be maintained. Dozens of people must know of its existence.

And who was more likely to have heard of its being there than someone way up in the hierarchy of the very organization that owned and operated it?

Sheffield.

The thought caused Mortimer's left hand to tighten on the steering wheel. He took a deep breath, let out a sigh, and considered the alternatives. What if he decided not to go to the safe house after all? He glanced down suspiciously at the map lying there on the seat, trying, it seemed to Mortimer, to look benign.

Where else could he go? He couldn't go back to the compound. He had heard that Sheffield had ordered men to return there early tomorrow to assure themselves that no one had survived. Perhaps Mortimer could find a place to hide out in the forest for a while. But what if Hawkin or one of his men tried to reach them? If the bad guys couldn't find them, neither could the good guys. Maybe that wasn't such a bad idea after all. And, when enough time had passed, they would come out of hiding.

But how would they contact Hawkin at that time? And how would they know where to go then? Most terrifying of all, how would they know who won? And if they didn't know had who had won, how would they know whether it was safe to come out of hiding?

These questions disturbed Mortimer, almost beyond his ability to retain composure.

Now, start over. I'm here in a government vehicle, in charge of protecting three ladies. The ladies' loved ones are in a fight for their lives. I've been told to deliver these ladies to a safe house. John Hawkin believes the house is safe. But he had an awful lot on his mind when I last saw him. Did he really have time to consider all of the possible ramifications of hiding these ladies there? Might he not have forgotten that the safe house was compromised somewhere along the way? Did he consider the possibility that Sheffield or one of his men might know about it?

What else can I do? Could I drive to the nearest town and contact the local law enforcement officials? Or should I head for the interstate and flag down a state trooper?

He thought for a while. Then his heart pounded as he remembered someone saying that Benson had informed the local and state law enforcement organizations that Chris, Jaime, and Becky were enemies of the government and dangerous. He wondered if he and the others had also been reported to those agencies. What if the officer they contacted took them into custody, and held them until getting further orders from the CIA? And what if the CIA official giving those further orders was Sheffield?

No, Mortimer thought, they had a lot better chance on their own than being in contact with anyone in an official capacity. Finally he decided he would do best, after all, to follow Hawkin's orders and hole up at the safe house.

He was glad he hadn't shared his thoughts with the others in that silent automobile. No sense filling their heads with additional doubts and fears. Better to let them think that once they reached the house, they would be fine until the good guys came for them.

What Mortimer didn't know was that both Sarah and Maria were thinking thoughts almost identical to those running through his mind. Gail was still savoring her newfound courage and, in a bizarre sort of way, almost looking forward to the next challenge.

Now that he had made the decision, Mortimer relaxed a bit, although the feeling of impending disaster continued to loom overhead. The remainder of the drive was silent and uneventful. Most of the route took them over back roads, some paved and some not. Eventually, the map brought them onto a state highway for a couple of miles, just before taking them onto a rough gravel road that wound down into a series of canyons. Those canyons were heavily forested, and twice Mortimer had to navigate his way across wide but shallow streams. The forest grew so thick that the moonlight filtered only occasionally through the dense canopy.

After six miles of winding through the forest, they came upon an open meadow covered with lush, tall grass, almost tall enough to reach the bottoms of the sedan's side mirrors. The dirt road was now barely discernable and apparently hadn't been used for quite some time. Twice Mortimer had to backtrack, not exactly sure where the road was in all that tall grass.

Just as everyone in the car had decided that they were lost, they caught a glimpse of the road where it re-entered the forest. Almost immediately, they came upon a small cabin so completely surrounded by trees that, even in the light of the sedan's high beams, it was difficult to see.

Hawkin had made a notation on the map that they would be able to identify the cabin by a triangle carved in the header beam above the front door. It was so dark that, as soon as Mortimer turned off the headlights, all was pitch black. He had to turn the headlights back on to find his way safely onto the front porch. There, in the glare of the headlamps, he was able, at close range, to make out the triangle. He traced its contours with his right index finger to assure himself that what he was seeing was accurate.

He motioned for the ladies to join him on the porch.

Handwritten notations on the map indicated that the front door key would likely be on top of the beam above the window to the left of the front door. But before Mortimer could begin searching for that key, the front door opened, yielding to the slight pressure that Maria accidentally placed upon it with her elbow as she stepped aside to allow Mortimer access to the window.

Maria gasped at the unexpected movement of the door and the realization that it was unlocked. That simple truth—that the door either was left unlocked or was unlocked by someone since its last use—was enough to add an entirely new and eerie feeling to an already scary situation.

Mortimer held up his hand to signal the ladies to remain still while he entered the doorway. He reached for a light switch and found none where he expected one to be. As he reached farther along the wall, groping for that much-needed switch, he suddenly found his fingers in contact with something furry. Reflexively he yanked his hand away and backed out of the doorway onto the porch. He remembered having seen a flashlight in the glove box. He went to get it.

He re-entered the cabin, shining the flashlight against the wall where he had encountered the furry something, taking care to keep his head protected by the door jamb. To his relief, the furry something proved to be a lynx pelt nailed to the log wall in typical backwoods-hunter fashion. He located the light switch but found it inoperative.

Mortimer invited the ladies into the room, where they found several candles and a kerosene lantern in the drawers and lower cupboard of the kitchen, along with two boxes of wooden matches. Before long, the main room was fairly well lighted, and a candle was burning in each of the two bedrooms and the only bathroom.

Sarah turned on a water tap at the kitchen sink. Water flowed out of the spout. Mortimer was confused because the water was on when there was no electricity. Certainly there was no municipal water supply this far out in the forest. The water must be provided by a well. But how could the well be pressurized without electricity? He suggested that the ladies make themselves at home while he went out to investigate the water-pressure dilemma.

Mortimer found a footpath that led a considerable distance away from the cabin. It was well-worn, however, and he assumed that it led to the well and, probably, the source of electricity for the cabin. After all, there wouldn't be light switches without lights. And there wouldn't be lights without some power source.

The path led Mortimer to a well pump. He followed a length of galvanized electrical conduit from the well farther into the forest. There he found a diesel-powered generator. The conduit and the generator were large enough for Mortimer to conclude that the generator was the source of power for the well pump and the cabin.

The well was attached to a pressure tank, which answered the question of how water pressure could exist without electricity. Not knowing how long the fuel in the diesel engine's tank had been there and not wanting to make any unnecessary noise, Mortimer decided against trying to start the generator until daylight. Besides, he didn't want to leave the ladies unattended for long.

Sarah had located plenty of sheets, blankets, and pillows in the bedroom closets and was helping Gail and Maria make the beds. They hadn't thought to stop along the way for food, and besides, there was no place to get food without going into one of the towns along the state highway. Doing so would have been time-consuming and dangerous. Luckily, they found several cans of soup in the pantry. That would have to do for now. Nobody was in much of a mood for eating, anyway.

They all did their best to keep the conversation pleasant, although nobody could fail to sense the undercurrent of worry that pervaded the cabin. Gail glanced at her watch and said the sun would be coming up in a couple of hours. They were painfully aware that their loved ones probably had arrived at the other safe house by now and were waiting for sunup to signal the commencement of whatever fate awaited them.

Drexel Farnsworth, Jr. had worked his way up the political ladder quickly. Early in his career with the CIA, he took notice of Frank Sheffield and identified with him at once. Sheffield was similarly impressed by Farnsworth. Within three months after Farnsworth joined the agency, they were lunching together regularly. They were kindred spirits. Farnsworth was probably the only person Frank Sheffield ever took a liking to—if you can call preparing to use someone mercilessly "liking" him.

Farnsworth reeked of yuppiness. He was educated in the Ivy League. He drove a BMW, which he always parked at an angle taking up two parking spaces. He wore black and white oxfords. He kept his hair slicked back to provide him with the harsh look he believed gave him a leg up on the competition.

At an early age, Farnsworth concluded that he was born with a form of genetic superiority that rendered him far too good to waste his time on any individual he chose to place in the category of "common man." What he didn't bother to notice was that he was regarded as a pariah by the vast majority of clear-thinking individuals who had the misfortune to cross his path.

Drex—as he requested that people call him—was on a fast track to the top. He knew who to shmooze, who to ignore, who to fear, and on whom to maintain files. His intention was to use Frank Sheffield until such time as he was ready to take over Sheffield's position.

This would take a lot of effort. But once he was there, he could use the awesome power of the federal government to enhance his cocaine-importing activities, which had made his trip through the Ivy League so easy and comfortable. The real question regarding his relationship with Frank Sheffield was, "Who is using whom?" Or in the immortal words of Aretha Franklin, "Who's zoomin' who?"

Earlier in the evening, just moments after Mortimer and the ladies had left the remains of the farmhouse, Farnsworth had arrived there. In fact, he arrived at the main gate only three minutes after Hawkin and his team left for the safe house. As Farnsworth approached the burned-out farmhouse, where he fully expected to find nobody, he caught a glimpse of distant taillights receding into the forest near the back gate.

Farnsworth had been ordered by Sheffield to head up the team that was scheduled to arrive shortly after sunrise to clean up the remains of the fire. Farnsworth decided to arrive a few hours before the other members of the team to see what he might dig up. He never knew when he might need some bit of evidence regarding the conduct of someone he intended to shove out of his way on the way up the political ladder.

He knew that Sheffield was totally unscrupulous. He knew enough about project Zephyr to realize that several powerful government officials had put their asses way out on a limb relative to whatever had happened at the farmhouse compound back in 1975. Nosing around the area before the clean-up crew was due to arrive might prove to be an advantage when the showdown between him and Sheffield came, as Farnsworth knew it undoubtedly would.

It was difficult for Farnsworth to decide whether to stay at the compound and investigate or whether to follow the receding tail-lights. Two factors swayed his decision.

First of all, the presence of a vehicle at a sensitive government installation, where he was assured that nobody would be, was tantalizing. Second, the taillights were moving and the farmhouse was not.

He decided to follow the sedan.

After having a chance to determine whether it was of any significance, he would still have time to return and search the compound before the cleanup team arrived.

Farnsworth flipped his cell phone open and placed a call to a sleeping member of the clean-up crew. He ordered the groggy man to delay the arrival of the crew for three hours. This would give Farnsworth plenty of time to pursue both opportunities.

Before leaving his home, Farnsworth had studied the map of the area surrounding the farmhouse compound. He always wanted to know the lay of the land. One never knew when one might have to make a hasty retreat. His study provided him with a basic understanding of the terrain and trails within twenty miles of the compound.

He decided to let the departing sedan have several minutes' head start. He didn't want to be detected by the driver of that vehicle. He knew there were no turnoffs between the compound and the state highway that led anywhere but to dead ends. The sedan eventually would have to pull onto the highway. And Farnsworth knew just where that would be. He decided to head out the front entrance and down the highway to the point where his quarry would come out. He calculated that he could get there a few minutes before the other car.

It proved to be no problem for someone of Drexel's superior intelligence to fall in behind Mortimer and the ladies without being noticed.

He followed them for quite a while. They turned onto a dirt road. He remained a good distance behind them as they wound down a long canyon, over two streams, across an open meadow, and finally, to the cabin. He managed to stay far enough behind them so they would not likely notice his headlights unless they were searching in earnest.

He didn't know exactly where Frank Sheffield was, but he knew the vehicle he was following was a loose end that Sheffield hadn't counted on. The existence of the sedan and its whereabouts would certainly be of interest to Sheffield.

Perhaps, with a little luck, he could win a few points with Sheffield. He could gather whatever tidbits of information he could glean from the presence of this vehicle in the midst of all this political intrigue and still get back to the compound in time to gather whatever else he could find to use against Sheffield before the cleanup crew made its appearance.

He calculated the time remaining and decided to stay hidden for a while and study the area thoroughly. This would still allow him plenty of time to dispose of whoever was inside that cabin. Just as he liked to know his terrain, he liked to know his victims. Surely, Sheffield would appreciate knowing that Farnsworth had eliminated these people. Who knows what they might be able to reveal about the farmhouse? He was fairly sure he could find out what these people knew before he killed them. This way, he could work his way more securely into Sheffield's confidence while gathering information to use against Sheffield later. Slick indeed.

If those jerks who snubbed him back in college could only see him now! But Farnsworth would take care of them later. There was plenty of time.

Just as the sun was rising over the ridge to the east, Farnsworth's cell phone rang. It was Sheffield.

"I've got a situation here," Sheffield muttered. "It seems some of the 'victims' of last night's little fire managed to escape. They're here now, threatening to attack us. Can you imagine that? A bunch of damn low-life civilians threatening to attack the CIA."

"What can I do to help?" Farnsworth asked, already strategizing his advantage.

"Get over to that farmhouse compound right away and see if you can find anyone. As near as I can tell, three or four women who were supposed to get cooked in that fire aren't here. They may be hiding someplace around there. Or maybe they're on the run. I want you to find them.

"Just in case these clowns are better than I think they are, it wouldn't hurt to have an ace up my sleeve, like being able to announce that we've got their women in custody."

Farnsworth gloated, "I'm happy to report that I've already got them in sight. I should have them in custody within the hour. I'll let you know when the task's complete. What's your cell number?"

Farnsworth jotted down the phone number Sheffield gave him. Then he sat back, waiting for a few more rays of sunlight.

Sheffield looked out through the front window of the Sleepy Hollow safe house and saw the troublemakers lined up barely within the forest's edge. He expected to receive a call from Farnsworth within the half-hour, announcing that he had the hostages in custody. Then Sheffield would have all the leverage needed to force Hawkin and his men to surrender. He had two women tucked away in the upstairs closet—the ones who called each other "Wendy" and "Grammy"—plus three or four more that Farnsworth was about to capture.

Mortimer couldn't sleep. Adding to the tension that almost anyone in his situation would feel, he had an inkling, sort of like when his knee told him a cold front was on the way. Something didn't feel right.

It was almost sunup. The sky to the east was already starting to brighten.

Mortimer decided to take a walk down to the diesel generator. It would be light by the time he got there, and he would see what he could do to get it started. He had decided that the generator was far enough away from the cabin so anyone in the cabin's vicinity couldn't hear it anyway. Whoever had set up this safe house had probably designed it that way on purpose. He pulled on his sneakers and slipped out the back door as quietly as he could. No need to wake the ladies.

The air was fresh and clear as Mortimer walked down the trail that led to the well pump and generator. The smell of aspen leaves on the moist soil brought a smile to his face. Under different circumstances, this would be paradise. He thought about his kids and his friends and what they must be doing now.

At least he had the ladies in a relatively safe place. The protection of their women was one less thing for the men to worry about as they confronted the bad guys. Mortimer felt proud. He was doing his part.

He spent several minutes tinkering with the diesel generator then realized he wouldn't be able to get it started without making a few adjustments. He needed a wrench and a small slot screw driver. Maybe he would find them in the car or in the cabin.

He had just started back along the trail when he heard a terrifying scream coming from the direction of the cabin. He hustled along the trail as fast as his stubby little legs could carry his portly old body, adrenaline coursing through his veins.

As he neared the area where the trail approached the cabin's back door, he was puffing like a steam engine. He stopped short, trying to decide what to do next. He looked around for anything that would help him understand what was happening.

Another scream pierced the air. It sounded like Sarah. He desperately wanted to rush into the cabin and put a stop to whatever was going on inside. But, he told himself, it wouldn't do anybody any good for him to fall into the same predicament that the others apparently were in. He had to think. He looked around frantically. What could he do?

Be smart, you old fool. Your family needs you. Don't mess this up.

He looked left. He looked right. He put his hands over his head in despair. He wanted to scream.

Do something smart. He fell to his knees and prayed. *Please, God, my family needs me. I don't know what to do. Help me be smart.* Then he stood up and took a deep breath.

He walked quietly to the window on the left, stood on his tip toes, and was able to get a look inside. He could see the entire room. There was one man. Only one man. Mortimer could handle one man.

But that man had a pistol. *And you forgot to take your pistol with you into the forest, you foolish old man.*

Sarah was on her knees, her hands tied behind her back. Apparently the man had managed to get the drop on the ladies before any of them could get to her pistol. He must have entered the cabin while the ladies were still asleep.

The man stood directly in front of Sarah, a couple of feet away from her. He slammed the side of his pistol into Sarah's cheek, then punched her in the other cheek with his fist.

This time Sarah didn't scream. She looked back at the man with rage in her eyes. He hit her again, on the side of her head this time. She fell forward.

Mortimer went crazy. His spindly legs carried him around the corner and onto the front porch faster than Mortimer knew he could move. Those legs were now a sprinter's legs. Mortimer kicked the door open, and it crashed against the wall.

The man spun around and faced Mortimer.

"Prepare to die, asshole," Mortimer screamed, as the door slammed shut behind him.

Farnsworth leveled his pistol at the forehead of the charging Mortimer Ziffel and started to squeeze the trigger.

Maria and Gail were too far away to do anything.

Sarah lay helpless on the floor on the ragged edge of unconsciousness.

At that very same instant, Big John Hawkin was chugging like a locomotive through the living room of a different safe house, grabbing Frank Sheffield's hostages and sprinting like a madman, serpentine style, across the agonizingly long meadow between the front porch of that house and the relative safety of the forest.

Just as the trigger of Farnsworth's Glock 357 Magnum was approaching the point of release, a booming voice rang forth just outside the window to Farnsworth's right. It was the loudest, deepest, most commanding voice Farnsworth had ever heard.

The voice roared, "What the hell's going on in there? Drop that weapon or you're a dead man!"

The shock of hearing that booming voice was enough to cause Farnsworth's trigger finger to finish its job. The Glock roared.

Fortunately, he turned his upper body to the right in response to the voice, just in time to send the bullet intended for Mortimer's head safely into the wall of the cabin.

Confusion swirled in Farnsworth's head. His jaw dropped.

In the time it took Farnsworth to turn to his right, blast a huge crater in the cabin wall, and look back at his intended target, the mighty Mortimer Ziffel made powerful contact between the top of his rock-hard forehead and the tip of Drexel Farnsworth's jaw.

Farnsworth melted to the floor.

Gail ran and picked up the pistol. She spun around, leveling it at Farnsworth, crouching in her best secret agent style. He didn't move. He was out cold.

Maria looked after Sarah while Gail ran to the kitchen and came back with three dishtowels, which she used to tie Farnsworth's arms and legs.

Slightly dazed from the bone-crunching contact his forehead had made with Farnsworth's jaw, Mortimer stumbled to the door to see who in the world was out there.

The porch was empty.

Mortimer looked left. He looked right. He saw nobody.

Then, above the breeze stirring across the meadow, he heard a voice. It was the sweet, soft, lovely voice of a young girl. He looked toward the sound of that familiar voice and there, at the edge of the forest, waving and smiling at him, stood Ellie, his baby sister.

He heard her say clearly, "I love you Morty. You're my hero."

Then she was gone.

Mortimer sank to the porch and knelt there, whispering, "I'm her hero; I'm her hero."

The ring of a cell phone startled everyone. Gail was able to locate the phone in Farnsworth's coat pocket. She flipped the cover open.

A voice boomed out of the earpiece, "Farnsworth, this is Sheffield. Where the hell are you? I need those hostages—now."

Gail placed the mouthpiece near her lips and stated sweetly, "I'm sorry, Mr. Farnsworth is unavailable. I believe he's on his way to prison. May I take a message?" She snapped the cover of the cell phone into the "off" position, her face graced with an impish smile.

Back at the Sleepy Hollow safe house, Frank Sheffield turned to two of his men with a look of shock on his face and commanded, "Gentlemen, we're out of hostages. Roll that damned machine gun onto the porch—now."

Mortimer sat on the floor of the cabin, Sarah's head cradled in his lap. Sarah looked up at him fondly.

He looked down at Sarah, tears in his eyes, and whispered, "I'm her hero."

Eddie Mercado

For several weeks after Eddie had suffered his severe and unexpected humiliation at the hands of Tim Lasher, he found himself in a state of abject confusion and wretched depression. Actually, Eddie couldn't remember ever being happy, at least not for more than a few minutes once in a rare while, but this was far beyond unhappiness.

By the time he was six years old, his basic personality had been contoured into a state of chronic and constant hopelessness. Much as a growing pumpkin that is placed inside a glass jar will ultimately assume the shape of that jar, Eddie's psyche didn't have a chance to grow into the normal healthy personality made available to him by the forces that orchestrate the incredible order of our exquisite universe.

Sadly for Eddie, his family had been evolving on a course of ever increasing dysfunctionality for several generations prior to Eddie's arrival on this physical plane. Even before Eddie's passage through the birth canal, his heredity had begun its inevitable destruction of his naturally healthy self-image.

Even while Eddie's tiny body was forming within his mother's womb, his psyche was being bombarded by almost overwhelming negativity. Eddie's mother knew absolutely nothing about nutrition. If someone had bothered to ask her to name the four food groups, she likely would have responded with something such as "Alpha Beta, Albertson's, Safeway, and Vons."

The unborn fetus of Eddie therefore had to survive and evolve on a diet of white bread, Coca Cola, milk, potato chips, and French fries. His tiny organs had to contend with regular doses of alcohol, aspirin, nicotine, and fluoridated and chlorinated water.

As a result of his mother's grossly inadequate and polluted diet during her pregnancy, Eddie slipped through the birth canal and into the outside world in a state of relatively poor health. Instead of greeting his new home with a healthy cry, Eddie arrived with a stomachache and a mild headache.

To make matters worse, Eddie was taken out of his mother's arms within minutes of his birth and subjected to an assortment of unnatural assaults upon his little body, including having some kind of liquid squirted into his sensitive eyes and being thoroughly inspected by a total stranger with rough hands. Worst of all, something sharp was inserted into one of his toes.

Then, instead of being returned to his mother's loving arms, Eddie was placed in some kind of container where he lay for long periods of time staring up into a source of bright, unnatural light. His brand new ears were assaulted repeatedly by the clanking and banging of an assortment of metal objects, punctuated by an occasional slamming door.

When Eddie at last was returned to his mother for the first time in what seemed like hours, he felt the warmth and comfort of her body. But he soon discovered that this was only a trick and that he was destined to be torn away from her often and placed again and again in that cold, uncomfortable box, beneath a source of unnatural light that assaulted his ears with an irritating buzzing sound.

Eddie did take consolation and comfort in being allowed to return to Mom several times each day, where he instinctively and joyfully found those soft, warm, nurturing breasts that told him, "You are loved, Eddie, child of the Universe."

Within a few days, Eddie was taken from the terror and loneliness of the box beneath the bright lights and delivered to a quieter place, where he was placed in a more pleasant box beneath a much softer, warmer light. For a few days he was more content. The room in which he now found himself was much more comfortable than the first one. More important, he spent a lot more time with Mom. And when the time came to return to the new box, he wasn't pulled away from Mom by a stranger. He was placed in the box by Mom herself, ever so gently. And Mom often stayed a while and looked down at him with love shining from her beautiful eyes.

Then one morning Eddie experienced a great shock. Until that terrible morning, whenever Eddie's tummy hurt, causing him to call out for Mom, he would be lifted to those wonderful breasts that would quickly make the pain go away. Even better than that, Mom would hold him safely while those warm breasts told him again and again, "Eddie Mercado, you are loved more than you will ever know."

But on this morning, something very wrong came into Eddie's life. When his little voice cried out for Mom, he wasn't lifted from the box. He wasn't held safely against her warm body. He wasn't placed against those loving breasts. Something cold and hard was placed in his mouth. He tried and tried to push it out. But Mom, his mother, the source of all that was good and wonderful in Eddie's life, was trying to hurt him with that terrible thing. He pushed and pushed against it, but Mom insisted. And Eddie, knowing that Mom really loved him, finally surrendered to her insistence and let the cold, unloving thing enter his mouth.

Then something warm trickled into Eddie's mouth. He knew instinctively that it didn't belong there. It didn't taste like the stuff from Mom's breasts. This stuff tasted foreign, almost as if God intended it for someone or something else. Eddie's tiny tongue pushed the stuff out of his mouth. Mom went back to where moms go when they're not shining their love light on their babies.

Eddie lay there for a long time, the pain in his tummy growing and growing.

After what seemed to Eddie like a long time, Mom came back, quietly and softly. *Mom's back. Oh yes, Mom's back! My mom, my mom with the soft touch and the shining eyes, and those warm, loving breasts is here. Mom's here to stop the pain in my tummy and the hunger in my heart.*

But then it happened again. The thing was there again. It was in Mom's hand. She was pushing it toward Eddie. And then it was in his mouth. The terrible stuff filled his mouth again. Before Eddie could push it back out, some of it slipped down his throat. Then some more. He swallowed several times. Then he noticed that the stuff made the pain in his tummy go away. He swallowed some more. Before long, his tummy was full. But it wasn't the same as when his tummy was full of the wonderful stuff from Mom's breasts. But it was better than the pain, *almost* better than the pain.

Then Mom was gone again. And in her place was the great sadness, the sadness that would haunt Eddie Mercado for much of the rest of his life.

Eddie didn't see much of Mom after that, except for a few minutes before he went to sleep at night. Every morning Eddie was taken to another place, where he saw lots of other people his own size. And there was always that terrible thing. He would suck on that thing to get rid of the tummy pain. But it never ever said, "Eddie, you are loved."

Nothing ever said that again.

Over the years Eddie learned that the magic he thought he remembered from somewhere long ago didn't really exist, mostly because adults told him that his friends he talked to in the spirit world were just in his imagination.

After a while, sure enough, they stopped being real to Eddie, and the magic went away.

Adults said a lot of bad things to Eddie. Eddie forgot those that weren't very important. But the really important things—such as that he was the reason Jesus had been killed on a cross—he couldn't forget. They told him that he was evil, that he was born with a terrible thing called "original sin," and that he would have to go to a place called "Hell" unless he did all the things adults told him to do. Not many of the things they told him to do made much sense. But Eddie was so afraid of going to Hell that he tried to do them.

As Eddie grew older, he found that there were more and more rules he had to follow to keep from burning forever in the all-consuming eternal fires. But he couldn't do all of those things. So finally Eddie decided he was destined to go to Hell.

After that, he grew angrier and angrier, until his poor tormented mind couldn't contain the rage any longer.

On Eddie's eighth birthday, a skinny, freckle-faced boy at his birthday party refused to eat any of the birthday cake. When Eddie's mom asked the boy why he didn't want to eat his cake, the boy said it was because it had been baked by a Mexican and his mother told him he mustn't eat anything touched by Mexicans because they're dirty.

Eddie looked up at Mom and saw a tear running down her cheek. He couldn't take his eyes off Mom's face. Suddenly, Eddie was an infant again. He was lying in the box, and the love was pouring out of those beautiful eyes. Then that single tear fell from Mom's cheek onto the birthday cake.

Eddie leapt across the table and attacked that skinny, freckle-faced kid, unleashing the rage and fury that had built up in him over all of those lonely, angry years. He no longer cared that he was born evil, that Jesus had died for him, that the magic had left him, or that there was no Santa Claus. He didn't care any longer that those warm, loving breasts had been replaced by that cold evil thing that made his tummy feel okay, but didn't soothe his heart. Eddie ripped loose with more wrath than he ever imagined existed.

The skinny, freckle-faced kid was taken to the hospital, and Eddie was punished. His mother made him apologize to the boy, even though he wasn't sorry at all.

Eddie had found a way not to feel the sadness for a while. For the first time since he was a tiny infant, Eddie felt good. He didn't feel the same contentment that had come from being close to those warm, loving breasts. But it did feel a lot better than when Mom made him drink from the cold thing called a bottle, a lot better than knowing that he was born in original sin, a lot better than the prospect of having his skin peel off in the fires of Hell.

Eddie Mercado had finally found himself. It wasn't his real self or the self he always dreamed he would be, but a self nonetheless. Eddie had found a self that could survive in spite of knowing that he was not loveable, in spite of knowing that he was born in sin, in spite of knowing that Mom didn't really love him, not really.

This self would have to do until someday, he prayed, when he would find his real self. Until then, Eddie would be the person the adults always told him he was, conceived in sin and evil through and through. After all, once you had killed Jesus, what more evil could you do?

He became the terror of his school, leader of those other angry young men who had been born in a state of original sin. And they'd get those other guys, the ones who were born into loving families where they were not told that they were born evil, who would never have to watch their mom cry over their birthday cakes.

During the summer before Eddie started high school, his family moved to Sprague. It took only a few weeks after school began for Eddie to seek out and proselytize six of the most emotionally disturbed young men in the school. Eddie's gang took care to torment the smallest and weakest kids, not wanting to risk any confrontation that might result in an unsatisfactory outcome. They picked on the least popular students, fearful that a victim with many friends might launch a retaliation involving numbers capable of overwhelming the Mercado gang.

For many months, Eddie and his friends rained down terror on the small, the weak, the unpopular, and the occasional geek. The school system was relatively ineffective in correcting the situation, given the state laws forbidding corporal punishment and the unspoken social sanction of that age group against "squealing."

This was an unfortunate circumstance, not only for the victims of Eddie's wrath but also for Eddie and his friends. As a consequence, they had no opportunity to change their ways, and any improvement to their self-image would be delayed for years. Eventually, correcting such abuses would be turned over to the judicial system, which could only result in the destruction of whatever trace of a positive self-image any of those young men still retained.

Little did Eddie know how fortunate he was to brush up against Jaime Lasher's arm on that fateful day outside the gym. The mortifying vengeance perpetrated upon Eddie and his friends by Tim Lasher sent Eddie into this most unsettling state of depression and self-doubt in his life. For the first time since Eddie had discovered the outlet for his deep-seated feelings of inferiority and rage, which was provided by his ability to outnumber and abuse the weak and helpless, Eddie could no longer avoid coming face to face with himself.

For days, he avoided school, preferring the detention sessions, which he knew he would ultimately have to face, to the humiliation of having to face his classmates, knowing that they *knew*. So Eddie spent most of his time sitting in a storm culvert under the interstate, face to face with the reality that he and his friends had been defeated by one gringo. Just one gringo. Eddie was unable to reconcile his self-proclaimed image as the toughest guy at Franklin High with the knowledge that he and three of his friends were overwhelmed by one white guy.

Eddie went through many of the emotional stages normally associated with a terrible loss, the same kind of mourning one goes through after the loss of a loved one. At first he entered into a state of total denial, searching for ways to rationalize his situation, trying to find some explanation for his defeat—other than the reality that he simply wasn't as tough as Tim Lasher.

Then he tried to convince himself that it didn't matter, that it wasn't really important to him to be the toughest. Then he became the victim, trying to convince himself that he would have won if he weren't a member of a minority race. That Tim Lasher had all of the advantages Eddie didn't. Lasher probably had the benefit of some expensive martial arts training or some boxing lessons that Eddie's family couldn't afford. Eddie even rationalized that his family wasn't able to purchase the nourishing foods that gringos eat.

Finally Eddie reached the moment of truth, the point always ultimately reached by those totally stripped of their emotional defenses, the moment where the ultimate decision has to be made, either to allow one's self to slip forever into the depths of neurosis and, ultimately, psychosis by continuing the charade that has rendered him or her practically dysfunctional or, to take "the empty-handed leap into the void," and come face to face with one's Higher Self.

Had Eddie Mercado been someone else, his decision might have been different. Each person will react in a totally different way to identical situations. For example, one faced with severe discipline will withdraw and comply, while another will assert himself and rebel.

Whichever of those roads is chosen will be the result of a very complex set of factors, some genetic, some societal, some physiological, and some apparent good or bad luck.

Sitting in that cold damp culvert beneath that interstate, Eddie wasn't even consciously aware that he was teetering on the very brink of a decision that would determine the outcome of the rest of his life.

As he sat there, in the midst of the deepest depression he had ever experienced, something told him that there had to be a way out of this trap, that there had to be a better way out than acting as if all of those terrible things that had been said about him were true.

His heart made a silent wish. He wished that everything in his physical reality would disappear and that he could start all over again, that Eddie Mercado could start with a clean slate, that he could be the sole determining factor in his world, that he could be free of those circumstances that had resulted in his sitting in a cold, damp culvert in a state of total disgrace with no possibility of a happy future.

Eddie directed that silent wish out to whomever or whatever was responsible for this world. He sent it out with more passion than he had ever experienced. At the same time, he wanted to scream his rage out to the world, to blame someone.

But, something caused him to remain silent, his lips pressed tightly together. Inside the depths of his tormented mind, Eddie Mercado was screaming, screaming with all of his might. *Help! Help, please help me, somebody.*

And those words, echoing down the labyrinthine corridors of his tortured mind did not go unheard.

A tear fell from Eddie's chin, the first tear Eddie could ever remember shedding. There followed another. He wiped his cheeks with his shirt sleeves.

Then a sudden calmness came over Eddie Mercado that had no logical explanation. Out of the depths of his utter sorrow, serenity had been born, strangely intertwined with some faint trace of hope, hope without reason, hope born of despair, hope born of hopelessness.

A shadow fell across the opening of the culvert—the opening that faced toward the west and the setting sun. Someone was standing in the opening of that cold, filthy culvert.

"Are you all right?" a gentle voice asked.

Eddie didn't know what to say.

A tiny girl stepped into the culvert. She walked slowly toward Eddie. She paused for a moment. Then she reached down and touched Eddie's shoulder. "Can I help you?"

Eddie looked up. "You're not afraid of me?" he asked.

The child smiled and leaned over. She touched Eddie's cheek so softly that he scarcely felt her tiny finger as she wiped away a small tear that lingered there.

"Why are you sad?" asked the girl. "Did somebody hurt you?"

Eddie swallowed hard and whispered, "Yes."

The girl reached out and wrapped her tiny arms around Eddie's head. He started to pull away, but something made him stay, something perhaps genetic or societal or physiological or maybe just good luck.

Eddie sat there, tears streaming down his face, and felt from that tiny child the love he had craved for as long as he could remember.

"It's gonna be just fine," said the little girl, as she held tight to Eddie.

Eddie hugged her back.

In that instant, Eddie's future was changed forever. Eddie Mercado finally took the empty-handed leap into the void.

Herbert Benson III

Herbert Benson sat silently in his living room, the window coverings drawn tightly against the setting sun. The room was dark, save for the dim light emitted from a small candle flickering in the far corner of the dingy room and the few traces of light that managed to slip through the tiny cracks between the window blinds and the wall.

The only sound was the muted squeak of a wheel spinning in the darkness, driven by a caged weasel attempting to buffer itself from the interminable boredom of its prison.

Three days earlier, Benson had abruptly terminated his relationship with the CIA with a cryptic, one-sentence letter of resignation. Since then, he had been sitting in utter and dismal silence in the tattered arm chair he had dragged home so many years ago from a garage sale.

For years Benson had sat in that chair most evenings eating Cheese-Its by the boxful and sharing them with his friends in the bank of cages stacked against the living room wall. In the early days, Benson would get up occasionally and pace back and forth in front of those cages, handing one cracker at a time to the eager weasels, who chirped their appreciation. In recent times he resorted to using a broom handle he had cut to a length of about four feet and to the end of which he had attached a clamping device fashioned from a wire coat hanger. He would place a Cheese It between two loops of wire and extend the cracker to within the reach of one of the weasels, who would snatch it from the clamp. With the assistance of this device, Benson was able to reach every one of his precious furry friends without having to rise from his chair.

For the past three days, the broom-handle device had remained in its resting place next to the old black-and-white, RCA, eight-inch television set. Benson was in such a state of deep thought that he didn't even notice that he had suspended his feeding ritual.

Fortunately, the weasels still had food and water in their cages.

While he had been away on duty at the farmhouse, Benson had arranged to have the old woman across the alley feed the animals. She had filled the food and water dispensers to overflowing just before Benson returned.

Now Benson was in a reverie, reviewing the highlights of his life from as far back as he could remember. He had gone through several rounds of depression, anger, sadness, and recovery. At the low points of his reminiscences, with almost unbearable self-recrimination and loathing, he concluded that his life was a complete waste of human capability and potential. At the occasional high point, he found himself torn between self-blame and accusing others for his desperation.

At the completion of each cycle, Benson rejoiced that there was still time left to make amends and to re-orchestrate whatever precious years remained in his life.

As the sun set in the west, the flickering candle flame in the corner of the room became the only source of light.

In less than another half-hour, the last trace of flame, clinging tenaciously to the candle's abbreviated wick, sputtered its final gasp and receded into oblivion.

Utter darkness. Total despair. Excruciating loneliness.

For the next two hours, Benson reviewed, in the musty alcoves of his tortured mind, the torment he had endured at the hands of the parochial school administrators, the executioners of his self-image. He thought of his years of empty solitude with a few caged weasels as his only contact with anything that faintly resembled a source of affection.

At last, he relived the infamy of his useless attempt to flee the onrushing threat of Frank Sheffield's government-issue, taxpayer-supported, BMW sedan and the excruciating pain and humiliation as the insistent beast drove his frantically fleeing body to the ground, the heat emanating from its oil pan melting the skin over his hamstrings to a blistering, agonizing gelatin.

The room was totally silent. The running weasel had long since fallen asleep.

Herbert Benson sat there, completely spent, absolutely exhausted.

Notwithstanding his physical state, he stood up, stretched, and shuffled over to the coat rack standing near the front door. Putting on his jacket as protection against the chill, he slipped out into the night.

When he returned, he had in his arms a black, zippered bag containing a rented VCR and a video of George C. Scott's rendition of *A Christmas Carol*.

Benson agonized for several minutes over how to attach the device to his antiquated black-and-white TV. Fortunately, the VCR came equipped with a Ziploc bag containing an assortment of adaptors, an eclectic combination and re-combination of which enabled Benson ultimately to achieve a clear picture of Mr. Scott on the television screen.

Benson hunkered down in front of the TV, assuming the posture of a youngster, lying flat on his tummy, with his chin propped up on his hands and his elbows spread wide. For two hours and twelve minutes, Benson lived the life of Ebenezer Scrooge, while tears streamed down his cheeks and an array of emotions attacked and cleansed his soul.

When Ebenezer awoke on Christmas morning to discover that the spirits had worked their miracles in one night, Herbert Benson experienced a rebirth of his own.

While Mister Scrooge was vowing to amend his life, Benson was doing the same with no less sincerity. When Tiny Tim finally looked into the camera and whispered, "God bless us, everyone," Benson mouthed those same words with such passion they sent a chill up his spine, a chill of joy the likes of which he had never before felt.

Herbert Benson emerged from "The Dark Night of the Soul."

When the credits finally scrolled up the black-and-white, eight-inch screen, Benson was already busy removing his beloved weasels from their cages and placing them gently in a gunny sack. He quickly delivered them to the area beneath the row of bushes from which he had first obtained them many years ago. He placed them there with great affection and took care to see that they had a supply of food and water.

That night Herbert Benson slept with more peace and comfort than he could ever remember.

He set out the next morning, seeking a meeting with John Hawkin. It took him three days to find Hawkin and to get through the maze of governmental red tape that surrounded the former Navy Seal. When, three months later, the dust had settled, Benson found himself a member of a top secret and select committee, operating directly under Hawkin's supervision, formed for the purpose of uncovering and prosecuting misconduct in previously untouchable governmental agencies.

Hawkin told Benson, "I wouldn't have recommended you for this position if I wasn't convinced that you could be trusted." Hawkin then fixed Benson with that look for which he was so well known and said, "But just in case I've misjudged you, I want you to know that any breach of your duties will be handled summarily by me personally."

Benson knew he had nothing to fear. A man doesn't get a second chance at life every day. "You have my word, Mr. Hawkin."

Benson couldn't resist the temptation to ask Hawkin why he entrusted him with the requested and obviously sensitive position after Benson's many known transgressions.

Looking Benson in the eye with utmost seriousness, Hawkin declared, "When I saw you climbing up that ladder to the second floor of the safe house, I knew."

Herbert Benson "…was as true to his word as any man had ever been."

Daryl Harrington

The computer's monitor flickered as the gigantic compressor of the building's air-conditioner kicked on fourteen stories overhead. It was after midnight, and the corridors were empty, although from the cubicle on Level Fourteen Minus, there was no way of ascertaining that fact. The swivel chair creaked as Daryl Harrington leaned back and stretched his arms overhead. It had been a long day.

He had planned on leaving the building at around 9:00 p.m. but hadn't even noticed that hour rushing past him as he pursued a cyber-trail into the depths of a top-secret corridor of the CIA's computerized filing system.

At the request of the President of the United States and based upon the recommendation of John Hawkin, Daryl was surreptitiously returned to his former cubicle with no record of his previous activities, no official title, and an unusually high security clearance.

His assignment was to uncover evidence of possible misconduct within various governmental agencies, report his discoveries to Hawkin, who then would review the findings and, if he thought additional investigation was appropriate, turn over those findings to the committee to which Herbert Benson III had been assigned. If that committee agreed that there were grounds for further action, a full-blown investigation would be initiated. Thus far, seven governmental employees, including two FBI agents and one CIA agent, had been dismissed or had criminal charges levied against them as a result of this program.

Daryl was pleased, for the most part. This kind of work fit in almost perfectly with his uncommon computer skills, his spirit of adventure, and his sense of justice. Besides, it isn't every day that someone with absolutely no political connections or without a sterling military record gets to work in a position dear to the heart of the President of the United States.

Best of all, Daryl thoroughly enjoyed working with Big John Hawkin. He was Daryl's kind of man; strong, tough, and honest and he had an attribute that was not often found in a man of Hawkin's stature—a big, soft heart.

Daryl's deep respect for Hawkin was what caused him to feel guilty from time to time. Daryl was not one to live by the rules. He especially resisted regulations that seemed to have no valid purpose. And, in his mind, the ultimate repository of useless rules was the Federal Government of the United States of America.

The guilt Daryl felt from time to time was the result of his propensity to bend and occasionally break the rules specified in relation to his position. Ordinarily, he would have no qualms about his occasional departure from the restrictions on his conduct. But his tremendous respect for Hawkin made his periodic transgressions more difficult to justify than they would have been otherwise.

Daryl had witnessed several instances in which the evidence he procured against some low-life government employee, although forwarded to the judicial system by Hawkin and his committee, resulted in nothing more than a slap on the wrist, usually because the culprit had powerful political connections.

So Daryl took it upon himself not only to search for evidence of misconduct but also to delve deeply into any details of a suspect's history that would indicate the likelihood of alliances with those perched high on the political ladder. If Daryl found that a suspect's conduct was particularly atrocious and that the transgressor had a reasonable chance of slipping through the proceedings unscathed, he sometimes buried his findings and took it upon himself to pursue the matter on his own. Thus far, four scoundrels had been undone by Daryl's old-fashioned form of retribution.

In one case, Daryl discovered that a particularly unlikable and obnoxious high-ranking member of the U. S. Senate was leaking information of a highly sensitive nature to a friend in the corporate world for their mutual financial gain. If this information fell into the wrong hands, it could seriously jeopardize the lives of numerous members of the military.

Although Daryl knew for a certainty that the senator was guilty as hell, he also knew that the evidence he discovered would not be enough to result in a conviction. Daryl, too, suspected that any actions taken by the committee in this regard would be brought to a quick and quiet halt by the senator's awesome power and his many contacts.

Daryl suspected that the senator was even capable of causing a formidable opponent to "disappear." He didn't want to endanger any of the committee members or risk embarrassing the President. So he

took steps to see that justice was achieved through his own unorthodox methods.

A bit more digging into the senator's past by means of Daryl's
substantial computer skills plus several months of "on the street"
detective work—a pastime that he particularly enjoyed—resulted in
his coming into possession of several photographs of the senator in
the company of numerous assorted and varied sexual partners. The
good senator was photographed performing acts that would make
Bill Clinton's oval office closet conduct look like a choirboy's picnic.

Daryl's research also revealed that the senator's rise to promi-
nence had resulted, in large part, from the substantial wealth of his
wife's family, the control of which remained in the hands of his wife's
father, who was a staunch Catholic and who regarded his only daughter as the apple of his eye.

Daryl sent copies of those photographs to the senator, taking
care to leave no fingerprints on them or the enclosed letter. He also
made sure there were no fingerprints or saliva on the envelope or the
postage stamps so that nothing could lead back to him. The letter
stated that the senator was being watched by a special task force
investigating corruption in politics and that, in addition to the photographs, the task force had uncovered the senator's connection to the
Ellsinore Corporation and its ill-gained profits.

The letter demanded that the senator stop all illicit activity
immediately, including cavorting behind his wife's back. It implied
that all of his activities since his twenty first birthday had been inves-
tigated and documented. It then demanded that the senator make
cash donations to a group of enumerated charities in an amount
roughly equal to triple the illicit profits he had made divulging governmental secrets to the Ellsinore Corporation.

Further, the letter stated that failure to comply would result in
copies of the photographs being delivered to several major newspapers and the senator's father-in-law. It also promised that proof of
his numerous treasonous acts would be forwarded to a congressional
committee formed to investigate conspiracies against the federal government. The letter did more than hint that the senator's best chance

to keep these matters from becoming public knowledge would be for him to resign his position.

Finally, the letter demanded that the senator use his abundant influence and numerous contacts with people in high places to force the Ellsinore Corporation into bankruptcy. It ended with the simple sentence, "We'll be watching."

The effects of that letter upon the nervous system of the senator, not to mention his digestive tract, were enough to guarantee his whole-hearted compliance with its demands. Within weeks the senator resigned his position, using a rather implausible explanation.

Shortly after that incident, Hawkin summoned Daryl to his office. He said simply, "Daryl, I've noticed that four prominent political figures have resigned unexpectedly and without a reasonable explanation during the six months since you began your duties down on Floor Fourteen-Minus. I also found four closed files in your computer records, each of which, strangely, involved one of those four prominent citizens. I couldn't help but notice that you appear to have discovered what I shall call 'unsavory' conduct on the part of those gentlemen.

"The information contained in your files, while compelling, would not likely have resulted in a conviction."

They sat there for several minutes in silence.

"That will be all," said Big John finally, with a look in his eyes that put an end to any guilt Daryl might have been inclined to indulge in at any time in the near future.

Daryl left that meeting itching for another adventure.

Now, several weeks later, Daryl sat alone shortly after midnight in the silence of his cubicle. He moved the cursor of his computer to the X in the upper right hand corner of the screen, intending to close the program preparatory to his departure for the night. At the last moment, his eyes happened upon an asterisk in the lower left hand corner of the page. He spaced down one line below the asterisk and found a cryptic footnote that would have had little meaning for anyone who hadn't been involved in the events at the farmhouse six months earlier.

Daryl Harrington leaned back in his swivel chair and smiled.

Douglas Seaborn

Douglas Seaborn's mother, Christine, was the oldest of seven children. She was born into a poor Mormon family, consigned by the edicts of their religion to eke out a living on a dry, wind-blown patch of desert in the Utah badlands.

At an early age, Christine had almost resigned herself to the life of grinding poverty that was her lot, her cross to bear, by virtue of the fact that she was born a sinner. In the secret depths of her soul, however, and contrary to the teachings of the elders of her church, Christine dared to hope there was more.

During the summer of her fifteenth year, a miracle found its way into Christine's desperate life. Had she not been conditioned at an early age to forsake her power, her magic, in exchange for a belief system that placed human beings in the position of victims of their circumstances, Christine would have known that her miracle was the result of her secret, fervent wishes, combined with a subconscious knowing that she still had the power. But to Christine it was a miracle.

In a rather brief time, an assortment of hormones and chemicals were released in her body, causing dramatic changes in her physical appearance. What had been, since her birth, a rather common body with an unremarkable face was transformed, almost before her eyes, into a radiant, voluptuous young woman. At first her parents tried to ignore the transformation, believing that physical beauty was a curse visited upon certain unsuspecting young ladies by Satan, likely the result of surreptitious impure thoughts.

When those rapidly unfolding pulchritudinal attributes finally became undeniable, Christine's mother sought to reduce their visual impact by dressing her daughter in loose-fitting, drab garments. In spite of her mother's most intense efforts, however, Christine still looked—as one young man commented in the high school locker room—"like a gunny sack full of wildcats."

Finally, when at age seventeen, Christine became the source of more furtive glances and locker room comments than the family could tolerate, she was sent away to live with her Aunt Harriet in Philadelphia. Christine's parents hoped that, in a city of sinners, her obvious physical "aberrations" would appear less outstanding. But what escaped them was that Aunt Harriet had undergone a transformation of her own. She had left the church and replaced the teachings of her former religion with a progressive and liberating spirituality.

Christine welcomed the opportunity to escape the boredom of the small town in which she had been reared. More important, it didn't take her long, with a few nudges from Aunt Harriet, to realize that her pulchritude might not be the curse it was labeled by the ladies of her former parish. She began to revel in the attention heaped upon her by the young men of the City of Brotherly Love, who silently and unanimously agreed that Christine's rapidly unfolding attributes were of a definitely positive nature.

She finally came to realize that her beauty was not only the source of a healthier self-image but, perhaps, a factor in the implementing of her constantly prayed-for escape from a life of demeaning poverty. All of the precepts of her former religion, which had been drilled into her youthful mind by so many well-meaning but misguided adults, fell away with surprising ease as Christine was exposed, with Aunt Harriet's enthusiastic complicity, to some of the wondrous joys of life.

By the time Christine reached her early twenties, she found herself courted by and married to one of the wealthiest men in Philadelphia. He was a good man and supported Christine's desire to use portions of their wealth to rescue her parents from their life of deprivation. The funds provided to her parents, while bringing an abundance of physical comforts into their home, unfortunately were not the least bit effective in uprooting the mental poverty that had been ingrained in them for decades. A visit to the luxurious new residence of Christine's parents in the suburbs of Logan, Utah, might have made one mindful of a rerun of a "Beverly Hillbillies" episode.

By the end of their second year of marriage, Christine and her husband found themselves in joyous anticipation of the birth of a child. Still contending with deep-rooted scars from her joyless childhood and blaming her parents in part for her having had to share what little there was with her siblings, she vowed that this child would be an only child. And this child would want for nothing.

Christine's efforts, although fueled by the best of intentions, did not have the desired effect. By the time young Douglas had reached the age of three, he had been pretty much bequeathed control of his tiny world. By the age of six, he had seized dominance over any child who had the misfortune of finding himself in Douglas's presence. At nine, he had taken tyrannical and irrevocable control of his parents and the household servants.

Shortly after his twelfth birthday, Douglas acquired a Havahart© animal trap, which he baited with nuts, apples, carrots, or chunks of tuna fish, to secure an assortment of chipmunks, squirrels, weasels, raccoons, and an occasional house cat, for the menagerie of critters he kept in a cage hidden beneath a makeshift shelter in the forest behind his parents' home. He spent hours torturing his hapless victims with a variety of devices and chemicals, his favorite of which was to douse the critter with lighter fluid and set it ablaze.

When the pleasure he derived from such activities began to lose its allure, Douglas found a new fiendish delight from enticing younger children to accompany him to his woodland hideaway, where they were forced to commit similar atrocities, under threat of having identical acts performed on their young bodies should they fail to carry out Douglas's orders. Each of those children left the scene with the unquestionable understanding that, if he would ever speak to another human being about these abuses, similar acts would be perpetrated upon his very person. None of those shattered children ever entertained the slightest doubt regarding the sincerity with which Douglas conveyed that message. The psychological damage done to those children and their progeny was immeasurable and far-reaching, probably having devastating effects unto the seventh generation.

Christine continued to cater to young Douglas's every whim. She no longer did this out of a desire to make his childhood better than hers but, instead, out of an overwhelming fear of her son's unrelenting temper tantrums, which carried the unspoken threat of unthinkable retribution.

Further, over the years, Douglas's behavior had been successful in driving a powerful and devastating wedge between Christine and her beloved husband. By the time Douglas reached the age of thirteen, his tyranny had caused his father to spend increasingly more time away from home, allegedly for the purpose of lengthy and important business trips but, in reality, as an escape from the terror Douglas continually visited upon the household.

Christine remained in that cold and lonely home with Douglas but spent as much time as possible out of his presence, entrusting his care, for the most part, to the nanny who had been courageously tending to him for some time.

Ultimately, Douglas was sent to a military academy, allowing his father a safe return to the family home. But Douglas was expelled from school for, among other things, the excesses he displayed in hazing the incoming students. Douglas now had attained an age that enabled him to make the choice practically, if not legally, not to return home. His parents didn't object. Under the pretext of fulfilling their parental duties, but really with the hope that Douglas would remain at a geographical distance, they mailed him a monthly check sufficient to satisfy all of his physical and financial needs.

Douglas, having taken to heart the notion that "knowledge is power"—or as interpreted by his warped mind, a certificate that purports the acquisition of knowledge is power—somehow made his way through a junior college with passable grades.

He managed to get himself admitted to a state university, where he graduated with a 3.7 grade point average, not the result of academic excellence but, rather, the result of his ability to cheat effectively on examinations and to badger smaller and brighter students into doing his homework.

Eventually, Douglas took refuge in the Central Intelligence Agency, where he discovered that his proclivity toward cruelty and violence could be vented in what he believed would be considered an appropriate venue. He had, he believed, a license to terrorize.

By the time Douglas Seaborn was selected to be a part of the team hastily formed by Herbert Benson III to handle the situation surrounding the farmhouse, as well as the renegade decoder from Level Fourteen-Minus, Seaborn was dangerously close to being expelled from, if not imprisoned by, the CIA as the result of repeated sadistic conduct far beyond what his superiors considered necessary to achieve the company's objectives.

———

A middle-aged cowboy sat in a booth in the back corner of the cocktail lounge, his old and weathered Stetson pulled low over his forehead, creating a shadow that entirely hid his handsome face. The sleeves of his shirt were rolled up to a point just below his elbows. Even with his upper arms covered, a casual glance at his forearms would indicate to any discerning observer that this was a man who had engaged in some serious physical activity. He held a bottle of Pacifico in his left hand. The fingers of his right hand drummed slowly on the table top. The cowboy's eyes were fixed on a group of five men seated on bar stools surrounding a tall table near the center of the room.

The décor of the lounge was a far cry from that of the bar the cowboy occasionally visited with his friends back home. This place spoke of money and privilege. A Pacifico here went for five dollars and came with a napkin that looked as if it were designed by one of those New York interior decorating firms that ran difficult-to-interpret ads in the *Home Beautiful* magazine his wife kept on the coffee table at home.

The objects of the cowboy's scrutiny were dressed in suits and ties and spoke boisterously with an air of self-importance befitting their assumed status on the social ladder. They didn't leave the lounge until after midnight. The cowboy had waited patiently, savoring the situation with eager anticipation.

Leaving a ten dollar bill on the table, he grabbed his Levi's jacket from the seat beside him and followed the men out into the parking lot as he'd done every Thursday night for the past four weeks. He stopped in the shadows, observing the men as they headed for their automobiles.

The tallest man, the one he had been watching most closely, walked quietly up behind two ladies who had just left the lounge and placed his hand on the shoulder of the one on the right. The woman turned around with a startled look on her face. The cowboy was too far away to make out what was being said. But he could just about imagine. His suspicions were confirmed when the lady slapped the man across the face with a wallop sufficient to be heard for quite a distance. In return, the man punched the lady with enough force to send her to the ground screaming. She sat up and wiped the blood from her lips.

The cowboy could barely resist the temptation to intervene. He restrained himself out of an intense need to remain undetected.

While helping her friend to her feet, the other lady shouted obscenities at the attacker. The women ran to their car and locked the doors while the man shouted something about the ladies having just missed an opportunity for the experience of their lives.

The cowboy clenched his fists and gritted his teeth. *Be patient, Hang on just a while longer.*

Everyone except the cowboy left the parking lot. He remained in the shadows, watching the tall man turn left, as the cowboy knew he would. The cowboy waited another minute, then climbed into his pickup and started the engine. He stared at his watch as another sixty seconds ticked by. He pulled out of the lot and turned left. He followed the barely used back road for four miles until it began its ascent up a two-mile rise to the top of a hill. He knew that beyond the crest of that hill, the road dropped for a mile and a half before crossing Fremont Avenue, the street upon which was located the apartment complex in which the tall man had lived for the past three years.

Slowing his truck, the cowboy turned off the headlights. Just as he'd anticipated, an automobile was stopped halfway up the hill. He pulled onto the gravel turnout, sheltered from view of the stalled automobile, just as he'd practiced a dozen times before. He removed his Stetson and pulled a black ski mask over his head and face. Then he picked up the 308 caliber sniper rifle resting on the passenger seat.

He opened the truck door, knowing that the dome light wouldn't come on. He stepped out, braced himself against the door frame, and raised the rifle's night sight to his right eye.

The tall man was out of his car, looking under the hood for some sign of the cause of the stalling of his automobile's engine. The cowboy had no problem waiting patiently. He had been through this scenario in his mind many times.

At last his quarry slammed the hood and started walking down the road toward where the cowboy stood behind the shelter of his pickup door. As anticipated, he was heading for the service station 1.3 miles behind the cowboy's pickup.

The cowboy allowed the man to walk about twenty paces before squeezing off a round from the old, reliable 308. The bullet struck the asphalt four inches from the tall man's right foot. The tar-coated gravel, so violently uprooted from the place it had remained undisturbed since the county road crew had laid it four years earlier, tore into the man's ankle, shin, and lower calf with terrible ferocity. He screamed in agony, dancing in circles on his left foot.

Instinctively, the man pulled his pistol from his shoulder holster, even before he was able to stop his dance. He spun around, dropped to the ground, and pulled the pistol's sights up to eye level, searching desperately for the source of the sound he knew so well.

Douglas Seaborn hadn't heard the report from a Winchester 308 sniper rifle since he had been on assignment almost ten years ago in Cambodia. The thought brought a smile to his face, in spite of the burning, throbbing pain in his right leg. Just the name "Cambodia" brought to mind dozens of teenage girls he had raped and brutalized during his eighteen-month assignment there.

Another round struck the asphalt just inches in front of and to the left of his face, sending numerous grains of sand deep into the epithelia of his face and forehead. It felt like an instant intense sunburn, numbed shortly thereafter by his body's defense mechanisms. He had blinked in time to prevent the sand from entering his eyes.

Seaborn looked around frantically, seeking a route of escape. He certainly didn't want to run toward the psycho hiding in the darkness downhill from him. He didn't dare run up the road behind him, where he would be a wide-open target for the several minutes it would take him to run the mile to the crest of the hill.

Beyond the edge of the road to his right was a steep uphill incline, created when the road had been cut through the pass. Trying to climb up that incline would also leave him exposed far too long. His only reasonable route of escape would be to head down the slope to his left, which appeared to lead into a deep ravine.

He rolled four times to his left and disappeared off the edge of the road, just as the cowboy knew he would. As soon as Seaborn was out of sight of the sniper, he struggled to his feet and headed farther down into the ravine as fast as his injured leg would allow. At the bottom, he found a stream. He turned to his left and ran uphill, attempting to distance himself from his attacker. He stayed in the middle of the stream, where he had to contend with slippery rocks but where he figured there would be fewer branches and other obstructions to block his progress.

The cowboy made his way down to the stream bed, anticipating his quarry's next move.

Seaborn ran upstream as fast as he could with due consideration for the likelihood of slipping on the moss-covered cobbles that lined the bottom. Several times he stopped and looked back through the darkness to see if he could detect some sign of his unknown assailant, his Smith and Wesson 38 special cocked and ready to fire.

The cowboy did his best to stay out of sight while remaining close enough to be able to make his move effectively at just the right time.

Seaborn stopped again, gasping for breath. He turned around to stare into the darkness downstream. He saw and heard nothing. The roar of a waterfall upstream easily concealed the sound of anyone moving in its vicinity.

As Seaborn stood there waiting for his respiratory system to recover from the oxygen depletion caused by the combination of the alcohol in his system, his uncommon physical exertion, and the adrenaline flowing through his veins, the cowboy managed to slip to within fifteen feet of the terrified agent.

As Seaborn turned to resume his climb, his right shin pressed against something that felt to him just like the numerous shrub branches he had been trudging through. His conscious mind didn't register this as having any significance. His subconscious mind detected a slightly different feel but was unable effectively to communicate it to his conscious mind because of the overabundance of stimuli assaulting his senses.

Leaning into his next stride, his shin pressed with more force against a length of clear fishing line filament, tripping several devices to which the filament was attached. The Smith and Wesson was torn out of his hand and slammed violently against a large steel disk attached to several aspen trees two feet away. A second later, about two hundred pounds of steel netting fell from ten feet overhead, pinning Seaborn to the ground and immobilizing his limbs.

The cowboy pounced on the terrified man, putting an end to Seaborn's futile attempt to bring his right hand within reach of the backup pistol strapped above his left ankle. The cowboy took a Ziploc bag from his jacket, ripped it open and removed a piece of cloth, forcing it over the agent's nose and mouth.

Seaborn struggled to keep from inhaling, having immediately recognized the familiar odor of chloroform.

✦ ✦

At first Seaborn thought he must be dreaming. Then the reality of his situation came crashing into his mind with the intensity of a perfectly placed blow from a sledge hammer. He was standing bolt upright at the very edge of a cliff, four to five hundred feet above a raging river. His arms and legs were immobile. What little he could see of his chest and shoulders informed him that he was wrapped in duct tape. His body was apparently wrapped from ankles to neck bringing to his mind the image of a mummy that had been painted silver-gray.

He felt pressure against the back of his skull. His finger tips told him that the cause of his erect posture was a length of rough wooden beam included within the mummifying web. As Seaborn hung there horrified, his upper body lurched a few inches forward, giving him a terrifying view of the face of the cliff upon which he was so precariously perched. He tried to see what was behind him, to no avail.

As he hung there over the precipice, a slight breeze buffeted his body, causing it to swing gently from left to right and back again. A strong feeling of vertigo ushered him to the very brink of a blood-curdling scream. He resisted that urge out of sheer terror that the slightest release of energy might tip, beyond the point of retrieval, the scales of whatever device held him so perilously suspended.

He continually replayed in his mind the frenzied plummeting of his body toward the rocks below. Not a single muscle in his entire body was at rest. Sweat dripped from the tip of his nose. Nausea caused bile to rise in his throat and pressed him to regurgitate the scanty contents of his stomach. He resisted the impulse with almost superhuman effort, as a result of the same impetus that had forestalled his compelling urge to scream.

The constraint of the duct tape surrounding his torso made it extremely difficult to breathe. He was able to take only small, shallow breaths, which he had to execute at the rate of about two per second to keep from losing consciousness. Suddenly, his upper body dropped several more inches, stopping abruptly, accompanied by a loud creaking sound. His body bounced up and down slightly.

Seaborn released the formerly sequestered scream with the hopeless rage befitting his circumstances. He slammed his eyes shut and squeezed them tightly as several more drops of perspiration trickled from his forehead.

Who the hell was tormenting him?

He caught a movement to his right. Turning his head, as imperceptibly as his constraints demanded, he saw someone. A black ski mask covered the man's face, but Seaborn could see the man was large and had massive arms. *Probably a body builder or some kind of martial arts freak.* No wonder Seaborn hadn't been able to free himself from the net dropped on him back in the ravine last night. The net itself felt as if it weighed a ton. But when the masked man jumped on him, Seaborn was totally immobilized.

"Do you believe in God?" asked the man.

"Yes," Seaborn gasped, as best he could with his diaphragm so severely restricted. "Why?"

"I thought you might want a minute to make your peace."

"Please, mister. Please. I don't want to die."

"Like Allen Crenshaw didn't want to die?"

"How do you know about Crenshaw?" Seaborn wheezed.

"I know all about you," taunted the masked man. "I know about how you tortured Jim Greenberg. I know about how you cut off Jerry Neibold's fingers, one at a time. Shall I go on?"

"No, please, mister, I was only doing my job. I work for the CIA."

"I know who you work for. Like I said, I know all about you. I've spent months visiting with dozens of your CIA buddies. It's amazing what a person can discover about someone by buying a few rounds of Jack Daniels for some of his associates, especially if those associates think he's a psycho. I've read the files. I've read your reports. I know you doctored most of them to hide the truth. It wasn't difficult to put two and two together and conclude that you're one of those sickos who delight in inflicting pain on others.

"I spent some time in Philadelphia, talking to a few of your relatives. Not a pretty picture, Douglas. Not the kind of childhood one would want his friends at the CIA to know about. I came across one of your old childhood playmates in Philadelphia. He's in an institution, very sick. Even though he doesn't speak well, I was able to get a feeling for your relationship with him. He seems to think you used forced him to soak animals with lighter fluid and set them on fire. Could just be the rantings of a crazy man, eh, Douglas? Only I found another of your childhood playmates who tells a similar story.

"I also know you've recently inherited several million dollars from your parents, who, I'm told, died under suspicious circumstances. You've been a bad boy, Douglas. A very bad boy. And now you're going to have to pay for your evil deeds."

Seaborn's upper body suddenly fell. His involuntary scream echoed down the canyon. The fall was stopped with such force that he felt the blood in his cheeks surge against the surface of his skin.

"Please, mister, please! I don't want to die!"

"How many times have you heard those words? How many times did Jerry Neibold beg for mercy when you were slicing off his fingertips?"

"I was just doing my job," Seaborn whined.

"Bullshit," yelled the masked man. "The CIA doesn't require, condone, or encourage torture, at least not in the situations in which you used it."

"Please —I'll do anything!"

A long silence ensued.

"You're a lucky man. You're damn lucky I'm not a psycho like you. If I were, I'd torch that worthless torso of yours just to watch your skin curl up.

"Tell you what, sicko. I'll give you one chance to save your hide.

"Then again, maybe I won't.

"In fact, the more I think about it, the more I think a nice little live cremation is what you deserve. It shouldn't take long to siphon a couple of quarts of gas out of my truck."

"No! No!" screamed Seaborn.

There was another long silence.

"Okay, one chance. But you'd better do exactly as I say. There won't be a second. I'm probably gonna regret not cooking your hide right here and now. But I'll give you this one chance because I'm a better man than you."

"Yes! Yes! You're a much better man than I am, much better. Please, what do you want?"

"I want you to answer every question I ask, without hesitation. Just remember—I know a hell of a lot about you. If you lie to me one time, you're history."

"Okay. Okay. Anything you say."

Another very long silence.

"Mister?" Seaborn inquired

Silence.

"Mister, are you there?"

Silence.

After another ten excruciatingly long minutes, Seaborn heard footsteps.

"Okay," said the masked man, "here are my questions."

"Where'd you go?" croaked Seaborn.

"Had to get a little gasoline," the man in the ski mask chuckled.

"Oh, dear God," screamed Seaborn, as loud as he could with such limited lung capacity.

"Just answer my questions."

The masked man silently pressed the "record" and "play" buttons on a portable tape recorder. He began shooting questions at Seaborn rapidly, personal questions, age, birth date, social security number, driver's license number, names of aunts, uncles, and cousins, details of cases in which Seaborn had been involved, details of the acts of torture he had perpetrated, names of others involved, names of his superiors, and on and on for forty-five minutes. Toward the end, Seaborn was volunteering information even before the man asked, as if he were purging his soul.

The recorder clicked off.

"What was that?" Seaborn shouted.

"Your death warrant," said the man, "your undoing.

"I've decided to release you. Not out of pity. Not out of the goodness of my heart, but because anyone as disgusting as you doesn't deserve to be released to the glory of the spirit world. You deserve to suffer on this plane for a long, long time.

"And I'm just the guy to see that you pay for your sins. Just remember that I know all about you. I've got a recorded confession regarding your numerous acts of torture, any one of which could put you in prison. I've got plenty of documentation confirming the contents of that confession. And you haven't got the foggiest notion of who I am.

"That's one of the disadvantages of your having abused so many people. Multiply that by the number of relatives each of your victims must have, who would love to see you fry, and you couldn't possibly find me before I'd have you crucified by the media, the CIA, and a congressional investigating committee that would love to receive a copy of this tape."

The man allowed Seaborn's head to drop another four feet, bringing his descent to a jarring halt at such a steep angle that the blood rushing to his head almost made him pass out. Seaborn shrieked.

"Just remember, I can put you back where you are at this moment any time I want. And next time, I promise you, there won't be a second chance. I've always got my siphon hose."

The man pulled Seaborn back up to a vertical position and then let him fall on his back.

Seaborn's skull cracked so hard against the two-by-eight to which he was taped that he saw stars. When he regained his senses, he realized that the duct tape had been cut in a line running from his sternum to his knees. For the first time in more than an hour, he was able to breathe somewhat comfortably. Glorious, blessed oxygen filled his lungs.

A minute later, Seaborn asked, "I've got to know, how the hell did you know my car would stop running where it did? And how did you know I'd head down to the stream? And that I'd run upstream? And what the hell did you use to yank my pistol out of my hand?"

There was no answer.

"Here are your first assignments," instructed the masked man. "Tomorrow you will turn in your written resignation to the CIA, citing as your reason a guilty conscience regarding unauthorized acts committed by you in the line of duty.

"Then you will begin, secretly and anonymously, making substantial contributions to every living person you ever abused. And, although the amends could never possibly be commensurate with the agony you caused, they had better be generous. I'll be watching.

"For those no longer living, you will provide benefits for his or her nearest living relative. One of your victims is related to me. You'd better hope you get around to making restitution to that victim before I decide you're not moving fast enough, or you'll find yourself hanging over another very high cliff. And when your inheritance is gone, I'll be back in touch with you with a list of public services you will be required to perform."

The masked man left Seaborn trying to free his ankles from the duct tape. Seaborn's head ached like hell.

Back in his truck, Clint Yarborough removed his ski mask and smiled at Maria. There was hardly any visible sign that her nose had ever been broken by Seaborn. Whatever trace there might have been was eclipsed by her radiant smile.

Maria had helped Clint plan the entire abduction. She had helped him calculate the exact amount of gasoline it would take to move Seaborn's vehicle from the parking lot of the cocktail lounge to approximately the mid-point of the two-mile uphill grade. This figure was calculated using figures from a mileage chart they found on the Internet. From the total amount of gasoline required, they subtracted the amount contained in the fuel injector lines of Seaborn's sedan, as disclosed by the mechanic's repair manual they consulted, plus an estimated amount in the main fuel line. They then filled a balloon with enough additional gasoline to get Seaborn halfway up the hill.

While Clint had been keeping an eye on Seaborn in the cocktail lounge, Maria had been busy in the parking lot cutting the fuel line of Seaborn's automobile between the gas tank and the engine, plugging, with a tiny cork, the portion of the fuel line still connected to the gas tank, and placing the neck of the gasoline-filled balloon, secured by a rubber band, over that part of the fuel line leading to the engine.

They had rehearsed the mission again and again until they felt certain they had accounted for any reasonable eventualities. They had obtained, from an automobile wrecking lot, a large electronic magnet, the kind used to lift automobiles. With the help of several friends, they had attached the magnet to a few sturdy aspen trees beside the stream they knew Seaborn would be following. The magnet was connected to a Honda generator placed about fifty yards away. When Seaborn tripped the fishing filament line, among other things, it flipped a switch that turned on the power to the magnet that yanked Seaborn's pistol from his hand with outrageous force.

That same fishing line released the hooks that were holding about two hundred pounds of metal netting above the spot where they knew Seaborn would be standing when his leg came into contact with the line.

Daryl Harrington, using his vast computer skills and CIA clearances, was immensely helpful in obtaining information regarding Seaborn's history, his contacts, his childhood friends, and his relatives. It wasn't difficult for Clint to follow those leads to an abundance of additional information about Seaborn.

Clint's and Maria's intentions were not to get even with Seaborn—although when Clint first saw Maria's broken nose and battered eye, he had a few brief, murderous thoughts. They knew the Universe would handle Seaborn's consequences to the extent that needed to be done. Their motivation was to put Seaborn in a position where he never again would harm anyone and where those who had suffered at his hands would receive some compensation for their suffering.

Maria slid across the seat of the pickup until she was as close to Clint as she could get. She wrapped her arms around her cowboy's neck and kissed him on the cheek. As always, he was her hero. They drove off into the sunset, knowing that a lot of good deeds were about to be done.

Grammy

Hazel Thatcher had been known by a variety of names in her seventy four years on this planet. Her first nickname was Hazy, bestowed upon her by her parents when she was a child. That name seemed to fit her just fine and stuck with her for many years.

The morning she walked out the front door of the old Victorian home where she grew up, on her way to her first high school class, she turned around and announced to her parents that, if it was all right with them, she would prefer to be called Hazel. From that moment on, Hazel it was, to her parents anyway

Hazel was always a feisty, but not an angry or rebellious, child. She tempered her energetic, aggressive disposition with an ever-present kindness that endeared her to all who knew her.

When she was twenty-five she married Roger, the man she fell madly in love with and who would become her lifetime partner. Roger was a handyman. He could repair any kind of contraption brought to him for fixing, and he did it with ease.

Although they never had much money, they lived well. Hazel prided herself on her homemaking but didn't let it become an obsession. She always had plenty of time for fun and an occasional adventure.

Roger never knew what she might be getting into next. He would laugh and say, "Ya never know what kind of excitement Hazel's gonna stir up."

Hazel was a darn fine gardener and a whiz in the kitchen, too. Roger never lacked for delicious, healthy food.

By virtue of her marriage to Roger, Hazel's name was changed from Thatcher to Higgins. She noted that the name "Hazel Higgins" seemed repetitive, "sort of like a name you might come across in one of them Rogers and Hammerstein musicals," she said. "But I like it, 'cause I got it from my Roger."

On their first anniversary, Hazel was well along with her first pregnancy. Once they got the process started, they "couldn't seem to turn the consarned thing off," as Roger would chuckle. Within five years they had four children.

Somewhere along the way Hazel naturally and appropriately came to be referred to as "Mommy." Even Roger called her Mommy, both out of habit and out of respect for the wonderful mother that Hazel was.

A little more than a decade later, "Mommy" began to give way to "Mom." Mom remained Hazel's official title for quite some time.

When Hazel was fifty, she heard, for the very first time, one of the softest, sweetest most gentle voices she could ever recall hearing. It spoke in a whisper, almost too faint to hear. The first name that reached the ears of Hazel Higgins from that precious source was, and has been ever since, Hazel's favorite name in the world, Grammy. The source of that heart-warming and tender utterance was none other than the most outstanding grandchild in the world, Wendy Eileen Strachan, daughter of Jerald and Sandra Strachan, formerly Sandra Higgins.

From that day forward, Wendy Strachan, the most perfect grandchild in the universe, held title to an irrevocable and permanent place in the warm and loving heart of Hazel Higgins.

Thereafter, by unspoken but clearly proclaimed and understood edict, Hazel, Hazy, Thatcher, Higgins, Mommy, Mom, was known as Grammy, the only name she would ever again use or recognize. Even her best friend, lover, and husband, Roger, knew her only and forevermore as Grammy.

Grammy led a nearly idyllic life. She loved being a homemaker and mother. She didn't have the slightest desire to enter the business world, although she likely would have become competent in that arena, too.

She was always happy. Roger often said that he couldn't ever remember Grammy being unhappy. People who knew her assumed that anyone with a life as pleasant and carefree as hers would naturally be happy. In Grammy's life, happiness was a given, with no possibility of any lesser condition ever being considered.

On a warm, clear, sunny Wednesday, at precisely 2:37 p.m., just twenty-three days after Grammy's sixtieth birthday, the world she had known and lived in was shattered beyond recognition. In seconds, Grammy's neat, safe, orderly world became suddenly foreign and unrecognizable. She knew where she was, but it didn't look right. Sounds seemed like words, but they didn't make sense. Everything in her presence took on a dreamlike appearance. Time moved erratically, paying no heed to the normal laws of nature. She tried to speak, to say something sensible. But there didn't seem to be any connection between her mind and her voice.

At exactly 2:36 p.m., Doctor Stanley Overton had finished a sentence containing exactly twenty seven words. When that sentence was complete, only three of those words remained in Grammy's mind. The words were so powerful and terrifying that they seemed to burn scars into her brain tissue. Tears poured from her eyes. The room began spinning. She grabbed the arms of the chair upon which she

THE UNDOING

was sitting, in an attempt to find some kind of order in her world. Her only words were, "God, no. Oh, God, no."

With almost super-human effort, she managed to retain consciousness. Her mind wanted to disappear. She wanted to spiral down into nothingness. She wanted to die.

But her Roger needed her, now, more than ever. She would hang on.

The three words that echoed and screamed down the corridors of her tortured mind were, "Roger. Cancer. Terminal."

With every ounce of courage her sweet grandmotherly mind could summon, she grabbed hold of herself, forced herself to regain composure, shut down the flow of tears, caught her breath, steadied herself, reached out for Roger's hand, and assured him, "It's going to be just fine, Roger. Don't you worry a bit."

She helped Roger to his feet and announced to Dr. Overton, "We're going home now. I'm taking my Roger home. We'll let you know in a few days if we need your help."

Grammy and Roger walked down that hall and never went back.

They spent the next three months reading everything they could find on cancer and its cure. They soon discovered that the conventional methods used to fight cancer were of little value and actually often did more harm than good. They came to realize that the human body has the ability to manufacture any chemical or hormone necessary to return the body to a condition of perfect health if we don't hamper the natural processes.

They convened a team of experts to advise them. The team consisted of a dietician, a bio-feedback expert, a chiropractor, an acupuncturist, a massage therapist, a colonics technician, a rolfer, and a medical doctor, one of those rare physicians who understands that those healing modalities that have so erroneously and unfairly been labeled "alternative healing" are every bit as effective, if not more so, than those used by allopathic practitioners.

Doctor Overton was upset when he heard of Grammy's and Roger's plans to handle the situation without surgery, radiation, or chemotherapy. He tried his best to reason with them. But the limitations of his education left him ill-prepared to counter the results of Grammy's and Roger's research.

He was totally shocked when, six months later, he was informed that Roger's "terminal cancer" was in total remission.

Roger lived another ten years, during which time he and Grammy stepped up their relentless pursuit of joy.

At seventy, Roger was struck down and killed by a drunk driver. Although his death was a terrible loss to Grammy, she was forever thankful for the ten additional years they had spent together. She was even more thankful that Roger died instantly rather than wasting away in a hospital bed, puking his guts out from chemotherapy, or having his body burned with radiation.

The close brush with cancer and Roger's sudden death combined to teach Grammy one of the most powerful lessons of her life. For as long as she could remember, she had assumed that she was happy because of the conditions of her life. But once those conditions changed drastically, she had to make a critical choice. The choice was either to enter into a life of misery over her loss or to find some way to be happy.

She chose happiness. And in doing so, she discovered a great truth: Happiness is not the result of having a good life. Having a good life is the result of choosing happiness. She learned that happiness is not a result. It is a choice. Finally, she realized that she had been choosing happiness all along. The wonderful life that she had enjoyed and that others labeled "lucky" was the result of Grammy's constantly choosing happiness, not happiness choosing Grammy.

At the age of seventy-four, only a few months after Grammy had the pleasure of traveling across an open meadow on the hip of Big John Hawkin, as several renegade CIA agents tried to mow them down with gunfire, Grammy was diagnosed with a terminal illness of her own.

Upon hearing the news, she paused for a few moments, looked the young doctor in the eye, and inquired, "Young man, how would you like to be part of a team exploring the leading edge of medicine?"

As the doctor stood there with his mouth open, Grammy turned, took Wendy Eileen Strachan and her handsome boyfriend Chris by the arms, and headed down the corridor with a big smile on her face, saying, "Come on gang; the game's afoot!"

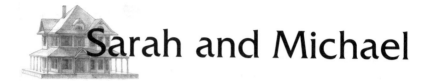

Sarah and Michael

Springtime came to the little town of Sprague softly and quietly. Within a fortnight, the morning temperatures had increased from the mid-60's to the mid-70's. The sun's arc on the horizon had risen several degrees, causing its rays to strike the lawn in front of the Lasher farm at an angle conducive to a substantial increase in the warmth that radiated upward from the rich, moist soil. Tiny traces of morning dew clung to the blades of grass.

As Sarah sat on the front porch of the old house, a gentle breeze ruffled the downy golden hair on her arms. The stirring was not enough to cause a chill, but sufficient to ensure that no pesky fly would attempt a landing. The cicadas had not yet begun their morning serenade.

On a small wooden table beside the porch swing rested an enticing glass of fresh-squeezed tangerine juice. A tiny drop of water that had condensed on the side of the glass trickled slowly down through the mini-droplets that had conspired to create a subtle fog on the outside of the glass.

Sarah's gaze wandered to the lush vegetation that bordered the bright blue sky on the far horizon. Dust still hung in the air above the gravel road where Michael, at the wheel of his old International pickup, had disappeared over the top of that same horizon only moments earlier.

She had awakened to the sound of the starter motor cranking the pickup's engine. She had wiggled her toes into her slippers, pulled on her flannel housecoat, and padded out to the kitchen. There on the breakfast table was a glass of juice that Michael had squeezed for her with a note reading, "Liquid sunshine for her royal majesty."

Now, as Sarah sat on the old wooden porch swing, luxuriating in the morning warmth and thinking of how very much she loved her Michael, the first subtle traces of longing began to play with her consciousness. At first those feelings didn't register in her awareness, most likely because they were so incongruous with the sense of well-being that pervaded her surroundings and her inner being. As she sipped on the sweet nectar, those longings gradually made the transition from subtle to undeniable. The comfort and peacefulness of her morning, combined with her warm and tender feelings for Michael, blended to produce what Sarah had heard referred to, in some long-forgotten song, as "bittersweet."

Sarah went inside and spent a while tidying the farmhouse, hoping that this would ease the melancholy she was feeling. But it didn't help. Finally, she decided to face it head-on and returned to her beloved swing.

The sun had risen to the point where its rays were falling on Sarah's shoulders, wrapping her in a comforting warmth. Just like a sad song that won't turn loose of you, the feelings of longing were so compelling that Sarah just had to pursue them to discover their source.

Certainly, being all alone for now was a contributing factor. Often when Michael was gone, she felt a strange combination of peaceful solitude and loneliness. But there was something more.

After pondering for a while, Sarah realized it was the farm itself, the cherished homestead where she and Michael had reared their two fine sons. She thought about the hard times they had gone through. She remembered the blazing hot summer when the entire corn crop was lost. She recalled how Michael survived that disaster with the grace and dignity that was such an integral part of his essence.

She thought about her sons growing up on the farm, how much fun they all had, and how hard those boys worked. At times Sarah had worried about them working much harder than most kids their age. But the results were undeniable: courage, integrity, loyalty, passion, and best of all, tenderness.

Sarah had watched Michael grow, too, from the cocky, feisty, aggressive young soldier she had fallen in love with to the solid, stable, reliable, gentle man with whom she had fallen into a different kind of love. This was a new kind of love that combined the passionate love she had first known with an even more comfortable, cozy kind of love.

She placed the empty juice glass back on the table, glanced at it contentedly, and surrendered to a gentle urge to take a walk in the morning sunshine. She took a few moments to replace her slippers and housecoat with her faded blue jeans, her old plaid work shirt, and her "tennies." She stepped off the front porch and began to walk along the maze of footpaths that had been formed over the years among the various buildings, pastures, orchards, gardens, and meadows that made up her beloved farm, her home. Those paths weren't the result of conscious planning. They evolved of necessity, formed by those countless footsteps laid down so lovingly and irrevocably by her men.

Even now Sarah could visualize the twins on either end of a bale of alfalfa on their way to one of the corrals, struggling against the weight that was more than their tender years could justify. She remembered the hours she spent looking out of the window above her kitchen sink, the window that Michael had so lovingly constructed so her basil and oregano plants would receive maximum sunshine in the mornings. So many times she looked out of that window, watching for Michael's return from a day's labor in the fields as the last traces of dusk surrendered to the darkness of night. The sense of joy she felt upon seeing the distant flicker of his flashlight illuminating the trail before him always made her heart smile. She imagined the lunch box dangling from his hand, the dust on his face streaked by the day's perspiration, and the unmistakable earthy scent of a wholesome, hard-working man.

How fortunate she was to have married a man who loved the earth! Michael was a man who worked hand-in-hand with Mother Nature to bring forth life from the soil. She was glad she hadn't married a man who would come home at night with the smell of city grime permeating his body.

Sarah always greeted Michael at the back door with a big hug. She savored his manly, musky scent, knowing that he soon would be washing it away. While Michael was singing his way through his nightly shower, his deep baritone voice booming out a favorite John Denver song, Sarah busied herself over the stove, doing her best to provide her men with something hearty, healthy, and tasty. Her most constant ingredient was love.

Now, as Sarah strolled along one of the paths, she found herself on the hillside behind the farmhouse, looking down at the pond where Michael often had taken Tim and Jaime swimming when they were children. She could almost hear them splashing and laughing in the cool water under the hot summer sun.

She came to the meadow where a small creek flowed from high up in the mountains to the east, cascading over the bright red and gold cobbles that lined its bottom, until the crystal clear waters were eventually deposited in the swimming pond. She sat down on the cool grass along the edge of the creek and thought about how Jaime often came back to the farmhouse late on a Saturday afternoon with a big grin on his face and a stringer of native trout hanging from his hand.

As she sat there listening to the rush of the water, she thought about the many Christmases she and Michael had enjoyed with their boys. Often, when the summer market for their produce hadn't been good, the only gifts under the tree were those made by hand. But the spirit was always the same, the laughter just as spontaneous and sincere. If the boys were disappointed by the lack of store-bought gifts, they didn't let it show.

Tears began to pool in Sarah's eyes, spilling over the rims and trickling down her cheeks. They felt cool on her sun-drenched face. Then she realized what else had been causing a tinge of sorrow to mingle with her joy. Her boys were gone. Yes, even though they both slept in their old beds almost every night, they were gone. In the place of those little boys there were now two men, young men for sure, but men nonetheless. And as such, they were now more interested in the allures of the outside world than they were in the simple pleasures of the farm.

Sarah had known all along that one day her boys would leave. Of that she had no doubt. She would have it no other way. They had lives of their own to lead, adventures to experience, mysteries to explore, loves to find. Yet, it all seemed to have come so fast. The time from childhood to adulthood seemed to take not much more than an instant. Her mother's heart could remember every scrape and bruise, every tear, every victory, every joy. All of those birthday parties rolled through her mind like a movie with bright colors, clear sounds, and strong feelings.

My how Sarah wished she could roll back the sands of time, to hold those babies in her arms again, to smell the sweet aroma of baby oil on those soft, pudgy little arms, to touch the fine, silky hair of those precious little heads, to hear their laughter, the soft, gentle, carefree laughter that only a baby can make, not yet hampered by the cares of life.

Sarah wiped a tear from her cheek and looked up at the puffy white clouds that floated in the southern sky. A gentle wind played with her hair and caused the dampness on her cheeks to grow colder.

As she sat there, mesmerized by the beauty of the southern sky, she thought of an old song entitled "Southern Cross." That song never failed to cause an unusual yet unnamed feeling to flow through her. It felt like sadness and strength and courage and longing all rolled into one. It made her think of the American Civil War and all of those brave young men who had died so painfully and needlessly. She tried to imagine what their mothers must have felt. But even beginning to think about it was more than Sarah could bear.

She stood up and walked across the meadow that led to the tree house the boys had built so many years ago. They called it "The Fort." By the time they were eight years old, they were whiling away countless hours in The Fort, doing what only young boys can do. By the end of their twelfth year, The Fort had become a thing of the past, their attention diverted to more social pursuits that involved bicycles and that took them away from the farmhouse and their parents more and more, but not away from Sarah's heart, never away from her heart.

Sarah sat on the floor of that weathered clubhouse with a decade's worth of dust accumulated on its gray wooden boards. She examined each of the souvenirs hanging on its walls with thumb tacks and pins and paper clips and rubber bands. There were baseball cards and photographs and treasures from the forest, placed there by tiny, joyful, loving little hands. The memories hung there, aging almost imperceptibly into the realm of the forgotten, but not by the heart of a mom, never forgotten by a mom.

Alone. How completely alone she felt, the aloneness that comes from knowing that nobody else will ever feel these same memories, never in exactly the same way. There was nobody with whom Sarah would ever be able to share them, these memories beyond expression, beyond words, so joyous and so sad, bittersweet.

She wandered along the forest path for hours, stopping occasionally to relive a memory, finding herself, finally, back at the farmhouse.

In the distance she heard the same old sound she had heard a million times before.

It was Michael, her sweet Michael, bouncing over the gravel road in his ancient International pickup, with paint so old and rusty a person couldn't tell if it was paint or bare metal.

He was coming up that familiar road they had traveled a thousand times for trips to town for groceries, supplies, and tools and for parties, graduations, funerals, and picture shows. Bouncing on that old spring-loaded seat with cracks in the leather was her Michael, sweet, honest, loving Michael, coming home to her as always.

He was ready and able to fill a part of the void Sarah was feeling, left by the years, by change, by the way things are, the way things so wonderfully are, a void provided by the Universe to make way for more wondrousness.

Sarah wondered what lay ahead. Maybe she would find wondrousness in a daughter-in-law or two, a grandbaby or two or more.

By the time Michael's truck was turning into the driveway, Sarah had made her way back to the front porch, having brushed the dust of the clubhouse floor off her blue jeans as she walked along the path. She had taken care to wipe the tears from her cheeks. She wouldn't want Michael to worry about her silly crying. She knew she couldn't explain why she had been crying in a way that Michael could accept without worrying.

Michael stepped out of the pickup and started up the long path leading to the porch where Sarah was swaying back and forth on the old wooden swing, the empty juice glass reflecting the shine of the late afternoon sun.

Under his arm he held a bright pink package with a red ribbon.

Oh my, what has my Michael gone and done now?

Then, before she could ask, she noticed headlights down along the road, barely visible in the growing dusk, lots of headlights. About twenty automobiles were moving slowly along the road. Sarah hadn't seen twenty automobiles on that road in a single day for as long as she could remember. Yet, there they were and all at the same time, coming down the road.

Michael reached the steps at the bottom of the porch. He stood there grinning like a kid who had just spotted a new bicycle beckoning to him from beside a Christmas tree. He said nothing.

"Michael?" Sarah asked.

He just smiled, with so much love that Sarah could not help but return a smile of her own.

The first car had just passed the mailbox and was turning into the driveway, followed closely by the others.

Sarah stood there, speechless.

Michael turned and faced the vehicles as they found room to park along the edge of the front yard.

Those cars were familiar. Why, there was Mortimer's old Plymouth. And there was the Datsun that belonged to Helen from down at Kelly's diner. And there was Chris in his Jeep with Wendy in the passenger seat and Grammy in the back, standing up and holding tightly to the roll bar. Then Sarah saw her Jaime in his new pickup with Becky snuggled up close to him.

They kept coming: Tim on his Harley with Becky's best friend, Rachel, on the back, and Daryl Harrington driving a white BMW convertible, and so many more.

What is this all about?

One by one they turned off their engines and got out of their vehicles. They all stood there in silence, smiling.

Then Michael, Sarah's wonderful Michael, turned to her and began in that deep baritone voice, "Happy birthday to you...."

The rest of those gathered along the edge of the front lawn joined in. They sang with such vigor and enthusiasm that Sarah was astonished.

"My birthday!" she shouted. "I forgot that today is my birthday. I didn't even realize what date this is!"

But Michael hadn't forgotten. Not her Michael.

Sarah ran down the steps into Michael's waiting arms. He set the present gently on the lawn and turned his Sarah around to face the crowd. She stood there in radiant, beaming silence as her many admirers finished her birthday song.

When the last note faded away, all Sarah could say was, "Thank you. Thank you."

The rest of the night was spent in festive partying and laughter. The food was superb. Sarah took plenty of opportunities to sneak little secret glances at her boys, her men. They were happy. They were in love. All was well. And Michael never looked so content, so vibrant.

Mortimer was the life of the party, bringing joy to everyone around him. Sarah knew he carried scars remaining from the deaths of his mom and dad and his sister Ellie. But he seemed to have risen above that terrible burden, especially in the past few months. The love he shared with so many people now seemed to flow with even less effort.

Sarah watched her boys interacting with the others. They were not children any longer but full-grown, capable young men. She looked with pride as her boys added life and warmth to the gathering. It was obvious that they were socially capable and well-liked. Most important, they liked themselves.

Yes, things had changed. Her boys were older. Even Michael was older. But all was well in Sarah's world. The memories would have to be just that—memories.

The guests had brought way more food and drink than they could consume that night. Sarah insisted that everyone take some home with them.

The last of the friends departed. The boys returned from driving Becky and Rachel to their homes. Michael and Sarah had finished the dishes.

As they had done so many times over the years, the Lasher family sat together on the front porch swing. Sarah and Michael were in the middle, Tim and Jaime one on each end, leaning in affectionately toward their parents. Jaime stroked his mother's hair as he'd often done when he was a young boy. Sarah held Michael's hand, thinking what a warm, friendly hand it was. Tim's mind drifted to thoughts of Rachel. He wondered if they might someday have a family. And would they be fortunate enough to find the kind of love his mom and dad shared?

Sarah knew it wouldn't be long before her boys would move out on their own. And, she thought with a trace of melancholy, that's the way it should be.

She sat there in that timeless swing, enjoying the warmth and closeness of her family, and reliving the events of the day. She had come to terms with the changes in her life. She and her men sat in contented silence, the only sound the creaking of the swing.

As she looked up at a full moon, all was well in Sarah's world.